DIAMONDS AND DEATH

A DCI TYLER THRILLER

MARK ROMAIN

Copyright © 2022 Mark Romain.
All rights reserved.
ISBN-13: 979-8-8432-5060-7

The right of Mark Romain to be identified as author of this work has been asserted by him in accordance with sections 77 and 78 of the copyright, designs and patents act 1988. This book is a work of fiction and any resemblance to actual persons, living or dead, is purely coincidental.

THE DCI TYLER THRILLERS

TURF WAR

JACK'S BACK

THE HUNT FOR CHEN

UNLAWFULLY AT LARGE

THE CANDY KILLER

DIAMONDS AND DEATH

WOLFPACK

Wishing the lovely Lynne Romain a speedy return to good health.

READER ADVISORIES

Language and opinions

The DCI Tyler Thrillers are set in the late nineties and early noughties, which means most of the detectives they feature would have joined the police in the eighties. In the interests of realism, the books contain language and opinions that were commonplace and acceptable at the time, but which would now be considered inappropriate and offensive.

Spelling and Grammar

Please note that this book is written in British (UK) English, and that many spellings in the UK differ from those in the USA.

1

MONDAY 1ST OCTOBER 2001

I fancy an ice cream

Slouched in the front passenger seat of the unmarked green Vauxhall Omega, DCI Jack Tyler fidgeted impatiently, then let out a long sigh of frustration. He hated traffic jams with a vengeance and, as they crawled along the A13 towards Barking at a snail's pace, he found himself wishing that he had taken the train instead.

Beyond the Omega's bonnet, three lanes of pollution belching vehicles stretched on for as far as the eye could see. They were all displaying red brake lights; a colour he felt aptly reflected the growing anger of the rush-hour travellers trapped inside them.

"Pity we can't find an excuse to use the blues and twos to get us through this," he said, staring at his driver longingly.

Beside him, DS Steve Bull smothered a grin. Jack 'I want it yesterday, if not sooner' Tyler wasn't exactly renowned for his patience but, if Bull switched on the lights and noise without a valid reason, and then had a prang, he would be the one who got into trouble with the Traffic Sergeant, not Tyler. "It's not as bad as it looks, guv," he said, letting Tyler down gently. "You watch, it'll soon start moving again."

"You really are a 'cup's half-full' type of bloke, aren't you, Stevie?" a sleepy voice announced from behind them.

Tyler glanced over his shoulder at the hulking figure sprawled across the Omega's rear seats. "Hello, sleepyhead! Finally surfaced from the land of Nod, have you?"

Sitting up sluggishly, DI Tony Dillon yawned, gave his head a good long scratch, then arched his back and treated himself to a full-on stretch.

Tyler couldn't help but grin. It was like watching a grizzly bear coming out of hibernation.

Unaware that he was being watched, Dillon smacked his lips together, then dry washed his eyes with the heels of his hands. "I wasn't sleeping," he insisted. "I was just resting my eyelids for a few moments."

Tyler snorted. "Yeah, right! You were snoring like a broken chainsaw within two minutes of us leaving The Bailey, and that was forty-five minutes ago."

The three detectives were travelling back to Hertford House, where they were based, after a stressful afternoon at The Central Criminal Court. What should have been a relatively short Plea and Case Management Hearing for an upcoming trial had deteriorated into a lengthy legal argument after the defence barrister kicked up a stink over the Crown's refusal to include the name of a snout – or Confidential Human Intelligence Source as informants were referred to these days – as part of the advanced disclosure package. The ensuing Public Interest Immunity hearing had been held '*In Camera*' – meaning the court had been cleared of all non-essential personnel and then locked – and it had stretched on for two whole hours before inevitably concluding in the only way that it possibly could, with the trial judge ruling in favour of the Crown's decision not to disclose the highly sensitive information.

Already losing the will to live by that stage, Tyler had then been forced to endure a gruelling meeting with Treasury Counsel and the instructing CPS lawyer, in which they had thrashed out the Special

Measures and security precautions that would have to be implemented when the CHIS, who had been relocated to another part of the country under the Witness Protection Scheme, finally gave his evidence.

By the time they finally escaped the imposing court building, it had been getting on for six o'clock, and traffic had been horrendous right from the get go.

Dillon tapped Bull on the shoulder. "How long till we get back?"

Bull glanced at his wristwatch. "No idea, but as I've been on overtime for the past hour, I don't really care."

A scowl darkened Dillon's broad features. "Lucky you."

Unlike constables and sergeants, officers of inspector rank and above were salaried, so whether he and Tyler worked eight hours or eighteen, they still got paid the same.

Meeting Dillon's eye in the rearview mirror, Bull gave him a smug smile. "Don't you *dare* start whinging about how hard done by you are, guv'nor," he warned. "It's not like anyone forced you to take promotion."

Dillon's sigh, short and sharp, was the sound of a man acknowledging defeat. "Yeah, I suppose so," he conceded. Leaning forward, he thrust his head between the front seats. "Can't you find an alternative route, Stevie? he asked, tetchily. "Only I've got things to do; places to be."

"Haven't we all?" Tyler observed drily, wishing he was back home, curled up on the sofa with Kelly Flowers, and not stuck in a tin can listening to their bickering.

Dillon pointed through the windscreen, towards a slip road about a hundred yards further along the dual carriageway. "Doesn't that exit take us off at Prince Regent Lane?"

"It does," Bull answered warily. "Why?"

Dillon's loud tutting implied it was a daft question. "Because, if we make a detour along Prince Regent Lane, we can head up to Barking Road, and get back to the office that way."

"I'm happy to do that if you really want me to," Bull said, although he didn't sound it, "but in my experience, P. R. Lane is likely to be gridlocked at this time of night."

Dillon wasn't going to be dissuaded that easily. "Well, it can't be any worse than this, can it, huh?"

Bull glanced sideways at Tyler, leaving the final decision to him. "Boss?"

Tyler shrugged. "Let's do it," he said. "We've got nothing to lose." And besides, it was better than listening to the big man whine.

The set consisted of a big four poster bed in the centre of a fake Georgian bedroom. Out of camera shot, four barn door lighting units, standing tall on their adjustable aluminium tripods, had been rigged up to ensure that the performers were evenly lit from every angle. Three video cameras, also mounted on tripods, were simultaneously filming the man and woman who were writhing around naked on the bed.

The director, a middle-aged man with a bulging waistline and a receding hairline, was prancing around the bed, being careful to remain out of shot while he gave explicit directions to the couple having sex, telling them what positions to take up, what parts of their bodies to touch, and even what facial expressions he wanted them to pull at any given point in time.

"And you'd be willing to let us have this place at a day rate?" Annie Jenkins asked. "Including access to the editing suite next door?"

Without taking his eyes off the cavorting couple, who were now doing it doggy style, the man beside her nodded. "As long as you give me exclusive distribution rights for the end product," he said with a slimy smile.

The tinpot studio was located above a video rental shop in Dalston, and the man she was speaking to was the proprietor, Pervy Pete Simpkins.

"Obviously, you can only have the studio on the days it isn't booked out by professionals," he added. "After all, I can't turn down the kind of money people like Cyril pay me, just so you can knock out your amateur home movies, can I?"

Annie looked at the two people going at it like rabbits on the bed; a skanky druggie and a local fitness instructor who was desperate to raise some cash to pay off his gambling debts. And then there was Cyril Cain, their overly enthusiastic director, who was shouting at them to hurry up and achieve a joint climax.

They were hardly BAFTA contenders.

"And what percentage of the turnover will we get?" she asked, eyeing him cynically. Pervy Pete was renowned for being a cheap-skate, and she fully expected him to try and knock her.

"Well," he said, licking his thin, cracked lips greedily. "I have a *lot* of overheads, so I couldn't give you more than thirty percent, and that's being generous."

Annie laughed. "Fifty-fifty," she demanded. "You forget, Pete, I work here, so I know exactly how much your overheads set you back."

A cunning smile spread across Simpkins' lizard-like face. "Sixty-forty," he countered, knowing he had her over a barrel. "Final offer."

"Deal," Annie said, offering her hand so they could shake on it.

Fifteen minutes later, after they had travelled less than two hundred yards along Prince Regent Lane, Bull shoved the gear selector into neutral and angrily yanked the handbrake up. "Well, that detour was *really* worth taking," he griped. As he had predicted, the roads were gridlocked in both directions.

Folding his arms, Dillon shook his head and tutted loudly. "I wouldn't have come this way if I'd been driving."

Bull's mouth compressed into an angry thin line. "Very funny."

Tyler glanced across at him. "Don't take the bait," he advised, aware that Dillon was deliberately goading Bull, just to get a reaction.

"At this rate, there won't be any point in going home, tonight," Dillon added, just to wind him up further.

Bull's grip on the steering wheel tightened, as if he were trying to strangle it. "You're very welcome to take over the driving if you think you can do any better," he smarted, glowering at Dillon in his rearview mirror.

Tyler held up a hand to silence them. "Tell you what," he said. "There's a really nice little fish and chip shop just along here. Why don't we stop off and grab some food?" He stared at each of them in turn. "It's got to be better than being stuck in this shitty traffic for the next hour, getting on each other's nerves."

"Yeah, why not?" Dillon said, coming around to the idea. "I'm starving, and I could really do with a cold drink."

"Hopefully, you'll choke on it," Bull said, cattily.

"Now, now, children," Tyler chided, feeling very much like a parent playing peacemaker between two squabbling siblings.

———

"Aidan, it's me," Annie said when her boyfriend answered the phone. "I've spoken to Pervy Pete, and he's agreed to let us use the studio. Better than that, we can start first thing tomorrow…. Yes, I know that doesn't give us much time to prepare… What…? Don't worry about the money. We only have to pay him a day rate, and we'll get forty percent of the profits from the film sales, and we get free use of the editing suite next door as well … Yes, of course I know how to do that. I've been helping Pervy Pete to splice these poxy porn films together for the best part of a year now; I'm better at it than he is."

Aidan's response was a surly grunt. *"I'm really not sure about this."* From the hesitancy in his voice, she could tell he was on the verge of chickening out.

"Look, we've discussed this at great fucking length," she responded, angrily. "It's a no-brainer. We'll be making a shit load of money for doing the things we enjoy doing anyway–" That wasn't quite true. He enjoyed their kinky little sex games; she just put up with them to keep him happy "–And you even admitted it would be a major turn on for you."

"I know," he whinged, making himself sound utterly pathetic,

"but what if anyone we know watches one of our films? Can you imagine how much grief I'd get from Carrie and Dazza if they ever found out?"

Aidan's family were strict Catholics who took a very dim view of promiscuity in any form.

Annie gritted her teeth, wishing he would grow a pair. She had far more to lose than he did, but she was still willing to take the risk. A former drug addict and prostitute, Annie Jenkins' life had been in ruins when she met Aidan, three years earlier. Social Services had just taken her baby daughter into care, having been tipped off by her bastard of a landlord that she was bringing clients back to her bedsit to service them. Whatever her shortcomings, Annie had loved Anabel with all her heart, and a part of her had died on the day they were parted.

Annie had turned her life around since then. She was off the gear, she had a steady relationship and a regular job at the video shop, and she had recently submitted a petition to the court, requesting visitation rights to her daughter. Aidan's family might be morally offended by them making a porno but, if the court found out, it would destroy her chances of gaining access to Anabel. "It'll only be two films," she said, trying to put his fears to rest. "Three at the most." She thought it wiser not to point out that they were only having to do this because he had got them into such dire straits financially.

"I know, but—"

"Look," she said, cutting him off before his spineless whinging became too much to bear, and she started telling him a few home truths. "We can wear wigs and makeup, disguise ourselves so that no one will recognise us, and we'll be using made up porn names so no one will ever twig it's us."

"Yeah, but what if—"

"Will you stop worrying about it, Aidan," she snapped. "I know exactly what I'm doing."

"Course you do," he said, nastily. *"I forgot that you used to be a skanky whore until I saved you from the street."*

His words stung worse than any slap could ever have done. "I've got to go," she said, feeling her eyes prickle with moisture. "My bus is coming."

Exactly forty minutes later, hunger sated, tempers improved, the three detectives emerged from the fish and chip shop to find that the roads in Newham were flowing much more freely.

As they made their way back to the Omega, Tyler spotted a mini-market with an illuminated ATM sign in the window. "I'm just going to nip in there and get some cash out," he told them, nodding towards the shop. "Won't be a minute."

"I fancy an ice cream, so I'll come with you," Dillon said.

Entering the mini-market a few seconds later, Tyler nodded politely at the middle-aged woman standing behind the counter. The vacant expression on her homely face suggested that she was either bored out of her wits or had recently undergone a frontal lobotomy.

What could only be described as elevator music was being piped out of the store's wall speakers. It was bland and boring, and would certainly discourage shoppers from lingering, Tyler thought, already fed up with it.

The mini-market consisted of a half dozen aisles, which were crammed together so tightly that there was barely enough room for two people to squeeze past each other if their paths crossed.

"Excuse me, where will I find the ice creams?" Dillon cheerfully enquired of the woman behind the counter.

She stared back at him with a gormless expression. "In one of the freezers at the back," she replied in a disinterested monotone.

Tyler nodded to himself. *Definitely a frontal lobotomy.*

Leaving Dillon to it, he crossed to the ATM at the front of the shop, adjacent to the counter. After checking the small print to confirm that they didn't charge for withdrawals, he slid his bank card in, entered his PIN, and pressed the 'ENTER' button. Selecting the twenty pounds option from the pop-up menu, he stepped back and waited for the machine to spit it out.

Glancing out of the window, Tyler noticed two mopeds pulling onto the pavement outside the mini-market. The *ning-ning-ninging* of their engines was irritatingly loud, and he wondered if they had been illegally tweaked to give them a bit more power?

Both riders were dressed in nondescript, baggy hoodies and loose-fitting jeans, and they seemed very 'eyes about', which instantly set alarm bells ringing inside his head. As he watched, one of the males dismounted. Leaving the moped running, he crossed to the plate glass window, pulled his visor up to reveal a spotty white face, and peered inside.

Tyler's eyes narrowed, and he wondered if they were on the prowl, looking for potential victims to follow off and rob? There was a big problem with youths doing that at the moment, he knew.

After a few moments, the spotty male pushed himself away from the window and returned to his ride. Clambering aboard, he said something to his companion, who promptly pulled out a mobile phone and made a call.

Shoving the two tens that had just popped out of the cash machine into the back of his warrant card, Tyler set off in search of Dillon. Annoyingly, there was no sign of his partner by the freezer cabinets but, on looking in the convex security mirror that hung in the far corner, he spotted Dillon's large frame sauntering towards the counter, ice cream in hand.

Making his way over to join him, Tyler glanced out of the shop window, hoping to catch another glimpse of the two dodgy looking moped riders. To his astonishment, he was instead greeted by the worrying sight of an old red Transit van reversing towards the mini-market at high speed.

"What the—"

Before he could finish the sentence, the plate glass window exploded, spraying the inside of the shop with jagged shards of flying glass.

Having knocked down a large section of wall, the van trampled over the crumpled aluminium window frame, and then bulldozed a tall magazine display case out of its way. Even after it skidded to a halt, sending debris flying in all directions, the driver continued to rev the engine into the red, filling the mini-market's interior with a thick cloud of toxic exhaust fumes.

Almost immediately, the rear doors sprang open and two burly masked men, both clad in dark overalls and steel toe-capped boots, emerged from within. One was carrying a sawn-off shotgun, while the other was clutching what looked like a heavy-duty angle grinder to his chest.

The man with the shotgun quickly weaved his way through the debris towards Dillon, who was crouching down by the counter, having instinctively taken cover when the world around him exploded.

The gunman raised his weapon and pointed the business end straight at Dillon's face. "STAY WHERE YOU FUCKING ARE," he yelled as glass crunched underfoot.

Hiding in the aisle, Tyler watched as a stunned Dillon slowly stood up and raised his hands above his head.

Behind the counter, the cashier was screaming hysterically. As the shotgun wielding raider advanced towards her, she started hopping up and down, as though someone had just slid a tray full of burning hot coals under her feet.

Swinging the gun in a pendulous motion between Dillon and the cashier, the gunman shouted, "SHUT UP! SHUT UP!"

The jarring sound of the angle grinder bursting into action drowned out the cashier's incessant screaming.

Unseen by the ram raiders, Tyler scuttled forward and risked a quick glance around the side of the aisle. The one with the angle grinder was kneeling down by the base of the ATM, with his back towards Tyler, and he was methodically cutting his way through the restraining bolts that secured the cash machine to the floor. White-hot sparks flew in all directions as he worked, lighting up the area around him like a miniature fireworks display.

The mini-market's door suddenly flew open, and the scrawny moped rider Tyler had earlier observed squinting through the window appeared carrying a set of heavy chains over his shoulder. Bypassing the man who was recklessly waving the sawn-off around, he rushed over to the ATM and started wrapping the chains around it.

As soon as the last securing bolt had been severed, the angry roar of the angle grinder came to an abrupt end, and Tyler found that he could actually hear himself think again.

The two raiders by the ATM climbed aboard the van and set about securing the chains to what looked like an internal winching mechanism. As soon as they were finished, the one in the crash helmet jumped down and disappeared through the shattered window to rejoin his fellow biker, who had remained outside to act as their lookout.

"Stay where you are and no one gets hurt," the raider with the sawn-off warned Dillon, before retreating towards the Transit.

It occurred to Tyler that, if he was going to do something, it would have to be now, before the gunman got into the van. From the frustrated expression on Dillon's face, he could tell the big man was thinking exactly the same thing.

Casting his eyes over the nearest shelves in search of an impromptu weapon, Tyler selected a large bottle of wine. It felt satisfyingly heavy in his hand, and he knew it would do the trick if he could just get it on target.

Waving to get Dillon's attention, Tyler pointed at the bottle, then mimed chucking it. Jerking his thumb over his shoulder at the retreating gunman, he held the bottle up to his head.

Dillon's eyes narrowed as he processed what Tyler was suggesting, but then he gave an almost imperceptible nod, indicating that he was up for it if Tyler was.

Tyler's palm suddenly felt sweaty, so he put the bottle down and wiped it on his trouser leg. After all, it wouldn't do for it to slip out of his hand as he threw it.

Grabbing the bottle firmly by its neck, Tyler stood up, sucked in air, and drew back his arm. The ram raider who had used the grinder so expertly was already inside the van, and he was holding out a helping hand to pull his comrade up.

As the gunman took it, Tyler threw the bottle with all his might.

It hurtled towards him at great speed, spinning madly as it went, but instead of striking its intended target, it sailed straight past the gunman's head and struck the man in the van squarely in the chest, sending him staggering backwards.

"Shit!" Tyler breathed as the startled gunman spun around to face him.

A split second later, the shotgun was pointing straight at his head. As Tyler's eyes widened in fear, the gunman pulled the trigger.

2

Not now, Adele!

Inside the Omega, Steve Bull switched the radio on, tuned it into Magic, and then reclined his seat. He figured that he had a few minutes of chill time before the others returned, so he might as well make himself comfortable while he waited.

Closing his eyes, he let out a world-weary sigh.

What a bloody long day it had been!

He couldn't wait to get home, slip out of his suit, and put his feet up for a little while. The boys were both out at football practice tonight, so he and his wife would be able to watch TV in peace and quiet for a change, instead of being constantly interrupted. Adele was doing him a spaghetti bolognaise for dinner, not that he was remotely hungry anymore, not after shovelling a large portion of cod and chips down his throat.

Closing his eyes, Bull clasped his hands across his chest and wriggled around in his seat until he was comfortable. He didn't bother looking up when he heard a high revving vehicle reversing at speed. After all, he was a detective, not a traffic officer.

Still fretting over the unwanted dinner that Adele was making him, Bull wondered if it might be worth giving her a quick call? If she hadn't already started cooking, he could tell her not to bother. That way he could have it tomorrow night instead. She would be okay with–

There was an almighty crash: glass shattered; metal distorted; a woman started screaming hysterically.

Bull sat bolt upright, his eyes springing wide open.

"What the…?"

No more than twenty yards ahead of him, an old Ford Transit van had just smashed through the front windows of the mini-market that Tyler and Dillon had entered a few moments earlier.

There was smoke and dust everywhere.

As Bull's eyes anxiously raked the market's interior in search of his colleagues, he prayed that neither of them had been standing near the windows when the van struck.

His initial reaction was that it had been a freakish accident, and that the van's driver had somehow lost control, but that idea was quickly dispelled when two masked men jumped out of the rear.

"Oh shit!" he breathed, realising that he was witnessing a ram raid.

The first man to emerge carried a sawn-off shotgun, and he peeled off to Bull's left, striding purposefully towards the counter, where all the screaming was coming from. As the dust began to settle, he spotted Tony Dillon crouching down in front of the counter. The big man stood up slowly, hands raised above his head.

He looked shell-shocked.

Bull's mobile burst into life, creating a very unwelcome distraction. Glancing down at the cupholder, where he had left his phone, he saw that his wife was calling him. She was probably ringing to see how much longer he would be.

Not now, Adele!

Briefly averting his eyes from the drama inside the mini-market, he reached down and killed the call. When he looked back up, he saw that the other masked man was using an angle grinder on the ATM, presumably severing the restraining bolts so that it could be loaded onto the van.

There was still no sign of Tyler, which was most disconcerting.

Snatching the mic from the Omega's dashboard, he pressed the transmit button. "MP, MP from Metro Sierra 93, active message. SO1 officers require urgent assistance at Matterson's Mini-Market in Prince Regent Lane, Newham. We've got two masked suspects inside the premises, and one of them's armed with a sawn-off shotgun."

Before the Information Room operator at New Scotland Yard could even acknowledge the call, a plethora of units were putting up to assist.

Although Bull hadn't noticed them at first, because there was so much else going on, he now became aware of the two moped riders waiting outside the mini-market. Their eyes were ping-ponging all over the place as they kept lookout.

One of them suddenly dismounted and ran to the front of the van. Reaching inside, he removed a bundle of heavy-duty chains, which he then carried into the mini-market, staggering under their weight. For some bizarre reason, instead of just stepping through the shattered glass window, the clueless moron jogged all the way over to the door and entered that way.

After assisting Angle Grinder Man to wrap the chains around the ATM, the pair of them jumped into the back of the van. It had to be equipped with an electric winch, Bull realised, because the ATM immediately started scraping along the floor towards the vehicle's interior.

Leaving his buddy to finish loading the ATM, Moped Man jumped down and ran back outside. Only this time, he had the sense to step through the shop window, instead of taking the circuitous route he had entered by. Mounting his ride, he revved the moped's engine until it sounded like a demented hairdryer.

Inside the shop, the shotgun wielding ram raider started making his way back towards the van, keeping the sawn-off trained on Dillon and the hapless shop assistant.

A sudden movement by one of the aisles caught Bull's attention. Craning his neck to get a better look, he caught a fleeting glimpse of Tyler's head as it poked around the corner.

Even from a distance, Bull could see the steely determination in Tyler's eyes. It was a look he was all too familiar with. "What are you up to, Jack?" he whispered. "Please, just this once, don't play the bloody hero."

No sooner had the words left his mouth than Tyler stood up and threw a wine bottle straight at the gunman, who was just about to climb aboard the Transit.

Bull didn't see where the bottle landed, but it clearly hadn't hit its intended target because the man holding the sawn-off instantly turned towards Tyler and, striding towards him, fired both barrels in quick succession.

———

Annie was fuming. She had taken a lot of shit from Aidan over the past three years. She had put up with the shameful way that he treated her; she had indulged his unsavoury sexual fantasies; she had even tolerated him stealing money from her purse to finance his burgeoning drug habit.

And what had he ever done for her in return?

Absolutely nothing, that's what.

The fact was, Aidan was a spiteful, manipulative bastard who got off on playing mind games with her. This wouldn't be the first occasion that he had agreed to something and then changed his mind at the last moment. She had always put up with it in the past, letting him walk all over her like the doormat he obviously thought she was.

But not this time.

In a foul mood, Annie unlocked the street door of her one-bedroom flat in Crondall Street, tossed her bag onto the kitchen table, and then took a deep breath. She held it in for several seconds, and then exhaled slowly. Steeling herself for the inevitable argument, she dialled Aidan's number.

"Now, you listen to me, Aidan McCullen," she said the moment he answered. "We're making this film whether you like it or not. I will *not* be—"

Aidan's manic laughter drowned her out. *"It's okay, babes,"* he cooed, seemingly unfazed by her ranting. *"Everything's sweet as a nut. I've thought it all through, and I'm up for it if you are."*

The slurred voice and chilled attitude could only mean that he was stoned out of his head. Annie groaned inwardly, resigned to the fact that she would have to take his acquiescence with a massive pinch of salt. Knowing him, he would probably change his mind again when the drugs wore off. Well, fuck him if he did, she thought, angrily tossing the phone onto the table. They desperately needed the money the porn films would bring them and, if Aidan wasn't prepared to participate in tomorrow morning's filming, she would just have to go through Pervy Pete's list of contacts and find someone who was.

As Tyler ducked down behind the nearest aisle, there was a deafening roar from the shotgun. The shelves immediately above his head were blown into a million pieces, and several bottles of wine exploded simultaneously, showering him with their contents. He instinctively wrapped his arms around his head as a shard filled sea of red liquid rained down upon him.

Almost immediately, he heard heavy footsteps and realised that the gunman was picking his way through the debris towards him. Wiping the wine from his eyes, Tyler scrabbled along the floor, half crawling and half running as he tried to put some distance between himself and the approaching gunman. As he reached the end of the aisle, his wet feet slipping and sliding on the linoleum flooring, there was another explosion.

Tyler instinctively threw himself to the right, landing flat on his face and sliding along the floor in an undignified heap. Behind him, the glass frontage of the freezer cabinet he had been standing in front of disintegrated, and the lights inside started flickering madly.

Springing to his feet, Tyler cautiously poked his head around the side of the aisle to find the gunman staring back at him from the other end. Breaking open the shotgun's barrel, the ram raider calmly ejected the two spent cartridges onto the floor, and then reached into his pocket in search of more ammo.

Tyler broke into a run. Head lowered, he charged along the narrow aisle, intent on rugby tackling the gunman to the floor before he could finish reloading.

Ahead of him, the ram raider's hand emerged from his pocket. In one fluid movement, he popped the two red cartridges it contained into the shotgun, snapped it shut, and raised his weapon.

Had his opponent been armed with a handgun, Tyler might still have made it, but the chilling thing about scatter guns was that you didn't have to be a particularly good shot to use them; all you had to do was point the damn thing in the general direction of your intended target and pull the trigger.

Behind his ski mask, the gunman smiled at Tyler.

Still running, Tyler braced himself for the inevitable impact that would surely end his life; waited for the ball bearings to tear his flesh apart, shredding him as effortlessly as they had the shelving above his head a few moments earlier.

He had investigated a lot of murders, and the thought that he was about to become a homicide statistic himself was too surreal to even contemplate. A detached part of his brain wondered who Holland would assign to run the case? Andy Quinlan would be a very good choice; calm, methodical, intelligent and dedicated. He would move heaven and earth to get justice for Tyler's grieving loved ones.

As the gunman's gloved finger tightened on the trigger, and Tyler drew what he feared would be his last breath, Dillon cannoned into the unsuspecting man with the force of an express train, virtually folding him in half as he lifted him off his feet.

One moment the ram raider had been standing there, pointing the sawn-off at Tyler's midsection; the next he had vanished, and the aisle was empty.

By the time that Tyler cleared the aisle, Dillon had the situation completely under control. He was sitting astride the gunman, who was now lying face down on the ground, one arm twisted so far up his back that it must surely snap at any moment. The shotgun had clattered along the floor when it had been dropped, and was now lying safely out of reach.

Behind them, the van's engine suddenly coughed into life.

Its wheels spun in place as they sought to gain traction.

Looking out of the shattered window, Tyler saw that the two moped riders were already long gone.

As the Transit surged forward, the glass and loose brick trapped beneath its chassis was churned up and sprayed in all directions.

"Don't just stand there gawping," Dillon shouted, raising a hand to shield his head from the flying debris. "Stop that bloody van!"

The words galvanised Tyler into action, and he sprinted over to the driver's door. Yanking it open, he saw a masked man sitting behind the wheel, revving the engine wildly.

Before Tyler could pull him out, the Transit broke free of the rubble and accelerated wildly, tearing the door handle from Tyler's grasp, and nearly breaking his wrist in the process.

Tyler was forced to jump backwards to avoid being sideswiped. "Fuck!" he yelled, tucking his throbbing wrist under his armpit as he ran after the fleeing Transit.

As the van bounced off the pavement to join the carriageway, the centrifugal force of its sharp right turn sent the unlocked driver's door flying into the side of a parked car before slamming it shut on the rebound.

Running flat out, Tyler gave chase, knowing it was probably pointless but too angry to even think about conceding defeat. Above the rasping sound of his own heavy breathing, the faint wail of distant sirens reached his ears. Backup was on its way, but it would arrive too late to prevent the van from escaping.

The sound of a horn being honked directly behind him made Tyler jump. Glancing over his shoulder, he saw a familiar head sticking out the driver's window.

"Get in the bloody car!" Steve Bull yelled, impatiently.

Tyler didn't need to be told twice.

No sooner had his rump touched the passenger seat than Bull activated the blue lights and two-tones, and floored the gas pedal. Tyler barely had time to close his door before the Omega surged forward like a rocket.

Beside him, Bull began animatedly sniffing the air, then wrinkled his nose in disgust. "You smell like a bloody brewery."

"Never mind what I smell like," Tyler snapped. "Just keep your eyes on the road."

Up ahead, the van was weaving all over the place, and Tyler wondered if this was because the heavy ATM hadn't been properly secured, and was now sliding from side to side every time the Transit changed direction.

"Don't you dare let him get away from us," Tyler snarled, wiping a line of perspiration and wine from his brow.

In front of them, the Transit kept jinking violently to its right, looking to overtake a slow-moving bus but being thwarted by a steady line of cars travelling in the opposite direction.

Bull risked another quick sideways glance at Tyler, and this time there was a wry smile on his slender face. "Why is it that there's never a traffic jam when you want one?"

Tyler grinned, appreciating the intentional irony in the comment. "Shut up and drive," he said, fondly.

At the first sniff of a gap, the van accelerated, just about squeezing itself between the lumbering bus and a row of parked cars, but losing both wing mirrors in the process.

Bull flinched as one of the dislodged mirrors bounced harmlessly across the tarmac and smashed into the Omega's front grill before spinning away into the gutter. "That bloke must have a death wish," he said, shaking his head at the man's reckless stupidity.

Bull waited for the gap to widen before pulling onto the wrong side of the road and accelerating past the bus. Although the van had opened up a healthy gap, he quickly closed it down again, slotting in behind the bandit vehicle as it sped towards Barking Road.

Tyler snatched the radio mic from its holder. "MP, MP from Metro Sierra 93, active message. We're chasing a red Transit van,

Prince Regent Lane towards Barking Road. It's one up, and it's just decamped from the scene of a ram raid."

"*Metro Sierra 93, that's all received by MP,*" the Information Room operator responded, calm as you like. "*Can you give me the vehicle's registration number for a PNC check, MP over?*"

Tyler would have been happy to oblige, but the van no longer had one. "Negative, MP. The number plate must have come off during the ram raid."

"*All received by MP. India 99, are you available to assist?*"

India 99 was the call sign for the Met's helicopter.

A tinny voice responded almost instantly. "*MP from India 99, yes, yes! We were already responding to the urgent assistance call to the mini-market, and we should be overhead in thirty seconds or so.*"

The noise of the rotor could clearly be heard in the background.

Tyler toggled the mic. "Nine-Nine, for your info, we're in an unmarked green Vauxhall Omega," he said.

"*All received by India 99. MP and all ground units, please be advised that we now have visual of the bandit vehicle and the perusing police unit, and are filming.*"

Up ahead, the van pulled out and blindly overtook a London taxi, ignoring the blaring horn and flashing headlights of the oncoming car it had just forced out of its way.

"He's definitely got a death wish," Bull repeated, easing past the taxi and gunning the accelerator to bring them back into contact.

Tyler nodded his agreement, then squeezed the press-to-talk button on the mic. "MP from Metro Sierra 93, we're just passing Belgrave Road on our offside, speed five-zero MPH and increasing."

"What the hell does he think he's playing at?" Bull wondered aloud. "He can't possibly outrun us in that thing, especially not with the helicopter above."

"What's he got to lose?" Tyler asked, rhetorically. It had been his experience that, when a fugitive's fight or flight instinct kicked in, reason went straight out of the window, and he had seen normally sane people take the most unbelievable risks in a bid to evade capture. "I suppose, from his point of view, he's looking at a good ten stretch if he gets caught, so he might as well take a few chances."

A hump back bridge was rushing towards them at frightening speed. The pedestrian-controlled traffic lights at its apex were red against them. Worryingly, a small group of people were already crossing the road.

Toggling the PTT again, Tyler spoke in a taut voice. "MP, the bandit's approaching red ATS. We've got stationary traffic in both directions and pedestrians crossing. Stand by…"

The van braked hard but, instead of stopping, it swerved left, mounting the pavement with a jarring thud. Its nearside panels scraped against a set of waist high metal railings, making a horrendous grinding noise and sending sparks flying everywhere, before straightening itself out.

As the van sped along the footway, Bull pulled onto the wrong side of the road and accelerated hard. Now separated by a line of stationary vehicles, the van and Omega raced along, neck and neck with each other. When the Transit's masked driver glanced sideways at them, Tyler only just about resisted the temptation to wave at him.

At the bridge's summit, the van skidded to a jarring halt. To his credit, Bull reacted incredibly quickly. Stamping on the brakes, he steered the Omega up onto the pavement and slewed it across the front of the now stationary van, effectively cutting off its escape route.

Tyler jumped out. Fuelled by adrenaline, he sprinted around the side of the van and set off after the driver, who had now decamped. His heart sank when he spotted the two mopeds that had been keeping lookout outside the mini-market waiting on the footpath, less than ten yards ahead of the running man.

Overhead, he could hear the distinctive *whup, whup, whup* of the helicopter and, on risking a quick glance upwards, he saw that India 99 was now hovering directly above them.

With a fearful glance over his shoulder, the fleeing Transit driver clumsily threw his leg over the seat of nearest moped. "Go, go, go!"

he screamed, tapping the rider on the back with great urgency to hurry him along.

Letting out an angry yell of frustration, Tyler ran after them, hands outstretched to drag the pillion passenger from the moped. He came tantalisingly close to succeeding but, as his fingers brushed against the man's overalls, the moped took off with a jolt, and he was left clutching at thin air.

3

I want my solicitor

Dillon looked up as the first uniform responders, their radios chattering away, charged through the mini-market's door. Outside, several more response vehicles were pulling up, their blue lights strobing brightly.

"Over here," he shouted as they were waylaid by the cashier, who had found her voice again and was rambling on about how terrible her ordeal had been. A sympathetic officer led her to one side, trying to calm her down, while the others, two men and a woman, ran over to offer Dillon assistance.

Kneeling by his prisoner, who still had an arm twisted behind his back and was now complaining about police brutality, Dillon reached into his jacket pocket and withdrew his warrant card. "I'm DI Dillon from the Homicide Command," he informed them. "This man's been arrested for armed robbery, and for attempting to blow my colleague's head off with that." He nodded towards the shotgun laying a few feet away as he spoke.

Following his eyes, the three officers glanced at the gun, then stared malevolently at the man who had tried to use it on one of their own.

"Don't suppose I could borrow some handcuffs?" Dillon asked, "only I seem to have left mine in my other suit."

The female officer in charge, a pretty brunette in her late twenties with the three chevrons of a sergeant on her epaulettes, removed a pair of rigid handcuffs from her utility belt. "You can borrow mine," she said. "As long as you promise *not* to run off with them." There was a note of warning in her voice, implying that she would hunt him down and exact a terrible vengeance if he did.

Dillon liked her sassiness. "Thank you, sergeant…?"

"Cotton. Lizzy to my friends."

Dillon smiled at her, and was pleased to see the tiniest hint of a blush appear on her face as she reciprocated. Out of habit, his eyes flew to her left hand, which he was delighted to see was ringless.

Police uniforms were notoriously unflattering, and the cumbersome Met Vests made everyone look shapeless but, from the graceful way that she moved, he could tell that Cotton was fit and athletic, unlike her colleagues, who both looked like they had been overdoing the doughnuts.

Accepting the Quick-Cuffs with a grateful nod, he applied them to his prisoner's wrists, ensuring they were securely fastened behind his back. The ram raider yelped, claiming that they were too tight, and that he could no longer feel his fingers.

His protests fell on deaf ears.

"Not so cocky now you haven't got a sawn-off in your hands, are you?" Dillon said, staring at him with utter contempt.

"I want my solicitor," the prisoner responded in a surly tone.

"Course you do," Dillon said. Standing up, he took hold of the prisoner's right elbow. "If one of you could help me get this piece of human flotsam to his feet, I'd be most grateful."

Lizzy Cotton stepped forward and, between them, they unceremoniously hoisted the prisoner into a standing position.

The man was droning on like a broken record, complaining that the cuffs were cutting into his flesh.

Dillon checked them. As he suspected, they were nowhere near as tight as the prisoner would have them believe, and he easily slid his little finger into the gap between the metal and the man's flesh to make sure, just as the Officer Safety Training manual stipulated.

At Dillon's request, one of the uniform officers stepped forward and used the pointy bit at the end of his handcuff key to double lock them. That would prevent the ratchets from working themselves any tighter.

Dillon roughly yanked the prisoner's ski mask off to reveal a pugnacious face covered by an unruly mop of ginger hair. Staring into hate-filled grey eyes, Dillon recognised the vindictive nature of the man, someone quick to anger and slow to forgive.

Lizzy Cotton winced when she saw the state of the prisoner's face; one eye was almost completely closed, his left cheek was a mass of purple bruising, and his top lip was so badly swollen that an onlooker could be forgiven for thinking that a whole bottle of Botox had just been injected into it.

"What happened?" she asked, glancing sideways at Dillon.

"He viciously assaulted my fist with his face," he replied, po-faced, "Several times."

"You hit me when I wasn't looking," the prisoner objected. "I'd like to see you try that when I'm ready for you."

Dillon's expression hardened. Clenching fists the size of small anvils, he took a menacing step towards the detained man. "I'm very tempted to uncuff you and give you a chance to put your money where your mouth is."

The prisoner blanched, took a backward step and averted his eyes. "I want my lawyer," he said, meekly.

"Tell you what, we'll call him for you once we arrive at the station," Cotton said, grabbing his arm and marching him out towards the waiting police van. "Between you and me," she informed him as she opened the rear doors for him to get in, "I reckon my colleague's done you a bit of a favour. At least now you'll have an excuse for being that ugly."

As the prisoner started yelling abuse at her, she slammed the doors in his face.

Standing behind her, Dillon nodded approvingly. He rather liked this woman.

———

As the mopeds took off, leaving him for dead, Tyler spun around and sprinted back towards the Omega. When he got there, he found that several marked units had arrived. Flashing his warrant card at the crew of a panda car, he ordered them to secure the van as a crime scene. Then, before they could ask any questions, he dived into the Omega. "Please tell me that Nine-Nine's still above those sodding mopeds?" he pleaded.

"It is," Bull confirmed, reversing off the pavement as he spoke. Shoving the selector into drive, he hit the horn to activate the two-tones, and set off towards Barking Road at breakneck speed.

The chase was continuing on the Main-Set, with the helicopter crew now providing a commentary from above.

"MP from India 99, we've got two mopeds making off from ground units in Prince Regent Lane. The second is two-up, and the pillion passenger's not wearing a helmet. They're currently heading East along Greenway towards the junction with Balaam Street. Stand by for a direction of travel... MP, both mopeds have now gone straight across Balaam Street and are continuing towards Upper Road... MP they've just turned their headlights off to try and shake us, but we're following them on the infra-red."

Tyler grabbed the mic, squeezed the PTT. "MP from Metro Sierra 93, if the mopeds split up, India 99 is to stay with the one that's two-up, and our priority is the pillion passenger, not the rider." Tyler desperately wanted all three suspects arrested, but the two moped riders had only played an ancillary role in the ram raid, whereas the pillion passenger had been up to his neck in it so, if things got sticky, he wanted everyone to know who they should focus their efforts on.

"That's all received by India 99."

"Do you know where we're going?" Tyler asked as Bull turned left into Barking Road.

"Sort of," Bull replied, which didn't inspire confidence.

"Both mopeds have gone straight across Upper Road, and are continuing along Greenway," the radio operator aboard India 99 transmitted.

Ground units with local knowledge of the area were rushing ahead of the fleeing mopeds to cover the various exits along Greenway, of which there were many, and the whole operation was being skilfully co-ordinated by the ultra-efficient operator at Information Room, who was giving a masterclass of calmness under pressure.

"What is this Greenway path thing they're on?" Tyler demanded.

"Not sure," Bull replied, overtaking several slower vehicles at the same time. "It's basically a combined cycle path and public footway, and it's surrounded by a large expanse of greenery. I think it runs from Beckton all the way over to Hackney, but I could be wrong."

Aboard the Met's AS335 Twin Squirrel helicopter, flying high above the fleeing mopeds, PS Phillip Webber focused his efforts on providing a detailed running commentary for the ground units who were rushing to contain the area, while his colleague, PC Keith Rowley, concentrated on following the suspects with the IR camera.

Down below, the mopeds arrived at a bridge spanning some railway tracks. Although the lead rider continued going straight, the second one branched off, taking a dirt track that wound its way down to the railway lines.

Webber tensed. "All units from India 99, be advised that the mopeds have just split up. The lead bike's continuing along Greenway towards Stratford High Street, but the second one's just veered left and is heading for the train tracks."

An authoritative voice erupted from the Main-Set speaker. *"India 99 from Metro Sierra 93, stay with the second moped. I repeat, stay with the second one."*

"Received by India 99," Webber acknowledged.

The railway tracks ran north to south, servicing trains on the National Rail, Docklands Light Rail and London Underground networks. The moped was now heading south, towards West Ham,

DIAMONDS AND DEATH

and Webber could see the station up ahead. Worryingly, two trains were just pulling into separate platforms.

"All units from India 99, the moped's heading straight for West Ham train station. A couple of trains have just pulled in and are about to start offloading passengers. We need to get ground units there ASAP, because if they manage to dump the bike and blend into the crowd leaving the station, we won't be able to distinguish who's who."

Inside the Omega, Tyler swore loudly and profusely. "How close are we to West Ham station?" he demanded.

Bull grimaced, then shook his head. "Not close enough."

With an agitated sigh, Tyler sagged back in his seat. "Get us there as quickly as you can," he said, suddenly feeling drained. He hated to admit it, but the ram raiders had planned the job, and their getaway, with military precision. As angry as he was, he couldn't help but admire their audaciousness.

The Main-Set crackled into life, and Tyler leaned forward to listen to the transmission.

"All units from India 99, the suspects have just ridden straight up onto one of the platforms. Stand by… All units, all units, it's a decamp. They're off on foot, running towards the station exit… They're merging into the crowd entering the station building and it's a loss, loss, loss."

"Damn!" Tyler growled, slamming a fist down on the centre console.

The radio became non-stop with frenetic chatter. Several marked units announced that they were pulling up on scene, and the local radio channel was linked to the Main-Set so that officers who were responding from other divisions could hear what was going on.

Tyler listened intently, feeling his heart rate increase as the tension mounted. "Come on," he willed them. "Put in a containment and stop everyone from leaving."

"MP from Kilo One," a new voice transmitted, and it sounded stressed.

Kilo One was the call sign for Forest Gate's pursuit car, which had been one of the first units on scene.

"Kilo One, go ahead, MP over."

"MP, we've got people spilling out of the station from two different trains that have just arrived, and we don't have enough officers to stop them all. Can the unit that originally put this chase up give us a detailed description of the two suspects, please?"

Tyler groaned. What could he tell them that would realistically help? "Units at West Ham station from Metro Sierra 93, both are IC1 males. The pillion passenger was tall and stocky, and he was wearing a ski mask and dark overalls; the moped rider was slim, and he was dressed in a dark, baggy hoodie and jeans." As a description, he conceded that it was next to useless, but it was the best he could do.

There was a pregnant pause, then the officer from Kilo One said, as tactfully as he could under the circumstances, *"...Er, yes, received. We'll do our best."*

Tyler cringed with embarrassment.

———

By the time the Omega pulled up outside West Ham station, the excitement had long since dissipated and the commuters had all been allowed to leave. Unsurprisingly, with the descriptions Tyler had provided being so vague, there had been no grounds to detain them.

A half dozen uniform officers had been deployed in a loose cordon to secure the station as a crime scene, and Tyler urgently sought out the skipper in charge. "I take it you had no luck finding the suspects?" he asked, holding out his warrant card for inspection.

The sergeant, a portly man in his mid-forties, raised an exasperated eyebrow. "Didn't exactly have much of a description to go on, did we, guv?" he pointed out.

Tyler glared at him. "Point taken. Have we found the moped yet?"

The skipper nodded. "Yep, it's lying on its side up on one of the platforms. I've got an officer standing watch over it."

"What about the rider's helmet and the passenger's overalls?"

"The overalls were stashed down the back of a cistern in the male toilets, and the helmet was lobbed over the fence by the exit. Landed in some wasteland on the other side." He pointed towards where a bored looking PC in a florescent jacket was standing with a crime scene log in his hand.

Tyler grunted. "I want it left in place till it's been photographed, then scenes of crime can bag it for us."

"That's the instruction I've already given," the skipper said, and the brusqueness of his tone inferred that he didn't need some jumped-up 'suit' from a Central Squad teaching him how to do his job.

"What about CCTV? Has anyone checked that yet?"

The skipper nodded. "We have, sir. There are cameras dotted along all the platforms and at various points inside the station building, but we can't access them tonight."

Tyler was about to tell him to get onto TfL and see if they could access the footage remotely, when Steve Bull gave his sleeve an urgent tug. "What?" he snapped, and immediately regretted doing so. His face softened, and he reached out to squeeze Bull's arm. "Sorry, Stevie."

"Don't sweat it," Bull said, making Tyler feel even more guilty over his outburst. "Thought you'd want to know; it's just come over the Main-Set that the other moped rider's been detained after stacking his bike in Stratford High Street."

That was good news, and it made Tyler feel slightly better about the two suspects who were still adrift. Hopefully, even if they weren't apprehended that night, the lab would retrieve wearer DNA from the discarded overalls and crash helmet, and they would be identified through that. In the meantime, it wouldn't hurt to start trawling through the various intelligence databases to identify the known associates of the two men who were already in custody, and start visiting them.

Tyler's phone rang and, on seeing the incoming call was from

Dillon, he excused himself from the uniform sergeant to answer it. The man didn't seem particularly sad to see him go.

"How are you getting on at your end?" he asked.

"*Fine,*" Dillon said. "*Well, apart from the fact that that nutty cashier tried to charge me for the ice cream I dropped when the van smashed through the window.*"

Tyler grinned, imagining his friend's indignant reaction to that. "Where are you taking your prisoner?"

"*He's on his way to Newham as we speak,*" Dillon informed him. "*I've told the escorting officers to seize all his clothing before he goes into a cell, and I've instructed that he's not to use the loo until GSR swabs have been taken from his face and hands.*"

Following the discharge of a firearm, gunshot residue often clings to the shooter's skin and clothing for several hours afterwards. Unfortunately, the criminals who used guns were becoming more forensically aware, and they were routinely requesting that they be allowed to go to the toilet the moment they arrived at a police station. When permitted to do so, they had taken to washing themselves in their own urine, which was very good at removing GSR.

"Well done," Tyler said. "I'm over at West Ham train station at the moment. The good news is that one of the moped riders has just been nicked. The bad news is that we're still two adrift, including the big bloke who was working the angle grinder. I'm just making sure that everything's under control here, then I'll make my way over to Newham, so we can write our notes up together."

"*That sounds like a plan,*" Dillon said. "*By the way, are we keeping this, or handing it over to the Flying Squad?*"

As the ram raiders had committed an armed robbery, the investigation fell squarely within the remit of SO8, the Flying Squad.

"Don't know yet," Tyler said. His instinct was to keep it, but he knew that his boss, DCS George Holland, would go into one if he did. "Probably not, but we'll see."

4

TUESDAY 2ND OCTOBER 2001

Diamonds

Annie Jenkins attached the large, strap-on dildo, pulling it as tight as it would go. Watching on expectantly, the spaced-out figure kneeling on the king-sized bed, waiting patiently on hands and knees to be done doggy-style, giggled expectantly.

Annie wore a bodice, stockings and suspenders, while her partner was clad in a shiny, all-in-one, black PVC cat suit and a pair of stilettos. The back of the suit had been cut out to expose pale, naked buttocks. Unlike some of the buxom porn stars Annie had previously worked with, this one was a scrawny looking thing with no boobs to speak of and long brown hair that hung down demurely over the face, shielding it from view.

Taking a toke from the spliff they were sharing, Annie checked the lighting, made sure that all three cameras were recording, and then clambered onto the bed to position herself behind her partner. She passed the spliff forward and waited while her co-star took a final drag before stubbing it out in the ashtray on the floor.

Enjoying a spliff to make them mellow seemed pretty tame in comparison to what had gone on in the old days, when Annie had been making these films on a regular basis. Back then, a lot of the performers, herself included, had taken a cocktail of drugs before filming, to give them a buzz and get them in the mood.

Annie snatched a tube of KY Jelly from the bedside table and squirted a large glob onto her hand. "Are you ready?" she asked.

The response was a throaty laugh, and a slurred voice confirmed, "I'm horny as fuck."

In addition to the cannabis, a half bottle of vodka had also been consumed since arriving at the studio, to help them relax.

"Okay, let's get into character then," Annie said. "Ready? Three, two one… and action!"

Adopting a seductive pose, Annie pouted at the camera, let out a low groan of fake pleasure, and leaned forward to coat her lover's anus with the lubricant.

The figure kneeling on the bed shuddered with delight, then bit down on the pillow in anticipation.

Annie carefully positioned the tip of the dildo against her partner's anus and began making little circles with the tip. "I want to ride you," she moaned. "I want to make you scream with pleasure."

"Put your big juicy cock deep inside me," her co-star's trembling voice responded, lustfully.

As soon as Annie obliged, the head on the pillow came up sharply, its owner gasping in pleasure. Inserting it deeper, Annie began to get into a rhythm that saw each forward movement met by backwards thrusting hips that were eager to meet the advancing sex toy.

"You're so sexy," Annie purred, slapping her partner's bony buttocks.

They were making the script up as they went along, and Annie made a mental note to have something prepared next time, as what they were saying to each other sounded a little repetitive and very cliche.

The moaning intensified as the dildo penetrated deeper, and Annie reached around her partner's front and began stroking non-existent breasts, while licking her lips erotically for the benefit of the camera. It had been a while since she had done this, and she was trying to remember all the tips she had been given for turning the audience on.

As she butt-fucked her partner, Annie wondered how many perverts would wank themselves off while watching this? The more the merrier, as far as she was concerned, as long as they were all paying her for the privilege.

Casper Wright exuded such an aura of menace that most people crossed the road to avoid him, and even those who were brave enough to hold their nerve studiously avoided making eye contact as they walked past, just in case he took it the wrong way and turned on them.

At six-feet-seven inches tall, the beady eyed albino was built like a brick outhouse. His shovel sized hands seemed disproportionately larger than the rest of his body, and they habitually hung down by his sides, creating an impression that he dragged them along the floor like a primate.

Stooping down to receive instructions from his much shorter associate, Fred Wiggins, the giant's face creased into a mask of intense concentration.

His hulking physique, broad sloping forehead, and Neanderthal mannerisms had made Casper the regular butt of jokes amongst the admin girls at the head office of Willard Betting. Behind his back, they sniggered at him and called him *The Missing Link*. Some of them even made little ape noises when he walked into the room, although they were always extremely careful to ensure that he couldn't hear them doing it; Casper wasn't exactly known for his sense of humour.

"So, you understand what I want you to do when we get there?" Wiggins asked in his gravelly Canning Town accent. He spoke slowly, as though addressing a child with learning difficulties. Blessed with the guile and cunning of a fox, the spindly gangster was the total antithesis of Casper, and he was the only person who could handle the volatile giant when he threw a strop.

Casper nodded slowly, digesting what he had been told. He rarely spoke, and when he did, his sentences tended to be short and simple.

Wiggins reached up and ruffled his hair. "Good lad," he said, as if addressing an obedient dog.

With Casper trailing along behind, Wiggins made his way into the open plan general admin area of Willard Betting's head office. As always, the room was a hive of activity, with people either rushing back and forth between their desks and the various filing cabinets that littered the room, or holding telephone conversations with clients, suppliers or branch managers. As in the betting shops themselves, there were notice boards listing the day's racing, taken from the trade issue of the *Racing Post*, and a bank of TV screens along the back wall, from which the racing could be viewed.

"Afternoon, Mr Wiggins," Carrie McCullen called out as he walked past the glass partition that separated her office from the open plan general admin area.

Carrie was Willard's PA. She was a very pretty girl, bubbly too, and although he knew that she 'batted for the other side,' Wiggins could never resist flirting with her. One day, he promised himself, by hook or by crook, he would find a way to get her into bed and show her what she had been missing for all these years. Pausing in the doorway, he fired a cheeky wink in her direction.

"Alright, gorgeous?"

Carrie responded with a saucy giggle, and waved him in. "Good thanks, how about yourself?" She had a strong Cockney accent, and the way she spoke always reminded Wiggins of Barbara Windsor.

Even though he was on his way out to do a job, and couldn't really spare the time to fraternise, her invite was too tempting to resist. "Couldn't be better," he declared, plonking himself down on the edge of her desk.

Carrie was typing out a document on company headed paper. On the pretext of being interested in its contents, Wiggins leaned over her shoulder, secretly hoping to grab a sneak peek down the front of her ample cleavage. "What are you typing, treacle?" he enquired.

Carrie's nose wrinkled. "Just a boring instruction from Mr Willard to all the branch managers."

The art of conversation was lost on Casper, so he took up station behind Wiggins and waited for them to finish talking, a silent automaton awaiting orders.

Having been unsuccessful in his attempt to ogle her breasts, Wiggins quickly grew tired of making idle chit-chat. Waving farewell to Carrie, he buttoned up his suit jacket and signalled for the white-haired giant to follow him.

"Frank the Tank's backing us up, and I've asked him to pick up the jewellery expert on his way over," Wiggins said as they passed through the service entrance at the back of the building and crossed the road towards his car.

Ignoring the vehicles whizzing by, Casper stopped in the middle of the road. A dark scowl blighted his features. "We don't need no backup," he protested, sounding like a petulant child.

Wiggins had expected this, and he knew exactly how to handle Casper's churlish reaction.

"I know we don't, old son," he responded with a kindly smile, "but Mr Willard insisted on it and, as we both know, it's not for us to question *his* decisions."

Casper thought about that for a moment, and then shrugged his enormous shoulders, a slow and ponderous movement that seemed to take ages to complete.

"I suppose," he mumbled, unhappily.

"That's the attitude, old son," Wiggins announced, playfully punching him on the arm. It was like hitting a telephone pole.

As he resumed walking, Casper seemed thoughtful. "Are we gonna be tooled up?"

"Yep. There's a shooter in the boot for you," Wiggins replied. "Frankie's bringing his own firepower."

That cheered the giant up no end. He liked guns. "Cool," he said, joining Wiggins by the rear of the car.

Wiggins opened the boot and removed a bulky object wrapped

in a cloth. He handed it to Casper, who snatched it from his hand and eagerly began unwrapping it.

"Remember, though," Wiggins warned with a stern wag of his spindly finger, "you don't use it unless I tell you to. Got it?"

Casper had once confided in Wiggins that inflicting pain on others always gave him a lazy-lob, and he'd naively asked if that was a normal reaction for someone in his line of work. Wiggins had responded diplomatically by saying, "It is for you, me old mucker."

The lumbering giant frowned, and then tucked the heavy calibre pistol into his waistband.

"Okay," he said, sounding a trifle disappointed.

Clicking the key fob to release the central locking on his gleaming Audi A4 Quattro, Wiggins chuckled to himself as he recalled the strange conversation. It was one of many they had had over the years.

Casper mimicked the laugh, not really understanding what was funny, but instinctively wanting to please Wiggins.

Frank the Tank Kyle was almost as broad as Casper but a few inches shorter. He was waiting for them in a little car park at the back of a rundown pub in Boleyn Road. In his mid-forties, he had a square jaw, a thick mane of wavy brown hair, and a neatly trimmed moustache. His day job was managing the Stratford branch of Willard Betting, but he was also one of Jonas Willard's most trusted enforcers.

"Alright boys," he greeted them cheerfully as he stepped out of his Merc, where he had been reading a copy of *The Sun* while awaiting their arrival.

His tight-fitting shirt strained at the seams as it battled to contain the powerfully built body within, and a thick gold chain hung gaudily from his neck. With a cocky grin, he strutted over to join Wiggins and Casper.

"Alright, Frankie?" Wiggins responded, reluctantly accepting the calloused hand that had been offered.

Kyle turned to the albino next. "Alright, Casper?" he said, holding out his hand.

Casper responded with a sullen nod, but said nothing, and Frankie's hand was left dangling in the air.

After an awkward silence, Kyle withdrew it and turned to Wiggins, clearly offended. "What's the matter with him?"

"Casper's not big on exchanging pleasantries," Wiggins said by way of explanation, then nodded towards a thin, elderly man with a long, bulbous nose and a thatch of untidy grey hair who was sitting in the front passenger seat of Kyle's car, watching them apprehensively through a pair of wire framed spectacles. "Is that the jeweller?"

Kyle nodded, still miffed that Casper had blanked him. "Yep. That's Avram. What he doesn't know about diamonds ain't worth knowing."

"I'm sure, but can he be trusted?" Wiggins asked, casting a sceptical eye over the aging jeweller, who promptly looked away.

"Avram's sound as a pound," Kyle assured him. "Mr Willard's used his services several times before and he's always proved very reliable."

Wiggins grunted. "Then you'd better call him over."

Kyle stuck two fingers in his mouth and whistled loudly.

Wiggins winced at the shrill noise, then gave Kyle a filthy look for making it.

When the old man looked up, Kyle made an impatient come-hither gesture.

The jeweller got out of the car. Dressed in a wrinkled black suit that looked two sizes too big for him, and clutching an ancient briefcase to his thin chest, he approached them with obvious trepidation.

Wiggins acknowledged him with a curt nod, at the same time clocking the black fabric kippah that adorned the crown of Avram's head. These skullcaps were worn by religious Jews, of which North London had a large population. "We'll take my car," he said, indicating for the others to get in.

Kyle made to open the front passenger door, but Casper placed a restraining hand on his arm.

"That's my seat."

Kyle released the handle and moved back. "Sure," he said, smiling placatingly. "No problem. I'll sit in the back with Avram."

The meeting had been arranged to take place in the back room of a seedy little snooker club above a row of dilapidated shops, halfway along Leytonstone High Road. They had agreed to meet there because it was located in neutral territory, which meant that neither side would have an advantage over the other.

A downwards facing video camera had been mounted on the wall above the entrance, and access to the club's interior was strictly controlled by a buzzer system operated from inside. Although this was ostensibly a security measure to deny access to non-members and rabble rousers, in reality it had been installed to prevent the police from being able to barge straight in if they turned up unexpectedly, as they were sometimes prone to do, either to conduct a random licensing visit or to search the hall for a local toerag who happened to be wanted.

Wiggins pressed the buzzer and stared up at the camera impatiently. Several seconds passed, then there was a dull zizzing noise and the heavy metal door popped open with a loud click. Closely followed by his two enforcers and Avram, Wiggins ascended the narrow staircase.

As they passed through the wooden swing doors at the top, the four men found themselves in a rectangular shaped, high-ceilinged room with a half dozen blacked out windows dotted along the side facing out onto the High Road. The lower half of the walls were wood panelled, while the top half had been painted the same shade of green as the snooker tables themselves.

The lighting had been turned down low in order to create the right atmosphere to play snooker. A line of eight full size, slate bed Riley snooker tables, each of which was illuminated by a low hanging light that shone down on the smooth green baize, were evenly spaced out along the centre of the room.

It was a few minutes shy of five o'clock, so only about half the tables were currently occupied, but it would get much busier as the evening progressed. There was a little bar at the far end of the room, and several punters were sitting at it, holding muted conversations. Eight small round tables, one for each snooker table, had been set up along the carpeted area that ran down the left-hand side of the hall, providing players with somewhere to sit and enjoy their drinks between shots.

They were greeted by the manager, who had been told to expect them. He was a shifty looking man of indeterminable age, with a balding head, a five o'clock shadow, and the bleary eyes of a heavy drinker. Reeking of cigarette smoke and cheap cologne, he showed Wiggins into a pokey little office at the rear of the hall, wedged between the stock room and staff toilet. The only illumination was provided by a weak desk lamp, so the edges of the room were ensconced in shadow.

As he passed through the doorway, Wiggins saw that his opposite number had already arrived, and had lost no time in making himself comfortable behind the rickety desk that dominated the room.

The air inside swirled with thick cigarette smoke.

The man he was there to negotiate with was a morbidly obese Turk, with a thick Saddam Hussein type moustache and a surly expression. Two unshaven goons, who were doing their best to look intimidating, flanked him, one on each side of the desk. They were big units, of roughly comparable size to Frank the Tank but, instead of having his wide shoulders, barrel chest and narrow waist, they had the big beer bellies of men who liked to drink too much and exercise too little. Wiggins was confident that Casper would quickly make short work of them both if things got physical.

Much to Wiggins' surprise and annoyance, three more Turks were lurking in the shadows over by the back wall. They were leaner, fitter, and they moved with the confidence of men who knew how to handle themselves.

It had been agreed that each negotiator would only bring two minders to the meeting, and Wiggins couldn't help but wonder if this blatant breech in etiquette signalled trouble.

Were the Turks planning some skulduggery?

He wouldn't put it past them.

As subtly as he could, Wiggins leaned in and nudged Casper. "Keep your eyes peeled," he whispered. "I don't trust this lot."

Casper grunted his understanding.

With a lazy gesture of his hand, the seated Turk indicated for Wiggins to take the empty chair on the opposite side of the desk, then blew out a thick plume of smoke from the Camel cigarette he was smoking. "Can I get you a drink, Mr Wiggins?" he asked in heavily accented English.

"No, thank you," Wiggins replied with a polite smile. "I'd rather we got straight down to business."

Casper hovered by his left shoulder, staring menacingly at the opposition, while Kyle silently took up station by the door, behind him and off to his right. The elderly jeweller, Avram, was standing immediately behind him, and Wiggins could tell he was scared from the ragged sound of his breathing.

"Very well," the Turk said, retrieving a black leather briefcase from the floor. He clumsily worked the clasps with his podgy fingers, and then pushed it open. From inside, he withdrew a small velvet bag that had been pulled together with a drawstring. "As you know," he said with a mirthless smile, "my uncle's business ventures don't usually include trading in precious stones."

Wiggins acknowledged his statement with a wry smile. The man sitting in front of him was Yusuf Kaya, and his uncle was Abdullah Goren, the leader of a powerful North London based Kurdish-Turkish crime gang. Their usual 'business ventures' consisted mainly of prostitution, protection rackets, gun running and the widescale importation and distribution of heroin.

The gems he was about to enter into negotiations over had come into Goren's hands by way of accident, and the gang leader was looking to sell them on as quickly as possible. If a deal could be struck, this was a transaction in which all parties concerned could walk away with a tidy little profit, and their respective bosses had tasked Kaya and Wiggins to work out the finer details and negotiate a price on their behalf.

Yusuf Kaya poured the stones out onto the desk. "Please feel free to examine them," he said, dropping the blue velvet bag back in the briefcase.

Without taking his eyes off Kaya, Wiggins snapped his fingers, and pointed at the diamonds.

Taking his cue, Avram timidly stepped forward. With a shaking hand, he placed his ancient briefcase on the desk, next to Kaya's much newer one. Opening it up, the gemologist removed a pair of cotton gloves and put them on. Then he removed a loupe – a special magnifying glass used to examine diamonds, gemstones and other jewellery. Taking his time, he proceeded to pick up random stones and look for blemishes and imperfections within them. As he had told Wiggins on the way over, while a fake diamond could be perfectly constructed, real diamonds will have small imperfections known as inclusions.

Muttering away to himself in Yiddish as he evaluated the gems, Avram quickly became so engrossed in his work that he forgot all about the other people in the room, all of whom were staring at him intently. When he had finished his inspection, Avram returned the loupe and his cotton gloves to his briefcase, which he then tucked under his arm.

Wiggins stood up. "I'd like a moment alone with my associate," he announced, beckoning for Avram to follow him. "You two wait here," he instructed Casper and Kyle, inferring that they should keep their eyes on the jewels in case the Turks tried to switch them while he was out of the room.

"Well?" he demanded as soon as he and Avram were alone.

Avram, whose skittish movements reminded Wiggins of a dormouse, nodded nervously, and then looked around to make sure they couldn't be overheard. "The stones are real, and very valuable," he confirmed.

Wiggins grinned. "Excellent," he said, rubbing his hands together greedily. "Right then, let's get down to brass tacks. How much are they realistically worth?"

Avram stroked the bristles on his pointy chin thoughtfully. "On the open market? Probably just north of a million and a half," he estimated.

The gemologist had very dirty fingernails, Wiggins noticed with some distaste.

"Forgive my directness," Avram said, meekly, "but I'm assuming the lawfulness of their current ownership is somewhat… questionable?"

"Is that a problem?" Wiggins asked.

The old jeweller shrugged, and his face took on a pained expression. "Only in so much as it will have an impact on what we can ask for them when we sell them on. Even so, I could probably still get you between eight and nine-hundred thousand for them."

Wiggins stared at him, wondering just how much the diamonds were really worth. He hadn't been born yesterday, and if the wily old jeweller was saying he could get Mr Willard the best part of a million quid for them, their true value was probably twenty to thirty per cent higher than Avram had told him, and the difference would go straight into his pocket.

"So, what's the most I should be prepared to pay for them?" Wiggins asked.

Avram wrung his hands together as he considered this. "I would start low, say two hundred grand, but be prepared to go up to four hundred. That would be a very fair price. Anything more will start to eat into your profits, and I would strongly advise against paying more than half a mil. Trust me, it won't be easy for the Turks to find another buyer who's willing to offer that much."

When Wiggins returned to the negotiating table, the Turk was impatient to seal the deal.

"So, are you satisfied the gems are real?" he asked, lighting up another Camel.

"I am," Wiggins said, "and I'd be willing to offer you two hundred large to take them off your hands."

Yusuf Kaya laughed loudly. A hard guttural sound, it was completely devoid of humour. "Yes, very funny. When you're finished making your little jokes, perhaps we could start talking seriously."

Leaning forwards, Wiggins adopted a conciliatory manner. "They're worth far more than that, old son, and I'm not denying it. The problem, as I understand it, is that stones of this quality will inevitably attract a lot of unwanted attention when we try to shift them on, which means we'll have to grease a lot of palms to persuade the greedy bastards who could make life awkward for us to turn a blind eye. That'll eat heavily into our profits."

"Not that heavily," Kaya said, eyeing him disdainfully.

Wiggins didn't reply. He just sat there, happy to let the silence stretch on.

After a few seconds, Kaya started to get a little restless. He glanced at his watch, which didn't bode well. "I don't have all day," the Turk said, impatiently.

"Very well," Wiggins said. He spread his arms magnanimously, as though he were about to make a huge concession. "I can go as high as three hundred, but that's pushing me right to the top of my budget."

With a sigh, Kaya picked up the velvet bag and began sweeping the diamonds back into it. "In that case, I fear there is no deal to be done here, and we must look elsewhere."

As the Turk made to rise, Frank the Tank whipped out a Colt Python .357 magnum revolver from the rear of his waistband. Pointing the six-inch long, stainless-steel barrel straight at Kaya's head, he said, "Nobody's going anywhere until Mr Wiggins says so."

Glancing back over his shoulder, Wiggins stared at him in open mouthed disbelief. What the fuck was the steroid taking imbecile playing at?

In the blink of an eye, the five Turkish bodyguards had drawn weapons of their own, and they were pointing them at Wiggins and his men.

Everyone apart from Avram, who had dropped to the floor in fear, seemed to be shouting at everyone else, and their raised voices quickly became a jumbled blur of angry noise.

In the ensuing chaos, Casper lunged forward, knocking the

Turk standing nearest to him out with a punch to the jaw that would probably have felled an adult rhino. Before anyone else could react, he rammed his own gun, a model 1911 Colt .45 semi-automatic, under Kaya's undulating chins, making him cry out in pain. At the same time, Casper's free hand gripped the Turk's greasy hair, savagely twisting his head sideways. "If anybody moves, I'll splatter his brains all over the fucking ceiling," the raging albino snarled.

Everyone froze.

Still pointing their guns at each other, they realised that they were locked in a standoff, and neither side wanted to be the first to blink.

Moving with exaggerated slowness, Wiggins raised his hands in what he hoped would be seen as a placating gesture. "Everybody needs to relax," he said, speaking softly in an effort to calm the situation down. "There's no need for things to get out of hand, and I'd like to suggest that everyone lowers their weapons so that Mr Kaya and I can continue talking."

Nobody moved; nobody spoke. The only sounds in the room were the gunmen's ragged breathing and Avram's terrified mewling. Outside, in the snooker hall, someone cheered, and this was followed by a bout of raucous laughter.

The eyes of the four Turkish gunmen who remained standing continuously flitted from Casper and their boss to Frank the Tank. Wiggins could almost hear the cogs in their heads turning as they tried to work out whether to do as he'd suggested, and lower their weapons, or open fire and hope for the best.

The room's atmosphere was charged with explosive energy, and all it would take to ignite it was a wrong word or a sudden movement. Fearing that the situation was fast becoming irredeemable, Wiggins turned to Casper. "Be a good lad and let Mr Kaya go," he instructed.

With a snarl, Casper's head spun in his direction, and he did not look happy.

Wiggins knew they would be lucky to survive the gun battle if Casper killed the Turk and, even if they did, the resulting fallout would spark a war with the Turkish mafia that Jonas Willard couldn't possibly hope to win.

Wiggins licked his lips. "Casper, listen to me," he ordered, locking eyes with the dim-witted giant as he spoke. "Remember what I said back at the office, that you were only to use the gun if I told you to?"

Casper frowned as he tried to recall the conversation, then nodded reluctantly.

"Well, I haven't told you to use it, have I lad, so be a good boy and let Mr Kaya go."

For a long moment, Casper stared at him defiantly. Then, with an angry grunt, he released his grip on Yusuf Kaya's hair and stepped back, lowering his gun. He glared at Wiggins with the petulant expression of a child whose favourite toy had just been confiscated as a punishment for bad behaviour.

His face ashen, Kaya slowly sat up and massaged the underside of his wobbly chin, in which an angry indent from the muzzle of Casper's gun could clearly be seen.

Wiggins turned to Kyle, who was still pointing his weapon at the Turks. "Put the bloody gun down, Frankie," he snapped, furious with the bodybuilder for nearly getting them all killed.

"But—"

"Just fucking do it!"

Wilting under Wiggins' fierce gaze, Kyle hesitantly lowered his gun.

Still massaging his flabby chin, Kaya waved for his men to do likewise, and everyone in the room breathed a sigh of relief as they stepped back from the brink.

"This is an affront to my honour," Kaya snarled, his jowls quivering with anger. "Never have I been so insulted."

Wiggins knew how seriously the Turks viewed matters of honour, and the last thing he wanted to do was trigger a blood vendetta. Taking a deep breath, and speaking with as much deference as he could muster, he said, "Mr Kaya, I'm deeply sorry for the unfortunate misunderstanding, truly I am." He paused long enough to fire another caustic look over his shoulder at Kyle before continuing. "To make amends, I would like to increase my offer for the gems to four hundred thousand pounds. That's far more than I was authorised to pay," he lied, "but, I think Mr Willard would want me to make this very generous gesture as a means of compensating you for being manhandled. Would that be enough to put things right between us, Mr Kaya?"

The Turk studied him through narrowed eyes. Still rubbing his neck, he glanced up at Casper, who scowled back hatefully. "That man is an animal," he hissed.

Wiggins smiled apologetically. "He was just doing his job, Mr Kaya, which is to protect me, so please don't take it personally. I'm offering you four hundred thousand, which is considerably more than you'll get elsewhere, and I'm only willing to stump up that much dosh to make amends for your being manhandled. So, what do you say? Do we have a deal?"

Although the four Turks had lowered their weapons, they hadn't put them away, Wiggins noticed, and they were now looking at Kaya for guidance. Wiggins' mouth ran dry. In the next few seconds, they would either cement the deal or there would be a bloodbath. The decision rested entirely in Kaya's hands.

On the floor, the Turk that Casper had hit a few moments ago stirred, and one of his colleagues rushed over to help him to his feet.

"You have the money with you?" Kaya asked.

Wiggins breathed a sigh of relief. "It's in the car. If we have a deal, I'll send one of my men to fetch it."

The Turk nodded, just once, and then winced at the pain the movement caused him. He glanced up at Casper again. "Very well. Send your lackey to fetch the money before I change my mind."

Wiggins pulled his blue Audi into the car park at the rear of the pub in Boleyn Road. Stopping opposite Kyle's Merc, he angrily yanked the handbrake up and killed the engine.

The journey back from the snooker club had been a tense one, and Wiggins had spent most of it venting his fury at Kyle over the hot-headed stupidity that had nearly gotten them all killed.

"Right, you musclebound cunt, get out of my motor," he said, scowling at Kyle in his rear-view mirror.

Kyle did as he was told, and then stood sheepishly by the side of the car. In his left hand, he clutched the black briefcase containing the gems, which Kaya had thrown in for free, and the bag containing the remaining cash from the half a million stake Willard had provided for their purchase.

"I'm sorry, Fred," he said, miserably. "I don't know how many times you expect me to say it, but–"

"Shut up," Wiggins snapped, cutting him off. "You," he said, pointing at Avram. "Go and wait by Frankie's car."

Watching the old Jew scuttle off, Wiggins got the distinct impression that Avram hadn't been able to get away quickly enough.

"You're a fucking liability, Frankie," Wiggins said once the jeweller was out of earshot, "and you're lucky I'm not letting Casper rip your empty head off for causing me so much grief today. Now, sod off home and make sure you put that cash back in the office safe first thing in the morning."

"I will," Frank promised, looking browbeaten.

"And keep those bloody gems somewhere safe until Avram finds us a buyer," Wiggins added.

"Don't worry about the diamonds, Fred," Kyle assured him. "I'll lock them away in the safe at my gaff and–"

Wiggins held up a hand to silence him. "I don't need to know where they are, you dickhead, just make sure that nothing happens to them, cause if it does, you'll end up wearing a concrete overcoat and propping up a motorway bypass somewhere between here and Birmingham, got it?"

Kyle swallowed hard, knowing that this was no idle threat. If the rumours were to be believed, Wiggins had already made several men who had displeased him or Mr Willard disappear.

"Yeah, no worries, Fred," he said, nodding vigorously to appease the other man. "They'll be safe as houses with me."

5

WEDNESDAY 3RD OCTOBER 2001

You almost burned the house down

Carrie McCullen was in a rush. She had overslept and was now in danger of being late for work, which wouldn't go down well. Mr Willard was a stickler for good time keeping. If she got a wiggle on, she might still just make it, but her tosspot twin brother was hogging the bathroom as per usual.

"How much longer are you going to be, Aidan?" she hollered, rapping on the door to get his attention.

"Sod off," came the surly reply from inside.

Arrogant, selfish bastard!

Carrie swallowed the waspish retort she so desperately wanted to shout, knowing it would only make matters worse. Taking a deep breath to calm herself, she thumped the door again, this time using the bottom of her fist instead of her knuckles. "Aidan, *please!* I'm going to be late for work."

A harsh laugh broke out behind the closed door. "Serves you right for sleeping in then, you lazy cow."

"I swear, I'll swing for that bastard one day," she muttered as she stomped back to her bedroom.

Plonking herself down on the end of her bed, from where she could keep an eye on the bathroom door, Carrie anxiously checked her watch. It was already half-seven, and she really needed to be out of the door by eight-fifteen at the absolute latest. By the time she showered, dressed and then applied her makeup, there would barely be enough time for breakfast, let alone to prepare a packed lunch for work.

Carrie could be quite feisty when provoked, and it required all her willpower not to start screaming at Aidan to pull his finger out. The only thing stopping her was the knowledge that, the more fuss she made, the longer the horrible little cretin would make her wait.

Eventually, the bathroom door opened, and Aidan emerged with a thick towel wrapped around his slender waist. Still wet from the long shower he had just taken, his hairless torso glistened with water.

Carrie hadn't seen him topless for quite some time, and she was startled to see how worryingly thin he had become. He looked emaciated. She blamed the drugs and alcohol for his weight loss; they had destroyed his appetite and turned him into a walking skeleton.

A cruel smile tugged at the corners of his mouth when he spotted her sitting on her bed.

"All yours, sis," he said, rubbing his closely cropped head with a hand towel.

Although they were twins, with her being the oldest by ten whole minutes, Carrie and Aidan were polar opposites, and they had grated on each other since the day they emerged from their mother's womb. Left alone together for more than a few minutes, the inevitable outcome was an acrimonious argument or a full-blown fight.

In their formative years, Aidan had acquired a well-deserved reputation for being lazy and disruptive, while Carrie had been a hard-working student who knew what she wanted from life and was prepared to sweat blood and tears to get it.

After leaving secondary school, Carrie had walked straight into a good job, and she had never known unemployment in all the years that had passed. Aidan, on the other hand, had drifted aimlessly from one low-income job to another, and she had lost count of the number of times he had been fired over his tardiness and slovenly behaviour. It didn't help that he was a heavy skunk cannabis user, or that he had started to use crack cocaine with increasing regularity. The excessive drug usage, coupled with his regular binge drinking, had taken its toll and, although he was only thirty-four, he looked much older.

Aidan's latest job involved him working as a warehouse man for a firm based in Houndsditch but, in the two months that he had been working there, he had already received a number of warnings for being late, and had recently been called in by his manager to discuss the alarming number of sick days he had taken off. If his past form was anything to go by, it wouldn't be long until his current employers decided that enough was enough and gave him the sack.

Carrie stormed out of her room, conscious that time was against her.

"No need to thank me," Aidan goaded, his voice dripping with sarcasm.

She flipped him the finger as they passed in the hallway.

"Drop dead," Aidan responded, slamming his bedroom door behind him.

"Arsehole," she shouted back, wondering why she had even bothered to waste her breath.

———

When Carrie emerged from the bathroom, fifteen minutes later, she immediately smelled burning.

"Aidan, can you smell that?" she called out in alarm.

There was no reply.

"Aidan?" Surely, he hadn't left for work already?

Carrie peered over the banister, and was horrified to see thin tendrils of smoke drifting up the stairs from the hallway below.

"Bloody hell!" she gasped, clutching her bathrobe to stop it from flapping open.

Running down the stairs as quickly as she could, Carrie followed the thickening trail of smoke into the kitchen, where she immediately saw the source of the problem. Unbelievably, a tea towel had been left next to a naked flame, and it had caught fire.

"Shit!" she yelled, furiously fanning the dense smoke with her free hand.

Holding her breath, she darted into the room and, being careful not to get herself burned in the process, plucked the burning rag from hob and threw it into the sink.

Ignoring her bursting lungs, and the fact that her eyes were stinging so badly she could hardly open them, Carrie turned the cold tap onto full. A strong jet of water burst out of the spout, and there was a long, angry hissing noise as the flames were doused.

Now that the immediate danger was over, Carrie hurriedly pushed open the window to ventilate the room. Unable to hold her breath any longer, she released it in a loud whoosh. As soon as she inhaled, the acrid smoke caught in the back of her throat, and she began coughing uncontrollably.

"Aidan," she called as she marched into the hallway.

Again, there was no answer.

Carrie opened the street door and greedily sucked in fresh air. When she finally managed to stop coughing, she returned to the kitchen to inspect the damage. Thankfully, the tea towel was no longer alight, although it was completely ruined. Still fanning the slowly dissipating smoke, Carrie turned the gas hob off and went in search of her brother, who was obviously responsible for the fire.

"Aidan!" she bellowed as she thundered up the stairs. "Where are you, you dim witted junkie?"

She pushed open his bedroom door without knocking. To her fury, her brother was slouched on his unmade bed, with a huge spiff in his mouth and a pair of earphones clamped over his head. His face was all but obscured by a giant cloud of greenish marijuana smoke.

As soon as she saw the empty bowl of porridge on the bedside table, she realised what had happened. Aidan had left the hob on after heating up the milk for his oats. They no longer had a working microwave to do that because he had blown it up the previous week by leaving a metal spoon in a bowl of soup he was preparing.

Aidan's eyes were glazed from puffing weed, and a look of drug induced confusion spread across his gaunt face as he turned towards her. Dragging himself into a sitting position, he pulled the cans from his head. "What's the matter?" he asked, his eyes vacant.

He sounded completely spaced out, she thought, shaking her head in disgust.

"You! You're the matter," she yelled. "You left the gas hob on after making your breakfast, you idiot, and a tea towel caught fire. It almost burned the house down."

Aidan stood up, struggled to focus his eyes. "Have you called the fire brigade?" he asked, striding out of his room and onto the landing.

Following behind, she shook her head. "No. I managed to put it out."

Aidan spun to face her. "If you've already put it out, what's the fucking problem?"

Carrie was enraged by his response. "YOU'RE THE PROBLEM!" she screamed. "You're a total liability. The week before last, you left the tap running in the bathroom sink and it overflowed, completely drenching the carpet and staining the plaster in the living room ceiling. Last week, you blew up the microwave by putting a metal spoon in it. I've had enough of this," she told him. "You either need to sort yourself out or find somewhere else to live."

Aidan's emaciated face flushed with anger. "This is just as much my home as yours," he snapped, covering her skin with little specs of spittle.

Carrie wiped her face. "That's where you're wrong," she told him, her voice acid. "When mum died, she left this place to me and Dazza, *not* you."

Damian and Doreen McCullen had purchased their three-bedroom council house in Ivy Street, near Hoxton Market, under the 'Right to Buy' scheme that had been introduced by Margaret

Thatcher's Conservative government in 1980. Sadly, Damian had died five years ago, succumbing to a fatal heart attack at the relatively young age of sixty-eight. Doreen had survived him by four years, but she had passed on nine months ago, following a short battle with cancer.

During the reading of their mother's will, their three children had been shocked to discover that Aidan had been excluded from the inheritance on the basis that he would squander his share on drugs and alcohol, and that everything had been split between Carrie and their older brother, Darren.

Darren had left home to join the army when he was eighteen. Having travelled the world and learned a trade as a mechanic, he had finally quit the military a couple of years ago, and had since opened up a small garage in Bethnal Green.

Carrie had fully expected him to pressure her into selling the family home so that he could get his hands on his share of the inheritance, but he had been more than happy for her and Aidan to continue living there.

Unfortunately, things had recently changed. Dazza's business was struggling and would probably go under without a large infusion of cash, and selling the house represented his only chance of saving it. Carrie had been exploring ways of buying him out, but this was proving extremely difficult as she couldn't get a big enough mortgage to do it on her own, and it now seemed likely that she would be forced to put the house on the market after all.

Aidan had never come to terms with being written out of his mother's will, and the mere mention of it was always enough to send him flying into a rage. Clenching his fists menacingly, he thrust his forehead against hers and forced her backwards until she collided with the wall.

"Go on," he ranted, his face contorting into an ugly snarl. "Bring *that* up again, why don't you? Rub my fucking nose in it like you always do." Without warning, he punched a section of wall a few inches away from her face, putting a large dent in the plasterboard.

Carrie screamed.

His eyes burning with hatred, Aidan drew back his fist to throw another punch, but then he seemed to think better of it. Letting his hand fall limply to his side, he spun around and strode into his bedroom, slamming the door behind him with such force that the frame shook.

Hot tears ran down Carrie's cheeks as she watched him go, and she reached out an unsteady hand for support, aware that her whole body was shaking violently.

"I fucking hate you," she heard him yell as she made her tearful way into her room to get dressed for work.

―――

Frank the Tank Kyle was mulling over the previous day's incident with the Turks as he unlocked the doors to the Stratford branch of Willard Betting. He had fucked up badly by drawing his weapon when he had; he realised that now, but he had meant well, like he always did.

Fred Wiggins was Jonas Willard's right-hand man and the heir apparent to his throne. Everyone on the firm knew that Willard was grooming Wiggins to take over from him one day. Despite knowing each other for several years, yesterday's outing had been the first time that they had actually gone out on a job together, and Kyle had so desperately wanted to impress him. Instead, his plan to make a name for himself, and enhance his reputation as a reliable hard man, had backfired, and he had nearly ended up getting them all killed.

After unlocking the shop, he opened up the alarm box and quickly entered the code to deactivate the central station alarm before it went off. The last thing he wanted, after everything else that had happened, was for the Old Bill to come flying over because they thought the place was being robbed.

Knowing that it was only a matter of time until he was summoned to head office to explain himself to Willard, Frankie had slept fitfully and, as he trudged up the stairs towards the manager's office, he yawned like a creaky door.

As Frankie placed the surplus hundred grand from the diamond purchase into his office safe, his mind turned to the little bag of diamonds at his house. He had locked them in his personal safe, next to the two hundred grand he had managed to scrape together for his and Morag's future. With all the new money laundering laws that had come into play, it was nigh on impossible to deposit large sums of cash into a bank account these days, unless you could provide an audit trail showing where it had come from, which of course, being a criminal, he couldn't. That was why he had invested in the Chubb. It was a top of the range model, and had come highly recommended by a safe cracking buddy of his. In addition to the Chubb, his house was fitted with an expensive alarm, which went straight through to the local nick, and there were good locks on all the doors and windows. Morag regularly complained that it was like living in Fort-fucking-Knox.

Kyle had barely sat down when the telephone on his desk started ringing. It was his private number too, not the outside line that punters used to reach him on. He stared at it in trepidation for a moment, then grabbed the receiver and jammed it against his ear.

"Hello? Frank Kyle speaking," he said, trying to inject a tone of carefree confidence into his voice.

The colour drained from his face the instant he heard his caller's voice.

He listened for a few moments, nodding respectfully every now and again. "Yes, Mr Willard. Give me ten minutes to get things up and running here, and then I'll be straight over."

―――――

Carrie had made it into work on time by the skin of her teeth, only to find that Willard was already in his office. He did that sometimes, got in before her, and she hated it because she liked to have a few minutes to sort herself out before she started running around for him.

Still upset over her fight with Aidan, she hurriedly prepared his morning coffee. Placing his favourite newspaper on the tray beside it, she put on a brave smile as she opened the door to his office and then breezed in as though she didn't have a care in the world.

"Good morning, Mr Willard," she announced, cheerfully. "You're in very early today."

"Morning, sweetheart," he replied, running a manicured hand through the thick mane of silver hair that was swept back from his wrinkly forehead. "Busy day, lots to do, so I thought I'd make an early start."

She carefully placed the tray on the edge of his desk and passed him his coffee and morning paper. "Is there anything in particular you require from me this morning?" she asked, determined to be as efficient as ever, despite everything on her mind.

Willard took a sip of coffee and nodded approvingly. "Very nice," he told her, reaching for the newspaper.

Carrie smiled at him. Despite his fearsome reputation, he had always behaved like the perfect gentleman towards her.

"I'm expecting Frank the Tank shortly," he said, flicking through to the racing section at the back. "Silly sod nearly got Fred and Casper killed yesterday, so I'm going to give him a bit of a bollocking."

"Oh dear," Carrie said, adopting a suitably concerned expression. She was one of only a handful of people at Willard Betting who knew about his illegal sidelines.

Carrie's father, Damian, had gone to school with Jonas Willard, and he had gone on to work for him for many years, reluctantly retiring six years ago when his health had started to deteriorate. Through her father, Carrie had known Willard for most of her life, which was why he hadn't hesitated to bring her into his inner circle, or 'the firm' as he liked to call it, when she started working for him.

Willard laughed, mirthlessly. "The useless wanker tried to do a Dirty Harry and stare down a bunch of horrible Turks that Fred was buying those diamonds I told you about from," he said by way of explanation.

"Did anyone get hurt?" Carrie asked. She didn't particularly care about Casper or Frankie, but she had a bit of a soft spot for Fred Wiggins. A few months back, when she was going through a particularly acrimonious split from a control freak of a woman called Stella Carter, Fred had unexpectedly come to her rescue.

Stella was a domineering woman who had treated Carrie more like a possession than a lover. After being dumped, Stella had refused to take no for an answer, and she had taken to stalking Carrie, ringing her at all hours of the day and night, randomly accosting her in the street, and even following her to and from work. One day, over a coffee in the staff kitchen, Carrie had broken down in front of Wiggins. Taking her to one side, he had listened sympathetically as she unburdened herself to him, then given her a big hug and told her not to worry; he would sort it out.

And he had.

The following day, he had dispatched Casper to have a quiet word in Stella's ear. Carrie had never found out what Casper said to her but, whatever it was, it had certainly done the trick, because Stella-the-nutcase-stalker hadn't bothered her once since then.

Having taken on the role of her unofficial protector, Fred had also offered to let Casper have a chat with Aidan about his increasingly churlish behaviour, but she had politely declined the offer – her brother might be a complete twat, but he was still family. Still, it was reassuring to know that, if things ever became totally unbearable, or if Aidan played hard ball by refusing to move out when she asked him to, she had an ace up her sleeve that she could play.

"There was a bit of a scuffle," Willard said, "but thankfully it all blew over. Frankie's looking after the gems for me until I can move them on."

"Wouldn't they be better off in the safe here?" she asked.

Willard smiled at her naivety. "I don't like to keep anything that might cause me grief with the local constabulary on the premises, if you get my drift," he said, tapping the side of his nose as he spoke. "Be a bit hard to explain a million quid's worth of dodgy gems to the Cozzers if they turned up, wouldn't it?"

Frank the Tank had a larger-than-life personality, and he was normally so loud and brash that you could hear him coming a mile away but, when he entered the admin office at Willard Betting's head branch that morning, he was displaying none of his usual swagger.

"Morning, Carrie," he said as he meekly presented himself before her desk. "Mr Willard's expecting me."

Carrie looked up from the letter she was typing. "Morning, Frankie," she said, offering him a little smile. "Why don't you have a seat, and I'll let him know you're here."

Kyle nodded, and retreated to the small cluster of easy chairs in the waiting area opposite her desk. The wooden frame of the tub shaped chair he chose was covered in cheap green fabric, and it was clearly designed for normal sized people, not massive bodybuilders like Frank Kyle. He squeezed himself into it with some difficulty, and then sat there with his hands clasped together in his lap, looking very uncomfortable.

"In a good mood today, is he?" he asked, sounding a little too hopeful.

"Would you like some coffee?" she enquired, deftly sidestepping the question.

Kyle shook his head, miserably. "No, ta."

Carrie picked up her phone, dialled Willard's internal extension number. "Mr Kyle's out here to see you, Mr Willard," she said when it was answered. She listened for a moment, and then her eyes drifted up to Kyle, who was staring back at her with nervous expectation. "I'll pass that on to him, Mr Willard," she said before hanging up.

As she cradled the phone, Kyle gave her a nervous smile. "That didn't sound too good," he said, clearly worried.

Carrie glanced over her shoulder to make sure that the door leading into Willard's office was closed properly, then leaned forward and lowered her voice conspiratorially. "Between you and me, Frankie, I don't think he's very pleased with you," she said quietly.

Kyle swallowed hard. "I fucked up yesterday afternoon," he

admitted, "and I don't think he's taken it too well." He looked through the glass partition that separated Carrie's office from the general admin area beyond, in search of Wiggins' door at the far end. "Is Fred in yet?" he asked.

"Haven't seen him."

Kyle sat in awkward silence for a few seconds, then cleared his throat. "I take it that the boss hasn't got Casper or a few of the other boys waiting to give me a good seeing to?" he asked. The words stumbled over each other in his eagerness to spit them out.

Carrie stared at him, earnestly. "Frankie, I think he's just going to give you a bit of a bollocking," she confided.

Kyle's relief was palpable, bringing a feeling without parallel. "Really?" A big sigh. "I was beginning to think that… Well, you know." He drew his right forefinger across his neck.

Carrie rolled her eyes. "Don't be daft. From what I can gather, no real harm was done."

Kyle immediately latched onto her optimism. "That's right. That's exactly how I see it. We had a bit of a result with the diamonds, only paid four hundred grand for them. They've got to be worth at least twice that much in resale value. I've got them locked away in the safe at my gaff until old Avram can find us a buyer."

"Will that take long?" Carrie asked.

Kyle shrugged. "I dunno. A few days, I should imagine. Why?"

"No reason," she told him. "Just curious how these things work."

Carrie's work phone rang, making them both jump. She scooped it up quickly. "Yes, Mr Willard?" A moment's pause, then her eyes locked with Frankie's. "Yes, I'll send him in right away… He'll see you now," she told Kyle as she hung up.

Frank the Tank stood up, adjusted his collar and tie, and then made sure his shirt was properly tucked in. "Wish me luck," he said as he reluctantly walked towards Willard's office door.

Wiping a sweaty palm along his trouser leg, he nervously rapped on the door.

"Come," Willard barked from inside.

Kyle took hold of the handle, paused long enough to take a deep breath, and then stepped inside to face the music.

After he'd gone in, Carrie sat in silence, mulling over the conversation they had just had. Then, grabbing her Bottega Veneta handbag, she set off for the powder room. She figured that Willard would be tied up with Frankie for a few minutes yet, and wouldn't require her services during that time.

The room was empty but, just to be on the safe side, she pushed open each of the three cubicle doors to make sure that no one was sitting inside. When she was satisfied that she really was all alone, she dug her mobile out of her bag and tapped in her older brother's number.

Her heart was beating fast.

"Hello, sis…"

"Listen, Dazza, I haven't got long, but I've just come into some very interesting information that could resolve the need for us to sell mum's house. If you're interested, pop around to mine after work tonight and I'll tell you all about it… No, I can't say any more now, not over the phone." She listened for a moment, cringing as her older brother bombarded her with pointless questions.

"Listen," she hissed, "I've got to go before I'm missed. I'll speak to you later." With that, she hung up.

After checking her hair in the mirror, Carrie returned to her desk.

She took a moment to centre herself, hardly able to believe the audacious plan that had sprung into her head following her conversation with Frank the Tank. Taking a deep breath, and aware that her hands were shaking from fear and excitement, she resumed typing the letter she had been halfway through.

Above the tap, tap, tap of her electric typewriter, Carrie heard Willard's muffled voice booming away as he shouted at his guest.

For the sake of her newly hatched plan, Carrie found herself hoping that she was right, and that Willard only intended to give Frankie a verbal reprimand, not have his arms and legs broken.

6

THURSDAY 4TH OCTOBER 2001

Intruders

A strong easterly wind hurried turbulent storm clouds across the East London skies as though they were late for an important appointment. Accompanied by ice-cold, sideways driven rain, it felt more like the middle of January than the beginning of October. It had been raining like this for several days now, and the drastic change in weather was a stark contrast to the glorious heatwave the city had basked in over much of the summer.

The silver Mercedes CLK Coupe turned off the main drag into a residential road in East Ham, not far from the A406 exit for Beckton Alps. It was a quiet road, not exactly run down, but definitely heading that way. About half way along, the car slowed and pulled onto the block paved driveway of a semi-detached house, one of many similar residences that lined the road. Its powerful halogen headlights illuminated the relentless rain, which was falling so hard that it bounced a good foot off the ground upon impact.

With its brake pads squealing, the Merc pulled under an aging carport at the side of the house and glided to a stop. The driver's door opened almost immediately and Frank Kyle clambered out. As he did, a big drip of water splattered his wide forehead. Wiping it away with his sleeve, he glanced up at the corrugated roof in search of the leak, just in time for another drip to hit him straight in the eye. Examining the structure, he spotted several nasty looking cracks through which water was pouring at an alarming rate.

Great!

Just what he didn't need! The old house already had a niggle list as long as his arm, without adding this to it.

Kyle's idea of DIY was knocking one out while looking at a porn mag, but his wife had thrown a serious strop when he'd suggested calling in the local handyman, claiming it would be a really good project for them to work on together. Kyle couldn't think of anything worse, but he had gone along with it to keep Morag happy.

With a final glance at the leaking roof, he grabbed his sports bag from the rear seat and slammed the door shut. Pulling the hood of his training top over his head, he made a dash for the porch, being careful not to step in any of the humungous puddles that had formed during this latest deluge.

Removing a small bundle of keys from his tracksuit pocket, Kyle let himself into the house. "Morag, I'm home!" he shouted from the hallway.

After wiping his feet on the heavy-duty doormat, Kyle deposited his gym bag on the polished wooden floor. The shoulders of his grey hoodie were soaked through, even though he'd only been exposed to the elements for a few seconds, so he pulled it off and tossed it on top of his bag.

Having avoided any serious punishment for messing things up with the Turks, Kyle was back to his usual cocksure self today, and he couldn't resist stopping in front of the big hall mirror to run through a well-rehearsed posing routine. His yellow Gold's Gym vest strained at the seams as he puffed out his V-shaped back and flexed his powerfully defined chest and arms.

"Looking good, Frankie boy," he purred, winking approvingly at his sunlamp tanned reflection. Allowing himself a final glance in the mirror, he set off in search of his beautiful young wife.

As expected, he found her in the kitchen, where she was busy preparing their evening meal.

Morag glanced over her shoulder and smiled at him as he entered the room. Even without makeup on, Kyle thought the pale skinned redhead was undeniably the most beautiful woman he had ever set eyes upon. They had met while holidaying in Ibiza two years earlier. He had expected it to be a one-night-stand but, despite her being twenty years his junior, something had clicked between them that night, and they had been inseparable ever since.

"You're back earlier than I was expecting," Morag said in her strong Shetlands accent. "I'm afraid dinner willnae be ready for at least another hour."

Kyle dwarfed his petite wife. Sidling up behind her, he wrapped his tree trunk like arms around her slender frame and pulled her into him, inhaling the orange scented fragrance of her shampoo and feeling very lucky to have her.

"That's okay, hon," he replied in a deep, gravelly voice. "It gives me time to have a shower and sort out a couple of things that the boss wants me to take care of." As he spoke, he leaned in and affectionately nuzzled his face against hers.

"Stop it!" she giggled, making a token effort to pull free. "You know that bloody awful moustache of yours tickles like crazy!"

Grinning at her protest, which had become something of an evening ritual between them, Kyle allowed his calloused hand to wander down to the huge bump that protruded from her stomach. "How's junior been behaving himself today?" he asked, gently caressing their unborn baby.

Morag groaned. "The wee bugger thinks my bladder's a frigging football, and he hasnae stopped kicking it all evening." She let out a long sigh. "Honestly, I'll be glad when he finally drops, just so I can go for more than thirty minutes without needing to pee."

Kyle gently kissed the top of her head. "Not long now," he soothed.

Morag snorted. "Not long? That's easy for you to say. You're no' the one who's got to endure another three months of torture!"

Kyle smiled. Although Morag frequently bemoaned the trials and tribulations she'd endured during her pregnancy, he suspected that she was secretly enjoying every moment of it.

Lifting her head, Morag sniffed the air, then wrinkled her pretty little nose in disapproval.

"I think you'd better go and have that shower, you stinking great brute."

Kyle laughed, heartily. One of the things he loved most about her was that she didn't mince her words. "Okay, luv," he said, obediently. "I'll see you when I've cleaned myself up and made a few calls." Giving her an affectionate pat on the rump, he turned to leave.

"And shave that horrible strip of bum fluff off your top lip while you're at it," she called after him.

"Not gonna happen," he replied, blowing her a kiss from the doorway.

The two men who had followed Frank Kyle home from his gym session in Stratford sat in their car, which was parked a few yards south of his driveway. They had been sitting there for just under an hour now, waiting for the right moment to make their move.

"We're lucky it's raining," the driver said, stifling a yawn. He was a stocky white male in his late thirties; barrel shaped, like he had swallowed a massive beer keg. "At least, with this shitty weather, there's less chance of anyone noticing us."

The torrential rain hammering the car's roof was making such a din that he could no longer hear the radio above it, and the continuous stream of water flooding the windscreen had totally obscured his vision of the target address.

His passenger, a wiry man with a spotty face and restless blue eyes, responded with a surly grunt. Although his given name was Paul Pickford, an untimely accident with a hedge trimmer a few years back had sent the little pinkie and ring finger of his left hand flying through the air like little chipolatas, and since then everyone had taken to calling him Fingers.

"I should bleeding well hope so, Dazza," he said, wiping a small circle in the condensation that fogged his window. "Cos, if you ask me, we've already been sitting here for way too long."

Darren McCullen stiffened. "Yeah, well, no one's asking you, are they?" he responded, sourly.

Fingers gave him a wounded puppy look. "Aww, don't be like that, Dazza."

Darren's face softened, and he leaned over to ruffle Fingers' hair. "Sorry mate, didn't mean to snap at you. Just a bit stressed at the moment, know what I mean?"

He had been on edge since Monday night's botched ram raid, convinced that it was only a matter of time until the Old Bill came knocking on his door and carted him off to jail. Carrie had assured him they had nothing to worry about; neither he nor Fingers had ever been arrested before, so the police wouldn't have their fingerprints or DNA on record. Even though he knew she was probably right, Darren couldn't shake the nagging fear that one of the Pevensey brothers might decide to cut a deal with the Old Bill in exchange for grassing him and Fingers up.

And then there was all the added stress involved with planning tonight's robbery. Despite his initial reservations, Carrie had convinced him that the reward was worth the risk; if things panned out, she had argued, he would be able to keep his business afloat without forcing her to sell the house she loved. Of course, if Jonas Willard ever found out, all three of them would be as good as dead, but he tried not to think about that.

Earlier that day, Carrie had called with the unwelcome news that the wily old Jew had found a buyer for the stones, and that Frank the Tank was due to drop them off the following morning, which meant that they either made their move tonight or not at all.

"That's okay, Dazza," Fingers said, smiling to show that no harm had been done.

"You're a good pal, Fingers."

The sudden, sharp trill of a ringtone made both men jump.

Leaning forward, Darren snatched his mobile phone from the cup holder in the centre console. "Hello…?"

He listened for a few seconds, ignoring Fingers, who was staring at him expectantly.

"Is it Carrie?" Fingers asked.

Darren held a digit to his lips, mouthed, "Be quiet."

He could hardly hear her over the rainfall.

"No, we haven't bloody done it yet," he snapped. "What? No, don't be daft… No, I'm not losing my bottle… Okay, okay, don't go on… Yes, I *know* tonight's our last chance…" An angry sigh. "Look, we'll do it right now, okay? Now, bugger off and stop bothering me." Killing the call, he tossed the phone onto the back seat. "Stroppy fucking cow," he grumbled, reaching for his balaclava.

"What did Carrie say?" Fingers asked, picking up on McCullen's mood change. "Is everything alright?"

A belligerent shrug. "She's worried that we're losing our nerve," Darren snapped. "Course, it's easy to be brave when you're sitting at home with your feet up, watching Coronation Street and painting your frigging toe nails. I bet she wouldn't be so cocky if she was here with us."

"Course not," Fingers agreed. "She'd be pissing herself."

Darren laughed. "Wouldn't she just!"

"Do you think the diamonds are definitely in there?" Fingers asked, pulling on a pair of black leather gloves. "I mean, what if Carrie's got it wrong, and he's left them in the safe where he works?"

"Only one way to find out," Darren told him, removing a pistol from his waistband and working the breech to chamber a round. The gun was an old Browning Hi-Power he had acquired in Germany during his army service. Before setting off, he had provided Fingers with an identical weapon, along with a crash course in how to use it. "Now, stop faffing about and put your bloody balaclava on. And remember, once we're inside, we don't say nothing about no diamonds. We've got to make it seem like we're only after cash, otherwise it'll be obvious that someone in the know put us up to this robbery."

When Aidan opened the street door, he was greeted by the sight of Annie standing in the pouring rain, her auburn hair clinging to her face like strands of wet spaghetti.

"Have you got the demo tape?" he demanded, seemingly oblivious to the fact that she was getting soaked.

"Yes, I've got it," Annie snapped as she pushed past him. "But I don't think this is a good idea. What if Carrie sees it?"

Slamming the door shut, Aidan watched his girlfriend struggle out of her wet coat and hang it over the kitchen doorframe to dry.

"She's gone over to Abi's, so she won't be back for an hour or two," he informed her.

Abi was Carrie's bestie, and she lived nearby.

"I don't see why you can't just wait till all the filming's done and the editing's finished," Annie complained, dripping water onto the floor as she bent to retrieve a VHS tape from her bag. "I mean, what's the point in even looking at the daily takes when most of them won't even make the final print?"

Snatching it from her hand, Aidan stomped into the lounge and sought out the video player. "Because I want to see everything that's filmed before Pervy Pete does, in case there's something I don't want left in there," he shouted over his shoulder.

Pressing the play button on the remote, he slung himself onto the couch and made himself comfortable. "Do you fancy a cup of tea?" he asked, as the first scene came on.

"That would be nice," she said, moving to join him on the sofa.

"Good. Make me one while you're at it," he told her with a smirk.

Halfway into a sitting position, Annie froze, then stood up again.

Aidan was laughing, like it was a big joke.

"The old one's are always the best," he chuckled as she set off toward the kitchen.

Morag Kyle was just getting ready to serve up their evening meal. She had heard her husband emerge from the shower a half hour earlier and, since then, he had been tucked away in the little room at the front of the house that he used as an office. She assumed he had been on the phone to his boss as she had heard him talking animatedly from time to time.

"I'm dishing it up," she shouted as she shovelled a large portion of organic wholewheat spaghetti onto his plate. When he didn't respond, she sighed, lowered the plate, and walked over to the hallway door. "Frank, dinner's ready in two minutes."

There was a sudden knock at the street door, loud and business like.

Morag's face fell. She hoped it wasn't the Jehovah's Witnesses who were canvassing the area. They were harder to get rid of than a dose of the clap.

"I'll get it," Frank called from the office, much to her relief.

Leaving him to deal with the unwanted caller, Morag finished dishing up and placed both plates on the table. As she poured them both a glass of wine to accompany their meal, she heard muffled voices coming from the hallway.

"Frank, hurry up! Your grub's getting cold," Morag shouted, wondering why he hadn't just told whoever it was to sod off. She had just taken a seat when her husband appeared in the doorway, his huge frame filling it.

"Finally!" she said, raising a fork loaded with spaghetti to her mouth. As their eyes met, she registered the troubled expression on his face. "What's the matter?" she asked, staring at him intently.

Before he could answer, Frank was violently shoved into the room, staggering forward until he collided with the dining table. As he straightened up, two masked men stepped into the kitchen and fanned out. Both had weapons. One, the larger of the two, was pointing his gun directly at her husband's spine.

"What's going on?" Morag demanded, half rising from her chair.

"Sit down," the slimmer of the two intruders snarled, briefly swinging the barrel of his gun in her direction. He had a coarse East London accent, very similar to Frank's, but much higher pitched.

Morag glanced at her husband for guidance.

Frank tapped the table, indicating for her to be seated. "It's alright, luv," he said, reassuringly. "I'm sure this is all just a big mistake."

"Shut up!" the skinny one demanded. Moving forward quickly, he pulled a chair out from under the table. It made a horrible screeching noise as he clumsily dragged it across the tiled floor. "Now, sit down and don't move," he ordered Frank, pointing towards the chair as he spoke.

Ignoring him, Kyle slowly ran his eyes over each of the masked men in turn, making the point that, guns or not, he wasn't intimidated by them.

"Do you pair of cunts know who I am?" he growled, "or who I work for? If you've got any fucking sense, you'll turn around now, and walk straight out of that door. Otherwise, I promise you, you'll both end up dead."

The skinny one shifted uneasily, and Morag could tell that he was rattled by her husband's threat, but the bigger one just laughed. Then, without warning, he lunged forward and pistol-whipped Frank across the top of his head.

Blood poured from the open wound.

"Sit down and shut the fuck up," the gunman yelled, "or I'll put a bullet in your pregnant wife's gut." Stepping back, he calmly pointed the gun at Morag's stomach and thumbed back the hammer to show he wasn't bluffing.

There was no mistaking the fear that appeared in Frank's eyes. Applying pressure to his bleeding scalp, he gently lowered himself onto the dining room chair. "Okay, okay," he said, suddenly eager to appease. "I'll do whatever you say. Just don't hurt her."

"That's better," the gunman said, nodding approvingly. "Now, where's the money?"

Frank seemed confused by the question. "Money? What

money?" he demanded. Blood from the ugly gash in his forehead was seeping through his fingers to stain the side of his face red.

The gunman responded with an impatient sigh. "Don't play silly buggers with me Frankie boy," he warned. "I know you've got a shit load of cash here, so stop wasting my fucking time and take me to it."

Frank's face darkened. "There's a couple of grand stashed away up in the bedroom," he said through gritted teeth. "It's all the money I've got."

The two gunmen exchanged knowing looks, then the stocky one laughed again. It was a grating sound, without humour. "Course it is," he responded sarcastically. Walking around the table with grim purpose, he delivered a vicious backhanded blow to the side of Morag's face, almost knocking her out of her chair.

Frank Kyle was out of his seat in an instant; incandescent with rage, he reached out to grab the throat of the man who had dared to strike his wife. "You're a walking dead man, you fucking cunt," he snarled.

Both gunmen turned their weapons on him. "Don't even think about it," the stocky one warned.

Frank hesitated. He would have gladly taken his chances against the intruders had Morag not been there, but he couldn't allow his ridiculous temper to endanger her or the precious cargo she was carrying.

"Don't be a bloody fool," the slimmer gunman warned, his voice a nervous squeal.

Breathing heavily, Frank Kyle slowly unclenched his fists. A vein pulsed in his temple as he forced himself to take a backwards step. No longer applying pressure to his head wound, blood was pouring freely from the jagged tear in his scalp, but he was oblivious to it.

"That's right, back off and be sensible," the man in charge said. "That way, no one gets hurt. Now, where's the money?"

Kyle stared at Morag for a long moment, then his shoulders

sagged in defeat. "It's in my office," he said, pointing towards the hallway.

The barrel-chested gunman glanced over his shoulder. "Show me," he ordered, beckoning Kyle forward with an impatient gesture.

Moving slowly, Kyle crossed the kitchen, passing between the two gunmen, whose weapons followed him every step of the way. "Don't worry," he told Morag as he left the room. "Everything'll be okay."

The space that Kyle had converted into his home office had originally been used as a dining room. It was roughly square in shape, with a big bay window overlooking the drive. It contained a cheap rectangular desk he had purchased from IKEA, and three dented filing cabinets. A natural recess in the far wall had been converted into cupboard space, with white, floor to ceiling, MDF doors that opened outward from the middle. The magnolia painted plaster walls were littered with gold framed photographs of varying sizes and shapes, each displaying a shot of Kyle, either competing at various bodybuilding competitions over the years or standing next to legends such as Arnold Schwarzenegger, Lou Ferrigno and Dorian Yates.

Kyle liked to listen to music while he worked, and an expensive Bose stereo system was neatly stacked in one corner of the room. Above it, several well stocked shelves contained a diverse selection of CDs. The floor was covered in a thick woollen carpet of speckled grey; tasteful but hard wearing.

Kyle walked over to the cupboard and pulled it open. The top half contained three shelves that were crammed full of dusty lever arch files. Beneath these, concealed by a little curtain, sat a large green safe. Without saying a word, Kyle knelt down, drew the curtain aside, and began turning the safe's tumbler, nimbly working his way through the combination.

"You're gonna regret doing this," Kyle promised as his temper bubbled. "If you go through with this, you'll be signing your own death warrant."

The safe's door popped open with a dull click.

"Why don't you let me worry about that," the gunman said, smugly.

Kyle shrugged his massive shoulders. "It's your funeral," he said. Reaching inside, he curled his fingers around the grip of the Colt Python .357 Magnum he kept hidden there, "but don't say you weren't warned."

Something in his voice must have given the game away, because the gunman suddenly stepped forward and rammed the muzzle of his weapon into the base of Kyle's skull. "Bring your hand out of there," he barked. "Do it now. Nice and slow."

Kyle tensed. After a moment, he released his grip on the revolver and slowly withdrew his hand, holding it open to show that it was empty.

The pressure from the gun eased off. "Good. Now, go and sit at your desk," the gunman ordered.

As Kyle stood up, a look of pure hatred crossed his face. "Just so you know, I'm gonna hunt you down and kill you," he promised. "What do you think about that?"

"I'm shaking all over," the gunman said, indifferently.

He waited until Kyle was sitting behind his desk, with both hands clasped on top of his head, before bending down to peek inside the safe. As he did, the sleeve of his top snagged on the sharp corner of the safe door, ripping the seam and exposing a heart shaped tattoo on the inside of his left wrist. The names Darren and Janice were inked in capital letters above and below it.

Kyle's eyes were immediately drawn to the tattoo and, as he silently read the names to himself, a cruel smile flickered across his face.

"You should be, *Darren*," he said, loading the name with menace, "cause you're going to spend the rest of your life looking over your shoulder until, one day, you find me standing there."

The gunman – Darren – reacted as though he'd been slapped.

"W–what did you just call me?" he stammered, sounding badly shaken.

Kyle sensed the man's fear, fed off it. Darren was right to be afraid. Kyle knew his first name now, along with the name of his woman. "You heard me, *Darren*. I know your name, and Janice's too, so it won't be hard for me to track you down." As he spoke, he unclasped his hands and spread them out wide.

"Put your hands back on top of your head," the gunman barked, trying to reassert his authority by upping the aggression.

Kyle responded with a frustrated sigh, but he did as he'd been told. "What's the point in going through with this?" he demanded, sounding almost bored. "I know your name now, so it's as good as over for you." He laughed, cruelly. "Do you honestly think I won't find you and kill you, *Darren*?"

There was a long pause. "Not if I kill you first," the man finally said.

For a split second, Kyle thought he must have misheard, then his eyes widened. "You wouldn't dare." Despite the arrogance in his voice, a little ripple of anxiety fluttered through his chest. He decided to make it clear to the gunman exactly what would happen if he were harmed. "Listen, you mug, Jonas Willard won't just wipe you out if you're stupid enough to harm me or my wife, he'll kill your entire fucking family as well."

The gunman responded with a resigned shrug. "You haven't given me a choice in the matter, have you? So, all things considered, I guess I'll have to take that chance."

Pointing the Browning at Kyle's large head, he pulled the trigger.

Inside the kitchen, where the second intruder was still keeping her a prisoner at gunpoint, Morag flinched as the deep boom of the gunshot shattered the silence. The man guarding her jumped too, and she could see that his gun hand was shaking.

"What was that?" she demanded, straining her neck to peer past him into the hallway.

"Shut up!" her captor yelled, glancing nervously at the door.

Morag could feel herself becoming hysterical. "Frank?" she screamed, fearfully. "Frank, are you okay?" Rising from her chair on shaky legs, she made a sudden dash for the door, but the masked man moved quickly to block her path.

"Sit down," he snarled, pointing his gun straight in her face.

Detecting movement at the edge of her vision, Morag looked up as the stocky gunman strode through the doorway.

He seemed very agitated.

"What's going on here?" he demanded.

"Where's my husband?" Morag shrieked, looking beyond him into the hallway. "What have you done to him?"

"Did you find the diamonds?" the skinny one asked, keeping his weapon trained on Morag.

"Shut up, you idiot," the stocky man snapped, "and lower that bloody gun." Pushing his companion's gun arm down, he barged past the smaller man and eyeballed Morag. "Apart from the safe, where does your old man stash his valuables?"

Morag's mind was all over the place. "Where's my husband," she sobbed, somehow finding the strength to remain upright when all she wanted to do was collapse in a heap on the floor.

The anger in the man's eyes was unmistakable, but there was something else there, too: fear.

Turning to his partner, he said, "We need to be quick in case any of the neighbours heard the shot and called the Old Bill."

Morag could hear the stress in his voice, and the thought that someone might have called the police gave her renewed hope.

The burly gunman suddenly grabbed her arm and began dragging her along the hallway, ignoring her feeble attempts to break free. When he reached the downstairs loo, he pulled open the door and glanced inside. "Perfect," he said, manhandling her into the tiny room. "Stay in there if you know what's good for you," he snapped, then jabbed her in the chest with a gloved finger. "I'm warning you, if you stick your head out of this carsey before I tell you to, I'll blow the fucking thing off."

With that, he slammed the door in her face.

Left alone, Morag lowered herself onto the toilet, buried her head in her hands, and burst into tears.

Beyond the toilet door, she heard the two intruders crashing around as they noisily ransacked the house. What would happen to her and her unborn child when they finished? Surely, if they had killed Frank, they couldn't afford to leave any witnesses behind?

Galvanised by an all-consuming desire to protect her unborn baby, Morag pressed herself against the door. Placing her ear against it, she listened carefully. From all the thumping around coming from above, it sounded like they had moved upstairs. If that was the case, she might be able to sneak out and make a run for it before they noticed. A loud crash from the kitchen robbed her of that hope. One of them must have remained downstairs, she realised.

Morag turned around to examine the double-glazed window above the toilet, wondering if that could be her way out. It was small, impossibly so. Surely, there was no way a person, even one as petite as her, could fit through that, especially not in her heavily pregnant condition? But the only alternative was to wait for them to come back and kill her.

With nothing to lose, Morag awkwardly climbed on top of the toilet and pushed open the small window. As she stuck her head out of the narrow opening, she was immediately assailed by the driving rain and biting wind.

"Please God, let me survive for the sake of our baby," she prayed aloud.

7

An unexpected caller

The sound of their doorbell being rung with great urgency nearly gave Mavis Charwood a heart attack. It was coming up to ten o'clock at night, which was when they normally retired to bed, and it was most unusual for anyone to be calling at such a late hour. "Who could that possibly be?" she asked her husband, Jim, who was sitting next to her on the sofa.

In addition to the bell ringing, their mysterious caller began thumping on the door with considerable force. "Do you think it's burglars?" Mavis asked, grabbing the remote control and muting the sound on the TV.

"I dunno," Jim replied, reaching for his walking stick with a gnarled hand.

"Maybe we should call the police?" Mavis suggested, levering herself out of the armchair. She hobbled across the living room as quickly as she could, but her dodgy hip was flaring up again, making her movements stiff and painful. Coming to a halt by the hallway door, her aging eyes squinted at the small opaque glass panel in their street door, then sought out the little table on which their telephone sat.

To her immense relief, all the bell ringing and door banging suddenly stopped.

The silence was wonderful.

"Do you think they've gone?" Mavis whispered, not knowing what to do for the best.

Jim shuffled over to join her, breathing heavily from the exertion. "I bleeding well hope so," he whispered, peering fearfully at the street door.

The silence was shattered by a distraught female voice. "Mavis! Jim! Please open the door!"

Mavis almost jumped out of her skin.

Moving to her side, Jim wrapped a protective arm around her bony shoulders.

"Mavis! Jim! Can you hear me?"

Mavis' hearing aid squealed loudly, and she quickly adjusted the volume control. The voice had sounded absolutely terrified, but it had also sounded vaguely familiar.

Was the accent Scottish?

Jim took a tentative step into the hall. "Who's there?" he demanded, doing his best to sound unafraid.

"It's Morag, from next door," the woman outside sobbed.

They both jumped when she poked the letterbox open and peered in. "Something awful's happened," Morag cried; she was clearly hysterical. "Please, Jim, I'm begging you, let me in."

Huddled together in the middle of the hall, Jim and Mavis shared a worried look.

The street door slammed with a dull thud, making them both jump. Worryingly, neither of them had heard it open. Aidan made a hurried grab for the remote control resting on the cushion next to him but, in his haste to reach it, sent it spiralling onto the floor.

"Shit!" he cursed, diving after it.

Somehow, he managed to press the stop button just before Carrie walked into the lounge. Sitting down again, he casually draped an arm around Annie's shoulders, doing his best to act naturally, and not like she had almost stumbled upon them watching home-made porn.

Carrie nodded amiably to Annie, but her demeanour instantly changed when she saw her brother.

"What you looking at?" he snapped, staring back with open animosity.

"Aidan," Annie chided him. "Don't talk to your sister like that."

Carrie held his eye a moment longer, her face taut with anger, then turned to Annie. "Has he told you what he did yesterday?" she enquired in a frosty tone. "The stupid git nearly burned the house down."

"Don't start," he warned. "I told you it was a fucking accident."

"It wasn't an accident," Carrie fired back. "It happened because you were stoned out of your head again, like you were when you blew up the microwave."

Aidan was on his feet in an instant. "Don't talk to me like that in front of my girlfriend," he snarled, taking a step towards her.

Annie rose, hurriedly inserting herself between them to prevent things getting out of hand. She had seen them fly off the handle at each other before, and it wasn't a pretty sight. "Why don't I put the kettle on, and make us all a nice cup of tea?" she suggested, placing a hand on Aidan's scrawny arm.

He shrugged it off.

Although Carrie looked scared, she was showing no signs of backing down. "What you gonna do," she goaded. "Prove to Annie what a big strong man you are by hitting a defenceless woman?"

Aidan's face flushed with fury, and he clenched both fists. "Don't fucking tempt me," he spat.

Annie could see that they were a hairsbreadth away from tearing into each other. "Please," she said, swapping Aidan's arm for Carrie's. "Let's me and you go in the kitchen and leave him to calm down."

Carrie looked at her, then at Aidan. "Yeah, you're right," she said. "He's not worth wasting my breath on."

Aidan resented the scorn in her voice, and he reacted by deliberately crashing his shoulder into Carrie's as he barged through them on his way to the door. "You make me sick, the pair of you," he snarled. "I'm going outside for a smoke."

The three-man crew of Trojan 501, the Armed Response Vehicle responding to the Charwood's 999 call, were greeted by an elderly man braving the rain from the edge of his driveway.

Clad in striped pyjamas and a brown dressing gown, their informant was leaning on his walking stick with one hand and holding an umbrella above his head with the other.

"Was it you who called the police, sir?" PC Matt Davies, the most experienced of the three firearms officers asked as he alighted the car.

"Yes, officer," Jim Charwood said, teeth chattering from the cold.

"Can you tell me exactly what happened?" Davies asked, pulling his Gore-Tex jacket tight around him and doing his best to ignore the driving rain.

Instead of answering, Jim glanced down at the soggy slippers on his feet. "Do you think we could talk inside?" he asked, indicating the open door of his house with a jut of his ancient chin. "Only my new slippers are getting ruined out here."

Davies wiped rain from his face. "When you dialled 999, you said something to the operator about your next-door neighbour being shot," he persisted. "Which house are we talking about?"

Using his cane, Jim pointed unsteadily towards the next house along. "That one there. His poor wife's inside my house if you want to speak to her. She's in a terrible state."

Signalling for his colleagues to nip off and carry out a quick recce of the property, Davies followed Charwood into his house.

They found Morag Kyle sitting in the lounge, hunched forward on the settee with a blanket wrapped around her shoulders. She glanced up as they entered the room, her eyes wide and fearful.

From the traumatised expression on her tear-streaked face, it was clear to Davies that she was in a state of deep shock. He noticed that her bottom lip was badly swollen. The dried blood, running from the corner of her mouth down to her chin, suggested that she had recently been on the receiving end of a heavy blow to the face.

Mavis was hovering over her, her wrinkly face plastered with concern. "Are you sure you don't want a nice cup of tea, dear?" she was saying.

Staring straight ahead, Morag shook her head sluggishly, and the effort of doing so seemed to exhaust her.

Turning the volume down on his personal radio, which was blaring away in his earpiece, Davies knelt down in front of her. "What's your name?" he asked, speaking softly so as not to alarm her unduly.

For a long moment Morag continued to stare straight ahead, as though she hadn't heard him speak. Then, moving in slow motion, she pivoted to face him and, from the puffiness around her red-rimmed eyes, it was clear she had been doing a lot of crying. Her brow knitted into a deep frown of concentration, as if the question was so complex that she needed time to process it. She stared at him listlessly. "My name's... My name's Morag. Morag Kyle."

Davies gave her a reassuring smile. "Morag, my name's Matt, and I need you to tell me exactly what happened tonight."

Morag's hands were worrying away at each other in her lap. "I– I was dishing up dinner when there was a knock at the door."

Her voice was so weak and tremulous that Davies had to lean in to catch the words. "Go on," he encouraged.

Swallowing hard, she continued reluctantly. "Frank answered it. The next thing I knew, two masked men were shoving him into the kitchen. They had guns, and they demanded to know where he kept his money." Her face contorted with pain as she recounted the story. "One of them hit me," she sobbed, subconsciously reaching a hand up to her injured face. "He threatened to shoot me if Frank didn't do exactly what they said."

Tears started to fall, and Mavis quickly handed her a tissue from the box on the sideboard.

"Take your time," Davies soothed, forcing himself to sound relaxed despite the urgency of the situation.

Nodding gratefully, Morag accepted the comforting hand that Mavis offered her, and then resumed her tale. "The one in charge took Frank off to the office, while the other one stayed with me." She paused for a breath, then squeezed Mavis' hand. "A few moments later I heard a gunshot. The man who had taken Frank away came back into the room, and asked me where Frank stashed his valuables. Then... Then, they locked me in the downstairs loo, warning me that, if I came out, they would shoot me. I could hear them ransacking the place, and I knew it was only a matter of time until they returned to finish me off, so I climbed out of the window and ran here to get help."

"Morag, did you actually see them leave the house?" Davies asked.

A shudder ran through her as she shook her head.

"You say they both had guns," Davies said. "Can you describe them?"

Morag thought about this. "They were like the ones cops use on TV, not the old-fashioned things you see in cowboy films."

Davies took this to mean they had pistols as opposed to revolvers. "Morag, I realise that this isn't easy for you, but I need to know if you saw or heard your husband again after the gunshot."

Morag's face seemed to cave in on itself, and her sobbing became more intense. "No," she wailed. "But I know Frank. If... If he was still alive, he would have called out to me."

Davies suspected that she was right, but he refrained from passing comment.

Morag stiffened, then let out a high-pitched howl of grief. "Oh God! My poor Frankie's dead," she cried, wrapping her arms around herself.

Sitting down beside her, Mavis began stroking her hair in an effort to comfort her, but Morag was inconsolable.

It quickly became apparent to Davies that he wasn't going to get much more from her. "Morag, I know you're struggling," he said, gently, "but, before I go, I need you to describe the layout of your house for me."

Squelching through puddles the size of small lakes, PC Davies and his two colleagues crossed the driveway leading to the Kyle's house in a running crouch. They paused when they reached the street door, which was slightly ajar.

Did that mean the suspects were still inside, or had they simply left it open when they fled the scene?

Trojan 502, their sister ARV, was making its way from Leyton to support them, but it was still several minutes away. In all good conscience, Davies knew they couldn't afford to wait that long. If Frank Kyle was still alive, and in desperate need of medical assistance, every second they waited for backup drastically decreased his chances of surviving.

Taking point, the stock of his Heckler & Koch MP5 cradled against his right shoulder, Davies gently pushed open the street door to Kyle's house.

The lights were on inside, but there were no sounds coming from within.

"ARMED POLICE!" he called out. "YOU IN THE HOUSE, COME FORWARD WITH YOUR HANDS IN THE AIR!"

Silence. Not even the sound of a TV or radio playing.

Davies repeated the command but, again, there was no response.

Adrenaline surged through him as he pictured the layout that Morag had tearfully described to him. Having scoped out the property while Davies was debriefing her, his colleagues had reported back that there were no obvious signs of anyone inside, at least not on the ground floor. So, unless the intruders were hiding upstairs, waiting to ambush them – which seemed highly unlikely – the premises was almost certainly empty.

"Stand by to make entry,' Davies whispered, glancing back over his shoulder.

Behind him, PCs Andrew Langworthy and Phillip Blair acknowledged him with a thumbs up sign, then readied themselves to move forward.

Thumbing the safety off his MP5, Davies cautiously stepped into the hall, which was square in shape and had four doors leading off it. The bulky ballistic body armour he had just donned was cumbersome, restricting his movement, but the metal plates inside felt reassuringly heavy, and he knew it would stop pretty much anything that was fired at him.

Either side of him, Langworthy and Blair fanned out as they advanced.

The door to their immediate left was closed. This, he knew from what Morag had told him, was the downstairs loo she had escaped from. He signalled towards it and Langworthy padded over and turned the handle.

As expected, the room was empty. Above the toilet, a small window was wide open, letting in rain, and Davies found himself marvelling that a heavily pregnant woman had managed to squeeze through such a small aperture.

Moving slowly forward, Davies came to another door, this one on his right. According to Mrs Kyle, this was her husband's office and, if her fears were grounded, it was where they would find his body.

The door was wide open and a light was on inside. Just beyond the office, further up on the right, he could see another closed door. That would be the living room. Opposite that, a wide staircase led up to the first floor, which was in darkness. At the far end of the hall, he could see into the kitchen through its open door. Two plates of uneaten food and two glasses of wine were clearly visible on the oak dining table.

Coming to a halt by the office door, Davies indicated for his colleagues to cover him while he went inside.

"ARMED POLICE," he yelled for a third time. "COME OUT

OF THE ROOM WITH YOUR HANDS ABOVE YOUR HEAD."

Predictably, there was no response.

Taking a deep breath to oxygenate himself, Davies peered around the door, sighting along the barrel of his weapon. Working on the assumption that someone could be lying in wait for him, his index finger hovered over the trigger, ready to return fire if he encountered an armed hostile.

Shit!

"CONTACT!" he called, aiming his weapon at a large figure slumped in a high-backed chair behind the desk. As his finger tightened on the trigger, Davies registered the small hole in the unmoving man's forehead. A nanosecond later, he spotted the blood and gore that plastered the headrest and a large section of the wall behind the desk. Apart from the unmoving man, who was staring up at the ceiling through unseeing eyes, the room was unoccupied.

Returning his finger to the trigger guard, Davies quickly crossed to examine the man, who he presumed was Frank Kyle. Up close, he saw that the back half of Kyle's skull was missing. It was blatantly obvious that he was dead, but he pressed two fingers into the side of his neck anyway, searching for a pulse in the carotid artery. It was merely a formality, but procedure required it to be done, and Davies was a stickler for procedure.

The body was still warm.

Seeing that Kyle was beyond help, Davies re-joined his colleagues in the hall. "We've got one fatality, single gunshot to the head," he informed them, grimly.

Outside, the wail of an approaching siren grew steadily louder, heralding the imminent arrival of Trojan 502.

With Langworthy covering the stairs, in case anyone tried to lay down a field of fire from above while their backs were turned, Davies and Blair systematically cleared the remaining downstairs rooms. As they regrouped to move upstairs, the crew of Trojan 502 arrived, doubling their firepower.

Detective Chief Inspector Andrew Quinlan, clad in a full set of barrier clothing, was met at the street door by Sam Calvin, the duty Crime Scene Manager. "What have we got, Sam?" he asked as he stepped inside the hall.

"You'll find the victim in the first room on the right," Calvin informed him, pointing towards the open door with his clipboard. "Looks like he was killed by a single gunshot to the head."

Like Quinlan, he wore a set of white Tyvek coveralls, a Victoria face mask, plastic overshoes and nitrile gloves.

Quinlan was the Homicide Command's on-call Senior Investigating Officer for East London, and he had been called back into work to take charge of the investigation. "You'd better lead the way," he said, gesturing for Calvin to precede him.

Inside the study, an SO3 photographer was busy taking preliminary record photography. The motor drive of his expensive camera whirled quietly as he snapped away, accompanied by the strobing effect of the attached flash.

"Ned, can you give us a minute, please," Calvin asked, placing a gloved hand on his shoulder to get his attention.

Ned Saunders stood up, smiling at them from behind his face mask. "Sure thing, Sam," he said, folding his tripod up and moving it out of the way so that Calvin and Quinlan could get closer to the body.

From behind his tortoiseshell framed glasses, Quinlan studied the corpse. "He's a big man," he observed. "Maybe even bigger than Tony Dillon."

Calvin chuckled. "I wouldn't go saying that to Tony if I were you," he advised.

"No, perhaps not," Quinlan agreed with a wan smile. He made a sweeping gesture towards the framed photos that adorned the walls. "Looks like our victim was a pretty serious bodybuilder. I wonder if he was on steroids."

Calvin responded with a disinterested shrug. At his stage, it didn't seem particularly relevant to the case, so he didn't care. "I guess we'll find out when the toxicology results come in," he said, dismissively.

Walking up to the desk where the victim sat, Quinlan spent a few moments studying the entry wound. "Do you think I'd be able to see all the way through if I peered inside?"

Behind his mask, Calvin grinned. "Why don't you give it a try?" he suggested.

Quinlan shuddered at the thought. "I think I'll pass on that one." Walking around the desk, he saw that the back of the dead man's head was a real mess. "Crikey! It's a good job his wife didn't find him," he said, grimacing at the carnage. Circling the desk until he found himself back where he'd started, Quinlan studied the victim's facial expression. "He looks really shocked, doesn't he? Like he wasn't expecting to be shot."

"I'm sure he wasn't expecting it," Calvin said. "He probably just thought they were here to rob him, not end his life."

Quinlan thought about that. "Was this a robbery gone wrong, or did they come here intending to kill him?"

Assuming the question was purely rhetorical, and not directed at him, Calvin remained silent.

Deep in thought, Quinlan moved to the centre of the room. "I didn't see any powder marks around the entry wound," he pointed out, "so I'm assuming the killer didn't shoot him at point blank range?"

Powder burns were caused by the muzzle flashes that occurred when the gases expelled from a gun's barrel combusted during discharge. Their presence would have indicated that the weapon had been in direct contact with, or in very close proximity to, the victim when it was fired.

"I agree," Calvin said.

"So, how close do you think the gunman was standing when he pulled the trigger?"

Calvin crossed to his side as he pondered this. "We found the ejected shell over by the wall," he said, pointing to Quinlan's left.

A clear plastic sharps tube had been placed over the casing to identify its location and prevent anyone entering the room from accidentally kicking it.

"Using the landing site as a reference point, I'm guessing that the shooter was standing in the middle of the room, pretty much where we are now," Calvin said. "Naturally, I've requested the attendance of a ballistics expert, so hopefully that will give us a clearer picture."

Crossing to where the spent cartridge had fallen, Quinlan knelt down to get a closer look. "The shooter used a pistol, not a converted Brocock?"

Converting easily obtainable Brocock replicas into live firing weapons had become big business for some of London's more entrepreneurial criminals. With the right equipment, a harmless replica could be converted into a real firearm, capable of discharging a .22 cartridge, in less than ten minutes, simply by using a decent quality household drill.

Calvin shook his head, emphatically. "Nope. The killer used a Section One firearm, a nine millimetre from the look of it, not a converted replica, and that makes me think the intruders were probably professionals, not just local oiks."

"I'll need the cartridge case checked for DNA and fingerprints before the FSS submit it to NABIS for ballistic comparisons," Quinlan told him, standing up as he spoke.

It was standard procedure for the Met's Forensic Science Service at Lambeth to have striation marks and hammer imprints run through the National Ballistics Intelligence Service – or NABIS for short – to see if they matched those of weapons that had been used in previous shootings.

"That goes without saying," Calvin replied in a narked tone that suggested Quinlan was trying to teach him how to suck eggs.

"Yes, of course," Quinlan said, realising that he had inadvertently caused offence. "Apologies, Sam. I wasn't trying to tell you how to do your job." He stepped away from the shell casing and turned his attention to the open safe. "Is there anything in it?" he asked.

"A loaded Colt Python .357 Magnum revolver," Calvin said.

Quinlan stared at him in surprise. "That's interesting."

The possession of handguns anywhere in the UK, apart from Northern Ireland, had been banned since the Dunblane school massacre in 1996, which meant the weapon stashed in Kyle's safe was an illegally held one.

"Is he a known villain?" Calvin asked.

"No idea," Quinlan admitted. "I've got people back at Hertford House running intelligence checks on him as we speak."

"Do you want to have a quick nose around the rest of the house before you go?" Calvin asked. It was a, not very subtle, hint that the SIO had taken up enough of his time and he wanted to get back to work.

Quinlan nodded. "I understand the place was subjected to a messy search?" he said. "So, maybe the killers didn't find what they were looking for in the safe?"

Calvin shrugged. "Who knows. Perhaps the victim's wife can shed some light on that when she calms down. Last I heard, she was so hysterical that the paramedics were talking about sedating her."

"I've sent a DC to the hospital with her," Quinlan said, "but I don't think we're going to get much sense out of her tonight if I'm honest."

"So, are you going to be keeping this case, Andy?" Calvin asked, more out of politeness than interest, "or are you just holding it until it's handed over."

Quinlan glanced over at the body, then sighed. Although this was a very interesting job, he sensed that this was going to be a complicated and protracted enquiry and, with an upcoming promotion board to prepare for, he really could have done without taking it on.

"No, I think I'm stuck with this one," he said, miserably.

8

FRIDAY 5TH OCTOBER 2001

Blagging a favour

Carrie had hardly slept a wink all night. How could she have, now that poor Frankie was as dead as a dodo and his heavily pregnant wife had been left a widow?

Frankie's murder had been the lead item on this morning's six o'clock news, which had started playing the moment her radio alarm clock had gone off; it wasn't a good story to be waking up too, not that she had actually been asleep.

Running a hand through her still damp hair, Carrie wondered what the hell Dazza had been thinking when he'd pulled the trigger?

Her plan had been so simple: take Frankie and his wife by surprise; hold them at gunpoint; steal the jewels and any cash that was floating about the house, then tie them up and get out without making any fuss. Willard would never have reported the robbery but, with Frankie dead, the police were now involved.

Bleary eyed from lack of sleep, she quietly closed the door to her house and crossed the road to Oberon House, the block of flats her brother lived in. Dazza's flat was on the ground floor, about halfway along the landing, and she could see that there was a light on in the kitchen, which meant that he hadn't left for work yet.

Good. She intended to give him a piece of her mind before he did.

Peering in through the kitchen window, she spotted her brother sitting at the table with his back to her, eating a slice of toast like this was just a normal day and he hadn't committed a cold-blooded murder the previous evening.

Dazza had rung her in a right flap after returning to the garage last night, and the agitated tone of his voice had instantly given away the fact that something had gone badly wrong. It had taken a bit of prompting on her part, but he had eventually confessed that there had been a 'slight hitch'.

A slight hitch? It was an absolute fucking catastrophe!

She tapped on the window, not wanting to disturb Dazza's other half, who was probably still fast asleep at this time of day.

Standing up, Dazza motioned her to go to the street door. "I wasn't expecting to see you up this early," he said as she barged past him and strode into the kitchen.

"Close the door behind you," she hissed when he followed her in.

After doing so, Dazza sat down and resumed eating his toast. She could smell the peanut butter it was coated in. "Fancy a brew, sis?" he asked, casually nodding towards the kettle. "I'm just about to make one for Janice anyway."

"No, I bloody well don't," Carrie snapped. She slid into the wooden chair opposite his and stared daggers at him across the pine table, waiting for an explanation. When it became apparent that she wasn't going to get one, she leaned forward and spoke in a strained whisper. "What the hell happened last night? Frankie's death's all over the poxy news this morning."

He had refused to go into specifics over the phone, limiting the information he had provided to the fact that he had been forced to shoot Frankie, and that he was dead.

Dazza's eyes shot up to the ceiling, as if afraid that Janice might overhear them. When Carrie opened her mouth to speak, he held up his hands to silence her. "Look, I'm sorry about what happened last night," he said through gritted teeth, "but I swear I didn't have any choice in the matter, not after he saw the tattoo on my arm."

Carrie was confused. "Tattoo? What tattoo?"

Darren rolled his left sleeve up and showed it to her. "This one," he said, holding his arm up for inspection. "It's got our fucking names on it, for Christ's sake."

Carrie was stunned. "The writing's tiny, Dazza. You don't honestly think he would have been able to read that, do you?"

"He *did* read it," Darren told her, his voice becoming increasingly strained with every word. "He even started calling me Darren, for fuck's sake, and he told me he was going to hunt me down and kill me. What else was I meant to do?"

Carrie's face had drained of colour. "That's why you killed him?" she asked, shaking her head incredulously. "Because he saw the names on your stupid tattoo?"

Angered by her naivety, Darren's face twisted into a contemptuous sneer. "You need to face up to the facts," he growled, leaning across the table to point an accusatory finger at her chest. "The moment that dickhead discovered our names, I had to kill him. If he'd survived, Willard would have come after all of us and, as much as you might like to kid yourself that he's got a soft spot for you because of dad, the truth is he would have had you snuffed out without batting an eyelid."

Carrie's indignation burned like fire. "How *dare* you pretend you killed Frankie to protect me!" she hissed, feeling tears of anger prickle her eyes.

Darren dry washed his unshaven face with shaking hands. "Look, sis," he said in a voice that trembled with emotion, "you might think you're a tough cookie, but the truth is, you ain't got a clue when it comes to the ways of the world. Bottom line is, if I hadn't killed that horrible fucker last night, he *would* have come after you, me, and Fingers, and he wouldn't have thought twice about slotting the three of us. Knowing that, who would you rather see in a wooden box: him or us? Because I had to make a split-second choice last night, and I chose him."

Carrie didn't know what to say. This wasn't her fault; she hadn't pulled the trigger, or even been anywhere near the house, so why did she feel so damn guilty?

She forced herself to think pragmatically; whether Frankie's death had been necessary or not, it had happened, and nothing could change that, so it was pointless to dwell on it or waste energy on self-recrimination. All that mattered now was them not getting caught. "Oh Dazza," she said, studying him through tear blurred eyes. "What have we got ourselves into?"

He reached out a calloused hand and squeezed her arm. "Don't worry, sis," he said, softly. "We've covered our tracks, so no one will ever be able to trace the robbery back to us."

Carrie shrugged his hand off, then dragged her sleeve across her face. "What have you done with the guns you and Fingers took on the job?"

"The guns are somewhere safe," he said, dismissively.

Carrie's eyes burned into his. "You need to destroy them," she warned. "If the Cozzers find them, they'll be able to link the pair of you to Frankie's murder."

Darren's voice hardened. "They won't find them," he promised, "so don't worry about it."

Carrie felt her cheeks flush. "What about the cash and jewellery?" she demanded, "or shouldn't I worry about those, either?"

Darren pinched the bridge of his nose, then exhaled slowly. "There was a bag of jewels in the safe," he said with forced patience, "but I haven't had a chance to sort through what's in it yet. What I have done is count the cash we found." A pause for effect. "Kyle had a couple of hundred grand stashed away."

Carrie's eyes widened. "How much?" she gasped.

"You heard me," he said with a mirthless smile. "Two hundred grand. We'll split it three ways, so I'll have enough from my cut to bail out my business even if we don't earn much from the jewels. That means you won't have to sell the house."

Carrie's mind was reeling; how had Frankie accumulated that much money? It had to be dirty, but was it his or was he just looking after it for Willard?

"We'll need to stash it somewhere safe," she said, thinking fast. "And, whatever happens, we'll need to be ultra-cautious. We can't spend a penny of it until after the heat's died down and we're in the clear."

Darren's lips compressed into an angry thin line. "Don't treat me like an idiot. I haven't even told Fingers how much money we got away with yet, that's how bloody cautious I'm being."

"I'm not treating you like an idiot," she snapped, then tempered her voice before continuing. "But you've grown reckless since you started hanging out with Gareth Pevensey, and I don't want you doing something that could land us all in the shit."

It was a veiled dig at the ram raids he had been committing with them.

"Yeah, well, him and his brother are banged up now, so you won't have to worry about that anymore, will you?"

Carrie checked her watch; it was getting on for seven. "I need to get a move on," she said, pushing her chair back and standing up. She was dreading going into work. Frankie had been a branch manager for one of their busiest betting shops, so everyone was going to be talking about his murder. "What time are you setting off?" she asked.

Darren shifted awkwardly in his seat. "I'm not going into work today," he said quietly.

Carrie's jaw dropped. "What?"

Darren gave her a shifty look, then stared down at his feet. "I said I'm not going into work today."

Carrie sat back down. "You're shitting me?"

A little shake of the head, but still no eye contact. "No. Me and Janice are going away for a few days, so that I can get my head together."

Carrie had to stop herself from leaning over the table and slapping him. "Don't you think it'll look suspicious if you don't show up?" she asked, struggling to control her temper.

"It can't be helped," he said, defiantly. "I booked the trip on Tuesday morning. I wasn't thinking straight after Monday night's ram raid went south." A guilty shrug. "Thought I'd better take Janice away for a few days, just in case it was the last chance I got for a while. Anyway, it'll be fine," he assured her. "I'll make sure that the cash and the jewels are well hidden before I go, and there isn't much going on at the garage anyway, so Fingers won't have too much to do."

"Tell me, Dazza," she asked, feeling betrayed. "Would you have told me about this little trip of yours if I hadn't come over to see you this morning?"

A pathetic shrug. "I was going to give you a call before we set off," he said meekly.

Carrie didn't believe that for one moment. "Course you were," said, spitting the words out contemptuously.

The guilt that flashed across his face confirmed her suspicion.

"You haven't said anything to Aidan about Frankie or the ram raids, have you?" Darren asked.

Carrie let out a harsh, mocking laugh. She wouldn't trust her twin as far as she could throw him. "Don't be ridiculous. That useless bastard would give us both up to Willard or the Fuzz if he thought there was any money in it for him."

Andy Quinlan poked his head around the door to Tyler's office. It was just after nine, and he had just come from briefing his team on the overnight murder of Frank Kyle.

"Morning, Jack."

Tyler looked up from the forensic report he had been reading. "Morning, mate," he replied with a warm smile. "I heard you took on a new job last night. Anything good?"

"It's quite an interesting one, actually," Quinlan said, flopping down into the chair opposite Tyler's desk and running a hand through his thick mop of black hair. Behind the glasses that gave him such a professorial look, his eyes were red rimmed and puffy. "A bloke in East Ham was shot dead by masked intruders, who then ransacked his house looking for money."

"You look shattered," Tyler observed. "Have you been here all night?"

Quinlan nodded. "I'm bloody knackered," he admitted, peering over Tyler's shoulder to take in the picturesque views that his window afforded of the A406 dual carriageway and the Barking gas works.

"I'm guessing this isn't a social call?" Tyler said.

"Afraid not," Quinlan confirmed with a wry smile "I'm hoping to blag a big favour and borrow some troops to help us out with the statement taking, the CCTV trawl and all the house-to-house enquiries."

Tyler's face adopted a pained expression. "But it's Friday, and we're off over the weekend so I was planning to let the team slip away at a reasonable time today," by which he meant he was going to let them slide a little early.

Quinlan had anticipated Tyler's reaction. It was POETS Day – Piss Off Early, Tomorrow's Saturday – after all, and he was prepared for it. "I fully appreciate that, Jack, which is why I'm offering the glorious incentive of one day's red time over the weekend to anyone who helps us out today."

Red time was double time overtime.

Tyler responded with a cynical laugh. They both knew that nothing attracted willing volunteers more than the offer of red time. "What's the deal?"

"Today's going to be a very long day, there's no denying that. As a caveat, anyone helping us out can work one day in red over the weekend. If we're half as busy as I suspect we're going to be, they'll probably be given the chance to work both days."

Tyler winced. "Sounds like this new job's going to cost you a few quid."

Quinlan nodded, resigned to the fact that his budget was going to take a bit of a pounding. "Can't be helped," he said, pragmatically.

"How many people do you need?"

"One DS and six DCs would be perfect," Quinlan replied, stifling a yawn. "Sorry," he said with an embarrassed grin.

Tyler sympathised in a way that few others would be able to. Senior Investigating Officers had to lead by example. During the early stages of a new job that meant being the first one into the office and the last out, and it was a delicate balancing act, giving your all to an enquiry without damaging your health in the process. "Leave it to me, Andy," he said. "Once I've canvassed the team, I'll send the money grabbing bastards who volunteer straight through to you."

Jonas Willard was sitting comfortably behind his expensive teak desk, immersed in the racing section in the morning paper while enjoying a cup of coffee, as was his wont most weekday mornings. The sixty-one year old looked up in surprise when Fred Wiggins burst into his office without knocking. "What is it, Fred?" he asked, annoyed as much by the lack of manners as the intrusion.

"Frank the Tank's been murdered, shot dead in his own home last night," Wiggins said without preamble.

Willard had been chewing on a large cigar but, on hearing that, he placed it in the ashtray next to his coffee cup. "Who did it?' he demanded, staring at Wiggins over the top of his square framed glasses. "Was it the Turks?"

After Frankie's incredible act of stupidity, which could easily have sparked a war between Willard's mob and the Turks, Wiggins had been all for having the idiot's legs broken, just to teach him a lesson, but Willard had decided against it, feeling that no real harm had been done. Perhaps he had been wrong?

Wiggins shook his head. "It doesn't sound like it."

Willard wasn't so sure. It struck him as a hell of a coincidence that Frank Kyle had been gunned down just two days after the fiasco with the diamonds, and he had never been a big believer in coincidences. "What *does* it sound like, then?" he asked, folding his newspaper and tossing it onto his desk.

"An old chum of mine lives opposite Frankie's gaff," Wiggins explained. "When he heard all the commotion last night, he started snooping around. The word on the street is that it was a couple of white geezers who broke in looking for money."

Willard remained sceptical. "Is that so?"

Wiggins could only shrug. "Well, my mate wasn't able to speak to Frankie's missus directly, seeing as the ambulance had already whisked her off to hospital by the time he went out, but he did manage to have a quiet word with the two old fogies who took her in and called the Cozzers. Morag – that's Frankie's missus – told them that the two slags who topped Frankie were white fuckers with local accents."

Willard slammed the bottom of his fist down onto the desktop with so much force that it rattled his cup and saucer. "Well, it's a fucking liberty and, whoever it was, I want them taken care of, pronto."

"Of course," Wiggins agreed.

"I mean it, Fred. No one steals from me, or kills one of my men, especially not on my own fucking manor."

"Don't worry, Mr Willard," Wiggins soothed. "Sooner or later, the soppy gits who did it will start blabbing; people like that always do. Once word gets out, someone'll grass them up to us."

Slightly mollified, Willard retrieved his cigar and resumed chomping on it. "And what about the diamonds that Frankie was looking after for me?" he asked between puffs. "Are they safe?"

Wiggins spread his arms apologetically. "Sorry, Mr Willard, I don't know the answer to that one."

"Well, don't just stand there like a spare prick at a wedding," Willard snapped. "Go and find out. If those murdering cunts have stolen my diamonds, I'll have them flayed alive while their families watch on."

"I'll make some calls," Wiggins offered.

Willard hammered his desk again, and this time the cup toppled over, spilling coffee all over his blotter. "Don't make fucking calls," he raged. "Get yourself straight over to Frankie's gaff and spin the place."

Wiggins flinched. Very few people scared him, but Willard did. "Mr Willard, Frankie's house is still a crime scene. I won't be able to get anywhere near it while it's crawling with Cozzers. Tell you what, let me make some discreet enquiries to find out where his wife is instead, then I'll go straight over and have a quiet word with her."

"You do that, Fred," Willard snapped. "If the bastards who topped Frankie didn't steal my diamonds, and they're still round his gaff, I don't want them falling into the hands of the Old Bill. I'll never get them back if that happens."

DS Charlie White was a diminutive Scotsman whose nose had been so badly broken during his youth that it was now noticeably out of alignment with the rest of his face, leaving him with a very nasally voice. Coupled with his strong Glaswegian accent, this could make him rather difficult to understand at times, especially when he was angry or stressed, because on those occasions he tended to speak much faster than normal. Charlie had been the only DS on Tyler's team to volunteer to work the weekend, and he now led a contingent of six DCs along the corridor towards Andy Quinlan's office.

"We've had a bit of a result here, if you ask me," he said, glancing sideways at DC Kevin Murray, who had also volunteered.

"I know," Murray grinned. The skeletally thin detective had messy brown hair and a goatee beard that took some of the sharpness out of his weasel like features. "With a bit of luck, all we'll have to do is a bit of CCTV collection. That'll be a doddle."

Following along behind them, DC Debbie Brown snorted. She was a short, buxom woman in her late thirties, with a plain but not unattractive face. "That's so typical of you, Kevin," she said, unimpressed by his brazen laziness. "We've not even started yet, and you're already trying to land yourself a cushy number."

Beside her, DC Dick Jarvis chuckled. Fresh faced and fair haired, he was considerably younger than the others.

Glancing back over his shoulder, Murray tapped the side of his skull. "That's the difference between you and me, Debs," he said with a smarmy grin. "I'm always thinking ahead."

It was a pity he wasn't always looking ahead because, as they turned the corner, he collided with Tony Dillon, who was coming the other way.

"Oomph!" Murray gasped as he was brought to a painful halt. Knocked off balance, he tottered backwards and would have fallen flat on his backside if Debbie Brown and Dick Jarvis hadn't reached out to steady him.

Bringing up the rear of the little group, DCs Jim Stone, an ex-paratrooper who was as hard as nails, and Paul Evans, a fiery Welshman whose two passions in life were rugby and football, burst into laughter.

Incensed by this, Murray shrugged off the supporting hands of his colleagues and spun to confront the idiot who had walked into him. His jaw dropped when he saw who it was, and he quickly swallowed the abuse that was about to leave his lips.

"Look what you've done," Dillon complained, staring down at the two empty polystyrene cups in his hands. A moment ago, they had been filled to the brim with steaming hot coffee, but the liquid was now a steaming puddle on the hallway's heavy-duty carpet.

Murray's face blanched. Dillon didn't have a very high opinion of him to start with, and this was hardly going to improve matters. "Sorry, boss," he muttered. "It's Debs fault for distracting me." Ignoring the indignant huff from behind, he quickly reached into his trouser pocket and fished out a couple of pound coins. "There you go," he said, holding them out for Dillon to take. "Let me pay for those spilt drinks."

Refusing the money, Dillon stormed off, muttering obscenities under his breath.

Murray watched him go, then shook his head. "Some people, eh? How ungrateful was he?"

With a face like thunder, Debbie Brown barged him out of the way and set off towards DCI Quinlan's office, her chin raised in haughty disdain.

Murray glanced at each of the others in turn. "What's her problem?" he asked, watching her storm off.

All morning, Carrie had been forced to listen to her colleagues discussing Frankie's murder amongst themselves in hushed whispers. A couple of the girls had even approached her to see if Mr Willard would be okay with them organising a whip round to buy Frankie's widow some flowers. She had promised to bring it up with him if and when the poxy newspaper reporters who kept ringing in to request a comment from Mr Willard stopped bothering her.

Willard had gathered everyone together at the start of the day to make an official announcement. As tragic as Frankie's death was, he had told them in a suitably solemn tone, it wouldn't affect the orderly running of the business, and their working practices would continue as normal, with Frankie's deputy stepping in to cover his role until a new branch manager could be recruited. Afterwards, Willard had retired to his office, where he had remained locked in muted conversation with Fred Wiggins ever since.

In the wake of the terrible announcement, the mood at head office had been very subdued, with everyone understandably shocked. Like Carrie, a few of the girls had already heard about it on the morning news, but most hadn't. Frankie had always been a popular figure, and more than a few tears had been shed for his passing.

A sudden buzzing caught Carrie's attention, and she glanced down to see her mobile vibrating its way across her desk. She winced when she saw that the incoming call was from Aidan.

What the hell did he want? She had purposefully avoided speaking to him since their bust up the previous night. The atmosphere at home had been terrible after that, with her giving him the cold shoulder, and him moping around the place in a sulk, acting as if he was the one who had been wronged, and not her. Annie had tried to act as peacemaker, but Aidan had grown angry with her, and had accused her of taking Carrie's side. Then, calling her every name under the sun, he had physically ejected her from the house.

Why Annie tolerated Aidan's appalling behaviour was beyond Carrie. Perhaps she only put up with him in the hope that the family court would take a more favourable view of her circumstances if she was in a steady relationship when her case was heard in a couple of months' time?

Looking around to ensure that no one was watching, Carrie snatched up her mobile and pressed the green button. "What is it this time, Aidan?" she hissed, keeping her voice low in case anyone overheard.

"I've been thinking," Aidan told her. "I don't reckon mum and dad were in their right minds when they made that will, and I'm going to hire a solicitor to challenge it."

He sounded agitated, and his voice was all slurred. She guessed that he was either stoned or drunk, possibly both. It was the only logical explanation for his paranoid ramblings.

Closing her eyes, Carrie screamed inwardly. When he finally shut up, she sucked in a deep breath and forced herself to speak calmly. "Look, Aidan, you do whatever you think is right, but *please* don't bother me while I'm at work unless it's an emergency."

"*This is an emergency,*" he yelled, flying off the handle. "*It might not be important to you, but it's fucking life or death for me. I know you and Dazza deliberately poisoned mum and dad against me, tricked them into writing me out of their will so that you could have more for yourselves, but I won't let you steal my rightful inheritance from—*"

Pressing the red button, Carrie ended the call. There was no way that she could have this bloody discussion with him now, even if she wanted to, which she most certainly didn't. Besides, what would be the point? Hadn't she already explained the situation to him a million times? Their parents had never consulted her or Dazza about cutting Aidan out of the inheritance, and it had been as much of a shock to them as it had to him.

Almost immediately, her mobile started vibrating again, sounding like an angry bee.

With a tortured groan, she glanced down at the caller ID. Sure enough, it was Aidan. After declining the call, Carrie powered her phone down, knowing that if she left it on, he would just keep ringing her.

Her timing was perfect because, a split second later, an unusually stern-faced Fred Wiggins emerged from Willard's office and walked straight past her desk on his way out, forgoing any of the usual pleasantries.

She watched him move through the main admin area and link up with Casper, who had only just arrived. After a quick word, both men set off towards the exit, their faces grim.

A little frisson of panic passed through her as she wondered what they were up to.

―――

Wiggins had finally managed to speak to his man on the inside, but the useless wanker had been about as much use as a chocolate tea pot. Wiggins wasn't interested in his flimsy excuses about another murder team investigating the case, and he had told him in no uncertain terms to find out if the diamonds were still at Frankie's gaff.

At least tracking Morag Kyle down had proved easy enough, as she was staying with Frankie's older sister, Pauline.

Pauline Kyle was a short stout woman with the stern face of a bulldog. Unlike Frankie, it could never be said that she resembled a tank, although there were probably grounds for comparing her to a smallish armoured car. After showing them into the living room and making them all tea, Pauline tactfully retreated to the kitchen with her two screaming brats in tow, in order to allow them some privacy while they talked.

"We're very sorry for your loss, Mrs Kyle, aren't we, Casper?" Wiggins told Morag, smiling sweetly in an effort to break the ice.

The two men were crammed together in a little two-seater sofa that was barely big enough to contain Casper's great bulk, without having to accommodate Wiggins as well.

Sitting opposite them in a frayed fabric armchair, and looking like she carried the weight of the world on her slender shoulders, Morag alternated between dabbing at her eyes with a little blue handkerchief and rubbing the huge bump protruding from her stomach.

Sitting with his hands clasped on his lap, the lumbering giant said nothing, so Wiggins gave him a subtle nudge in the ribs.

"Yeah. Sorry for your loss," Casper dutifully blurted out, even nodding like he meant it.

"Thank you," Morag said, her voice quivering with raw emotion.

Wiggins had insisted that the intimidating albino should sit down beside him to put Morag at ease. However, after several minutes of being crushed, he was bitterly regretting the decision.

"Mr Willard wanted me to pass on his sincere condolences," Wiggins continued, fidgeting uncomfortably to try and restore the flagging circulation to his legs, "and he wants me to assure you that you'll be well taken care of. You know, financially speaking. He's gonna make sure Frankie gets a proper send off, so you won't have to worry about funeral costs or anything like that."

Morag managed a weak smile. "That's very kind of him," she sniffed.

Wiggins took a sip of the tepid tea that Pauline had made them, grimaced, then cleared his throat. "This is a little awkward," he said, placing his cup and saucer on the small table beside the sofa, "what with poor Frankie's body not even being cold yet, but I really need to ask you some questions about what happened."

"They were wearing masks, Mr Wiggins, and everything happened so quickly," Morag blurted out. "I didnae even see their faces–" Her voice suddenly cracked, and she choked back a giant sob. "Sorry," she said, visibly shrinking into herself. "It's just a bit too painful for me to talk about it at the moment."

Casper sighed impatiently, letting Wiggins know he was getting bored.

"I've only got a few questions," Wiggins promised. "Start by telling me what colour these two slags–er–I mean these two blokes were?"

"They were white."

"Are you sure about that? Is it possible that they were, oh, I don't know, Turkish?"

"They were definitely white folk, Mr Wiggins," she insisted. "Their balaclavas had big eye and mouth holes in them, and I could clearly see their skin through those. Maybe their complexion wasnae as pale and pasty as mine," she said, holding an anaemic looking arm up, "but they defiantly wasnae foreigners."

Wiggins paused a moment, processing what she had said. "If it's not too much trouble," he finally said, "I'd like you to describe these two blokes for me. Do you think you could do that?"

Morag responded with an almost imperceptible nod, then dabbed each of her eyes in turn.

Wiggins was a hard man; he was cold and cruel, and could be totally ruthless when it was necessary, but even he couldn't help but be moved by her obvious pain. "If it's any consolation, luv," he said softly, "me and Casper won't rest until we've delivered their worthless heads to Mr Willard on a platter, and I don't mean that in a metaphorical sense, either."

Morag managed a tearful smile. "Frankie's lucky to have friends like you and Mr Willard," she sobbed. "He would be very grateful for everything that you're doing for him."

Wiggins brushed the comment aside. "It's the least we can do," he said. "Now, if you don't mind, tell me what they looked like."

Taking a deep breath, Morag forced herself to relive the night of her husband's murder. As she spoke, her face contorted with pain. "There were two men, both dressed in dark clothing and wearing balaclavas." Her breathing grew faster, became more ragged. "The one in charge was about six foot tall, and he was barrel chested. No' a bodybuilder like my Frank, but big nonetheless. The second one was a few inches shorter, and skinny. I got the impression he was a lot younger."

Wiggins leaned forward. "What makes you say that?"

Morag shrugged. "I cannae really say. Maybe it was the way he deferred to the bigger guy, and he seemed so nervous, like he didnae really want to be there."

"We're nearly finished," Wiggins promised her. "I just need you to tell me exactly what these bastards said to Frankie before they killed him?"

Morag thought hard. "They asked him where he kept his money... He tried to fob them off by saying he had a couple of grand stashed away in the bedroom, but the big one just laughed, like he knew better, and then he threatened to shoot me if Frankie didnae play ball and tell them where the cash was." Tears were running freely down Morag's face now. "The big one hit me," she whispered, instinctively reaching up to touch the side of her face.

Wiggins' mouth compressed into a thin line. "Fucking liberty," he said, shaking his head in disgust. "He'll pay for doing that," he promised.

"My Frankie was so brave," Morag sobbed. "He only opened the safe to protect me. I swear he wasnae going to give into them until they threatened to kill me."

Wiggins leaned forward, partly to comfort her, partly to ease the pain of being crushed by Casper. "He was a brave bloke, Mrs Kyle," he agreed. "No one could ever dispute that."

Morag smiled proudly. "Aye, he was. He really was... The bigger of the two men led him away at gunpoint, and then a few seconds later, there was ... there was a shot. I didnae see Frankie again after that." Unable to continue, Morag buried her head in her hands and the floodgates opened.

Exchanging a quick look with Casper, who remained totally indifferent to Morag's suffering, Wiggins levered himself out of his seat and crossed to her side. Kneeling down, he placed an awkward hand on her shoulder in what he hoped was a comforting gesture. "Just one more question," he said, softly. "Did Frankie ever say anything to you about any diamonds?"

Morag stared up at him, face blotchy, eyes red, nose running. "F–Frankie told me he was l–looking after some diamonds for Mr Willard," she stammered.

"What about the two slags who topped him, did they mention them?"

A frown of fierce concentration creased Morag's forehead.

"Now that you mention it, I'm pretty sure that the smaller of the two men did say something about diamonds, but I cannae recall exactly what it was."

That was interesting.

"I don't suppose you know where the diamonds are now, do you luv?" Wiggins asked, trying not to sound too eager.

Morag shook her head. "They were in the safe, last I knew." With that, she buried her head in her hands again, and began crying uncontrollably.

Alerted by the sound of her wailing, Pauline Kyle gingerly poked her head around the kitchen door. "Is everything all right, Mr Wiggins?" she asked, nervously.

Wiggins stood up, straightened his tie. "Poor little cow's heartbroken," he said, beckoning her into the room.

Pauline rushed over to Morag's side. Kneeling down, she wrapped a protective arm around the girl's shoulders. "It's alright, Morag," she said, close to tears herself. "We're all hurting, but we'll get through this together cause that's what families do."

Wiggins signalled for Casper to stand up. "We'll see ourselves out," he said, producing a business card from inside his jacket. "Someone will be in touch with you to sort out the funeral arrangements, Mrs Kyle. In the meantime, if you remember anything that might help us track down the cockroaches responsible for doing this to Frankie, give me a call on this number." When Morag didn't look up, he handed the card to Pauline for safekeeping. "One last thing," he said, pausing by the doorway. "Me and Mr Willard would be very grateful if you didn't mention anything about the diamonds to the Old Bill."

9

Sun, sea and sangria

Charlie White and Kevin Murray hadn't been given the cushy number that they had been hoping for. Instead of bumbling around in search of CCTV, they had been dispatched to collect Morag Kyle from her sister-in-law's house, where she had been staying since her release from hospital, with instructions to take her to Plaistow police station and conduct a lengthy key witness interview with her on tape.

"Well, so far this isn't going quite the way I'd envisaged it," Murray complained as he pulled the battered old pool car up outside a mid-terraced house in Canning Town.

"Aye, I was thinking the same thing," White agreed, double checking the address against the one he'd scribbled in his daybook to make sure they were at the right place.

When Murray switched off the ignition, the car began to judder violently.

"This thing really needs to be scrapped," White said, waiting for the shaking and rattling to stop before opening his door.

"I had the same problem with an old banger I owned in my late teens," Murray informed him, getting out to the accompaniment of rusting door hinges and creaking springs. "Turned out the bolts connecting the lower swing arm to the gearbox were loose."

White stared at him blankly. "I havenae got a clue what you're talking about."

Murray pointed at the gleaming Audi A4 Quattro they had parked behind. "Pity we can't be given one of them," he said, staring enviously at the car.

"In your dreams," White scoffed.

The hinges on the gate had dropped, and it dragged noisily along the floor as Murray pushed it open. The front garden had a postage stamp sized lawn, which was full of weeds.

"As she's a fellow Jock, it's probably best if I let you do all the talking," he said, smiling sweetly.

White laughed. "Fine by me. It'll be nice to have a cultured conversation for once, instead of having to make boring small talk with an ignorant Sassenach like you."

Before he could ring the bell, the street door opened, and White found himself standing face to face with a short, slim white man who looked very dapper in an expensive business suit. In his late-thirties, the man had intelligent eyes, but there was a cruel cunningness in them that made White instantly distrust him.

"Can I help you? The man asked, clearly surprised to find them standing there. He had an East London accent, White noticed, and his tone, although not exactly hostile, could hardly be described as friendly.

White produced his warrant card. "I'm DS White from the Homicide Command, and I'm here to see Mrs Morag Kyle."

Glancing over his shoulder, the man spoke to someone standing in the hall behind him. "Casper, be a good lad and let Pauline know that the police are here, would you?"

There was an animal like grunt from within, and a large shape detached itself from the surrounding shadows and went off in search of Pauline Kyle.

"I take it this is in relation to Frankie's murder," the man in the doorway asked, leaning against the frame and crossing his arms.

He had neatly manicured fingernails, White observed, wondering what he did for a living.

"Aye, that's right," White confirmed.

"Are you any closer to catching the slags that did it?" the man asked.

White's eyes narrowed. "I'm sorry, you are?"

The man extended a hand. "Fred Wiggins, area manager for Willard Betting. Frankie was the manager at our Stratford branch. I was just carrying out a welfare visit on behalf of the company."

"I see," White said, thinking Wiggins had a grip like a wet lettuce. "The honest answer to your question, Mr Wiggins, is no, but it's early days yet. We'll get the people responsible; you can be sure of that."

Wiggins responded with a crocodile smile. "I'm sure you will," he purred, releasing White's hand.

There was a commotion behind him, and a woman in her early forties appeared in the doorway.

"I'm Pauline Kyle, Frankie's sister," she told the officers. She was a bit dumpy, with short hair and a harsh, lived-in face, and she gave the impression that she would give as good as she got in an argument.

White went through the rigmarole of showing his warrant card and identifying himself all over again. "My condolences for your loss," he told her, when that was done. "Would it be possible for us to come in and speak to Morag?"

"Of course," Pauline said. Stepping aside, she unfolded her chunky arms to let them pass but, before White could enter, Fred Wiggins stepped into the front garden.

"Right then, Pauline, we're going to scoot off and leave you in peace."

"Right you are, Mr Wiggins. Thanks again for stopping by," Pauline said, nodding deferentially.

"My pleasure," Wiggins told her with a friendly smile.

As he set off along the garden path, a huge man, with pale skin and short white spikey hair, appeared in the doorway behind him, completely filling it. Scowling at the two police officers through little piggy eyes, he squeezed himself through the door and lumbered off after Wiggins.

White watched him go, marvelling at the man's size. He was a good five inches taller than Tony Dillon, and was almost twice as wide.

Wiggins and his ape-like crony walked over to the Audi Quattro. The former got in without a backward glance, but the albino stopped and stared back at them hatefully before climbing in.

Murray leaned in close enough to be sure that Pauline Kyle couldn't overhear him. "Look at the size of that ugly fucker."

White nodded, grimly. "You wouldn't want to meet him in a quiet street on dark night, would you?"

"I wouldn't want to meet him anywhere, under any conditions," Murray said as the Quattro pulled away.

"Are you coming in, or what?" Pauline demanded impatiently. Her tone was noticeably cooler than the one she had reserved for Wiggins. "Only it's bloody cold out here, and you're letting all my heat out."

"Sorry," White said, walking towards the door.

Pauline's eyes followed the two detectives across the threshold. "Morag's in the living room at the end of the hall," she told them, indicating that they should go on ahead. As the detectives squeezed by her, Pauline's nose turned up in disgust, as though they had simultaneously broken wind in front of her.

When Carrie turned her phone back on, an hour later, she was unsurprised to see that she had a half dozen voice mail messages waiting for her. No doubt, these would all contain more of Aidan's disjointed ramblings. She was in desperate need of a coffee, but she decided to pop to the loo first and listen to Aidan's ranting messages before deleting them.

Locking herself in a cubicle, she sat down and clamped the Motorola against her ear. Yep. Sure enough, the first five were from her twin brother, and they were full of vitriol and rancour. He sounded even more spaced out than before, which probably meant that he had stayed in bed, smoking skunk, or possibly crack cocaine, and hadn't gone into work again.

The last one, however, was from Dazza, who was calling from Stansted Airport of all places. It seemed that he hadn't told her the whole truth earlier that morning, when he'd reluctantly revealed that he and Janice were going to go away for a few days so that he could clear his head.

She had understood him to mean that they were booking into a little B&B somewhere in the UK, like they normally did when they went on holiday, not sodding off abroad.

Dazza's message informed her that they were actually on their way to Tenerife, not Bognor Regis, for two weeks of sun, sea and sangria.

Two-fucking-weeks!

Was he completely off his trolley?

Carrie was so flabbergasted by the news that she had to replay the message twice more before it finally sank in. In the background, she could hear the airport announcer calling passengers to their flights, so there could be no doubt that he really was calling from Stansted.

She could just about accept his desire to whisk Janice off for a few days in the aftermath of Monday's botched ram raid, when he'd mistakenly believed that his collar was going to be felt at any moment, but he knew better now, and jetting off on a two-week jolly in Spain the morning after he'd killed one of Jonas Willard's men was pure madness!

She tried to call him back, but he had switched his mobile off, presumably for the flight. Carrie's hands were shaking with rage as she dialled the landline number for Dazza's garage. It was answered after the fourth ring.

"McCullen's Garage, Paul speaking."

"Fingers, it's Carrie. I've just had a message from Dazza to say he's on his way to Tenerife for a fortnight in the sun. Please, tell me this is a fucking wind up?"

"Hello, Carrie, luv," Fingers said, sounding subdued.

"Don't give me all that 'hello luv' bollocks," she snapped. "Is it a poxy wind up or not?"

As soon as the words left her mouth, she felt terrible. Fingers was probably the meekest person she had ever met, and having a go at him was a bit like kicking puppies.

"What can I tell you?" Fingers moaned, sounding thoroughly miserable. *"He's got that useless git, Terry Marshall, covering for him while he's away. The first I knew about it was when Tel-boy waltzed in this morning and told me that Dazza had fucked off on a last-minute holiday."*

Carrie was stunned. Running a hand through her hair, she wondered if she was the only sane one left in the family. "It's not your fault," she told him after a moment's reflection. "Listen, Fingers, if that jumped up tosser, Marshall, tries giving you a hard time while Dazza's away, let me know and I'll put him in his place."

"Thanks Carrie," Fingers said, sounding very relieved.

"And Fingers…?"

"Y–yes, Carrie?"

Her voice turned to steel. "Make sure you keep your bloody gob shut about what happened last night, got it?"

"I will, Carrie," he promised, and she could hear the fear in his voice. *"I won't say a dicky bird to anyone."*

After hanging up, she stormed out of the cubicle, washed her hands and returned to her desk. She was so fired up that she completely forgot about the coffee she had promised herself.

Behind her, Willard's door opened.

Glancing over her shoulder, Carrie saw him standing there in his overcoat, with a leather satchel tucked under his arm and a stout Malacca gentleman's umbrella in his hand.

"Going out, Mr Willard?" she asked, trying not to show how flustered she was by his sudden appearance.

"I've got an unavoidable business meeting with a couple of shysters who run a second-rate dog track down in Kent," he told her. "They're trying to put a bit of business my way, and from what I've heard so far, it could be quite lucrative."

At their last Christmas do, Willard had ended up getting rather tipsy. In an unusually gregarious mood, he had regaled Carrie with tall stories about race fixing in the bad old days. He had revealed how a dog's fur would be dyed to disguise it, and how it would then be entered under a false name; how coats would be swapped in the traps at the last minute, so that the dog who was odds on favourite to win finished last and the dog that everyone expected to bring up the rear won the race; and of how dogs who were stand out favourites would occasionally be given a Micky Finn to slow them down.

"I didn't think you did business with people like *that* anymore," Carrie said, wondering why a man who owned a successful chain of betting shops and a lucrative building firm would want to put his hard-earned reputation on the line for the sake of earning a few extra quid? It wasn't as if he needed the money. Willard was worth millions from his legitimate business ventures, and that was without taking all the dirty cash that he raked in from his criminal activities into account.

Willard responded with a guilty shrug. "Carrie, sweetheart, it's the villain in me. I could never resist the temptation to get involved in a bit of larceny." With that, he gave her shoulder a paternal squeeze and then set off towards the door.

"Good luck," she called out after him.

Willard stopped by the door, then turned around to face her. "Tell you what, Carrie, as I won't be coming back to the office today, why don't you knock off at three, and start the weekend early?"

"Really?"

"Absolutely."

"Thank you," she said, blowing him a kiss.

As he'd done since she was a little girl, he made a big show of grabbing it out of the air and placing it against his heart. With a farewell wave, he passed through the general admin office and walked out of the door at the far end.

As soon as he was gone, the smile fell from Carrie's face and she sagged back in her seat, feeling utterly exhausted. A girl she quite fancied had invited Carrie to join her and a few of her friends for a drink that evening, but Frankie's murder had put a bit of a dampener on the idea. As she sat there, taking stock of the situation, she began to think that it might actually do her some good to let her hair down for a little while. Plus, being able to finish work at three meant that, instead of rushing home, doing a quick change and then shooting straight out, she would have time for a luxurious soak in the bath before getting ready.

On a whim, Carrie picked up her mobile and rang Abigale Stanwick, her best friend who, by a happy coincidence, also happened to be a brilliant hairdresser. "Hi, Abi," she said when her friend picked up. "I was just wondering if you could do me a humungous favour and fit me in for a quick wash and trim this afternoon... I finish at three, so I could be at yours for half past, if that's any good? It is, oh that's perfect. Thanks, hon." Carrie blasted a few air kisses down the line. "Love you, babes, see you later."

———

Standing in a shop doorway opposite Willard Betting's head office, Stella Carter fidgeted restlessly. Not only were her feet aching like hell, but she was in desperate need of a wee. She had been waiting there for half an hour, but there was still no sign of Carrie.

To help her blend in with the rush-hour crowd, Stella was wearing a vintage check panelled gabardine trench coat, a knitted scarlet dress, and a pair of smart shoes she had dug out from the bottom of her wardrobe. The heels were only two-inches high, but they felt weird on her feet, and she could hardly stand up in them, let along walk in a straight line. Stella hated wearing makeup, but she had gone overboard with it today, smothering her blotchy skin with foundation, blusher, eyeliner and mascara. She felt like a Barbie doll, but the disguise was a necessary evil because, whatever else happened, she couldn't afford to be spotted by Fred Wiggins. That would trigger another visit from the terrifying albino, and she still had vivid nightmares about their last encounter, and all the terrible things the foul creature had threatened to do to her if she ever contacted Carrie again. There had been no doubt that he meant it; the sinister giant had radiated craziness like the sun gave off heat.

Where the fuck are you, Carrie?

Buses came and went with boring regularity, and the numbers at the bus stop dwindled and then swelled again as newcomers arrived to take the places of those who had departed.

Checking her watch again, Stella began to fret. Carrie rarely worked beyond five, and she *never* stayed later than half past. It was almost that now.

Being without Carrie was like suffering withdrawal from an all-consuming addiction. Every day, Carrie was the first thing that Stella thought about upon waking, and the last thing she thought about before going to sleep. She spent most of her waking hours trying to devise a scheme to persuade Carrie to give her one last chance at making their relationship work.

Stella had just about been coping, taking things one day at a time, until a chance encounter with one of Carrie's friends that morning had sent her emotions spiralling into a dangerous freefall. The woman's name was Sharon, and she was a bartender at *The Merry Fiddler* pub near Broadway Market. They had bumped into each other at their local Tesco store, and Sharon had casually mentioned that Carrie was going out with a group of friends that evening, including a woman she had developed a crush on. The revelation that Carrie had the hots for another woman had knocked Stella for six, and she had stormed out of the store in tears, leaving her half-full shopping trolley to roll down the middle of the freezer aisle unattended.

A frizzy haired woman emerged from Willard Betting, and Stella instantly recognised her as one of the admin girls from Carrie's office. As she crossed the road towards the bus stop, Stella struggled to recall her name.

Jane? Joanne?

It was something like that.

Jesse? Judy?

Stella waited until the woman joined the back of line, and then tagged on behind her.

Joan!

That was her bloody name.

Gently tapping her shoulder, Stella smiled a friendly greeting when the startled woman turned around. "It's Joan, isn't it?" she enquired, cheerily.

Stella had a deep voice for a woman, and twenty years of chain smoking had made it raspy.

Joan nodded cautiously, not showing any sign of recognition. "Sorry, do I know you?" she asked, nervously.

Stella smiled disarmingly, trying to put her at ease. "I'm a friend of Carrie's," she explained. "I think she introduced us once." Stella doubted that Joan would enquire after her name but, on the off chance that she did, Stella had already decided on an alias.

Joan relaxed slightly. "Oh, I see." A guilty shrug. "I'm very sorry, but I don't remember you," she confessed with an apologetic smile.

"That's okay," Stella said, waving a dismissive hand through the air. "Just finished work, have you?"

Joan nodded, a nervous movement that made her mop of frizzy hair rock backwards and forwards like it had a life of its own. "Yes, thank God," she said, blowing out her cheeks. "What about you?"

Stella nodded back. Giving it a moment, she adopted a thoughtful expression. "I don't suppose Carrie's still in the office, is she?" she asked, trying to keep her tone light. "Only, I might see if she fancies stopping off for a quick drink if she is."

Staring at Joan intently, Stella held her breath as she waited for an answer.

Joan shook her head, sending her hair into a sideways rocking motion. "No, she got away early today, lucky thing." She sounded envious. "Mr Willard was out of the office for most of the day, so he let her slide at three." A long sigh. "Wish he'd done the same thing for me."

A bus trundled along, and the people standing in front of them started shuffling forward. Joan followed suit. "We can try and grab a seat together if you like?" she offered with a weary smile.

Stella shook her head. "Sorry, I'm waiting for a different bus." She was crestfallen to have missed Carrie. What was she going to do now? She had to do *something* to stop her from going out with another woman.

Looking back over her shoulder, Joan gave her a little wave as she boarded the bus.

Stella responded in kind, but her mind was elsewhere. As soon as the bus pulled away, she spun on her heel and stomped off in the direction of her moped, which she had left in a nearby street.

Carrie had changed her mobile number after the separation, so Stella couldn't even ring her, but she just *had* to speak to her tonight, before it was too late. Carrie was hers, and Stella had no intention of sharing her with anyone else. There was only one thing left for her to do: she would have to go round to Carrie's house and confront her, and to hell with the consequences.

Annie was doing the washing up when her mobile started ringing. Drying her hands on a tea towel, she hurried over to her bag and dug it out, expecting the call to be from Aidan. He hadn't spoken to her since their fight the previous night, when he had kicked her out of his house. Thankfully, they hadn't had any filming scheduled for a couple of days, so his histrionics hadn't left her out of pocket.

To her surprise, the caller ID showed the incoming call was from Carrie, which was most unusual as Carrie rarely ever called her. "Hi, Carrie," she said, injecting a smile into her voice. "To what do I owe the pleasure?"

"*What the fuck is this disgusting porn video I've just found doing in my house?*" Carrie demanded aggressively.

Annie's heart missed a beat. Before he'd thrown her out last night, she had pleaded with Aidan to return the VHS tape to her, but he had been in one of his belligerent moods, where you just couldn't reason with him, so he had flatly refused. Even as he'd manhandled her out of the door, she had warned him to hide it somewhere safe overnight, and not leave it out where his narrow-minded sister could find it. His response had been to swear at her, and tell her what a worthless whore she was.

"Carrie, I–"

"*Shut up, you perverted bitch!*" Carrie yelled. "*My sicko brother has enough issues to deal with, without you corrupting him with this filth.*" Each word was peppered with disgust. "*What's wrong with you, Annie? I mean, what were you thinking of, filming yourself ramming a giant dildo up someone else's arse? Is that really how you get your kicks?*"

Although Carrie swore like a trooper, she was a bit of a prude when it came to discussing sex, and it really rattled Annie to hear her using such descriptive language. Her comments made Annie feel physically sick, and for a moment she thought she would actually die of shame.

"Carrie, please–"

"*Shut up and listen,*" Carrie cut in, her voice as cold as ice. "*You're no longer welcome in my house, you slut, I'll be telling my worthless brother exactly the same thing the next time I see him.*"

"Please, Carrie–"

It was too late; Carrie had already hung up.

Annie immediately tried calling her back, but the line was engaged. With a growing sense of unease, she wondered who Carrie was calling.

Aidan, perhaps?

Or her best friend, Abi?

Maybe she was ringing Darren?

What if she were ringing Social Services, to tell them what an unsuitable mother Annie was? How would that affect her chances of getting Anabel back?

Annie's hand was shaking as she dialled Aidan's number. The call went straight to voicemail; probably because Carrie had got through first, and was giving him his marching orders.

In a state of shock, Annie wandered through to the lounge and sank into the sofa. Burying her face in her hands, she began to sob uncontrollably.

This would ruin her life.

Carrie was a terrible gossip, and she would tell everyone she knew about the tape and what it contained.

Everyone!

She would vilify Annie, destroy her already brittle reputation, and poison the few friendships she had worked so hard to establish since getting her act together.

Any chances she might have had of being granted visitation rights, and eventually full-time custody of her baby, would be blown out of the water.

Maybe, if Annie promised never to release the film, and explained that she had made it out of desperation, because of the terrible financial mess that Aidan had gotten them both into, Carrie would forgive her and keep schtum?

A harsh laugh erupted from Annie's lips; it was a desperate sound, devoid of any hope. The truth was, short of killing Carrie, there was no way of preventing her from revealing Annie's shameful secret to the world.

10

SATURDAY 6TH OCTOBER 2001

Lucinda wants a cab

Elvis Winters sagged back in the controller's swivel chair and let out a long sigh. It was just coming up to ten o'clock, but it felt so much later. He glanced out of the glass plated windows into Hoxton Market, bored out of his brain and wondering how he was going to get through the night shift if things didn't liven up.

The minicab firm he worked for was located near the junction with Ivy Street, at the top end of the market. It was a good location, and they usually picked up a fair amount of passing trade, but tonight business was painfully slow, which was highly unusual for a Saturday.

Resisting the urge to put his feet up on the already cluttered desk, Elvis stared at the phone, willing it to ring.

Three bored looking drivers were slouching on the old leather sofa opposite his desk, listlessly watching the wall mounted TV while waiting for a fare. A talent show was on, but so far, all the contestants had been rubbish.

"Man, they're really scraping the bottom of the barrel this week," Elvis said. "I reckon there's more talent in one of my turds than there is on that stage."

"If it doesn't pick up soon, I'm going to call it a night and go home," Eric Hammond, the man sitting nearest to Elvis, complained. In his late forties, Eric was a skinny Mancunian with more stubble on his face than there was hair on his head.

Sitting next to him, Tony 'Tubsy' Peters grumbled his agreement. He was too busy stuffing crisps into his mouth to actually speak. Of a similar age to Eric, Tubsy was originally of West African descent, although you'd never know it from his East London accent. Despite its loose fit, the brightly coloured baroque print shirt hanging over his jeans did little to conceal a bulging stomach the size of a small hill.

Elvis sucked through his teeth. "Just be patient, you two," he rebuked them in his strong Jamaican accent. "Mark my words, it'll pick up soon."

As if on cue, the telephone rang. Elvis gave them an 'I told you so' look as he scooped up the receiver. "Easy Cars, Elvis speaking. How can I help you?" he said, reeling off his usual spiel in the sing-song voice he used whenever he answered the phone.

He listened for a few moments, made a note in the register of the caller's name, telephone number and address, then hung up. "There you go, Eric. Some woman called Lucinda McLean wants a cab to take her down to the canal. She'll be here in five minutes, and she's all yours."

Eric turned his nose up at the offer. "A cab to the canal? Seriously? That's only a five-minute trip. The fare will barely cover the cost of the fuel."

Elvis spun his high-backed chair in a full circle, lifting his feet off the floor so that it would go faster. "It's a start though, innit?" he said when he was back facing the others.

"Yeah, mate," Tubsy chipped in. "Beggars can't be choosers."

"Sod off, the pair of you," Eric said, crossing his arms sulkily.

Laughing loudly, Elvis took his chair for another spin.

It was closer to ten minutes than five, but eventually the little bell suspended above the cab office door chimed as a skinny white female pushed it open. She stumbled halfway in, then stopped abruptly as one of the wheels on the large suitcase she was dragging along behind her became wedged underneath the doorstep's overhang.

The three drivers watched her struggle in silence for a few seconds, finding the sight of her tugging and groaning but getting nowhere far more interesting than the juggling act on the TV screen.

In the end, Tubsy stood up and did the gentlemanly thing by helping her to free it. "There you go," he said, relieving her of the handle and pulling it across the threshold.

"Thank you," the woman responded, breathing heavily from her exertions. Her voice was low and raspy, like she smoked far too many cigarettes.

"Are you after a cab?" Elvis asked from behind his desk.

She nodded demurely, being careful to avoid making eye contact with him. Her face was obscured by a mass of long brown curls that hung all the way down to her slender shoulders. "My name's Lucinda McLean, and I called ahead."

Elvis glanced across at Eric, gave him a knowing smile. "This one's yours bruv, remember?"

Following Elvis' line of vision to where Eric was sitting, Lucinda acknowledged him with a raised hand.

Eric's first impression was that Lucinda was in her late thirties or early forties, but he was rubbish at gauging people's ages so he could be well wide of the mark. Besides, with so much makeup on – it looked like it had been slapped on with a gardening trowel – how could anyone really tell? And what had she been thinking when she'd applied her lipstick? She had gone totally overboard with it, making herself look more like *The Joker* from *Batman* than Julia Roberts in *Pretty Woman*.

Elvis coughed to get his attention and, when Eric glanced in his direction, he made a shooing gesture with his hands.

Eric didn't take the hint. "I honestly don't mind if one of you two wants to go instead," he offered the other drivers, looking down the line at each of them in turn.

"You're alright, mate," Tubsy said.

Stan Pilkington, the third driver, didn't even bother to respond. His eyes were glued to the screen, and the preforming dog that was doing a little sequence of pirouettes for its master.

Elvis began drumming his fingers on the desk, slowly at first, then with increasing speed.

When it became clear that neither of the other drivers was going relieve him of the fare, Eric stood up, wincing as his knees clicked.

Elvis stopped drumming and started tapping his watch instead.

Eric blanked him. He appreciated that time was money, but they were hardly busy, so Elvis the slave driver could go and do one. He stretched lazily, then turned towards the waiting customer.

"This way, miss," he said, opening the door.

Dragging her unwieldy suitcase behind her, Lucinda followed him out into the street.

Once outside, Eric pointed towards a red Vauxhall Cavalier parked outside a neon fronted pizzeria on the opposite side of the road. "That's my cab over there," he said.

Without a word, Lucinda set off towards it.

Beneath her leather bomber jacket, she wore an all-in-one jumpsuit, the legs of which spouted ridiculously wide bell bottom flares. It was made from a thick velvety material that hadn't been fashionable since the late seventies. In fairness, Eric decided, the outfit might have suited a woman with a more curvaceous figure but, on someone with no boobs whatsoever, and a backside like an IKEA flatpack, it looked dreadful.

The expression 'mutton dressed as lamb' sprang to mind.

When they reached the car, he opened the boot so that she could put her bulging case inside.

The first droplets of rain were starting to fall.

Glancing up into the night sky, Eric grimaced. "Looks like we're in for more bad weather," he said, just to make conversation.

Lucinda didn't answer. She was far too busy trying to lift the case into the boot, but it was too heavy and cumbersome for her to manage on her own.

"Let me help," Eric said, taking one side from her.

Between them, they manhandled the case into the car's boot but, even with them sharing the lifting, it proved surprisingly difficult.

When they had finished, Eric slammed the boot shut. "Blimey," he said, wiping his brow with the back of his hand. "What have you got in there, a dead body?"

The woman responded with a nervous laugh. "No, nothing like that."

Before he could ask any further questions, she opened the rear passenger door and got in.

The rain was falling a little harder now, so Eric followed her lead. Slipping behind the wheel, he pulled on his seatbelt and started the diesel engine. "So, where do you want me to take you?" he asked.

"I want you to drop me in Dunston Road," she said. "It's not too far from here. I can direct you if you don't know the way."

Eric had been driving a minicab for six years now, and he knew this area like the back of his hand. "That's alright, I know it," he replied, brusquely.

They drove in silence along Hoxton Street. With it being night-time, pretty much everywhere was closed and shuttered up, although the pub on the corner of Stanway Street was open for business, as was a rival minicab office and a couple of late-night cafés and bars. None of them seemed particularly busy, though.

Turning left at the junction with Falkirk Street, Eric continued past the Shoreditch campus of Hackney Community College, then made another left turn when he reached Kingsland High Street.

"Are you sure you want Dunston Road, not Dunston Street?" he asked, deciding to show off the full extent of his local knowledge.

"They're right next to each other and people often get them confused."

"Dunston Road, please," she confirmed. "You can drop me by the bollards."

Two minutes later, Eric drew up by a line of bollards protecting the pedestrianised area beneath the railway bridge at the junction with Acton Mews. He even braved the rain to help her haul her heavy suitcase out of his boot, nearly giving himself a hernia in the process.

To his surprise, she gave him a crisp new ten-pound note and told him to keep the change.

For a moment, he watched the strange woman as she dragged her case along the canal path towards Haggerston, then he got back in his car

Spinning the Cavalier around, he set off on a reciprocal route back towards the office.

Stopping for the give way sign at the junction with Kingsland Road, Eric glanced in his rear-view mirror, and was just in time to catch a fleeting glimpse of Lucinda McLean and her suitcase as she stepped out of the warm, yellow glow of a street lamp and was swallowed up by the surrounding darkness.

11

MONDAY 8TH OCTOBER 2001

I want to report my sister missing

When Carrie still hadn't arrived at work by half past nine, Jonas Willard started to get very annoyed with her. Not only was he still waiting for his morning coffee and newspaper, a routine that was set in stone, but he had appointments lined up throughout the day and he needed her help to prepare for them.

It definitely wasn't a good start to the week.

Fred Wiggins' policeman contact had finally managed to confirm that no diamonds had been found inside Frank Kyle's house, but there was still no news on where they might be, or who the two scumbags who had stolen them and killed Frankie were.

Muttering under his breath, Willard checked his calendar, just in case Carrie had booked time off and he had forgotten about it. As he'd thought, there was nothing listed.

"Right, sod this for a laugh," he said, pushing his chair back and standing up.

Sticking his head around the admin office door, he scoured the open plan room until he found the person he wanted, then bellowed, "Joan!"

A frizzy mop of brown hair popped up from behind a computer screen several desks along. "Yes, Mr Willard?" its nervous owner responded, meekly.

Joan Spinney was a rather plain woman with the waif like figure of someone who burned calories at an alarming rate. The forty-three year old mother of two managed the admin team for Willard, and it was her responsibility to stand in for Carrie whenever she was off.

"Has Carrie phoned in sick today?" he barked, angrily chomping on his cigar and staring at her as though it was her fault that his PA was AWOL.

Joan seemed bewildered by the question. "No, Mr Willard," she said, shaking her head.

Breathing out a frustrated sigh, Willard made an impatient come-hither gesture. "Right, you'll have to drop whatever it is that you're doing and cover for her till she shows up."

"But I–"

"Chop, chop," Willard snapped, clapping his hands to chivvy her along.

Joan's shoulders slumped in defeat. "Yes, Mr Willard," she said, logging off from her computer.

Willard watched her in stony silence, puffing agitatedly on his cheroot as she gathered up her things.

"About bloody time," he complained when she finally trudged over to Carrie's desk. "Firstly, I need you to sort me out my morning coffee and newspaper," he told her, huffily. "Then, I need you to get on the blower and find out why she hasn't come in."

"Yes, Mr Willard," Joan responded, dutifully.

Back in his office, Willard snatched up his phone and dialled Wiggins' extension number. "Fred," he said the moment it was answered. "Get your arse over to my office, now." Without waiting for a reply, he slammed the phone down.

The day was not going how he had planned it.

Jack Tyler had just been called down to Detective Chief Superintendent George Holland's office on the ground floor of Hertford House. No reason had been given for the early morning summons, and he wondered if that meant he was in the dog house. The only possible reason he could think of, for Holland having the hump with him, was his continued involvement in the ram raid investigation from the previous week.

As per Holland's explicit orders, they had written up their arrest notes and handed the case over to the Flying Squad. However, on the quiet, Tyler had maintained contact with the DI in charge, and he had been receiving regular updates on the progress they were making, not that there had been much of that. The Transit van and mopeds used by the raiders had all turned out to be stolen vehicles on false plates. There was no CCTV footage of the thefts, and no fingerprints or DNA had been recovered from the vehicles themselves. It transpired that the two males who had been arrested so far – the shotgun wielding thug from inside the mini-market and the rider of the stacked moped – were brothers, Gareth and Peter Pevensey. The former, an ex-soldier, had no previous form, while the latter had stacks of it. Neither had said a single word during interview, and they had refused to name the other two gang members.

Tyler had asked to be informed when the outstanding suspects were finally identified, so that he could tag along for the arrests.

Had Holland somehow found out about this?

Was he calling Tyler down to tell him to drop it?

He was greeted by Holland's long-term staff officer, DS Derek Peterson.

"Morning, Derek," Tyler said, risking a quick glance down the end of the Command Team corridor, where Holland's office was located. "Any idea what he wants me for?"

Peterson was an affable man in his late fifties. Well-liked by everyone on the command, he had a big heart and an even bigger waistline, and he had influential contacts all over the Met, which made him a very useful person to know.

Peterson had been due to retire the previous year, having completed his thirty years' service but, with two kids from his second marriage still attending university, he had decided to stay on until they graduated, in order to save eating into the lump-sum pay-out that formed part of his pension package.

"Morning boss," Peterson replied with a warm smile. "He's calling all the DCIs down, one at a time, to tell them about some filming that's going to be occurring over the next few weeks."

Tyler groaned. Not *that* again! A TV company was making a documentary about one of Holland's old cases, and for the past few months a researcher called Imogen Askew had been periodically floating around the building, making a right nuisance of herself. Now, it seemed, the research phase had ended and the cameras were about to start rolling. "I suppose it's too late to submit a quick four-ten and ask for a couple of weeks annual leave?"

A F410 was the form used to make all applications for time off.

Peterson responded with a throaty laugh. "Not a snowball's chance in hell," he said, relishing the look of misery that appeared on Tyler's face. "Between you and me, you're not the first SIO to ask me that today," he confessed.

"No, I don't suppose I am," Tyler said, drily.

At the far end of the corridor, Holland's door opened and Andy Quinlan emerged. He had a face like a slapped arse, Tyler noticed, which was most unlike him.

"He said to send you straight in," Quinlan informed Tyler on his way out. No greeting. No smile. Just a glower.

Tyler frowned. That really wasn't like Quinlan, a man who was renowned throughout the command for his good manners.

"Your turn," Peterson said, gleefully nudging Tyler's elbow.

Tyler scowled at him accusingly. "You're bloody well enjoying this, aren't you?"

"Someone's got to," Peterson chortled.

Tyler stomped off along the Command Team corridor, grumbling to himself about the inconvenience of having a film crew at Hertford House.

"Come in," Holland shouted as soon as he rapped on the door.

Blowing out his cheeks, Tyler steeled himself for whatever was to come. Turning the handle firmly, he stepped into the lion's den.

From behind his desk, Holland's craggy face broke into an affectionate grin. "Ah, come in Jack, have a seat."

Three chairs had been arranged in front of Holland's desk, but two of them were already taken. Imogen Askew occupied the first, legal pad opened on her shapely knee, pen poised, ready to make notes. Tyler couldn't help but wonder if the pen was surgically attached, because he didn't think he had ever seen her without it.

Tyler had first met Askew the previous month, while his team had been investigating The Candy Killer murders. While researching one of Holland's old cases, she had come up with the idea of filming a fly on the wall type documentary about the Homicide Command, and rumour had it that Holland was very much up for this, and had approved the request.

Askew was undeniably a strikingly attractive woman, with shoulder length blonde hair, perfect teeth and a body most models would have killed for. "Nice to see you again, Chief Inspector," she said in her oh-so posh voice.

"Miss Askew," he said, nodding impartially at her.

Askew's green eyes were regarding him with open amusement, which really irritated him. Tyler knew that this was all just a big game to her. She knew he didn't like her being there, and she also knew that there was absolutely nothing he could do about it.

Checkmate to her.

"And I believe you've already met Terri Miller, who will be the show's presenter," Holland said, indicating his second visitor.

Miller was in her early thirties, slim, with light brown hair and a little button nose. Behind her large brown eyes, there was a keen intellect and, from previous experience, he knew that she was driven by an insatiable desire to succeed.

Miller stood up and reached across the top of Askew's head to offer her hand. "It's nice to meet you again, Jack," she said, smiling like she was greeting an old friend.

Tyler had first encountered Terri Miller back in November 1999, when she had been a rookie reporter working for *The London*

Echo, and he had been leading a high-profile investigation into the Whitechapel murders, which had been committed by a clever, resourceful and totally deranged serial killer. Miller, in her enthusiasm to get a scoop on her Fleet Street opposition, had trampled all over one of the crime scenes, which hadn't endeared her to either Tyler or Tony Dillon.

Afterwards, Miller had capitalised on her limited involvement with the investigation by writing a best-selling book about the killings; the publicity she had received from that had quickly helped her to become an established investigative journalist, and she had since gone on to become a much sought-after TV presenter.

"Hello, Miss Miller," Tyler said, reluctantly accepting her manicured hand. "It seems congratulations are in order. You've obviously come a long way since the last time we met."

She gave him a self-deprecating smile. "And I've learned a lot too, like how important it is *not* to piss off SIOs by contaminating their crime scenes."

The candidness of her comment surprised him, and Tyler couldn't help but smile. "I'm glad to hear it," he said, releasing her hand and sitting down.

"I'm calling all the SIOs down this morning to meet Terri and Imogen," Holland explained. "As of tomorrow, they and their film crew will be working out of the next office along from Derek Peterson's, here in the Command Team corridor. They're going to be with us for six weeks, so you'll undoubtedly be seeing rather a lot of them in that time."

I bloody well hope not!

Tyler raised an eyebrow but said nothing.

"At the moment, Terri's people are following Andy's team while they investigate the East Ham murder from last week, but your team are next in the frame to take on a new job. When one breaks, I've given Terri's people carte blanche to shadow you throughout the investigation."

Tyler felt his heart sink. He leaned forward in his chair. "Sorry boss, but for the sake of clarity, when you say carte blanche, what exactly do you mean by that?"

Holland regarded him with a degree of sympathy "Jack, I know it goes against your instincts to trust the media, but everyone involved in the show's been thoroughly vetted, and they've all signed legally binding confidentiality agreements, which means they can't broadcast or publish anything without first clearing it with both us here at KZ and the solicitors at NSY."

Tyler's mouth curled down in a sneer; Holland obviously had a lot more faith in that working than he did.

Holland's voice became firmer. "The bottom line is that I need you to buy into this, because it's happening whether you like it or not. The film crew have an access-all-areas pass, subject to the usual restrictions around not letting them go anywhere that would jeopardise the integrity of the investigation, contaminate evidence or put them at risk. The final decision on where they go and what they see will be yours, naturally, but I'm expecting you to do everything you can to facilitate their filming."

It was only when his jaw started to ache that Tyler realised how hard he was gritting his teeth. Holland and the two media representatives were all staring at him, waiting for him to give an assurance that he would do exactly that. Instead, he acknowledged the instruction with a curt nod.

"Well, in that case, ladies," he said, standing up. "I guess I'll be seeing you around."

No wonder Andy Quinlan's face had resembled a smacked arse when he left Holland's office a few minutes earlier, Tyler suspected his own countenance sported a very similar expression as he closed the door behind him.

"I know you won't like me saying this," Fred Wiggins said, choosing his words carefully, "but don't you think it's a little bit odd that Carrie hasn't shown up today?"

"What do you mean?" Willard snapped, although he knew exactly what his lieutenant was alluding to.

"Well, it stands to reason that whoever stole those diamonds and topped Frankie was tipped off by someone inside the firm. All I'm saying is that, apart from you, me, Casper and the old jeweller, Carrie was the only person who knew those diamonds were being kept at Frankie's house."

Willard scowled at him. "And you think that, because Carrie hasn't come in today, she must be the leak?"

"It's possible. All I'm saying is—"

Willard blew out a stream of smoke, then jabbed his cigar in Wiggins' direction. "Now you listen to me, Fred," he growled, cutting him off mid-sentence. "That girl's father and me were good friends. I've known her since she was a baby, and I'm telling you, she wouldn't sell us out. So, stop talking complete and utter bollocks and concentrate on finding the cunt who stole my diamonds."

Wiggins' face remained impassive. "No offence, but if this were someone else, other than Carrie, would you still be saying that?"

Willard jumped up, absolutely livid, and pointed towards the door. "You cheeky, disrespectful git! I told you, Carrie's like family to me, so watch your mouth. Now, go on, sling your hook before I lose my rag with you."

Wiggins left the room with his tail between his legs.

After he'd gone, Willard sat there fuming.

Jonas Willard was a man who prized loyalty above all else. As far as he was concerned, it was perfectly acceptable to steal from the government, the church, or anyone else for that matter, but you never stole from your own people.

These days, he had more money than he knew what to do with, but that hadn't always been the case. Willard had grown up in the poverty of an East London slum, and his family had barely had enough money to put food on the table some days. Everyone he knew had been involved in one kind of villainy or another; it was just the way things were back then, but they had a code they lived by; they stole from everyone around them, but they never took anything from their own.

It just wasn't done.

During the early 50s, when Willard had still been at school, his father had worked in the tote offices at Newmarket racecourse.

During the holidays, young Jonas had sometimes accompanied him there. The flamboyant and colourful bookies, with their expensive clothes, opinionated views and ready cashflow, had made a very big impression on him. Over time, he had come to see the profession as a means of escaping poverty.

Quickly mastering the basics of how the betting system worked, young Jonas started running a book at school. The other kids only made small bets, ranging from tuppence ha'penny to a shilling, but it all added up, and he soon started to turn a tidy profit.

Being a clever lad, he enlisted the services of the school bully, Damian McCullen, to make sure that none of the punters had second thoughts about paying up when they lost, or got any funny ideas about muscling in and taking over his operation.

He and McCullen had instantly clicked, becoming firm friends. To this day, Willard maintained that putting Damian on a retainer had been one of the shrewdest business moves he had ever made.

After leaving school, Willard applied for a job with one of the nation's biggest bookmakers. Having breezed the maths test and interview, he was offered a position as a settler. There followed three months of intensive classroom training, at the end of which he was awarded a three-year contract.

Eventually, Willard decided that it was time to take the plunge and set himself up as an independent bookmaker. He purchased his first betting shop for less than two thousand pounds and, over the next couple of years, acquired four more. Remembering how well Damian McCullen had served him at school, Willard had sought him out and offered him a similar role. When Willard had started to dabble in loan sharking, and other side lines that were highly illegal, McCullen had served as his right hand man and head enforcer.

After many years of faithful service, Damian's health had eventually started to suffer, forcing him to step down. Before retiring, Damian had suggested that his protégé, Fred Wiggins, was the ideal candidate to replace him, which was why Willard now found himself so angry with his right-hand man. By suggesting that Damian's daughter would ever do the dirty on them, Wiggins was being disloyal to his mentor's memory.

Shrouded in a thick fog of cigar smoke, Willard leaned back in his chair. As much as it galled him to admit it, Fred had been right about one thing: had they been discussing anyone other than Carrie, he would have been very suspicious. With a sigh, he picked up his phone. "Joan, have you managed to track down Carrie yet?" he asked.

"*Sorry, Mr Willard,*" Joan replied, sounding harassed. "*I've rung her several times but her mobile phone seems to be switched off. I'll keep trying and let you know as soon as I hear anything.*"

Willard hung up, feeling strangely unsettled. This really was out of character for Carrie. Maybe she had been involved in an accident? Maybe she had been hospitalised through illness? Maybe she had run off with his fucking diamonds?

Stop it!

He picked up his phone again, and this time he dialled Wiggins' extension. "Fred, Joan still can't raise Carrie, so I want you to pop round to her place for me, just to make sure she's okay."

It was just after nine that evening when Aidan McCullen, Annie Jenkins, and Abigale Stanwick entered the waiting area at City Road police station in Shepherdess Walk.

Aidan had always fancied Stanwick, but she was immune to his charms, to the point of barely acknowledging his existence whenever they met. Now in her thirties, he secretly thought that she was hotter than ever, with perfect teeth, perfect skin, and a perfect hourglass figure, which had become even more eye catching since she had treated herself to a boob job a couple of years earlier.

While Annie was something of a 'Plain Jane' who rarely wore make-up, always opted for cheap, non-branded jeans and baggy sweatshirts, Abi always dressed like a supermodel, choosing clothes that accentuated her voluptuous figure, wore intoxicating perfume, and had men drooling over her wherever she went. Casting a lascivious glance in her direction when no one was looking, Aidan imagined her starring in one of their home-made porn films, but the lustful leer vanished from his face when he saw the queue in front of them. Without breaking stride, he did an abrupt U turn and headed back towards the door.

Stanwick grabbed him roughly by the arm. "Where the hell do you think you're going?" she snapped, dragging him back inside.

"Ouch," he complained as her fake nails dug into his skin. "Let go. I'm not waiting here for hours on end. Let's come back tomorrow when it's quieter."

Stanwick tightened her grip. "Don't be so bloody lazy," she scolded. "Your sister's missing and we need to report it *now*, not tomorrow. Tell him, Annie."

"Abi's right," Annie said, unenthusiastically. "Let's just get it over with."

Aidan opened his mouth to protest, but the steely glint in Stanwick's eyes convinced him there was no point. "Fine," he sulked, flopping down on a wooden bench next to an elderly woman with an old Jack Russell sitting on her lap.

The glassy eyed mutt had matted fur, stank of urine and looked like it was on its last legs, but it was still feisty enough to growl at him when he looked at it. Rubbing his arm, which was smarting from where Stanwick had pinched him, Aidan shuffled sideways along the bench to put some space between them.

"Oh, don't mind Freddie, dear," the old woman said with a toothless smile. "He's all bark and no bite, aren't you, my lovely?"

As if determined to prove her wrong, the old dog immediately launched itself out of her arms, scuttled across the bench on stiff legs, and tried to sink its remaining teeth into the arm of Aidan's jacket.

"Gerroff," Aidan shouted, jumping up before the snapping dog could get a proper grip.

"Freddie, you're such a naughty boy," his owner admonished as she scooped the still snarling terrier up and returned him to her lap. "I'm very sorry," she told Annie. "He's normally so well behaved."

Freddie was panting heavily, clearly worn out by his exertions, and he flopped down on his owner's lap, looking pleased with himself.

Examining his jacket for puncture marks, Aidan glared angrily at the dog, cursing it under his breath.

"That's okay," Annie said with an understanding smile. "No harm done."

Aidan wasn't so sure about that but, before he could give the old crone a piece of his mind, she was called into the front office by the constable on desk duty.

By the time they were actually seen, it was getting on for half past nine.

"It's alright for you," Aidan griped as Stanwick ushered him into the front office ahead of her, "but I've got work in the morning and I don't want a late night."

"Stop whinging," she hissed, placing her hand in the small of his back and shoving him forward.

"How can I help you?" the young officer behind the counter asked. The Velcro name badge on his blue NATO jumper read: Constable Maxwell. Although his smile was cordial, he sounded totally disinterested.

Stanwick looked at Aidan, nodded encouragingly for him to speak.

Realising that there was no way out of this, Aidan rested his bony elbows on the counter and let out a little sigh of defeat. "I'd like to report my sister missing," he mumbled.

"What's your sister's name, sir?" Maxwell asked.

"Carrie McCullen. I'm Aidan, this is my girlfriend, Annie, and this is my sister's best friend, Abi."

Maxwell acknowledged Annie and Abi in turn, but allowed his eyes to linger a fraction longer than was necessary on the latter. "How old is Carrie, Mr McCullen?"

"She's thirty-four, the same age as me," Aidan said, quickly adding, "We're twins."

Maxwell raised a surprised eyebrow, having obviously thought that Aidan was much older. "And when did you last see her?"

Aidan was busy studying his fingernails, which had been chewed down to the quick. "Friday afternoon," he replied, charmingly spitting a slither of nail onto the station floor. "Can't remember what time."

Maxwell grimaced, but refrained from passing comment.

"She popped round to my place at about three-thirty," Stanwick cut in. "Some girl she fancied had invited Carrie to join her and a few mates on a girlie night out, so she wanted me to do her hair for her."

"I don't suppose you know their names by any chance?" Maxwell asked.

Stanwick shook her head. "No. Sorry, I don't. They weren't Carrie's usual crowd, I'm afraid."

"And what time did she leave yours?" Maxwell enquired. As he spoke, he opened his notebook and began jotting some details down.

Stanwick frowned. "She left mine at four-fifteen, so she would have been home by four-thirty at the latest."

"She came through the door at about twenty-five past four," Aidan confirmed. "As soon as she got in, she went upstairs for a soak in the bath, and she was still up there when I went out at five-thirty."

Maxwell was keen to pin down the last confirmed sighting. "Did you see her again after that?"

Aidan gave a brisk shake of his head. "Nope. I met a mate at the social club in Pitfield Street. We played snooker for a few hours. I got home sometime between nine and ten, I think, but I wasn't feeling very well so I went straight to bed, stayed there until the following morning."

"I don't suppose *you* know who she was meeting?" Maxwell asked.

"Nah, mate. No idea."

"So, none of you have heard from Carrie since she went out on Friday night?" Maxwell confirmed.

"No," Annie and Aidan said together.

"I tried to ring her before going to bed on Friday night," Stanwick interjected. "But she didn't answer, so I sent a jokey text, asking how the date was going. She never messaged me back, though."

"What time would that have been?" Maxwell enquired.

Stanwick shrugged. "About eleven-thirty, I think."

Aidan's expression suddenly became solemn. "The point is, she didn't come home, and none of her friends have seen or heard from her since then. We know this because we checked in with them all before coming here."

"And she didn't turn up for work this morning," Stanwick chipped in. "She loves her job and never goes sick, so this really isn't like her. In fact, Aidan told me her boss was so worried this morning that he sent someone around to check on her welfare. Isn't that right, Aidan?"

Aidan pulled a sour face. "Right couple of charmers they were," he said with a shudder.

Ignoring him, Maxwell addressed his next question to Stanwick. "What does Carrie do for a living?"

"She's the PA for Jonas Willard, the bloke who runs Willard Betting," she told him.

Maxwell grunted, made a note. "Have you tried ringing her?"

Aidan rolled his eyes theatrically, then slapped the palm of his hand against his forehead. "Well, duh! Why didn't we think of that?"

His flippancy put Maxwell's back up. "No need to be sarky, mate," he said, making it clear he wasn't impressed.

Annie scowled at Aidan, then smiled apologetically at Maxwell. "Sorry," she said, with a sheepish smile. "He really didn't mean to be rude. We're just a bit on edge because we're so worried about Carrie."

Maxwell fixed Aidan a with a cold, hard stare, but his face softened a moment later, when he turned his attention to Stanwick. "Does Carrie have any underlying heath or mental health issues that would put her at risk?"

Aidan stiffened. "What exactly are you implying?"

"For instance," Maxwell continued, ignoring the interruption, "is she a diabetic who's gone off without her insulin? Or is she suffering from depression and possibly suicidal?"

Aidan opened his mouth to say something, but Annie quickly placed a restraining hand on his arm.

"No. Nothing like that, officer," Stanwick assured Maxwell. "Carrie's fit and healthy and perfectly happy. This really is totally out of character for her."

Maxwell thought hard. "I take it she hasn't been having any problems with anyone, like a violent ex-partner or a stalker, perhaps?"

Aidan, Annie and Stanwick all exchanged unsure glances. "Not exactly," Stanwick said, hesitantly. "Not recently, anyway."

12

WEDNESDAY 10TH OCTOBER 2001

The body in the canal

Regent's Canal carves an 8.6-mile winding route through London that begins at Paddington in the west and crosses to Limehouse in the east. There are twelve locks and three tunnels to be negotiated along the way, although only two of the latter are generally acknowledged as such, with many people incorrectly assuming that Eyre's tunnel beneath Lisson Grove is actually a bridge.

At 15:40hrs on what was turning out to be a very blustery afternoon, Alec Du Plessis' barge, *The Springbok*, arrived at Acton's Lock, which runs parallel with Broadway Market in Hackney, and is approximately 2.5 miles from the Limehouse Basin.

The Springbok was a ten year old P.M. Buckle 50' Semi Trad Narrowboat designed in a forward layout, and he had been living aboard her on a full time basis for the past seven months, since taking early retirement from his job as a civil engineer following the tragic death of his beloved wife, Trudy.

The River Authority classed Du Plessis as a 'constant cruiser', which simply meant that his boat wasn't registered to a home mooring and was obliged to make a progressive journey along the waterways without remaining moored at any one location for too long. He was currently heading towards the Limehouse Basin, where he had pre-booked a berth for a couple of nights so that he could catch up with an old friend on the first, and enrol himself on a Ripper tour through the streets of Whitechapel on the second.

Originally from South Africa, Du Plessis had emigrated to the UK with his parents during the early fifties and, although he had lived in England for the majority of his life, he still retained a trace of his boyhood accent and a passion for the great outdoors.

With no family ties to restrict hm now that his wife had passed on, Du Plessis had rented out his large, four-bedroom house in rural Essex for a whole year and purchased *The Springbok* with a view to exploring the canals and waterways at his leisure while he rediscovered himself and came to terms with his grief.

Some of the more naive live-aboard boaters that he had encountered during his travels had allowed themselves to be carried away by the romantic misconception that they were buying into an idyllic and peaceful lifestyle, but Du Plessis had done his homework carefully before swapping his spacious house, which was equipped with all the luxury mod-cons anyone could ever want, for the minimalistic, semi-nomadic existence of life aboard a cramped narrowboat with only the most basic amenities and very little storage space.

Zipping up his red Helly Hansen sailing jacket to protect himself against the biting wind, Du Plessis grabbed the windlass winch he would need to work the lock controls off the sideboard. Before setting off, he slipped a fluorescent life jacket over his coat. It was a tight fit, but wearing it was a necessary safety requirement for a man who had never learned to swim.

Like many narrowboats, *The Springbok* had a canvas cratch cover erected over the front deck. This not only provided Du Plessis with additional storage space, but it also made for a useful wet weather changing area. The downside was that it also made getting on and off the boat that much harder. In order to go ashore, Du Plessis had to simultaneously duck under the cratch cover and step two feet over the hull side in order to reach the canal towpath. When he first moved aboard, he had found this an incredibly tricky manoeuvre, but now it was second nature to him, and he didn't give it a moment's thought as he jumped off the boat and tied the rope off on one of the stumpy little bollards that projected out of the canal towpath. After checking it was secure, he set off towards the Lock Master, who was waiting for him over by the lower gate controls.

Locks worked by adjusting the levels along different stretches of water to allow canal boats to travel up or downhill. Du Plessis currently was travelling uphill and, as the water inside Acton's Lock was set against him, he would have to drain it before he could continue his journey.

"Afternoon," he called out as the Lock Master came forward to meet him by the controls to the lower gate.

"Good day," the Lock Master replied. He was a thin man in his mid-fifties, with a scruffy mop of grey hair and a couple of days' worth of stubble covering the weathered skin of his face. Like Du Plessis, he wore a lifejacket over a waterproof jacket, which had a 'Canal & River Trust' logo embossed on it. Nodding in a friendly fashion, the Lock Master said, "If you want to work the lever on this side, I'll do the one over there for you."

Thanking him, Du Plessis crossed to the lock controls and attached his windlass to the top. He waited until the Lock Master had traversed the walkway to the other side of the canal and signalled that he was ready, then he began cranking away at the mechanism to open the paddles that were fitted into the lock gates. Almost immediately, the water level inside the lock started to recede.

The paddle controls at some of the locks Du Plessis had passed through had been stiff and unwieldy, and it had required a lot of effort to open them up, but this one seemed pretty smooth, and he hardly even built up a sweat as he turned the winch.

It took a few minutes for the water to drain down to the level that *The Springbok* was moored at but, once it did, the pressure equalised and he was able to push open the gates with ease.

Returning to his boat, Du Plessis carefully navigated her inside the lock, stopping by the sign that read: 'KEEP BOAT FORWARD

OF THE CIL MARKER'. To take her any further into the lock would have risked the bow being hit by the top end gates when they opened.

After tying her off, Du Plessis returned to the towpath to close off the paddles and shut the lower lock gates. That done, he made his way over to the controls for the top end gates. Using his windlass, he began cranking away for all he was worth. As well as pouring in through the gate paddles, water at this end of the lock was admitted via an underground pipe called a culvert.

As Du Plessis winched away, he caught a glimpse of something dark and heavy bobbing around in the murky water below. It had obviously been dragged into the lock by the water flooding in through the paddles or the culvert. The bulky object was drifting down the side of *The Springbok*'s hull, but then it disappeared from view, presumably having been sucked under by the current.

Du Plessis had seen so much rubbish dumped in the canal during his travels that he didn't give it a second thought at first, but then it resurfaced a few yards further along, and he saw that it was a wheeled suitcase.

"Disgraceful," he muttered under his breath, wondering why people couldn't just take their unwanted junk to a local authority tip instead of polluting the canals and riverways with it.

Laziness, he fumed; that's what it all boiled down to.

As water continued to flood into the lock, churning the silt up, the suitcase started to get bumped around a bit. Du Plessis watched as it spun around and was dragged under again. As it tumbled along, he could hear it repeatedly banging against the underside of his boat.

A few seconds later, the suitcase surfaced again, but so did something else. Exploding out of the water like a submarine surfacing from the deep, a pink mannequin was catapulted from inside the case, landing in the water with a little splash.

Du Plessis waited until the lock had fully flooded, and then walked over to the edge of the towpath to get a better look at the mannequin.

The Lock Master appeared by his side. "What you looking at?" he enquired, peering down into the water with him.

"Looks like some idiot's dumped a tailors dummy in the canal," Du Plessis told him.

The Lock Master sighed his disgruntlement. "What's wrong with these bloody people?" he complained. "They make my life hell, polluting the water like this. Honestly, I had to fish a shopping trolley out last week, nearly put my back out in the process."

Du Plessis made what he hoped was a sympathetic noise. "I think the case it was in has become snagged on something under my boat," he said, kneeling down to get a better look.

Looking up and down the canal, the Lock Master saw that several vessels were now patiently waiting their turn to pass through the lock. "Give me a minute," he said, grumpily. "I've got a boat hook in the office; I should be able to drag it clear with that."

Unable to do anything until the Lock Master returned with his hook, Du Plessis picked up a handful of small stones and started using the dummy for target practice. He was a fairly good shot, and he managed to hit it in the shoulder with his very first attempt.

"Ha! Strike!" he grinned as it started rocking in the water. The grin turned into a frown as the mannequin wobbled unsteadily and the right shoulder briefly rose above the waterline.

Mannequins didn't normally have bones poking out of the tops of them, did they?

Wondering if he had merely imagined it, or if his old eyes were starting to play tricks on him, Du Plessis threw another, bigger stone, but this one missed completely.

Du Plessis swore.

He was just taking aim with his third missile when the Lock Master came jogging over.

"There you go," he said, breathlessly handing the long boat hook to Du Plessis. "We've got a bit of a queue building up so we'd better get a move on."

Accepting the boat hook, Du Plessis leaned forward and tried to nab the mannequin, but it stubbornly resisted his best efforts to snare it.

"Here," the Lock Master said, holding his hand out impatiently. "Let me try."

"Be my guest," Du Plessis replied, handing the boat hook over.

While the South African dusted himself down, he listened to the Lock Master grunting and groaning as he attempted to do what Du Plessis had been unable to.

"Gotcha!" the Lock Master suddenly whooped.

Du Plessis watched as the mannequin was dragged clear of *The Springbok* and pulled towards the towpath.

Lying flat on his chest, the Lock Master extended his arm over the edge and grabbed the mannequin by one of its shoulders. He immediately recoiled, letting out a little scream of fright as the mannequin slipped back into the water with a soft plop.

"What's wrong?" Du Plessis asked, alarmed by the horrified look that had appeared on the other man's face. He assumed something sharp was protruding from the dummy, and the Lock Master had caught his hand on it.

"That ain't no tailors dummy," the Lock Master told him with a shudder. He stared down at his hand as though it had become contaminated.

"What else could it be?" Du Plessis said, laughing at him.

"It felt like flesh to me," the Lock Master said, his face pale with shock.

Looking down into the water, Du Plessis saw that the mannequin, which had been floating face down up to that point, had now turned over, exposing a good-sized pair of breasts and a trimmed thatch of pubic hair.

"Oh my God," he breathed, realising that the gruesome object was actually the dismembered torso of a white female.

Just before 6 p.m., a green Vauxhall Omega pulled up at the edge of the outer cordon. A crowd had already gathered and, although most of the onlookers would genuinely be curious as to what was going on, Tyler knew from experience that a few ghouls would be secreted in amongst them; sick fuckers who got off on seeing dead bodies and other morbid sights.

Leaving Bull to park up, Tyler and Dillon alighted the vehicle and made their way over to the officer running the scene log. Flashing their warrant cards, they gave him their details and passed through the outer cordon onto the towpath.

Less than thirty yards further along the canal bank, they spotted Juliet Kennedy, the on-call Crime Scene Manger, standing by the stern of a riverboat called *The Springbok*. She was clad in a baggy white Tyvek suit, plastic overshoes and nitrile gloves. Looking over in their direction, Juliet raised a purple hand in greeting and waved them over.

Police divers from the Met's Underwater Search Unit, having been called out from their base at Wapping police station to retrieve the torso from the lock, were immersed in the water, searching for the missing head and limbs.

"Afternoon, gentlemen," Juliet said as the two detectives reached her side. Hands on hips, she smiled at them from behind her mask. "This one's certainly a bit different from the run of the mill stabbings and shootings we usually get."

Dillon grimaced. "It's definitely a human torso, then?" he asked, looking like he would rather be somewhere else.

"It most certainly is," Kennedy confirmed, "and the quicker you stop faffing about and put your barrier clothing on, the quicker I can take you over there and show it to you." Her tone implied that it would be a real treat for them.

"I can't wait," Dillon replied, unenthusiastically accepting the bundle of protective clothing she had just thrust into his hands.

Tyler flashed him a sympathetic smile, thinking how ironic it was that someone who hated the sight and smell of death as much as Dillon had chosen to apply for a posting on the Homicide Command.

Taking a set of barrier clothing from Juliet's outstretched hand, he set off in pursuit of his friend, who had wandered a short distance away. As Dillon tore open the plastic wrapping to get at his overalls, Tyler placed a hand on his shoulder. "Dill, why don't you wait here, mate? There's no need for both of us to go over to the body."

Dillon responded with a gloomy shake of his head. "Thanks, Jack," he said, wobbling unsteadily on one foot as he attempted to slide his left leg into the Tyvek overalls, "but I'll have to see it when I attend the mortuary for the SPM, so I might as well bite the bullet now."

A Special Post Mortem was required in all cases where a suspicious death occurred, and protocol dictated that a Detective Inspector had to be in attendance when it was carried out.

Much to his delight, Dillon had managed to avoid making any trips to the mortuary for the past four months because, since her promotion to DI, Susie Sergeant had volunteered to cover the SPM for every new job they had taken. Unlike Dillon, Susie wasn't remotely fazed by the gruesome sights and smells that accompanied the process. Unfortunately for him, Susie was currently away on her three-week inspector's course at Hendon, which meant that he would have to step up to the plate this time around.

As the wind changed course, the sound of a heated argument reached their ears. The ruckus was coming from the direction of the outer cordon. Glancing over his shoulder, Tyler groaned out loud when he saw Imogen Askew going toe to toe with the officer on cordon duty. She was insisting that they be allowed to pass, and he was giving her short shrift.

A large, hairy, scruffily dressed man, who bore a striking resemblance to the cartoon character, Captain Caveman, was standing docilely behind Askew, an expensive looking video camera dangling from his right hand.

Turning around so that his back was towards them, Tyler ducked his head down and hurriedly ripped open the plastic wrapping of his Tyvek overalls. If he could get them on and slip his Victoria mask over his face before she spotted him, she wouldn't be able to recognise—

"DCI Tyler! Jack!"

Tyler's shoulders slumped, and he swore under his breath.

Perhaps, if he pretended that he hadn't heard her, she would give up and go–

"DCI TYLER!"

Everyone inside the cordon stopped what they were doing and looked, first at her, then at him.

"Bollocks!" Tyler muttered. Putting on a brave face, he turned around and gave her a jaunty little wave. "Miss Askew, what a surprise," he said, walking towards her. He wasn't lying – it *was* a surprise, an unpleasant one, but still a surprise.

Arms folded, a look on her face like she had just been chewing a wasp, Imogen glared at him as he made his way over. "Will you please tell this *jobsworth* that we're allowed inside the cordon?" she demanded, barely able to contain her burgeoning frustration.

"We?" Tyler enquired innocently, just to be awkward.

Imogen's eyes narrowed into little slits. "Me and Bear," she snapped, indicating Captain Caveman with an angry jut of her pretty chin.

From beneath the mop of shaggy brown hair and overgrown beard, Tyler glimpsed a flash of teeth, and realised that Bear was smiling at him.

Constable Jobsworth was giving Tyler a 'surely not' stare, convinced that the media woman was trying to put one over on him.

Pinching the bridge of his nose, Tyler let out a little sigh of defeat. "Give the cordon officer your names and contact numbers for the log," he said, resentfully. "Once they've done that, they can be admitted into the outer cordon," he told the stunned constable.

Imogen gave him a triumphant smirk of one-upmanship, which put Tyler's back right up. "Just to be clear," he said, deciding to lay down the law at a very early stage, "you're only here under sufferance, and if you put one foot out of place – one bloody foot – I will have you removed. Is that clear?"

Imogen stiffened, clearly unaccustomed to being spoken to in that manner. "Perfectly," she said, her tone glacial.

Constable Jobsworth was nodding approvingly.

"You won't even know I'm here," Bear promised, affably. He had a thick Brummie accent.

"Follow me," Tyler ordered, heading back the way he had come.

Breaking into a jog, Imogen quickly caught him up. "Why didn't you tell me you were taking a new job?" she demanded as they made their way over to where Dillon and Kennedy were watching them with growing interest. "George *told* you that I was to be informed at once."

Tyler bristled. *George?* She was on first names with Holland now, was she?

"Don't expect me to come looking for you every time something breaks," he told her. "In your line of work, you snooze, you lose. I would have thought that, working for Terri Miller, you would have learnt that by now."

Behind them, Tyler could have sworn that Bear chuckled.

Imogen must have heard it too, because she whipped her head around and glared at her shaggy haired companion with malice.

Bear, very wisely, made himself busy fiddling with his camera controls.

The torso, its skin prune-like from prolonged immersion in the water and bleached white from blood loss, was now laying on a thick plastic sheet twenty feet inside the inner cordon.

A black, wheeled suitcase sat on the towpath beside it, a small pool of water slowly forming beneath it. Two heavy duty refuse sacks, a clear one for recycling and a black one for general household waste, had been placed next to it, each secured in place by a rock to prevent it from being blown away. The bags were flapping angrily in the wind, as though desperately trying to escape their captivity. The printed letters 'LBH' – which stood for 'London Borough of Hackney' – could clearly be seen on the transparent recycling bag.

"Let me get this straight," Tyler said, having just listened to the account that Kennedy had provided regarding the afternoon's gruesome discovery. "The torso was inside the suitcase, which came into the lock when the sluice gates were opened, and then smashed into the underside of that boat–" he nodded towards *The Springbok* " causing it to burst open. Is that right?"

"They're called paddles, I'm told, not sluice gates, but otherwise that's right."

"And the refuse sacks?"

A shrug. "We think the body was wrapped in them, but came out when the case was ripped open. We won't know for sure until the lab results come back, but as the bags were stuck to the suitcase's zipper, it seems very likely."

DNA testing of the plastic bags' interiors would quickly reveal whether or not the torso had been inside them. If they were really lucky, the bags might even contain some of the killer's DNA, deposited there when he placed the dismembered body inside.

In addition to DNA testing, the bags would also be examined for fingerprints and microscopic fibres.

Tyler stroked his chin, thoughtfully. "I don't suppose we've got any idea where the suitcase went into the canal?"

"Not at the moment," Kennedy informed him. "The Lock Master reckons it could have been chucked in nearby, or a couple of miles away."

Tyler tutted bad temperedly. That wasn't helpful. Not in the slightest. He couldn't close off the whole canal as a crime scene.

"Any idea how long it's been in the water?" he asked. The corpse didn't look particularly bloated, and there were no obvious signs of putrefaction, so he doubted it had been submerged for too long.

Kennedy shrugged, made a show of blowing her cheeks out. "Three to five days at the most, maybe not even that long."

"Has an FME attended?" Tyler asked. He was referring to a police surgeon, or Forensic Medical Examiner as they were officially known.

"Yep. The locals called one out, and she pronounced life extinct at 17:00 hours."

Interestingly, even when it was blatantly obvious that someone was dead, the police were still required to have this officially confirmed by a qualified medical practitioner.

"Did the FME give any indication as to how long the victim's been dead?"

Kennedy's Tyvek suit made little crinkly sounds as she shook her head. "Of course not," she chucked. "Apparently, the FME's professional advice to the first responders was that, when we find out who the victim is and when she was last seen alive, we would know that she was killed sometime between then and when she was found."

Tyler gave her a rueful smile. "You can't fault that logic, I suppose, but it doesn't really help me."

"No, it doesn't," Juliet agreed. "We'll just have to wait and see what the pathologist and forensic anthropologist have to say about time of death when they examine the torso."

Tyler studied the murky waters of the lock. Although the torso had been recovered from there, it didn't necessarily follow that the head and missing limbs would be, and that worried him greatly. "Have the divers given an estimate of how long it'll take them to finish searching the lock?"

Kennedy winced. "The problem is, there's zero visibility underwater, which means all the searching's got to be done by feel alone, and that could easily take them a couple of days to complete."

Tyler swore under his breath. If the USU divers, resembling giant frogs as they blindly groped their way around the bottom of the lock, didn't find the remaining body parts in there, the search radius would have to be extended to cover the waterway on either side of Acton's Lock.

Unzipping his Tyvek overalls, Tyler pulled out a crumpled Computer Aided Dispatch message from his inside jacket pocket. Grumbling under his breath, he unfolded and reread it carefully. It gave the location of the crime scene as Acton's Lock and, in brackets, stated that this was lock number seven of twelve along Regent's Canal.

"You do realise that, if the missing body parts aren't recovered in there, all the water between locks eight and six will have to be searched, and maybe even dredged?" he told her.

"I'm trying not to think that far ahead," Juliet admitted.

They both knew that it would be a massive undertaking, potentially lasting several weeks, and it would cause untold havoc for anyone needing to use the waterways.

Doing his best not to dwell on the logistics, or the cost implications, of running such a lengthy operation, Tyler knelt down beside the torso and carried out a visual examination of the unidentified victim.

"Is that a scar?" he asked, pointing at a diagonal line on the torso's right side, just above the hip.

"I think it is," Juliet said, leaning forward to get a better look. "Looks to me like she's had her appendix removed at some point."

Tyler made a mental note of it, knowing that any marks, scars or tattoos might give them a vital clue in solving the mystery of the torso's identity.

"Juliet, can you arrange for DNA swabs to be taken from the torso and rushed straight up to the lab?" he asked. "Obviously, I'll need you to make sure that they're fast tracked."

If the victim's DNA was held on the national database in Birmingham, either because she had a criminal record or had provided a sample for elimination purposes at some point, they should be able to establish her name within forty-eight hours. If not, he would request that a familial search be run, to see if anyone related to her was in the system, but that would be costly, and take a lot longer to complete. And, of course, there was no guarantee that any of her relatives would be known to police anyway.

Kennedy gave him a jaded smile. "Let me guess, you want the results back yesterday, if not sooner?"

Behind his Victoria mask, Tyler's face took on an injured expression. "Am I really *that* bad?"

"Yes," she said, sternly. "You bloody well are." When she continued, her tone had softened and the affection in her voice was unmistakable. "But, as you're also my favourite SIO, I'll put in a call and see if I can pull some strings."

That mollified him, as she had known it would.

"Any idea what the cause of death was?" Tyler asked as he stood up.

"Not yet. There are no obvious penetrative wounds to the front or sides of the torso. I'm just waiting for the SO3 snapper to get here. Once she's been photographed in situ, we'll flip her over and examine her back properly."

"What about age?" Tyler asked next. "Any idea how old she was?"

Kennedy shrugged. At least one shoulder did; the other stayed exactly where it was. "Somewhere between twenty and forty would be my best guess, but until a forensic anthropologist takes a gander, we won't know for sure."

Tyler was finding the whole experience slightly surreal. He had seen plenty of bodies over the years, ranging from ones that looked like they were merely sleeping, to those that were horribly mutilated or badly decomposed. Regardless of how peaceful or ghastly their appearance had been, he had never had any trouble thinking of them as another person, a living entity like himself, with thoughts and feelings, hopes and desires. The unsettling thing about this case was that, without its head and limbs, the body in front of him just didn't seem real, and he was really struggling to think of it as a human being.

He ran his eyes over the torso again, in case he had missed anything the first time around. The exposed flesh at the sites where the head and limbs had been severed appeared more grey than red, and he could see bits of jagged white bones protruding from inside. Bits of loose skin surrounded each of the wounds, and these were flapping about in the wind. There were lots of nicks visible in the flesh, and some in the bones, suggesting that the killer hadn't had an easy time of dismantling her.

"It's weird," Dillon said, taking a cautious step closer. "She looks just like the pig carcasses I used to see hanging in my local butcher's shop window when I was a kid."

Tyler nodded his agreement. "I was thinking exactly the same thing," he admitted, grimly.

"DCI Tyler!"

Tyler cringed. It was Askew again, and her whiny voice was really beginning to irritate him. He stood up, lowered his mask. "Yes, Miss Askew, what is it now?"

Imogen was standing twenty feet away, barred from proceeding any further by the inner cordon tape and the burly PC stationed there.

"Surely, if we put on one of those silly paper suits, we can come over and have a closer look?"

"No."

Her brow morphed into a frustrated frown. "But George said—"

"George isn't here; I am. The answer is no."

Waiting behind her, Bear looked mildly amused, as if he were secretly enjoying the experience of seeing her not getting her own way for once.

Imogen harrumphed loudly, then delved into her bag. "We'll see about that," she muttered angrily as she rummaged around inside. After several seconds of frantic searching, she finally dug out her phone. "Ah-ha!" she said, staring at it triumphantly.

Tyler left her to it. If she planned to ring George Holland every time that he denied one of her requests, she was going to be spending a lot of time on the phone.

Two men wearing barrier clothing wandered over, both lugging heavy bags. After checking in with the cordon officer, they slipped under the tape and made their way over.

"Evening, guv'nors," Kevin Murray said, nodding respectfully. Dumping his exhibits bag on the floor, he massaged the small of his back for a few seconds, then wandered over to take a closer look at the body. "Here, Ned, grab an eyeful of this," he called to the photographer, who had just started to unpack his equipment.

Looking up from his camera bag, tripod in hand, Ned Saunders sauntered over to stand by Murray's side. "Evening, Juliet, Mr Tyler, Mr Dillon," he said, nodding to each of them in turn.

Murray elbowed him to get his attention. "Oi, what do you call a man with no head, no arms or legs, and no torso?"

Ned frowned, then shrugged.

"Dick!" Murray said, laughing at his own joke.

When no one else joined in, he pointed to his genitals. "Dick, get it? Because that's the only part of him that's left."

13

If you don't believe me, smell my fingers

Imogen was waiting to ambush Tyler and Dillon the moment they left the inner cordon. "DCI Tyler, can I have a word, please?"

To Tyler's surprise, her confrontational attitude seemed to have mellowed somewhat. "Of course," he responded with a strained smile. The cynic in him suspected that, having made the call, she hadn't received the unconditional backing from George Holland that she had been expecting, and so she was now trying a different approach.

"Look, I know we haven't got off to the best of starts," she said with a deprecating smile, "and most of that is probably my fault."

Most?

Tyler said nothing, but his raised eyebrow spoke volumes.

"Okay, fine," she conceded. "It was *all* my fault. At times I can be a bit pushy." A guilty shrug, then spreading her arms in a conciliatory gesture, she admitted, "My enthusiasm sometimes gets the better of me."

Tyler remained silent. He wasn't going to let her off that easily.

"Anyway, I wanted to apologise for being a little overzealous, and ask if we can put it all behind us and start over again?"

Tyler felt a subtle elbow in the side from Dillon, who was standing beside him, waiting to be formally introduced. He mentally rolled his eyes, aware that his friend had been trying to engineer an opportunity to speak to Askew for weeks. "Imogen, have you met my partner, DI Tony Dillon, yet?"

Dillon stepped forward, extending a paw like hand. "Call me Tony," he said, flashing her a debonair smile.

Imogen ran her eyes over him, and Tyler got the impression that she liked what she saw.

"I've seen you around the building," she said with a coy smile, "but we haven't actually met."

Resisting the urge to poke his finger down his throat at the sight of their overt flirting, Tyler was struck by an inspirational idea. "Dill, why don't you give Imogen an overview of the case while I nip off and get things organised?" he suggested.

Dillon looked at him, then at Imogen. "Well, I…"

"That's fine by me," Imogen said, quickly. She beckoned the cameraman over. "Would you mind if Bear filmed you while you're briefing me?"

Dillon blushed. "I suppose that would be okay," he said, glancing at Tyler for confirmation.

"Well, as long as the camera lens is fully insured," Tyler said. "After all, let's be honest Dill, your face is more likely to break mirrors than hearts."

———

Having successfully offloaded Imogen Askew and her hairy cameraman on Dillon, Tyler put in a call to the Intel Cell at Hertford House. The telephone was answered on the second ring, and he found himself listening to the dulcet tones of his lead researcher.

"Intel Cell, Dean Fletcher speaking."

"Deano, it's Jack Tyler. I'm down at Regent's Canal and I need you to run some urgent checks for me in relation to the new job. Have you got a pen ready?"

There was a brief pause, during which he heard papers rustling as Fletcher fumbled about in search of a biro. *"Okay, got one,"* he said a few moments later. *"What can I do for you?"*

Tyler was extremely grateful that Deano hadn't wasted precious time bombarding him with pointless questions, even though he must have been desperate to know what was going on down at the scene.

"I need you to get me a list of all the female Mispers from Hackney and Whitechapel divisions. All we've got to go on with this torso is that it belongs to a white female, aged somewhere between twenty and forty. She doesn't have any tattoos or other distinguishing marks, but she does have an appendectomy scar on the right side."

As he spoke, he could hear Dean's pen scratching against paper as he wrote the information down.

"Okay, leave it with me, guv. It shouldn't take too long to get that information."

"Thanks, Deano."

"Sounds like we've got our work cut out with this one."

Tyler tried to think of something positive to say, but failed miserably. "I've got to be honest; I think it's going to be a very challenging case."

"A bit stumped, are you?"

"Not nearly as stumped as the victim," Tyler said. He couldn't help it; the words just came tumbling out.

Dean laughed, and then told everyone else in the office what the boss had just said.

Hanging up to the sound of their laughter, Tyler walked over to join Steve Bull, who had now donned a Tyvek suit and was squatting down by the torso, watching on in morbid fascination as Juliet Kennedy and Kevin Murray began swabbing it.

"Doesn't look real, does it?" Bull said, looking up at him.

Tyler shook his head, sadly. "No, it doesn't, but unfortunately it is."

A wave of guilt washed over him as he recalled the tacky joke he'd just made to Dean, about the victim being stumped. Looking down at her now, it felt like a pretty tasteless thing to have said, but he consoled himself with the knowledge that gallows humour, as inappropriate as it might seem to an outsider, was an important safety valve; a coping mechanism without which most police officers – himself included – wouldn't be able to do the job.

"Yeah, but where do we even start?" Bull asked. "I mean, although the torso was found here, it could have been dumped into the canal miles away."

"I know," Tyler replied, glumly.

"What do you want me to do first?" Bull asked, looking a little overwhelmed.

Tyler thought hard. "Arrange for someone to take the Lock Master and the bloke from the barge to the nearest nick and obtain key witness statements from them. Once that's done, contact the relevant waterways authority and see if they can give us a steer on which direction the other body parts are likely to be travelling in." He glanced at the stretches of canal either side of the lock. "The way I see it, the suitcase containing the torso was swept into the lock from the Haggerston side, not the Limehouse one, so I'm minded to move in that direction first, if we have to extend the search radius."

Bull nodded. "Makes sense," he agreed. "I'll have a quick word with the Lock Master. If he can't give me the info about the canal, he'll definitely be able to point me in the direction of someone who can."

Tyler looked up at the sound of an approaching car. It was a battered Vauxhall Astra, and it pulled up next to the Omega. A moment later, Colin Franklin and Paul Evans alighted. Tyler waved at them and indicated for them to remain where they were.

"I'll let you crack on," he told Bull. "I need to get Colin and Paul briefed, so they can get the CCTV trawl underway."

Fred Wiggins knocked gently on Willard's office door, then waited to be called in. "It's probably nothing," he said, closing the door behind him, "but I just heard on the radio that a woman's body was found in Regent's Canal earlier this afternoon, down by Broadway Market in Hackney."

Leaning back in his chair, Willard blew out a thick plume of cigar smoke, then shrugged indifferently. "So…?"

Wiggins paused, looking uncomfortable.

"Spit it out," Willard snapped. "I haven't got all day."

"Well," Wiggins said, hesitantly, "Carrie went missing on Friday evening, and no one's seen hide nor hair of her since then. Her wanker of a brother, Aidan, reported her missing so the family are obviously worried about her. When I heard about the body, it got me thinking: What if she didn't do the dirty on us? What if she just got mega pissed on Friday night and ended up face down in the drink?"

Willard considered this, and the sour expression on his face told Wiggins that he was having trouble deciding which outcome would be more palatable to him.

"Make a couple of calls and bottom it out," Willard said tersely. "Let me know as soon as you hear anything."

Wiggins nodded. "I'll get straight on it," he promised.

―――

Tyler stripped out of the restrictive barrier clothing, scrunched it into a ball, and threw it into the back of the Omega. Closing the door with a clunk, he crossed to Franklin and Evans, who were both leaning against the side of their pool car, patiently waiting to be briefed.

"Right, boys," he said with a world-weary sigh. "Let me apologise in advance, because you're going to have your hands pretty full with this one."

Their faces clouded over but they said nothing.

"I need you to scope out the canal footpath from here, all the way down to Kingsland Road." He pointed to the west, and they followed his finger with their eyes.

"How quickly do you want all this done?" Evans asked.

"Today, if possible."

The furtive look the two detectives shared told Tyler that that they were unhappy, and he couldn't really blame them; it was a tall order.

"I don't mean to sound negative, boss," Franklin said. He was an athletic black man of thirty, who had recently passed his sergeant's exams. "But that's just too much work for the two of us. If you're serious about covering that much ground today, you're going to have to find us some more people to help out."

Tyler winced. It was a perfectly reasonable request, but one he suspected he wouldn't be able to accommodate. "I'll try, Colin," he promised, "but there's so much else to do that I think we might struggle on that front."

As they set off, Tyler checked his watch, wondering how much daylight they had left. As if reading his mind, Juliet Kennedy appeared at the outer cordon perimeter and beckoned him over.

"Jack, I've ordered some arc lighting for when it gets dark. It should be here within the hour."

Tyler smiled his gratitude. "Thanks, Juliet." At least that was one less thing for him to worry about.

Annie Jenkins was curled up on the sofa in Aidan's living room, watching the early evening TV. She had recently finished eating her dinner, and the tray containing her dirty plate and utensils was resting on the cushion beside her.

The sound of the downstairs toilet flushing preceded Aidan's arrival in the living room. He had only arrived home from work a few minutes ago, and was still wearing his overalls, which were stained and grubby.

"I hope you washed your hands," she said, thinking he had appeared too soon after flushing to have realistically had enough time to do so.

"Course I did," he said, flopping down next to her. "If you don't believe me, you can smell my fingers." As he spoke, he extended his right hand towards her face.

Annie instinctively leaned back. "Get away from me you dirty git," she snapped, turning her mouth down in disgust.

He reacted by shoving his fingers right under her nostrils and wiggling them. Annie jerked sideways to avoid them, crashing into the tray and nearly knocking it onto the carpet. Luckily, she managed to grab it at the last moment.

Aidan seemed to find this hilarious. Tilting his head back, he laughed uproariously. "Leave it out," he told her. "I only had a piss."

"That's not the point," she said, primly.

That afternoon, she had finally finished editing their first porn film, adding some bland background music and the title credits. The production might not be up to Steven Spielberg's standards, but the kinky niche scenes it contained would make it a sure-fire best seller, Pervy Pete had assured her. She had shown it to him before leaving work and, while he thought it was still a little rough around the edges, he had seemed reasonably impressed.

With Pervy Pete handling the packaging and distribution side of the business, she should be able to sit back and rake in the profits. Except she couldn't relax, not with Carrie discovering the VHS tape that Aidan had stupidly left in the video player overnight.

After receiving Carrie's call, Annie had wandered around the flat in a state of agitation, not knowing what to do for the best. In the end, she had waited until she was sure that Carrie had set off on her night out, and had then sneaked over to the house, letting herself in with the emergency key the family kept hidden under a flowerpot.

Thankfully, the offending VHS tape had still been sitting on top of the video player, and she had been able to recover it without any further drama. She hadn't told Aidan about the clandestine visit. He was a funny sod, and he would have gone into one if he'd known that she had entered his house without permission, even though it was his fault that she had been forced to take such drastic action in the first place.

As time passed, Annie was becoming increasingly confident that Carrie hadn't spoken to anyone about the porn film's discovery before her disappearance. Stanwick would have been the first person that Carrie confided in, but she hadn't acted any differently to normal when they attended the police station to report Carrie missing on Monday night.

More importantly, Annie hadn't heard anything from her solicitor to suggest that Social Services had been informed. If word had reached them, she was sure they would have reached out to her by now, demanding to know if there was any truth in the allegation.

Maybe, she was going to get away with—

"I'm starving," Aidan said, dragging her away from her thoughts. "What have I got for dinner?"

"You've got sausage and mash, the same as me."

Aidan turned his nose up. "Again?" A petulant sigh of disappointment, like it was all she ever fed him. "Well, the mash better not have lumps in it, like it did last time," he complained, as ungrateful as ever.

On screen, a kid in an advert took a large bite from a juicy hamburger, munched away for a couple of seconds, and then smiled into the camera like it was the best thing he had ever tasted. "I would have much preferred a burger and chips," Aidan said, staring at the screen enviously.

"Well, tough," she snapped, annoyed by his ingratitude. "You'll have what you're given and like it."

The local news came on. As soon as the opening music faded, the camera panned out and a serious faced female presenter began reading from her autocue.

"Good evening. Reports are coming in that a woman's torso has been found in a stretch of Regent's Canal in East London. The gruesome discovery was made earlier this afternoon by staff at Acton's Lock, which runs parallel with Broadway Market..."

"Jesus!" Annie said, glancing sideways at Aidan.

He didn't respond, but she noticed the colour had drained from his face, and realised he was thinking exactly the same thing that she was. "Oh my God, it's Carrie, isn't it?" she whispered, reaching over to squeeze his trembling hand.

Terry Marshall had badgered Fingers into accompanying him to the little pub down the road from the garage for a quick pint after work. Fingers didn't like Terry, and he certainly didn't want to go drinking with him, but Marshall had refused to take no for an answer, making him feel like a lightweight for showing reluctance.

Marshall had gone to school with Darren, and he liked to make a big thing about being older and wiser than Fingers. He was always giving it large when they were alone, boasting that he was a seasoned man of the world, and mocking Fingers for being an immature little boy.

As Fingers trudged along behind Marshall, he wondered why he had allowed himself to be bullied into going to the pub, when all he really wanted to do was go home.

Because I'm a bloody doormat, that's why.

Well, that and the fact that he had been determined to prove that he was as much of a man as Marshall.

The pub was called *The Black Horse*, and it was, to put it mildly, a bit of a dive, frequented by local villains, down and outs, and other unsavoury characters who had nowhere better to go. As Fingers followed Marshall into the bar, all conversation stopped, and he felt every eye in the room turn on him. Their hostility was palpable, and he froze on the spot, trying not to succumb to the urge to turn around and leave. Marshall must have been aware that his guest would be greeted with suspicion, but he continued to the bar without a backwards glance. When he finally turned around, it was clear that he was enjoying Fingers' discomfort.

Wanker!

"I dunno about you, Fingers," Marshall said after letting him stew a moment longer, "but I'm gagging for a pint."

As soon as the other patrons realised that Fingers was with

Marshall, who was obviously a regular, they immediately lost interest in him, and the atmosphere became a little less tense.

Cringing at the horrible stickiness of the threadbare carpet, Fingers crossed the room to join Marshall at the bar. The older man had found a small gap between two groups of scruffily dressed men, and Fingers slotted into it, being careful not to bump into anyone in case it triggered a confrontational response.

The bar was dimly lit, and the air stank of spilt ale and stale cigarette smoke. There was also a vague scent of herbal cannabis. Fingers ran his eyes over the room, but couldn't work out where it was coming from. Then he spotted two men in stained blue overalls sitting at a nearby table, and clocked the spliffs in their hands. He vaguely recognised one of them as a fellow grease monkey who worked at a rival garage a couple of streets away. When the man glanced up, their eyes met and Fingers nodded amiably, but the man instantly looked away.

"My round," Marshall announced genially. Leaning on the bar, he waved at a buxom woman who had just finished serving another customer at the other end of the counter. She lazily acknowledged him with a hand that was festooned with bulbous rings, more closely resembling a knuckle duster than a collection of jewellery.

"Evening, Maureen," he said when she ambled over a few seconds later.

"What can I get you, Terry?" She made the request sound like a terrible inconvenience.

Unperturbed by her lack of warmth, Marshall flashed her a brilliant smile. "I'll have a pint of Guinness," he told her, then raised an enquiring eyebrow at Fingers.

"A pint of lager, please," Fingers said, smiling politely.

With a sullen grunt, Maureen bent down and retrieved two glasses from a shelf beneath the bar, then sauntered over to the pumps. "Do you boys want any nuts or crisps to go with your drinks?" she enquired as she poured.

"I'll have a packet of dry roasted nuts," Marshall said, "and some change for the slot machines." He slapped a ten pound note down on the bar as he spoke.

Once they had their drinks, Marshall signalled for Fingers to follow him over to the far end of the room, where three brightly coloured gaming machines stood in a neat row. Two men in their sixties, one short and stocky, the other tall and skinny, were busy playing the first two machines, but the third was free.

"Anyone mind if I jump on this one?" Marshall asked. Downing half of his pint in one go, he put the glass down on an unoccupied table adjacent to the fruit machines.

Both men grunted their indifference.

Wiping the froth from his lip with the back of his hand, Marshall belched loudly. Then, with a grin of anticipation, he inserted a coin and pulled the lever. "Come on, baby," he purred as the machine dinged and flashed and a bugle played a jaunty little tune.

The elderly beanpole standing next to him gave him a smug look. "You're wasting your time on that one," he remarked as Marshall inserted another coin. His name was Arthur Brownlow, and he still sported the same Teddy-Boy quiff that he'd had since his late teens.

"Why's that then, Arthur?" Marshall asked as he yanked down the lever a second time.

Arthur tapped his coat pocket, and change jingled inside. "I had a good win on it not long before you arrived, didn't I, Vlad?"

The thicker set man standing to Arthur's left nodded. "Da," his deep voice confirmed. The greying moustache above his top lip was almost as thick as the yard broom Fingers used to sweep the garage floor, and a thick mane of salt and pepper hair was swept back across his broad Slavic forehead. The military style RAF greatcoat he wore was totally at odds with the faded jeans and snazzy trainers beneath it.

Vlad tore his eyes away from the gaming machine long enough to smile at the two newcomers, revealing a mouth full of wonky yellow teeth. The sight made Fingers think of the rows of subsiding gravestones he'd seen at Manor Park cemetery when they had buried his grandmother earlier that year.

"Perhaps best you give up now and go home," Vlad suggested.

Marshall chortled. "You won't get rid of me that easy," he told the Russian. Pulling the lever again, he watched eagerly. A few seconds later, the spinning icons came to rest with two matches. Marshall let out a little yelp of delight and began jabbing the nudge button for all he was worth, trying to make it three in a row. "Come on, come on, come on," he coaxed.

Fingers watched on indifferently, wondering how soon he could make his excuses and leave.

"Fuck," Marshall growled when he didn't win anything. He retrieved his pint glass from the table and downed the remaining liquid, then handed it to Fingers. "Your round I believe," he said without looking up from the screen. "I'll have the same again. Vlad, Arthur, fancy a drink? My mate's buying."

It was gone eight by the time that Tyler and Dillon arrived back at Hertford House, and Imogen Askew and her cameraman had virtually sat on their bumper for the entire journey back. After missing the earlier call-out, she had made it clear that she didn't intend to let either of them out of her sight again. Dillon had been very happy to hear that; Tyler, not so much.

"Those two are following us around like a bad smell," he complained as they swiped into the building.

Dillon smiled. "She's not that bad when you get to know her," he said, glancing over his shoulder at Imogen.

Tyler rolled his eyes. "You're not thinking with your brain when it comes to her, are you?" he remarked, drily.

Dillon had the good grace to laugh.

Upon entering the office, Tyler made his way straight over to the Intelligence Cell. "How are you getting on with those Misper reports?"

Dean was standing by the printer. Grinning at them, he hoisted a stack of forms aloft. "Just printing the results out now," he said. "Give me five minutes to get them in order, then I'll bring them through."

Face flushed from having just run up a flight of stairs, Imogen attempted to follow the two detectives into Tyler's office but, as she reached the door, he held out a hand to stop her.

"Sorry, Imogen, can you give us five minutes to have a quick chat?" he asked, forcing a friendly smile onto his face. "Help yourself to tea or coffee while you wait, and I'll give you a shout when we've finished."

"Oh, okay," she said, sounding a little deflated.

As she turned away, Tyler grinned inwardly. It was clear that she had wanted to say more, but had exercised restraint in the hope of making a good impression on him. Closing the door behind him, he walked over to his desk. Flopping down in his high-backed chair, he rested both elbows on his desk and began massaging his temples. "I've got the headache from hell," he announced, miserably.

"Tell you what, why don't I go and make us both a brew?" Dillon offered, heading for the door.

Tyler smiled his gratitude. "Good idea, and I wouldn't mind a couple of chocolate biscuits if there are any left."

As soon as he was alone, Tyler pulled his collar loose, then sagged back in his chair and stared into the middle distance, lost in thought. As much as he hated to admit it, solving this case was going to be an uphill struggle. He didn't want to sound like a defeatist, especially not when the investigation had only been going for a few hours, but one word kept popping into his mind:

Sticker!

Ignoring his throbbing head, Tyler opened his Decision Log and commenced his opening entry. He outlined the nature of the call-out, what had been found at the crime scene, and recorded that his first priorities were to identify who the victim was, where she had been killed, how she had been transported to the canal, and from which point along the towpath she had been thrown into the water.

Like any of that was going to be easy!

The act of dismemberment had probably been committed out of necessity, because there was no other way for the killer to remove the victim from wherever he had murdered her without drawing attention to himself. That much made sense, but why go to all the trouble of concealing the torso in a suitcase? Having already double wrapped it in refuse sacks, presumably to prevent any leakage, why not just bundle it into the boot of his car and drive it to the canal during the dead of night?

The most likely answer was that the killer didn't have access to a vehicle.

Perhaps he didn't even possess a driving licence. Not everyone did.

He?

Tyler had automatically assumed that the killer was male, even though there was no evidence to support this. True, statistically speaking, the vast majority of dismemberments *were* carried out by male killers, but there were also some well documented cases in which female murderers had gone down that road. Annoyed with himself for jumping to unsupported conclusions, he vowed to keep an open mind from now on.

He wondered if the killer – be they male or female – had wheeled the suitcase from the crime scene to the canal? That would have taken some nerve but, if the killer didn't have access to a car, what other choice would they have had?

Tyler made a note to remind whoever ended up viewing the CCTV to be on the lookout for anyone towing a suitcase behind them.

After completing four whole pages of notes, he lowered his pen and massaged the back of his neck.

What was keeping Dill?

The big lug had been gone ages, and Tyler was gagging for the coffee he'd been promised. He stood up and stretched, then wandered over to the door. Looking out, he was miffed to see his friend standing over by the urn, chatting to Imogen-bloody-Askew, and the pair of them were flirting outrageously.

Tyler rapped on the window and angrily beckoned Dillon over, then stormed back to his desk, where he began rummaging through the drawers in search of some pain killers. Digging out a couple of paracetamols, he popped them into his mouth and began crunching angrily.

A moment later, the door crashed open and Dillon entered, carrying two steaming mugs of coffee. "There you go," he said, kicking it shut with his heel.

"You took your time," Tyler complained, snatching the mug from his friend's hand and taking a sip to wash the tablets down.

Before Dillon could respond, there was a polite rap on the door, and Dean Fletcher poked his head in. "Got the Misper details you wanted," he announced cheerfully.

Tyler pointed to a seat. "Come in and make yourself comfortable."

"What have we got?" Dillon asked, lowering himself into a chair to the researcher's right.

Taking his time, Dean adjusted his reading glasses. "Eight white females between the ages of twenty and forty are currently reported missing at Whitechapel, and a further six are missing from Hackney."

Tyler leaned forward, resting his elbows on his desk. "I suppose it could be worse," he said, sounding cautiously optimistic. "How many of them were reported missing within the last month?"

"Three from Whitechapel, and two from Hackney," Dean informed him. "The rest of the reports are all between four months and two years old."

"How many of them are shown as having appendectomy scars?"

"Only two."

Holding out his hand, Tyler impatiently beckoned for Dean to pass over the relevant reports. "Show me," he demanded excitedly.

The first report had been filed at Bethnal Green police station three weeks earlier. It related to a thirty-two year old woman called Rhoda Sinclair, who had gone missing from her council flat in Roman Road after a bust up with her long-term partner. There was a long history of domestic violence between them, and she had left him several times before, only to eventually return so that the cycle could repeat itself all over again.

Tyler paraphrased the last entry on the back of Sinclair's form F584, which stated that she had rung her parents on Sunday morning to inform them she was staying with a friend in Margate. "Was this friend ever spoken to, to confirm this?" he asked Dean.

The researcher shrugged. "Dunno, boss. I left a message for the Misper unit an hour ago, seeking clarification on that point, but they haven't got back to me yet."

Tyler glanced at his watch. "Dill, give them a quick bell and light a rocket under their arses."

"You'll find their number on my desk," Dean said as Dillon stood up.

"Hang fire," Tyler said before the big man had taken two steps. "I've just read the marks and scars section of the report, and it says that Rhoda Sinclair has a large, clover shaped birthmark right between her shoulder blades, which our victim most definitely doesn't."

Dillon returned to his seat.

Tyler picked up the second report. "This one relates to a thirty-four year old woman called Carrie McCullen, who went missing on Friday night," he read aloud. "She was reported missing at GD on Monday evening by her brother, his girlfriend, and her best friend."

GD was phonetic code for City Road police station in Shoreditch.

"Under distinguishing marks or scars, it lists an appendectomy, nothing else." He looked up, shrugged. "This one seems much more likely," he said. "Let's get someone straight over there to speak with the family."

As the others filed out of the room, Tyler tried to imagine how their unidentified victim's next of kin would be feeling right then. They would be trapped in a limbo of sorts, he guessed, still daring to hope that their loved one was alive, while secretly fearing the worst. The not knowing would be pure agony. The dreaded confirmation of death, when it finally came, would bring a strange sense of relief, because it would mean that they could start moving forward, although how anyone who suffered such a tragic loss ever did that was beyond him.

A half hour later, Kelly Flowers pulled the pool car up outside a line of terraced houses in Ivy Street. Leaning over the steering wheel, she stared at the house numbers through the dirty windscreen. "I think it's the end one," she said, squinting to be sure.

In her late-twenties, Kelly had shoulder length brown hair, symmetrical features and a smile that Jack Tyler regularly informed her melted his heart every time he saw it.

"Yep, that's the one," Debbie Brown confirmed, opening her door to get out.

From somewhere deep within the council flats across the road came the sound of a large dog barking. This was immediately followed by a man's voice, harsh and angry, shouting for it to shut up.

Two gangly teenagers, one black, the other white, were standing outside a house two doors along, and they regarded the detectives with hostile eyes.

Clicking the fob to activate the central locking, Kelly pulled her coat tight to ward off the cold. "I think we've been made," she said, nodding towards the teenagers.

Debbie waved at them, received a scowl in return. "Yep. I think it's safe to say our cover's blown," she said with a grin.

Kelly stopped to study the gleaming red Mini in the driveway. The car was immaculate inside and out, and it was obviously someone's pride and joy.

Carrie's, perhaps?

"I have a feeling this is going to be a very awkward discussion," she said.

"Just a bit," Debbie agreed with a grimace.

"I'm happy to take the lead," Kelly offered as they reached the door, not that she had the slightest idea how best to inform someone that their missing relative's dismembered torso *might* or *might not* have been discovered in a suitcase that had been found in a canal lock.

Debbie shrugged, amenably. "Let's just see how it goes."

"Okay," Kelly said, thinking that Debs was probably right. Taking a deep breath, she rang the bell. "Here goes."

The street door opened almost instantly, as if the occupants had been standing behind it, waiting for them to knock, and they found themselves standing face to face with a man and a woman, both of whom were staring at them expectantly.

Caught off guard, both officers hurriedly produced their warrant cards. "Good evening," Kelly said, fixing each of them with a polite smile. "I'm DC Flowers and this is DC Brown. We're from the Homicide Command and we're here in relation to—"

"It's about Carrie, isn't it?" the man interrupted. His face was intense, and he had the sallow complexion of a drug user.

Kelly opened her mouth to speak, but the woman beat her to it.

"You got here very quickly," she said, sounding impressed. "We only phoned the station five minutes ago."

Kelly and Debbie exchanged a confused look, wondering what was going on. "Do you think we could come inside?" Kelly asked. "It might be better if we discussed this in private."

They were shown through to the living room and invited to take a seat. There was a sofa and two armchairs to choose from.

"Would you like anything to drink, tea or coffee?" the auburn-haired woman asked them, and Kelly could see that she was a bundle of nerves.

"Never mind all that," the male snapped, impatiently. "Is it Carrie or not?"

Sitting down in one of the armchairs, Kelly opened her daybook on her knees. "Before we get into any specifics, can I confirm that you're Carrie's brother?" she enquired of the man, who was so tense that it seemed likely he would explode at any second.

An agitated nod. "That's right. I'm Aidan. This is my girlfriend, Annie."

"Please, Aidan, take a seat," Kelly said, pointing towards the sofa.

When he didn't move, Annie gently took his arm and led him over to it. They sat down together, and she gripped his hand in hers, interlocking their fingers and squeezing tightly.

"You said you called the station a few minutes ago," Debbie said. "Can you tell us what that was in relation to?"

"We saw the news on the telly," Aidan said. He was twitching now, finding it increasingly hard to sit still, and Kelly wondered if he was in need of a fix.

"Is it true what they said on TV?" Annie asked in a quivering voice. "Did someone really chop her up?" With that, her face crumpled and the waterworks started.

Wrapping a protective arm around his girlfriend's shoulders, Aidan glared at them angrily, as though it was their fault that she was crying. "Now look what you've done," he growled.

Kelly had taken an instant dislike to him but, as a FLO, it was her role to support the family and facilitate communication between them and the SIO, so she couldn't afford to let her feelings get in the way of that. "Aidan, I know this is a very difficult time for you and Annie, but—"

"Just answer the damn question," he snapped. "Was that my sister you pulled out of the canal or not?"

Kelly took a deep breath, exhaled slowly. "The truth is, we don't know," she said, candidly. "All we can tell you at the moment is that the torso belongs to a white female, aged between twenty and forty, and it has an appendectomy scar."

Aidan bowed his head, and an anguished sigh escaped his lips. "Carrie had her appendix removed when she was in her twenties," he informed them, and the abject misery in his voice told her that he was resigned to the fact that Carrie was dead.

As much as she hadn't warmed to him, Kelly felt his pain. "Look, I think you need to prepare yourself in case it does turn out to be Carrie but, until we get DNA confirmation, we won't know for sure. My advice would be not to jump to any conclusions just yet, in case it's not her."

Annie wiped her eyes. "That's why you're here, isn't it?" she said, blinking back the tears. "To get something of Carrie's with her DNA on it."

Kelly looked her straight in the eye. As a FLO, it was paramount that she was always completely honest with the family, even if that meant telling them something they didn't want to hear. It was the only way to establish a bond of trust. "Yes, it is," she said softly. "I'm so very sorry, and I wish there was some way that we could make this easier for you, but there isn't."

"What exactly do you need?" Aidan asked.

"We'll need to take Carrie's hairbrush or toothbrush with us, preferably both. The lab will compare DNA samples from those to ones taken from the torso."

Aidan's eyes narrowed. "And how long will this take, exactly?"

"We've been assured that the process will be fast tracked," Debbie said, speaking for the first time. She had a matronly manner about her that brokered no argument, and Kelly noticed how wary Aidan seemed of her.

"I'll get them for you," Annie said, standing up on shaky legs. She had to prise her hand away from Aidan's, and he clung on to it for as long as possible.

Kelly also stood. "Actually, if you don't mind, it would be better if you showed me where they are, so I can formally seize them and produce them as my exhibits."

"Oh, okay," Annie said, looking utterly depressed. "If you'd like to follow me."

With Imogen Askew and her hairy cameraman sitting directly opposite him, Tyler felt extremely self-conscious as he listened to the update from Kelly Flowers but, having only just allowed them into his office, he couldn't really shoo them out again.

"So, what do you think?" he asked, turning his back on his audience so they couldn't see the strain on his face.

"Hard to say," Kelly replied, her voice deliberately noncommittal.

Tyler desperately needed a steer from her because he had a *big* decision to make, and her sitting on the fence like this wasn't going to cut it for him. "I hate to pressure you, but I'm going to need more than that," he told her, trying not to let the urgency he felt show in his voice. "What's your gut telling you, Kelly?"

There was a pregnant pause, and then he heard footsteps, followed by a door being closed.

"Sorry, Jack," she said, lowering her voice to a whisper. *"I couldn't speak freely because the family were within earshot, so I've just popped out to the street for a bit of privacy. If you want my honest opinion, I reckon Carrie McCullen is looking like a pretty good fit for this."*

He was relieved to hear that. "Yeah, I think so, too," he admitted.

Tyler crunched the numbers in his head. Carrie's toothbrush and hairbrush would go up to the lab that evening, but it was unrealistic to expect any results back in anything less than thirty-six hours. The question was: did he wait for the DNA findings to come back before pulling the trigger, or did he act now, on the premise that they had identified their victim?

What to do? What to do?

If he went with a hunch, only for it to turn out that Carrie wasn't their victim, he would have wasted precious time chasing shadows. That could prove disastrous. But, if he didn't act fast to preserve her house as a crime scene, and it turned out that she *was* their victim, then there was a substantial risk that any evidence it contained would be contaminated or, worse, completely obliterated.

Tyler groaned inwardly; the press would have a field day with that one, and it would sound terrible at court if they ever got the case to trial. Either way, his reputation could end up in tatters.

What to do? What to do?

There was no way of knowing for sure, so he was just going to have to make a judgement call and live with the decision if it turned out to be wrong.

"Jack? Jack, are you still there…?"

"Sorry, Kelly," he said with a heavy sigh. "I was miles away."

Tyler sat up straight, having made his decision. "Okay, look. I'm going to work on the presumption that Carrie McCullen's our victim, and act accordingly." He knew it was a big call to make, but it just felt like the right thing to do; besides, getting justice for the victim and her family was far more important to him than his reputation. "Will her family grant us voluntary authority to search the house, or do I need to get a Section 8 PACE warrant organised?"

On the other side of the desk, wedged between Imogen and

Bear, Dillon was staring at him intently. When their eyes met, the big man arched an eyebrow, which seemed to beg the question: 'Is there something I need to know?'

Tyler held up a finger, urging patience. In the background, he could hear Kelly talking to Carrie's brother and his girlfriend, but he couldn't make out any of the words being spoken. Then she was back on the line.

"Jack, they're willing to sign off on a voluntary search. I'll fill out the Book 101 accordingly."

"Excellent," Tyler said. "I'll have Steve Bull cobble together an exhibits officer and a CSM and get them straight over to you to take charge of the scene."

"Care to tell me what's happened?" Dillon asked the moment he killed the call.

Imogen leaned forward, equally interested. "Yes, I'd like to know, too."

I bet you would!

"Nothing's happened," Tyler told them. "Kelly's gut tells her that Carrie McCullen is our victim, and I agree with her, so I'm going to treat her house as a crime scene."

"Sorry, I don't understand," Imogen said, sounding totally bamboozled. "If there haven't been any new developments, how can you jump to that conclusion?"

"It's a necessary precaution," Tyler explained, annoyed that he should have to do so. "Statistically speaking, most murder victims are killed by someone they know, not by strangers. Statistics also tell us that our victim was most likely dismembered where she was murdered, not elsewhere so, if we proceed on the basis that Carrie was probably killed by someone she knew, we also have to assume that the most likely place for it to have happened was her home, which is why we need to treat it as a crime scene."

"I guess that makes sense," Imogen conceded, still processing the information, "but we still don't know that this girl, Carrie, is our victim."

"No, we don't," Tyler accepted. "But she fits the profile, both in terms of the appendectomy scar and with regards to the amount of time that's passed since her disappearance."

Imogen had been making notes as he spoke. "Are you going to make a public announcement that she's the victim?"

Tyler shook his head, emphatically. "No. Until such time as it's confirmed by a DNA match, all we can say is that we're trying to establish, one way or another, whether a woman who went missing last Friday is our victim. In the meantime, we're maintaining an open mind and will continue to explore all possibilities."

Imogen took a moment to digest what she had been told. "So, basically, what you're saying is that you think – but don't know – Carrie McCullen is your victim, so you're going to start doing all the things you would if you knew for certain that she was, but you're still going to be doing all the things you would have done if she wasn't?"

Tyler nodded. "That's about the size of it."

Imogen seemed genuinely impressed. "But won't that stretch you very thin on the ground?"

"It's going to be very resource intensive," Tyler confirmed with a wry smile, "which is why I'm just about to make myself very unpopular with George Holland by disturbing him at home to request some additional staff."

"Would it be possible for you to explain all that to me again?" Imogen asked, and there seemed to be a new found respect in her voice, "but with Bear filming you."

Tyler was already on his feet. "I'd love to," he fibbed, "but I've got a search team to organise, and a difficult call to make to DCS Holland."

Imogen's face clouded with disappointment.

"However, I'm more than happy for DI Dillon to stand in for me," he said, patting his friend on the shoulder.

As Tyler walked past Imogen, she reached out and placed a hand on his arm. "Jack, would it be okay if Bear and I accompany the search team tonight? I promise that we won't get in their way."

Tyler had been half expecting this. Out of principle, he wanted to refuse, but he didn't think he could. "I suppose so," he said, nodding reluctantly. "DS Steve Bull's going to be in charge, so you'll have to follow his orders, and he'll have to clear it with the family first. If they say no, you don't get to go inside."

"Thank you," she said, and he was surprised by the warmth in her voice. Perhaps Dill had been right; perhaps she wasn't that bad once you got to know her.

The bell sounded for last orders.

"Your round, mate," Marshall said, elbowing him in the ribs. The four men were crammed into the little booth opposite the slot machines, Fingers and Marshall on one side, Arthur and Vlad on the other.

Fingers said nothing, but inwardly he was fuming. This was the fourth time on the trot that Marshall had declared it was his bloody round. Apart from buying him a pint when they first arrived, Marshall hadn't put his hand in his pocket once, and Arthur and Vlad hadn't either.

They were ponces, the lot of them.

With a resigned sigh, Fingers slid out of the cramped booth. "Same again?" he asked through gritted teeth. He was even angrier with himself for letting them get away with it than he was with them for taking liberties with him.

"Cheers mate," Marshall said in a slurred voice. After four pints, he was a little the worse for wear. "And I'll have a whiskey chaser if you don't mind, just to round the night off."

Fingers did mind, but he was too timid to say so.

"Da," Vlad said, echoing the sentiment. "If we have chasers, mine is large vodka." He pronounced it, 'wodka'.

Arthur shook his head. "Just a pint for me," he half said, half burped. "I don't go in for spirits."

"And make sure you have one yourself," Marshall said generously, as though he were paying for it.

Fingers set off towards the bar without saying a word, consoling himself with the knowledge that his nightmare trip to the pub was nearly over. In a few short minutes, the boozer would close, and he would finally be free to go home. While he was waiting to be served, he spotted Marshall heading for the men's room on unsteady legs. "Bloody wanker," he muttered under his breath.

Arthur appeared at his side. "Alright, lad," he said with a friendly smile. "Thought I'd come and give you a hand to carry the drinks over."

Fingers nodded his thanks. "Cheers, Arthur. Very kind of you."

Arthur leaned against the bar and studied him carefully. "Terry reckons your boss has sodded off to Tenerife for a couple of weeks," he said, conversationally.

Fingers harrumphed. It was a sore point and he didn't want be drawn into talking about it.

Arthur gave him a sly smile. Ignoring the 'no smoking' sign on the wall behind him, he lit up and took a deep drag from his fag, coughing as the smoke worked its way deep into his aging lungs. "That's better," he said, exhaling thin tendrils of smoke from both nostrils. "Business must be blooming good if he can afford to do that, especially as he's paid Terry way over the odds to cover for him."

Fingers stared at him, blinked hard. "Has he?" he demanded. "I didn't know that."

Arthur nodded, sagely. "Oh yeah," he confirmed, his cheeks hollowing as he took another drag. "You know what a big trap Terry's got. Been bragging about it to anyone who'll listen. Why would your boss do that, then?" he asked, then barked out a short humourless laugh. "Suddenly got money to burn, has he? Thought his business was doing badly?"

The taunting angered Fingers. "Yeah, well it won't be when we sell off the diamonds," he responded defensively and without thinking. As soon as the words left his mouth, he realised the enormity of his mistake.

It was too late. Arthur's ears had already pricked up. "Diamonds? What diamonds would that be?" he asked, showing far too much interest for Fingers' liking.

"I–er–I…" Fingers stammered, and the more flustered he became, the harder he found it to think clearly.

"Where's my Guinness?" Terry Marshall's voice boomed from the direction of the men's room, from which he had just emerged. A moment later, he had crossed to Fingers' side. Wrapping an arm around his scrawny shoulders, he gave Fingers a drunken squeeze of affection and then released him. "He's a good lad," Marshall told Arthur.

Pulling free, Fingers turned to address the jaded looking barman who was waiting to take his order.

Arthur tapped him on the shoulder. "What diamonds?" he persisted. The cigarette hanging from the corner of his mouth bobbed up and down as he spoke, dislodging a half inch of ash, which fluttered down into his lap. Pulling a face, he brushed it away with nicotine-stained fingers.

"You must've misheard me," Fingers said, glancing nervously at the older man. "I said Daimler's, not diamonds. Dazza owns a small fleet of Daimlers, which he rents out for weddings and the like. He's going to sell them to raise some funds."

Arthur's eyes narrowed, suspiciously. "I know what I heard," he insisted, bullishly.

The barman returned with their order.

"What's all this about a fleet of Daimlers?" Marshall asked, looking very confused.

Before any further questions could be asked, Fingers thrust their drinks into their hands and shooed them away.

Watching them wander back to their seats, he removed a twenty from his wallet and handed it over. As he waited for his change, he was conscious of Arthur's eyes burning into the back of his head. With any luck, the old codger would have forgotten all about their conversation by morning, and no real harm would have been done.

14

THURSDAY 11TH OCTOBER 2001

Operation Haddonfield

The office meeting began at eight o'clock on the dot. Clutching a mug of coffee to his chest as if it was a shield that would protect him from all the stress that the coming day promised to bring with it, Tyler ensconced himself in his usual spot, sitting with his back to the tea urn.

Sitting to his immediate left, Dillon looked like he was ready for whatever the day might throw at him. Tyler, on the other hand, looked like he was ready for bed.

George Holland had elected to join them this morning, and he was sitting to Tyler's right, back stiff, legs crossed at the ankles, face sombre. He hadn't smiled once since arriving.

He's probably got the hump because of all the extra officers I've requested.

Most of Tyler's team had pulled their chairs into a tight cluster around him, but the officers seconded from other teams were milling around in their respective little groups, making the place look untidy.

Tyler tried to block Imogen Askew and her shaggy companion from his thoughts. He had deliberately turned his chair to one side, so at least they weren't directly in his eyeline. Bear, who actually seemed like quite a pleasant fellow when you got him on his own, was squinting through the eyepiece of his video camera, which was mounted on a large tripod at the back of the room. His tongue protruded from the side of his mouth like some giant, hairy dog, and a fierce frown of concentration marred his brow as he made his final checks. To Bear's credit, he had warned Tyler that whenever the light on top of his camera was glowing red, it meant that he was filming, and it was doing that now, as Holland had given them permission to film the entire briefing, much to Tyler's annoyance.

Imogen had taken up station directly behind Bear and, from that vantage point, she was imperiously watching over proceedings. As always, a pen and pad were glued to her hand in case she needed to make notes.

"Let's begin," Tyler announced, and the isolated pockets of conversation that had broken out around the room rapidly faded into silence. "For those of you who don't know me, I'm DCI Jack Tyler, and I'm the Senior Investigating Officer. The big lug sitting to my left is DI Tony Dillon. He's the deputy SIO and not, as you could easily be forgiven for thinking, my minder."

A few people chuckled, but not many.

Tough audience, Tyler thought. He normally got a far better reaction when he cracked that gag. Perhaps he needed some new material? "As you all know," he continued, "the dismembered torso of a white female was dragged from Acton's Lock in Hackney yesterday afternoon. It was inside a suitcase, which sprung open when it became entangled with the hull of a barge passing through the lock. The torso doesn't have any birthmarks or tattoos, but it does have an appendectomy scar on its right side."

As he spoke, his eyes slowly traversed the office, and he was pleased to see he had their undivided attention. Even Kevin Murray was hanging onto his every word, which was virtually unheard of. Of course, Tyler was acutely aware that their interest stemmed from the fact that dismemberment cases were incredibly rare in the UK, and had absolutely nothing to do with his mesmerising skills as an orator.

"On Monday evening, a thirty-four-year-old white female called Carrie McCullen was reported missing by her brother, Aidan. Apparently, Carrie went out with a group of friends on Friday evening, but didn't return home. In common with the torso, Carrie has an appendectomy scar on her right side. DNA samples were taken from the torso, and these are being compared to control samples from Carrie's tooth and hair brushes. We've been assured that the results will be back with us by tomorrow morning at the very latest."

He glanced over at Juliet Kennedy, who was sitting in the first row, and was rewarded with an affirmative nod.

Predictably, Juliet was dressed to the nines, with her makeup immaculately applied and not a single blonde hair out of place.

A hand belonging to one of the officers Holland had drafted in to assist them went up at the back of the room. Tyler didn't recognise the man, and assumed he must be fairly new to the command.

"Yes?"

"DC Ian Yule, sir, from team six," a slim man in his early forties announced in a boring monotone. He was wafer thin, with a droopy little moustache and a comb-over that was fooling no one but him. Either he had really bad dress sense or he had got ready in the dark, Tyler decided, because his suit jacket didn't match his trousers and he was wearing odd socks.

"Aren't you worried that we could be jumping the gun by assuming this McCullen woman's our victim?"

Tyler raised a condescending eyebrow.

Aren't you worried about going out looking like that?

"Well, Ian," he responded, addressing Yule with more diplomacy than would have been the case had there not been a film crew present. "It's a gamble. If I'm wrong, we will have wasted precious time but, if I'm right, we'll have given ourselves a massive head start. I'm hoping it's the latter. What about you?"

That seemed to throw Yule off his stride. "Oh, I, er... Well, obviously, I'm hoping for that, too."

Tyler's smile didn't go anywhere near his eyes. "I'm glad to hear it. Now, if there are no more interruptions, we've got a lot to get through. Kevin, talk us through the crime scene at Acton's Lock, please."

Murray cleared his throat. "In addition to the torso, we recovered a wheeled suitcase and two London Borough of Hackney refuse bags; one made of clear plastic, the other of black. They've been put in the drying cabinet downstairs. As soon as they're ready, I'll get them up to the lab for DNA and fingerprint testing. I found a label in the suitcase, and we've obtained the manufacturer's details and a batch number from that." He held up a cautionary hand. "Before anyone gets too excited, the case looks quite old, so I wouldn't hold out too much hope of tracking anyone down from it."

A collective sigh of disappointment went around the room like a verbal Mexican Wave.

"As you know, boss," Murray continued, "the torso was photographed and swabbed at the scene. It was then carted off to the hospital for radiography and PMCT testing. Juliet's probably better placed to explain what that all means than I am."

In the front row, Juliet stifled a yawn, patted her hair to make sure it was still in place, then opened her daybook. "Basically, I managed to pull some strings and get a post mortem CT scan performed as well as standard X-Rays. The CT imaging will help the pathologist and forensic anthropologist to differentiate between the perimortem trauma that occurred at the time of death and the subsequent injuries caused during the dismemberment process."

Nodding his thanks to her, Murray took up the narrative again. "After the medical imaging was completed, the torso was transported to the mortuary. The SPM's scheduled to start at eleven, and I'll be attending that, along with Juliet and Mr Dillon."

Tyler thanked him, then turned to Dick Jarvis. "What came out of the key witness interviews from last night?"

Clearing his throat self-consciously, Jarvis quickly glanced down at the notes on his lap. "To be honest, guv, they didn't add anything more to the narrative than you already know. Alec Du Plessis noticed the suitcase when it became entangled with his boat, and then saw the torso spring out of it. Freddie Harris came over to see what was going on, and then they both tried to pull it out of the lock but failed miserably. When they realised it was a human torso, and not a tailors dummy, they called the locals, who called us."

"The dive team didn't finish searching the lock until the early hours," Tyler told the room. "Unfortunately, it didn't contain any additional body parts."

"I'm not surprised," Murray said. "The case was only just about big enough to hold the torso, so the killer wouldn't have been able to fit anything else inside."

Tyler turned to Steve Bull, who had been tasked with liaising with the dive team skipper and the waterways authorities. "What's the plan of action for the divers today, Steve?"

"They're going to start searching the section of canal between Acton's Lock and Queensbridge Road this morning," Bull told him. "The general consensus of opinion is that the torso was the body part to reach the lock, so the other bits will almost certainly still be on the Haggerston side of the canal."

Tyler thanked him and moved on. "Okay, that brings us to CCTV," he announced, casting a sympathetic glance in the direction of Colin Franklin and Paul Evans. "How did you get on with that, last night?"

"We checked out all the properties along the towpath between Acton's Lock and Queensbridge Road," Franklin informed him. "This morning, we're planning to cover the area between Queensbridge Road and Kingsland High Road. Trouble is, most residents are likely to be out at work, so I don't know how much luck we'll have."

"All we can do is try," Tyler encouraged. "The good news is that Mr Holland has drummed up some additional staff to assist you with the CCTV, and they'll be at your disposal all day."

Next, Tyler's eyes sought out Kelly Flowers and Debbie Brown. "Kelly and Debs are the two FLOs assigned to the family," he informed the room. "Last night they visited Aidan McCullen at the house he shared with Carrie in Ivy Street. How did that go?"

"Aidan and his girlfriend, Annie Jenkins, were both understandably very upset," Kelly said. "We obtained Carrie's tooth and hair brushes from them for DNA comparisons, and they granted us permission to search the house."

"Any problems with getting them to agree to that?" Dillon asked.

"Aidan wasn't too keen initially," Kelly said. "Fortunately, Annie was much more reasonable, and she managed to talk some sense into him."

Tyler's eyes narrowed. "Can you think of any reason for his reticence?" he asked, wondering if that meant the man had something to hide.

"He's a lazy, selfish bastard," Debbie said, bluntly. "I just don't think he liked the idea of being inconvenienced."

Kelly snorted. "I think it's more likely down to the fact that he's a junkie and he was worried we'd find his stash if we searched the place."

"Either way, he sounds like a complete wanker to me," Dillon said, shaking his head disapprovingly.

Tyler shot a worried glance at the video camera and saw that the red light was still on. He inwardly cringed, hoping that his friend's tactless comment wouldn't make the final cut.

"He was a grade A arsehole, guv," Debbie Brown confirmed, triggering an outbreak of laughter.

Tyler mentally rolled his eyes, hoping that little pearl of wisdom would be edited out too. He would have to have a word with the team, warn them to watch their Ps and Qs when Imogen and her cameraman were around.

"Anyway," Kelly was saying, "Aidan's agreed to move in with Annie for a few days, while we examine the house forensically."

Fixing his sights on George Copeland, Tyler said, "How's that coming along?"

Copeland was a well-upholstered man in his forties, and by far the most experienced Advanced Exhibits Officer on the team. "It's a three-bedroom terraced house, clean, and generally well maintained," he informed them in an accent that hailed from the Holme Valley in West Yorkshire.

Tyler smothered a smile. Whenever Copeland spoke, he

pictured him standing at a bar, with a flat cap on his head, a pint of Yorkshire Bitter in his hand, and a Whippet sitting by his feet.

"I could see that all the surfaces were dusty and contained micro-fibres," Copeland continued. "To me, that suggests there hasn't been a hurried clean-up, which–"

"Which we would expect to see if it was the dismemberment site." Tyler finished the sentence for him.

Copeland hesitated, then nodded. "Aye. Sorry, I know that's not what you want to hear, but…" He let the words taper off, effectively finishing the sentence with a shrug of resignation.

Tyler smiled his understanding. "George, I'm not trying to fit a square peg into a round hole. If it isn't the dismemberment site, the sooner we confirm that, the sooner we can stop wasting time and move on."

"If Carrie McCullen *was* dismembered there," Copeland said, "it would have had to have happened in either the kitchen or the bathroom."

"What makes you say that?" The unexpected interruption had come from Imogen.

"Well, lass, both rooms have tiled walls and lino on the floor, so it would be relatively easy to clean up any blood spillage afterwards, and there's just about enough space in either one for a body to be chopped up in."

"Did you do any presumptive testing last night?" Tyler asked.

"I couldn't see any blood in the kitchen, so I didn't do any testing in there, but I found what appeared to be minute traces of blood staining up in the bathroom. There was a tiny spot on the vanity unit mirror, and a second spot on the cold tap in the bath. I carried out presumptive tests on these, and they both came back positive for blood. Obviously, without sending the samples off for analysis, I can't say who it belonged to."

"Interesting," Tyler said, stroking his chin thoughtfully. He stopped doing that when he remembered that the camera was trained on him, worried that the gesture might come across as being too clichéd.

"Not necessarily," Juliet warned. "If it *is* Carrie's blood, there could be any number of legitimate reasons for it being there and, as there's only a couple of random drops, it doesn't prove anything."

Tyler nodded, conceding it was a fair point. "So, what happens next?"

"We'll carry out a more thorough examination of the house today, Hemastix testing a lot more surfaces and checking everything under UV light conditions," Copeland informed him. "That'll give us a better indication, but we won't know for sure whether or not the body was dismembered there until we Luminol the place."

Luminol was a chemical that reacted with the iron in haemoglobin, and it glowed blue under ultraviolet light whenever blood was present, even if a serious attempt had been made to wash it away and it was no longer visible to the naked eye.

"And when will that be?" Tyler asked.

Copeland deferred to Juliet Kennedy, who bathed Tyler in an indulgent smile, like a protective mother wanting to let her over enthusiastic child down gently.

"Let Sam and George get all the basics done today, and I'll try and organise the Luminol treatment for tomorrow. If not, it'll definitely be done the day after."

Tyler nodded, not happy but resigned to the fact that this was going to be a slow burn. "Fine," he huffed. "In the meantime, I want Aidan's key witness interview completed this morning. Until we track down the people she went out with on Friday night, he's the last known person to have seen her alive, and I want a detailed account from him regarding that."

"He'll be at work until three," Kelly pointed out.

Tyler's jaw tightened. "Do you have a contact number for him?"

"Uh-huh," Kelly replied.

"Good. Ring him up and tell him that you need to meet him straight away," he said, tetchily. "This won't wait, so don't take no for an answer. If he's worried about getting into trouble at work, tell him we'll square it with his boss."

"Okay," Kelly said, exchanging a dubious glance with Debbie.

"Right, where's Reggie hiding?" Tyler demanded, scouring the room for his telephone expert.

A pudgy hand shot into the air from the middle of the back row. "I'm over here," Reg Parker announced, giving him a little wave.

"Reg, I want Carrie's mobile phone billing, call and cell site data obtained ASAP. Go back a week before her death, just in case we need to look for historic contact or movement patterns. Make sure the TIU knows how urgent it is."

The Telephone Intelligence Unit was based at New Scotland Yard, and it acted as the link between the investigative teams and the various industry service providers.

"I will, boss," Parker assured him.

"Reg," DCS Holland said, speaking for the first time. "Tell them this is a Cat A enquiry, and if they need me to speak to anyone to oil the machinery, I'm quite happy to do that."

"Leave it with me," Reg said, beaming at him in anticipation of his empowerment. "I'll throw your name into every conversation I have and use it shamelessly to get whatever we need."

Laughter broke out. Even Holland joined in, but Tyler could tell that he was slightly worried that Parker might abuse the privilege.

"Reg, use Mr Holland's name sparingly," he cautioned. "Having his support doesn't give you carte blanche to demand anything you want."

"Yes, boss," Reg said, sounding properly deflated.

―――

"Are you absolutely sure, Fred?" Willard asked. He had been enjoying a very pleasant breakfast with his trophy wife in the kitchen of their lavish house in Millionaire's Row, Chigwell when the call from Wiggins came in.

"Positive, Mr Willard. I've just been down there to confirm it for myself. According to the nosey neighbours who live next door, the Cozzers turned up late last night, kicked her fuckwit brother and his girlfriend out, and then turned the place into a crime scene."

Willard closed his eyes as a wave of sadness engulfed him. He had known Carrie since she was a babe in swaddling, and she was more like a favourite niece to him than an employee. In many ways, having her around had almost been like having Damian back, so similar were they in their mannerisms.

Her unexplained disappearance had concerned him greatly but, unlike Fred Wiggins, he had never seriously entertained the idea that it was connected to Frankie's murder and the theft of his jewels.

Willard reached under his glasses and wiped moisture from his eyes. "So, the body that turned up in the canal; that was definitely her, was it?"

His wife looked up from her newspaper upon hearing that, and gave him a quizzical look.

There was a long pause at the other end of the line, then Wiggins said, *"I'm sorry, I know how fond you were of her…"*

Willard didn't like his wife knowing too much about the darker side of his business, so he stood up and walked away from the table. Opening the French doors, he stepped out onto the garden patio, where he could speak freely. It was chilly out there, but he found the coldness invigorating. "I want to know who did this to her, Fred," he said, his voice trembling with rage. "And when you find out, I'm going sort the horrible little cock sucker out myself."

"Is that wise, Mr Willard?" Wiggins cautioned. *"Wouldn't it be better to let me and Casper take care of it for you like we always do?"*

"No!" Willard snarled. "This is something I need to take care of personally, not just for little Carrie's sake, but to honour Damian's memory."

The meeting had been going for well over an hour now, and people were flagging, but the end was in sight so Tyler pushed on. "Whitey, I want you to shoot over to Carrie's place of work at some point today. Speak to her colleagues. Find out if she's been acting out of character lately, or if anything's been troubling her."

"Leave it wi' me," Charlie White replied.

Turning to Dean Fletcher, Tyler said, "I want research dockets on Carrie, her brother Aidan, Annie Jenkins, and this Stella Carter woman who's mentioned on the missing person report as her troublesome ex."

"Boss, she's got another brother called Darren," Debbie Brown chipped in. "He's a few years older than the twins. Apparently, he's on holiday at the moment, flew out to Spain on Friday morning"

Tyler hadn't been aware of the older brother's existence. However, if Debbie was right about Darren McCullen flying out on Friday morning, he couldn't possibly be a suspect.

"Is it worth even bothering with him if that's the case?" Fletcher asked, understandably keen not to take on any more work than was absolutely necessary.

Tyler turned to DS Chris Deakin, the Office Manager. "Chris, raise the action but don't allocate it yet. We'll review it in a few days' time."

"Fair enough," Deakin said.

"Carrie owns a little Mini, which I'm reliably informed is still parked outside the home address," Tyler continued. "Dean, can you run a retrospective ANPR search through NADAC?" NADAC was the National ANPR data centre. "I want to know if it's had any hits within the past seven days."

"Yeah, no problem," Dean said, making a quick note.

Tyler paused to draw breath. "Okay," he said, after consulting his notes. "Let's run through today's main priorities. One: we identify and seize as much CCTV as possible. Two: the divers search the canal between Acton's Lock and Queensbridge Road for missing body parts. Three: we debrief Carrie's family, friends and colleagues to see if we can piece together her last movements and identify any possible suspects. Four: Reggie will obtain Carrie's phone data, and the Intel Cell will put the research dockets together." As Tyler spoke, he ticked each point off on his hand. "Five: We run financial checks on Carrie. I want to know if any of her accounts have been accessed since her disappearance on Friday, on the off chance that her killer stole her bank cards and has been withdrawing money ever since."

"I take it that the financial stuff will be down to me?" Chris

Deakin asked. He was a qualified Financial Investigator and had previously served on the Fraud Squad.

"I'm afraid so," Tyler confirmed.

"Thought as much," Deakin said with a wry smile. "I'll get onto it this morning."

"Okay, before I hand you over to DI Dillon and DS Bull to go through individual taskings, are there any questions?" Tyler glanced over at Ian Yule, wondering if he would be stupid enough to raise his head above the parapet a second time, but he was sitting quietly with his hands clasped in his lap.

"Ladies and gentlemen," Tyler said, bringing the meeting to a close, "I'm sure the most important question on your minds is what code should you use for all your overtime and expense claims. The answer is: Operation Haddonfield."

Grinning like a naughty schoolboy, Charlie White scribbled the operation title onto the front of his daybook, as did almost everyone else in the room.

15

Come on, you slacker!

Wiggins tapped out a message to his man on the inside.

'Any update on who topped Frankie yet? Mr W getting impatient. Also, need to know name of torso from canal and who is responsible. Call me when you can.'

He read it over to make sure that he was happy with the content, then pressed send. It was infuriating that he couldn't just ring the man, but he had to be ultra-cautious. It had taken him years to cultivate a cop, and he couldn't afford to let his impatience endanger his prize asset. Wondering when he would hear back, and knowing that it could take hours, he was startled when his phone pinged less than thirty seconds later.

. . .

'No news on who topped F. Will speak to mate on team today to see if any developments. No official confirmation on torso ID yet. DCI thinks her name is Carrie McCullen. Will let you know when DNA results come back.'

"Shit," Wiggins said as he read Carrie's name. He felt a tiny twinge of guilt for having suspected her of doing a runner because she had been involved in Frankie's death and the theft of the diamonds. Willard had been right to chastise him; Carrie was Damian's daughter, a trusted member of the firm, and he should have known better than to have ever doubted her.

The Coroner's Court in Poplar High Street was a sombre red brick building with stone dressings, a tiled roof and stucco covered eaves. The mortuary was located at the rear of the building, tucked out of the way.

Having found a rare parking space outside the front, Dillon and Murray made their way around to the side entrance. The journey from Hertford House had been made in strained silence, with neither man making much of an effort to engage the other in small talk.

Dillon pressed the buzzer, then gave his hands a brisk rub to warm them up, wryly reflecting that the temperature was almost as chilly as the atmosphere inside the car had been.

After being buzzed in, they ascended to the first floor, where Juliet was already waiting for them, having made her own way over.

Dillon had prepared the official briefing document for the Home Office Forensic Pathologist, and he gave Juliet a copy to read through, just in case there was anything she felt should be added.

The Coroner's Officer, an ancient PC who looked like he could soon be occupying one of the mortuary freezers himself, made them a cup of instant coffee, which they accepted gratefully.

Leaving Juliet and Murray to chat amongst themselves, Dillon wandered over to the window, trying not to think about the grisly sights he would shortly have to endure. Subconsciously patting his jacket pocket, he was comforted by the reassuring bulge of his little jar of Vick's nasal gel. He would insert a liberal amount up each nostril before the procedure began, in the hope that it would filter out the cloying stench of death and disinfectant that always pervaded the mortuary.

For him, the stomach-turning smell was the worst thing about post mortems. It lingered in the hair and on the skin for hours afterwards, and no matter how hard he scrubbed himself in the shower, he could never quite rid himself of it.

"Good morning, everyone," an authoritative female voice announced from the doorway. Spinning around, Dillon was greeted by the sight of a slender woman with short black hair. She appeared to be in her early forties, and she was dressed in a grey business suit and white blouse. She had an intelligent face with well-defined, attractive features, and a welcoming smile.

As she entered the room, Juliet detached herself from Murray and greeted her warmly. "Stephanie, lovely to see you again," she said, extending her hand.

Reluctantly, Dillon wandered over to join them.

Juliet made the introductions. "Stephanie, this is DI Tony Dillon, the Investigating Officer. Tony, this is Dr Stephanie Tolpuddle, our pathologist."

"Pleased to meet you," Dillon said, shaking her hand. It was smooth and delicate, like that of a piano player.

Tolpuddle regarded him with an amused expression. "You're the detective who doesn't like dead bodies, aren't you? Juliet's told me about you."

A blush started in Dillon's neck and worked its way upwards until his entire face was the colour of a lobster.

"I, er…"

Tolpuddle laughed. It was a nice laugh; the sound of someone who enjoyed life and possessed a deliciously wicked sense of humour. "Don't worry, I won't make you stand too close to the cadaver while I work," she promised.

That was a relief; some pathologists, like Creepy Claxton, insisted that the DI in attendance be glued to their side while they dissected the corpse.

Dillon handed over the briefing note. "I prepared this for you," he told her, his face still burning with embarrassment.

"Excellent," Tolpuddle said. Removing a pair of tortoiseshell reading glasses from her jacket pocket, she adjourned to a chair to read through the document.

As soon as she was out of earshot, Dillon gave Juliet a traitorous glance. "I can't believe you told her that," he whispered.

Juliet grinned at him. "Being squeamish is nothing to be ashamed about," she teased.

"I am *not* squeamish," he insisted.

Juliet patted his arm. "No dear, of course you're not," she said in a patronising tone.

The two-man crew of the British Waterways dredger slowly chugging its way along Regent's Canal towards Acton's Lock were on their way to carry out a routine clear-up operation that had been pencilled in several weeks ago and, as they were only going to be dredging water on the Old Ford side of the lock, there was no danger of them interfering with the ongoing police operation.

Their flat-bottomed boat resembled a floating skip, and it was fitted with an excavator. Conventional dredging consisted of scooping up the sediment that had formed on the bottom of the canal and removing it for disposal but, before they could begin doing that, Cliff Hayter and Billy Bowman would need to clear all the floating rubbish that had accumulated against the side of the lock.

"Look at all that shit," Hayter said to his colleague as the lock came into sight. There was a huge cache of rubbish crammed against the side of the lock, mainly consisting of discarded refuse sacks.

Drawing the dredger alongside the towpath, so that his workmate could jump ashore and tie her off, Hayter put the engine into idle. "There's a lot more than I was expecting from the briefing," he complained, stepping out onto the deck to survey the floating debris.

Both men wore regulation attire, which consisted of bright orange jackets with fluorescent stripes, waterproof trousers, approved safety boats and flotation devices, which was just a fancy way of saying lifejackets. They also wore white hard hats of the type normally seen on building sites.

Running his eyes over the smelly mound of soggy bags, Bowman pushed his hard hat back on his head and let out a dejected sigh. "Right, I suppose we'd better get started," he said, donning a pair of heavy-duty gloves.

In his late thirties, Bowman was tall and gangly, with stooped shoulders. He leaned down and hoisted up the first black sack, tossing it into the hold of the dredger. Several more followed in quick succession.

"Feel free to join in anytime you like," he told Hayter, who had only just finished putting his safety gloves on.

"Alright, Speedy-bloody-Gonzales! Give me a chance," Hayter responded, reaching down to grab a sack. It was much heavier than he had been expecting and, as he lifted it up, the black plastic tore.

He swore as it slipped out of his hand.

Bowman had already thrown three more sacks into the dredger. "Come on, you slacker! Get a move on!" he chivvied his colleague.

On his second attempt, Hayter decided to play it safe and grab the bag with both hands. It contained something long and cylindrical, like an extra-large draft excluder but much heavier. As he raised it up onto his right shoulder, in readiness to catapult it into the dredger, the damn thing folded in the middle and he nearly dropped it again. Scrabbling to keep it from falling into the water, he clumsily ripped the black plastic bag wide open. Fortunately, there was another refuse sack inside – this one transparent – or he would have been covered in whatever ghastly contents it contained.

Hayter frowned as he stared through the clear plastic. Unless he was very much mistaken, he was looking at a human hand. "What the fuck!" he yelled, dropping the sack like it had just burned him.

"What's the matter, now?" Bowman demanded impatiently. He paused long enough to glare disapprovingly at Hayter before lobbing another refuse sack into the dredger's hold.

Hayter leaned forward and pulled the sack out of the water for a third time. Placing it on the canal towpath by his feet, he gingerly peeled back the remaining black plastic, to expose the clear bag within. There was no doubt about it; the bag contained a human arm, hand at one end, mutilated stump at the other. "Jesus!" he breathed, feeling his legs go weak.

Kelly ushered Aidan McCullen into interview room number two at Shoreditch police station, and followed him in. The threadbare carpet was so badly stained from all the drink spillages that it was no longer possible to distinguish its original colour. Shaking her head in disgust, Kelly decided that she definitely wouldn't be applying the five second rule to any food dropped on that!

Bolted to the floor, a sturdy wooden table took up most of the available space, with the only other items of furniture being four tatty wooden chairs and an overflowing wastebin.

"Take a seat," Kelly instructed, pointing towards the two chairs furthest away from the door.

Aidan hesitated for a moment, then flopped down and sulkily crossed his arms. He wiggled his bony butt around on the non-existent padding for a few seconds, trying to get comfortable, then gave up and slouched sideways against the wall.

The single fluorescent light suspended from the ceiling gave the room a yellowish tinge, making Aidan's already sallow complexion appear almost waxen. "I hope you realise that dragging me away from work like that could cost me my job," he complained, sourly.

Kelly smiled; said nothing. He had been making a major drama out of providing a statement about his sister's disappearance since they'd collected him from his place of employment, half-hour earlier.

Kelly and Debbie slipped into the equally uncomfortable seats opposite him. "I explained everything to your boss," Debbie told him equably, "and he was absolutely fine with it, so stop worrying."

Aidan harrumphed. "It won't be fine at all," he predicted, pessimistically. "The miserable bastard's been looking for an excuse to sack me for ages, and you just gifted him one."

The two detectives shared a glance; Aidan was really trying their patience.

"And why would he want to sack you, Aidan?" Kelly asked as she unwrapped two audio cassettes and stuck them into the tape deck. The plastic coverings went onto the floor beside the wastebasket, along with all the others.

A petulant shrug. "He's got it in for me because I've been late a couple of times and I've had to take some sick days here and there," he said, sounding hard done by.

The two detectives stared at him without a shred of sympathy.

"Aidan, Debbie and I are going to take a statement from you," Kelly explained. "Because you're the last known person to have seen Carrie alive, the whole process will be tape recorded to protect the integrity of the process, and to prevent anyone from suggesting that we primed you or put words into your mouth. Are you okay with that?"

"But I'm not the last person to have seen her alive," he protested. "Her mates, the ones she met up with, are. You need to do this with them, not me."

Kelly raised a hand to silence him. "Once we track them down, we'll be doing this with them too but, for now, you're the last person we can conclusively say saw her alive before her death."

Another shrug, this one tinged with impatience. "I suppose so," he replied, begrudgingly accepting her point. "Let's just get it over with, shall we? I've got better things to be doing."

Biting her tongue, Kelly pressed the record button. After buzzing for several seconds, the machine started blinking to show that it was working properly.

Kelly began by stating the day, date, time and place that the interview was being conducted, and then went on to outline who was present. She repeated the explanation she had given before they started, about why the recording was necessary, and then asked Aidan to describe, in as much detail as he could remember, his interactions with Carrie on Friday 5th October, the day that she had gone missing.

Aidan sniffed, then wiped his runny nose against the back of his hand. "Not a lot to tell, really," he said, unhelpfully. "She'd left for work before I got up, so I didn't see her until she got back, about half-four, or thereabouts."

Kelly sat in silence for a couple of seconds, waiting for him to elaborate, but he showed no inclination to do so. "Is that the normal time she gets back from work?" she prompted, while Debbie made the notes from which his statement would be drafted.

Aidan responded with a bored shake of his head. "Nah, she usually works till five, half-five, but her boss let her go early on Friday. She told me she stopped off at her mate's gaff on the way home, to get her hair done."

"Was there any particular reason for her doing that?" Kelly asked, after ascertaining the friend's name and address.

Aidan shrugged. "Carrie was always vain. She wanted to look her best, probably because she was going out that night with her mates."

"Can you tell us where Carrie was going, or who she was meeting?" Kelly encouraged.

Aidan made a big show of thinking about this, then blew his cheeks out as though the effort had exhausted him. "She reckoned she was meeting up with a few friends, don't know where, probably at *The Merry Fiddler* or somewhere like that." He shrugged, disinterestedly. "She might've said, but I wasn't paying that much attention."

"And that was the last time you saw her?"

Aidan nodded. "That's right. I went out to meet a friend. We played snooker in the club around the corner. Left the house about five, and got back sometime between nine and ten. I was still suffering from the man-flu I'd had all week, so I dosed myself up with *Night Nurse* and went to bed early. Slept like a log. Didn't get up till late on Saturday morning, then I mooched around at home all day, then had another early night."

"How well would you say you and Carrie got on?" Kelly asked, changing the subject slightly to shake things up.

"We got on okay," he said, guardedly. His eyes flickered to his left as he spoke, only for a millisecond, but that was long enough to convince Kelly that he was lying.

"Weren't you concerned that Carrie hadn't come home?" Debbie asked, unable to prevent a smidgen of irritation from creeping into her voice.

Aidan laughed. It was a cruel, heartless sound. "What am I, her bloody keeper? No, I wasn't concerned. Why would I be? She's a big girl, and she stays over with friends sometimes, so I just assumed she was doing that."

"So, when *did* you first start to become concerned?" Kelly asked. So far, Aidan was proving to be spectacularly unhelpful.

Aidan shifted his weight, turned side on and leaned an elbow on the table. "I went over to Annie's for dinner on Sunday afternoon," he informed them. "When I mentioned that Carrie hadn't been home since Friday, she thought it was a bit odd, so we tried ringing Carrie, but her phone was dead. Neither of us were too concerned, but then her best mate, Abi, called me on Sunday afternoon. She was worried because my sister hadn't messaged her back since Friday night. Abi insisted that we ring all her friends, you know, to see if any of them knew where she was, but none of them had seen her. Annie thought the same as me, that she was just spending a few days with a friend, but Abi wouldn't let it go."

Debbie frowned at him. "Didn't it bother you that her phone was dead when you tried ringing her?" she asked.

Aidan shook his head. "I just assumed the battery was dead. It was only when Carrie didn't show up for work on Monday morning that I started to take things more seriously." A lackadaisical shrug. "I mean, that really wasn't like her, and that's when I started fretting that something might be wrong."

"So, whose idea was it to report Carrie missing?" Kelly asked.

Aidan's eyes volleyed nervously from one detective to the other. "Well, it was a joint decision, really," he told them. "I mean, Abi suggested it, but me and Annie were totally on board with the idea."

Debbie raised a sceptical eyebrow. "I'm sure you were," she said, somehow managing to keep the cynicism from her voice. "We're going to need the names and telephone numbers of everyone you and Annie rang about Carrie," she told him. "We'll also need the details of anyone else you spoke to about Carrie's disappearance before reporting her missing"

Aidan stiffened, then fixed her with a hostile stare. "Why? Do you think I'm lying or something?"

"Of course not," Kelly placated him. "We just have to be thorough, that's all."

Tyler looked down at the bag on the towpath. Through the transparent plastic of the LBH refuse sack, he could make out the misted pink V shape of a woman's arm, bent at the elbow. The victim's right hand was pressed tight against the plastic, as if trying to claw its way out.

A British Waterways dredger was moored off to his right, and the two crewmen who had made the macabre discovery were watching him with interest from inside the pilot's cabin.

A half dozen black sacks were sitting in the dredger's hold, and Tyler estimated there was probably three times that many still floating in the water alongside Acton's Lock. All of them would have to be thoroughly checked by a police search team before they could be removed, just in case there were any more body parts hidden amongst them.

Staring down at the bagged limb, Tyler swore profusely. Its discovery this morning had massively complicated things and, as a consequence, he would have to rethink his whole search strategy. He had convinced himself that the torso had been the first part of

Carrie's dismembered body to enter Acton's Lock from the Queensbridge Road side of the canal but, in order for it to have travelled this far along the canal, the arm would have had to have gone through before it, which begged the question: how many other body parts had also passed through the lock.

Although the Waterways Authority had been really supportive, he knew that his having closed off the stretch of canal between Acton's Lock and Queensbridge Road was causing a logistical nightmare, and he dreaded to think what would happen if he extended the blockade all the way back to Old Ford.

Was it even viable to do that?

He honestly didn't think it was.

That was a problem he would have to address later; right now, he had to focus on this latest crime scene. With Kevin Murray tied up at the Special Post Mortem, and George Copeland busy processing Carrie's home, the only other Advanced Exhibits Officer on his team was Dick Jarvis, and he was currently chatting to Cynthia Alderton, the on-call Crime Scene Manager.

Alderton was a beanpole of a woman in her early forties, whose angular face was set in a permanent scowl. Despite her intensity, which could be a little overpowering at times, Tyler had always found her to be ultra-efficient and very professional.

Joining them by the cordon perimeter, Tyler removed the Victoria mask covering the lower half of his face and sucked in the cold, crisp air.

"Morning, Cynth," he said with a weary smile.

Looking up from her clipboard, Alderton fixed him with her trademark piercing stare. "Morning, Jack. What can I do for you?"

"I was just wondering what the plan was for processing the scene?"

Alderton's eyes bored into his. "The plan is to have the remaining bags photographed in situ, then removed and searched one by one."

She hadn't blinked once, which he found very off-putting. Feeling as though he had somehow been drawn into a staring competition, Tyler tried not to blink himself, but failed miserably.

"Got something in your eye?" Alderton asked, with an amused smile.

Tyler responded with a question of his own. "Have you had a chance to examine the severed limb yet?"

Alderton nodded, just the once. "I gave it a quick once over when I arrived," she told him. "It's the right arm of a white female. The ball joint is still present, which suggests that it was pulled out of the torso."

Tyler grimaced. "Sounds absolutely gross," he said, glancing over his shoulder at the bag. "Could you see if any of the fingers had rings on them?"

Alderton's brow creased into a studious frown and, for a split-second, Tyler thought that she was finally about to blink.

When she didn't, the disappointment was overwhelming.

"Actually, there was a yellow metal signet ring on the little finger," Alderton informed him. "I couldn't be sure, because it was difficult to see into the bag, what with all the condensation inside, but I think it might have had initials on it."

Now that was interesting.

Excusing himself so that he could make a private call, Tyler dug out his mobile and rang Kelly's number. Unfortunately, it went straight to answerphone, which probably meant that she was still taking Aidan McCullen's Key Witness statement. He tried Debbie's phone next, but got the same response. Ringing Kelly back, he waited for her answerphone to kick in.

"Kelly, it's Jack. Listen, I'm back down at Acton's Lock, where the victim's right arm has turned up. Can you ask Aidan if Carrie wore a signet ring on her right hand and, if so, whether it was initialled? I'd really appreciate it if you can ring me back with the answer as soon as possible." He was about to hang up, then remembered to add, "Love you loads."

———

It was almost midday when Stella woke up, and her return to consciousness was greeted by a splitting headache and a lurching stomach. She had drunk herself into oblivion the night before, just as she had the night before that. In fact, she had been hitting the bottle pretty hard since Friday night. It was the only way she could stop her mind from dwelling on the terrible things she had said and done to the woman she loved.

Every time she thought about their fight, her stomach knotted. She really hadn't set out to hurt Carrie, but the vile insults spewing from her former girlfriend's mouth had pushed her over the edge, causing something inside her to snap. Reeling from the hurtful accusations levelled against her, Stella's volatile temper had gotten the better of her and she had lashed out.

Stella had been ravaged by guilt and remorse ever since, and she would have given anything to turn back the clock and undo the harm she had done. Of course, she knew she couldn't do that, and her way of dealing with it had been to hide herself away in her flat and drown her sorrows in booze. She hadn't been out; hadn't showered or got dressed; hadn't even watched TV.

Pushing the bed covers back, Stella sat up groggily. The sudden movement made her feel dizzy, and she closed her eyes until the horrible spinning sensation passed. Her pounding head felt like it was going to explode at any moment, and she very nearly succumbed to the urge to lie back down. Instead, uttering a low, pitiful groan, she stood up and staggered into the toilet, moving with the exaggerated slowness of a zombie.

Her tongue had been replaced by a piece of old cardboard, her throat was parched, and her lips were so dry that she could hardly open them. Dropping her pyjama bottoms around her ankles, she delicately lowered herself onto the toilet. Clasping her aching head in both hands, Stella leaned so far forward that she nearly folded herself in half. "I want to die," she moaned.

She was so badly dehydrated that she only just about managed to squeeze out the tiniest trickle of wee.

No more booze, she promised herself.

After pulling her PJ bottoms back up, Stella flushed the chain and washed her hands. Moving on autopilot, she lurched along the hallway of her one-bedroom flat until she reached the kitchen at the far end.

Holding the kettle under the cold tap, she winced at the incredibly harsh sound the water made as it gushed out.

Too loud! Too loud!

Her ears begged her to make it stop. Granting them their wish, she switched the kettle on.

Coffee would help.

Coffee and painkillers.

Moving gingerly, Stella fished out the little bottle of paracetamol from the cupboard under the sink and tipped a couple of tablets into her outstretched palm. She poured herself a glass of water to wash them down with, grimacing at their bitter taste.

Stella made her coffee extra strong and very sweet. Carrying it into the lounge, she curled up on the faux leather sofa and tucked her feet beneath her. The room was a perfectly nondescript place, possessing no character whatsoever. There was a chill in the air, but she didn't have the money to waste on heating, not when a jumper would to the trick just as well. Clutching her coffee to her chest, and savouring its warmth, she decided that she would shower and get dressed as soon as she finished her brew.

It was time to stop hiding, and start facing the world again.

As she took her first sip of coffee, the torturous images returned. The disjointed memories, played out in slow motion, were of Carrie falling to the floor after she had been hit. They flashed into her head unbidden; a graphic succession of snapshots, depicting her former girlfriend wide eyed with shock, face covered in blood. Scrunching her eyes shut, Stella shook her head to banish the nightmarish visions.

Stop it! Stop it! STOP IT!

As the burning liquid landed in her lap, Stella's eyes jolted wide open, and a startled gasp escaped her lips. Looking down, she saw that she had spilled her coffee all over her PJs. With a shaking hand, she quickly deposited her mug on the nearby table and started brushing at her clothes.

The sobs, once they started, wouldn't stop.

"Oh, Carrie," she wailed. "I'm so sorry."

Out of nowhere, a hot wave of nausea washed over Stella. Ignoring the jarring pain in her head, she sprang to her feet and made a frantic dash for the door, clamping her hand over her mouth as she ran.

She only just made it to the toilet before throwing up.

Aidan called Annie the moment he was out of the police station. "Listen up," he said as soon as she answered. "I've just been given the third degree by the Filth about my movements on the day Carrie disappeared."

Annie gasped. *"Why, surely, they don't suspect you, do they?"*

Aidan shook his head. "Nah, course not. They're just going through the motions. Thing is, it got me thinking. They're searching my place at the moment, but what if they decide to spin your gaff as well for some reason?"

"Why would they want to do that?" Annie asked. He could hear the confusion in her voice. That and fear.

"How the fuck would I know," he retorted, angrily. "But, if they do, they'll find all the working copies of the film we've made, and then we'll get done for making and distributing porn."

"I'm not sure we've actually done anything illegal," Annie said, but she didn't sound overly confident.

"Well, maybe we haven't," he shot back, "but do we really want to take that chance? Besides, if those bastards at Social Services find out what we're doing, your chances of getting your kid back will be well and truly fucked."

At the other end of the line Annie sucked in air. When she spoke again, her voice was tremulous. *"What should I do?"*

She was really starting to try his patience. "You gather everything together, and I'll have a think about where we can stash it till all this fuss about Carrie blows over."

"What about all the covers I've had printed for the boxes?" she asked. *"Do we need to hide them, too?"*

Aidan pinched his nose. She was as thick as two short planks. "No, just leave them out for the pigs to find," he said, sarcastically, before exploding, "Yes, of course we bloody well do, you dozy cow."

Tyler popped his head around the door. "How's it going?" he enquired with a friendly smile. Having just returned from the canal, he had decided to check in on Andy Quinlan to see how his team were progressing with the job they had picked up the previous week.

Sitting behind his desk, half hidden by an untidy mound of paperwork, Quinlan looked up and groaned. "Don't ask," he said, tossing aside the report he had been reading.

Tyler winced. "Oh dear, like that, is it?" As if by magic, he produced two Styrofoam cups. "I come bearing gifts," he said, handing one over. "There you go, a large Cappuccino with no sugar, just the way you like it."

"Very kind of you," Quinlan said, accepting it gratefully.

Easing himself into a chair, Tyler took a sip of his latte, then licked the froth from his top lip. "Come on then, tell Uncle Jack everything."

Quinlan grimaced. "There's nothing to tell. Despite all the resources being poured into it, we're getting nowhere fast."

"No suspects yet?"

Quinlan barked out a humourless laugh. "I wish!"

"Have forensics turned anything up at the house?"

"Nope," Quinlan said, shaking his head sadly.

"What about ballistics?"

"The murder weapon was a nine-millimetre semi-auto. I've had the NABIS results back, and all they tell me is that it hasn't been used in any previous crimes. We recovered a loaded .357 Colt Python Magnum revolver from Kyle's safe, but the serial number had been ground out, so there's no way to trace it. It's covered in the victim's fingerprints, but that doesn't help us. Again, all NABIS can tell me is that it hasn't been used in previous reported crimes."

"Sounds like this Kyle bloke was a bit of a bad boy," Tyler observed. "Did he have much form?"

"Absolutely none," Quinlan said.

"What did his wife say about the gun?"

"She claims to have no knowledge of it, and the FLO says she comes over as very believable, so who knows?"

Tyler felt his pain. "How about CCTV?"

Quinlan laughed. "Can you believe it, there's no CCTV coverage in or near the victim's road."

Tyler was running out of suggestions. "Anything from the phones?"

Quinlan picked up a manila folder, waved it in Tyler's direction, then threw it back down onto his desk. "I've obtained three months' worth of call and cell site data for the victim and his wife, and there's nothing in it that remotely helps."

"Have you run a financial on the victim?"

"Yep. Frank Kyle was the branch manager at Willard Betting's Stratford office. He had a few quid in the bank, but nothing that would ring alarm bells or indicate he was living beyond his means. All his financial transactions were perfectly normal; wages in, bills out, that kind of thing. The safe in his home office was open when we arrived, and his wife said the intruders kept asking where he kept his cash and other valuables, so they were obviously after money."

"Do we know how much cash was in the house?"

Quinlan shrugged. "His wife reckons a couple of grand. Nothing that would justify killing him over."

Tyler winced. It sounded like the enquiry was stalling, and he wondered if Quinlan had already started to fear that the case would turn into a sticker. "He might not have a record, but did he have any affiliations to organised crime?"

Quinlan responded with a bittersweet laugh. "He worked for Jonas Willard, so yes, although there's no evidence to suggest he was actually involved in anything shady himself."

"What's Willard's deal?" Tyler asked, wondering if it could have any bearing on Carrie's murder – she had worked for him too, after all.

Quinlan shrugged. "Hard to say with any degree of certainty. In years gone by, he was implicated in loan sharking and race fixing amongst other things, but nothing was ever proved. These days, he runs a series of betting shops, owns a building firm, and has shares in various other legitimate business, but word on the street is that he also has his grubby little fingers in all sorts of nasty pies as well. Unfortunately, he's a very shrewd operator, always distances himself from being hands on, so there has never been any evidence against him."

Tyler shrugged. "If Kyle's murder isn't linked to organised crime, then maybe it really was just a robbery gone wrong?"

"That appears to be the case," Quinlan said, guardedly. "But I plan on keeping an open mind until we can confirm that, given Kyle's links to Willard."

"Well, it certainly sounds like a very interesting job, Andy," Tyler said, trying to cheer him up. "I'm sure if you keep chipping away at it, something will eventually give."

"Let's hope so," Quinlan said, stoically. A frown suddenly marred his features. "Considering that both our victim's worked for Jonas Willard, do you think there's any way that their murders could be connected?"

Tyler considered the question for a moment before answering. "I've obviously wondered the same thing myself," he admitted, "but they met their respective ends in drastically different circumstances, so I very much doubt it."

Quinlan sipped his coffee, then forced a smile. "Yeah, that's my take on it, too. How are you getting on with Little Miss Pushy and her hairy cameraman, by the way?" he asked, changing the subject.

Tyler shrugged. "To be fair, despite my initial misgivings, they seem to be behaving themselves so far, and I've managed to palm young Imogen off on Tony Dillon, so at least she's not getting under my feet anymore."

Quinlan smiled, knowingly. "Yes, I saw them chatting down in the canteen this morning. They seemed very pally, I must say."

"The randy sod's in his element," Tyler admitted.

The conversation was interrupted by the trill of Tyler's mobile. "Excuse me," he said, taking the call.

"Boss, it's Colin here," Franklin said as soon as he answered. The excitement in his voice was unmistakable. *"Thought you'd want to know, I'm down by the canal, and I've found a flat with a covert camera overlooking the towpath. I've viewed the overnight footage for Friday and Saturday nights on fast forward, and I think I've found something important."*

16

The shifty wee git knows something

Having phoned ahead to let them know that he was coming, Charlie White wasn't remotely surprised to find that someone was waiting for him when he walked into Willard Betting's head office. No sooner had he shown his warrant card to the receptionist, than a frizzy haired rake of a woman walked over and asked him to accompany her upstairs.

Clad in a beige woolly cardigan with faded leather elbow pads, his guide introduced herself as Joan Spinney and explained that she was temporarily performing the role of Mr Willard's personal assistant.

After making him a cup of bland instant coffee in the tiny staff kitchen, Spinney turned to face him with a troubled expression. "Can I ask you a question?" she enquired, hesitantly.

"Aye, of course," White replied, hoping it would be something banal.

Spinney cleared her throat, then said timidly, "The torso they found in the canal yesterday, was it… Was it Carrie?"

White took a slow sip of his brew, smiled wanly. "We don't know yet," he told her, earnestly.

Spinney's brow furrowed. "But it could be?"

He nodded, cautiously. "Aye, it could be. Why do you ask?"

An awkward shrug, like she was struggling to find the words. "I didn't think anything of it when I saw the story on the news last night," she said, starting slowly but gathering speed as she got into her stride. "But, well, when you rang and said you were from the murder squad, and that you wanted to speak to Mr Willard about Carrie, it seemed obvious that the two things had to be connected."

"Is that the general consensus of opinion around here, that Carrie's disappearance is connected to the torso we fished out of the canal yesterday afternoon?"

Spinney shook her head firmly. "Not that I'm aware of. Knowing this lot, a juicy bit of gossip like that would have spread like wildfire."

With time to kill before his appointment with Jonas Willard, Spinney offered to give him a quick tour.

"Who amongst the staff would you say were Carrie's closest friends?" he asked as they strolled through the admin office, tracked by every eye in the room.

The question got Spinney all flustered. "Oh, well, I wouldn't say that Carrie was friends with anyone in particular, to be honest," she responded. "Friendly, yes. But *not* friends."

White stopped by a wall that was covered from top to bottom with TV screens, all of which were showing different sports channels. "And what about you, Joan? Would you describe you and Carrie as friends?"

Spinney shook her head, sending her frizzy hair swishing from side to side. "No, not really." The statement was followed by a hesitant shrug. "I mean, we liked each other, and all that, but we weren't friends per se."

"So, she never confided in you about her personal life, never mentioned anything about having relationship problems, or falling out with anyone?"

Spinney seemed genuinely surprised by the question. "Good gracious, no! Carrie was a *very* private person, and she was fiercely protective about her personal life."

"Have you ever met any of her family?"

"One of her brothers picked her up from work a couple of times, when her car was in the garage earlier this year, and I said hello to him in passing. I don't know if that counts?"

White wasn't sure that it did. "Do you know which brother that was?"

Another shake of the head, another sideways swish of the hair. "Sorry, I don't. He was a tall man though, and very stocky. I vaguely recall her telling me that he used to be in the army."

That would be Darren, the one who was away on holiday, White decided.

They resumed walking, with Spinney now guiding him back towards Willard's office.

"What about her friends, or her love interests, I don't suppose you ever met any of those?" White asked.

Sashaying between two desks, Spinney glanced back over her shoulder. "Well, it's funny you should ask that," she said. "I bumped into a friend of Carrie's at the bus stop across the road last Friday." A deep frown appeared on her forehead. "At least she said she was a friend. She claimed that Carrie had introduced us once, although I didn't recognise her."

"If you didnae recognise her, what made you talk to her?" White asked, confused.

"It was her who spoke to me," Spinney corrected him. "She was behind me in the queue, and she asked if Carrie was still in the office, said something about seeing if she fancied grabbing a drink. I must admit, when I told her that Carrie had left early, she seemed very disappointed."

"Did you get her name, by any chance?" White asked, mentally crossing his fingers.

Spinney sat down behind her desk. "Sorry, I didn't ask, and she didn't offer." A cordial smile. "Would you like another coffee while you wait?"

The first one had been hideous, so he politely declined. "Can you at least describe this woman for me?"

Spinney's mouth formed a little moue as she considered this. "Umm, she had brown hair that fell below her shoulders, and she was wearing a trench coat over a dress."

"What about her age, her height, or her accent?" White prompted.

Spinney thought some more. "At a guess, I'd say she was in her late thirties, but she was wearing so much makeup that it's hard to be sure. She was about five-eight or five-nine, I think, but she had heels on, so they would have made her seem taller. I think she had a local accent, like Carrie's."

White hurriedly scribbled this down in his daybook. "Anything else you can tell me about her?"

Spinney's head tilted to one side as she considered this. "The thing that struck me the most was how deep her voice was. In fact, I remember thinking that she sounded like one of Marge Simpson's sisters."

White gave her a blank look. "I'm sorry, I don't watch the show."

Spinney seemed shocked. "Really? I thought everyone watched *The Simpsons*!"

White shrugged. "Aye, everyone but me, it seems."

"Her voice was deep, like she smoked fifty ciggies a day," Spinney explained. "That's how Marge's sisters sound in *The Simpsons*."

"Ah," White said, as the penny dropped. "I see. And you're quite sure you hadnae met her before?"

"Positive," Spinney confirmed. "The only acquaintance of Carrie's that I ever met was her girlfriend, and that was just the once. I can't remember her name, but she was a very butch woman." She lowered her voice, sounded a trifle embarrassed. "If I'm honest, I mistook her for a man when I first saw her; she was so masculine in her mannerisms, and she had really short hair. It was only when Carrie introduced us that I realised she was female. I felt terrible. The clothes didn't help, I suppose. She was dressed in jeans, a parka coat, and bovver boots, like the Mods used to wear when I was younger."

White flexed his fingers, which were starting to cramp from all the writing he was doing. "When exactly was this?"

"It was at last year's Christmas do. Come to think of it, she had a very deep voice too."

White was reasonably confident that the 'butch' woman from the Christmas party had been Stella Carter, but who was the friend Spinney had spoken to at the bus stop?

Could they possible be one and the same person? Their descriptions were very different, so it seemed highly unlikely, but Spinney *had* told him that they both had deep voices, and the fact that they did was ringing alarm bells.

"Did Carrie tell you that she split up from her girlfriend a few months ago?" White asked, studying her face carefully.

"She didn't tell *me*," Spinney said, loading the final word with emphasis.

White instantly picked up on this. "Oh, who did she tell, then?" he asked quickly.

Spinney's eyes darted everywhere, checking that that no one was close enough to overhear what she was about to say, then she leaned forward and lowered her voice. "You didn't hear this from me, but you might want to have a quiet word with Fred Wiggins. I saw Carrie crying on his shoulder a couple of months back. They were in the staff kitchen, and they shut up when I walked in, but not before I heard him telling her that he would sort out whatever it was that was bothering her. It might not be connected, but the timing would fit."

White made a mental note. "Thank you," he said, smiling his gratitude.

"Remember," she warned him. "You didn't get that from me."

White tapped the side of his disfigured nose. "You can rely on my discretion," he promised.

The phone on Spinney's desk chirped, making her jump.

Picking it up, she listened for a few seconds. "Yes Mr Willard," she said, deferentially. "I'll show him straight in." Hanging up, she looked over at White. "He'll see you now," she told him.

Standing up, Jonas Willard walked around his desk to greet Charlie White, his hand extended in welcome. "Nice to meet you," he said in a gruff but friendly tone. "Sorry about the wait, but my boring conference call dragged on for bloody ages."

"Nae worries," White told him with a polite smile.

Although Willard was in his early sixties, he looked as fit as a fiddle. Slim, with a thick mane of silver hair, his charcoal business suit was exquisitely tailored. Tony Dillon had a penchant for such things, and he would have probably been able to identify the tailor just from the cut of the cloth, but Charlie White was strictly an M&S man, and didn't have a clue; all he could tell from looking at the material was that it was expensive.

"Thank you for seeing me at such short notice," White said as he took the chair Willard had indicated for him to sit in.

The wood panelled room smelled of Cuban cigars and expensive cologne. As Willard returned to the padded leather chair behind his mahogany desk, there was a brisk rap on the door.

"Come in," Willard barked.

Fred Wiggins entered the room. Casting a disdainful glance in White's direction, he crossed to stand by Willard's shoulder. Like his boss, Wiggins was wearing an expensively tailored business suit. If the power dressing was meant to convey class and sophistication, they had both wasted their money as far as Charlie White was concerned. No matter how hard thugs like Willard and Wiggins attempted to gloss over it, their true nature always shone through in the end, exposing them for the pondlife they really were.

"This is Fred Wiggins, my head of security," Willard said, making the introductions. "I've asked him to sit in with us in case he can be of assistance."

White thought back to their previous encounter at Pauline

McCullen's house, and wondered where the albino man mountain who had accompanied him on that occasion was hiding today. Hopefully, he was locked away in a metal cage in the basement.

While Wiggins wasn't the tallest or the broadest, he had an undeniably imposing presence, and White decided there was something inherently dangerous about him.

"We've already met," White said, nodding a lukewarm acknowledgement, which was grudgingly returned.

Willard arched an eyebrow. "Is that so?" In an instant, the fake bonhomie evaporated and his eyes became cold and hard.

Wiggins nodded, unenthusiastically. "This is one of the officers who came over to speak to Morag Kyle while me and Casper were round there, carrying out a welfare visit," he explained, his eyes holding White's.

"So, you're one of the detectives investigating Frankie's murder, are you?" Willard asked, leaning forward to study the detective with renewed interest.

White shook his head. "I worked on the case for a couple of days, that's all," he explained. "I'm on a different investigation now."

"You mean you're working on Carrie's murder?"

"I'm investigating the murder of a woman whose torso was found in Regent's Canal yesterday afternoon," White corrected him. "Her identity hasn't been established yet."

Willard's nostrils flared with anger. "Don't play word games with me, sunshine," he snapped. "You think it's Carrie, don't you? Why else would you be treating her house as a crime scene? And why else would you be here, poking your nose into my business?"

White stiffened. How did Willard know that Carrie's house was a crime scene? It wasn't public knowledge, so where was he getting his information from?

"We're looking into the possibility that Carrie is our victim," he admitted, guardedly, "but I cannae say any more than that at this stage."

"What are you doing here then?" Willard growled. "Is Carrie's murder somehow related to Frankie's? Is some horrible cunt knocking off my staff? If you've found out that someone's got a blood vendetta against me, I've got a right to know about it."

Yep, White thought smugly. No matter how hard they tried to hide behind the wafer thin veneer of respectability that they crafted for themselves, their true natures always shone through in the end, and they always reverted to type when provoked.

He raised his hands in a placating manner. "It's no' a line of enquiry we're pursuing at this time," he said, trying to be diplomatic, "but if you have any information that supports what you've just said, I'd be very interested to hear it."

"Very funny," Willard snapped. Still scowling at the detective, he yanked open a desk drawer and removed a thick cigar. Raising it to his nose, he sniffed appreciatively. Like most premium cigars, it had a closed head, and Willard expertly used a double-bladed desktop cutter to make an incision before lighting up. Puffing on the massive cheroot, he blew an angry succession of smoke rings into the air above his desk.

"We don't have any information to suggest that's the case," Wiggins said, to fill the awkward silence that had befallen them. His voice was calm, his response measured. "But I'm sure you can understand why Mr Willard would be concerned. After all, two of his staff have been brutally murdered within a very short space of time."

"Aye, I get that," White allowed, "but we're trying to help; we're no' the bloody enemy."

"No one said you were," Wiggins said, treating him to a frosty smile. "Now, time's cracking on, and we're all busy men, so why don't you just tell us exactly what you want?"

White nodded; the sooner he got out of there, the better. "Until we get the DNA results back, we won't know for sure if the torso we fished out of the canal is Carrie's, but it seems likely that this will turn out to be the case, which is why we're treating her house as a crime scene—"

"So, you *do* think that's where she was killed?" Willard interrupted, puffing away like an out-of-control steam train.

"Not necessarily," White cautioned. "There's nothing to suggest that's the case, but we have to start somewhere."

"Do you have any idea who might have done this to her?" Willard asked, staring at him intently.

White gave him an economical shake of his head. "Not yet, but it's very early days. We were hoping you might be able to help us out with some background detail. Did Carrie have any enemies? Had she been experiencing any problems, romantic or otherwise, with anyone who might have wanted to harm her?" He made a point of staring straight at Wiggins during the latter part of the question.

"Carrie was a terrific girl, and everyone loved her," Willard insisted. "She was the daughter of a dear friend of mine, and I regarded her as family."

"Our records show that Carrie had an acrimonious split from her former girlfriend, Stella Carter, a few months ago," White said, trying to introduce the subject in a tactful way. "Her brother tells us that she refused to take no for an answer and began stalking Carrie, making her life hell. Were either of you aware of this?"

Willard shook his head emphatically. "I'd have had the little slag spoken to if Carrie had told me she was having a hard time," he snarled.

Remaining silent, Wiggins looked away, and his body language suddenly became very guarded.

It was as good as a confession.

The shifty wee git knows something.

17

There have been some developments

Grunting from the unexpected effort it required, Arthur Brownlow prised open the stiff door to the telephone kiosk and stepped inside. Turning his nose up at the rancid smell of urine wafting up from the floor, he pulled some change from his pocket and inserted a 20p coin into the receptacle. Unfolding a creased scrap of paper, he dialled the number that was scribbled on it.

The phone seemed to ring forever before finally being answered.

"Hello?" The voice was aggressive, untrusting.

Arthur licked his lips nervously. The contact who had given him this number had warned him that there would be consequences to pay if he was wasting Wiggins' time. "Good afternoon, can I speak to Mr Wiggins, please?"

A long pause, then, *"Who wants him?"*

"I… Just tell him it's in relation to the reward he's offering for information about the missing diamonds."

"I'll decide what I tell him." The confrontational voice snapped,

making it clear he called the shots, not Arthur. *"Now, do you have a name, soppy bollocks, or shall I hang up?"*

Arthur swallowed hard. "My name's A–Arthur," he stammered, "and I've got some information about the diamonds Mr Wiggins is offering the reward for."

"Yeah, you said that already," the voice pointed out, unimpressed. *"What I want to know is, what information have you got?"*

Arthur shook his head, then remembered the man he was talking to couldn't see him doing it. "Nah, sorry," he said, defiantly. "I speak to Mr Wiggins, no one else."

The sound of a bad-tempered sigh. *"If you say so, pal. But, get this: If you're wasting his time, I will personally track you down, cut your gonads off, and then feed them to you. Savvy?"*

A chill ran down Arthur's spine, and he swallowed hard. "I–I'm not wasting his time," he assured the scary man. "He'll definitely want to hear what I've got to say."

'Right then, give me a number and he'll call you back when he returns," the voice told him, sounding mildly mollified.

That threw Arthur; he didn't like mobile phones, they were too complicated to use, and the only landline he had access to was the one in the reception area of the halfway house he had been released to from prison three weeks earlier. "Well, I don't actually have a phone myself," he said, lamely. "I'll just have to call back when Mr Wiggins is in. When's the best time to do that?"

"What do you mean, you don't have a phone? Don't you have a mobile?"

Arthur's back went up. "No. I don't. I can't work the bloody things."

There was an awkward silence as the man at the other end of the line considered this.

'Alright. phone back tomorrow morning, between ten and twelve," he eventually said, and then hung up.

Cradling the receiver, Arthur leaned against the side of the phone box and let out a long sigh. "Bloody hell," he said to himself as he pushed open the heavy door and stepped into the street. "That geezer was hard work."

Waiting for a gap in the traffic, he crossed the road and went into *The Black Horse*, where he found Vlad sitting alone at the bar. "Evening, you horrible old Russki git," he said by way of greeting. Sliding onto the stool next to him, he gave his friend a sly grin. "I've just had a bit of good news, Vlad, so let me buy you a drink to celebrate."

———

As Tyler ran his eyes over the officers assembled before him, he was struck by how haggard they all appeared. Yesterday had been gruelling, but today had been significantly harder, and tomorrow would probably be even worse. Unfortunately, that was always the way it went when a new job broke. Maintaining momentum was all-important and, no matter how fatigued they became, they had to keep pushing themselves.

Not everyone had made it back in time for the evening meeting, but most were there, including DC Ian Yule, the dreary man with the personality bypass and weird dress sense.

At the back of the room, Bear – Tyler made a mental note to find out what the man's real name was – had already set his video camera up on its tripod, and the little red light was on, signalling that it was recording. Sitting next to him, Imogen Askew looked like she was struggling to stay awake.

Welcome to the world of homicide investigations!

"Okay, let's begin," Tyler announced.

The room lapsed into silence.

"I'll try and keep this as brief as possible," he promised, "but there have been some developments during the day, which you all need to be aware of."

That got their attention, and some of them even started to look mildly interested.

"Let's start with the SPM. Kevin, talk us through how that went."

Murray cleared his throat. Unlike Dillon, who had showered and changed immediately upon his return, he was still wearing the same suit that he had worn during the Special Post Mortem, and every time he moved, those sitting closest were treated to the unpleasant whiff of decaying corpses. "The pathologist was Dr Stephanie Tolpuddle," he began, staring straight into the camera lens instead of at Tyler. "Although she found extensive bruising on the torso, there were no penetrative wounds so, at this stage, the cause of death remains indeterminable."

"I'm over here, Kevin," Tyler said, wishing Murray would stop fixating on the bloody camera.

Murray's head pivoted 180 degrees, and he gave Tyler a sheepish smile. "Sorry, boss." He began checking through his notes in a flustered manner. "Er, where was I? Oh yeah... Dr Tolpuddle suspects that the victim was either strangled or suffered blunt force trauma to the head."

Tyler had already figured that much out for himself. "Did she tell us anything about the victim that we didn't already know?" he enquired testily.

Murray quoted from his notes. "The torso weighed thirty-one kilos. There were no obvious signs of natural disease. There were no obvious signs of sexual interference. There was no indication that any restraints had been used on the torso, although that doesn't preclude the possibility of them being used on the limbs. The torso was naked when it was found, but the victim was definitely wearing a bra at the time of her death. This was established by bloodline imprints around the area where her bra would have been in contact with the skin. Dr Tolpuddle found considerable evidence that the head and limbs had been severed messily, as if hacked at by someone who didn't have a clue what they were doing." He helpfully mimed a series of vicious chopping actions as he spoke.

Tyler grimaced at the thought, and saw a number of other people doing likewise. His reaction was a good thing, he told himself. The day that he stopped being shocked by the terrible atrocities he investigated on the Homicide Command would be the day he considered applying for an alternative posting.

"Dr Tolpuddle identified a number of aborted attempts to cut through the bones at the shoulders and at other locations," Murray continued, "and there were a couple of nasty horizontal nicks to the victim's vagina where the hacksaw, meat cleaver, or whatever her killer used to dismember her, went off course."

Hearing a muffled gasp from the back of the room, Tyler fired a quick glance in Imogen Askew's direction, and saw that her complexion had suddenly taken on a greenish tinge. By contrast, it was impossible to gauge Bear's reaction; there was so much hair covering his face that all Tyler could make out was a pair of green eyes and a large nose.

A hand went up.

Tyler groaned when he saw it belonged to DC Yule.

"Yes, Ian?"

"Am I right in thinking that, if we don't recover the missing body parts, we might never be able to prove the exact cause of death?"

Delivered in monotonic dreariness, the question grated on Tyler and, if the murmurs of discord rippling around the room were any sort of barometer, he wasn't the only one to be affected that way.

"Possibly, Ian. Why?"

"Well, I was just wondering, if we can't prove cause of death, how will we prove murder?"

"Shut up, Vic," a bored detective yelled from the back of the room. Tyler didn't recognise the speaker's voice, but it definitely didn't belong to anyone on his team, and he wondered why the heckler had addressed Yule as Vic?

"It's a fair question," Yule insisted.

It wasn't, but with the camera rolling, Tyler had no choice but to humour him. "In my humble opinion, having been an SIO on the Homicide Command for the past three years, people who die of natural causes don't normally end up dismembered. Of course, with your vast experience, you might know better?"

Yule's face turned pink, and he suddenly seemed far less confident. "Well, I…"

With a little growl of impatience, Dillon suddenly leaned forward. "DC Yule, how long have you been on the command?"

"Four weeks," Yule replied, wilting under Dillon's fierce stare.

"In that case," Dillon said, scathingly, "my advice to you would be to keep your eyes and ears open and your mouth shut while you learn your trade, instead of making silly comments and getting on everyone's nerves. Do you think you can manage that?"

Yule nodded, meekly. "Yes, sir. Sorry, sir." His face was now a vibrant shade of red.

Tyler found himself taking pity on Yule. His attempt to impress had backfired, and he was now in danger of becoming a laughing stock amongst his colleagues. "For the record, Ian, I've known cases where the offence of murder was proved even though the victim's body was never found so, even if we don't recover the head or the rest of the missing limbs, murder is still very much on the table."

"Yes, sir," Yule muttered, looking like he wanted the floor to open up and swallow him.

Someone sitting behind him disguised the word 'wanker' with a loud cough, and this triggered an outburst of laughter that Tyler silenced with an angry glower.

"Settle down," he ordered, and the room immediately fell silent. "Right, Steve, how did the divers get on?"

Bull groaned. "They've been searching the canal all day," he said in a voice as flat as his mood. "So far, all they've got to show for their efforts is a rusted bicycle frame, a mangled shopping trolley and the chassis from a stolen moped. It's going to be a painfully long process, if you want my honest opinion."

"Well, the divers might not have had any luck," Tyler said, "but a British Waterways dredger found a bag containing the victim's right arm this morning. Dick, for the benefit of those who haven't heard about this yet, can you talk us through it?"

Dick Jarvis fastidiously shuffled his notes. "As the boss said, a dismembered right arm was discovered by the crew of a dredger clearing refuse from the water by the side of the lock."

"Just to clarify," Tyler interrupted, "we're talking about the water that leads from Acton's Lock to Old Ford, not the Queensbridge Road side where the divers are searching."

He nodded for Jarvis to continue.

"The arm was double bagged, just like the torso. The exciting news is that there was a signet ring on the little finger, which had the initials CM engraved on it."

Tyler interrupted again. "We've confirmed that Carrie McCullen wore a gold signet ring on the little finger of her right hand, and her initials – CM – were etched into it."

A ripple of excitement passed through the room.

Jarvis cleared his throat. "As happened with the torso, the arm was photographed in situ, and then taken for X-rays before being transferred to the mortuary. The SPM won't be held until Saturday morning, but that's purely because we need Dr Tolpuddle to perform it for continuity reasons, and she's unavailable until then."

Tyler smiled his thanks. "Finding the arm on the other side of the lock presents us with a dilemma," he informed them. "Ideally, in light of its discovery, I would prefer it if the canal was closed off between Old Ford and Kingsland Road, so that we can search both sides of the lock properly, but that's simply not realistic, not when it could take a couple of months to do that."

"Perhaps we should put the dredger crew on a retainer, instead," White suggested. "See if they can find the missing body parts for us."

Tyler chuckled. "Perhaps we should, especially as they're going to be in the area anyway."

"We could run a book on it," Reg Parker suggested from the back of the room. "You know, to see who recovers the most body parts, the divers or the dredgers."

"Nothing like a bit of healthy competition to motivate the buggers," Bull added with a wry smile.

Tyler held a finger to his lips to quell the banter. "Whitey visited Carrie's workplace today," he informed the room, then stared enquiringly at the Scotsman. "How did that go?"

Charlie White stood up and looked around the room. Dressed in his customary winkle pickers and drainpipes, Tyler couldn't help but compare his skinny, bowed legs to a chicken's wishbone.

"I spoke to Carrie's boss, Jonas Willard, his head of security, Fred Wiggins and a few of her co-workers," White told the room. "The most helpful person I met was Joan Spinney, the woman who's taken over as Willard's PA. She told me two things of interest. Firstly, a couple of months ago, she walked into the staff kitchen to find Carrie crying on Fred Wiggins' shoulder. They both clammed up when they saw her, but no' before she overheard Wiggins saying that he'd take care of whatever was bothering Carrie."

"For those of you who are assisting us from other teams," Tyler cut in, "Stella Carter is Carrie's ex. According to her brother, she took to stalking Carrie after being dumped."

A deep frown had appeared on Bull's forehead. "Why would Stella care what this Wiggins bloke said?"

"Fred Wiggins isnae a very nice man," White told him. "Trust me, if he ordered Stella to back off, she'd be a right loon not to heed the warning."

Dillon placed a hand on Tyler's arm. "Wasn't the bloke who was shot dead in East Ham last week also an employee of Jonas Willard?"

"His name's Frank Kyle and he was one of Willard's branch managers," Tyler confirmed. "I've spoken to Andy Quinlan about this, and we don't think the two cases are connected."

Dillon spread his arms in a questioning manner. "It's a bit of a coincidence though, isn't it?" he persisted. "Two of Willard's employees being murdered less than a week apart."

"It is," Tyler allowed. "But it's looking very much like Frank Kyle's murder was a professional hit, which might or might not be connected to Willard's underworld dealings, whereas Carrie's murder has all the hallmarks of being intensely personal."

"What reason did Wiggins give for Carrie crying on his shoulder?" Kelly asked.

Charlie White gave her an apologetic shrug. "I couldnae ask him about it. No' without revealing my source, and Spinney made it very clear that she didnae want anyone knowing she'd supplied the info."

"You did the right thing," Tyler assured him. "Now, what was the second thing that Spinney told you?"

"Aye, well, Spinney reckons she only met Carter once, very briefly, and that was at last year's Christmas party. She described her as being very butch, to the point that she originally mistook her for a man. Oh, and she has a deep voice, apparently."

A cruel chuckle escaped Bull's lips. "Everyone's got a deep voice compared to yours, Whitey," he teased. "You sound like you're on helium most of the time."

"It's because his trousers are too tight," Dillon said, pointing at White's legs. "Those bloody drainpipes are cutting off the circulation to his nether regions."

White was about to unleash a sarcastic rejoinder when Tyler raised a warning hand. "Let's just crack on, shall we, Charlie?" he said, conscious that the sooner they finished, the sooner he could send them all home.

Mumbling something under his breath about his legs being perfectly normal, White picked up his daybook and flicked through the pages until he found the relevant entry. "Spinney mentioned a woman who approached her while she was waiting for a bus on Friday evening and asked her if Carrie was still at work."

Dillon raised a questioning eyebrow. "I'm guessing you're about to tell us that this woman was Stella Carter?"

White hesitated. "Spinney didnae seem to think so, and the description she gave me of the two women was very different, but folk *do* change the way they look, and Spinney *did* say that they both had deep voices."

Bull snorted. "We can't assume this woman was Carter just because she had a deep voice."

"You can assume what you want," White bristled, "but my gut tells me it *is* her. And even if I'm wrong, there's definitely something very dodgy about her." Removing a VHS tape from his man bag, he crossed to where the TV-video combo was mounted on the wall.

"See what I mean about his trousers being too tight?" Dillon observed.

"Not as tight as you are, when it comes to putting your hand in your pocket," White countered, sparking an outburst of laughter. Giving Dillon a smile of one-upmanship, he continued, "I spotted a CCTV camera outside Willard's office on my way out, so I popped down to the local CCTV control room and retrieved the footage for last Friday." He hit the play button, and the screen flickered into life. "That's the head office of Willard Betting, and this wee wifey is Joan Spinney," he said, tapping the left of the screen, about halfway down, as a skinny white woman with frizzy hair emerged from a doorway.

On screen, Spinney crossed the road to a crowded bus stop on the other side.

"Now pay attention to the woman loitering in the doorway behind the bus stop," White instructed.

On cue, a smartly dressed woman stepped out of the doorway and sidled up behind Spinney. The two women engaged in a short conversation, which ended abruptly when a bus pulled up and Spinney got on. The other woman watched it go, then turned around and walked off.

"This woman," White said, pointing at the screen, "told Spinney she was waiting for a bus but, as you've just seen for yourselves, she most definitely wasnae."

"Where are you going with this, Whitey?" Bull asked, still not seeing how it was relevant to the investigation.

"Bearing in mind that we know Carrie was previously being stalked by Carter, to the point where she had to get someone to warn her off, my take on this is that it's way too much of a coincidence that Carrie disappeared a few short hours after Carter was waiting to ambush her as she left work."

"But we don't know that's definitely Carter," Bull objected.

Standing up, Dean Fletcher passed forward an A4 colour printout of Carter's most recent custody imaging photo. "Perhaps this image will help solve the riddle?'

White snatched it from his hand, studied it for a moment, then stared intently at the blurred woman on screen. Then with a muted sigh of frustration, he passed it across to Tyler. "It's no good, I cannae tell from this," he said, miserably.

Tyler studied the head and shoulder shot carefully before comparing it to the flickering image of the woman on screen. "You're right," he said, passing it to Dillon. "This photo doesn't help one way or the other."

"Is that the only image of her we've got?" Dillon asked, passing the photo to Steve Bull, who took a quick glance, shrugged, and then handed it to the person sitting next to him.

"Afraid so," Dean Fletcher confirmed.

"I don't want anyone to dismiss Charlie's theory out of hand," Tyler cautioned, "because it fits in with what Aidan's been telling us, and it gels with another development that occurred today. Colin, would you be kind enough to play the canal footage for us."

Weaving his way through the detectives, Franklin deftly inserted a VHS tape into the player. "The clip I'm about to play you comes from a covert security setup we discovered in a house in Dunston Road earlier today. The camera overlooks a small stretch of canal path behind it, running between Kingsland Road and Queensbridge Road."

He pressed play and the screen flickered into life, revealing a low-resolution image. A digital display in the top right-hand corner of the screen timed the clip at 22:30hrs on Saturday 6th October, 2001.

"I've checked the camera's time stamp against the talking clock, and it's ten minutes fast," Franklin informed them, by which he meant he had dialled the number for TIM, the talking clock, and had compared the time the live feed showed on screen to the actual time.

Moving forward, Franklin tapped the screen. "This gap in the railings is an entry point onto the canal path from the pavement in Dunston Road. In a few moments, I want you to study the woman who comes into shot from the right of the screen."

"Can someone quickly turn off the lights?" Tyler asked, hoping that would make it easier to see the picture definition.

Dick Jarvis obliged, and the room was plunged into darkness.

At precisely 22:31 hours, a slim woman with shoulder length dark hair walked into view, awkwardly dragging a wheeled suitcase behind her. When she reached the gap in the railings, she descended the ramp onto the towpath and continued walking in the direction of Acton's Lock.

"Play it again," Tyler asked as soon as the clip had finished.

Franklin obliged, and they all eagerly watched the brief segment a second time.

Afterwards, Franklin partially rewound the tape, freezing it at the point where the woman reached the gap in the railings. "That's the clearest view we get of her," he informed them.

White squinted at the screen. "That could easily be the same woman who accosted Spinney outside the bus stop," he announced, excitedly.

"It could be," Bull allowed, "but it could also be someone completely different."

"They're definitely very similar in appearance," Tyler said, leaning forward to get a better view.

"It might be worth bringing in a gait analyst to compare the way the two women walk," Dillon suggested. "That might give us a definitive answer."

"It's definitely something to keep in mind," Tyler said, "but it's a bit early to be going down that road just yet."

Jarvis switched the lights back on.

"Kevin, how similar is the case she's dragging to the one we recovered from the lock?" Tyler asked.

"It looks identical," Murray said, "and she was clearly struggling with it, as though it was very heavy."

"How much did you say Carrie's torso weighed?" Tyler asked, stroking the bristles on his chin thoughtfully.

"Thirty-one kilos."

That would certainly make it unwieldy.

"Okay, so I think we can all agree that this is a breakthrough," Tyler said. "I'm confident that the woman dragging the suitcase is our killer, and that she's on her way to dump Carrie's torso into the canal."

"Do we think the torso was the first section of Carrie's body to be removed from the dismemberment site?" The question had come from Imogen Askew at the back of the room.

"It would make sense," Dillon said, smiling at her. "It's the biggest, heaviest part, so moving it would have involved the greatest risk."

"I agree," Tyler said, then paused for a moment, gathering his thoughts. "Carrie was either murdered late on Friday night or during the early hours of Saturday morning. It seems likely that her killer was someone she knew, and that the murder occurred inside a premises. I doubt this was a premeditated act, and I think the killer, who it now appears was female, found herself in the unenviable position of not being able to dispose of the body without first chopping it up."

"It would have taken her quite a while to do that," Dillon observed, "so she must have been confident that the body wouldn't be discovered before she had finished."

"I discussed time frames with Juliet earlier," Tyler informed his colleagues. "She reckons it would have taken three or four hours to chop the body up, and another couple of hours to bag it, which would take us well into Saturday morning, even if she had started the dismemberment process straight after killing Carrie."

"If the murder wasn't premeditated," White said, "it would have taken her some time to cobble together all the things she needed to chop the body up."

"I agree," Tyler said, "which means it could have actually taken her most of the day to get the job done."

"It makes sense that the killer would have waited for the cover of nightfall before dumping the various body parts," Dillon said, "so the canal footage would fit perfectly with the theoretical timing we've just discussed."

"It would," Tyler said, nodding thoughtfully. "After disposing of the torso, she would have had to make a number of further trips to get rid of the remaining body parts, assuming she dumped them one by one, and I don't think she could have done that in one night."

"Maybe she went back on Sunday evening?" Bull speculated.

"My thoughts, exactly," Tyler said. "Colin, I want all the CCTV from Kingsland Road to be reviewed, to see if we can pick this woman up entering Dunston Road on Saturday night. We already know where she entered the canal towpath, so you'll also need to look for potential CCTV opportunities in the vicinity of all the exits between Dunston Road and Acton's Lock. With any luck, we might be able to pick up our suspect as she leaves the canal. And I'm afraid you'll have to repeat the process for Sunday evening too, just in case Steve's right, and she did end up going back the following night."

"What do we have on Carter, from an intel perspective?" Dillon asked.

"She's known to the system," Fletcher told him. "She was nicked several times during her late teens and early twenties, but only for possession of cannabis. Her most recent convictions relate to the harassment and assault of a former girlfriend, Justine Woods. The stalking MO in that case pretty much mirrors the way she treated Carrie. Despite putting Woods through a living hell, all Carter received was a suspended sentence, a restraining order and a psychiatric referral."

"How long ago was this?" Tyler asked.

"Three years."

"Pull the case file from archives," he instructed. "If Carter's our killer, we can use her previous behaviour towards Justine Woods as bad character evidence."

"We should probably trace the doctor who dealt with her psychiatric referral as well," Dillon suggested. "The hospital probably won't grant us access to Carter's medical records without a production order, but that's fine. If she becomes a suspect, we'll have no trouble getting one of those."

"Dean, do we have a current address for Carter?" Tyler asked.

"Well, we have a last known address, but that was three years ago, so gawd knows if it's still current."

"I want someone around there, first thing in the morning," Tyler said.

"I'll go," Charlie White volunteered.

"I'll go with him," Murray said.

"Chris, raise an action for yourself to initiate a financial investigation on Carter. With a bit of luck, her finances will reveal that she popped into Travis Perkins on Saturday morning to purchase a hack saw."

"Sorry to interrupt you," Fletcher said, "but I forgot to mention that I've found a mobile telephone number for Carter. I don't know if it's still in use, but I've given it to Reggie."

"Thanks, Deano," Tyler said, then turned to Parker. "Reg, can you obtain subscriber details, billing and cell site data, ASAP."

"I'll submit the requests first thing in the morning," Parker promised.

"Just to be clear, we're not formally declaring Stella Carter a suspect, are we?" Bull asked.

Tyler shook his head. "No. For the moment, she's purely a person of interest." He checked his watch, conscious that they had been going for a long while. "Before we call it a day, what's the latest with the phones?"

"Carrie's phone data came back earlier this evening," Parker informed him with a yawn. "I haven't had time to go through it in any detail yet but, on first glance, there doesn't seem to be anything unusual in it. There are a few calls between her and her two brothers, and some others from friends and work. There are five voice mails from Aidan's number, and one from Darren's. I've requested recordings of those, but it might be a couple of days before we get them. I checked the number Dean gave me for Stella Carter against Carrie's call data, but it doesn't show up. That said, Carrie's current number is only three months old, so it looks like she changed it after splitting up from Stella. I'll get onto the service providers in the morning to find out what her previous number was, then order a shed load of call data for that."

"Have you had a chance to look at the cell site data, in order, to plot Carrie's movements on the day she died?" Tyler asked.

Reg nodded wearily. "There was a call from Carrie to Annie Jenkins at 19:03 hours. That was handled by the mast servicing both their home addresses. There's also a missed call and a text message from Stanwick, timed at 23:30 hours. The message just enquires how the date was going. Carrie's phone was in the vicinity of a mast located in Pitfield Street when she received it, which would suggest she was heading home."

"I want someone to speak to Stanwick tomorrow morning, to

see if she can shed any light on this so-called girlie night out that's mentioned in the Misper report," Tyler instructed. "Right, that's all for tonight. Get yourselves off home, and try and grab some much-needed sleep."

The cheeky sods were up on their feet and heading for the door before he had even finished speaking. Ian Yule was the first one out, head bowed in shame.

"I want everyone back in the office for eight o'clock sharp," Tyler shouted as they bottlenecked at the door.

A middle-aged detective with a craggy face and an enigmatic smile wandered over to where Tyler was sitting. His name was DS Jim Cuthbert, and he had joined the command around the same time as Yule. "Don't mind Vic," Cuthbert said.

Tyler immediately recognised his voice as belonging to Ian Yule's heckler.

"It's nothing personal," Cuthbert assured him. "Vic pisses off everyone he meets like that."

Tyler didn't doubt it for a second. "Why do you call him Vic?" he asked.

Cuthbert arched an amused eyebrow. "We call him that because he gets right up your nose."

Tyler chuckled, thinking it was one of the most fitting nicknames he had ever heard. As he headed back to his office, with Dillon trailing along behind, his mobile phone began vibrating inside his pocket. Pulling it out, he thumbed the green button. It was Juliet Kennedy. *"Jack, I've just received a call from the lab. The DNA comparisons have come back as a perfect match. Carrie McCullen's definitely our victim."*

Wiggins glanced at the screen of his mobile, which showed him the incoming call was from a withheld number. "Hello...?" he answered, warily.

"It's me," the caller said, his voice hushed, as though he was afraid of being overheard.

"About bloody time," Wiggins complained. "Mr Willard's been asking me if I'd heard from you."

"Yeah, well, I have to be careful. Besides, there hasn't been much to report. I spoke to my mate on the team investigating Frankie's shooting, but they haven't got a clue who's behind it or where the diamonds have been outed."

Wiggins' face darkened. "That doesn't help me, does it?" he responded, tetchily. "We pay you a lot of money every month to be kept in the loop about matters that might affect our business, and it doesn't seem to me that you're doing much to earn it, if you get my drift."

"I'm doing all I can," the caller said, defensively.

Wiggins pinched the bridge of his nose, where a headache was starting to form. "So, if you haven't got an update about who topped Frankie and stole Mr Willard's diamonds, what are you bothering me for?"

"I've got some hot off the press news on the torso murder. The DCI thinks she was killed by an ex-girlfriend called Stella Carter. He's having her researched, and as soon as I get an address for her, I'll ping it over."

"Don't bother, I already know where to find her," Wiggins said. "She's a complete psycho bitch. I had to get Casper to have a word with her after they split up, to stop her from pestering Carrie."

The caller laughed. *"So, you're sending one psycho to deal with another! Makes sense, I suppose."*

Wiggins didn't share his amusement. "Is she definitely responsible?" he asked, knowing what Willard would want done if she were.

There was a pause. *"Dunno. I'd wait until I can firm it up before unleashing Casper on her if I were you, just in case it turns out to be a red herring."*

Wiggins responded with a surly grunt. "Yeah, all right, but be quick about it. Mr Willard wants whoever did this punished, and he's not a patient man. And, while you're at it, find out who killed Frankie and stole those fucking diamonds or you'll have some explaining to do about why we're keeping you on the payroll."

18

FRIDAY 12TH OCTOBER 2001

Sounds like a plan

The din from the alarm sounded like a ship's foghorn stuck on repeat. Groaning in dismay, Tyler lifted his head off the pillow and squinted through bleary eyes at the display.

06:00 hours.

That couldn't possibly be right, could it? He had only closed his eyes a few short seconds ago.

Moving on auto pilot, he groggily reached out and groped around for the off button.

Beside him, Kelly stirred, then moaned. "Will you please turn that wretched thing off!" she pleaded.

"I'm trying," Tyler grunted, frantically pressing every button he could find.

The noise seemed to be getting louder, as though the alarm was becoming increasingly annoyed with them for ignoring it.

With an angry growl, Kelly rammed her head under her pillow. "Jack!"

"I'm trying," he repeated, finally finding the snooze button. Silence!

Tyler breathed a sigh of relief.

Peeking out from beneath the pillow, Kelly stared at him through puffy eyes. "Please tell me that I don't have to get up yet," she half pleaded, half yawned.

Tyler threw the quilt back and kicked his legs over the edge of the bed. "You don't have to get up yet."

"Really?" Kelly asked, sounding surprised.

Tyler shook his head, sighed regretfully. "Sorry, babe, I was being facetious. We've got to get ready for work."

Her pillow hit him in the back of the head. "Wanker!"

"Kelly, I—"

The pillow struck a second time. "Shush! You shower first, and I'll nap until you're finished"

Slipping into his tailored suit jacket, Dillon smiled warmly at Imogen Askew. It was already a quarter past six, and he wanted to be in the office for seven-thirty, which meant that he was going to have to get a move on. "Are you ready?" he asked.

Sitting at his dining table, Imogen didn't look remotely ready. She hurriedly gulped down the last of her coffee, then sagged back in her chair. "How do you do this day in, day out?" she asked, stifling a yawn. "I feel like death warmed up."

"We work long hours when a new job breaks," he told her with an apologetic shrug. "It's the nature of the beast. Sometimes it only lasts a few days; sometimes it goes on for weeks."

Imogen shuddered at the thought. "I couldn't do it," she said, shaking her head emphatically. "I'm not much of a morning person, and doing this for weeks on end, would kill me."

"You sound like Jack," he said with a wry smile. "And I'll tell you exactly what I always tell him: mornings are the best time of the day."

Imogen's mouth twisted downwards. "I bet that goes down like a lead balloon," she observed, drily.

Dillon smiled, held out a hand, which she accepted gratefully. "It does," he admitted.

A knowing snort escaped her lips. "Thought so."

As she stood up, he enveloped her in his arms. "Thank you for last night," he said, kissing her gently on the lips. "It was… amazing."

She responded with a crooked grin. "It wasn't *too* bad, I suppose," she allowed, wrapping her slender arms around his wide neck and kissing him again.

"I take it you don't want to share a lift in with me?" he asked as they untangled themselves from their embrace.

Imogen gave him a bittersweet smile. "Don't take this the wrong way, but I think it's better we go in our own cars. After all, we don't want people to start talking about us."

Dillon was more than happy with that. He very much doubted that Tyler would approve of him 'sleeping with the enemy'.

After the previous evening's office meeting had concluded, they had lingered in the car park while everyone around them jumped into their cars and sped off like contestants in *The Whacky Races*.

The sexual chemistry between them had been tangible from the first moment they met and, although it was getting late, Dillon had been unable to resist inviting her to go for a drink. To his delight, she had gladly accepted. Afterwards, they had gone back to his place for a nightcap, but they had ended up sharing something far more intimate than a cup of cocoa!

Later, as they lay entwined in each other's arms, she had drifted straight off to sleep. Envying her, Dillon had lain there wide awake, unable to make his mind switch off. After a while, his thoughts had turned to his love life. Most people he knew of his age were either married or in a steady relationship, yet he remained stubbornly single. Unlike Tyler, who couldn't wait to start a family with Kelly, the idea of being in a long-term relationship, with all the baggage that came with it, frightened him, which made him wonder if he had underlying commitment issues?

Probably, he admitted to himself.

The only woman he had ever considered settling down with was Emma Drew, the bubbly mortuary assistant he had dated a couple of years back. They had met during the Whitechapel murders, and had ended up seeing each other for several months afterwards, which was by far the longest period that Dillon had ever spent with one woman. Although he had never confessed it to anyone else, not even Jack, he had actually started to think she might be the one; the person he wanted to spend the rest of his life with. Unfortunately, just as he was coming round to the idea, she had dropped a massive bombshell on him with the heart wrenching news that she had been offered a once in a lifetime job opportunity in Canada, and she was moving abroad.

The pain of losing Emma had cut deep and, although he had put on a brave face, he had sworn never to allow himself to become that attached to anyone else ever again. But when he had glanced down at Imogen, thinking how beautiful she looked, he had felt something stir deep within himself. It was probably just indigestion, he had told himself, but what if it was something more… what if, in the ridiculously short space of time that he had known her, Imogen Askew had somehow managed get around the defences he had put in place to prevent himself from getting hurt again?

Kelly was dozing in the passenger seat, while Tyler listened to the radio. Notwithstanding Kelly's sporadic outbursts of snoring, each of which completely drowned out the DJ's voice, he felt this was a far more civilised way to start the day than being subjected to Dillon's relentless early morning cheerfulness.

When the ads came on, Tyler glanced down at his watch. The Luminol treatment of Carrie's house was scheduled to begin in an hour or so, and it would be interesting to see if the process unearthed anything remotely incriminating. He doubted it would, but it needed to be done, even if only for elimination purposes.

On the radio, *Spitting in The Wind* by Badly Drawn Boy began to play.

Kelly's eyes flickered open. "I like this one," she mumbled, sleepily. "Can you turn it up?"

The song had originally been titled *Pissing in the wind* but, before being released back in April, it had been re-recorded with a more radio friendly lyric to ensure that it received air play. As Tyler obliged, he couldn't help thinking that the original title more aptly reflected the way that things were going with the investigation at the moment.

Charlie White had pulled up outside a local café so that Kevin Murray could nip in and grab them a quick bite to eat before their search for Stella Carter began in earnest.

When Murray returned a few minutes later, he handed White a large, greasy bundle and a Styrofoam cup containing a frothy coffee. "I got you the same as me," he declared cheerfully.

"And what exactly is that?" White asked, staring at the offering with mild concern.

"It's a bacon, egg and sausage roll," Murray said, salivating at the thought.

White gingerly unwrapped the package. "This looks like a heart attack on a plate," he complained.

"It's not on a plate," Murray pointed out. "It's in a bag. Now, stop pretending to be worried about your health, and stuff it down your throat." Leading by example, he took a huge mouthful from his own roll, jettisoning great splodges of tomato sauce out of the sides.

Making a series of appreciative noises as he munched, Murray shovelled one gigantic bite after another into his mouth until it was all gone. After wiping little dribbles of butter and ketchup from his chin, he took a large slurp of his coffee, then smiled encouragingly at his companion. "Come on, Whitey, eat up. A fried breakfast will set you up nicely for the day ahead."

The sun was shining, and not so much as a single cloud obscured the vibrant blue sky above Regent's Canal as the British Waterways dredger, some three quarters of a mile east of Acton's Lock, slowly chugged its way towards Old Ford.

Even though it was only nine-o'clock, Cliff Hayter and Billy Bowman had dispensed with their heavy jackets in favour of T-shirts. Hayter checked his watch, then poked his head out of the wheelhouse at the stern of the vessel. "Fancy a brew?" he called to his compatriot.

Billy Bowman, standing at the dredger's bow and surveying the water ahead of them for floating debris, had never declined a cup of tea in his life, so he smiled over his shoulder and raised an enthusiastic thumb. "Sounds like a plan," he called back.

He studied the intricate multi-coloured graffiti on one of the walls they passed. It was really quite skilful, he thought, unlike the giant ejaculating penis that had been painted in bright red on one of the metal bridges they had recently passed beneath.

A bobbing object off to his right caught his eye. Sure enough, it was another refuse sack. The canal was littered with the bloody things. Grabbing his boat hook, he moved to the starboard side of the boat and leaned out to nab it as they went past. Bowman was a seasoned hand at retrieving debris from the water while on a moving boat, and he snared it expertly.

"Come to daddy," he said as he hoisted it out of the water.

The bag, was surprisingly heavy, and the plastic split as he pulled it out of the canal, revealing a clear bag inside.

There was something scarily familiar about it.

"Oh shit," he said, gingerly lowering it onto the deck beside him.

"Tea's up," Hayter called from the wheelhouse.

Bowman ignored him. Bending down, he carefully peeled more of the outer black refuse sack away. His heart lurched as he caught sight of the contents.

"We need to moor up," he shouted to his partner.

Hayter stuck his head around the wheelhouse door. "What?"

Feeling sick, Bowman pointed towards the towpath. "We need to make an urgent stop."

As the dredger altered course, heading for the shore, Bowman stared down at the gruesome sight, and found himself mesmerised by the single painted toe protruding from the clear plastic bag like it was sticking out of a pair of laddered nylons.

The last known address for Stella Carter was a second floor flat in a tidy little block situated on the corner of Hoxton Market and Hemsworth Street, opposite St. Anne's of Hoxton church.

Entry was controlled by a buzzer system, but thankfully a middle-aged woman was keying herself in just as they arrived, so the detectives were able to ride her slipstream into the building.

The door to Stella Carter's second floor flat was opened by a slim framed Indian male in his mid-twenties. He was wearing an orange and black striped shirt that looked like it had started its life as the fabric on the back of a deckchair. As soon as he saw them, a worried expression appeared on his pockmarked face, and his wispy moustache twitched nervously.

"Yes, can I help you?" he asked in heavily accented English.

A petite woman in a gaily coloured sari appeared at his shoulder, looking equally concerned.

White produced his warrant card. "We're police officers," he explained, "and we're looking for Stella Carter, who we understand resides here."

On seeing their identification, the pair visibly relaxed.

"I thought you were bailiffs," the man said by way of explanation. "You see, the woman you are after has not resided here for two months, but we keep getting bills for her, and we have had three very unpleasant visits from debt collection agencies. It has been most stressful."

"I'm sure it has, Mr…?"

"My name is Amir Patel, and this is my wife, Jasmin."

The woman nodded meekly, then smiled at them. "Would you like to come in?"

White smiled back at her. "That's most kind of you, Mrs Patel, but we really need to find Ms Carter. I don't suppose you have a forwarding address for her, do you?"

"I have tried asking the landlord if he has a forwarding address," Patel explained in his singsong voice, "but he is telling me that he does not." He spread his arms and gave them a 'what can I do?' shrug, then his face lit up as an idea occurred to him. "Maybe there is something you can do to stop them bothering me?" he asked, hopefully.

Thanking him for his time, the detectives beat a hasty retreat before they could be dragged any further into the Patels' tale of woe.

"Well, I suppose we should try knocking at the rest of the flats," White said as they descended the stairs to the ground floor.

"I suppose so," Murray responded, unenthusiastically, "but we both know it's going to be a complete waste of time."

The inside of the telephone kiosk was even more stinky than it had been last time, Arthur noted, wondering if a local tramp had taken to using it as a personal urinal. Being careful not to step in one of the wet patches that had pooled in the corners, he noticed a copy of yesterday's *The Sun* lying open on the floor.

Arthur twisted his head to get a better look at the page three model smiling up at him, admiring her obvious assets. When he finally got his hands on the reward money Wiggins was offering, he decided that he would treat himself to a classy call girl who looked just like that, and sod the expense. It would make a very pleasant change from the pasty skinned skanks he was forced to use for sexual gratification at the moment, with their missing teeth, deflated tits and track-marked arms.

It was just after ten and, putting his reading glasses on, Arthur commenced dialling Fred Wiggins' number. Unlike last time, when it had taken ages for someone to pick up, his call was answered on the second ring, catching him off guard.

"*Yes?*" Authoritative and measured, this man's voice was far more refined than the brute he had spoken to last time.

The old Teddy Boy took a deep breath, steadied himself before speaking. "Er, good morning to you," he said in his best telephone manner. "My name's Arthur, and I'd like to speak to Mr Wiggins, please."

"*You're speaking to him. What is it you want?*"

Arthur licked his lips greedily. This was it, the moment of truth, when he discovered just how valuable the information he was selling really was. "Word on the street is that you're interested in information about some missing diamonds, and that there's a handsome reward for anyone who can help you recover them."

"*And you think you're that person, do you, old son?*" Wiggins asked. There was a note of scepticism in his voice, as if he was fed up with people making promises and then failing to deliver on them.

"I do," Arthur confirmed, proudly.

Wiggins merely grunted. "*And what exactly do you know about the diamonds?*"

Arthur had been expecting Wiggins to sound pleased, excited even, but he didn't; he just sounded bored. Maybe, the information wasn't as valuable as he had been led to believe?

"Well, I bumped into a fella in the pub the other night. We got chatting, as you do, and he mentioned something about him and the bloke he works for coming into a bit of money when they sell off some diamonds. When I asked him what he meant by that, he got all nervous like, then tried to tell me I'd misheard him, but I hadn't. He definitely said diamonds."

There was a long pause, during which Arthur could hear Wiggins' steady breathing. Not wanting to appear too keen, he waited patiently for the other man to speak.

"*Okay, you've piqued my interest,*" Wiggins eventually admitted. "*What's this geezer's name, and where can I find him?*"

Arthur hesitated, not wanting to cause offence, then said as tactfully as he could, "No disrespect, Mr Wiggins, but if I just tell you, how do I know I'll still get the reward money?"

Wiggins' laugh oozed contempt. *"Don't you worry about that,"* he said, dismissively. *"If what you're telling me is true, you'll be well looked after."*

"But—"

Wiggins spoke over him, angrily. *"Don't fuck me about, sunshine."*

Arthur froze, not knowing how best to respond. He didn't want to share his precious knowledge until he had a big wad of readies in his hand, but Wiggins wasn't a man to upset, and if Arthur didn't play ball, there was every chance that he would send one of his goons over to beat the information out of him. Then, instead of a big payoff, all he'd have to show for his efforts would be a load of broken bones.

In the end, Arthur's desire to continue breathing without the aid of a ventilator overcame his natural greed. Hoping that Wiggins really would be as good as his word, he said, "The bloke's name is Fingers, Mr Wiggins. He's a grease monkey, works with a bloke called Terry Marshall in a garage in Cudworth Street, just down the road from *The Black Horse* pub."

"I know the pub. What's this tin-pot garage called? There are loads of them around there."

Arthur panicked because his mind had suddenly gone blank. "Dunno, Mr Wiggins."

An impatient sigh, signalling that Wiggins was losing patience with him. *"And do you happen to know the owner's name, Arthur, because, so far, you haven't exactly impressed me?"*

Arthur's aging brow creased into a fierce frown of concentration as he tried to recall the man's name. The relief, when it finally popped into his head, was indescribable. "His name's Darren," he said quickly. "Darren McCullen."

———

Abigale Stanwick ran her business from her home in Whiston Road. "I'm a freelance beautician and hairdresser," she explained as she showed Paul Evans through to the kitchen. "I've cancelled all my morning appointments, but I've got to pick my daughter up from school at midday, so I hope that's going to be enough time."

"I'm sure it will be," he said with a smile.

"Coffee?" she asked.

"Please," Evans replied, gratefully.

Sliding onto a stool by the kitchen peninsula, he studied Stanwick as she poured water into the percolator. She reminded him of a Barbie doll: slim, pretty, hair immaculately styled, with tasteful highlights, make-up applied to perfection, and dressed in tight fitting, designer label clothing. Her appearance was faultless, but everything about her seemed either contrived or augmented. Hair extensions; false eyelashes; veneers on her shiny white teeth; stick-on nails that were more like talons; silicone implants that made her cleavage so top heavy that it looked unnatural. Up close, her face had a decidedly plastic sheen to it. He could see that she had been injected with Botox to reduce the wrinkles in her forehead and collagen to make her lips fuller.

It was a great pity really, because underneath all the artificial add-ons, she seemed like a really nice person.

"How do you take your coffee?" she asked.

"White, two sugars," he told her, opening his battered daybook to a blank page. "If it's okay with you, I'll make some notes as we speak, and then I'll draft a statement for you to sign from them."

Stanwick shrugged, indifferently. "Whatever you think best," she said, taking a seat opposite him.

"Am I right in saying that you and Carrie were best friends?"

Stanwick nodded, and he could tell she was trying not to cry. "We've been besties since primary school," she said with a sad smile. "We just clicked, and we've been inseparable ever since. I–I can't believe that she's gone."

"What can you tell me about Carrie's brothers?" he asked, just to distract her.

Stanwick looked up at him, and he noticed that she had unnaturally blue eyes. Could they be coloured contact lenses? He had read somewhere that such things were available these days.

"Carrie's older brother's called Darren. He's a nice lad, used to be in the army, but now runs a garage over in Bethnal Green. She's got a twin brother called Aidan, but he's a total tosser."

Evans smiled at the description, which perfectly mirrored Kelly Flowers' opinion of the man. "Was she close to her brothers?"

"She was very close to Darren, but not Aidan. Those two fought like cat and dog. Honestly, it's a miracle that they never killed each other. Apart from being a complete waste of space, Aidan's got a bee in his bonnet because their mum cut him out of her will, so the house went to Carrie and Darren when she died, and he ended up without a pot to piss in." Her tone suggested Abigale thought he had got exactly what he deserved.

Evans raised an enquiring eyebrow. "I should imagine that caused a considerable amount of tension between them, especially as they lived together under the same roof?"

Stanwick managed a smile. "That's the understatement of the year. Aidan was constantly bleating on about it. At one point, he even threatened to get a solicitor and take them to court to challenge the will."

"Was Carrie worried about that?"

Stanwick shook her head, and smirked. "Aidan spunks all his money on drugs, so everyone knew it was empty talk."

Evans scribbled down some notes, then looked up at her. "What can you tell me about Carrie's ex? I believe her name was Stella."

Stanwick blew out her cheeks, then walked over to the percolator. Standing with her back to Evans, she poured their coffee into mugs. "What a complete and utter bitch she was," she said venomously. After adding milk and sugar, she handed him his drink and then sat down again.

"I take it that you didn't like her, then?" Evans enquired, drily.

"I don't think there's ever been anyone I liked less," Stanwick replied, candidly.

"Did Carrie ever talk to you about her relationship with Stella?"

Stanwick took a sip of her coffee, being careful not to smear her lipstick. "We were like sisters, so she told me everything. I could see that Stella was wrong for Carrie, right from the off, but she was too smitten to listen to me. By the time that she saw sense, it was too late and she was stuck in an abusive relationship."

Evans' cup paused halfway to his mouth. "Abusive? In what way?"

Stanwick's face darkened, and Evans could sense the anger simmering away just beneath the surface.

"In every way. Physically, mentally, emotionally; Stella put her through absolute hell." She shook her head sadly. "They were together, on and off, for about ten months in total, I think. Carrie tried to end things with her several times, but always ended up taking her back because she felt sorry for her. In the end, it became too unbearable, and she dumped Stella about two or three months ago."

Evans' pen was going like the clappers. "Did she say why?" he asked without looking up from his notes.

Stanwick responded with a mirthless laugh. "Stella was a horrible, *horrible* person; she was controlling and manipulative, and she was insanely jealous, always accusing Carrie of having affairs with other women, which she never did. She even thought that something was going on between me and Carrie at one point, which was just ridiculous. Carrie used to come around to see me in tears, nursing black eyes and bruised ribs. She would have purple marks all over her arms and legs, from where she'd been punched and kicked by Stella. She always made pathetic excuses for her injuries, out of embarrassment I think, but it was obvious to me that her psycho-bitch girlfriend was knocking her about."

Evans nodded, thoughtfully. The more he heard about Stella Carter, the more he fancied her for Carrie's murder. "Do you have a telephone number for Stella, or know where she lives, by any chance?"

Stanwick shook her head. "No. Sorry. She used to have a flat near Hoxton Market, but I heard she gave that up after they split up. Now that you mention it, I don't think I've seen her around the area since Carrie got someone to scare her off."

Evans' eyes widened. "What do you mean by that?"

Stanwick hesitated before answering. "I probably shouldn't have said anything about that," she said, guiltily. "I don't want to get anyone in trouble."

Evans treated her to his most engaging smile. "You won't be getting anyone in trouble," he assured her. "But it would really help us to know who scared Stella off for Carrie, just in case they know where she's living now."

Stanwick thought about this for a few seconds, chewing her bottom lip anxiously. "She spoke to a friend at work, a bloke called Fred. Apparently, he's well connected, has friends in all the wrong places, if you get my drift. He sent some big albino geezer around to have a quiet word with Stella. I don't know what was said, but whatever it was did the trick, because the rotten cow never bothered Carrie again after that."

19

I don't think she's the full shilling

"Did she tell you the name of Carrie's new love interest?" Tyler asked. He was fielding a call from Paul Evans, who had just finished with Abigale Stanwick.

There was a pregnant pause.

"Abi reckons that Carrie was unusually coy with her about the new woman. Apparently, she wanted to see how the night out went before going into any detail about her, just in case it didn't pan out."

"Great," Tyler said, his voice acerbic. "So, we still don't know the name of the girl Carrie was seeing."

"We don't," Evans allowed, *"but I'm just on my way over to Broadway Market to see if I can track down someone who does."*

"That sounds promising," Tyler said, perking up a little. "Who is it?"

"Abi told me about a woman called Sharon Peacock. She works as a part time barmaid at The Merry Fiddler pub. Apparently, she knows the woman

Carrie was meeting, and it was her who introduced them. I've got her address, and I'm going to see if she can put us in touch with her mate."

"Let's hope she can," Tyler said, feeling frustration swell inside him. "Ring me straight away if you manage to get her details."

"Will do, boss," Evans promised. *"Oh, and as I'm going to be in that neck of the woods, I'll pop into The Merry Fiddler and see if I can grab a copy of their CCTV."*

Dressed in a baggy Hawaiian shirt, shorts and flip flops, Darren McCullen plonked himself down on a stool at the hotel bar and ordered a round of drinks. It was far too hot for his liking, humid too, and it was only mid-morning, so it was going to get a hell of a lot worse before it got any better.

Wilting under the oppressive Spanish heat, he grabbed a serviette from the counter and mopped his brow, wishing that he'd chosen somewhere cooler to go on holiday.

He had left Janice laying on a sunbed by the pool, doing her impression of a beached whale. To be honest, he was glad to get away from her for a few minutes, because she had been doing his head in all week. He had been hoping to book a few excursions while they were there, explore the island, see the local culture, and do all that other touristy stuff, but all she wanted to do was split her time between the crowded pool and the nearby beach.

Janice hadn't taken it too well when he'd pointed out that she resembled an overcooked lobster. Well, he thought haughtily, when she started crying that she was burnt to a crisp, she had better not expect any sympathy from him.

The massive TV on the wall behind the bar was tuned into Sky News, and he watched it while the sluggishly slow bartender prepared their drinks. He had periodically checked the news but, so far, there hadn't been anything more about Frank Kyle's murder.

He had tried ringing Carrie's number several times since his arrival, but her phone was constantly switched off, and he figured she was deliberately blanking him because she was annoyed with him for flying out to Tenerife.

Great arcs of sweat ringed his armpits and, as Darren tugged at the neckline of his shirt, trying to get some air circulating around his body, the swarthy looking barman reappeared, handing him his pint of lager and a Piña colada for Janice. It had come in a big fancy glass, with a chunk of pineapple, a little umbrella and a straw. She would love that, the pretentious cow. He smiled his thanks and muttered, "Gracias."

Picking up their drinks, Darren was just about to leave the bar when a photograph of Carrie appeared on the TV screen. He instantly recognised it as one that had been taken a couple of years previously, before their mum had died. Carrie was smiling in the photo, looking like she didn't have a care in the world.

Despite the oppressive heat, a chill ran down his spine. Why was his sister's face suddenly plastered all over the TV screen? Returning the drinks to the counter, he asked the barman to turn up the volume.

"...*Officers from New Scotland Yard's Homicide Command have today released the identity of the dismembered female torso that was discovered in Regent's Canal on Wednesday afternoon. Carrie McCullen, a bubbly thirty-four year old from Hackney, had been reported missing from her home near Hoxton Market by her twin brother two days earlier...*"

Feeling his legs buckle, Darren clawed at the polished counter to stop himself from falling. With his free hand, he grabbed the nearest bar stool and collapsed onto it. "This can't be real," he said, staring up at the widescreen TV in horror.

His mind was reeling.

On screen, a chilly looking reporter was addressing the camera from the side of Regent's Canal. In the background, several police forensic officers in baggy white suits and face masks were sifting through a pile of black plastic sacks that had been stacked by the side of a lock. A dredger with an excavator on the front was moored just beyond them.

"...*since the chilling discovery of Carrie's torso, on Wednesday afternoon, two further body parts have been recovered. Yesterday morning, a bin liner containing Carrie's right arm was retrieved from near Acton's Lock and, this morning, her right leg was found floating three-quarters of a mile further along the canal…"*

Darren clamped a hand to his mouth to prevent an anguished scream bursting out. Carrie was dead; her body chopped into little pieces. What kind of a sick fuck would do something like that?

His shock turned to sadness, and then to rage. With that came the burning desire to avenge her death; to bring unimaginable pain and suffering to whoever had caused it.

Without conscious thought, he clenched his fists, and it was only when he registered the searing pain in his palms that he relaxed his hands. Looking down at them, he saw deep indentations from where his nails had dug into the skin.

Take a deep breathe, calm down…

He couldn't. His emotions were spiralling out of control. All it would take was for someone to look at him in the wrong way, or say something flippant, and he would tear their throat out.

Calm down! Breathe!

He opened his mouth, tried to suck in a lungful of air, but nothing happened.

He began to hyperventilate.

Breathe…

The fact that Carrie had been dismembered could only mean one thing: Jonas Willard had learned of her involvement in Frank Kyle's murder, and he was sending a very clear message to her co-conspirators: we know who you are, and we will be coming for you next.

Breathe…

Stars exploded in front of his eyes, and the world around him began to spin. Feeling dizzy, he sagged forward, resting his head on the bar.

Breathe…

Red faced, eyes bulging, Darren finally managed to draw breath. For a few moments, all he could do was sit there, doubled over, his chest heaving.

Eventually, he felt strong enough to stand. Ignoring the strange looks he was attracting from other holiday makers and the Spanish barman, Darren rushed into the lobby in search of a payphone.

"Your drinks, Señor!" the barman called after him.

Darren didn't give a toss about the damn drinks. He needed to speak to Fingers urgently, to warn him that Willard was onto them. As soon as he'd done that, he would see about booking a flight home.

If Jonas Willard wanted a war, Darren McCullen would oblige him. Willard might be a big-time gangster, but he had picked the wrong fucking person to mess with this time.

He knew there was no point in running from Willard; the man had eyes everywhere, and his people would eventually find Darren and Fingers, wherever they went. The only way to stop that from happening was to put a bullet between the aging mobster's eyes.

As he lifted the telephone receiver, Darren found himself struggling to cope with the crushing guilt. Carrie had died because of his greed and stupidity; it was all his fault, and the soldier in him swore that he would avenge her or die trying.

Imogen Askew looked at Bear and shook her head in dismay. "What on earth are you doing?" she asked as he repeatedly tugged at his crotch.

They were standing on the canal towpath, a few yards away from the bag containing the severed right leg. The cameraman flashed her a sheepish smile, then resumed his fumbling with the tight-fitting overalls that Juliet Kennedy had given him upon their arrival a few minutes earlier.

"Why don't they make these things bigger in the crotch?" he complained, tugging the material down again. "I daren't lift my leg or I'll be cut in two."

Watching on in amusement, Dillon gave him a look that was one part grin and two parts eye-roll.

"You shouldn't have let them into the inner cordon," Bull chastised him. "*He* won't be happy." The 'He' in question was

Jack Tyler, who had been forced to remain at Hertford House to brief Holland, rather than attend the latest crime scene with them.

Dillon swatted Bull's concern aside. "He'll be fine about it," he said, hoping that was true. With Imogen batting her eyelashes at him in a most provocative manner, he had reluctantly agreed to allow her and Bear to accompany them into the inner cordon, as long as they promised to behave in an exemplary fashion and follow his instructions to the letter.

"Stop fiddling with your dangly bits and get a shot of the bin liner," Imogen snapped, growing impatient with her cameraman.

Grumbling under his breath, Bear reluctantly raised the camera to his shoulder and began filming.

"Would you mind standing by the bag?" Imogen asked Dillon. "That's it. Now, look down, as though you're assessing it for evidence or something. That'll look good on camera."

Dillon cringed with embarrassment, but obliged.

"Brilliant," Imogen beamed. "Now look thoughtful, as though you're working something out in your head."

Dillon bent forward, frowned.

"She said look thoughtful, not constipated," Bull said, laughing at him.

Dillon stood up. Clenching his fists, he stared pointedly at Bull. "Don't you have somewhere else to be?"

Bull shook his head, clearly enjoying Dillon's discomfort. "Wouldn't miss this for the world," he said, smiling sweetly.

Dillon was about to come back with an acerbic retort when his mobile started ringing. Unzipping his Tyvek overalls as he walked away, he pulled out his phone and rammed it against his ear. "DI Dillon."

"Boss, it's Colin here."

Franklin sounded excited, and Dillon hoped that meant he was calling with good news.

"How can I help you, Colin?"

"Sorry to disturb you, but Mr Tyler's still in a meeting with the DCS, and I need some advice. I've just found some footage of the woman with the suitcase

getting out of a minicab in Dunston Road, a couple of minutes before the clip we have of her walking along the canal towpath."

"How do you know it's a minicab?" Dillon asked.

Franklin chuckled. *"I'm a skilled detective, remember?"*

"No, seriously, how do you know."

"It's got the company details written across the rear doors, and a big illuminated taxi sign on the roof."

Dillon rolled his eyes. *Skilled detective, my arse!*

"The company's called Easy Cars," Franklin continued. *"I'm guessing they're a local firm, as they have an 0207 telephone number. Dean's just running the numberplate through the PNC for me, so I can get the registered keeper details. What I need to know is, do you want me to send someone over to the R/K's address once we've got it?"*

Dillon considered this for a moment. "Yes, do that. And get Deano to run the car through the insurance database to see if it has a hire and reward policy, and who that actually covers to drive the car." It wasn't uncommon for a hire and reward car to be registered to one person but used by another, and this simple check could save them a lot of time if the two were based at different locations. "Lastly, find out where the cab office is, and send someone straight over there. With any luck, they'll have a record of who ordered the cab. Oh, and make sure whoever goes also checks the cab office for CCTV."

"Will do," Franklin said. *"Once I've done that, I'm going to try and track the cab backwards using local authority CCTV."*

Hanging up, Dillon walked over to where Bull was standing. Imogen had grown tired of waiting for him, and she and Bear had wandered off to do some filming further along the path.

"Anything interesting?" Bull asked.

Dillon nodded. "Yep. Colin's found CCTV of our female suspect getting out of a cab in Dunston Road a few minutes before we picked her up on the towpath."

"Do we know the name of the cab company?" Bull asked. Prior to joining the Homicide command, or AMIP as it had been known back then, he had been based at Hackney Borough, and he knew the area well.

"They're called Easy Cars, I think."

"I know them," Bull told him. "They're a reputable firm, based at the top end of Hoxton Market if memory serves."

Dillon arched an eyebrow. "Doesn't Carrie live in one of the roads off Hoxton Market?"

"Ivy Street," Bull confirmed. "It's runs between the top end of Hoxton Market and Pitfield street."

"Bit of a coincidence, don't you think?" Dillon said, tilting his head to one side.

"Too much of a coincidence, if you ask me," Bull agreed.

———

"Thank you for seeing me at such short notice," Evans said as he followed Sharon Peacock up a steep flight of creaky stairs to her flat. It was located above an off-licence, about halfway down Broadway Market, a few doors along from the pie and mash shop. The flat's decor was old, and the wallpaper faded, but at least it was clean and tidy.

Peacock led him past the lounge into a small kitchen at the back of the property.

"Fancy a cuppa?" she asked, pulling the tie-cord of her pink dressing gown tight as she filled the kettle. She was a busty blonde, in her late thirties, with a heart shaped face and a happy-go-lucky smile. Gigantic hooped earrings dangled from her lobes, swinging wildly every time she twisted her head.

A ginger cat appeared from nowhere and started brushing itself up against her legs and purring loudly.

Pulling a wooden chair out from beneath a small pine table against the wall, Evans sat down. "Yes, please. Strong, with two sugars."

The cat eyed him for a moment, and then jumped onto his lap. It padded around until it was comfy, and then settled down, looking out over his knees.

"Don't mind Clarence," she said, smiling at Evans' obvious discomfort. "He's very friendly."

"I can see that," Evans said, wishing the cat would sod off.

Clarence was going nowhere. Dribbling worse than a teething child, he was repeatedly digging his very sharp claws into Evans' legs.

"I think he's taken a bit of a shine to you," Peacock said, opening a squeaking cupboard above the fridge.

"Lucky me," Evans replied, wincing as the fidgety cat continued to use his thighs as a pincushion.

Peacock produced a large box of Twinings flavoured teas. "What d'ya fancy, then?" she asked, enthusiastically holding the box out for his inspection. "I've got black, green, herbal, lemon, a few other fruit infusions if you'd prefer one of those…"

Evans grimaced, apologetically. "I'm more of a PG Tips kind of bloke to be honest," he told her, wishing he'd declined the offer.

Peacock turned her nose up at his lacklustre response, having obviously mistaken him for a fellow connoisseur. "I might have a few supermarket value teabags somewhere," she said, reopening the cupboard.

"I don't want to put you to any trouble," Evans said, quickly.

"It's no trouble," Peacock assured him. Going up on tiptoes, she rummaged around the far recesses of the top shelf for a few seconds, pulling a succession of weird expressions as she searched.

"Aha!" she suddenly announced, and a look of triumph spread across her face as she withdrew her hand. It quickly faded when she saw the sorry state of the lone teabag. It was a crumpled, manky looking thing that had become wet at some point, and then been allowed to dry out. Peacock looked down at it, then at him. Holding it up for inspection, she gave him a deflated shrug. "Sorry, this is all I've got left."

"That'll be fine," Evans said, just to be polite.

Peacock shook the teabag to make sure it was still structurally intact, then brushed it against her dressing gown to remove the cobwebs that had attached themselves to it.

"Yeah, it looks alright to me," she said, tossing it into a cup and pouring a liberal amount of hot water in after it. "So, what can I do for you?" she asked, adding a smidgeon of milk and two large teaspoons of granulated sugar. A quick stir, and then she handed it to him.

"I'm investigating the murder of a woman called Carrie McCullen," he began, and then winced as the cat dug its claws in again. "Her torso was dragged out of Regent's Canal on Wednesday afternoon."

Peacock's face clouded over, and she nodded sombrely. "Poor Carrie," she said, taking a sip of her tea. It smelled minty. "I've been following the story on the news. I was so shocked when I realised that it was someone I knew. You just don't expect it, do you?"

"How well did you know Carrie?" Evans asked, wondering if he should be brave and try the tea, now that she had gone to all the trouble of making it for him. It didn't actually look *too* bad, and he was thirsty.

Peacock's face scrunched into a sad frown. "Not that well. She was a regular at the pub I work part time in and, like all good barmaids, I made a point of getting to know the regulars because it's good for business."

"So, you weren't friends?"

Peacock shook her head. "Not friends, no. But she was a nice person, and we got on pretty well."

"When was the last time you saw Carrie?"

"She came in on Friday night," Peacock said without hesitation. "She was with several other girls. They stayed till about eleven, and then left."

"Did they all leave together?"

Peacock shrugged. "Not sure. I was pretty busy for the last hour or so, so I didn't actually see any of them go."

That was a pity.

"I'm led to believe that Carrie might have become romantically involved with one of these girls, and that you might be able to give me her details?"

The touch of a smile twisted Peacock's mouth upwards. "I presume you're talking about Trisha Perkins?"

Evans' face was devoid of expression. "I don't know. Am I?"

"Me and Trish went to school together," Peacock informed him.

"We were really close during our teens, but drifted apart when she moved down to Devon in her early twenties. We've stayed in touch over the years, exchanging Christmas and birthday cards, and sharing the odd phone call, and she always pops into the pub for a proper catchup whenever she's in London. Her poor old mum's been ill with cancer recently, so Trish has taken a month off work to look after her while she undergoes chemo. I introduced her to Carrie a couple of weekends ago, and they really hit it off, but I'm not sure it was ever going to go anywhere."

"Why do you say that?" Evans asked.

Peacock shrugged. "Trish will be going back to Devon in a couple of weeks' time, when her mum's well enough to look after herself again, so it would have to be a long-distance relationship if they were going to start seeing each other properly, and I don't have a lot of faith in those, do you?"

Evans didn't know how to answer that one. "I don't suppose you know Carrie's ex by any chance, do you?"

Peacock's eyes narrowed. "Stella? Yeah, I know her. Why?"

"We're very keen to talk to her, just to get some background information and such."

Peacock was giving him a strange look. "They split up a few months ago," she told him. "As far as I know, Stella hasn't seen Carrie in ages."

Evans shrugged. "Yeah, well it's just a belt and braces approach really," he lied. After all, he could hardly reveal that Stella was a person of interest, and likely to become a nailed-on suspect in the not-too-distant future.

"I bumped into Stella on Friday morning as it happens," Peacock said, reaching across to ruffle one of the cat's ears. "We were both doing our weekly shop in the big Tesco store in Morning Lane." She gave him a coy look. "She's a bit of a strange one, that's for sure," she said in a tone that implied Stella had issues.

"How so?" he asked, smiling politely while wishing that the cat would go and sit on her lap instead. His trousers were covered in long ginger hairs now, and he suspected they wouldn't be easy to get rid of.

Peacock raised a forefinger to her temple and started making little circles in the air. "Well, let's just say I don't think she's the full shilling, if you get my drift."

He raised an eyebrow, inviting her to expand on her observation.

Peacock was happy to oblige. "One minute she was chatting away happily, like everything was all hunky-dory. Then, for no obvious reason, she just stormed off, leaving her half-full shopping trolley in the middle of the aisle. I mean, who does that?"

Evans shrugged. "Did you say anything to upset her?"

"Me?" Peacock demanded indignantly. "All I said was—" She broke off mid-sentence, and bit her lower lip. "Oh dear, I've just realised why she was so upset," she confessed, having the grace to look embarrassed. "I might have mentioned that Carrie fancied another woman, and that she was going out with her and some other mates that evening. In hindsight, I suppose that could be considered a bit insensitive of me, although I didn't mean it to come across that way."

"I'm sure you didn't," Evans consoled her. She didn't come across as the malicious type, someone who would deliberately say something to stir things up, but she was certainly a bit ditsy, so he had no trouble believing that she would open her mouth before engaging her brain. "I don't suppose you can give me Stella's current address or telephone number?"

Peacock shook her head. "No. Sorry. Friday was the first time I'd seen her since they split up, but she hasn't got a car, so she must live local to Morning Lane."

"What about Trish? I take it you can put me in touch with her?"

"Of course," Peacock said, eager to please him. "I'll just grab my mobile from the lounge," she said with a smile. "Be back in a jiffy."

As soon as she left the room, Evans shooed the cat off his lap and started brushing at his trousers. "Look at the mess you've made, you dirty git," he said, unimpressed.

Clearly offended by the eviction, Clarence's green eyes studied him with haughty disdain, and his tail swished angrily.

Having retrieved her handbag from the lounge, Peacock dumped it on the kitchen table and rummaged through it until she found her mobile, which she dangled triumphantly in front of his face. "I'll give her a ring now, and you can speak to her direct."

"That would be very helpful," Evans said, crossing his legs to prevent the recently displaced cat from jumping back up.

20

Better out than in, right?

A fierce frown of concentration had drawn Jonas Willard's eyebrows together to form one continuous line along his forehead. Sitting opposite him, on the other side of the polished teak desk, Fred Wiggins waited in silence for his boss to make a decision. Although he was growing impatient, he knew better than to interrupt Willard while he was mulling things over.

"And your contact was absolutely sure, was he? Carrie's brother, Darren, is behind the theft of my diamonds?"

"That's how it's looking," Wiggins said, being careful to keep his voice neutral. The old man had been very upset to learn that Carrie had been confirmed as the source of the leak.

Willard locked eyes with his subordinate. "And you think Carrie deliberately passed the information to him, and that she betrayed me, stabbed me right in the fucking back?" His voice was simmering with barely controlled anger.

Wiggins knew he would have to be very careful with how he

framed his response. "I'm not saying that she was involved," he replied, diplomatically, "or that she even knew her scumbag brother was behind the robbery. All I'm saying is that Carrie was the leak. It's quite possible that she just mentioned it in passing, thinking she could trust him, and that Darren McCullen betrayed her as much as he did you."

Willard nodded, liking the sound of that. "Yeah, that's what I think, too," he said, sounding slightly mollified.

Wiggins had guessed the conversation would proceed along these lines. Willard had never shared the affection he felt for Carrie with either of her siblings, and he would have no qualms about hurting either of them.

"So, let me get this straight," Willard said. "Darren McCullen owns the garage this bloke Arthur told you about, and these other fuckers, Fingers and Marshall, work for him?"

Wiggins nodded, but remained silent, knowing it would be better to allow Willard to reach his own conclusions without trying to influence the outcome.

"Well, we know only two people carried out the robbery," Willard said. "That much was confirmed by Frankie's wife. And didn't she say that one of them was a skinny fucker, like this Fingers bloke?"

His face impassive, Wiggins nodded again.

"But there could have been a third cunt waiting outside for them in a getaway car?"

For the third time on the trot, Wiggins, head bobbed up and down in agreement.

Willard puffed agitatedly on his cigar for a few seconds, causing the tip to glow bright red. "It seems to me that, whether he was there or not, McCullen would have been behind it," he eventually said.

"I can't see how he wouldn't have known about it," Wiggins agreed.

Leaning back in his padded leather chair, Willard grunted, then took another long drag on his cigar, before blowing a thick stream of smoke up toward the ceiling.

"What do you want me to do about it?" Wiggins asked.

Standing up, Willard stubbed the cigar out in the ashtray on his desk. "I've made my decision," he said with an ominous sense of finality. "Grab them all. Torture the truth out of them, and then, once you've got my fucking diamonds back, kill all three of those horrible cunts and put them in a concrete coffin."

Wiggins rose from his chair, bowed deferentially. "Leave it to me," he purred.

Having failed miserably in their efforts to track Stella Carter down, White and Murray had been allocated a new task. Their latest mission was to locate Eric Hammond, the mini-cab driver who had taken Carrie's killer to Dunston Road on Saturday evening.

Unfortunately, there was no sign of Hammond's red Cavalier outside his address in Malvern Drive, a tree lined residential road that mainly consisted of large Georgian style terraced houses.

They tried knocking at his door anyway, but there was no reply.

"We're no' having much luck today, are we?" White said, with a disgruntled sigh.

Closing the garden gate behind them, Murray opened his mouth to complain.

White cut him off with a raised hand. "I'm no' in the mood to put up wi' you moaning about this being a wasted journey," he warned.

Murray huffed, then lapsed into silence.

"We'd better try knocking on the neighbours' doors," White said. "Maybe one of them knows where Hammond is."

Ten minutes later, they were back in the pool car, none the wiser.

"I suppose we'd better pop over to the cab office he works from," White said, starting the car.

Murray's stomach gurgled loudly. "Let's go via the nearest Maccy Dees," he said, rubbing it. "I'm bloody starving."

White glanced at him disbelievingly. How could someone who was so painfully thin need to eat so much food?

"What?" Murray demanded, defensively. "It's not my fault I've got a fast metabolism and need to eat regularly."

It was getting on for two o'clock by the time they pulled up outside Easy Cars, but there was no sign of Hammond's Cavalier there either.

"Will you hurry up and finish your sodding burger, so we can go in and find out if he's working today," White snapped.

Murray shot him an injured look.

"Just eat," White said, gesticulating for him to hurry up.

With a humungous burger in one hand, and a thick shake in the other, Murray's arms made alternative trips to his mouth. "I'll end up with indigestion, rushing my food like this," he protested, spraying the centre console with bits of burger bun.

When he had finally finished, he crumpled the wrapping into a ball, tossed it over his shoulder onto the back seat, then let out a long, undulating burp.

Fanning his nose, White gave him a withering stare.

"What?" Murray protested, staring back indignantly.

"You're gross," White informed him.

Shifting all his weight onto one buttock, Murray pulled a straining face as he passed wind. "Better out than in, right?"

White was too busy holding his breath to respond.

Exiting the vehicle as quickly as he could, White set off towards the cab office, with Murray trailing behind.

The door opened to the accompaniment of a bell going ding-a-ling overhead.

On hearing the bell, the cab controller looked up from the newspaper he was reading and gave them a warm smile of welcome that showcased his gleaming white teeth. He was a middle-aged black man with short dreadlocks and a perpetually happy face. According to the badge he wore, his name was Elvis Winters.

"Afternoon, gents," Elvis declared in a rich Jamaican accent. "If you're after a cab, I'm afraid you might have a bit of a wait. All of my drivers are out at the moment."

White flashed his warrant card at him. "I'm DS White, this is DC Murray. We're from the Homicide Command, and we're looking for a man called Eric Hammond. I understand he works here?"

A look of concern appeared on the controller's face, putting a dent in his smile. "Is Eric in trouble?" he asked, anxiously.

Squinting at the name badge, White shook his head. "Not at all, Mr Winters. He's a potential witness in a case we're investigating, that's all."

Worry turned to relief. "Bliss," Winters said, then added, "Call me Elvis, named after Costello not Presley. Eric's out with a fare at the moment, but he should be back within the next fifteen minutes or so." Swivelling in his chair, he indicated the radio setup on the table behind his desk. "Do you want me to call him for you, and tell him to hurry up?"

White shook his head. "That's okay, we'll wait."

Adjourning to the window overlooking the market, White ran his eyes around the room, checking for cameras. He immediately spotted the small wall-mounted camera over the door, and there was another, this one at the back of the room, facing forward. "Tell me, are these cameras working?" he asked, pointing at each of them in turn.

Elvis nodded. "They are," he confirmed. "Can't be too careful around here, know what I mean?"

White knew exactly what he meant. "Elvis, while we're waiting for Mr Hammond to come back, do you think it would be possible for us to view the footage from last Saturday night?"

Elvis frowned, thoughtfully. "I suppose so," he said, and then gave them a lopsided grin. "As long as I can work out how to play it."

White walked over to the desk. "I'll also need to go through your register, just to see who ordered cabs that evening."

"Yeah, no problem, man," Elvis said. Reaching for the book, he rapidly flicked through the pages until he came to the relevant one. "Here you go," he said, sliding it across the counter.

Wiggins parked the Audi on the double yellow lines outside McCullen's Garage in Cudworth Street. It was right on the corner of Collingwood Street and, like all the other units in the road, the front of the premises protruded some twenty or so feet beyond the old railway arches that were set into the railway viaduct behind it.

McCullen's Garage was a cramped, shoddy looking place. The brickwork at the side of the building badly needed repointing; the corrugated metal roof was riddled with orange rust; everything about the place, from the oil-stained pavement outside, to the dark and dingy interior, proclaimed it to be a tinpot operation.

According to a flaking blue sign suspended above the wide shutters, the garage specialised in MOTs, services, crash repairs and engine rebuilds. Wiggins had made a few discreet enquiries, and the word on the street was that the business was losing money hand over fist.

Behind him, Casper pulled up in a white Ford Transit van. Basher Nolan was sitting beside him in the passenger seat. With his crinkled bald head, cauliflower ears, broken nose and scared face, he resembled a battered crash test dummy.

Basher had once been a professional wrestler, but had failed to make it to the big time. He had then tried his hand at bare-knuckle fighting, but hadn't been too successful at that either. By his own admission, he wasn't a particularly skilful boxer, but he had a jaw like granite, and, as his face bore testament, he could take an awful lot of punishment. A big unit at eighteen stone, Basher's preferred tactic in the ring had been to lean on his opponents until they ran out of steam, and then clobber them into unconsciousness. Now, well past his prime, he scraped a living by performing whatever funny business Wiggins put his way and doing door security at low-brow nightclubs.

Most people in the underworld circles he moved in believed that Basher had earned his nickname because he was handy with his fists, but the truth was that he had been given it at school, when one of his friends had caught him bashing one out in the boy's toilets during playtime.

Mickey Mulligan, another reliable hood Wiggins sometimes farmed out dirty work to, was sitting in the back of the van, on the long bench behind the driver's seat. Mulligan was an ex-squaddie and, while he didn't have Basher's physical presence, he was very handy in a fight. Plenty of people had underestimated Mickey, only to end up face down on the floor, lying in a pool of their own blood, and wondering what had happened.

Alighting the Audi, Wiggins signalled for the others to remain in the van until he called them in. He adjusted his tie, fastened the top two buttons of his jacket, then strolled into the garage, being careful not to scuff his shiny shoes on the uneven, filthy floor.

Inside, there were two hydraulic ramps with work pits beneath them. A dirty VW Transporter occupied one of these, and it had been raised into the air. Standing in the pit below, a skinny young man with greasy hair and a spotty face was banging away at the underside of the vehicle. All that was visible of him was his head, shoulders and arms, both of which were extended above his head. He held a hammer in his right hand, but it was the other one that drew Wiggins' attention. Even from a distance, he could see that some of the fingers were missing from it.

A predator's smile crept across Wiggins' face as he made his way over to the young man, who was grunting and groaning from his efforts. An ABBA song was booming out over the radio, and the boy was singing along, doing his best to murder the tune.

Space was at a premium inside, and the industrial shelving surrounding the work bays was banged out with tools, boxes of car parts, a selection of exhaust systems, and two giant stacks of tyres.

There was a cramped office at the back, and Wiggins spotted a burly man in oil-stained blue overalls standing inside, with his back towards the open door. That, he presumed would be Terry Marshall. A telephone receiver was clamped against his ear, and it sounded like he was quoting a prospective customer a price for some new tyres.

Wiggins came to a halt beside the pit Fingers was working in. "Alright, me old son?" he enquired, pleasantly.

Fingers jumped at the sound, then looked up. "Sorry," he said. "Didn't hear you come in. If you want to pop over to the office, Terry will sort you out as soon as he's finished on the phone." Smiling politely at Wiggins, he raised the hammer to resume his work.

"Actually," Wiggins said, before Fingers could commence banging again, "it's you I wanted to talk to."

Fingers frowned at him. "Me?" he asked, sounding confused.

The poor boy definitely wasn't the sharpest knife in the drawer, Wiggins realised as he beckoned him out of the pit with a crooked forefinger. "Yes, I was hoping we could step outside, so I can discuss a little problem with you." A conspiratorial smile. "I think you might be just the person to help me with it."

Lowering his hammer, Fingers climbed out of the pit and reached for a cloth. Wiping his oily hands, he set off toward the office. "I'll need to clear it with Terry, first," he announced over his shoulder.

Wiggins sighed. He had hoped to lure the little mechanic outside before Marshall finished his telephone conversation. That way, the boys could have taken care of them, one at a time, with a minimum of fuss. Realising that this wasn't going to be possible, he withdrew his mobile phone and pressed speed dial for Casper.

"Casper, old son, can you and Basher pop inside and take care of these two grease monkeys for me... Yes, just the two of you. You can leave Mickey with the van."

Tyler had just sat down at his desk with a cup of coffee and a sandwich when his mobile phone rang. He looked at it then groaned. "There's no peace for the wicked," he told Kelly Flowers, who was sitting opposite him.

"*Boss, It's Charlie,*" the Scotsman's excited voice announced as soon as he answered. "*Me and Kev are down at the cab office in Hoxton*

Market, and we've found a couple of interesting leads that you need to know about."

Tyler took a large bite from his sandwich. "I'm all ears," he said, munching away.

"*Firstly, there's a record of a woman who gave her name as Lucinda McLean phoning in on Saturday night and booking a cab to take her down to Dunston Road. The controller on duty now was working that night, and he's confirmed that she came to the cab office with a heavy suitcase, and that Eric Hammond was the cabbie who drove her to the canal. Elvis – that's the controller – remembers taking the call. She said she would be with them in five minutes, but actually took nearer ten. And get this, he reckons she had a really deep voice.*"

Tyler grinned, exposing a mouth full of half chewed bread and cheese, which he promptly swallowed.

Lucinda McLean had a deep voice, just like Stella Carter.

"Have we managed to get an address or telephone number for her?" he asked, anticipation building as he waited for a response.

"*Yep. We've got both,*" White said, triumphantly. He rattled off the address and telephone number, so that Tyler could get the Intel cell to start researching them. "*As soon as we finish here, we'll go and recce the address.*"

"That's great news," Tyler told him. "What's the second lead?"

"*The cab office has a really good quality CCTV system, and Elvis has burned me a copy of Lucinda coming in wi' her suitcase in tow. I'm a hundred percent certain that it's the same woman from the canal towpath footage Colin showed us.*"

"Can you see her face?" Tyler asked.

"*Afraid not,*" White said, sounding disappointed. "*She didnae look towards either of the cameras, and her hair was hanging down over her face, so we havenae got a clear shot of it.*"

That was disappointing. "Have you spoken to Hammond yet?" Tyler asked, wondering if he should have him brought in for an E-fit.

"*No. We're just waiting for him to come back from a job, but he should be here any minute now.*"

In the background, Tyler heard a bell go ding-a-ling, then White was speaking again. *"Well, well, well. Speak of the devil, and all that… Boss, our wee man just walked in, so I'll have to jump off the phone."*

"Fair enough," Tyler said, "but call me back after you've spoken to him. In the meantime, I'll get Dean to run some preliminary checks on the address and telephone number you've given me."

"Can I help you?" Terry Marshall asked as he emerged from the pokey little office. His enquiring expression quickly morphed into one of alarm as Wiggins' two enforcers sauntered in and took up station on either side of their boss.

Wiggins gave him a wolf like smile. "Nah, you can't help me," he said, amiably, "but you can help yourself by being a good little boy and coming quietly."

"I ain't going nowhere, mate. Now, fuck off or I'll call the police." As he spoke, Marshall puffed out his chest in an act of defiance, but the fear in his eyes exposed the bluff for what it was.

Wiggins shook his head in mock despair, then pointed at Marshall. "Casper, be a good lad and teach this gobby little worm some manners."

As Casper lumbered forward, the colour drained from Marshall's face. "Wait," he said, hastily raising his hands to placate the advancing giant. "Can't we talk this through?"

Wiggins smiled indulgently, then said, "We'll talk later, I promise. And when we do, you'll tell me everything you know about Mr Willard's diamonds."

Confusion competed with fear on Marshall's face. "Diamonds? I don't know anything about any—"

Before he could complete the sentence, Casper charged him.

With a little squeal of fear, Marshall turned and made a desperate dash for the office.

Casper gave chase, his massive hands extended to grab him.

As he reached the office door, Marshall suddenly stopped, then jinked violently to his left, slipping under Casper's outstretched arms.

Snarling with rage, the albino's momentum propelled him into the office, where he collided with the desk, shunting it backwards into the wall.

Basher, who had remained by Wiggins' side, moved sideways to intercept Marshall. "Not so fast, you little shit," he growled, extending his arm in a clothesline manoeuvre from his wrestling days. The jarring impact lifted Marshall off his feet and sent him tumbling backwards to land in a crumpled heap on the hard concrete floor, where he groaned, rolled onto his side, and then stopped moving.

With the three men all focused on Marshall, Fingers made a run for the door.

If he hadn't collided with the shelves, knocking a load of tools onto the floor, he might have escaped unnoticed. As it was, he made enough noise to wake the dead.

Spinning around, Wiggins caught a fleeting glimpse of the mechanic's back, and then he was gone. "Mickey, stop that little shit!" he yelled, hoping the ex-squaddie was within earshot.

Glancing at the unmoving form on the floor, he turned to his two goons. "Basher, load that wanker onto the van. Casper, go and help Mickey grab the other one."

———

Slipping his mobile into his jacket pocket, Charlie White turned to address the startled looking man who had entered the cab office a few seconds earlier, and who was now being questioned by Kevin Murray.

Clad in that season's Manchester United home jersey, the skinny cab driver kept shooting furtive glances at Elvis, as though seeking reassurance that he wasn't in any trouble.

"It's Mr Hammond, isn't it?" White asked, offering his hand.

Hammond licked his lips nervously. "Yeah, that's right," he confirmed in his thick Mancunian accent.

Treating him to a friendly smile, White placed a hand on his shoulder and gently steered him back towards the door. "We're going to need a statement from you," he explained. "But first, we need to take a look in the boot of your car. Is it parked out the front?"

Hammond hesitated, then nodded. "What do you wanna look in my car for?" he demanded, skittishly. "There's nothing in it that shouldn't be there."

Leaving White to mollify him, Murray went ahead to retrieve his evidence bag from the boot of the pool car.

"You took a woman to Dunston Road on Saturday night," White explained. "She had a heavy suitcase with her, and it went in the boot of your car."

Hammond nodded in vague recollection. "Yeah, so?"

"That woman and her suitcase are of interest to us, and we need to see if there's any trace evidence from where the case has been in your car, that's all. You're no' in any trouble, and this isnae anything to worry about."

Hammond's relief was palpable. "I do remember her," he said, visibly relaxing. "Weird one, she was. Face all plastered in makeup, and her suitcase was so heavy that I nearly did myself an injury getting it in and out of the boot. Mind you," he said with a rueful smile, "she was a good tipper, I'll say that much for her."

Hammond led White over to where his red Cavalier was parked, and opened the boot, which was empty.

The interior was neat and tidy, White thought, as was the rest of the car. Hammond obviously took pride in his job.

"When was the last time you washed the motor?" Murray asked. He had slipped into a set of white overalls, and had donned nitrile gloves and a face mask.

"I put it through the car wash yesterday as it happens," Hammond said. "Looks more professional if I keep it clean."

"When was the last time you hoovered out the boot?" Murray asked.

Hammond frowned. "Not done that for a good couple of weeks," he admitted.

Murray leaned in and methodically shone his pen torch around the interior. "That's interesting," he said a few seconds later.

"There's some dark staining on the carpet. I'll Hemastix it just in case."

"Just in case of what?" Hammond asked, suddenly alarmed.

"Just in case it's blood," Murray told him.

Hammond's face blanched. "Blood! Why would there be blood in my car?"

Murray ignored him. He was too busy preparing the test.

While he did that, White borrowed the torch from him and shone the beam inside the boot. Hammond tried to take a sneak peek, but White held up a hand and waved for him to step back. "Could you just wait over there until my colleague's finished."

The carpet was a very dark colour to start with, so the staining that Murray had spotted didn't immediately jump out at him but, upon closer inspection, White was able to make out the marginally darker splodges scattered around the boot's interior.

"You did bloody well to spot that," he said, impressed.

A moment later, Murray was back by his side, holding the equipment he needed to carry out the presumptive tests. "You'll have to shine the light for me while I work," he instructed White. "I'll be swabbing several areas, starting at the back and working forwards."

Hemastix are basically reagent strips that were originally designed to test for blood in urine but, because they are so quick and easy to use, they can also be utilised to great effect as a presumptive blood test at crime scenes. The test itself is conducted by applying a drop of deionised water to the padded end of the Hemastix, and then rubbing the stain in question. It can take anything up to sixty seconds for the reaction to occur. If the test is negative, there will be no change in colour to the Hemastix; if it turns orange or green, that denotes a positive result, while blue indicates a very strong trace of blood.

Murray carried out several tests, one at the back of the boot; one at the front, and one in the middle. Within thirty seconds, all three Hemastix turned a strong shade of blue.

"Bingo!" Murray said, smiling at White from beneath his facemask.

"What does that mean?" Hammond asked, worriedly.

"It means," White said, apologetically, "that we're going to have to seize your cab and have it towed to the car pound, so that the crime scene team can properly forensicate it."

Hammond looked like he was going to cry. "But that cab's my livelihood. How am I going to make a living without it?"

Fingers instinctively turned right as he bolted out of the garage. Head down, he ran blindly, giving no real thought to where he was going. All that mattered was giving the thugs who were after him the slip.

They had to be Jonas Willard's men. There was no other explanation for it, which meant that the old man had somehow worked out that he and Dazza were responsible for the death of one of his men.

Reaching the end of the road, Fingers skidded to a halt, trying to decide whether to head left into the estate or go right and leg it through the viaduct?

The Black Horse stood directly in front of him, and he briefly considered seeking sanctuary in there, but then dismissed that idea for fear that the criminal scumbags who frequented it would hand him straight over to his pursuers.

"Fingers, you alright, mate?" a slurred voice called out, making him jump.

The sound had come from his right, and he spun in that direction to see Arthur the old Teddy Boy and his Russian mate, Vlad, staggering along the tunnel towards him, both as pissed as farts.

His stupid response to Arthur's goading the other night came rushing back. *"...Yeah, well it won't be when we sell off the diamonds..."* Grinding his teeth in anger, he realised that the old man must have sold him out to Willard's men.

Glancing back over his shoulder, Fingers spotted two of Willard's goons running full pelt towards him. The first was a slender man with short dark hair and hooded eyes. He looked fit and formidable, and there was something about his deportment that reminded Fingers of Dazza.

Another ex-squaddie, perhaps?

The second man was the lumbering albino who had attacked Marshall. Built for strength, not speed, he was lagging a good ten yards behind his fleet footed companion.

Ignoring Arthur and Vlad, who were giggling away to themselves as they beckoned him to join them for a quick pint, Fingers ran across the cobbled road and started scaling the seven-foot-high meshed fence that had been erected between the end of the pub and the start of the railway viaduct. Slinging a leg over the sharp spikes that protruded from the top, Fingers cautiously stood up, steadying himself against the viaduct wall with one hand. Swaying dangerously, he groped for a handhold in the brickwork above his head. It would be a dangerous climb, but if he could reach the top of the viaduct, some twelve feet above him, he would be able to make good his escape along the railway tracks.

Looking down, Fingers heart sank as the ex-military type sprinted across the road after him. The fucker was fast, and there was a grim determination about him that Fingers found deeply unsettling.

Taking a deep breath, and praying that he wouldn't fall and kill himself in the process, Fingers launched himself into the air, making a desperate grab for a protruding ledge a few feet above his head.

21

O ye, of little faith!

Darren McCullen was waiting to board his plane at Tenerife South – Reina Sofia – Airport. To his relief, he had managed to purchase a ticket on the early evening flight to Stansted without any trouble. Standing in line, his passport held at the ready, he slowly inched his way towards a bored looking immigration official who was giving the travel documents presented by passengers heading onto the tarmac no more than a cursory glance. Security here was a lot less strict than it had been on the way out. All airports in the UK had been placed on a heightened state of alertness as a result of the four coordinated suicide bombings that al-Qaeda terrorists had carried out in America the previous month.

It really worried him that he hadn't been able to get in touch with Fingers, to warn him that Willard was onto them. The boy was a nightmare when it came to his mobile phone, and he often forgot to take it with him when he went out, but there was no answer at the garage either, and that was most unusual.

When he'd broken the news of Carrie's death to Janice, she had been all for flying back with him, and she hadn't taken kindly to being told that he had only been able to purchase one ticket, so she would have to remain behind until her scheduled flight home the following week.

It weighed heavily on him that, at some point, he was going to have to tell Janice about the ram raids and the robbery, and the man he had killed during it. He was going to have to find a way to explain that his sister had been murdered because he had stolen from Willard, and killed one of his men in the process. What would she think of him? How could he possibly expect her to continue loving a man like that? The shame made him feel physically sick.

If he succeeded in killing Willard, he would be a wanted man, and he would have to set himself up in a country that didn't have an extradition agreement with the UK. How would she react to that? Would she go with him, or walk away in disgust? He consoled himself with the thought that, if she decided to remain by his side, they would never be short of cash, and they would be able to live out their life in exile in relative comfort. After all, with Carrie dead, their parents' house was all his. On top of that, there was his share of the 200K they had stolen from Kyle's house. By his calculations, after giving Fingers his third, he would be left with a little over 133 grand. Then there was the money he would get for the stolen gems. They had to be worth a small fortune. Hell, they might even be worth a *large* fortune!

All week long, Janice had been raving about the heat and the sunshine, and saying how, if she ever won the lottery, she would relocate to warmer climes on a permanent basis. Well, if things worked out, it looked like she was going to get her wish.

———

Clinging to the protruding ledge above his head, Fingers blinked sweat and brick dust from his eyes. He was painfully aware of his out-of-control legs swinging below him. A nervous downwards glance revealed the ex-military type thug was climbing the fence quicker than a rat going up a drainpipe. At this rate, the man would be upon him in seconds.

Somehow, Fingers' right foot stumbled across a large gap in the crumbling brickwork and, cramming his toes deep into the crevice, he was able to take some of the burden from his trembling hands.

Something hard brushed against his heel. Looking down, Fingers was horrified to see that his pursuer had now reached the top of the fence and was leaning out into space, trying to grab him.

The thug was precariously balanced, with a foot wedged either side of a series of spikes that resembled razor-sharp maple leaves. Moving slowly, and with great caution, he gradually raised himself into semi-standing position.

Fingers hoped the bastard would slip on one of the spikes and give himself a serrated metal enema.

As his pursuer lunged at him for a second time, Fingers used the crevice as a springboard, propelling himself upwards with all the strength he could muster. Thrusting his upper body onto the ledge, he clung on for all he was worth.

I've made it!

A powerful hand wrapped itself around his ankle and began pulling him back down.

"Let go of me," Fingers screamed, kicking out wildly.

The thug pulled again, much harder this time, and Fingers was dragged backwards at an alarming rate. Another tug like that and he would surely go over the edge.

Fingers lashed out in panic, kicking at the hand clamped around his ankle. Below him, there was a sudden scream of pain, and the man's grip became noticeably weaker. Another downwards stomp, and Fingers' ankle was suddenly free.

Hauling his legs onto the ledge, Fingers lay there, his chest heaving. Several seconds passed before he was able to drag himself into a standing position. Keeping his back to the wall, he risked a quick downward glance, just as his pursuer launched himself into the air and grabbed the brickwork either side of Fingers' feet.

Fingers reacted by stamping on the nearest hand, and his efforts were rewarded by a surprised scream of pain. Better still, the hand fell away, leaving its owner dangling by one arm.

"I'll kill you, you little fucker."

You've got to catch me first, Fingers thought, bringing his heel crashing down on the man's other hand.

There followed a surprised howl of anguish as his pursuer's grip was broken and the man suddenly found himself plummeting towards the pavement below.

Fingers jumped up and grabbed the metal framework of the bridge. Hauling himself over the top, he dropped down onto the train tracks and started running flat out.

With ballast crunching underfoot, Fingers stumbled along the tracks, keeping one ear cocked for pursuers, and the other for approaching trains. In the distance, he spotted a staircase that appeared to lead back down to ground level, and he wearily made his way towards it.

The metal stairs clanged as he hurtled down them, and he winced at the noise, afraid that it might draw unwanted attention.

Seconds later, he found himself in Hemmings Street. There was no sign of his pursuers, so he cut through the side streets, making his way towards Bethnal Green Road.

He had to assume that they knew where he lived, so he couldn't risk going back home, but he had an elderly aunt who only lived a few streets away, and she would let him stay with her for a few days, while he figured out what to do.

All in all, it had been a pretty good day, Tyler thought as he wrote up his Decision Log. Despite his initial fears that this case might turn into a sticker, they were making really good progress, and he was becoming increasingly confident of solving it.

They could now prove that Carrie's killer, a woman calling herself Lucinda McLean, had taken a cab from Easy Cars in Hoxton to Dunston Road on Saturday night. Dragging her heavy suitcase behind her, she had then walked along the canal path. They had captured both events on CCTV.

He was toying with the idea of having an E-fit composite created from the combined descriptions of the cab office staff, although none of the men had managed to get a good look at her face. Hammond, who had spent more time with her than any of the others, had unhelpfully suggested they should circulate an image of a stick insect with The Joker's face on it.

The positive result from the Hemastix testing Murray had carried out in Hammond's boot was promising, and the Cavalier had been lifted to Charlton Car Pound, where it would be forensically examined the following day. Tyler was quietly confident that the blood in the boot would match Carrie's DNA profile.

Hammond was understandably upset about the seizure, but there was nothing they could do about that. Hopefully, his insurance would cover the hiring of an alternative vehicle until it was returned. If not, it would serve him right for making stupid comments about circulating drawings of stick insects with the faces of comic book villains.

Annoyingly, but unsurprisingly, the address and telephone numbers that Lucinda McLean had supplied the cab company with had turned out to be fictitious. Tyler suspected the name was, too.

He had instructed Reg Parker to obtain subscriber and billing details for all incoming calls to Easy Cars between 8 p.m. and 9 p.m. on Saturday night. Once that information was available, Tyler planned to dispatch officers to each of the callers' addresses in the hope that one of them would belong to the mysterious Lucinda.

They had established that precisely eight minutes had elapsed between Lucinda ordering the cab and arriving at Easy Cars. Calculations were being carried out to determine the distance an average person walking at normal speed could travel in that time, which would give them the radius between the dismemberment site and the cab office and show them where to focus their efforts.

The phone on his desk burst into life, shattering his train of thought.

"DCI Tyler."

"Boss, it's Paul Horley over at Eagle House. Wasn't sure you'd still be in the office, but thought I'd give it a try, just in case." Horley was the Flying Squad DI investigating the ram raids.

Tyler chuckled. "Paul, I'll probably still be here at midnight, the way this job is going. What can I do for you?"

"As you know, we didn't get any matches for the wearer DNA we obtained from the crash helmet and overalls the local plod recovered when the ram raiders decamped at West Ham station a couple of weeks ago."

Tyler responded with a noncommittal grunt. He did know that, and he had suggested that the Flying Squad resubmit them for a familial test, but this hadn't been actioned as far as he knew.

As if reading his mind, Horley chuckled. *"Anyway, as the bastards tried to blow your brains out, which means we're looking at the attempted murder of a police officer in addition to armed robbery, I eventually decided to follow your advice and re-submit them for a familial search."*

Generally speaking, whenever a DNA sample was run through the National DNA Database – which had been given the ever so catchy acronym, NDNAD – the computer was only instructed to search for exact matches. However, by extending the search parameters, it was also possible to identify people in the system who shared some, but not all, of the genetic markers being sought – in other words, relatives of the test subject.

It worked like this: Human beings share one half of their genes with their father and the other half with their mother, so a familial search for a male relative yielding a match of sixteen markers would indicate a 99.9 per cent probability that the two individuals were father and son. If a significant number of markers – but less than fifty per cent– matched, it would suggest that they were related, but not as father and son.

"Anyway, the result just came in and, guess what…?"

"Don't tell me you got a hit?" Tyler said, feeling a jolt of excitement sizzle his veins.

"We did," Horley confirmed, and Tyler could almost hear the smile in his voice.

"And here's the weird part…" Horley stopped speaking long enough

to hum the theme from *The Twilight Zone* "...*It looks like the suspect's connected to the murder you're working on.*"

Tyler sat up straight. "In what way?" he asked, not liking the sound of that.

"*Your victim's name's Carrie McCullen, right?*"

"That's right," Tyler responded with studied neutrality.

"*She has a twin brother called Aidan, right?*"

"Again right. Again, why?"

"*There's a close familial match between the wearer DNA we recovered from the overalls and Aidan McCullen, whose DNA is on record as a result of his various drug convictions. Not enough matching markers for it to be his dad, mind you, but it could easily be a brother or an uncle.*"

Tyler's brow furrowed as he tried to recall the family tree from Carrie's research docket. "I don't think there are any uncles," he said. "In fact, I think his brother, Darren, is the only surviving male relative Aidan has. At least, he's the only one that we know of."

"*I don't suppose you've researched Darren McCullen, have you?*" Horley asked. If a docket already existed, it would save him from having to commission one.

"No, sorry. He flew out to Tenerife with his girlfriend, Janice something-or-other, on the day that Carrie was killed, so he can't be a suspect in her murder."

"*When are they due back?*" Horley asked.

"They're not due back until next Friday, which is...." Tyler's eyes shot to the calendar on his desk. "...the nineteenth."

"*I don't suppose you have a description of him, and a current home address, do you?*"

"I'm pretty sure all of that will be in the system," Tyler said, confidently. "Give me ten minutes to cobble everything we've got together, and I'll call you back."

"*Cheers, boss. In the meantime, I'll get someone here to start drafting an All-Ports Warning. That way, he can be detained when he flies back into the country. The good news, if he's not due back until next Friday, is that there's no panic to get it up and running.*"

They both knew it could easily take a couple of days for the

Home Office to get the All-Ports Warning circulated at their end, so that a detention marker would flash up at immigration control when Darren McCullen presented his passport for examination.

"Will you get a ticket to spin his drum while he's away, or wait until he comes back and search it under Section 18 after you've nicked him?"

"*Haven't decided yet,*" Horley said. "*I suppose, with him out of the country, there's no real rush. If there's any evidence in his flat, it isn't going anywhere. Besides, if we get a warrant to turn the place over now, it might alert the moped rider, and we still don't know who he is.*"

"Well, good luck," Tyler said. "Make sure you keep me in the loop."

———

The van pulled up outside *The Black Horse* and Basher jumped out. He frowned when he saw Mickey writhing around on the floor, clutching his ankle. Standing beside him, Casper watched on, unmoved by his suffering.

"What happened to the grease monkey who did a runner?" Basher asked, opening the side door to reveal the unconscious form of Terry Marshall inside.

"The fucker got away," Casper growled. Hauling Mickey to his feet, he shoved him into the van, making impatient tutting noises as the ex-squaddie gingerly lowered himself onto the bench seat traversing the back.

Mickey's face contorted with pain as he tucked his injured hand under his armpit. "Any chance I can sit up front?" he pleaded, "only I think my wrist might be broken."

"No," Casper said, and slammed the door shut.

"Where to?" Basher asked as Casper clambered into the passenger seat beside him, making the van rock under his weight.

Casper shot him a venomous look, as if it were Basher's fault that things had gone pear shaped. "Let's do a quick circuit and see if we can pick that little twat up," he suggested. "If not, we'll take this one—" he jerked a thumb over his shoulder at Marshall "—back to the warehouse."

As the van pulled away, Casper's phone started ringing. "Yeah?" he said, after pressing the green button. He listened for a few moments, and then a nasty smile lit up his pale face. "Be there in five," he said. Hanging up, he turned to Basher. "Right, Fred's just spotted our boy waiting at a bus stop in Bethnal Green Road. He wants you to drop me off so I can join him, then you're to get this piece of shit straight back to the warehouse."

The Major Incident Room – or MIR as it was more commonly referred to – was where all the information and documentation coming into an enquiry was processed, evaluated and subsequently stored. Everything was entered into a database called HOLMES, an acronym that stood for Home Office Large Major Enquiry System. It was, in essence, an ingenious electronic filing cabinet that was capable of searching and cross referencing data at the press of a button.

Tyler was sitting in the MIR with Dillon, Steve Bull and Chris Deakin, going through all the actions yet to be allocated. It was a laborious task, and it wasn't being made any easier by Bear looming over them while he filmed their conversation.

"Cut!" Imogen said, interrupting Tyler halfway through a sentence.

He glared at her, took a deep breath, and then calmly continued what he was saying. "So, once that's done, we can kill any remaining actions to do with processing Carrie's house as a crime scene."

"Sorry, Jack," Imogen said, pulling a pained expression and wringing her hands together contritely. "Would you mind saying that again for me while Bear films you from a different angle?" She gave him an ingratiating smile that just made her look constipated.

Tyler harrumphed. "Fine," he said, and waited patiently until Bear had found a more suitable location on the opposite side of the room before repeating it all over again.

"Perfect," Imogen said, beaming at him. "You have a very strong presence on camera," she added.

Tyler ignored the compliment, convinced that she was only trying to butter him up.

They all looked up as Paul Evans came rushing in. His face was flushed, and he was slightly out of breath.

"There you are," he said on spotting Tyler. "I've been looking everywhere for you."

Tyler spread his arms, smiled magnanimously. "Well, now that you've found me, what can I do for you?"

Evans held up a VHS tape. "This is the CCTV from *The Merry Fiddler* for last Friday night," he said, waving it about triumphantly. "You're definitely going to want to see what's on it."

Tyler was intrigued. "Best you set it up to play, then," he suggested.

Evans led them all back to the main office, where he commandeered the TV-video combo, which had been tuned to the Sky News channel.

Tyler grabbed a seat and pulled it close to the TV. Dillon, Bull, and Deakin joined him there.

Bear padded across the room with his camera at the ready, while Imogen stood directly behind him, so that she could whisper instructions while he was filming.

Puzzled by the sudden flurry of activity, pretty much everyone else in the room wandered over to see what was going on. Ian Yule and Jim Cuthbert, two of the officers assisting from team six, had been chatting to Dean Fletcher in the Intel Cell but, like everyone else, they tagged along. "What's going on?" Yule asked.

Bull shrugged. "Apparently, we've had a development with the CCTV."

Smothering a smile, Tyler noticed that Yule's jacket and trousers belonged to the same suit today; even his socks matched.

Standing beside the TV, Evans inserted the tape, then grabbed the remote. "This footage is from inside *The Merry Fiddler* pub at 19:00 hours on Friday night," he explained, pressing the play button.

As the screen burst into life, he pointed towards a door that had just opened to admit a pretty woman with a voluptuous figure. She was dressed in tight black trousers, a sparkling red blouse, and a black leather jacket, and she was carrying a Bottega Veneta bag. "That's Carrie McCullen entering the pub," he told them.

Everyone instinctively leaned closer; they had all seen the photographs of Carrie's dismembered torso and severed limbs, but this was their first look at the person she had been.

Tyler made a mental note of the clothing Carrie was wearing. As soon as the showing was over, he would ring George, who was still down at her address, and ask him to check through her belongings to see if any of it was there. If it was, it would tell them that she had returned home prior to her murder.

On screen, a smiling Carrie wandered over to a group of five other women, all of a similar age, who were sitting at a table towards the rear of the pub. They all seemed pleased to see her, smiling and waving excitedly. One of them stood up, gave her a big hug and then planted a great big smacker on her cheek.

"The woman who just hugged her is Trisha Perkins," Evans said. "According to Sharon Peacock, who I took a statement off earlier today, she was Carrie's new love interest."

Stepping away from Perkins, Carrie sat at the table with her back to the door.

"Right," Evans said, fast forwarding the footage. "I'm going to skip forward half an hour, to 19:30 hours."

When the tape resumed playing, Evans tapped the screen with his finger. "Now, pay attention to the woman who comes in, has a quick nose around, and then leaves."

As he finished speaking, a scrawny white woman with short dark hair, wearing a battered bomber jacket, faded jeans and bovver boots, entered through the same door that Carrie had used.

Tyler recognised her instantly, from the mug shot Dean had shown them of Stella Carter.

So, that's what she looks like in the flesh.

"That's Carter," Dillon blurted out beside him.

On screen, Stella crossed to the middle of the pub, then ran her eyes over the various tables, until they came to rest on the one Carrie and her friends occupied. The anger on her face was clear for all to see, Tyler thought, but there was something else too; a look of betrayal. She spent several seconds clenching and unclenching her fists while staring daggers at her former lover, then spun around and stormed out of the pub.

"Well, the fact that Carter's still got short hair is a bit of a bummer," Steve declared, sounding thoroughly miserable. "It means she can't possibly be the same woman who approached Joan Spinney after she left work, or the woman who dumped Carrie's torso into the canal."

"Not necessarily," Tyler cautioned. "Her general physique's the same, so she could have been wearing a wig to disguise herself in the other clips."

Dillon considered this. "Hmmm, maybe it's worth calling in that gait expert after all?" he suggested. "You know, to compare the way that the women in the various clips walk."

"Well, I didn't think you wanted him to compare the size of their noses," Tyler said with a grin.

"Is that it?" Deakin asked, sounding disappointed.

The Welshman shook his head as he ejected the tape, then grinned mischievously. "O ye, of little faith!" He deftly inserted another VHS cassette into the machine. "I'm now going to play you two clips from a local authority camera in Westgate Street. It covers the pub entrance, and you can also see sections of London Fields and Broadway Market. This first clip is timed at 19:28 hours."

Evans pressed play, then tapped the top right of the screen with his pen, where a moped was parked on a public footpath at the entrance to London Fields. "That's Carter, sitting on the moped."

As they watched, she removed her crash helmet and ran a hand through her short dark hair. Sliding off the moped a moment later, she left the helmet on the seat and crossed to the pub. She was only inside for a couple of minutes, then she came back out and walked back to her moped.

Evans fast forwarded the tape. "Basically, she sat on her moped until closing time, which is when Carrie and her friends left the pub.

That's the clip I'm going to show you now, and it's timed at 23:00 hours."

He pressed play, and the screen flickered into life to reveal a group of women spilling out of the pub. Standing in a huddle, they seemed to take ages to say goodnight to each other.

"You'll notice that Stella's still sitting on her moped, watching them," Evans pointed out.

She was, and she had put her helmet back on, so Carrie wouldn't have recognised her, even if she had bothered to look in that direction, which she didn't.

After a while, three of the women peeled off, heading towards Well Street, leaving Carrie and Trish behind. After waving them off, Carrie slipped an arm around Trish's waist, and the pair of them sauntered off towards the market. They didn't seem to be in any hurry, and were laughing and smiling, as if they were really enjoying each other's company.

It was sad, Tyler thought, that Carrie's happiness was due to be short lived, and that, before the night was out, she would be brutally murdered.

A few moments after the two lovebirds disappeared into Broadway Market, Carter kickstarted her moped, and followed them.

Evans killed the tape. "I managed to speak to Trish Perkins earlier," he informed Tyler. "She reckons that they walked as far as the cab office at the end of the market. From there, they got a cab back to Pitfield Street."

"Did Trish say anything about being followed?" Tyler asked.

Evans shook his head, emphatically. "No, but they were probably too wrapped up in each other to notice anyone else."

"What happened when the cab dropped them off?" Dillon enquired.

"Trish is staying at her mum's flat in Clinger Court, which is where the cab dropped them off." Evans explained. "She reckons they had a little kiss and cuddle, but decided against seeing each other again as Trish is going back to Devon in a couple of weeks, so there was no hope of a long-term relationship. The last time she saw Carrie, she was walking along Pitfield Street towards Ivy Street. It's not far, only a few hundred yards away."

"Have you taken a statement from her yet?" Tyler asked.

Evans shook his head. "I've arranged to do it tomorrow morning," he said.

22

Welcome back to the UK

The van pulled up outside the old warehouse, which was located on an industrial estate on the outskirts of Barking. Leaving the engine running, Basher jumped out and undid the padlock securing the two heavy metal shutters for the loading bay, then pulled them apart until there was a gap wide enough for the van to be driven through.

Once the van was safely tucked away inside, he closed the shutters behind him. After locking them from the inside, he crossed to the cluster of ancient light switches and clanked them all down. After much flickering and some very unhealthy clicking sounds, the fluorescent strip lighting twenty odd feet above his head burst into life. Filled with the bodies of countless dead insects, they illuminated the bay in a dull yellow glow.

Several identical vans to the one Basher had just driven inside were parked up. Unlike his, they had all been reversed in so that their back doors were level with the raised walkaround area that was used for unloading.

When Basher yanked open the side door, Mickey was sitting there with a face like a smacked arse. Terry Marshall was still lying face down on the floor, but his hands and feet were now tightly bound with gaffer tape. He looked up as the door opened, and Basher saw that his face was tearstained. "What's the matter with him?" he asked.

Mickey hobbled out of the van, testing his injured ankle before putting any weight on it.

"I had to give him a bit of a slap because he wouldn't stop whinging."

Basher tutted. "Bit harsh, innit? Hitting a bloke who's tied up."

"It was alright for you, sitting up front with the radio on," Mickey said, defensively. "You didn't have this spineless wanker doing your head in."

"Yeah, well, cut him a bit of slack. He'll be dead soon."

Marshall started crying at the mention of his impending doom.

"Shut up!" Mickey snarled, leaning into the van.

Basher placed a restraining hand on his arm. "Temper, temper. C'mon, let's get him into one of Casper's little holding rooms, and then we can have ourselves a nice cup of tea."

"I could murder a brew," Mickey said, longingly.

Basher chuckled. "Me too." He nodded at the mewling figure in the back of the van. "And then we can murder him."

"What is it?" Wiggins said, clamping his phone to his ear. Driving one handed, he pointed at the stereo with his eyes.

Sitting next to him, Casper took the hint and turned the volume down.

"It's me," his man on the inside said, speaking hurriedly. *"I need to be quick, so listen. It's definitely looking like Stella Carter's the one who murdered Carrie. We've got her on CCTV, following Carrie to the pub, then waiting for her to leave. Mr Tyler's pulling out all the stops to find her, so you had better move quickly if you want to get your hands on her before he does."*

"Don't you worry about that," Wiggins assured him, then added, "I take it he still doesn't know where she lives?"

"*No. They haven't got a clue, so you've probably got a couple of days before they track her down.*"

Hanging up, Wiggins turned thoughtfully to Casper. "We've got a slight problem."

The albino arched an eyebrow, said nothing. His job was to follow orders, not find solutions to problems.

"Remember that bitch who gave Carrie such a hard time after being dumped?"

Casper frowned for a moment, trying to recall her name, then nodded slowly.

"Well, it looks like she's the one who topped Carrie, which means we're gonna have to nab her before the Cozzers do, or Mr Willard will be most displeased."

Casper licked his lips. "Can I hurt her this time?"

Wiggins held up a warning finger. "I don't mind you being a bit rough with her," he said sternly, "but Mr Willard wants to have the pleasure of dispatching her himself, so don't go overboard. And, whatever you do, don't mark her face. Got it?"

Casper nodded, obediently. "When do you want me to go after her?"

Wiggins glanced sideways. "Let's sort these two grease monkeys out first, then you can grab the psycho bitch in the morning."

Casper's eyes glazed over in anticipation.

A few seconds later, the Audi pulled up outside the loading bay, and Wiggins gave two short honks of his horn to let Basher know he was there.

Almost immediately, the metal shutters began to concertina open.

The warehouse was owned by a building company that Willard had controlling shares in. It was mainly used as a storage facility, but there was a self-contained unit at the rear that was strictly off limits to the day-to-day staff who worked there. Not even the site manager had keys to access that part of the building.

The off-limits area had been specially configured to act as a mini prison, and it contained three holding cells, an office with its own kitchenette, and a long, sterile torture chamber where anyone who had been stupid enough to step out of line could be properly punished or – if their transgression merited a more severe response – permanently eradicated.

As soon as the shutters had opened wide enough, Wiggins reversed the Audi in and parked up next to the Ford Transit.

"All go according to plan, Fred?" Basher asked as he pulled the shutters together.

Wiggins smiled. The naive little mechanic had lowered his guard the moment he boarded the bus, convinced that the danger had passed. They had followed it at a safe distance, biding their time until he got off. Casper had then tailed him through the side streets, keeping in touch via their phones. That had enabled Wiggins to get ahead of him, and they had jumped him as he cut through a darkened alley.

"It couldn't have gone smoother," Wiggins said, as Casper hauled the boy from the boot and started dragging him towards the corridor that led down to the holding cells.

―――

Fingers' eyelids flickered open, but there seemed to be three of everything in front of him. Trying to focus only made matters worse. Afraid that he was going to throw up, he scrunched his eyes shut for a couple of seconds, then cautiously tried again. Things were less blurry, but his mind was too numb to process the constant stream of information his senses were bombarding it with. He felt confused, disorientated by his surroundings.

He was being dragged along a dimly lit corridor with concrete walls.

Was this a prison?

Had he been arrested?

He vaguely remembered getting off the bus after escaping from the garage. There was a fleeting image of him cutting through the alley that led to the road his aunt lived in, and then…

Oh God!

A feeling of abject terror washed over him as everything came flooding back.

Halfway down the alley, he had suddenly become aware of someone running up to him from behind. He had spun around to confront what he assumed were muggers, and that was when the terrible pain had exploded inside the back of his skull, sending the world around him into sudden, total darkness.

"Ah, you're awake, are you, old son?" a friendly voice enquired of him. The sound reverberated off the walls.

A moment later, the smiling face of the suited dandy who had approached him in the garage appeared above him, looking down. "Between you and me, I thought you were going to be out for a lot longer than this," the dandy informed him, conversationally. He glanced sideways, nodding to someone standing just beyond Fingers' vision. "Casper here, hit you quite hard, didn't you, old son?"

Had he detected a note of rebuke in the dandy's voice?

Fingers' eyelids were suddenly very heavy, and a warm fuzzy feeling washed over him.

"Oh dear," he heard the dandy say. "I think I might have tempted fate by…"

The rest of the sentence was lost on Fingers, who had already lapsed back into unconsciousness.

Crying silently to himself, Marshall sat on the edge of a slim cot that was bolted to the wall of his tiny cell. There was no mattress or bedding, just a metal frame with jagged screws around the edges. The springs of the frame were digging into the soft flesh of his legs and buttocks, but it was better than the alternative, which was sitting on the cold concrete floor.

After getting him out of the van, they had half carried, half dragged him to a hidden recess at the far end of the loading bay. Opening a metal door, they had taken him along a dark corridor, into a brightly lit rectangular room. There was no furniture in it, and the walls and floor appeared to have been scrubbed clean because the place had the same antiseptic smell of a hospital corridor.

Looking around, he had noticed a large, wall mounted circular hose on the far wall. At first, he had thought that was odd, but then he had noticed the concrete floor sloped down gently from the walls towards the centre of the room, where two metal drains had been installed for water to run into. Why the room should need a hose and a drainage system had been completely beyond him.

Making him stand in the centre of the room, right between the two drain covers, they had forced him to undress, laughing at his obvious embarrassment, and his pathetic attempts to hide his shrivelled manhood from them. Once they were happy that he wasn't concealing anything, they had allowed him to put his underpants back on, although that was the only garment he was permitted to wear. They had forced him to stand there in the freezing cold for what seemed like hours, but had probably only been minutes. He had spent that time pleading with them, begging them to release him, and swearing on his honour that he wouldn't go to the police or tell anyone else what had happened.

They had just stared at him in frigid silence, mocking him with their eyes.

Then, the one with the injured wrist – the one called Mickey – had proceeded to hose him down with a powerful jet of ice-cold water. Marshall had been driven back into the far corner by its power, and he had cowered there, enduring the relentless onslaught for several minutes.

Whenever Marshall had cried out for them to stop, the water had been turned off immediately, but then the bald-headed bruiser had beaten him about the arms and legs with a long rattan cane until he fell to the floor. The fat man had then waded into him with a series of savage kicks, shouting for him to get to his feet. As soon as Marshall complied, his attacker had retreated, and the water torture had resumed.

After the third time of calling out, Marshall had learned to keep his mouth shut.

By the time they had finished with him, Marshall's entire body had been covered in a criss-cross network of livid red welts, and he had been so exhausted that he could no longer stand unaided. That was when they had thrown him, dripping wet, into the windowless room he now found himself trapped in. Their parting words had been a grim warning that he should think very carefully about what he told them when the questions started.

"W–when w–will that b–be?" he had sobbed, his entire body shivering violently from cold and exhaustion.

The big, bald-headed man had responded with a blasé shrug. "Mr Wiggins'll be here when he's good and ready. If you know what's good for you, you'll tell him exactly what he wants to know. If not…" He had shaken his head, as though the alternative were too terrible to contemplate.

The door had been slammed in Marshall's face, plunging the tiny room into darkness, and he had been left alone to ponder his fate.

He had no idea how much time had passed since then. It could have been minutes; it could have been days. Wrapping his arms around his battered body, Marshall gritted his teeth together to stop them from chattering. Every inch of his body was throbbing in pain, and he really didn't think he would be able to survive another round of their inhumane punishment.

The worst thing was, Marshall had absolutely no idea where they had taken him, or why he was there. All he knew was that he was in deep, *deep* shit, through no fault of his own.

Groping around in the dark, hoping to find something he could use as a weapon, he came across a plastic bucket. At first, he wondered what it was doing there, but then it dawned on him that this was his latrine, should he need to go to the toilet.

From somewhere outside his cell, there came the harsh metallic sound of a door being unlocked. Then came the sound of footsteps, slow and plodding.

They stopped by the next cell along to his.

A man began talking, his words muffled but his tone jovial and friendly. The voice didn't belong to either of the thugs who had brought him there. Putting the bucket down, Marshall stood up, wincing at the effort. Moving awkwardly, he limped over to the heavy door and placed an ear against it.

The voice came again, and the words were just about discernible as the man outside said, "Oh dear, I think I might have tempted fate by speaking too quickly…"

———

The flight from Tenerife had been a total nightmare from start to finish. As Darren walked into the arrivals' hall at London Stansted Airport, feeling utterly exhausted, the relief of having landed safely was palpable.

He should have that known it was going to be a bad trip when the family from hell plonked themselves down in the seats directly behind his. Loud, annoying, with two young kids who were unable to sit still for more than five seconds at a time, they had already driven him to distraction by the time the plane taxied along the runway.

He could forgive the brat who had deafened him with its ear-piercing screams during take-off and landing; the changes in cabin air pressure affected some people very badly. What he couldn't forgive was the non-stop fidgeting, the constant complaining, and the way the little shit sitting behind him had repeatedly kicked the back of his seat during the flight. If it hadn't been for the fact that Darren couldn't afford to draw any unwanted attention to himself, he would have turned around and threatened to strangle the useless father if he didn't pull his finger out and get his offspring under control.

And then there had been the turbulence; Darren had never experienced anything like it. He had ridden smoother rollercoasters.

The screams of frightened passengers had resonated up and down the plane, and even the normally smiling cabin crew had seemed unusually tense.

Of course, the kids behind him had cried and kicked out in fear, and their useless mother had been terribly airsick, spewing her guts up as the aircraft repeatedly dropped through air pockets and was buffeted all over the place, rocking, dropping and shuddering as if it was about to fall out of the sky.

"Good evening, sir. Where have you travelled from today?" the immigration officer asked when he presented his passport.

"I'm flying in from Tenerife," Darren said, wearily.

The officer checked the personal details page for a watermark, then studied the photograph and compared it to Darren's face. "Good trip, was it?" he asked, sliding the travel document into a machine for it to read the electronic biodata it contained.

"Lovely," Darren said, accepting his passport back.

"Welcome back to the UK," the immigration officer said, already assessing the next passenger in line. "Have a safe onward journey."

"So, I've identified Stella Carter's old telephone number and ordered three months' worth of data for it, but I don't think it's going to help us," Reg said. "I've also managed to get copies of the voicemail messages that had been left on Carrie's phone. Four are from Aidan, and one is from Darren, but there's nothing in them that would help us identify her murderer."

"Pity," Tyler said, sounding disappointed.

Reg was keen to press on. "Let's get to the exciting stuff. As you know, even though Lucinda McLean gave a him false telephone number, the cab controller logged the exact time of her call. Having gone through the incoming call data for the cab office, I've identified that the call was made from a mobile ending in 657."

Tyler arched an eyebrow, impressed. "That was quick work. Have you put in a subscriber check for it yet?"

"I have," Reg confirmed, "and I used Mr Holland's name to have it fast tracked, so I've already got the result."

"Please tell me you have a name and address for me," Tyler implored him.

"I'd love to," Reg said with a sad smile, "but I haven't. The number belongs to an unregistered Pay As You Go SIM."

A Subscriber Identity Module – commonly referred to as a SIM card – is a tiny chip that acts as the phone's brain. A mobile phone telephone number is attributed to this, and not the handset.

Tyler flopped back in his chair, swore under his breath. He should have known this was going nowhere; whenever Reggie had a big reveal to make, he always made a habit of dragging the proceedings out for as long as possible before finally spilling the beans.

"Well, that was a bit of an anti-climax," Tyler grumbled, unable to hide his disappointment.

A cryptic smile crept across Reggie's cherubic face. "I've not finished yet," he said, insinuating there was more to come.

Ah, so he *was* doing his usual grandstanding, Tyler thought. "I haven't got time for this, Reggie," he said, sternly.

Reggie chuckled, swatted the rebuke aside. "You always say that." He slid a sheet of paper onto Tyler's desk.

"What's this?" Tyler asked, scooping it up. The document contained the name and address of a shop – a mini-market from the sound of it – in Hackney.

"I asked my contact at the TIU to speak to the service provider for me, and he got them to check their distribution records to see if we could identify where the SIM was sold."

There followed an annoying pause while Reggie let the excitement build. It was infuriating, but Tyler bit his tongue, knowing it would only take longer if he started getting all gnarly with him.

"Turns out it was one of a batch that was sent to a mini-market in Hoxton at the beginning of the month," Reggie announced, triumphantly. "Our suspect purchased the SIM for the 657 number from the address in your hand on Saturday morning."

Tyler beamed at Reggie, instantly forgiving his irritating flair for the dramatic. Scooping up his phone, he jabbed in the five-digit internal number for Steve Bull, then waited impatiently for the phone to be answered. "Stevie, Jack Tyler here. I need you to rustle up a couple of people to shoot straight down to a mini-market in Hackney... Why? Because it's where Lucinda McLean purchased a SIM card for the mobile she used to ring Easy Cars on Saturday night... Yes, of course it's bloody urgent!"

He hung up, shook his head. *Is it urgent?* What a daft question!

"You've done well," he said, smiling up at Reggie.

"Oh, I've done better then well," his preening phones expert asserted with a distinct lack of modesty. "After the subscriber check results came in, I got to thinking. Why just buy a SIM card, and not get a handset to go with it as well?" He looked at Tyler expectedly, and the twinkle in his eye made it clear that he wanted his boss to answer the question for him.

"Because she already had a handset to put it in?" Tyler suggested, after a moment's reflection.

Reggie's face broke into an enormous grin. "That's right," he said, approvingly. "The question is, whose handset was she using?"

As the penny dropped, Tyler sat bolt upright, snapped his fingers. "You think she put the new SIM in Carrie's handset to make the call?"

"I don't think," Reg said, solemnly. "I know."

Tyler spread his arms in perplexity. "How could you possibly know that?"

Reg was in his element now. "Carrie was tied into a two-year monthly contract with her phone, which meant that I was able to obtain her handset details through the service provider. Then, it was a simple matter of running a cross network search to see if it had ever been used with any other SIM cards, and..." he let the sentence taper off.

"And this revealed that the SIM for the 657 number had been used with Carrie's handset on Saturday night," Tyler said, filling in the blanks.

"Voilà!"

Tyler shook his head in awe. "Reggie, you're a star," he said, mock bowing to show his appreciation.

"It was nothing," Reg said, lapping the praise up.

Something was wrong.

The shutters to McCullen's Garage had been pulled down, but neither of the padlocks had been applied, and the alarm hadn't been set either. If it had been, the little light on top of the alarm box would have been flashing blue. Fingers was the most conscientious bloke he had even known, and he would *never* have left the garage without first making sure it was properly secured.

Darren's hand instinctively sought out the butt of the Browning Hi-Power tucked into the rear waistband of his jeans. After satisfying himself that no one was watching the place, he stepped out of the shadows and hurriedly crossed to the garage, keeping his head down as he walked.

Raising the shutters as quietly as he could, he ducked beneath them as soon as they were waist high. With a final glance back into the street, to make sure that no one had seen him, he pulled them back down, then groped his way over to the lights and turned them on.

A VW van was raised above one of the service pits, which immediately rang alarm bells inside his head. Fingers knew better than to leave a vehicle up there overnight.

Darren tiptoed over to the office, and saw that the desk had been rammed up against the shelves behind it, and a load of invoices had been scattered all over the floor. Either it had been ransacked or a fight had taken place in there. Willard's men had obviously beaten him there, but what had they done to Fingers and Terry?

After catching the Stansted Express back to London, Darren had picked up his car from Oberon House and then driven straight to the nearby allotments where he had buried the two handguns. The money and jewels from the robbery were buried there too, but they were in a separate hole.

Darren had dug up both bags.

He had hidden the diamonds and cash beneath the spare wheel of his car. They should be safe enough there, at least in the short term. From the other plastic bag, Darren had removed the pistol that Fingers had carried during the robbery, before returning the gun he had shot Frank Kyle with to its hole, praying that it would never be found.

The army had taught him to take good care of his weapons so, upon returning to his car, he had field-stripped and cleaned the handgun. Satisfied that the Browning would work without jamming when the need arose, he had placed it inside the glove compartment for ease of access.

After leaving the allotments, he had driven first to Fingers' flat, and then to Marshall's. Both men lived alone, but there had been no answer at either address, and their neighbours claimed not to have seen them since they had left for work that morning. The garage had been his last hope of finding them safe and well. Not knowing what else to do, Darren set the alarm and locked up.

As he was leaving, the old hippy who made wicker furniture in the next unit along stuck his head out and beckoned him over. The man's name was Vince, although with his shoulder length silver hair, unkempt beard and bulging eyes, he had always reminded Darren of the seventies TV character, Catweazle. An assortment of beads hung from Vince's neck, tattoos took up every inch of available skin on his arms, and a large spliff protruded from the corner of his mouth at a jaunty angle.

"Oi, Dazza, what the fuck went on in your garage earlier?" he demanded, blowing a long tendril of greenish smoke into the evening air.

"What do you mean?" Darren asked, feigning ignorance.

The old man gave his knotted hair a vigorous scratch. "I was getting ready to make a delivery a few hours ago, when Fingers bolted out of the garage. Poor sod looked like he was bricking himself, and there were two proper dodgy looking blokes hot on his heels." Vince gave him a sly grin. "What was that all about? Has he been shagging one of your customer's wives or something?"

"Dunno, mate," Darren said, shrugging his shoulders. "I've just got back from abroad, so I haven't seen him yet."

"Well, I wouldn't worry too much," the old man said, seeing the look of worry that had appeared on Darren's face. "Fingers took off like a rocket, so I doubt they managed to catch him." With a friendly nod, he turned to go back into the warmth of his unit. "Tell the randy sod to keep his pecker in his trousers from now on," he said over his shoulder.

"Just a minute, Vince," Darren said, placing a hand on his bony shoulder. "What did they look like, the two geezers who were chasing him?"

The old man frowned thoughtfully. "Let me see," he said stroking his bristly chin. "One was just a normal sized bloke, fit looking, hard face. The other was a fucking monster, with white hair and pale skin."

Darren felt his breath catch in his throat. The second male had to be Casper Wright, Fred Wiggins' psychotic albino enforcer.

"What about Terry Marshall?" Darren asked. "Was he there when all this was going on?"

"Dunno," the old man said, indifferently. "I didn't see him, and the garage was closed up by the time I got back from making my deliveries."

Feeling deeply troubled, and praying that Fingers and Terry were okay, Darren returned to his car to try and work out his next move. If Willard's men had captured them, they would undoubtedly torture them to find out where the diamonds were.

The sad thing was, Fingers had no idea where Darren had hidden the cash and the jewels, so he had nothing useful to give Willard. Ironically, even if he had known, Darren had already dug them up.

As upset as Darren was about Fingers, he felt even worse about Terry Marshall; the bloke was a gobshite and a wanker, but he didn't deserve to die because of that. Willard's people wouldn't believe him when he protested his innocence and, by the time they figured out that he was actually telling the truth, he would be a battered and broken wreck of a man. And then he would be dead.

Killing an innocent man wouldn't bother Willard or his cronies; all they would care about was making sure the murder couldn't be traced back to them.

In a moment of weakness, Darren wondered if he should just catch the first available plane back to Tenerife now that he had the cash and the jewels, purchase a couple of fake passports for himself and Janice, and go into hiding. Then he remembered his vow to avenge his sister, and fire burned in his stomach.

23

SATURDAY 13TH OCTOBER 2001

A human jigsaw puzzle, minus some of the pieces

Stella Carter studied her raw-boned figure in the full-length mirror in her bedroom. While some women were fortunate enough to have curves in all the right places, she didn't have curves *anywhere*. The first girl that she had ever gone out with, after officially coming out in her mid-teens, had told Stella that she had nipples like mosquito bites and a bum like a deflated balloon. The spiteful observation, intended to be hurtful because Stella had just broken up with her, hadn't bothered her in the slightest; she was what she was and she couldn't change that.

Likewise, when people had taunted her about her sexuality or her boyish appearance over the years, or used hateful, demeaning slurs like dyke or rug muncher, their pathetic insults had been like water off a duck's back to Stella. She really didn't give a toss what anyone else thought because she was completely comfortable with her sexuality.

"Why do you always have to dress like a boy?" her horrified mother had demanded when she was twelve.

"Maybe I am one, at least on the inside," Stella had taunted just to ger a rise out of her. Deep down, she had felt like there was an element of truth in what she had said: she looked like a boy; wore her hair short like a boy; acted like a boy; dressed like a boy, and even fancied girls, just like most of the boys she knew.

So what?

That was just who she was.

It didn't bother her, so why should it bother anyone else?

Turning away from the mirror, Stella pulled a black T-shirt over her head, slipped into her skinny fit jeans, and then sat down on the edge of the bed in order to pull on the rainbow striped socks that Carrie had bought her during their one and only Christmas together. The vibrant memory made her very emotional, and she blinked away the moisture that was forming in her eyes, annoyed with herself for letting her nostalgia get the better of her. As she shoved her right foot into its Doc Marten, a giant teardrop splattered against the boot's toecap. Sniffing loudly, she angrily dragged the back of her hand across her eyes to stem the flow, but it was as if a dam had burst, and a deluge of tears rolled down her face.

She understood that her weeping had been triggered, not by sentimentality, but by gut-wrenching guilt. She had spent much of the past week in a drunken stupor, drowning her sorrows by pouring so much vodka down her throat that, in the end, there had been more alcohol in her body than blood. She had stopped binge drinking a couple of days back, and the vivid flashbacks that accompanied her new found sobriety were becoming more and more frequent, intruding into her consciousness with bone jarring clarity, blurring the lines between past and present.

Burying her head in her hands, Stella let out a low moan as she relived last Friday night all over again. She had followed Carrie and the drunken floozy she seemed so besotted with away from the pub, keeping a discreet distance and praying that an opportunity would present itself for her to get Carrie alone.

All she had wanted to do was talk.

Not fight; just talk

The sight of them, being all touchy feely with each other as they frolicked their way along Broadway Market, had enraged Stella.

She had followed the cab they had taken, convinced that Carrie was planning to take her back to the family house in Ivy Street, to fuck her in the very same bed she had shared with Stella up until a few short months ago.

After the cab dropped them outside Clinger Court in Pitfield Street, they had started smooching. The sight of Carrie playing tonsil tennis with another woman had incensed Stella to the point that she had seriously considered mowing them down with her moped. Thankfully, the embrace had ended before she succumbed to the temptation.

And then the chance she had been waiting for had presented itself. Waving goodnight to her girlfriend, Carrie had tipsily set off towards home.

Stella had waited until Carrie reached the junction with Ivy Street before approaching her. By then, her mood had become so dark that she was unable to control her temper, and the arguing had started almost straight away. And then… And then, she had done the unthinkable. In her anger and frustration, she had lashed out at Carrie.

A knock at the door interrupted Stella's turbulent thoughts.

Ramming her left foot into the other boot, she quickly tied the laces up.

There was another knock, more insistent than the first.

"Hang on!" she yelled. "I'll be there in a second."

Rushing along the hallway, Stella wondered who could possibly be calling so early in the morning. The post man, perhaps, with a recorded delivery?

Slipping the latch off, she fumbled with the Yale lock and pulled the door open.

The colour drained from her face as she stared up at the monstrous hulk filling the doorway.

"Hello, Stella," Casper said with an ominous smile. "Did you miss me?"

"It's me," his inside man said. As per usual, he was speaking in a hushed whisper, as though afraid he would be discovered at any second. "*Just finished the morning meeting, and thought you'd want to know that the DCI has sent a couple of detectives over to see you.*"

Wiggins' eyes hardened. "To see me? What for?"

"*They've spoken to Carrie's best friend, Abi, and apparently Carrie told her that you sent your crazy albino over to scare Stella off when she wouldn't stop pestering her after they split up.*"

"Yeah, so?"

"*They think you might know where she lives, and they're desperate to find out so they can nick her for Carrie's murder.*"

Wiggins smiled. He did know where Stella lived. Having just received a call from Casper, he also knew that she was no longer there. In fact, she was currently in the back of a Ford Transit, on her way over to the warehouse, where she would remain until Mr Willard popped over and ended her miserable life. Then, her worthless corpse would go into a large steel drum, to be shipped off to a building site in West London on Monday morning, where it would become part of the foundations of an office block that was being erected there.

"They're wasting their time," Wiggins told his contact.

They were, but they were also wasting his. He had been about to drive over to the warehouse himself, to interrogate the two grease monkeys. Now, thanks to the impending visit from the Cozzers, he would have to postpone that conversation until after he had completed his rounds of Willard's betting shops.

Like the good foot soldiers that they were, Basher and Mickey had remained at the warehouse overnight to nursemaid the prisoners. He had checked in with them earlier, to confirm that his instructions had been followed to the letter.

Last night, the two murdering thieves had been stripped naked, given a good soaking, and then repeatedly beaten with rattan canes to soften them up. He had learned this method from a book he had read about Gestapo interrogations during World War Two. Humiliated, exhausted, covered in cuts and bruises, they had then been left in a freezing cold cell overnight, with no light, no food or water, and no company other than their own terrified thoughts.

Wiggins was hoping that the experience had softened them up, and that the wankers would be tripping over themselves in their eagerness to avoid further punishment.

All he needed was the location they had hidden the diamonds in. Once the gems were recovered, he would have no further use for either of them, and they could be disposed of.

Although more than a week had passed since the robbery at Frank's house, Wiggins was confident that McCullen's crew still had the gems in their possession. They were low calibre criminals, which meant they were incapable of sourcing a buyer without outside help. They would need to reach out to a well-connected fence, and there weren't as many of those around as most people thought. If they had already made an approach, Avram would have heard about it, but there hadn't been any whispers about a large cache of jewels being made available for sale on the black market.

Wiggins had promised Casper that he could have some fun with the prisoners once they had outlived their usefulness. Of course, Casper's interpretation of fun would involve him beating them to pulp, but that was absolutely fine by Wiggins; it would save him the cost of two bullets, and it would send out a very poignant message to anyone else who might be getting ideas above their station.

No matter how many times he adjusted the lumbar support or recline controls, Darren just couldn't get comfortable. Arriving just before dawn, he had found himself a nice little spot in the cul-de-sac opposite Fred Wiggins' home address, and had tucked the Ford Scorpio in behind a little Alfa Romeo.

He had only been there once before, to pick Carrie up from a New Year's Eve party so that she wouldn't have to worry about getting a cab home.

Stifling a yawn, Darren rubbed his eyes with his knuckles.

Having not slept for the best part of twenty-four hours, he was physically shattered and emotionally drained. He was also ravenously hungry, and his stomach was making loud rumbling noises, demanding to be fed. He had grabbed a dried-out sandwich and a beer on the flight, but he hadn't eaten or drunk anything since, and he would have happily killed for a cup of coffee and a bacon butty.

He was also in desperate need of a piss.

There was a BP garage just around the corner, but he couldn't risk making a trip there, just in case Wiggins left while he was gone. Lowering the window to let some fresh air in, he cursed himself for not having stocked up on food and drink before beginning the stakeout, and for not bringing an empty water bottle along so that he could relieve himself without having to get out of the car. It had been a schoolboy error on his part but, in his defence, he had been in such a state of shock since learning of Carrie's murder that he hadn't been thinking straight.

Truth be told, he still wasn't.

Unable to postpone nature's call any longer, Darren slid out of the car, wincing because his limbs were stiff from hours of inactivity. After a quick check to make sure that no one was watching him out of their window, he hurriedly unzipped his fly and began urinating against a wall. Halfway through, the sound of an approaching car engine grabbed his attention.

"Shit, shit, shit!" he muttered, willing himself to finish.

The last thing he needed was for an indignant resident to return home while he was still taking a leak. Unfortunately, his bladder had other ideas, and it completely ignored the mental command.

A blue Ford Escort drove along the main road, slowing as it went past Wiggins' house. Coming to a halt, there was a grinding noise as reverse gear was selected, and then it backed into a space outside Wiggins' front door.

Two suited men got out. One had big ears, a disfigured nose, and bowed legs, while the other was fairly nondescript. It could not have been more obvious that they were police officers had they both been wearing neon signs across their chests and had flashing blue lights strapped to their heads.

Thankfully, neither man looked in Darren's direction.

Instead, they walked straight up to Wiggins' door.

Finally, the stream reduced to a trickle, then a few wayward drips. Giving himself a little shake, Darren tucked his manhood away, zipped up his jeans, and quickly returned to his car to observe what happened next.

Wiggins opened his street door to find Charlie White and another detective standing there. Even though they had already met, the Scotsman produced his warrant card and identified himself.

Wiggins smiled to himself; Cozzers were such predictable creatures.

Somehow, he managed to mask his contempt. "To what do I owe the honour of this surprise?" he asked with a gracious smile. Had this actually been a surprise, he most certainly would not have been smiling.

"Morning, Mr Wiggins," White said, his face impassive. "We need to ask you a couple of questions regarding a woman called Stella Carter. Have you heard of her?"

Wiggins made a show of considering this. "The name does sound vaguely familiar," he conceded. "Didn't she used to go out with Carrie?"

"Aye, she did," White said. "Do you mind if we pop in and have a wee chat with you about her?"

Wiggins shook his head, regretfully. "I'm afraid that won't be possible," he told them. "I'm about to go to work, but I'm happy to answer your questions out here, if that's alright?"

He could tell that it wasn't but, out of principle, he wasn't going to let the Cozzers into his home without a warrant, even if he didn't have anything to hide. The smell of pig took ages to clear, and he'd rather not have his house polluted by it.

"Carrie told one of her friends that you arranged for someone to have a quiet word with Stella, to get her to stop pestering Carrie after they split up," the man standing beside White said. He had a Welsh accent, Wiggins noted.

"Carrie's friend is mistaken," Wiggins said, firmly. "What I actually said to Carrie was that, if it ever got too much for her, she should tell me, and I would have a word with Stella on her behalf, but she never asked me to do that, so I assumed everything had sorted itself out." Wiggins could tell that they didn't believe him but, so what? "Will there be anything else?" he asked, blithely. "Only I'm already running late for work, and Saturday tends to a very busy day in the betting industry, so I need to crack on."

"Aye, one more question," White said, staring at him intently. "Do you have an address for Stella Carter?"

Again, Wiggins made a great show of considering this, when in truth he was thinking about what he was going to have for breakfast. "I believe she lived in the flats opposite St. Anne's church in Hoxton Street," he said after a moment's contemplation. "I don't know the number, but I think it was on the second floor."

The detectives thanked him, then left.

Closing the street door, Wiggins retired to his front room to watch them from behind the safety of his net curtains. The two detectives stood by their car for a few moments, deep in conversation. Then, the little Scotsman made a quick call on his mobile, presumably ringing in the results of his unsatisfactory conversation with Wiggins.

Wiggins checked his watch and smiled. After doing the obligatory round robin to check up on Willard's string of betting shops, he would have plenty of time to head over to the warehouse to question the grease monkeys. They had the warehouse to themselves until Monday morning, so there was no rush, and the longer he left them to stew in their own fear, the quicker they would break.

He pulled out his mobile and rang Basher's number. "Basher, me old son, there's been a slight change of plan and I'm gonna be a bit delayed getting there. I want you to take both grease monkeys out of their cells and chain them up, then give the fuckers another good soaking and work them over with the batons." It was an escalation on the previous night's torture, and it would take their suffering to the next level. By the time he got there that afternoon, they should be begging him to listen to their confession.

Not long after the Cozzers left, Wiggins came out of his house and climbed into a gleaming Audi Quattro that was parked a few doors further along the road.

It struck Darren that Wiggins didn't seem particularly flustered by the early morning visit from the police, and he wondered what the two detectives had wanted.

Had they called in connection to his sister's murder?

Perhaps, they had spoken to him about something else; Frank Kyle's shooting, for instance?

The Audi's throaty engine coughed into life, and Wiggins gunned the accelerator several times, taking the rev counter into the red.

Flash git.

The neighbours would love that.

A moment later, the car took off like a rocket.

Pulling out from behind the Alfa, Darren turned left at the main road, which was thankfully clear of traffic, and slotted into place thirty yards behind him.

Every time Darren closed his eyes, he saw the smiling picture of Carrie they had shown on TV. She would never smile like that again, he thought with a heavy heart. She would never do anything again. She was gone forever, reduced to a memory.

A lump formed in Darren's throat as he recalled the last time that he had visited their dying mum in hospital. She had been receiving palliative care by that stage, and had been doped up to the eyeballs with morphine to ease the pain. While Carrie popped out to get them both a coffee, he had sat there, holding her frail hand in his, not knowing what else to do. Fighting back the tears, he had prayed for the end to come quickly and be peaceful. During her last few moments of lucidity, before lapsing into a coma, his mother had made him promise that he would look after Carrie; that he would always be there when his sister needed him. He blinked away the tears that stung his eyes, shamed by the knowledge that he had failed his mother miserably in that respect.

He had failed Carrie, too.

The pain was suddenly too much for him to bear, and he howled like a wounded animal. Darren wanted to lash out; to kill the people responsible for Carrie's death, and he would, he promised himself. He would kill each and every one of them. But first, he would do everything within his power to rescue Fingers and Terry Marshall.

Darren was so wrapped up in his thoughts that it didn't immediately register when Wiggins' right-hand indicator started blinking. Slamming on the brakes to avoid overshooting the junction, Darren was forced to wait for a gap in the oncoming traffic before he could follow. By the time he turned into the road, there were several cars between himself and Wiggins.

Darren cursed his wandering mind. He would need to pay attention from now on; no more sudden lapses of concentration or he would lose his quarry.

―――

Sergeant Patrick Docherty was the police Dive Supervisor in charge of the Underwater Search Unit, and today was the fourth day they had been engaged in Operation Haddonfield. So far, the only body part that the divers had recovered was the torso itself, and they could hardly take any credit for that, seeing as it had actually been discovered by the Lock Master. All they had done was pop down to the scene and retrieve the bloody thing from the water.

Docherty was a proud Irishman who had served on the Underwater Search Unit for just over ten years, and it really galled him that an untrained dredging crew from the British Waterways Authority had managed to stumble across two of the victim's limbs in recent days, while his divers had been working their proverbial socks off in the freezing cold water, operating by feel alone, with nothing to show for their efforts other than a mild case of chilblains.

Working in a zero-visibility environment was fraught with

danger, but few people seemed to appreciate the inherent risks his divers had faced every day. Claustrophobia; disorientation; the risk of illness from water pollution or impalement from sharp debris. The canal bed was littered with used syringes, broken shards of glass, and sharp metal objects protruding from the silt, just waiting to impale the unwary diver.

The sarky skipper in charge of the local plod performing cordon control along the canal bank had taken to bursting into raucous chants of "Two-nil to the dredgers," every time he saw Docherty. It had been mildly amusing at first, but now it was starting to seriously piss him off so, when a diver suddenly stuck his head out of the murky water and shouted, "Find!" Docherty rushed over to the edge of the canal, praying that it would actually be a missing body part, and not another bloody shopping trolley.

The diver in question, Marcus Radley, was one of Docherty's most experienced officers, and he was holding aloft a three foot long, boomerang shaped object that was wrapped in a black plastic refuse sack.

"Think I've got something this time, sarge," Radley shouted, excitedly.

"Hurry up, then," Docherty called, impatiently beckoning the diver to come ashore.

As Radley pushed the object ahead of him in the water, Docherty studied it carefully. It certainly looked promising, he thought, daring to hope.

The dive team were all on double time overtime today, and Docherty thought it would be very fitting if they could justify their extra pay by finally producing the goods.

Donning a pair of nitrile gloves, Docherty reached out to accept the waterlogged bag from Radley, carefully pulling it out of the water and setting it down gently on the canal towpath.

It certainly felt heavy enough to be a human limb, he thought, and then felt a sudden twinge of guilt for being so pleased by the prospect of finding a severed body part.

Like all divers, Docherty was a licensed search officer, and he was acutely aware that a pivotal part of his role was to recover exhibits without compromising their evidential integrity.

A lot of water was leaking out of the black plastic bag and, on closer inspection, he saw that there was a jagged tear in the underside, where the plastic had been snagged by something on the canal bed. Peering through the tear, he saw that there was a second, transparent plastic bag inside. His heart rate began to climb. The right arm and right leg recovered by the dredgers, had also been wrapped that way.

The inner bag was too badly misted for him to see the object within clearly, but there could be no doubting the distinctive shape of the human arm, the bend in the elbow, and the hand at the end. "Looks like it's two-one," he announced proudly. "Well done, Marcus. You've just got us back in the game."

24

You're doing it again, knobhead

As Tyler opened the passenger door to the Omega, a battered Astra drew level with them in the car park at the rear of Hertford House. Sitting in the passenger seat, Jim Stone unwound his window. "Boss," he called out, signalling for Tyler to wait.

"What is it?" Tyler asked.

Stone jumped out. "We've just got back from that mini-market in Hoxton," he said. "Turns out it does have a CCTV system installed, but it's one of these new-fangled digital machines, and the proprietor can only play back footage from the last forty-eight hours on site. He tried calling out an engineer to download the stuff we're interested in, but one isn't available until the middle of next week."

Tyler snorted. "I'm not waiting that long," he said, belligerently. "Get onto Newlands Park, see if they can send someone out for us. I need to know whether our suspect was caught on camera when she purchased that SIM card."

"Already done it," Stone said. "Trouble is, even they can't do it before Monday morning."

Tyler shook his head. "Well, that's just marvellous," he growled, getting into the Omega. "Give them a call back, make sure they know this is a Cat A enquiry, and throw Mr Holland's name into the mix, see if that oils the machinery."

"I'll try," Stone said as Tyler slammed the door. "But I'm not sure it will make any difference."

Stella cried out in pain as Casper dragged her from the back of the van by the scruff of her neck, spitefully digging his rock like fingers into her soft flesh, just for the fun of it. With her hands still tightly bound behind her back, she was in no position to resist, not that she would have been able to do much against the hulking brute, had they been free.

"Move," he said, giving her an unnecessarily hard shove.

Stumbling forward on wobbly legs, Stella fell to her knees, ripping her jeans on the rough concrete and grazing the skin beneath.

"Get up," he snarled, as if it were her fault that she had taken a tumble.

"Give me a second," Stella pleaded. Her entire body was shaking from fear, and it felt as though all of her bones had vanished, leaving behind a quivering mass of jelly that was unable to support itself.

With a sigh of irritation, Casper yanked her onto her feet and frogmarched her through the loading bay until they reached the recess at the far end.

At first, she wondered why he was taking her into a dead end, but then she spotted a reinforced metal door protruding from the surrounding brickwork.

Ignoring her pitiful wailing, he shouldered open the heavy door and shoved her ahead of him along a narrow corridor until they arrived at an identical door at the other end.

"Get in there," he growled, pushing it open.

When Stella didn't respond immediately, he placed a massive hand in the small of her back and propelled her forward.

"I said, get in."

Crashing through the door, Stella fell hard, smashing her chin into the floor. The pain was so intense that she almost passed out.

"Pathetic," she heard the albino say.

Awkwardly twisting herself up onto her knees, Stella gingerly moved her throbbing jaw up and down, then side to side, praying that it wasn't broken. She stood up clumsily, tottering like a drunk until Casper reached out a hand to steady her.

Looking up at her new surroundings, Stella's breath caught in her throat, and she instinctively took a backward step as her brain struggled to process the information her eyes were sending it.

"No," she muttered, her voice hollow and breathless.

Before her, two badly beaten men had been suspended from the ceiling by thick metal chains and were swinging in little circles, with their feet dangling several inches above the concrete floor. Clad in nothing but their boxers, both were battered and bleeding, and their harrowed faces seemed bereft of hope.

The strain on their arms must have been unbearable, she thought, shuddering at the gruesome sight. Their wrists were tied with what looked like electrical cable. One end of an S shaped meat hook had been inserted through their bindings, while the other end had been looped through the chains. Stella could smell their sweat; she could smell their fear, too.

Standing to one side of the slowly spinning captives, two bare chested men were staring questioningly in her direction. The first was a massive man with a bald, crinkly head. The water hose in his right hand trailed all the way back to a tap in the side of the far wall like a long green snake. The second man was leaner, more muscularly defined, and his left wrist was heavily bandaged. In his right hand, he held a three-foot long rattan cane, which he twirled intermittently like a wannabe majorette.

It was evident that the two captives had just been given a good soaking, and one of the men, the slimmer of the two, was sobbing quietly. The bulkier man hanging next to him seemed too exhausted to cry. His mouth sagged open like he had suffered a stroke, and his half-open eyes were unfocused.

"What is this place…?" Stella asked, fearfully.

No one answered, but they didn't really need to, for Stella already knew that she had just passed through the gates of hell.

"You got her, then?" the bald man remarked casually, speaking as if Casper had just popped out to purchase a newspaper, not kidnap a woman from her flat in broad daylight.

"P–p–please," the bigger of the two men hanging from the ceiling suddenly stammered, his trembling voice barely audible. "P– please… make them stop."

With heart wrenching shock, Stella realised that he was addressing her. Her eyes welled, but there was nothing she could do to help him. She opened her mouth to speak, but her throat constricted and no words came out.

The man with the rattan cane tutted. "You've been told not to speak unless you're spoken to," he said, shaking his head in disapproval.

The hanging man's head slowly twisted in the direction that the reprimand had come from. "I–I'm sorry," he gasped.

"You're doing it again, knobhead," the bald man snapped, nodding to his accomplice, who stepped forward and administered a sharp blow to the prisoner's ankles with the cane.

The noise resonated around the enclosed room like a pistol shot, and Stella involuntarily flinched.

The man's anguished scream was far louder.

Stella screwed her eyes shut. "Dear God have mercy," she prayed aloud.

When Casper heard this, a delighted laugh escaped from his lips. "He ain't gonna help you," he scoffed.

Unfastening his seatbelt, Tyler stepped out of the Vauxhall Omega, which Bull had parked next to a white Leyland lorry containing all of the dive team's equipment.

It was another nice day, warm and dry, so he left his coat in the car.

After booking in with the cordon officer, the two detectives made their way over to join Cynthia Alderton, who was once again the on-call Crime Scene Manager, by the inner cordon.

Tyler removed his sunglasses, tucked them into the top pocket of his suit jacket. "We've got to stop meeting like this," he said, just about resisting the urge to wink at her.

As intense as ever, Alderton's eyes seemed to penetrate him like an X-ray, and he

reminded himself not to get drawn into another staring competition with her. There was no point; her eyelids were obviously super-glued open.

"Morning, Jack," she said, briskly handing him a set of barrier clothing to put on. "The divers have recovered the victim's left arm for us this morning," she explained as he donned the white Tyvek coveralls. "About time they found something," she added, speaking quietly so that the Dive Supervisor, who was only standing a few yards away, wouldn't hear.

Was that an attempt at humour?

Tyler wasn't sure.

"Did you just crack a joke?" he asked.

If she had, her face hadn't caught on to it yet. Maybe she had been born without the ability to blink *or* smile?

Now, there was a thought.

Alderton responded with an eyebrow shrug. "Don't sound *too* surprised," she told him. "I have been known to do that from time to time."

"You *do* know it's okay to smile when you make a joke, don't you, Cynth?" he pointed out, just in case she didn't.

"Ha-ha," Alderton responded, drolly. "Now, get a move on."

When Tyler was fully kitted out, she led him over to the

towpath, where the bin liner containing Carrie McCullen's left arm awaited them.

Tyler knelt down and studied it in solitude for a moment, then looked up at Alderton. "I was beginning to think that all of the missing body parts had already passed through Acton's Lock," he confessed. "I was even toying with the idea of pushing the divers over to that side of the canal." A rueful smile. "I'm glad I didn't, now."

Dick Jarvis meandered over. Also clad in full barrier clothing, his arms were laden with several bulging exhibits bags. "Only a leg and the head to go now," he said, cheerfully. "Then we'll have the full set."

"Anything you can tell me from what you've seen so far?" Tyler enquired of Alderton.

She shook her head in a single economical movement. "I'm not going to touch anything until the record photography has been completed," she told him. "There's a snapper en route from Amelia Street as we speak. All I can confirm for now is that this is the dismembered left arm of a white female and, like all the other body parts, it has been wrapped inside two bin liners."

Tyler nodded. He hadn't expected her to say anything else, and he would just have to be patient, not that he was very good at it.

"Okay," he said, standing up and dusting his knees down. "I'll leave you and Dick to process the scene. Give me a call if anything significant comes to light."

As Tyler turned to go, there was a sudden flurry of activity in the water. He turned in time to see a diver surface and raise a Neoprene gloved hand, waving it to get the Dive Supervisor's attention.

"Find!"

Several of the diver's colleagues were rushing towards the water's edge to assist their colleague and, his interest piqued, Tyler decided to join them. In truth, he wasn't overly excited by the development; it would probably turn out to be another false alarm, a bloody bicycle frame or old lawn mower, something banal like that.

As he got nearer, Tyler was able to see that the diver was holding onto a black bin liner, pushing it ahead of her towards the shore.

The sight triggered a little surge of adrenaline. "Surely not," he muttered to himself.

Was it possible that, after going several days without a single find, the dive team had just made their second discovery of the morning?

"Excuse me, please," the Dive Supervisor, a fit looking skipper with mousy hair and a soft Irish accent, said as he barged past Tyler.

He was grinning from ear to ear, Tyler noticed.

Bending down at the water's edge, the Dive Supervisor assisted the diver to haul the waterlogged black bin liner out of the canal. "What have we got this time, Sarah," he asked the diver as she climbed out of the water, assisted by another member of the team.

"Pretty sure it's the missing leg," she said, breathlessly.

"Oh, you little beauty!" the Dive Supervisor said to the bag, before punching the air like he'd just scored a goal in a cup final. "Two all!" he grinned, doing a little jig. "Honour is most definitely restored."

Cynthia Alderton materialised beside them, appearing out of nowhere and hovering over the bag like a floating beanpole. "When you've finished your little Riverdance routine, Mr Flatley, I'd be grateful if you could kindly move aside," she said, her voice acid.

The dive skipper promptly ceased his celebrations and stepped clear, not wanting to incur the wrath of the scary Crime Scene Manager.

Alderton knelt down beside the bag to carry out a visual examination, her attention completely focused on the dripping bag on the towpath.

"It's the right size and shape for a human leg," she told Tyler. "And the outer bin liner is identical to the ones used on the other body parts. It even has the same LBH markings." Being extremely careful, she gently probed the bulge within with her nitrile gloved hands. "Mm-hmm, uh-huh. Yes, I can clearly make out the shape of the thigh, the knee, the calf and ankle, and lastly the foot," she said, nodding to herself as she spoke.

A moment later, Alderton stood up. "Well done," she said to the female diver, who acknowledged the compliment with a little smile.

Tyler left her to it; Alderton was going to be very busy, and the last thing he wanted to do was get in her way while she worked.

On his way back to the car, he made a small detour to where the Dive Supervisor was now writing up his notes. "Skip, I'm DCI Tyler, the SIO," he said, extending his hand.

"PS Docherty, sir," the Irishman said, taking his hand and holding it firm.

Tyler gave him a lopsided grin. "I noticed your little celebration, just now."

Docherty's face instantly glowed red. "Sorry, sir," he said, sheepishly. "Didn't mean to get carried away, but I was getting a little worried that we were going to be outdone by the bloody dredgers."

Tyler laughed. "Like you said, honours are even now. Anyway, I just wanted to thank you and your team for all your hard work this week, and to say that there's a bottle of whiskey in it for whoever finds the head."

Docherty's eyes lit up. "Well, I'm certainly partial to a wee dram. What brand are we talking?" he enquired.

Tyler shrugged. He didn't know much about these things. "I'll let whoever finds the head pick." Patting the affable sergeant on the shoulder, he set off in search of Steve Bull. "I'd much rather my hard-earned money was spent on buying booze for the USU, and not the Waterways Authority," he called over his shoulder.

"We'll do our best, sir," the dive skipper shouted.

Tyler had no doubt that they would.

Dillon found himself back at Poplar mortuary for the SPM of Carrie's recovered limbs. As before, Dr Tolpuddle was presiding, and she was being ably assisted by an Anatomical Pathology Assistant called Sue Livermore. It was a fitting name, Dillon thought for someone who spent their working days surrounded by body parts and freshly harvested organs.

Livermore was a smiling woman in her early thirties, with copper coloured hair, pale skin, and green eyes. She was quite pretty, he thought, and she had a shapely enough figure, but she wasn't a patch on Emma Drew, the girl who had once held the position. Surprisingly, thinking about Emma hadn't elicited the little stab of pain it usually did, and he wondered if that was down to Imogen Askew. Surely, he couldn't be developing actual feelings for her, could he? He hardly even knew her.

In addition to Dillon, the pathologist and her assistant, Juliet Kennedy and Kevin Murray were also present in their respective capacities as CSM and Advanced Exhibits Officer. Nerdy Ned Saunders, the happy-go-lucky snapper from SO3, was lingering in the background, waiting to be called forward to carry out the record photography.

The visitors all wore the compulsory green gowns, masks and overshoes, while Tolpuddle and Livermore wore surgical pyjamas and Wellington boots. Both wore surgical caps, and they had Victoria masks hanging loosely under their chins.

On Tolpuddle's instruction, Livermore removed the drawer containing the torso from the freezer. From another draw, just above it, Livermore withdrew two severed female limbs, and these were placed on the pathology table next to Carrie's torso.

At first glance, the three separate body parts all seemed mutually compatible, and Dillon thought that it was just like looking at a human jigsaw puzzle, minus some of the pieces.

"Okay," Dr Tolpuddle said, cheerfully. "Let's get this party started, shall we?"

She turned on the dictation device that would be recording all her findings, made her preliminary introductions, and then turned to Murray, smiling at him from behind her mask.

"If you would be so kind as to swab each of the limbs and the torso for DNA comparisons," she said.

These would be submitted to the lab for official confirmation that all the body parts they were going to be examining did, in fact, belong the same victim, and had not been conveniently cobbled together from leftovers to form a Frankenstein's monster.

Once that had been done, Nerdy Ned was called forward to take a number of photographs, each one carefully set up by the pathologist. The limbs were photographed at various angles, both on their own and next to the joint in the torso they had been separated from. A metal ruler was incorporated into each frame to show the angle and depth of the various hacking cuts, and to demonstrate the mechanical fit between the limbs and the body they had been parted from.

Dillon watched on in morbid fascination, hating every second of it but transfixed by the clinical precision with which Tolpuddle worked.

"Right, so far so good," she announced when Saunders stepped back. "I'm going to carry out a visual examination of each limb next, starting with the right arm." She studied the limb carefully, giving them a running commentary as she went. "I see no evidence of any defence wounds on the arm, and there are no injuries to the wrist that would suggest she was tied up prior to her death." Tolpuddle bent forward, squinted. "There does appear to be some bruising on the elbow, but this is likely to have occurred post mortem. If you'd care to come closer, you will see that the whole of the ball joint is present, which suggests that it was pulled out of the torso."

Having been invited to come over and take a closer look, Murray, Kennedy and Nerdy Ned couldn't get there quick enough. Dillon hesitated a moment, before reluctantly bringing up the rear. As much as he was dreading it, he knew he would have to feign an interest – especially after Juliet had told Stephanie Tolpuddle how squeamish he was – or he would look weak. The others were all leaning over the arm, peering at the ball joint and nodding enthusiastically as Tolpuddle talked them through the separation process. Cringing inwardly at the vivid description she was painting, Dillon held his breath and followed suit.

Having gone through the motions, Dillon retreated from the pathologist's table the moment he felt it safe to do so without losing face.

Shooing the others away several seconds later, Tolpuddle

resumed her examination of Carrie's right arm. "The nails are relatively short, and they are painted red. I note that the toes on the leg we are going to examine afterwards are also painted the same shade of red. I can't see any obvious detritus beneath the fingernails to indicate our victim tried to fight her attacker off, but we will take some scrapings anyway, and these will be submitted for DNA testing." Standing back, she invited Kevin Murray to take the samples.

When he had finished, Livermore weighed the arm, proclaiming that it was 2.3 kilos.

In addition to the DNA samples taken at the beginning of the SPM, some deep muscle tissue was also taken to assist with the identification of the arm.

It was getting on for three when a tired and dishevelled Colin Franklin rapped on the door to Tyler's office. Like everyone else on the team, Franklin had been working incredibly long hours since the job had broken, and all he wanted to do was go home, crawl into his nice warm bed, and sleep for a week.

"Come in," Tyler shouted, beckoning him in with a flourish of his hand. Since returning from the canal, he had been locked away in his office, updating his Decision Log and reviewing the various statements that had come in during the week.

Franklin gratefully accepted the chair that Tyler pointed to. Opening his day book, he fumbled through his notes, yawning repeatedly as he searched for the right page.

"What can I do for you, Rip Van Winkle?" Tyler asked, staring at him in amusement.

Franklin tried to prevent himself from succumbing to another cavernous yawn, but failed miserably. "While you were down at the crime scene this morning," he said drowsily, "I managed to find snippets of footage showing Stella's moped following Carrie and Trish's cab from Broadway Market to Clinger Court in Pitfield Street. I even managed to get a clear view of the moped's registration number but, when Deano ran it through the PNC for me, it was shown as having no current keeper."

Tyler's face creased in disappointment. "What about the insurance database? Did he try that?"

Franklin nodded, wearily. "He did. There's a policy for the moped in Carter's name, but the address on record is the flat she used to live at in Hoxton, so it hasn't helped us to identify where she's living now."

Tyler swore under his breath. Carter was proving to be very elusive. The good news was that the moped was actually insured in her name, so at least they could now conclusively link her to it. "Okay," he said with a brittle smile. "Thanks for the update."

Franklin wearily rose to his feet. Stifling yet another yawn, he shuffled off towards the door like an old man.

"Colin," Tyler called after him.

"Yes, boss?"

"You look fit to drop. Why don't you take a short break?"

Franklin shook his head. "I'd love to, but there's too much to do, and—"

Tyler held up a hand to silence him. "Make yourself a strong cup of coffee, then go and get some fresh air for fifteen minutes. That's an order. You're no good to me if you fall asleep on the job."

Franklin opened his mouth to protest, realised that Tyler was right. "Yes, boss," he sighed, conceding defeat.

25

As you wish

Wiggins was in a really foul mood by the time he finally reached the warehouse. The idiot they had promoted to replace Frank the Tank at the Stratford branch was proving to be utterly useless, and Wiggins had spent the morning sorting out the string of fuck ups he had made since his arrival. The man would have to go, he decided, but that was a problem for another day. Right now, he had far more pressing matters to attend to.

"I was beginning to think you weren't coming," Basher said as he entered the office. He was sitting in a leather armchair, drinking coffee and watching TV. Opposite him, on a matching leather sofa, Casper and Mickey were huddled together, stuffing their faces with takeaway food.

"Been a shit day," Wiggins said, flopping down in a vacant armchair and smoothing an imaginary crease out of his trousers. "Have the grease monkeys spoken yet?"

Basher shook his head. "The arrogant little shits are both denying knowing anything."

After consulting his watch, Wiggins clapped his hands to get their attention. "Right, I'm gonna have a quick word with the nutjob who killed poor Carrie. While I do that, drag those fuckers out of their cells and get them chained up again. It's time to show them we mean business."

Leaving the others to sort out the male prisoners, Wiggins unlocked the cell containing Stella Carter. In the dimness within, he could just about make out her forlorn shape on the bed. Her knees were tucked up beneath her chin, and her arms were wrapped tightly around them.

Upon her arrival, her clothes had been taken from her, and she had been thrown in the holding cell wearing nothing but her panties and bra. Her ribcage was so bony that it reminded Wiggins of a xylophone. What a stunner like Carrie had ever seen in this car crash of a woman was beyond him.

Carter stared back at him with big, fearful eyes and, from the light filtering into the cell from the corridor, he could tell that she had been doing a lot of crying.

Wiggins eyes narrowed as he clocked the huge hand shaped mark across the left side of her face, and the nasty graze on her chin. That was Casper's work, no doubt. The sight angered him. Hadn't he specifically instructed the stupid oaf not to mess up her face?

As her terrified gaze settled on him, she seemed to shrivel in size.

Wiggins' mouth twisted downwards in contempt. "Not so tough now, are you?" he sneered. "You're lucky that Mr Willard wants to deal with you himself," he said. "Otherwise, I'd happily let Casper rip your fucking arms off for what you did to that poor sweet girl."

"Please," Stella sobbed. "I know it was wrong of me to go near Carrie again, and I should never have hit her, but–"

"Shouldn't have hit her?" Wiggins spluttered, incredulously. "You didn't just *hit* her though, did you, you mad psycho bitch? You fucking well *killed* her, and then you chopped her body up into little pieces."

Carter's eyes widened in shock. "What? I–I didn't kill her," she stammered, shaking her head in fierce denial. "I would never have—"

Wiggins had heard enough of this tripe. In two angry strides he was upon her, grabbing her short hair and viciously banging the back of her skull against the wall.

Stella cried out in pain and shock, and her eyes seemed to glaze over.

Unable to stop himself, Wiggins dragged her from the cot, and threw her roughly to the floor. Stella tried to fend him off, but he was too strong, and he just swatted her hands aside. She screamed at him, begging him not to hurt her, but he was far too angry to listen. With a guttural snarl of rage, he kicked her twice in the stomach.

Curling into a tight ball, Stella began making retching noises.

Standing above her, breathing heavily from his exertions, Wiggins ran his fingers through his hair, smoothing it back down into place. Tucking his shirt back in, and adjusting the knot of his tie, he paused by the cell door. "I'm gonna enjoy watching you die," he promised.

Stella slowly dragged herself into a sitting position, wiped a string of drool from her lips.

"I–I didn't kill Carrie," she panted, clutching her stomach. "I–I loved her."

Wiggins spat on her, then slammed the door shut behind him.

———

Darren pulled over a discreet distance away from the warehouse that Wiggins had recently entered. The service road it was located in was full of similar places, although most of the others were in a state of disrepair, looking as though they had been closed for some time and were awaiting demolition.

Surrounded by wasteland, the industrial area was close to the sewerage works at Barking Creek, and the stench, when the wind changed direction, was overpowering.

Darren had begun to have serious doubts that Wiggins would

ever lead him to Fingers and Marshall but, unlike the other venues that Willard's head of security had visited, this place showed potential. It was exactly the kind of out of the way location he imagined a gangster would use if he wanted to torture information out of someone.

To Darren's disappointment, Wiggins reappeared after a few short minutes. Striding purposefully towards his car, he clicked the fob to release the central locking. However, instead of getting in and driving off, Wiggins merely retrieved a petrol can from the boot, then hurried back inside.

Darren waited a few minutes, then set off on foot to carry out a quick recce.

The warehouse was a two-storey brick-built building with a flat roof. About twelve feet above ground level, a row of opaque windows ran the length of the main building. Above these, the walls were covered in sheets of thick corrugated green metal, which ran all the way up to the roof.

The concrete frontage was easily wide enough to accommodate three lorries at a time. Access to the internal loading area was controlled by black metal shutters, which were closed at the moment, preventing him from seeing inside. There was a windowless, metal door next to the shutters, and it was through there that Wiggins had entered. A yellow sign was affixed to the back of it, proclaiming that 24-hour CCTV was in operation. Looking around, Darren saw that there were cameras mounted on the walls at each end of the building, pointing inwards towards the loading bay doors, but he doubted anyone was actually watching the monitors.

Keeping the Browning tucked against his right leg, Darren crept up to the door and gently tried the handle.

It was locked.

He placed his ear against it and listened, but the thick steel prevented any internal sounds from filtering out. With a frustrated sigh, he set off to explore the rest of the building's perimeter. To the right of the warehouse, there was a service road leading down to a car park at the rear, but a padlocked wrought iron gate, about eight feet tall and topped with wicked looking spikes, prevented unauthorised entry.

The single storey extension at the side of the main building was windowless, and contained no doors. Then he spotted a solitary drainpipe, old and rusting, about halfway along. It was worryingly loose and moved freely when he gave it a little tug. Still, if he wanted to get a peek at the car park, shimmying up that seemed a lot less risky than scaling the spiked fence on the other side of the building, so he decided to try his luck.

Tucking the pistol into the front of his jeans, Darren clambered up the drainpipe, which groaned and creaked and threatened to come away from the wall at any second. On reaching the flat roof, he looked around, hoping to find a skylight from which he could look inside.

He was out of luck.

The car park was an empty concrete strip that ran the length of the building, with spaces marked out in orderly white lines. They were all empty. A barbed wire topped fence around the perimeter kept the overgrown jungle beyond from encroaching onto the property.

Darren spotted three windowless fire doors in the back wall of the warehouse: one in the extension; two in the main building. They were all made from reinforced steel, so there was no chance of him gaining access through any of those.

With a growing sense of frustration, Darren slithered down the wobbly drainpipe, then crept back to his car, feeling that he had already chanced his arm enough.

He reclined his seat and settled down, knowing that he might be in for a very long wait.

———

When Wiggins returned with the petrol can, he was pleased to see Fingers and Marshall swinging from the ceiling, their bare feet dangling inches from the cold concrete floor. Battered and bruised, both men looked utterly exhausted.

Good.

That should make his task easier.

Goosebumps peppered the prisoners' naked flesh, and Marshall's teeth were chattering uncontrollably.

"Good afternoon, lads," he said, smiling pleasantly. "I won't keep you *hanging* around for too long."

Standing between the prisoners, Basher laughed at the joke. "Good one, Fred," he said, nodding approvingly.

Lowering the petrol can to the floor, Wiggins strolled over to the prisoners, coming to a halt directly in front of them. Their sweat and piss-stained bodies were kicking up badly, and the odour caught in the back of his throat, almost making him gag.

"Before we start," he said, genially, "I want to give each of you one final chance to tell me where the diamonds you stole from Frank Kyle's place are hidden?" He looked expectantly at each of them in turn.

Staring down at the floor, Fingers said through gritted teeth, "I don't know what you're talking about. We didn't steal no diamonds."

The boy was certainly spirited, Wiggins thought. Under different circumstances, he would have found the quality admirable.

Not today, though.

Wiggins tutted, waving an admonishing finger from side to side like a metronome. "As commendable as it is, me old son, that attitude of yours is going to get you both killed."

"You're going to kill us no matter what we say," Fingers shot back, defiantly.

Wiggins couldn't help but smile. The boy had a point.

He turned to Marshall. "What about you?" he asked, casually. "Are you gonna tell me what I want to know, or are you as brave as your scrawny little mate, here?"

With an effort, Marshall lifted his head and stared into Wiggins' eyes. "I s–swear to you that I *didn't* steal any d–diamonds, and I don't even know who Frank Kyle is," he sobbed, blathering like a frightened child.

"Is that so?" Wiggins mocked, thinking that the man was spineless, and would be easy to break.

Marshall stared at him imploringly, his watery eyes pleading. "I s-swear it is."

Turning his back on the prisoners, Wiggins stood in silence for several seconds, deciding his next move. From the descriptions that Morag Kyle had provided, he was confident that Fingers was the intruder who had remained with her in the kitchen. While it was possible that Marshall had been the fucker who shot and killed Frankie, he clearly wasn't the brains behind the operation, therefore he was the most expendable of the two men hanging before him.

"Casper, bring the metal tray over," he shouted.

A few seconds later, Casper appeared from the office carrying a three-foot square metal container that was about three inches deep. The inside had black staining, as though it had been set on fire at some point. He placed it at Wiggins' feet.

After retrieving the petrol can, Wiggins unscrewed the lid and poured a liberal amount into the tray. "Put that under Marshall's feet," he said.

Grinning excitedly, Casper carefully slid the tray along the floor until it came to rest directly beneath Terry Marshall's dangling feet.

Marshall's toes were no more than an inch above the liquid.

"No, please…" Marshall begged, squirming ineffectually to break free of his wrist bindings. The violent thrashing of his desperate movements caused the cable ties to cut deeper into his flesh, and little trails of scarlet began to run down his arms towards his elbows.

Immune to his protestations, Wiggins turned to Casper, who was staring at him expectantly. "Would you like to do the honours, old son?"

It was, he knew, a stupid question.

Nodding eagerly, Casper removed a small box of matches from one of his trouser pockets.

"No, no, no…" Marshall's sobs became increasingly hysterical as he realised what was about to happen to him.

Casper struck a match and held it up before Marshall's eyes.

Smiling evilly, he waited until it had burned nearly all the way down before tossing it into the tray of petrol.

With a loud whoosh, the tray's contents caught fire, and the resulting flames leapt up to enshroud Marshall's feet.

Casper seemed spellbound by the intensity of the fire, and the catastrophic damage it was already inflicting to Marshall's lower legs.

Wiggins couldn't help but notice the growing bulge in the albino's trousers.

Sick fucker!

Mickey and Basher had retreated to the office, having less of a stomach for this kind of torture than the albino. Wiggins didn't blame them; he was only staying where he was because he had to.

The dancing flames continued to devour the feet and lower legs of the man suspended above them, eating away the exposed flesh of his ankles with an insatiable appetite. Screaming in insufferable agony, Marshall drew his knees up to his chest, desperately trying to escape the searing heat rushing up from the floor.

On seeing this, Wiggins nodded at Casper, who immediately stepped forward and struck Marshall across the body with the long rattan cane, forcing the air from his lungs.

Stunned by the unexpected blow, Marshall's body went limp, and his feet plummeted into the heart of the flames. His body jerked and spasmed uncontrollably as his burning flesh popped and crackled under the intense heat. Letting out a string of anguished howls, Marshall thrashed around until one of his feet collided with the tray's rim, overturning it.

The rolling sea of liquid fire quickly spread outwards, forcing Wiggins and Casper to jump out of its way.

"Get the bloody fire extinguisher," Wiggins bellowed, his voice competing with Marshall's incessant screams.

From within the office, Mickey appeared, carrying a large red extinguisher, which he immediately turned on the spreading pool of petrol, covering it with a film of foam and dousing the flames.

"What the fuck happened?" Mickey asked, when the fire had been extinguished.

"That stupid wanker kicked the tray over," Wiggins said, indicating Marshall with an angry jut of his chin.

Marshall's smoking figure now hung limply, and Wiggins realised that he had passed out from the excruciating pain. His blackened feet and smouldering shins were covered in a mass of ugly blisters, and the skin around his ankles had completely burned away, leaving the bone and muscle beneath painfully exposed.

Wiggins winced at the stomach-turning sight.

The stench, when it reached him, was enough to make him dry heave. He had once heard a fireman say that human flesh smelled like pork when it was cooked, and he now knew that it was true. Turning to Fingers, who was crying uncontrollably, he said, "What happens to him next is entirely up to you. You can spare him any further suffering simply by telling me what I want to know."

His eyes full of hatred, Fingers shook his head, vehemently. "You're going to kill him anyway, you fucking cunt," he cried.

"You're right, I am," Wiggins admitted with a sad smile. "Look, we both know this poor sod's fate is already sealed but, if you tell me what I need to know, I promise you he won't be made to suffer any more than he already has."

Fingers twisted his head away, doing his utmost to avoid looking at the smouldering ruins that had once been Marshall's legs, and trying his hardest to block the man's horrific injuries from his mind.

Wiggins shoulders slumped in defeat. "Very well," he said with weary resignation, "but, what happens next is completely on you."

He walked over to the petrol can, gave it a loud shake.

Fingers flinched at the unmistakeable sound of petrol swishing around inside.

Wiggins deliberately took his time walking over to Marshall, so that Fingers would have a chance to consider the ramifications of his decision. Ignoring the dreadful smell of burnt flesh, Wiggins raised the can and poured the remainder of the petrol over Marshall's head. It splashed down over his shoulders, soaking his entire body.

Thankfully, Marshall was unaware of what was happening to

him, having lapsed into a catatonic state as a result of his terrible injuries.

"Give me the matches," Wiggins demanded of Casper. He held his hand out impatiently.

A look of hurt passed over the albino's face, but he sulkily complied.

Wiggins held the matchbox against Fingers' ear and shook it.

Fingers recoiled at the sound.

"Last chance," Wiggins warned.

Fingers closed his eyes and bit down on his lips, signalling his intent to remain silent.

"As you wish," Wiggins said with a hint of sadness in his voice. Then, he struck the match.

After finishing the SPM on the arm, Tolpuddle called a fifteen minute break so that everyone could pop to the loo and stretch their legs. Livermore very kindly provided hot drinks for everyone, and Dillon accepted his gratefully.

When he had arrived at the mortuary that morning, the sickly sweet blend of death and disinfectant had seemed overwhelming. Now, a couple of hours into the process, it was barely noticeable.

Then it was time to get started on the leg.

Deep joy!

Before starting, Dillon jabbed another blob of Vicks up each nostril to help filter out the worst of the horrible smells.

And then Tolpuddle was talking into her recorder again.

The leg weighed in at 3.6 kilos.

A circular mark was noted at the top of the inner calf, and this was examined further using UV light sourcing.

"Do you think it's a bite mark?" Murray asked, craning his neck to get a closer look.

In front of him, Nerdy Ned was busy snapping away.

Tolpuddle shook her head. "I don't think so," she said, running a gloved finger over the surface of the mark. "There are no indentations, or obvious tooth imprints, and the skin hasn't been broken. We'll DNA swab it for saliva to be sure, and we'll also have the photographs Ned's just taken examined by a forensic odontologist, but I'm fairly confident it's just bruising."

There were areas of red marking on the outside of the leg. "I think these are likely to be ante-mortem bruises," Tolpuddle said. "They are consistent with a fall, but could also have been the result of our victim being kicked. Once the forensic anthropology has had a chance to examine all the body parts, we'll sit down together, go through all the X-rays and CT scans, and present our combined findings."

Contact had already been made with one of the UK's leading forensic anthropologists, and copies of the X-rays, scans and SPM reports were being sent to her to review before eventually travelling down to London to carry out her examination. It had been unanimously agreed that there was absolutely no point in her doing that until all – or at least as many as possible – of the outstanding body parts had been recovered.

As with the arm before it, deep muscle tissue samples were taken to assist with the identification of the leg.

Between them, the two post mortem examinations had taken a little over five hours, and all Dillon could think about was getting back to Hertford House and jumping under the shower.

26

You're useless at football

It was getting on for five when Dean Fletcher rapped on Tyler's office door. "Mind if I have a quick word?" he asked.

Tyler lowered his pen, waved him in.

"When Colin gave me the registration number for Carter's moped earlier, I took the liberty of having a retrospective ANPR search run on it, just to see what it threw up," Dean informed him.

"And...?"

"Well, I've just gone through the results they sent me, and there's a disproportionately high amount of ANPR hits from a camera in Morning Lane. We're talking several times a day, most days of the week." He handed Tyler the printout. "I've highlighted the relevant entries in yellow," he explained. "Now, I'm not an analyst, but I reckon she must live pretty close to where the camera's located, and it's picking her up every time she leaves home or returns."

Tyler hungrily ran his eyes over the data. "I need to look at this on a map of the area," he said, standing up. "Can you print me one out?"

"Already got one on my desk if you'd care to join me," Dean said, beckoning for Tyler to follow him.

A few seconds later, the two men were huddled over a map of Morning Lane and the surrounding side streets. Dean pointed out the location of the ANPR camera with a stubby forefinger. "Now, this could be a case of me adding two and two and getting eight, but the ANPR team sent me through a series of stills, along with the raw data, and it looks to me like the moped is indicating to turn right in some of these pictures." As he spoke, he handed Tyler several stills of the moped approaching a junction.

"Where is that?" Tyler asked, after examining them.

"The moped is in Morning Lane, and I think it's signalling to turn into Belsham Street, which is right opposite the Tesco store where Sharon Peacock bumped into Stella on the day that Carrie went missing."

Tyler looked at him. "That's a bit of a coincidence, isn't it?"

Dean nodded. "I think so. And it struck me that, if Stella was going shopping in Tesco, she would have walked there, not taken her moped, so it must be fairly close to where she lives."

Tyler picked up the phone on Dean's desk and tapped in the extension number for the CCTV viewing room. "Colin, Jack Tyler here. Have we got any CCTV coverage of the Tesco store in Morning Lane? I'm particularly interested in the junction with Belsham Street, which is located directly opposite."

"I'm pretty sure there's a local authority camera covering the junction," Franklin told him. *"I'll have to check to be certain, but it should only take me a couple of minutes."*

"Do that, please, and call me back as soon as you find out." Hanging up, Tyler returned to the map, deep in thought.

Dean peered over his shoulder. "What are you thinking?"

"I'm thinking that it might be worth doing a street search to look for Carter's moped."

The telephone rang.

It was Franklin, calling for Tyler.

"That was very quick," Tyler said, impressed. "What coverage have we got?"

"*There are two cameras covering the junction you're interested in, once facing in each direction,*" Franklin informed him. "*The good news is that both cameras are within the download parameters you gave me, so we already have the footage here.*"

That seemed too good to be true.

"Grab a pen," Tyler said, feeling his excitement mount. "I'm going to give you some dates and times, and I want you to view the two Morning Lane cameras for those periods. You'll be looking for Stella Carter on her moped, and she'll either be turning into Belsham Street or pulling out of it."

He reeled off the information from the ANPR list that Dean had given him. On a whim, he also asked Franklin to add the date that Stella had bumped into Sharon Peacock. "If you find her on that day, she'll probably be on foot, not on her moped."

"*How quickly do you need this?*" Franklin asked, and there was a note of trepidation in his voice.

Tyler grinned. "Yesterday, if not sooner."

Terry Marshall lay on his cot, whimpering quietly to himself in a state of agitated delirium. He was lucid one second, confused the next, and he was having a little trouble deciding whether he was actually awake, or if this was all simply a terrible nightmare from which he would be roused from at any moment.

Running his eyes down the length of his body, he saw that his lower legs were being ravaged by fire, and he recoiled in fear, drawing his knees up to his chest and screaming hysterically.

Make it stop! Please, make it stop!

He wasn't sure if he was shouting the words at the top of his voice, or just thinking them.

No one came to help, so maybe it was just the latter?

The room was filling with thick cloying smoke, and he was struggling to breathe.

The burning petrol was a living thing; a malevolent entity consuming everything in its path. The heat from those flames was unbearable, like sitting too close to a bonfire, only a thousand times worse.

Risking another downward glance, he was horrified to see that the flames had now reached his lower abdomen. Below that line, all he could see was the white of his bones, which were protruding from the charred meat that surrounded them.

The pain, as his skin sizzled and popped like sausages on a barbecue, was indescribable. The flames rose higher and higher, until he could feel the skin peeling from his face, coming away in great strips. He writhed and twisted, a last desperate attempt to break free from the chains that held him. Surrounded by thick, acrid smoke and red-hot flames, he opened his mouth for one last scream but, as soon as he did, the living fire invaded his lungs, roasting him from the inside out.

Oh God, it hurt so much!

As Marshall's eyes flew open, the powerful images dissipated into nothingness. Gulping in air, he realised that he was frantically patting his face and body, trying to put out the non-existent flames.

He wasn't on fire; it had all been a terrible dream.

Dizzy with relief, his chest heaving, he collapsed back on the cot, too exhausted to move.

He remained perfectly still for several minutes; his limbs too heavy to lift. Eventually, his breathing and heartbeat slowed, and he began to feel a little stronger.

With great difficulty, he reached down and gingerly explored his fire damaged legs. There was surprisingly little pain when he touched them, which he hoped was a good sign, signifying that the burns were not that serious after all. Had he been more knowledgeable about such things, he would have realised that quite the opposite was true; the real reason for his lack of pain was that the nerve endings had all been destroyed after the first fifteen seconds or so of being cooked.

In the darkness, the flesh of Marshall's ankles and calves felt like mottled candle wax, and he dreaded to think what the wounds would look like in daylight. Perhaps it was a blessing that his cell was pitch-black, so that he couldn't actually see the full extent of his burns. The smell wafting up from them was truly awful, and he began to worry that gangrene would set in if he didn't receive medical assistance very soon.

Forcing himself up into a sitting position, he tried calling out for help, but his vocal cords seemed to have stopped working, so all that came out was a feeble croak.

Marshall had never felt so dehydrated; it was as though he hadn't tasted water for a whole year. He tried licking his cracked lips, but his swollen tongue seemed to have lost the power of movement.

As Marshall laid back down again, a feeling of utter hopelessness washed over him. He was going to die in this darkened room, and there was absolutely nothing that he could do about it.

Fingers awoke from his uneasy slumber with a start. Scrabbling backwards into a sitting position, his back pressed tightly against the rough cell wall, he shuddered as he recalled how close Terry had come to being set alight a second time. The match had been inches away from his petrol-soaked form when Fingers had screamed at Wiggins to stop, promising to tell him everything he wanted to know, as long as he didn't harm Marshall.

Smiling victoriously, the arrogant bastard had made a big show of blowing out the match, before issuing orders that Marshall was to be returned to his cell.

Fingers had registered the intense disappointment on the albino's face as he unchained Marshall, and it had sickened him to realise that the giant had actually been looking forward to the spectacle of seeing the mechanic being turned into a human torch.

Afterwards, when they were alone, Wiggins had turned to Fingers. "For a moment there, I thought you were going to let me turn your flabby mate into Guy Fawkes," he confessed with an amused grin.

"What... what's going to happen to him now?" Fingers asked, still reeling from the horrors he had just witnessed.

Wiggins chuckled, evilly. "Best you worry about what's going to happen to you," he advised, giving the side of his aquiline nose a knowing tap. "Now, let's get down to business. I want to know the names of everyone involved in the robbery at Frankie's place."

Fingers' shoulders felt as though they were going to pop out of their sockets at any moment. He grimaced with pain, then broke into a wracking cough. He had inhaled so much smoke that his chest felt incredibly tight, and he was finding it increasingly difficult to breath.

"It was... It was m–me and... me and Darren," he stammered, before coughing so hard that he nearly brought up a lung.

Churning this over, Wiggins interlocked his hands behind his back and completed a contemplative stroll around Fingers. When he was facing his prisoner again, he nodded thoughtfully. "And who slotted Frankie?"

Fingers closed his eyes, prayed for forgiveness. "Darren," he said, his voice little more than a tormented whisper.

"And what about Carrie?" Wiggins demanded, completely unmoved by the other man's suffering. "Was she involved? Did she tip you off that the gems would be there?"

Fingers hesitated. He now knew that Carrie was dead, so admitting her involvement couldn't possibly harm her, and yet it went against the grain to do so. "I–I don't think so," he lied.

Wiggins didn't like wishy-washy answers. Stepping forward, he grabbed the prisoner's greasy hair and jerked his head backwards. "What exactly do you mean by that?" he snarled.

"I–I mean that D-Darren never told me where... where he got the info from," Fingers hissed through gritted teeth.

Wiggins released his grip, stepped backwards. "And where are the diamonds now?"

When Fingers didn't answer immediately, Wiggins punched him

hard in the solar plexus, sending him swinging in little circles and making the chains above him rattle loudly.

Fingers gasped as the air exploded from his lungs. He retched several times, but there was nothing in his stomach to throw up. Struggling for breath, he felt a wave of heat rush over him as the world started to spin.

"No, no, no," Wiggins said, angrily. "Don't you *dare* pass out on me."

That was the last thing that Fingers remembered before waking from the hellish nightmare a few moments earlier.

He wondered how long had he been back in his cell.

Minutes?

Hours?

Fingers knew that he didn't have much time to come up with a plan. As he saw it, his only chance of escape lay in fooling Wiggins into thinking that he could take them to the diamonds. The problem was, Fingers had no idea where they were. Dazza kept their hiding place a secret, even from Carrie.

But Wiggins didn't know that.

If Fingers could trick them into taking him somewhere public, he might be able to distract them enough that they would let down their guard, which would enable him to do a runner. It was a risky plan, and probably a hopeless one, but Fingers was as good as dead anyway, so he had nothing to lose and everything to gain.

Having made up his mind, he crossed the darkened room and banged on the door. "Hello," he shouted. "I wanna speak to Mr Wiggins."

It had taken Franklin just under two hours to view all of the footage relating to Belsham Street and Morning Lane that Tyler had expressed an interest in. His findings had made for interesting reading, and Tyler was now convinced that Stella either lived in Belsham Street itself, or in the council estate abutting it.

Most officers were still out on enquiries, but Tyler had managed to scrap together a half dozen detectives at short notice. Assembling them in his office for an urgent briefing, he gave orders that everyone – himself and Dillon included – were to get themselves down to Belsham Street as quickly as possible, so that they could conduct an impromptu street search for Carter's moped.

Imogen and Bear had tagged along, and Tyler was secretly fuming with Dillon, who had suggested they jump in with them.

"There's the ANPR camera," Dillon said as they cruised along Morning Lane. "And there are the two CCTV cameras covering the junction with Belsham Street."

Tyler grunted. He was about to point out that he didn't need a running commentary, when he realised that Dillon had been highlighting the camera locations for Imogen's benefit, not his.

He signalled right, waited for a gap in the oncoming traffic, and then steered the BMW into Belsham Street. It was a residential street, with parked cars lining both sides of the road.

The sprawling council estate to their right mainly consisted of high-rise blocks and maisonettes. Tyler's heart sank when he saw just how big it was, and he felt his earlier optimism drain away. "A pound to a penny, she lives in there," he said, miserably.

"Bound to," Dillon agreed. "It's called Trelawney Estate, if anyone's interested," he informed their guests.

Despite the relative lateness of the hour, a large group of prepubescent children were playing football on the grass area outside one of the tower blocks. Laughing and squealing as they ran around, they all seemed to be having a great time, and Tyler envied them their innocence.

With a cynicism born out of policing deprived inner London areas his entire career, he wondered how many of them would be allowed to lose that innocence naturally, and how many would have it cruelly stolen from them?

Some would have parents who were alcoholics or drug addicts.

Others would be suffering from physical or emotional abuse.

Most would have been potty mouthed before they were potty trained.

He wondered how many of them were already being coerced

into carrying drugs for the elders on the estate because they couldn't go to jail if they were caught in possession of them?

Tyler believed that all children were born pure, but far too many had their inherent happiness and goodness corrupted by an early exposure to the evils of the world. Advertising; peer pressure; perceived social status and family influence all played their part, as did a large number of other factors. Considering that he had spent much of his career dealing with violent thugs, drug dealers, and the monsters who killed and tortured others for fun, he still emphatically believed that not everyone who did a bad thing was a bad person. He had once asked Kelly if that made him a naïve fool. No, she had assured him; it made him a good man.

The left side of Belsham Street housed several industrial premises but, beyond those, there was a long row of terraced houses, some of which had been converted into flats if the buzzer systems on their street doors were anything to go by.

"I'll take a quick drive around the block," Tyler said, continuing slowly. Five minutes later, having completed a circuit that took them past more council estates and commercial premises, they returned to Belsham Street, and Tyler found a space to pull into. Opposite them, the game of football was still going strong.

"As we drove by earlier, I think I might've spotted a moped nestled between two vans," Bear said. "I mean, I only got a fleeting glance, and it might have been a motorbike, not a moped."

Tyler pulled out. "Let's have a look, shall we? You'll have to tell me where to stop."

Bear leaned forward, sticking his big, hairy head between the front seats like a shaggy dog. "There," he said a few seconds later, excitedly pointing to his left. "Between those two parked vans."

Tyler feathered on the brakes as they drew level. Sure enough, a little moped was tucked between a Mercedes Sprinter and a Bedford flatbed lorry. "Well spotted," he said, applying the handbrake.

Dillon was already out of the car. Striding to the rear of the moped, he checked the registration number against the one written in his daybook. Looking up a moment later, a big grin spread across his broad face, and he gave Tyler a thumbs up. "We've only gone and found it," he beamed.

Imogen opened her door. "Quick," she said to Bear, "let's get a shot of it."

As Tyler joined his colleague, a football came sailing through the air towards him. He deftly sidestepped it, and it bounced onto the pavement before rolling into the gutter.

"Oi, mister, can we have our ball back?" a cheeky looking oik with a dirty face called from the other side of a low brick wall that separated the council estate from the street beyond. The boy's light blue, crew neck jumper had a school crest on its left breast, and was covered with thick splodges of mud from where he had been rolling around on the grass with his mates. His grey shorts, which also had grass stains on them, were undoubtedly also a part of his school uniform. Reminding Tyler of a character from the *Just William* books, the little ragamuffin had mischievous blue eyes, and his short, dark hair was sticking up at all angles.

Smothering a smile, Tyler dreaded to think what his mother would say when he returned home in that state.

"Come on then," the boy said, impatiently placing his hands on his hips. "Kick our ball back."

Tyler grinned at him, then chipped the ball into the air and began playing keepie-uppie, seeing how many times he could kick the ball without it dropping to the floor. He only managed three.

The kid didn't seem very impressed.

"What team do you support?" Tyler asked, going for a second attempt.

"Spurs," the boy shouted back, proudly.

Tyler pulled a discouraging face. He was an avid Arsenal fan, and Tottenham Hotspur were their North London rivals. "They're rubbish," he said. "You should support a proper team like Arsenal." The ball fell to the floor again, but at least he had managed five goes this time around. Making sure that no cars were coming, he kicked the ball back over the wall. Unfortunately, a gust of wind caught it, and sent it tumbling in the wrong direction from the one he had intended it to travel in.

Embarrassing!

The kid had the audacity to raise his middle finger at Tyler. "You're useless at football," he shouted as he turned to run after the ball, "and so are Arsenal."

As Tyler watched him go, a lopsided grin spread across his face. That was when he noticed the wall mounted CCTV camera pointing straight at them from the tower block.

27

Ooh, you're a naughty one!

"So, let me get this straight," Willard said, speaking into his mobile phone in hushed tones. He had adjourned to the men's room of the swanky little restaurant his trophy wife had dragged him out to, so that he could take the incoming call in private. "You're seriously telling me that hard-nosed bitch has got the bare faced effrontery to deny killing poor little Carrie?"

"That's right," Wiggins confirmed.

Willard felt his blood pressure climb several notches. "Fucking liberty," he fumed, looking around for something to hit out at. "I'm not having that."

He spotted a trash bin in the corner, and gave it a good kick, sending used paper towels sprawling all over the tiled floor.

"I'm sure she'll tell us the truth before too much longer," Wiggins assured him.

"Oh, she will," Willard promised, ominously. "Mark my words, she'll be singing like a fucking canary by the time I'm finished with her. And what about that horrible little slag, Fingers? Has he finally admitted that it was him and Darren McCullen who stole my diamonds and topped Frankie?"

"Yep."

"And I take it Darren's the cunt who shot Frankie?"

"According to Fingers."

Willard looked around for something else to lash out at, but there was nothing, so he booted the overturned bin again, sending it clattering into one of the cubicle doors. "And he's adamant that this Marshall wanker had nothing to do with it?"

Wiggins paused before answering. *"That's what he says, but I'm not sure I believe him."*

Willard grunted. He didn't really give a damn, one way or another. "And now that you've explained the error of his ways to him, our digitally challenged friend's offering to take you to the spot where Darren buried the gems, is that right?"

"That's right."

That was good news, at least.

Willard pulled one of his precious cigars from his breast pocket, sniffed it longingly, wishing that he could light up right there and then. Unfortunately, a smoke alarm had been fitted in the ceiling, and the bloody thing would give him away.

"Why can't he just tell you where they are?" he demanded.

"He reckons Darren buried them at an allotment, and that he would need to point out the exact spot or we'd never find it," Wiggins explained, calmly.

"Yeah, but is he telling you the truth, Fred, or just stringing you along with a load of old bollocks?"

"Only one way to find out, I guess," Wiggins said, pragmatically. *"I'm going to wait a couple of hours, till it's nice and quiet, then we'll stick him in the back of the van and get the little toerag to take us there. If he's fucking us about, he knows what will happen to him."*

Willard emerged from the men's room. Looking across the restaurant to the packed bar, he smiled at his much younger wife, who was happily chatting away to another woman. She caught his eye, smiled back, then resumed talking.

"Listen, Fred, I'm stuck at some poncy restaurant, having dinner with a couple of my wife's wanker friends, but we'll be finished soon, so I'll bung her in a cab and come over there myself."

"There's no need for—"

"If I say there's a need, then there's a fucking need," Willard snapped, cutting him off.

"Yes, of course," Wiggins said quickly. *"I just meant that—"*

"Listen, Fred," Willard interrupted. "First, I'm gonna finish my fancy overpriced meal, then I'm coming straight over there. The way I see it, I might as well take care of that horrible slag, Stella, tonight. Her attitude has given me the right hump, and if I don't take it out on her, I'll only end up having a go at the missus. Besides, I want to be there when you recover my diamonds. In the meantime, if you don't need Marshall anymore, you might as well let Casper take care of him, if you get my drift."

Wiggins certainly did.

―――

It had taken some doing, but Franklin had finally managed to track down the estate caretaker who, after much cajoling, had grudgingly agreed to turn out on a Saturday night to grant them access to the estate's CCTV room.

"Dunno why you couldn't just wait till Monday morning," he complained as he switched the bank of viewing monitors on. "I was just about to pop down the pub for a game of billiards."

"It's very important," Franklin assured him. "I wouldn't have asked, otherwise."

The caretaker, a pencil-thin man of late middle age, with greying hair and a surly, unshaven face, snorted derisively. "My bloody game of billiards was important, too," he objected. "Nobody seems to care about that, though." As he spoke, he called up the live-time view from the camera Tyler had noticed earlier.

On screen, Franklin could see Tyler, Dillon, the pretty reporter and the hairy cameraman, clustered around Carter's moped.

"This the one you wanted?" the caretaker asked.

Franklin nodded. "That's the one. Now, I need to play the footage backwards, starting from ten minutes ago."

Shaking his head at the perceived unreasonableness of the request, the caretaker's nicotine-stained fingers fumbled with the controls. "How long's this gonna take?" he demanded, once the footage was playing.

"Can we swap places?" Franklin asked, shooing him out of his seat. "It'll be a lot quicker if you let me do it."

"Be my guest," the caretaker said, prising himself out of the chair. He stood up slowly, rubbed his lower back, then grimaced. "Right, I'm gonna go and make myself a brew," he said, fixing Franklin with a gnarly stare. "I'll be back in fifteen minutes. You'd better be done by then."

"We're going to canvass all these houses," Tyler told the four officers who had just joined them. He handed out copies of Stella's latest custody imaging photo, which Dean had printed off for him. "Remember to play down why we're looking for her," he reminded them. "If anyone asks, we're just trying to locate her as she might be a witness to an ongoing investigation."

When the others left, Tyler turned to Dillon, who was having a cosy conversation with Imogen. Those two were getting far too friendly for his liking.

"Right, Dill," he said, interrupting the love birds. "Let's start with the obvious place, shall we?" He indicated the black door immediately behind the moped. "I reckon there's a fairly good chance that she parked the bloody thing right outside her flat, don't you?"

Dillon glanced at the moped, then at the door behind him. It had four separate buzzers affixed to the wall beside it. "It would make sense," he agreed, walking over to examine the nameplates below the buzzers. Two of them were vacant, the other two contained the occupiers' names. "Who shall we try first?" he asked. "Edith Martin or Agatha Simpkins?"

Tyler shrugged, impatiently. "Just press them all, and we'll see what happens."

Dillon obliged, jabbing all four buzzers, one after the other, with a large finger.

A crackle of static from the speaker, then a brittle female voice, spooked by someone calling at such a late hour. "Yes, who is it?"

"It's the police," Dillon explained. "Can you open the door for us, please?"

"The police?" the woman sounded alarmed. "What's happened? What's wrong?"

"Nothing's wrong," Dillon assured her. "We're just making door to door enquiries and need to speak to all the residents. We won't take up much of your time."

The crackling ceased.

Silence.

Dillon and Tyler exchanged confused looks.

Dillon was just about to press the buzzers again, when the street door opened a few inches, and a withered face appeared in the gap.

"Hello," Dillon said, producing his warrant card for inspection and treating the wary pensioner who was peering out at him to his most charming smile. "We're trying to trace this woman," he said, holding up Stella's mug shot. "She's a potential witness in a very important case, and we believe she lives somewhere around here. I don't suppose you recognise her, do you?"

The door opened wider and the silver haired occupant, who must have been in her late seventies if she was a day, ventured forward on stiff legs. "Give it here," she said, extending a liver spotted hand. "Can't see too good without my glasses."

She snatched it from his hand and held it close to her face, squinting and frowning. "That's Stella," she said after a couple of moments. "Lives in the flat opposite mine."

"Is she inside her flat right now?" Tyler asked, speaking for the first time.

The old woman eyed him with suspicion. "And who are you?"

"This is my much uglier partner," Dillon said with a cheeky grin.

That drew a gummy smile. The old woman might not have any teeth left, Tyler thought, but she clearly still possessed a good sense of humour.

"Ooh, you're a naughty one," she cackled, relaxing now that she knew Tyler wasn't a mad axe murderer.

Imogen, who seemed to be permanently attached to Dillon's side, joined in.

"Isn't he?" Tyler said, drily.

There was a twinkle in the old woman's eyes as she gave Dillon and Imogen a knowing look. "You've got yourself a handsome fella there," she told Imogen, assuming they were a couple. "Take it from me, you ought to hang onto that one."

Imogen gave Dillon a gushy look.

Dillon blushed.

Tyler rolled his eyes. "Sorry to interrupt," he said, tetchily, "but is Stella in her flat now?"

Annoyed with him for spoiling the moment, the old crone glared at Tyler, then shook her head. "No," she said frostily. "She hasn't come back since she went out with that big, white haired bloke this morning."

Tyler frowned. "What time this morning?"

She shrugged. "I dunno. Early."

"What did this man look like?" Dillon asked. "You said he was big, but what else can you tell us about him?"

"He wasn't just big," she said. "He was a lot taller than you, and bloody enormous with it." She spread her arms out wide to demonstrate the width of his shoulders.

"Have you ever seen him before?" Tyler asked.

The woman shook her head, emphatically. "No, never. But they must be pretty friendly though, because he had his arm wrapped tightly around her waist when they left, and she was leaning right into him."

"I don't suppose you saw what vehicle they got into, did you" Dillon asked, hopefully.

"I did," the old woman said, treating him to another toothless smile. "It was a white van, and it was parked just over there," she said, pointing to her left. A frown marred her ancient forehead, and she began scratching her head thoughtfully. "Come to think of it, it did seem a bit odd that she got into the back of the van, not the front."

Tyler's phone went off. "Excuse me a moment," he said, stepping away.

"Boss, it's Colin," Franklin announced the moment he answered. His voice was taut, excited, and Tyler instinctively knew that he had found something important. He felt his heartbeat spike with anticipation.

"About half-eight this morning, a white Ford Transit pulled up a couple of doors further along from where the moped's parked," Franklin said. *"A gigantic albino, not just big, but brick-shit-house big, got out and went to the house immediately behind the moped. He spent a minute or so fiddling with the lock, then went inside. A couple of minutes later, he reappeared with Stella Carter. There's something very wrong about the way they leave. She looks out of it, like she's been drugged or something. He's got his right arm wrapped tightly around her waist, and her feet are dragging along the pavement like she can't walk under her own steam. He manhandled her into the back of the van and slammed the doors shut. He had a shifty look all around, as though making sure that no one had seen him, then climbed in the front and drove off."*

That gelled with what the old woman had just told them. From the way Franklin had described things, it didn't sound like Stella had left of her own accord. He wondered who the giant albino was, and what he wanted with her.

"I don't suppose you managed to get a clear view of the van's number plate, did you?"

"No, this camera only affords me a side on view of the van," Franklin told him. *"But both ends of Belsham Street are covered by local authority cameras so, once I get back to base, I should be able to pick it up leaving, and get the registration number from that."*

"Okay, get the caretaker to burn you off a copy of that footage, then head back to KZ. As soon as you get that registration number, ask Dean to run it through the PNC and ANPR databases."

Returning to where Dillon and Imogen were still talking to the old lady, Tyler examined the front door. Sure enough, there were fresh scratch marks around the lock, suggesting that it had recently been picked. That explained how the albino had gained entry, but where had he learned the skills to do something like that?

"Dill, call the others back," he said, straightening up. "We've found out what we needed to know. Get on the blower to the locals, and arrange for a PC to come and stand on the door till we can get a Section 8 PACE warrant organised. Stella's flat's a potential crime scene, so we'll have to hang onto it for a while."

———

Annie Jenkins ushered Kelly Flowers and Debbie Brown into the living room of her flat, which was located at the other end of Hoxton Market to the house Carrie had shared with her brother.

Looking as miserable as ever, Aidan was sitting on the sofa, drinking a can of lager. "What do you want?" he demanded with open hostility.

"We're here to give you an update, and to ask you a few questions," Kelly informed him.

"Please sit down," Annie said, indicating the two armchairs on either side of the settee. "Would you like a drink?"

Kelly shook her head, smiled appreciatively. At least one of them had some manners. "That's very kind of you," she responded, "but we're fine."

"What's this update, then?" Aidan asked, using the remote control to mute the TV.

Annie sat down beside him. Leaning her head against his shoulder, she reached across and took his free hand in both of hers.

"The DCI has asked us to let you know that we've discovered some CCTV footage of a white woman dragging the suitcase containing Carrie's torso along the canal towpath, last Saturday evening," Kelly told them.

Annie's hands flew to her mouth to stifle a gasp, and the colour drained from her face.

Aidan's jaw tightened, a nervous tick began in his right eye, and the can in his hand began to shake so much that he was forced to put it down. He hurriedly tucked both hands between his thighs to conceal this from the detectives.

Their shocked reaction was completely understandable and, even though she didn't like him, Kelly felt a pang of sympathy for Aidan.

"You... you think a woman killed my sister?" he asked in a hoarse voice.

Kelly nodded, solemnly. "Yes, we do."

Aidan sunk back into his seat, and shook his head, disbelievingly.

"We've managed to track her back to a cab office in Hoxton Market," Debbie said, taking up the narrative. "We've even got CCTV of her going into the cab office with the suitcase."

Aidan had gone a deathly shade of white. "Do you... do you know who she is?" he asked.

"She ordered a cab under the name of Lucinda McLean," Debbie said, studying them both carefully for a reaction.

Annie gasped, looked sideways at Aidan, who looked like he was going to throw up.

"Does that name mean anything to either of you?" Kelly asked.

Aidan just stared at her.

Tearing her eyes away from Aidan, Annie shook her head. "No, we don't know anyone by that name, do we, Aidan?"

After a moment, Aidan seemed to snap out of his trance. "What? N–no. No, we don't," he said, dry washing his face with a trembling hand.

"I've been authorised to play you a short clip of the footage of Lucinda in the cab office, to see if that jogs your memory," Debbie said, withdrawing a VHS tape from her bag. She held it out to Aidan, nodded towards the video player. "Would you mind doing the honours for me?"

For a moment, Aidan remained rooted to the spot.

The detectives were both staring at him quizzically, and the atmosphere quickly became strained. Then, Annie nudged him in the ribs, which seemed to break the spell. With a little gasp of surprise, he jumped up and snatched the VHS cassette from

Debbie's outstretched hand. Kneeling down by the TV, he inserted it into the video and pressed the play button.

As the thirty-second long clip began to play, Aidan stood up and cupped his hands to his mouth. Unable to drag his eyes away from the screen, he watched, mesmerised, as Lucinda entered the cab office, struggling to get the suitcase inside.

"Do you recognise her?" Debbie asked him, her voice filling with compassion.

Still staring at the TV, Aidan shook his head.

"What about you, Annie?" Kelly asked.

Annie opened her mouth, closed it again. Swallowed. She suddenly looked ill. "No," she said, weakly. "I'm sorry, I don't."

Kelly exchanged a subtle glance with Debbie, who gave her an almost imperceptible nod to continue. "I can't go into the details of how or why," Kelly said, "but we think that the woman in the footage could be Stella Carter, Carrie's ex-partner. If we're right, then it would follow that she's using the name 'Lucinda McLean' as an alias to cover her tracks."

Aidan blew his cheeks out. "I–I can't believe this," he stammered.

Annie was sitting rigid, and all colour had drained from her face.

Kelly smiled, sympathetically. "It's a lot for you to take in," she said.

"Have you spoken to Stella yet?" Annie asked, her voice brittle

Kelly shook her head, regretfully. "We're actively searching for her," she explained, "but she seems to have dropped off the radar at the moment."

Light from the corridor spilled in as the cell door was opened, illuminating the unmoving figure on the cot within its harsh yellow glow. Standing in the doorway, Casper turned his nose up as the putrefied stench of burnt flesh assailed his nostrils. "Get up," he ordered, fanning his nose.

Marshall didn't respond, but the gentle rise and fall of his chest told the albino that he was still alive, just sleeping.

Stepping into the room, Casper pulled on a pair of heavy-duty rubber gloves. Wiggins had promised him that he could have some fun with this one, but there would be no satisfaction in what he was about to do unless Marshall was conscious throughout.

He nudged the prisoner's arm. "Get up," he repeated, louder this time.

Again, no response.

Slipping his hands under the sleeping man's armpits. He unceremoniously dragged him off the cot and out of the cell.

Marshall's charred feet left behind a gory detritus of blood, pus and flaking skin as they slid along the hard floor. Looking back at the disgusting snail trail, Casper felt an irrational spike of anger, knowing that he would be the one who Wiggins lumbered with mopping it all up afterwards.

As they reached the brightly lit torture room, Marshall finally stirred. A moment later, his eyes flickered open and he moaned something unintelligible.

"About bloody time," Casper said, willing him to regain his senses.

Mickey and Basher were leaning against the far wall, watching him, while Fred Wiggins was in the office, speaking to Mr Willard on the phone.

Three circular steel drums, each with a 212 litre storage capacity, had been lined up against the rear wall. They were empty at the moment but, before the weekend was over, they would contain the bodies of the three prisoners. Then, on Monday morning, the drums would be loaded into the back of a Transit van and driven across London to a building site that was having its foundations laid during the coming week. The galvanised clamping rings on the tight-fitting circular lids would ensure that the drums remained airtight once sealed, so there was no danger of any nasty smells escaping during transport. The foreman at the building site was on the firm, and he would ensure that no one went near the drums until he was ready for their contents to be dumped into the wet concrete of the building's foundations.

Frustrated that Marshall had lapsed into silence again, Casper leaned down and slapped his face.

Nothing. No reaction at all.

Basher walked over and handed him a capsule of smelling salts, which Casper accepted without a word. Breaking it open, he waved it under the unconscious man's nostrils.

Marshall reacted at once, violently twisting his head to one side as he tried to avoid inhaling the fumes, but Casper mirrored his movements with the vial, making sure that he couldn't escape.

After a few seconds, Marshall's eyes flickered open and he looked up at Casper in confusion. "W–where am I?" he croaked.

Casper ran cold eyes over the broken body, gauging the injured man's reserves. He could tell that Marshall wouldn't be able to take much punishment and, in all probability, would pass out as soon as Casper began.

It was a great pity.

With a regretful sigh, he realised that there was no point in even trying to have any fun with this one, so he might as well just get on with it, and put the mangy cur out of its misery.

Raising a size fourteen foot high above Marshall's head, he brought it thundering down, driving the heel of his industrial work boot into the centre of Marshall's terrified face with all his might.

28

One thing at a time

It was a few minutes after nine when Franklin strode into the main office. Dillon and the pretty media lady who seemed to have been shadowing him for the past few days were chatting by the tea urn, and he nodded a polite acknowledgement to each of them, but they were too absorbed in each other to even notice.

"Dean, I need you to run me an urgent PNC check," he shouted from halfway across the room.

Looking up, Fletcher raised an enquiring eyebrow, then extended a hand for the scrap of paper Franklin was waving in his direction.

"It's the registration number for the van that Stella Carter was shoved into after being snatched from her flat," Franklin explained. "The boss also wants it run through ANPR."

Tapping away at his keyboard, Dean grunted an acknowledgement. "One thing at a time," he said, calmly.

The keeper details came up on screen a moment later, and Dean pressed the print button to produce a hardcopy. "It's a white Ford Transit, registered to a building company based in Barking," he said, looking up at Franklin.

Grabbing the printout, Franklin thanked him and headed straight for Tyler's office. The door was open, so he walked in without knocking. "Boss, I've got the registered keeper details for the van that was used to abduct Stella."

Tyler held out a hand. "This is a local address," he said, after reading it.

Franklin nodded. "Do you want me to arrange for a local unit to drive-by and see if it's there?"

"That would be very helpful," Tyler said. "While you're at it, can you dig out the key-holder details for me, in case we need to gain access?"

"Of course," Franklin said. "I'll get right on it."

"Oh, and ask Deano to do some flash research on the company, just to see if there's anything dodgy about it."

"Will do," Franklin shouted over his shoulder on his way through the door.

"Colin," Tyler shouted, calling him back a second time.

"Yes, boss?"

"Where's the footage of the albino putting Stella Carter into the back of the van? I'd like to see it, and I think it would be a good idea to play it for the rest of the team too, on the off chance that someone recognises him."

"It's downstairs in the CCTV room," Franklin said, wearily. "Give me five minutes to speak to Dean and phone the local nick, then I'll pop down and grab it.

"So, are you going to invite me back to your place again, tonight?" Imogen asked, smiling coyly at Dillon, who was making them both a much-needed cup of coffee. He stiffened, then looked around the room to make sure that no had overheard her comment.

Imogen laughed at his obvious unease. "Relax," she chided him softly. "I checked to see that we were alone before speaking."

"I would like that very much," he admitted, "but won't you need to go home and collect some fresh clothes, first?"

Imogen gave him a resolute shake of her head. "Nope."

Dillon frowned at her, his square face showing confusion.

"Whenever I go on an assignment," she explained, realising that he didn't have a clue what she was getting at. "I always pack a 'go bag' and leave it in the boot of my car in case of emergencies. It's filled with a few toiletries, a pair of PJs, several days' worth of underwear and a couple of spare blouses." An indignant frown drew her professionally plucked brows together. "Don't tell me you hadn't even realised that I'm wearing a different blouse today?" She stared at him incredulously, then tugged at her collar. "I mean, it's a completely different colour."

Dillon busied himself pouring out their coffee so that he wouldn't have to look at her. "I've had a lot on my mind," he said, lamely.

Imogen rolled her eyes, tutted. "Some bloody detective you are," she laughed, accepting the mug he offered her.

"Right, listen in, you lot," Tyler announced when Franklin returned with the CCTV from Trelawney Estate. "Colin's going to play us a short clip of a massive albino manhandling Stella Carter out of her flat in Belsham Street and into the back of a Ford Transit van. I want you all to have a good look at him. If anyone recognises him, it would be really helpful."

He nodded to Franklin, who pressed the play button. As the tape was coming to an end a couple of minutes later, the office door flew open and Kevin Murray rushed in, closely followed by Charlie White.

"Sorry we're late," White said, breathlessly. "We've been busy logging all the exhibits into the cage downstairs."

Indicating for them to be seated, Tyler instructed Franklin to replay the clip.

Almost immediately, Murray stiffened in his seat. "I know him," he spluttered, sounding surprised. "He's the ape who was with what's-his-face at thingy's house."

"Can we have that in English, please?" Tyler asked, testily.

Murray muttered an apology. "He was at Pauline Kyle's house last week, when me and Whitey went round there to collect Morag Kyle for Mr Q's team. It was the day after her husband was shot dead."

"Do either of you know his name?" Tyler asked, signalling for Franklin to play the clip a third time.

Both men shook their heads.

"All I can tell you is that he was with Fred Wiggins, following him around like a trained attack dog," White said, then frowned in thought. "But I bet Mr Q's Intel Cell will know who he is."

"Any idea why one of Wiggins' thugs would want to abduct Stella Carter?" Tyler asked.

White nodded, uncomfortably. "Aye, I have. Willard told me that Carrie was like family to him. If he's worked out that Stella killed her, he'll want something done about it."

"You think he'd take the law into his own hands?" Imogen asked, sounding surprisingly naive.

White laughed. "People like that dinnae give a toss about the law, Miss Askew. If he blames Stella for Carrie's death, he'll want his own personalised brand of justice dished out."

Tyler considered the implications of what White was telling him. If the Scotsman was right, he had to assume that Stella Carter's life was now in imminent danger, making her abduction a threat to life kidnapping.

Great!

With everything else that was going on, that was the last thing he bloody well needed.

PCs Kevin Greenway and Angela Oaks had been making their way back to the station when the control room ordered them to detour to the old industrial estate near Barking Creek, in order to see if a Ford Transit that had been involved in a possible abduction was parked outside one of the warehouses. Although they were due to finish their shift at ten, they still had three crime reports to enter onto the system, so there was no way they were going to get off on time as it was, and this pointless diversion would only delay them further.

"I don't know why this rubbish call couldn't have waited for night duty to roll out," Greenway complained, pulling the Immediate Response Vehicle into the industrial estate. In his late twenties, he was the senior of the two by five years, both in terms of age and police service.

"You heard the skipper," Oaks said, pragmatically. "It might have been involved in the abduction of a woman from a flat in Hackney."

Greenway had dealt with calls like this before, and they almost always turned out to be a load of old tosh. "Might being the operative word" he said, dismissively.

"I know, but we have to check it out. Besides, it'll only take a couple of minutes," Oaks said, trying to placate her irritable partner. "We'll do a quick drive by to see if it's there and, when it's not, we can Foxtrot Oscar back to base."

Foxtrot Oscar was a police expression meaning to 'fuck off.'

"Knowing my luck, it'll be there and we'll be tucked up dealing with it for half the sodding night," Greenway complained. He was a glass half empty kind of guy, and he always assumed the worst.

Oaks smothered a smile; it was a bit like working with a younger version of Victor Meldrew. "Let's worry about that if and when it happens," she suggested.

Driving slowly along the potholed service road that led through the estate, the Astra's headlights scythed a path through the darkness ahead of them. Most of the buildings were boarded up and, of those that weren't, very few had any identifying names or numbers outside, which made finding the place more complicated than it needed to be.

"See," Greenway grumbled. "I knew it wouldn't be straight forward; nothing ever is."

By a process of elimination, they eventually excluded all the other warehouses until they were left with one. "This has got to be the place," Greenway said, peering into the night.

There were no lights on inside the building, and all the doors and windows appeared secure. There was no sign of the van outside, although a very nice Audi was parked on the forecourt, right in front the metal shutters.

"What's a car like that doing round here?" Oaks asked, reaching for her radio.

"What are you doing?" Greenway demanded, staring at her accusingly.

"Chillax," she told him. "Just gonna do a quick car check to make sure that Audi's not nicked."

Leaving her to it, Greenway eased himself out the patrol car. Hands in pockets, he wandered over to the warehouse, where he carried out a token check of the shutters and door, just to be sure that they really were secure. That done, he wandered over to the side of the building. An eight-foot metal gate, which had a series of nasty looking spikes protruding outward from the top, prevented him from gaining access to the car park at the rear.

On his way back to the Astra, he gave the Audi a quick once over. If it was stolen, he would expect to find a popped door lock or smashed quarterlight, and for the ignition to be barrelled, but everything appeared intact.

"Well?" he asked, sliding behind the steering wheel a few moments later. "Is it nicked?"

Oaks shook her head. "Nah, there are no reports on it. It's registered to some local bloke called Fred Wiggins. Does it look like it's been tampered with?"

"Nope, and the doors and windows to the warehouse are all secure too, so I guess we can be on our way."

Now that they were free to go, his mood had lightened, she

noticed, pulling her seatbelt on. "Of course, the van could be parked around the back, out of sight," she pointed out, just to wind him up. "And the poor cow who was bundled into it could be trapped inside the building, being tortured as we speak."

Greenway slipped the Astra into first, then pulled away with a little wheelspin. "You've been watching far too many cop shows on TV," he told her, throwing in an exaggerated eye roll for good measure.

Darren's eyes followed the departing patrol car's tail lights until they disappeared around the corner at the end of the service road. His own car was tucked down the side of the alley that ran between the two buildings opposite Willard's warehouse. With its engine and running lights off, it blended into the surrounding darkness and, although both officers had looked straight at him at one point or another, neither had seen him.

Darren was becoming increasingly convinced that Fingers and Terry were inside the warehouse, but getting in was proving to be a major problem as the place was as impregnable as a fortress. If he couldn't go in to them, he would just have to make them come out to him, he decided. All he needed was a distraction to lure them into the open.

But what…?

It would have to be something pretty big to get their attention.

Slumping back in his seat, Darren's bloodshot eyes came to rest on the Audi. It was undeniably a magnificent piece of machinery, worth a small fortune, and it was probably Wiggins' pride and joy.

He sat up straight, his heart racing.

Suddenly, he knew exactly what to do.

Dean Fletcher popped his head around Tyler's door without knocking. "Just heard back from the locals with the result of the call-on we asked them to carry out at the warehouse," he announced.

Tyler had been locked in conversation with Dillon. He sat up, lowered his pen, and rolled his aching neck muscles. "Do tell," he said, staring expectantly at his lead researcher.

"There's no trace of the van," Dean said, flatly. "The building was in total darkness, and all the shutters were pulled down, so they couldn't tell if it was inside. Oh, and they couldn't access the car park at the rear of the building either, because the gates to the service road were locked."

Tyler cursed under his breath, thinking that the call-on had been a complete waste of time and energy. "So, basically, what you're saying is that we're no clearer about where the van is now than we were before the local plod attended the warehouse?"

Dean shrugged, lamely. "All they can say is that there was no sign of the van outside. Apparently, there was a nice motor parked on the forecourt, but the engine was cold, so it had obviously been parked there for quite a while."

"Who's it registered to?" Tyler asked, his interest piqued.

The question seemed to throw Fletcher. "I don't know if they even bothered to do a car check on it," he admitted, seeming a trifle embarrassed for not having thought to ask them.

Tyler sighed.

If you want something done properly, do it yourself…

He stood up, grabbed his suit jacket from the back of his chair. "Come on, Dill," he said, irritably. "Let's pop down there and check out the place for ourselves."

Dillon looked crestfallen. "Really?"

Halfway through slipping his jacket on, Tyler cast him an accusatory stare. "Yes, really!"

"But I need to go through all the outstanding actions and work out tomorrow's tasking priorities," Dillon objected.

With a loud harrumph, Tyler swatted the protest aside. "You can do that when we get back. We'll only be out for half an hour." Without waiting for a reply, he stormed out of the office.

Dillon glanced sideways at Dean Fletcher, gave him a defeated shrug, and followed suit.

Perched on the end of his cot, Fingers was so nervous that he could hardly sit still. Little jolts of adrenalin surged through him every time he heard a noise outside his cell. Wringing his hands together to stop them from shaking, he contemplated his chances of getting away. The odds were heavily stacked against him, he knew, but he had decided it was better to go out fighting than to just roll over and die.

After offering to take Wiggins to retrieve the diamonds, his clothes had been returned to him, and he had dressed in the darkness, wincing as the material brushed against his battered body.

After much consideration, Fingers had decided to take them to the allotments near Darren's estate in Pitfield Street. He had chosen the allotments purely because he knew the layout pretty well from all the times that he and Darren had assisted the late Mrs McCullen to dig it up in preparation for planting her crops. The place was surrounded by thick brambles and shrubbery, but Fingers knew where most of the gaps were and, more importantly, where they led to, so that should work in his favour, especially in the darkness.

A sudden noise outside his cell door made him jump. It was the grating sound of a bolt being slid back. Backing away from the door, he took a deep breath and steeled himself for whatever was to come. A second later, the heavy metal door swung open to reveal Mickey standing there. He was holding a large mug in his bandaged hand. "Brought you a cup of tea," he said, hobbling into the cell on his dodgy ankle.

Fingers hoped it hurt like hell.

"Thank you," he croaked, avoiding eye contact as he reached out to accept the offering.

The tea was hot and sweet, and it burned his cracked lips as he sipped it, but he didn't care; it was the first liquid to have passed his lips since his arrival at the awful place.

DIAMONDS AND DEATH

Clutching the mug in both hands, and savouring the warmth it gave off, Fingers drank the contents as quickly as he dared. When he was finished, he held the cup out for Mickey to take.

"Come on," the thug said, indicating the open door with a jerk of his head. "Mr Wiggins wants to talk to you in the main room."

After the stygian darkness of his cell, the harsh light of the corridor seemed blindingly bright, and Fingers raised a hand to shield himself from the worst of it.

Mickey laughed at him. "Come on," he said, grabbing the sleeve of Fingers' jacket and giving it a hard tug.

Stumbling along the corridor on stiff legs, his eyes compressed into thin slits, Fingers saw that Marshall's cell door was wide open. Had he not been squinting to protect his eyes from the harsh light, he would also have noticed the gore ridden trail along the floor. "Where's Terry?" he demanded, dragging his heels.

"He's in his drum," Mickey replied with a sneer.

The comment confused Fingers. Was Mickey being serious? Had they allowed Marshall to go home?

Before he could say anything more, a woman's voice came from behind the cell at the end of the corridor. Weak and reedy, it was full of fear. "Please, help me," it pleaded. "I didn't do it; I didn't kill Carrie!"

Fingers froze on the spot. "Who's that?" he demanded, "and what did she mean about not killing Carrie?"

Mickey released his arm long enough to slap him around the back of the head. "Save your questions for Mr Wiggins," he ordered, before grabbing Fingers arm even tighter than before, and frogmarching him into the main room.

When Fingers caught sight of the two sets of chains dangling from the ceiling, he instinctively wrapped his arms around his body, and tried to ignore the lingering smell of burnt flesh.

Wiggins was standing by the office door, talking into a mobile telephone. To his right, Basher was leaning nonchalantly against a wall, awaiting instructions. To his left, the sinister albino was watching him through dead eyes.

"Where's Terry?" Fingers asked, directing the question at Wiggins.

Wiggins raised a finger to his lips, indicated for him to be quiet. "Yes, Mr Willard," he said into the phone. "I'll send someone straight out to open the door for you." Terminating the call, he nodded towards Basher. "The boss is about to pull up outside," he said, pocketing the mobile. "Go and let him in."

With a grunt, Basher levered his large bulk off the wall and set off towards the loading bay.

"Where's Terry?" Fingers asked again, managing to inject more confidence than he actually felt into his voice.

Wiggins stared at him for a long moment, and there was an amused glint in his eye. Then he crossed the room to where three steel drums stood against the far wall. They hadn't been there earlier, when Fingers and Marshall were being tortured. Wiggins sat down on the nearest one. "Let's just say, he's around," he said, smiling cryptically.

Fingers nodded towards Mickey. "He said he's gone home."

"No," Mickey corrected. "I said he was in his drum."

Casper began to chuckle. Even Wiggins laughed. They looked at each other, as if sharing a private joke.

"What have you done with Terry, you cunt?" Fingers heard himself shout, and he was surprised at the anger in his voice.

Mickey stepped forward, delivered a hard uppercut to Fingers' jaw. The mechanic fell to the floor. Letting out a low moan, he curled into a ball.

Mickey drew back his good foot, lined up a to kick Fingers' head.

"That's enough," Wiggins said sharply.

Mickey lowered his foot. With a surly glance over his shoulder, he backed off.

Fingers stood up groggily, spitting blood from a cut lip. Massaging his aching jaw, he glared at Mickey for a moment, then turned to face Wiggins. "You still haven't answered my question," he said through gritted teeth.

Wiggins stood up. "Marshall's not your concern any longer," he said, and there was a dangerous edge to his voice. "The only thing you need to worry about is taking us to those diamonds." Walking over to Fingers, he cupped the mechanic's face between his hands. Then, staring deep into the prisoner's eyes, he leaned forward until their noses were almost touching. "Do you understand?"

"Y–yes," Fingers muttered, knowing that he would die a horrible death if his plan didn't work.

29

Thanks for the advice

Shaking the can, Darren sprinkled the last remaining drips of petrol over the roof of Wiggins' expensive Audi. He couldn't wait to see the look of horror on the bastard's face when he came rushing out and saw his precious vehicle covered in flames. With any luck, it would be the last thing that he saw before Darren put a 9mm bullet between his eyes.

Having decided that a car fire was the best way to draw Wiggins out, he had driven to the nearest garage in order to purchase the cannister and fill it with petrol. When he'd returned, after an absence of nearly fifteen minutes, his heart had been in his mouth. Thankfully, the Audi had still been there, parked exactly where he had last seen it.

When the petrol can was empty, Darren tossed it into the shadows. He was fumbling for the matches in his pocket when he heard the sound of an approaching vehicle. Fearing it was another patrol car, he scuttled across the service road and ducked into the alley his car was parked in. Leaning against the wall, he waited for the car to drive past but, to his horror, the engine note changed as the approaching vehicle slowed and then stopped.

Shit!

Risking a quick glance around the corner, he was shocked to see Jonas Willard walking from his Bentley Arnage towards the warehouse. A fat cigar protruded from the corner of his mouth, its tip glowing in the darkness like a demented firefly.

Before Darren could react, the door next to the shutters opened, flooding the forecourt with light, and the old man disappeared inside.

Reaching for the handgun tucked into his waistband, Darren broke into a run, hoping to reach the door before it closed.

A large man with a wrinkled dome poked his enormous head out of the door, quickly looked left and right, then pulled it shut with a dull thud.

Darren was still too far away to be confident of hitting him, so he held his fire. His blood was up by the time he reached the door, and he seriously considered shooting the lock off and following them in, but the damn thing was made of thick steel, and he didn't know if that would actually work.

He glanced over at Wiggins' car, torn between setting it alight as originally planned or delaying the arson attack to see what happened next. Willard was bound to come out soon and, from a tactical perspective, he decided that it made a lot more sense to find a suitable hiding spot, from which he could lay down an effective field of fire, and then mow the bastard down when he reappeared.

Darren spotted two industrial sized wheelie bins leaning against the wall between the loading bay shutters and car park entrance. Hurrying over to them, he pulled the nearest bin forward a couple of feet, creating a space that was just about big enough to accommodate him. Wincing as his knees clicked, he squeezed into the smelly gap and settled down for an uncomfortable wait.

―――

Basher escorted Willard through the loading bay towards the concealed door at the far end. "This way, sir," he said, deferentially.

"I know the fucking way, you moron," Willard snapped, wondering why Fred Wiggins had sent this buffoon to admit him, instead of coming himself.

He pushed through the heavy soundproofed door, annoyed that Basher hadn't opened it for him, then stomped along the narrow corridor with a thick plume of cigar smoke trailing behind him like an ethereal snake. He heard Basher cough as he inhaled it in, and shot the oaf a scathing look. "What's the matter with you?"

"Nothing," Basher said, quickly.

A dyspeptic grunt signalled Willard's growing displeasure. When he reached the door at the other end, he made a point of stopping, and staring up at the hired muscle expectantly. To his great irritation, instead of taking the hint, Basher just came to a halt a couple of steps behind him. Willard angrily jabbed the cigar towards the other man's chest. "Well, don't just stand there like a gormless halfwit," he roared. "Open the bloody door."

Flinching at the outburst, Basher hurried to oblige. "There you go, boss," he said, stepping smartly aside so that Willard could squeeze past him.

The white walled torture room contained four men, all of whom looked in his direction as he entered. Willard recognised Wiggins, his pet enforcer, Casper, and another rent-a-thug whose name escaped him. Nodding a terse acknowledgement to them, he turned his attention to the fourth man, a skinny little runt with worried eyes and a couple of fingers missing from his left hand.

"Well, well, well," he purred, running predatory eyes over the frightened man. "You must be one of the horrible cunts who stole my diamonds and slotted poor Frankie."

Fingers said nothing, but his Adam's apple bobbed up and down nervously as he swallowed.

Willard broke into a hyena like grin. "What's the matter, son? Cat got your tongue?" As he spoke, he took several slow steps towards the terrified man, whose retreat was prevented by Casper. Willard laughed at the scrawny man's distress, then took a long drag on his cheroot. "You better not be dicking us around about where the gems are hidden," he warned, simultaneously expelling smoke from his mouth and nostrils like an angry dragon. "Cause if you are, I will personally cut off your balls and feed them to you."

Standing behind Fingers, Casper grinned widely, as though that was something he would very much like to see.

Willard sniffed at the air around him, then wrinkled his nose. With a look of disgust, he turned to Casper. "Someone needs to rustle up some air freshener pronto, to get rid of that fucking stench."

Casper gave Mickey a delegatory look, making it clear he considered the request beneath him.

Mickey's shoulders slumped, and he set off towards the office.

Casper watched him go with a cold smile of satisfaction.

"Now," Willard said, turning to Fred Wiggins. "Before you fetch me my diamonds, I want to have a word with that horrible slag who offed poor little Carrie."

Fingers watched as Fred Wiggins guided Willard towards the cell corridor like he was some kind of celebrity guest. Casper followed behind at a respectful distance, saying nothing.

For a fleeting moment, Fingers wondered who Stella was, but then he turned his mind to his own predicament.

Mickey had returned from the office, carrying a large can of air freshener, which he vigorously proceeded to spray around the room. The lavender scented cloud spread outwards like a burst of radioactive fallout, covering everything in its path. Before long, Basher and Fingers were both choking on the fumes.

"Alright," Basher complained, coughing loudly. "No need to go overboard with it."

"Just doing as I was told," Mickey sulked, letting off another burst.

Fanning his nose, Basher set off towards the door to the loading bay. "I'm going to have a quick dump," he said. "Make sure you keep an eye on *him* while I'm gone."

"Thanks for the advice," Mickey replied, his voice dripping with sarcasm. "I would never have thought of doing that otherwise."

Without looking back, Basher raised his right hand and extended the middle finger.

"Same to you," Mickey called after him.

Basher made a point of leaving the heavy door open, presumably to dissipate the overpowering lavender fragrance.

With Willard, Wiggins and Casper all busy down the cells, and Basher taking a shit, that only left Mickey to worry about, and he had an injured ankle, so he wouldn't be able to run very fast.

This could be it, Fingers realised; this could be the moment he had been waiting for. Fidgeting restlessly, he wiped his sweaty palms against the side of his legs. Then, without conscious thought, he took a tentative step towards the door to the loading bay.

"Oi, where do you think you're going?" Mickey barked, eyeing him suspiciously.

"Just trying to get clear of that disgusting air freshener you sprayed everywhere," Fingers said, daring to take another couple of steps as he spoke. He could see into the narrow corridor now, and another step gave him a clear view into the loading bay beyond it.

Fingers licked his lips nervously. He needed to make a decision: make a run for it now, or bide his time and hope for a better opportunity later. There was no sign of Basher, which hopefully meant that he was already in the loo, sitting in trap one with his shreddies around his ankles.

Was it possible that Basher had been stupid enough to open the shutters before buggering off to the toilet?

Please, God, let that be the case!

Growing more determined by the second, Fingers glanced over his shoulder, hoping he'd put enough distance between himself and Mickey to have a fighting chance of outrunning him, but his guard had doggedly kept pace with him, and was still standing close enough to grab Fingers if he attempted to do a runner. Even with the injured wrist, Fingers knew that Mickey was more than a match for him if they got into a tussle. He needed to distract the man; take him out of action for a few minutes.

But how?

His eyes flickered towards the cell passage but, thankfully, the soundproofed door was still closed, and he knew from his time in captivity that, when you were down there, you couldn't hear anything that happened out here.

Trying to act nonchalantly, and not like a jittery prisoner who was about to make a run for it, Fingers turned to face Mickey. Self-consciously clearing his throat, he said, "I was just thinking, Casper should have sent Basher to get that air freshener, not you."

Mickey's eyes narrowed. "You taking the piss, or what?" he demanded, curling his one good hand into a fist.

Fingers shook his head. "No, of course not," he said with a disarming smile. "I just meant that you're obviously a lot savvier than Basher, so you shouldn't be doing the menial jobs." He paused for a breath, shrugged. "Just my opinion, for what it's worth."

Mickey nodded with alacrity, clearly liking what he had heard. "You're not as stupid as you look," he said approvingly, and Fingers was relieved to see his hand unfurl.

"It's obvious you're the brains and he's the brawn," Fingers continued, trying to butter him up.

"Yeah, you're right," Mickey said, puffing his chest out. "You'd have to get up very early in the morning to outsmart—"

Fingers kicked him hard in the balls, enjoying the sensation of the other man's testicles squishing against his instep.

Mickey's eyes bulged, and his hands flew to his genitalia. With a high-pitched whimper, he dropped to his knees, collapsing in on himself like a deflated balloon.

Hoping he had kicked his captor so hard that the bastard now had three Adam's apples, Fingers cast a final nervous glance towards the cell passage door, then made his break for freedom.

Behind him, Mickey tried to shout a warning, but all that came out was a strangled groan.

Reaching the loading bay a few seconds later, Fingers skidded to a halt, his head panning from side to side as tried to get his bearings.

The van was parked facing inwards, approximately fifteen yards ahead of him, and there was no sign of Basher.

He grinned.

That was good.

Then he saw that the shutters were still closed.

The grin vanished.

That was bad.

Very bad.

In the distance, he heard Mickey shouting the alarm. The bastard had finally found his voice again. Knowing he didn't have long, Fingers darted for the door next to the shutters.

Behind the van, the door to the men's room opened and Basher appeared, still doing up his fly. His jaw dropped when he spotted Fingers at the door.

"What the…?"

Leaving the sentence unfinished, he set off after Fingers, just as Mickey hobbled into the loading bay, still clutching his injured private parts.

With the gangsters closing in on him, Fingers grabbed the door handle and twisted it hard.

C'mon, c'mon…

As soon as he felt the locking mechanism release, Fingers pushed against the metal door, but it refused to budge. "No, no, no," he panted, firing a nervous glance over his shoulder.

He tried the handle again, then threw his shoulder into it.

Nothing happened.

Fingers couldn't understand why the door wasn't opening. It seemed as desperate to keep him trapped inside as he was to escape.

Had he not been in such a terrible state of panic, he would have realised that the door opened inwards, not outward, and that the only thing preventing his egress was the fact that he was pushing instead of pulling.

Fingers risked another glance over his shoulder.

Basher was charging towards him, gaining speed with every lumbering step.

Mickey was also closing in on him, half running, half hobbling; his beetroot face contorted with pain.

Both men were shouting at Fingers to remain where he was.

Paralysed with fear, Fingers pressed his back against the cold metal door, knowing that the two thugs were seconds away from tearing into him like the attack dogs they were.

And then it hit him; he had been pushing when he should have been pulling.

Spinning around, he grabbed the handle again, this time yanking it inwards with all his might.

Please, please, please!

Suddenly, the door was wide open and he was running through it.

I've done it! I've—

Rugby tackled from behind, he went down hard, faceplanting the concrete. The jarring impact forced the air from his lungs with a loud whoosh.

Overcome by panic, Fingers instinctively tried to kick out, but strong arms were tightly wrapped around his knees, pinning him down.

"Stop struggling, you little git," he heard Mickey grunt.

Someone grasped his ankles in a vice-like grip, and began dragging him backwards. Ignoring the excruciating pain, as the side of his face was scraped across the uneven forecourt, Fingers tried to claw his way to freedom.

I can do this...

At which point Mickey rabbit punched him in the back of the head, and his limbs went all wobbly.

They had him, he realised, as Basher leaned down to grab him by the scruff of the neck with one hand, and the seat of his pants with the other.

"Nooo!" he screamed as he was carried back inside.

30

This conversation isn't over

Stella had taken to grinding her teeth together to stop them from chattering. Her skin was covered in goosebumps, but she knew her uncontrollable shivering was as much down to shock as it was the biting cold temperature of the cell they had thrown her into.

Truth be told, she didn't know how much more of this treatment she could take before she cracked up. Moaning softly to herself, she rubbed her arms vigorously in an attempt to generate some heat, but it didn't seem to help in the slightest.

A cold draft constantly whisked around her ankles, but she couldn't tell where it was coming from. Not knowing what else to do, she stood up and began exploring the tiny cell by feel, letting the pads of her fingertips trace the course outline of the concrete walls until they came to the metal door. After making a circuit of the room, she sagged back onto her cot.

"Please, God," she begged in a breathless rasp. "Please don't let them kill me"

She almost jumped out of her skin when the bolt to the cell door was drawn back. With a soft creak, the heavy door swung inwards, flooding the tiny space with harsh yellow light from the hall.

By shielding her eyes against the savage glare, Stella could just about make out the three silhouettes filling the doorway. One of them was at least twice the size of the other two; it was Casper, she realised with a sense of impending doom.

"Get up," an unfamiliar male voice demanded. It was coarse, authoritative, and quivering with barely suppressed anger. When she didn't respond immediately, the man who had spoken snapped his fingers impatiently, and Casper stepped forward.

The sadistic albino grabbed her hair so tightly that Stella feared it would be torn out by its roots as he manhandled her into a standing position. Such was the pain that she forgot all about covering her modesty. Instead, with a scream of agony, she dug her nails into the soft flesh on the underside of his wrist in an attempt to make him release her.

Casper merely laughed at her feeble efforts. He was still laughing when he slammed her head against the wall.

Pain exploded inside Stella's cranium, bringing with it a terrible blinding whiteness. As if a switch had been flicked, turning off all her motor responses, Stella's arms flopped down to her sides. Her legs gave way at the same time, and she would have fallen had Casper not intervened by wrapping a massive arm around her waist.

In her semi-conscious state, Stella was vaguely aware of someone speaking to her, but the voice was badly distorted, like a recording that had been slowed down. Eventually, she managed to translate the strange sounds into words.

"Stand up and stop playing silly buggers," an authoritative voice was telling her, like she was doing this on purpose. She tried to speak, but the only thing to come out of her mouth was a long string of dribble.

A hand slapped her face, jarring her head sideways. "Open your fucking eyes," the man who had struck her said. He was wearing a very strong cologne, and his breath reeked of cigar smoke.

Stella hadn't even been aware that they were closed, but she tried to obey. Anything to stop him from hitting her again. When she eventually managed to prise them open, a well-dressed man in his early sixties, with swept back silver hair and designer glasses, slowly came into focus.

"Do you know who I am?" His tone inferred that she should.

Stella shook her head, and immediately regretted it as a wave of nausea washed over her. "N–no," she stammered, afraid to upset him in case he hit her again.

The man's mouth turned down in a disapproving sneer, and he shot a glance at Fred Wiggins. "Didn't you tell her I was coming over to see her?" he demanded, clearly miffed that she didn't know who he was.

Wiggins nodded, appeasingly. "Of course, Mr Willard."

Willard rammed a cigar into his mouth, took several agitated puffs, then blew a stream of thick smoke straight into Stella's face.

She coughed, tried to turn her head away, but was too weak.

"Now you listen here," Willard said, emphasising each word with a jab of his cigar. "Carrie was like family to me, and I'm gonna make you pay for what you did to her."

Tears spilled down Stella's face. "Please," she sobbed, her eyes wide with fear. "I swear I didn't kill Carrie. I loved her with all my heart, and I would never have—"

Willard slapped her. "Shut up," he snarled. "Don't you dare even say that poor girl's name in front of me."

"Do you want to take care of her now?" Wiggins asked.

Willard paced up and down in agitation for several seconds, puffing on his cigar. "No. Let's get the diamonds back first, then we can get rid of the other one at the same time."

They were going to kill her in cold blood. The realisation made Stella's blood run cold. "You're making a terrible mistake," she said in a trembling voice.

Willard turned on her, his eyes blazing with righteous anger. "No, *you're* the one who made a terrible mistake," he yelled, covering her face in spittle. "Those fucking grease monkeys thought they could get away with killing one of my men and stealing a million quid's worth of diamonds from me. They were wrong, and they're going to die for their mistake. You thought you could kill someone I care about and get away with it. Well, missy, you were fucking wrong too, and for that, I'm going to do you the very big honour of topping you myself."

"But I *DIDN'T* kill her," Stella screamed. "Why can't any of you get that through your thick skulls?"

For a moment, Willard's lips compressed into a thin angry line, then he bared his teeth in anger. "What's wrong with you?" he snarled, throwing his arms wide in disgust. "I know you killed her. The police know you killed her. Why can't you at least have the guts to confess your fucking crime, you spineless skank?"

"Because I didn't do it," Stella sobbed.

Willard slapped her face, hard. "This conversation isn't over. I've got a little bit of business to take care of first, then I'm coming back to continue it. Mark my words, before you die, you *will* confess to killing Carrie."

Squatting behind the large wheelie bin, his legs stiff from lack of movement, Darren tensed when he heard the door open. Pulling the gun from his waistband, he checked the breach to confirm that a round was chambered. Thumbing the safety off, he held the Browning in a two-handed grip with both arms extended in front of him. If either Willard or Wiggins emerged, he would shoot first and worry about the consequences afterwards.

A slender man suddenly burst out of the door, running as though his life depended on it. Darren instinctively tracked him with the gun. He didn't recognise the badly battered face until its owner moved into the light, and then recognition dawned; he was looking at Fingers.

His heart leapt with joy. Fingers was alive!

But how had he managed to escape?

The elation was short lived as a second man dived through the open door, wrapping his arms around Fingers' knees and bringing him down to the floor.

Despite landing heavily, Fingers immediately began thrashing round, desperately trying to shake off the man holding his legs.

Darren was conflicted. He ached to rush forward and assist his friend, but he knew that doing that could scupper everything, so he forced himself to hold his position, at least until the situation became a little clearer.

A large, bald-headed man lumbered out of the warehouse, puffing and panting like he had just run a half marathon. Bending down, he grabbed Fingers ankles and began dragging him back inside. The man who had tackled Fingers to the ground released his legs, then scrabbled forward on all fours to deliver a hard punch to the base of his skull.

Fingers immediately went limp.

Letting the prisoner's feet fall to the floor, the bald man took two steps forward, grabbed Fingers' collar in one hand and the belt of his trousers in the other, then lifted him clear of the floor. In this manner, he carried Fingers back into the warehouse.

Looking up and down the service road, to make sure that they hadn't been seen, the man who had rugby tackled Fingers brought up the rear. As the heavy door started to swing shut behind them, Darren jumped to his feet and sprinted towards it. Just before it closed, he stuck his fingers over the latch to prevent the lock from engaging.

Trembling with anger, Darren waited several seconds, then gently opened the door a couple of inches. It was pretty dark inside, and deathly quiet.

Pulling the door open a little wider, Darren risked a quick glance inside. An unattended Ford Transit was parked in the middle of the loading bay, and there were several similar vans parked a little way off to its right.

The two shits who had dragged Fingers back inside the warehouse were nowhere to be seen, which meant they had already relocated to another part of the building.

With a growing sense of urgency, Darren ran his eyes over the loading area. There were two doors directly behind the nearest van, but they just led to the staff toilets. To his far right, beyond the small fleet of vans, he spotted a set of swing doors that seemed to lead into the main building. To his left, at the other end of the bay, there was a large recess, but that appeared to be a dead end.

He set off towards the swing doors to his right. They seemed the most likely place for the thugs to have taken Fingers. He had only taken a couple of steps in that direction when a high-pitched scream rang out from behind him.

Darren spun around.

Another scream, this one weaker. Unless he was much mistaken, the noise was coming from the recess on the other side of the loading bay.

As he crept towards it, several agitated voices became audible. The dominant one was angry, its tone scolding; the other two were meek, apologetic, almost whiney.

Darren couldn't make out the exact words being spoken, but the cutting tone made it clear that someone was being severely reprimanded.

Peeking into the recess, Darren discovered a metal door. Had it not been wedged open, he would never have heard the screams that attracted his attention.

A narrow corridor, some twenty feet long, lead to an identical door, which was also wedged open. Beyond this, Darren could see a group of men milling around in the centre of a well-lit, rectangular room.

Jonas Willard, Fred Wiggins and Casper were facing towards him, while the two thugs who had just prevented Fingers' escape were standing with their backs to him. Heads bowed submissively, both men were being given a mega bollocking by Fred Wiggins.

Lying motionless on the floor between them was his friend, Fingers.

Darren took a deep breath to calm his nerves. Wiggins, Willard and Casper were his primary targets, but he didn't have a clear shot at any of them yet, so he needed to be patient for a few seconds longer, just until he had an unobstructed line of fire, then he would be able to avenge Carrie and rescue Fingers.

Sulking from the massively unfair bollocking that Wiggins had just given him, Basher stomped off to wait in the van. He was feeling exceptionally hard done by.

Why had *he* been made to share the blame for something that was entirely Mickey's fault?

If *he* hadn't come out of the toilet when he had, the devious little grease monkey would probably have gotten clean away.

If anything, Wiggins should have thanked him, not humiliated him in front of Mr Willard.

And Mickey should have spoken up for him, put Wiggins straight, but he had just stood there holding his balls and staring down at the floor like a naughty schoolboy. So much for him being a mate!

As he emerged into the loading bay, still grumbling to himself about the injustice of the situation, something cold and metallic was rammed into the crook of Basher's neck.

"Don't move or I'll blow your fucking head off," an angry voice hissed from behind him.

Basher froze.

A calloused hand grabbed his left shoulder and steered him away from the door, before spinning him around to stand with his back against the wall. Before he could speak, the muzzle of a black handgun was rammed under his chin, forcing his head upwards so that he was staring up at the ceiling.

"Easy," he said as his assailant's other hand began patting him down for weapons.

"Shut up and stand still."

"You're making a big mistake," Basher said through gritted teeth.

"That so?" the man asked, straightening up.

Basher instantly recognised him from the photo he had been shown of Darren McCullen. He frowned, confused. Wasn't McCullen supposed to be in Spain?

"Now listen carefully," Darren growled. "We're going back inside, and if you make a noise or a wrong move – if you so much as fart or twitch in a way that I don't like – I *will* kill you. Do you understand?"

Basher indicated his acquiescence with a submissive nod of his head.

Without warning, Darren spun him around and faceplanted him into the wall. Basher grunted with pain as his face was squished against the cold hard concrete, then a second time as the barrel of the gun was shoved into the base of his spine.

Wrapping an arm around Basher's neck, Darren tucked in behind him, using his body for cover. Pulling him away from the wall, he pointed him towards the corridor.

"Move."

Basher did as he was told, walking very slowly. His mind was racing as he tried to figure out a way to forewarn the others. As they entered the corridor, he could hear his comrade's voices up ahead. Straining his neck muscles against the arm compressing his windpipe, Basher sucked in some much-needed air.

"Nice and steady," Darren warned, grinding the gun deeper into his back.

Wiggins looked up as Basher stepped into the room "What the fuck do you want?" he demanded. "I told you to sod off and wait in the..." His voice trailed off as he noticed the arm around Basher's neck.

Pushing Basher roughly aside, Darren stepped out from behind the human shield and levelled the gun at everyone in the room. "Nobody fucking move!" he yelled.

Nobody did.

"Well, well, well," Willard said, puffing out thick tendrils of smoke. "Look who it is."

"Shut up," Darren warned him.

Willard smiled cockily, as if he was the one holding the firearm, not Darren. "This is all very nice and cosy," he said. "Saves me the trouble of having to come looking for you."

Darren ignored him. "Fingers, get up, mate," he said, trying to keep his voice steady.

At the sound of his name, Fingers groaned, lifted his head off the ground. "D–Dazza?" he moaned, trying to focus bleary eyes.

"Yes, mate," Darren said with a reassuring smile. "It's me. I've come to rescue you."

The albino took a menacing step forward, his mouth curled downwards in a sneer.

"Stay where you are," Darren shouted, aiming the Browning at his centre mass.

"Do as he says," Wiggins instructed, raising a hand to stay the giant.

Darren swallowed hard, acutely aware that he needed to act fast, before he lost the tactical advantage. "Fingers, you need to get up and come over here," he said, injecting some urgency into his voice. He could already see it in the eyes of the three goons; they were calculating their chances of overpowering him.

He hated to admit it, but if they all rushed him at the same time, their odds were bloody good.

"Get up, Fingers," he yelled.

Fingers nodded, before slowly pulling himself onto his knees.

"One of you help him," Darren ordered.

Basher made to step forward, but Casper got there first. His piggy eyes never left Darren's as he bent down and hoisted Fingers into his arms as effortlessly as if he were carrying a child.

"Where do you want him?" he asked, taking a step towards Darren.

"I don't need you to carry him for me," Darren snapped. "Just help him to stand on his own two feet, then move aside."

Casper's smile was cold and calculating, and it sent a shiver down Darren's spine. "Do it now," he said, beginning to panic. With Fingers cradled in the giant's arms, he couldn't risk shooting Casper. The albino seemed to have realised this too, for he took a couple of steps forward, holding Fingers in front of him.

"Put him down, right now," Darren said, backing up a step to maintain the distance between them.

"Whatever you say," Casper grinned, but instead of lowering Fingers to the floor, he hurled him through the air towards Darren.

Unable to move aside, Darren's hands instinctively came up to protect himself. A second later, Fingers clattered into him, sending him staggering backwards. The impact caused the gun to discharge, sending a bullet hurtling towards the ceiling. Inside the windowless room, the noise of the discharge was deafening.

Nimbly stepping over Finger's, Casper was upon Darren in an instant.

Darren attempted to turn the gun on him, but the fast-moving giant grabbed his wrist in both hands, squeezing it in a vice like grip.

Darren didn't bother wasting time trying to free his gun hand. Instead, he punched Casper hard, connecting with the point of his lantern like chin. Darren was a strong man, and the blow would have sent most people reeling, but the giant merely shrugged it off.

If anything, being hit just seemed to make him angrier.

Undeterred, Darren hit him again, with so much power that one of his knuckles shattered. Casper's head was jarred violently backwards, and when he straightened up, baring his teeth in a ferocious snarl, Darren was gratified to see they were coated in blood. Feeling the giant's grip weaken, Darren began forcing the gun's muzzle inwards, so that it was pointing towards his opponent's midsection. Fear flashed across Casper's eyes. He might be tough, but he wasn't bullet proof and he knew it

Darren grinned. He was going to enjoy this.

A blow from out of nowhere struck Darren just above the temple, rocking his head sideways. It had been delivered by Basher. A second swift punch followed the first, this time catching him on the cheekbone. There was a sickening crunch as he felt the right side of his face implode where the bone had just fractured. Blood exploded from Darren's nose and mouth as he sagged to the floor, his face a battered and pulpy mess. As he fell, he was dimly aware of the gun being wrenched from his hand.

A boot landed in his stomach, knocking the air from him.

"That's enough," he heard Willard say as he teetered on the verge of consciousness.

The attack stopped at once.

Curling himself into a tight ball, Darren lay there, sucking in air. It was over.

He had failed Carrie; he had failed Fingers.

He spat out a globule of blood, ran his tongue around the inside of his mouth. One tooth was loose, another chipped. "Bastards," he managed to say before passing out.

31

What more could you ask for in a sidearm?

Willard stood over Darren McCullen's beaten body, staring down at him impassively. Fingers was cradling his friend's head in his lap, and looking very sorry for himself.

"What I want to know," Willard said, addressing the question towards Fred Wiggins, "is how did this horrible cunt manage to get into my building without any of us knowing."

Wiggins regarded Basher and Mickey with cold, accusing eyes. "Did you make sure that the door was closed after nearly letting our guest escape?" he asked, icily.

Basher stiffened at the implication. "Yeah, we did," he insisted, mortally offended that Wiggins should automatically assume this was his fault.

"We definitely did," Mickey chipped in.

Wiggins continued to stare at them.

"We checked it," Basher reiterated, his cheeks glowing red.

On the floor, Darren let out a low moan, then squirmed in pain.

Fingers stroked his head, soothingly.

"He's coming round," Basher said, happy to have a reason to deflect the conversation away from him and Mickey.

Darren's swollen eyes flittered open. "Fingers," he muttered.

"It's alright, Dazza," Fingers said, softly. "I've got you."

Darren tried to sit up, but he just didn't have the strength.

Willard walked forward, gave Darren a little nudge with the toe of his shoe. "Now you listen here," he said, gruffly. "I know that you and this little wanker playing Florence Nightingale slotted Frankie Kyle and stole my diamonds, and I want them back, pronto."

"Fuck off," Darren spat, staring up at him defiantly.

Willard laughed. "You've got some balls, I'll give you that," he said with grudging admiration. "The way you said that reminded me of your dear old dad."

Removing a silk handkerchief from his top pocket, Willard knelt down and offered it to Darren. "Let's make this as easy on everyone as we can, shall we?"

Darren swatted the hanky away. "You know what you can do with that," he snarled.

Willard stood up, tutted disapprovingly. "If there's one thing I can't stand," he said, holding his hand out impatiently for the Browning. "It's bad fucking manners."

Snatching the gun from Mickey, he balanced it in the palm of his left hand for a moment, testing its weight. "Good gun, the Browning," he said. Releasing the magazine, he deftly checked to make sure the bullets were seated correctly, then reinserted it. "It's one of the most popular single actioned, hammer fired semi-autos ever made," he continued, admiringly. As he spoke, he expertly worked the breech to check that a round was chambered. "Fitted with a thirteen-round magazine, it's accurate, easy to fire, and aesthetically pleasing." He casually pointed the gun at Darren's right knee. "What more could you ask for in a sidearm?"

Squeezing the trigger, he sent a 9mm parabellum bullet crashing into Darren's kneecap.

"Jesus," Basher said, jumping back in surprise.

Wiggins belatedly raised his hands to his ears.

As the round shattered bone, Darren raised his head to the ceiling and let out a tortured scream. Rolling around in agony, he clutched his ruined leg as blood spilled out from between his fingers to pool on the floor.

Fascinated, Casper took a step closer to inspect the catastrophic damage.

The bullet had sent splinters of blood-soaked bone spiralling through the air to splatter the legs of those standing closest to Darren. When Wiggins noticed the blood and gore staining the bottom of his suit trousers, his face darkened. "Oh, for fucks sake," he cursed, bending down to dab at the worst of the detritus with a handkerchief.

Willard laughed. "Don't worry, Fred, I'll pay for them to be cleaned."

Wrapping his arms around Darren's shoulders, Fingers tried to comfort the former soldier.

As his sobbing gradually abated, Darren stared up at Willard with hate filled eyes.

"Now," Willard said, conversationally, "are you going to tell me what I need to know, or are we going to have to waste more bullets?"

Dillon pulled onto the warehouse forecourt and coasted to a halt a short distance away from the blue Audi. It had now been joined by a second car, a swanky red Bentley with a private number plate.

Behind the two expensive cars, the warehouse was in total darkness, as were all the other buildings in the service road they had just driven through.

"God, this place is like a ghost town," Dillon said, switching the pool car's engine off.

Grunting his agreement, Tyler pulled out his mobile and dialled the office number.

"Deano, Jack Tyler here. How long till the key-holder arrives?"

"*Sorry, boss,*" Dean said, sounding very frustrated. "*I've been ringing him non-stop since you left, but the bugger isn't picking up.*"

"Well, keep trying," Tyler instructed, grumpily. "But if you don't get an answer in the next few minutes, have someone from the local nick pop around to his home address and light a rocket under his arse."

"*I'll try,*" Dean promised, "*but it's coming up to ten o'clock, so it's changeover time, and they won't send someone out till the night duty parade is over.*"

Tyler glanced down at his watch. He hadn't realised just how late it was. By the time night duty paraded, then sorted out their cars, it could easily be another fifteen minutes before any of them got around to actually leaving the nick. "Let me know as soon as you get any joy," he said, beginning to think that coming to the warehouse hadn't been such a good idea after all. "Did you find out who the Audi belongs to?"

"*I did,*" Dean confirmed. "*It's registered to our old friend, Fred Wiggins.*"

Tyler raised an eyebrow. He hadn't been expecting that. "Are you sure?" he queried.

"*Positive.*"

"I need you to do me a PNC check on another car that's turned up," Tyler said, and reeled off the Bentley's registration number.

He listened as Fletcher's fingers efficiently tapped the digits into his keyboard. "*Hmmm,*" the researcher said a few moments later. "*This one belongs to Jonas Willard.*"

Tyler thanked him and hung up. "You'll never guess who these cars belong to," he said, opening his door.

"Go on then, enlighten me," Dillon said, following him out of the car.

"The Audi's Fred Wiggins' and the Bentley belongs to Jonas Willard."

"Now that *is* interesting," Dillon said. "What could they be up to, meeting at an out of the way place like this, late on a Saturday night?"

"Something highly illegal, I suspect."

They walked over to the Audi.

Cupping his hands against the windows, Tyler peered in. Almost immediately, he withdrew his hands, sniffed them. "Is that—"

"Petrol...?" Dillon said, finishing the sentence for him. "Yes, it is, and it smells like someone's doused Wiggins' car in a couple of gallons of the stuff."

Tyler noticed that the floor around the car was also quite wet. "If the size of this puddle is anything to go by, I make you right," he said, walking over to the Bentley to see if it had received a similar treatment.

"The Bentley looks dry," Dillon said, as if reading his mind.

"Do you think we disturbed the culprits before they could get around to torching it?" Tyler asked.

"I don't know," Dillon said, striding back to their car. "But we should probably take a quick look around, just in case they're hiding nearby." He returned a few moments later carrying a Maglite torch. "I'm going to check out the two buildings opposite," he said, turning the torch on.

Tyler pulled out his phone. "Be careful," he warned, "something's not right here."

Walking back to their car, he dialled the office number a second time. "Dean, it's me again. I need you to scramble a team together for me on the hurry up... No, I don't know what we've got yet, but something here is very wrong... Yes, two car loads should be plenty. Tell them all to bring their PPE, just in case and, while you're at it, request a dog unit to help us search the warehouse and surrounding area...Yes, I need all this done on the hurry up."

"No signs of anyone lurking over there," Dillon said as he rejoined his friend a minute later.

"Let's reposition our car," Tyler said. "If that Audi goes up, I don't want our vehicle anywhere near it."

He waited while Dillon relocated the pool car a safe distance away. When the big man returned, they set about checking the warehouse shutters.

"These look secure enough," Dillon said, shining his light over them.

"Shine the light on the door," Tyler said, pointing to the solid metal door just to the left of the shutters.

Dillon ran the beam over the lock, which appeared intact. "No sign of a break in," he said, giving the door a little push. To their surprise, there was a little click, and it opened inwards a couple of inches.

The two detectives exchanged a look of puzzlement.

"The latch couldn't have caught properly the last time it was closed," Dillon said, then smiled mischievously. "Shall we go in and have a little nose around?" Without waiting for an answer, he pushed the door open a little wider, revealing a large, unlit loading bay. A lone Ford Transit had been abandoned in the middle, but there were a number of other vans parked in a neat row off to its right.

Peering in, Tyler tried to make out their registration numbers, but it was too dark inside for him to be able to see clearly.

Dillon pointed at the nearest van; unlike the others, it was parked facing inwards, and it seemed out of place. "That *has* to be the van we're after," he whispered, taking a tentative step forward.

"Probably," Tyler agreed, placing a restraining hand on his friend's arm. "But I think we should wait for the cavalry to arrive before going in."

A frown of impatience marred Dillon's broad forehead. "Why?"

"Why? Because there could be half a dozen thugs in there, all of them extremely dangerous, that's why!" Tyler hissed, annoyed at having been forced to explain the obvious.

"Yeah, it's probably wisest to wait for backup," Dillon agreed, and then he stepped through the door anyway.

After a makeshift tourniquet had been applied to Darren's leg, he and Fingers had been unceremoniously dragged into the loading bay and dumped into the back of the waiting Ford Transit van. With their hands securely tied to a metal clasp on the side of the van, there was no chance of them doing a runner.

Darren's battered face was drenched with sweat as they lay huddled together on the cold plastic sheeted floor, and his breathing was coming in strained gasps.

Fingers was eyeing him with growing concern. "Hang in there, Dazza," he encouraged, worried that his friend was going to pass out.

Leaning his head on the smaller man's shoulder, Darren placed his mouth against his friend's ear. "Listen to me," he hissed, conscious that they might not be left alone for much longer. "I'm fucked, but there's still a chance for you. Promise me that, if you get a chance, you'll make a run for it."

Fingers stiffened, pulled his head away and stared at him in horror. "Don't talk like that," he insisted. "We're both going to make it. All we need to do is keep our cool. When we get to the allotments, we can create a diversion and escape."

Darren's face hardened. "How the hell did you know where I'd hidden the stuff?" he demanded, eyeing his friend suspiciously.

Fingers stared at him blankly. "What are you talking about?"

Darren gritted his teeth as another wave of pain washed over him. "How did you know I'd buried the stuff at the allotments?" A few minutes earlier, when Willard had threatened to shoot Darren a second time, Fingers had thrown himself prostrate across his friend's body and screamed that he wouldn't take them to the allotments to recover the gems if they killed Darren.

Fingers shook his head in bewilderment. "I had no idea where you'd hidden the stuff, Dazza." A lame shrug. "I just picked the allotments because I thought I might have a chance of escaping from there."

Despite his appalling injuries, Darren couldn't help but laugh at the irony of the situation. "You still might have," he said, wearily resting the back of his head against one of the van's cold metal panels. "I buried the gun I used to kill Frank Kyle there too. If we can con them into letting us dig that up, we might still come out of this alive."

A sudden noise from the loading bay, stealthy footsteps and

agitated whispering, alerted them that someone was moving around out there.

"Shhh," Darren cautioned. "They're coming back."

———

"Dill, come back," Tyler hissed, angrily beckoning his mule-headed partner to return.

Halfway across the loading bay, Dillon raised a finger to his lips, shooed him, then carried on walking towards the van.

Rolling his eyes in exasperation, Tyler reluctantly stepped into the loading bay after him. It was a big open space with very high ceilings, and every step he took seemed to echo around him.

With his torch now switched off, Dillon's great bulk was a dark shape that glided eerily through the surrounding shadows like something out of a vampire film.

"Will you come back?" Tyler hissed, feeling his temper rise.

"Shhh!" Dillon responded stubbornly. "I just want to check out the van's index number."

With his nerves on edge, Tyler waited for his friend to return, praying that they wouldn't be discovered.

Dillon was looking very pleased with himself as he grabbed Tyler's arm a few moments later and guided him back outside. "That's definitely the van the albino used to abduct Stella," he whispered, excitedly.

They retreated to the pool car, from where they could keep watch on the warehouse without being seen. As soon as he closed the door, Tyler pulled out his phone, dialled the office again. "How long till the troops get here?" he asked as soon as Dean Fletcher answered.

"They should be with you any minute now, guv," Dean said. *"You've got two car loads, and Steve said to tell you there's a dog unit en route too."*

"Good. Give them a ring for me, and let them know we're parked outside two derelict buildings directly opposite the target warehouse."

"Right," Willard said to the four men gathered around him. "Time's cracking on. Fred, you and Casper had better shoot off and get my diamonds." He glanced down at his Rolex. "I want to be back home in bed having a bunk up by midnight, so don't dilly-dally."

Basher cleared his throat. "What about me, boss?"

The corners of Willard's mouth were tugged down in a derisive sneer. "You can make yourself useful by opening the loading bay doors for Fred. After that, you and Mickey can start cleaning up that mess." He pointed at the blood on the floor. "And, while you're at it, the drum with the stiff in it needs to be moved into the loading bay, so that it's ready to go straight in the back of the van when these two get back with my diamonds."

Willard accompanied Wiggins over to the van, pulling him aside as he was about to climb into the front passenger seat. "I mean it, Fred," he warned. "I'll be seriously pissed off if those grease monkeys give you the run around."

"Don't worry," Wiggins assured him. "I won't let you down."

"Here," Willard said, handing over the Browning Hi-Power. "Take this, just in case."

As soon as Basher had finished opening the shutters, Casper reversed the van backwards.

Willard waved them off. "And remember," he shouted after them. "I want to be in the loving arms of my missus by midnight, so pull your sodding finger out."

"Heads up," Tyler said, giving Dillon's arm an urgent nudge.

In front of them, the warehouse shutters were starting to open.

Beside him, Dillon was having a guarded telephone conversation with Imogen Askew. Conscious that he wasn't alone, the big lug was trying to be circumspect, but subtlety had never been Dillon's strongest point, and he was failing miserably. Despite their coded speak, Tyler had managed to work out that she was planning to spend the night at his friend's place, and that this wasn't the first time it had happened.

Dillon was still talking into the phone, so Tyler nudged him again, much harder. "Dill, we've got movement," he said, irritably.

Dillon looked up, and his eyes widened. "Got to go," he told Imogen, then hung up. Handing his mobile to Tyler, he began frantically patting his pockets for the car keys. "Where did I put the damn things?" he said, starting to panic.

Tyler dumped Dillon's phone in the storage pocket of his door, then had a rummage around the car to help him find them. "Have you checked the ignition?" he asked, tetchily.

The transit reversed out of the loading bay, then made a U turn on the forecourt. With the albino driving and Wiggins sitting next to him, it set off along the service road.

Dillon let out a huge sigh of relief as he finally found the keys, then contorted himself into a most uncomfortable position to drag them out of his trouser pocket. "What do you want to do?" he asked, inserting them into the ignition and starting the car.

Tyler caught a fleeting glance of Jonas Willard peering out of the loading bay doors as a big, bald headed bruiser closed them for him.

"Jack…?"

"We'll have to split up," Tyler said, unhappily. He didn't like the idea, but there was no alternative. "Follow the van. When it stops, call in some backup to help you turn it over. I'll wait here for the others, then we'll search the warehouse." With that, he opened his door and slid out.

Watching his friend drive off, he hoped the night wasn't about to go pear shaped on them.

Just then, the first drops of rain began to fall.

Tyler raised his eyes heavenward. "Terrific," he said, despondently.

32

Thanks for the lumber

Three sets of headlights made their way towards him, bumping up and down as the cars they belonged to traversed the pothole ridden service road.

The rainfall was getting steadily worse, and Tyler stood huddled between the two buildings opposite Willard's warehouse, collar turned up as he tried to shelter from the worst of it.

It had been a full five minutes since Dillon had taken off after the van containing Wiggins and the albino, and he wondered if they had reached their destination yet.

Stepping out of the darkness as the small convoy pulled up, he waved to Steve Bull who was driving the lead vehicle.

As his team spilled out of the first two cars, faces taut, eyes alert, Tyler was surprised to see Jim Cuthbert and Ian Yule were nestled among them, and he found himself hoping that Yule would have the good sense to keep his big gob shut, and not say something inherently stupid that would instantly piss off everyone around him.

"You okay, boss?" DC Jim Stone asked.

"I'm fine, Jim," Tyler said, giving him a thumbs up.

As the eight officers gathered around him, he was pleased to see that they were all wearing their Met Vests and PPE, and several of them were carrying hand held radios.

The doors to the third car opened, and Imogen Askew and Bear alighted from within.

Tyler's face darkened, and he cursed inwardly. The last thing he wanted when they raided the warehouse was to have a camera crew present.

Leaving Bear to grab his video camera from the back seat, Imogen rushed over and squeezed his hand affectionately. "Are you okay, Jack?" she asked, seeming genuinely relieved to find that he was still in one piece.

"I'm fine," he reassured her, not that she was listening.

"Where's Tony?" she asked, looking around anxiously.

"He's following a suspect vehicle that left the warehouse a few minutes ago," Tyler said.

Imogen's jaw tightened, and her mouth withered into a paper-thin line of annoyance. "And you let him go on his own?" she demanded, sounding horrified.

Tyler resisted the urge to roll his eyes. "Yes, but don't worry. He's a big boy, and he can take care of himself."

"That may be," Imogen argued, "but—"

Tyler raised both hands to placate her. "Please, Imogen. We know what we're doing." Giving her a reassuring smile, he grabbed Bull's arm and dragged him aside. Lowering his voice, he said, "Have you received any updates from Dill yet?"

Bull shook his head. "Maybe he phoned the office. Do you want me to give Dean a ring and find out?"

Tyler shook his head. "No. I'm sure he's fine," he said, trying not to think about the massive albino driving the van. Even Dillon would have his hands full against that one. "Let's crack on with the search."

Stone had retrieved a large crow bar and a sledge hammer from the boot of his car, and Kevin Murray was struggling under the weight of an Enforcer.

"We brought these with us," Stone said, helpfully. "In case we have to force entry."

"Very considerate of you," Tyler acknowledged with a tense grin, "but I'm hoping we won't need them." Mentally, he crossed his fingers that the door he and Dillon had gained access through earlier, which they had deliberately left ajar when they left, was still open, and that Willard hadn't closed it after the van left. "Right, listen in," he said, beckoning them all closer. "A few minutes ago, the van used to abduct Stella Carter left the premises behind me with Fred Wiggins and Casper Wright on board. DI Dillon's following them, and the plan is that he'll call in for backup when it reaches its destination. In the meantime, Jonas Willard's still inside, and we have to assume that Carter's being held there against her will. The intention now is to effect entry under Section 17 of PACE to secure Carter's safety and arrest the people responsible for her abduction."

The Police and Criminal Evidence Act – PACE – provided police with powers to enter premises without a warrant under specific conditions, one of which was to save life and limb.

"To that effect," Tyler continued, "everyone found on the premises is to be arrested on suspicion of kidnapping and false imprisonment." He ran his eyes over the assembled detectives, to ensure that they were following him, and was annoyed to see that Cuthbert was in the process of typing out a text instead of listening to him. "What are you doing, Jim?" he demanded angrily. He had expected better of Cuthbert.

Jumping at the sound of his name, Cuthbert looked up, then shifted uncomfortably as all eyes turned upon him. "I–"

"Put the phone away," Tyler said, his voice simmering with anger.

Cuthbert licked his lips nervously, and for a moment he looked like he was considering arguing the point, but then nodded, guiltily. "Sorry, boss," he said, popping the phone inside his jacket pocket.

Tyler's eyes lingered on the man a moment longer. "No one uses their phones until we're inside and the building is secure," he said. "Got it?"

Cuthbert's head bobbed up and down in acquiescence. "Yes, sir," he said, meekly.

"Do we know the layout of the building?" Bull asked.

Tyler shook his head, apologetically. "We've tried to get in touch with the key-holder, but the bugger's not picking up."

"Are there any guard dogs roaming free?" Stone asked.

Tyler shrugged. "Not as far as I know, but I can't categorically say one way or another."

"I've requested a dog unit," Bull said, "but it was a good fifteen minutes away, the last I heard. Do you want to wait until it arrives before going in?"

Tyler shook his head. "We're not waiting."

"Is there a way we can cover the back of the premises; in case anyone tries to escape via the rear?" The question had come from Ian Yule.

"Good question," Tyler said, giving credit where it was due.

Yule positively beamed at the compliment.

"The short answer is, no," Tyler told him. "We can't get round the back because there's a big gate, with fuck-off spikes sticking out of the top, so we'll just have to wing it and hope for the best." He paused to wipe a splodge of rain from his face before continuing. "It's dark inside the warehouse. If you've got torches, bring them. Now, unless there are any more questions, let's do this."

There were none.

Several officers ran back to their vehicles to retrieve torches. When they returned, he paired them off and told them to stick with their respective partners when they went in.

"Shall I go with Ian?" Cuthbert asked.

Tyler shook his head. "You can go with Jim," he said, nodding towards Stone. "Ian, you can pair off with Steve Bull."

Bull gave him a look that said, 'Thanks for the lumber.'

Once they were ready, Tyler led them over to the warehouse, where they formed up in a line with their backs to the wall.

Tyler gave the metal door next to the shutters a gentle push. To his delight, it was still ajar. Raising a finger to his lips to ensure silence, he stepped inside.

Being careful to keep a couple of vehicles between them at all times, Dillon followed the van as it chugged along the A13 towards central London. He had no idea where Wiggins and the albino were going, but he hoped they weren't planning to wander too far afield.

Oncoming headlights made the tiny specs of rain that constantly peppered his windscreen gleam like little diamonds. He flicked the stalk to the right of the steering wheel, and the wipers juddered across the screen, clearing them away. As the rainfall slowly intensified, his finger retuned to the stalk with increasing frequency.

The albino's driving was a lot more sedate than Dillon would have expected it to be. Adhering strictly to the speed limit, he never once came close to going through an amber light, let alone running a red. He didn't even sound his horn when a boy racer, who was switching lanes with reckless abandonment, forced him to brake fiercely to avoid rear ending the idiot. Dillon felt sure the albino was only exercising so much restraint because he was desperate not to draw the unwanted attention of a passing police patrol.

Passing the exits for Plaistow and Canning Town, the van trundled on towards the Blackwell Tunnel, and Dillon sincerely hoped they wouldn't be going south of the river.

Like the model driver he was pretending to be, the albino gave a signal in plenty of time when indicating his intention to turn right onto the A12 towards Hackney.

"Where the hell are you taking me?" Dillon wondered aloud.

Inside the loading bay, Tyler's team fanned out. Several of them had their extendable metal batons racked, he noticed.

"Boss, there are some swing doors over there," Jim Stone whispered, pointing in the direction that his torch was shining.

Tyler nodded. "Steve, you and Ian stay with me. The rest of you spread out and search the warehouse, but be careful. These people are bloody dangerous. If anyone locates the suspects, get straight on the radio."

Stone signalled for the others to follow him and set off towards the swing doors at a jog.

"Imogen, why don't you and Bear stay with us," Tyler whispered as the film crew made to tag on behind the others. "You can get some footage of the loading bay, and I'll let you go forward once the place has been secured."

Askew's mouth compressed into a thin line, as he'd noticed it did whenever she was about to argue with him.

"I'm sorry, but I have to consider your safety and the security of the operation," he said firmly, cutting her off before she could voice her objections.

She folded her arms huffily, then thrust her chin into the air. "That's so unfair."

The unexpected sound of a heavy door opening behind them ended the conversation. As they all spun in that direction, a shaft of light shone out of a recess at the opposite end of the loading bay, slicing through the surrounding darkness to create a triangular wedge of yellow. There followed the distinctive squeaking of unoiled wheels, accompanied by loud grunting noises and constant swearing.

Holding a finger to his lips, Tyler signalled for Bull to kill his torch, and they all padded across the loading bay towards the source of the noise. A moment later, a lean, muscular man with short dark hair moved into the light, emerging from a door that had been concealed from view by an overlapping wall. He was pushing an ill-behaved L shaped hand-trolley ahead of him, cursing every time it banged into a wall or didn't turn where he wanted it to. One wrist was heavily bandaged, and Tyler wondered if that was affecting his ability to steer the thing.

Ian Yule raised the radio he was carrying to his lips, but Bull placed a restraining hand on his arm, whispered, "Wait till the boss gives the word."

The trolley had a large steel drum on it, which wobbled with every change of direction. With a curse, the man pushing it reached out a bandaged hand to stop it from toppling off.

"Why the fuck Basher couldn't have done this, I'll never know," Tyler heard him grumble to himself.

As he set off across the loading bay, Tyler stepped out of the shadows to confront him. "Police," he said, holding his warrant card up. "Stay where you are."

"Shit!" the startled man exclaimed, nearly jumping out of his skin.

Bull shone his torch in the man's face as he and Yule joined Tyler.

Shielding his eyes, the man's gaze nervously darted left and right as he took in the situation and weighed up the odds against him. Then, with a defiant roar, he shoved the trolley forwards, ejecting the steel drum, which toppled onto its side and gathered speed as it rolled towards them.

"We're being raided," he shouted over his shoulder, before turning around and running back the way he had come.

The heavy steel drum clattered towards them, gaining momentum as it bounced and clattered its way across the floor. Tyler was agile enough to hurdle it, and he immediately set off in pursuit of the fleeing suspect. Although Yule attempted to do likewise, his foot smashed into the top of the drum, catapulting him forward to land in a crumpled heap. The radio tumbled from his hand and skidded across the floor.

"Are you okay?" Bull asked, having done the sensible thing and sidestepped the speeding drum, which was now slowing down as it rolled harmlessly towards the centre of the loading bay.

"I–I'm fine," Yule said, retrieving the radio.

Ahead of them, Tyler followed the limping suspect into a narrow corridor.

"We're being raided," the suspect was repeatedly shouting, no doubt to warn his comrades.

Tyler burst out of the corridor into a well-lit rectangular room to find Jonas Willard and a huge bald-headed thug in a black T-shirt, whom he immediately recognised as the man who closed the shutters after the van left, standing by the doorway of what looked like an office, a little way off to his right.

On seeing Tyler, Willard bolted into the room, swiftly followed by the man the detective was chasing. However, the bald-headed man, who was as tall as Tyler and almost twice as wide, made no attempt to run. Instead, he came forward in a wrestler's crouch to engage Tyler, his massive hands curling and uncurling as he came.

"Stay where you are," Tyler ordered.

"Fuck you," the bald man replied, angrily. Then, with an animal like roar, he lowered his head and charged.

―――

The rainfall had increased considerably, and the staccato patter as it bombarded the car's roof was getting on Dillon's nerves. The Astra's ineffective wipers had smeared a film of dirt and grime across the driver's side of the windscreen, making it increasingly difficult for him to see out of. Like almost everything else on the ancient car, they needed replacing. He jabbed the wash button on the end of the stalk but, predictably, the water reservoir was dry.

Unable to stop for fear of losing sight of the van, Dillon was forced to complete the remainder of the journey with his neck craned over to his left, so that he could peer out of the passenger side of the windscreen, which was much cleaner.

Eventually, the van pulled into a small parking area outside a large plot of council run allotments, coming to a stop by the wrought iron gates.

Driving straight past the van, Dillon kept a careful eye on his rearview mirror, just in case it did a sudden U-turn and went back the other way.

The lights went off and the doors opened.

Satisfied that the van was going nowhere, Dillon pulled into a council estate a hundred yards up on his left, and spun the car around. Turning his headlights off, he crawled back to the junction and peered out.

In the distance, Wiggins and the albino were standing by the van's rear doors. Looking around furtively, they could not have looked any more suspicious if they had tried.

"What are you up to, you nasty pair of reprobates?" Dillon pondered, wiping a circle in the condensation that had already started to form on his window so that he could see them a little clearer. As he watched, Wiggins nodded to the albino, who opened the back doors. A moment later, a slender man in his twenties, wearing the overalls of a mechanic, was dragged out by the scruff of his neck.

"Hello," Dillon said, sitting up a little straighter. "Who are you, then?"

The albino reached into the Transit a second time, this time pulling out a much larger man who was struggling to put any weight on his right leg, and was having to lean heavily on his slender companion for support as he hobbled clear of the doors.

Before shutting them, the albino reached inside to retrieve a shovel.

Dillon began to feel uneasy. He began patting his pockets for his mobile phone, growing increasingly flustered when he couldn't find it. The last time he recalled using it was when he had been chatting to Imogen back at the warehouse, and he had handed it to Jack so that he could search for the car keys.

Shit!

Jack had never returned it.

"Oh no," he moaned, checking the cup holders on the off chance that Tyler had put it in there. They were full of all sorts of rubbish, most of it sticky, but there was no trace of his phone.

Dillon's heart sank. How was he going to summon help without it? He looked up and down the road, hoping to spot a telephone kiosk. Of course, there were none, and the clapped out heap he was driving wasn't equipped with a Force Main-Set.

"Fuck!"

The four men were slowly moving towards the allotment gates. With Wiggins in the lead, and the albino bringing up the rear, it was glaringly obvious that the two men sandwiched between them were prisoners. As they turned side on, Dillon spotted the tourniquet that had been applied above the right knee of the limping man's bloodstained leg.

Why would Wiggins need two prisoners, one of them clearly badly injured, to help him break into an allotment?

It made no sense whatsoever.

Think, Dill! Think!

Okay, they had a shovel so, presumably, they were there to bury something or dig something up? As they didn't appear to be carrying anything, Dillon assumed it had to be the latter, unless Wiggins was planning to kill the prisoners and bury them there? That was absurd. If he had wanted them dead, Wiggins would have killed them back at the warehouse.

No, they had to be there to dig something up, but what?

33

Stand still and fight

Tyler just about managed to duck under the haymaker that Basher threw at him, but Ian Yule, who was following close behind, wasn't so lucky. As the punch caught him in the forehead, Yule staggered backwards, as if he'd just been shot. Landing heavily on his posterior, he skidded along the floor until he collided with a wall.

Jumping over Yule's inert form, Steve Bull swiftly brought his metal baton crashing down into the bald man's shoulder, while shouting, "GET BACK!"

To Bull's horror, the baton simply bounced off the thick muscle with a dull 'thunk.' He immediately went for the follow up strike, but Basher intercepted the incoming blow before it could build up any momentum and, wrapping a massive hand around the detective's wrist, wrenched the baton from his grasp.

"Shit!" Bull cursed, backing away nervously.

Behind them, Yule had risen to his feet, and he now staggered into the room, baton raised. His comb-over was flapping down limply by the side of his head, leaving the shiny pink top of his head exposed.

Catching Bull's eye, Tyler jerked a thumb over his shoulder, towards the open door of the office behind him. "Willard's in there," he said, tersely. "Get after him, and take Ian with you."

Bull stared back uncertainly. "But—"

"Just do it."

Grabbing Yule's arm, Bull dragged the still groggy detective towards the office, pausing only long enough to scoop up his baton. "I hope you know what you're doing," he said, shooting Tyler a worried farewell glance.

So do I, Tyler thought.

A spiteful smirk made its way onto Basher's face. "You just made a big fucking mistake, pig," he crowed, "cos I'm gonna rip you up for arse paper."

With that, he charged.

During his younger days, Jack Tyler had been a carded ABA boxer of some distinction, and he had comfortably won the heavyweight division of the prestigious Met Police Lafone Cup during his probation. As Basher hurtled forward, he instinctively slipped into 'fight mode,' raising his guard and moving onto the balls of his feet.

Tyler was a southpaw, meaning that he led with his right, and he was a counter puncher by nature, so the other man coming onto him like this suited his style of fighting perfectly.

Basher's opening punch clumsily telegraphed his intentions.

Tyler sidestepped smartly to his right and countered with a savage hook to the ribs. It was a solid blow that would have dropped most men to their knees.

Basher merely grunted his surprise, retreated a step, then came in again.

A right cross this time, followed by a wild left hook. Both punches were amateurish; both missed by a country mile. Undeterred, Basher advanced, robotically repeating the same combination over and over again as if they were the only two punches in his repertoire.

He soon became boringly predictable.

"Stand still and fight," Basher bellowed, already puffing heavily from his exertions.

Instead of retreating when the next punch was thrown, Tyler feigned left then sidestepped to his right, letting fire with a crisp uppercut that connected with Basher's chin, jarring his head backwards at terrific speed. It was a textbook perfect punch, landed with considerable force, and it should have ended the fight there and then, but it didn't.

Staggering backwards, Basher shook his glistening head, spraying beads of sweat in all directions, then angrily spat out a thick glob of blood from his bleeding mouth. "I'm gonna make you pay for that," he promised. Extending his arms, he ran forward with the intention of trapping Tyler in a bearhug.

Retreating to the centre of the room, Tyler circled his opponent, keeping him at bay with a vicious succession of well executed jabs. The bigger man grew increasingly frustrated as his face took the brunt of the punishment. Before long, one eye had puffed up into a thin slit, and blood was flowing freely from his nose and mouth.

"Stand still, you faggot," Basher wheezed.

Tyler smiled inwardly. Not a chance, he thought, skipping back from another clumsy attempt to grab him.

Tyler had once read an interesting medical study that compared the density of the various bones in a typical human skull, and he recalled that the average thickness for the temporal bones had only been 4mm, which he figured was considerably thinner than the granite like jaw of his opponent. Deciding to find out, he waited for Basher to lunge forward again, then let fly with a vicious two punch combination; the first blow struck him cleanly on the left temple, the second on the right. As the punches connected, Basher's eyes bulged, and he staggered sideways, first one way, then the other. He took a drunken step towards Tyler, who paused long enough to marvel at the fact he was still standing, then promptly rectified the situation by kicking him as hard as he could in the testicles.

With a strangled groan, Basher's eyes crossed, and he dropped to his knees. He remained there for a moment, rocking from side to side, then pitched forward onto his face.

Breathing heavily, Tyler glanced down at his knuckles, which were swollen and sore, but nowhere near as swollen and sore as his opponent's battered face.

"Looks like I didn't make a mistake after all," he told the prostrate man.

With Yule bringing up the rear, Bull cautiously entered the office, expecting to come face to face with Jonas Willard and the suspect with the bandaged wrist. To his great surprise, there was no sign of either man. His eyes raked the room, taking in every detail. There were no windows, no doors other than the one he had just come in through, nowhere obvious for them to hide.

So, where were they?

A large mahogany desk sat against the far wall, with a high-backed swivel chair behind it; a comfortable looking sofa had been positioned opposite a big TV on the far side of the room; there was even a neat little kitchenette in one corner, equipped with all the mod-cons. There were a couple of small storage cupboards too, but neither of them was anywhere near big enough for one normal sized person to hide in, let alone two.

They had gone; vanished.

How was that possible? Willard was an aging gangster, not Harry-sodding-Houdini!

"Am I going mad?" he said, scratching his head.

Behind him, Yule walked over to the leather sofa. Rubbing his bruised forehead, which had a lump coming up on it the size of a boiled egg, he sat down on the padded arm to catch his breath. As he did so, it moved gently on its casters, sliding a foot or so to the right.

"Are you okay?" Bull asked, walking over to join him.

Yule nodded. "Fine, thank you," he replied, trying to brush his comb-over back into place.

Bull noticed a breeze around his ankles. Looking downwards to locate the source, he realised that it was coming from behind the sofa. Pulling Yule onto his feet, he shoved the sofa away from the wall, revealing a large ventilation shaft. The wire mesh cover had been removed, and this was now leaning against the wall. It was easily large enough for someone to crawl through; even the ape that Tyler was fighting could've managed it.

"The cunning bastards," Bull said, with grudging admiration.

Dropping to his knees, he poked his head in. Sure enough, the mesh cover at the other end had also been removed, exposing the floor of the car park behind the building.

In the distance, Bull could see two sets of legs running hell for leather across the tarmac.

"Where's Willard, and what are you doing down there?" Tyler's voice demanded from the doorway.

Bull jumped at the sound. Banging his head against the top of the shaft, he swore profusely. Wincing at the pain, he rubbed the back of his skull, then peered back through the ventilation shaft again. "It's Willard, he's getting away."

Tyler's eyes narrowed. "Through there? Are you serious?"

Bull nodded. "It leads out to the car park."

Crossing the room in three quick strides, Tyler bent down to see for himself. "Ian, get on the bloody radio," he snapped. "Get the others back here, pronto."

Yule nodded. Raising the radio to his lips, he began talking urgently.

"I'm going after them," Bull said, entering the tunnel on all fours.

"Be careful," Tyler shouted after him.

"They're on their way," Yule said. Kneeling down, he reluctantly crawled into the shaft after Bull.

"Wait," Tyler said, holding out his hand. "I'll need your cuffs for the prisoner."

Struggling under Dazza's considerable weight, Fingers was doing his best to support his friend through the uneven terrain of the allotments. Behind them, Fred Wiggins illuminated the way with a torch while complaining non-stop about the weather. Casper, as silent as a statue, brought up the rear, carrying a shovel and the bolt cutters he had used to cut through the chain at the main gates.

The soil was already getting slippery underfoot, making it increasingly difficult to stay upright, and Fingers was afraid that he and Dazza would collapse in a tangled heap of arms and legs at any moment. Dazza was finding every step incredibly painful, and his moans were becoming steadily louder as they moved deeper into the allotments.

"Can't you shut him up?" Wiggins hissed, pulling his collar up.

"He's in pain," Fingers said, protectively. He didn't know what Wiggins was so worried about. It wasn't as if there was anyone around to hear Darren's sobbing.

Wiggins grunted, brushed a stream of rain from his face. "He'll be in a lot more pain if he doesn't shut the fuck up."

"How much further?" Fingers whispered as soon as Wiggins had dropped back out of earshot.

"N–not far," Darren replied through gritted teeth. Despite the tourniquet, his entire lower leg was now soaked in scarlet, and his normally full face, with its ruddy complexion, appeared unnaturally gaunt and deathly pale.

Fingers was growing increasingly concerned about the severity of the blood loss. Darren was starting to ramble incoherently, becoming disorientated and confused. It was only a matter of time until he passed out. If they hadn't recovered the jewels by then and, more importantly, the second gun, Fingers dreaded to think what would happen.

―――

Steve Bull emerged from the ventilation shaft into the pouring rain, staggered to his feet and set off after the fleeing gangsters, both of whom had now reached the fence surrounding the car park perimeter.

Beyond the fence, an untamed jungle of brambles, nettles, thorn bushes and tightly clustered shrubbery stretched on for as far as Bull could see. If they could lose themselves in that, they had a half decent chance of evading capture.

Instead of scaling the high fence, as he had fully expected them to, Willard and his sidekick began pulling up a stretch of wire mesh fencing from the ground.

Ignoring the cold water flooding into his shoes, Bull splashed through the puddles after them. As he ran, he unclipped the pouch containing his CS canister. He hadn't dared use it inside the warehouse, for fear of incapacitating them as well as the bald thug they we trying to arrest. Here, in the open, there were no such concerns, and he would be free to spray the two fugitives to his heart's content if they tried to resist.

Neither man had looked back yet, and they seemed totally unaware that he was closing in on them. Hopefully, it would remain that way until it was too late for them to do anything about it. Detaining Jonas Willard was his priority, Bull decided. Willard was the big fish; the man calling the shots.

"Wait for me," Yule's voice cut through the night air behind him, shattering the silence.

Bull cursed as the two men kneeling by the fence whipped their heads around to look in his direction. Their eyes widened in fear, and they immediately redoubled their efforts. A moment later, Willard was dropping onto his stomach and crawling through the gap while his subordinate held it up for him.

"Shit, shit, shit!" Bull swore.

The man with the bandaged wrist was standing up now, turning to confront him. He glanced back over his shoulder, as if calculating his chances of following Willard through the gap in the fence before Bull reached him. Clearly, he decided they were poor, because he clenched his good fist and moved forward to attack.

While he wasn't as imposing as the humungous slob that Tyler had taken on, the man was still considerably bigger than Bull, and he looked like he knew how to handle himself.

Bull didn't hesitate.

He didn't waste time giving a warning.

He simply raised his right hand and depressed the CS trigger with his thumb, aiming the jet at the advancing man's chest, and then guiding it upwards till the liquid hit him full in the face.

The man stopped in his tracks, clawed at his face with his hands, then let out a high-pitched scream as the chemical agent began to work on the mucus membranes of his eyes and nose. He staggered forwards, then backwards, becoming disorientated.

"Stand still," Bull shouted, giving the standard post CS exposure instructions. "You've been sprayed with CS incapacitant. Do NOT rub your eyes."

The man was screaming with pain. His eyes were glued shut, and he was rubbing them furiously, completely ignoring the instruction he had been given.

"Stop rubbing your eyes," Bull shouted.

"Aargh! Argh! AARGH!"

'Walk towards my voice, stepping away from the area contaminated by CS," Bull said, firmly.

"Aargh! Argh! AARGH!"

Instead of walking, Mickey tried to run, crashed straight into the fence, ended up on his backside.

Bull shook his head, left him to it.

"Where did the old man go?" Yule asked, appearing by his side.

Bull pointed to the gap in the fence. "He went through there."

Yule nodded, then set off after him.

"Wait!" Bull called, but it was too late. Like a bumbling idiot, Yule ran straight through the area contaminated by CS spray. By the time he reached the fence, he was already starting to show signs of distress.

"Are you okay?" Bull asked.

"Fine," Yule called back.

Tears were running down his cheeks as he lifted the wire mesh, then shimmied under it with surprising agility. He stood up on the other side, looked left and right through bleary eyes, then set off to his left.

A moment later, there was a startled scream, followed by the sound of falling.

Then thrashing.

Then screaming and thrashing.

Bull ran over to the fence, peered through, saw Yule lying in a tangled heap, having somehow managed to ensnare himself in thick strands of bramble, which were wrapped around his face and body like barbed wire.

Bull winced, placed his hands on his hips, then raised his eyes heavenward in disbelief.

"Aargh! Argh!" Mickey cried out behind him, but with marginally less urgency than before.

"Oh, do shut up," Bull said.

The constant stream of rain water running down Dillon's neck sent an icy chill through him. His clothes were soaked through, and his expensive brogues, now completely waterlogged, squelched with every miserable step he took.

Without his mobile, Dillon had no way of summoning the help he needed to make an arrest. He was angry with Jack Tyler for not returning it to him, and even angrier with himself for not having noticed its absence until it was too late.

From his hiding place in the shadows, Dillon glanced over at Wiggins and his enforcer, who had taken shelter under the overhang of an old shed. A few yards ahead of them, McCullen was sitting on the mud, getting drenched, while his little friend dug hole after hole.

Presumably, when they dug up whatever it was that they were looking for, they would return to the van and drive back to the warehouse in Barking.

Once he was happy that they really were on a reciprocal route, Dillon planned to break off and find a telephone box. If India 99 was still up, it might be able to locate the van en route and guide ground-based units in to intercept it. If not, he would have to settle for forewarning Jack so that a reception committee would be waiting for them.

He wished that something would hurry up and happen soon, before he caught his death of cold.

―――

Fingers was knee deep in a large hole. It was the fifth one he had dug since their arrival at the allotments. Darren was half sitting, half laying on the muddy, uneven floor to his right, beside the ever-growing mound of earth that Fingers' efforts were creating. He was shivering from the cold.

A few yards to the south of them, Wiggins and Casper sheltered beneath the overhang of a wonky shed.

"How much longer?" Wiggins demanded, shining the torch straight in Fingers' eyes and destroying his night vision.

Fingers raised a hand to block out the light. "I'm going as fast as I can," he said, petulantly.

"I didn't ask how fast you were going," Wiggins snapped, wiping rain from his face. "I asked you how much longer it would take."

Fingers shrugged. "Hopefully not too much longer," he replied, sullenly, "but it's hard to be sure exactly where I should dig in the dark."

That wasn't true; he knew exactly where to dig. Darren had pointed out the spot soon after their arrival, but he had then done the weirdest thing and ordered Fingers to waste some time by digging several fake holes first. Fingers had been mystified by the instruction, but he trusted Darren, so he had gone along with it without question. After the first two holes had been dug, Willard and Casper had come rushing over, pushed Fingers out of the way and looked inside, hoping to see the bag of stolen gems laying there.

Naturally, they had been disappointed.

They had responded far less enthusiastically after he finished digging the third hole, and they hadn't bothered to check the fourth hole, preferring to stay dry and take Fingers' word that it was empty. Fingers stood up straight, massaged his aching back. "Are you sure you don't want to see for yourself?" he asked Wiggins.

"Is the hole empty?"

"Well, yeah."

"Then I don't need to get wet, do I?"

"Maybe I'll try digging a few feet to the left?" Fingers offered. "I know it's around here somewhere."

Wiggins spread his arms. "Sure, take your time," he responded, sarcastically. "It's not like I've got anything better to be doing, is it?"

Fingers glared at him hatefully, but said nothing. Picking up the shovel, he started digging again, only this time, he was standing directly above the buried handgun.

Before long, the tip of the shovel hit something.

Fingers froze, glanced sideways at Darren.

"Easy," the former soldier whispered. "Pass it to me slowly, so as not to draw attention."

Giving him an almost imperceptible nod, Fingers leaned down and pulled the plastic bag free from the surrounding earth.

"What's that?" Wiggins asked, pushing himself away from the rickety old shed and taking a half step towards him.

"Just a rock," Fingers replied, quickly tossing it onto the pile of earth beside Darren before Wiggins could switch his torch on.

Wiggins stood there for a moment, as if caught in two minds about coming over to see for himself. Then, with a bored shrug, he retreated back out of the rain. "Get on with it," he shouted, brushing water from his sleeves.

With a meek nod, Fingers resumed digging, but he was no longer paying attention to what he was doing. Instead, his eyes were riveted on Darren as he awaited further instructions.

After firing a nervous glance in Wiggins' direction, Darren hurriedly unzipped the bag and removed the Browning he had used to shoot Frank Kyle. A slow smile played across his face as he met his friend's eye. "Call them over. Say you've found something," he whispered, thumbing back the hammer and tucking the gun against his leg to shield it from view.

Fingers stopped digging, stood up, opened his mouth to shout, but nothing came out. He took a deep breath, cleared his throat. He was soaked through and shivering from the cold. "I–I think I've found something," he said in a tremulous voice.

"Like what, another rock?" Wiggins asked, not moving.

Fingers shook his head, spraying rain from his face. "N–no, I think I've found the bag with the gems."

Wiggins sprang to attention. "Why didn't you just say so," he growled, pushing himself away from the shed and striding purposefully towards the prisoners.

Casper followed behind at a more sedate pace, reluctant to abandon the relative dryness of the shed's overhang again until he was sure that the diamonds really had been found.

When Wiggins reached the halfway point between the shed and where Darren was lying, the former soldier whipped his hand up, revealing the gun. It took a moment for Wiggins to register the Browning's presence but, when he did, he jolted to a slippery halt, his eyes showing fear.

Squinting down the barrel, Darren cupped his left hand around the base of his right, to steady his aim. "This is for my sister," he said, before pulling the trigger.

Click.

That was it. No explosion; no ball of flame from the gun's muzzle.

Just the dull metallic click of a misfire.

Jim Stone was standing over Basher, who had now come round and was sitting with his back against the wall, feeling very sorry for himself.

A slender paramedic in her thirties, with kind eyes and a caring face, was squatting down beside him, giving him the once over. "Where does it hurt?" she asked him, wincing at the sight of his battered and bloody face.

"Everywhere," Basher moaned. His hands had been cuffed behind his back, so he couldn't point.

"Can we remove the restraints?" the female paramedic asked.

Stone shook his head, emphatically. "No, he's dangerous."

Her partner stood by her shoulder, staring at the handcuffed thug with far less sympathy than his colleague had displayed. "What did he do?" he asked Stone.

The detective shrugged. "Well, apart from just trying to beat my boss to death, he kidnapped a girl, beat the shit out of her, then locked her up in a cold, unlit cell and left her to freeze in nothing but her underwear."

The female paramedic stiffened on hearing that. When she next addressed the patient, her tone was far less friendly. "What day is it?" she asked Basher, shining a pencil torch in his eyes to check pupil dilation.

"My balls hurt," he whinged.

"I'm sure they do," she said, indifferently, "but what day is it?"

'Saturday," he said, miserably.

"Who's the Prime Minister?"

Basher frowned, deep in thought. "Tony Blair," he said after a moment, then added, "I didn't vote."

The paramedic smiled, seemingly satisfied. "I don't think there's any lasting damage," she said, standing up, "but as he lost consciousness for a while, we should probably pop him along to the hospital to get him checked out properly."

Stone grunted. He had been expecting her to say that. "I'll have to arrange for a guard to go with him," he said. "He's under arrest."

"I didn't do anything," Basher protested, glancing from Stone to the paramedics. "This is all a big mistake."

34

You're safe now

When Kevin Murray and Jim Cuthbert were sent to investigate the cell passageway, they found the doors to two of the three cells wide open. A sinister looking trail of what could only be dried blood led from the middle cell. It ran the length of the corridor where, for reasons yet to be established, it ended abruptly.

"It's the police," Murray called out loudly, just in case anyone was hiding in one of the cells.

Beside him, Cuthbert shuddered. "I get the feeling something very bad has gone on down here."

The first cell stunk of sweat and fear; unpleasant but not unbearable. Murray shone his pen-torch inside, taking in the fact that there were no windows, no lights, not even a toilet. He focused the beam of his torch on the slops bucket in the far corner, then turned his nose up at the smell wafting from it.

They moved on to the second cell, being careful not to step in the bloody trail that led from within. The overpowering stench of burning flesh hit them the moment they stepped inside.

The colour drained from Cuthbert's face, and he began to gag. Covering his nose, he retreated to the corridor, retching all the way.

Remaining behind, Murray shook his head contemptuously. As an Advanced Exhibits Officer, he was used to dealing with death in all its unpleasant glory, which wasn't to say that he enjoyed it or found it easy, just that he got on with it because that was his job.

In the unventilated space, the stench was utterly repugnant, but he forced himself to block it out and examine the cell for evidence. He shone the yellow beam from his pen-torch over the cot first, noting that the wire mesh crisscrossing the frame contained blobs of congealed blood and bits of flaked skin. He examined the wall next, and found that it was covered with red smears.

"Jesus," he breathed, wondering what had gone on?

Returning to the corridor a few moments later, he ran his eyes over Cuthbert, who was standing with his back pressed into the wall, head tilted upwards as he gulped in air.

"Are you okay?" he asked.

Cuthbert nodded, wiped his mouth with his handkerchief. "Sorry," he said, having the decency to look embarrassed. "It was the smell that did it."

When they opened the door to the final cell, they found Stella Carter cowering inside.

Murray scooped up her clothing, which had been dumped in a pile outside the door, then handed it over to her, averting his eyes from her semi-naked body, but not before he clocked the angry purple bruising that covered most of her abdomen and one side of her torso.

"T–thank you," she sobbed, accepting them with a trembling hand.

They gave her time to get dressed, then ushered her out of the cell.

Squinting against the harsh corridor light, Stella wrapped her arms tightly around her body. She shuddered and choked back a sob when she saw the blood trail on the floor.

"Be careful not to walk in that," Murray instructed.

Carter's eyes darted from one officer to the other, and it was clear that she was absolutely terrified. "W–where are the people who did this to me?" she asked.

"Don't worry about them," Murray said with surprising tenderness. "You're safe now."

She stared at him suspiciously, as though it had just occurred to her that he might be in league with her captors. "Who–who are you?"

Both men were wearing Met-Vests with the legend "POLICE' plastered across the chest, and Murray had made a point of calling out that they were police officers as they entered the cell passageway, but he could see that she was in shock, so he produced his warrant card for her to inspect.

Carter's lips moved soundlessly as she read it, then compared the photo it contained to the man standing in front of her. Tears were running down her cheeks as she nodded her acceptance.

"Wait here a moment, please," Murray said, leaving her with Cuthbert while he stepped into the cell to carry out a flash search. "Can I confirm your name?" he asked when he returned a few moments later. Although he recognised her from the custody imaging photos he had been shown, the formalities still had to be observed.

"My name's Stella… Stella Carter," she said, meekly.

Murray nodded, satisfied. "Stella, I'm arresting you on suspicion of the murder of Carrie McCullen. You don't have to say anything, but it may harm your defence if you don't mention when questioned something you later rely on in court. Anything you do say may be given in evidence. Do you understand the caution I've just given you?"

Carter was shaking her head with increasing desperation. "No, no, no…"

Murray frowned. "Are you saying you don't understand it?" he asked, wishing she would just stay silent, like most people did when they were arrested for murder.

"I–I'm saying I didn't kill Carrie," she stammered. "I loved her;

she was my world." She looked him straight in the eyes as she spoke, as though it was imperative that he should believe her.

Murray shrugged. Whether she did it or not was for others to decide, not him. "Come on," he said, gently taking hold of her arm. "There's a couple of paramedics outside. We'll get them to give you the once over before we head off to the nick."

The Browning Hi-Power was a remarkably reliable sidearm but, like any semi-automatic weapon, it could still suffer a temporary stoppage that rendered it inoperable.

When Darren heard a dull click instead of the loud bang he had been expecting, he instantly realised that the gun had suffered a firing malfunction and launched into the appropriate clearance drill. Keeping his eyes locked on his intended target, he tapped the magazine baseplate hard with his left hand to make sure that it was properly seated, then racked the slide to clear the chamber and cycle a new round. The process took no more than two seconds to complete, but that was enough time for Wiggins and Casper to dive for cover.

Before Darren could bring the gun to bear on either of them, they spun on their heels, with Wiggins veering off to the left and Casper to the right. Slipping and sliding in the gooey mud, they scuttled back to the shed.

Darren pulled the trigger twice, aiming a double tap at Wiggins receding centre mass. This time, instead of a worthless click, he was rewarded with the satisfying sound of the weapon barking. The first bullet thudded into the mud by Wiggins' feet, kicking up a great big chunk of earth, while the second whipped harmlessly past his head to embed itself in the side of the shed.

"Shit!" Darren yelled, awkwardly levering himself up to get a better aim.

He let out a howl of frustration as both men disappeared from view behind the shed.

Darren strained his ears, but the only noises he could hear came from the relentless rain and his own ragged breathing. Wiping his brow, he thought the situation through. The shed was the only cover for some distance, and Wiggins and Casper were trapped behind it. At some point, they were going to have to make a break for it and, when they did, he was confident that he would be able to pick them off.

"Not so fucking brave now, are you?" he shouted, his words echoing through the night air.

Silence.

No threats; no sarky come backs. Just two spineless killers cowering behind a shed in the driving rain, like rats hiding from the exterminator. It might have been funny if it hadn't been so pathetic.

He waved Fingers over, signalled for his friend to help him to his feet.

"She liked you, Fred," he shouted at Wiggins. Tears prickled his eyes as he spoke. "She thought you were an okay guy."

Leaning heavily on Fingers for support, Darren began hobbling towards the shed. If the rats wouldn't come to him, he would have to go to them.

"Dazza, we need to get away," Fingers cautioned.

"Come out and face me, you fuckers," Darren shouted, weaving the gun from one side of the shed to the other.

Suddenly, Wiggins head popped out from behind the shed. His right hand followed, and it was holding something. There was a muzzle flash, followed by a sharp crack, and then Darren was staggering backwards, clutching his stomach. He fell to the ground, pulling Fingers down with him.

With his lips drawn back in a snarl of agony, Darren glanced down at his left hand, which was covered in red. The pain in his stomach was unbearable, as though someone had just slit it open and poured red hot coals inside.

"Dazza, you're hit!" Fingers exclaimed, staring at the spreading bloodstain in shock.

Wiggins fired off another shot, and the bullet thudded into the earth a few inches to the left of Finger's foot.

"Run!" Darren told him.

Fingers shook his head, determinedly. "I'm not leaving you." Clambering to his feet, he grabbed hold of Darren's left arm and tried to pull him up.

Two more shots exploded into the ground to their right.

"Run," Darren repeated. Slapping Fingers' hands away, he raised the Browning and returned fire.

Three bullets slammed into the shed, forcing Wiggins to retreat behind it for cover.

Darren looked up at fingers, who was still fussing over him. "Get away from here," he panted, clutching his stomach with one hand while keeping the gun levelled at the shed with the other. "I can buy you some time, but you'll need to be quick."

Fingers was still shaking his head, but there was far less certainty in the movement now. "But I—"

"Run, damn it," Darren shouted. He laughed mirthlessly, then said, "There's no point in us both dying."

Fingers stared at him for a long moment, then his bottom lip started quivering as he accepted the inevitability of the situation. Fighting back tears, he leaned down and squeezed Darren's shoulder. "Okay, I'll go, but only to get help."

"Good lad," Darren said, smiling through the pain to reveal blood-stained teeth. With a heavy heart, he watched Fingers for a moment longer, then turned to face the shed.

"Come on then, Fred," he shouted through a coughing fit. "Let's do this." When he wiped his mouth, the back of his hand came away coated in frothy blood.

Blood loss was making Darren extremely light headed, and he wasn't sure how much longer he could hold out. Forcing himself into a sitting position, he stuck his injured leg straight out in front of him. His foot had gone numb, and he couldn't even feel his toes anymore.

Darren found himself struggling to draw breath, and his vision was beginning to dim. He squinted at the blurred outline of the shed, trying to get it back into focus.

Stay awake!

The gun in his hand was becoming increasingly heavy, and it was all he could do to keep his arm extended.

He was tired, so tired.

Suddenly, his hand was in his lap, and his head was on his chest.

He forced his eyes open.

Stay awake! You can sleep when you're dead!

Wiggins burst out from behind the shed, his gun arm extended. He was firing indiscriminately as he ran, and his efforts were wildly off target.

The Browning held thirteen rounds. Wiggins had fired three earlier on, and Darren counted another four as Wiggins ran towards him in a crouch, zig-zagging after every couple of steps to make himself harder to hit.

Under normal circumstances, the sideways jinking wouldn't have made much difference to Darren, who was an excellent shot, but with his vision blurred, and the ground beneath him pitching and rolling like a rough sea, he was finding it incredibly hard to take aim.

And then, out of the corner of his eye, he spotted Casper making his move. The albino bolted out from behind the opposite side of the shed. Moving forward in a lumbering crouch, he was trying to circle wide so that he could come at Darren from the side.

Although Casper was dangerous, he was unarmed, which made taking care of Wiggins the absolute priority. Lining the gun up on Wiggins, Darren blinked away the rain, drew in a deep, gurgly breath, held it for a moment, then released it slowly as he squeezed the trigger.

He missed.

Darren fired again, missed again.

What was wrong with him?

He fired again, and again, becoming more and more flustered.

Wiggins was firing at him as he ran. Bullets thudded into the ground all around Darren, but none of them came close to hitting him.

Darren's fourth shot found the target. Wiggins screamed in pain.

His arms flew out to the sides and he toppled forwards to land face down in the mud.

Darren kept the Browning trained on him, just in case it was a rouse on Wiggins' part, and he was only pretending to be hurt.

A sudden noise to his right startled him. A part of his brain registered the sound of heavy footsteps squelching through the mud, but he reacted far too sluggishly, which allowed Casper to reach him before he could bring the pistol up.

Grinning with evil intent, the albino swatted his gun arm aside and punched him in the face.

The Browning spun out of Darren's hand as he fell sideways onto the floor. He tried to lift his head, which had landed in a dirty puddle, but he just didn't have the energy. Turning his head to the side to avoid inhaling the water, Darren found himself staring directly at Fred Wiggins' body, which was lying motionless a few feet away from him.

Casper was staring at it too, but with complete detachment. After a moment's hesitation, he crossed to where his boss was laying and rolled him over. He examined the chest wound, felt for a pulse, then retrieved Wiggins' Browning.

Standing up, the giant checked that the muzzle hadn't become blocked with mud when Wiggins went down, then worked the slide to confirm there was a round in the chamber. He seemed in no particular rush as he walked back to where Darren was lying. Placing a massive instep under Darren's body, he flipped him over onto his back.

Looming over Darren, he smiled pleasantly. "I've always wanted to see what happens to a man's head when you put a bullet into it at point black range," he said, pointing the gun at Darren's skull.

35

I'm gonna break you in half

The search for Willard was well under way. The helicopter had been refuelling when the call for assistance came out, but it was now en route to them and, when it arrived it would search the wasteland abutting the warehouse using thermal imaging.

In the meantime, a dog unit had been deployed, entering the wasteland via the gap in the car park fencing. So far, it hadn't managed to pick up his scent.

Sitting in the back of a marked police van, Mickey was refusing to give his name. No one cared; his fingerprints would be in the system. The escorting officers were just waiting for the control room to call them back with instructions on where to take him.

Basher, also under arrest but unfit to be taken straight to a police station, had been placed in the back of an ambulance and carted off to hospital with three escorting officers in attendance.

A second ambulance had been called for Stella Carter, who had collapsed shortly after being released from her cell. As she was under arrest for Carrie's murder, Tyler had been forced to send a couple of escorts with her, which had depleted his limited resources even further.

Ian Yule had also required medical attention. After taking a tumble during his ill-fated pursuit of Willard, the accident-prone detective's face, neck and body were crisscrossed with a network of nasty looking lacerations. During his efforts to extricate himself from the brambles, Yule had somehow managed to roll into a mass of stinging nettles. By the time he had finally freed himself, his entire body had been covered in an angry rash that seemed to be getting worse by the second. In addition to intense itchiness and pain, he was also complaining of tightness in his chest and throat, and his lips and tongue seemed a little swollen. The paramedic examining him suspected that he was having an allergic reaction to the nettle rash, so he had joined the growing list of people requiring hospital treatment.

"Probably the safest place for him," Bull had remarked as Yule was wheeled out to the waiting ambulance.

There was no arguing with that.

Now that the initial drama was over, the warehouse annexe had been turned into a full-blown crime scene.

"I'd say this place has been used as a modern-day torture chamber," Juliet Kennedy proclaimed upon her arrival. "I reckon prisoners were hung from these chains and subjected to various forms of abuse and maltreatment." She paused to sniff the air, then pulled down her mask. "Can't you smell it?" she asked.

Tyler frowned, sniffed the air around him. "I can mainly smell strong disinfectant," he said, then had another sniff. "Also, there's a faint whiff of petrol... and something else, cooked meat, maybe?"

She raised a questioning eyebrow. "How many fatal house fires have you attended, Jack?"

The penny dropped. Tyler sniffed again, less enthusiastically this time. "You think that's human flesh I can smell?" he asked, turning his nose up.

"Almost certainly," Kennedy said.

"You can't seriously think they've been burning bodies in here?" Tyler scoffed, looking around the room.

Contrary to popular belief, it wasn't that easy to dispose of a body by setting it alight. Crematorium incinerators reached staggeringly high temperatures, and even then, parts of the skeletal structure generally remained intact. These had to be raked from the cremator and placed in a machine known as a cremulator to grind the remaining bones down into a granular ash.

"I'm not suggesting that they burned dead bodies here, you great doughnut," Kennedy said, addressing him in her usual irreverent tone. "What I'm saying is that the evil bastards strung their victims up and then tortured them with fire."

"Ah," Tyler said, blushing. That made much more sense. Inviting Kennedy to join him, he crossed to the two large circular drums by the far wall. "When we arrived, one of the men we've since arrested was wheeling a drum like this into the loading bay," he said, thoughtfully. "We never did check to see what was inside it." As he spoke, he gave each of them a little shove to test their weight. Then, unfastening the galvanised clamping rings, he pulled the lids off, looked inside.

They were empty.

A truly horrible thought suddenly occurred to him. The blood and gore leading from the middle cell suggested that someone had recently been tortured here, and Willard's men had still been cleaning the mess up when the detectives arrived, which begged the question: where was the victim?

Not in the cells.

Not in any of the vans.

Not anywhere else in the building.

Acting on impulse, Tyler set off towards the loading bay. "Come on, you two," he said, beckoning Murray and Kennedy to follow him with a crooked finger.

Placing her hands on her hips, Kennedy remained where she was. "I really haven't got time to go exploring," she said, tartly.

Tyler glanced back over his shoulder. "Make time," he said, firmly.

Kennedy and Murray exchanged glances, shrugged in unison, then did as they had been told.

Out in the loading bay, they found the drum that Mickey had tipped over lying on its side by one of the vans.

Tyler grabbed the side of the steel drum, tested the weight.

It was heavy.

Very heavy.

His mood darkened. "Give me a hand," he said to Murray.

Between them, they manhandled the drum upright, grunting from all the effort it took.

"Is there a point to this?" Kennedy asked, staring at him in exasperation.

"I have a horrible feeling there is," Tyler said.

After taking a moment to catch his breath, he undid the clamping ring, which came away with a soft hiss. Hoping that his suspicions were unfounded, Tyler pried the lid off.

The smell hit them at once.

Tyler turned his head away, took a deep breath, then forced himself to look inside. The drum contained a man's mangled body. The head, which sat at an unnatural angle to the shoulders, was a bloody mess. It looked as though someone had stamped it into a pulp. An eye had popped out under pressure, the victim's nose had imploded, and several teeth were missing.

Although Tyler couldn't see any charred flesh, the smell of burning was unmistakable.

"How did you know?" Kennedy asked.

Tyler shrugged. "Someone was obviously tortured in that room very recently. I figured that, if the poor bugger had died, there wouldn't have been enough time for them to get rid of the body before we turned up, so it still had to be on the premises somewhere."

"Do we know who he is – or rather, who he was?" Kennedy asked.

Tyler shook his head, sadly. "No, but whoever he was, he didn't deserve that." He pulled out his mobile. "I'd better let Steve Bull know that the two male suspects need to be further arrested on suspicion of murder."

"Get Stevie to seize their clothing and footwear," Kennedy said, looking at the corpse. "Someone stamped on this man's head, quite a few times by the look of it, so there will definitely be trace evidence on their trousers and in the soles of their shoes."

―――

Still pointing the gun at Darren McCullen's head, Casper teased, "Maybe, before I blow your head off, I'll have a little fun, teach you a lesson for what you did to Fred."

He began reciting the nursery rhyme, '*Eeny, meeny, miny, moe*' in a singsong voice. As he spoke, the barrel began moving slowly down Darren's body, pausing first at his shoulder, then at his elbow. It lingered there a moment, before continuing downwards towards his good knee. When it eventually came to rest, the pistol was pointing straight at his left ankle.

Casper thumbed back the hammer. "Let's start at the bottom and work our way upwards, shall we?" With that, he pulled the trigger.

At which point, Dillon lunged forward and brought the heavy bolt croppers he had found by the side of the shed crashing down into his wrist.

As metal slammed into bone, Casper let out a piercing scream, and the pistol flew out of his hand to land in the nearby mud. The bullet thudded harmlessly into one of the many mounds of earth that Fingers had dug up.

With a snarl of primal rage, Casper spun to face Dillon.

Before Dillon could utter a word, Casper lowered his head and charged, slamming his shoulder into the detective's chest. The impact carried both men to the floor. Twisting and turning in a clumsy backwards somersault they grabbed at each other, each one trying to get the upper hand.

Both men ended up flat on their backs several feet apart.

Dillon scrabbled to his feet first. Wiping mud from his eyes, he crouched in readiness for the next attack.

Casper was a little slower getting up, but not by much. Staring hatefully at the detective, his little piggy eyes scanned the surrounding area for the gun he had dropped, but there was no sign of it. Clenching his fists, he advanced on Dillon. "I'm gonna break you in half," he promised.

Dillon said nothing, preferring to let his actions speak for him. The fact that Casper was a good five inches taller than him, and probably had a fifty-to-sixty pound weight advantage, didn't faze him in the slightest. He had fought big men before, Claude Winston and Samuel Adebanjo to name but two, and he had always come out on top.

As Casper shuffled forward, Dillon circled to his right, kept going until he had placed himself between the albino and Darren McCullen.

"You can't hide from me," Casper snorted, mistaking his evasive moments for fear, when in fact Dillon had simply been seeking out firmer ground, so that he wouldn't slip and slide all over the place while they fought.

"I'm a police officer," Dillon said. "I'm arresting you for the kidnap of Stella Carter, and for the unlawful possession of a firearm with intent to endanger life."

Casper raised a white-haired eyebrow in surprise, then burst out laughing. He shook his head at the policeman's stupidity. "You think being a pig's gonna save you from me?"

Dillon's face remained impassive. "Don't be a complete arsehole. The game's up; you're nicked."

Casper wasn't going to let anyone speak to him like that. With a snarl of rage, he barrelled forward, throwing a succession of clubbing punches at the detective's head.

The suddenness of the attack caught Dillon off guard, and he leapt back, only narrowly avoiding the first two. The albino was surprisingly fast, considering his size, and Dillon was forced to absorb the third and fourth blows on his forearms, which he had raised to protect his head.

The power behind the punches was incredible, like nothing he had ever experienced before. As Dillon was rocked from side to side by their impact, he could literally feel the bones in his body rattling.

Although the ferocity of the giant's attack had taken him by surprise, Dillon managed to slip under the fifth punch and counter with a savage uppercut of his own, which caught the advancing man in the ribs. It was a good shot, delivered with perfect timing, and it should have dropped him to his knees and left him gasping for breath, but Casper didn't even break stride. To Dillon's dismay, he showed no sign of having noticed the punch, let alone being hurt by it.

As Casper made a grab for him, Dillon hit him again, this time unleashing a solid right that crashed into the side of his jaw with a jarring thud. He was rewarded by a satisfying 'Oomph' as the albino staggered backwards, looking noticeably shaken.

When Casper looked up, his lips were drawn back in a snarl, and Dillon was pleased to see that his eyes registered pain and something else… Wariness, perhaps?

Shaking his head to clear it, Casper came at him again. This time, leading with a clumsy front kick, which he aimed at Dillon's solar plexus.

Dillon skipped back, made an X with his forearms to block the kick. The albino had enormous feet, like Ronald MacDonald, and Dillon guessed that his shoe size had to be a UK fifteen or sixteen. Trapping his opponent's foot, he violently twisted it, hoping to snap his ankle.

With his arms flailing wildly, Casper tottered several steps to his left, like a kid playing hop-scotch in the school playground. Somehow, against all the odds, he remained upright.

Dillon gave his humungous foot another almighty tug, this time pulling the albino completely off balance and sending him sprawling onto the muddy floor.

Casper scrabbled backwards, trying to put some distance between them so that he could stand up.

Dillon wasn't in the mood to play fairly, so he ran forward and booted the albino straight in the side of the head, as if he were taking a penalty kick.

It was like kicking a concrete football.

It was a blow that would have snapped the neck of any normal man, hospitalised him at the very least, but the albino just shook his head groggily and tried to stand.

"Stay down," Dillon panted. His foot was throbbing so badly that he wondered if he had broken some of the bones in it.

Casper defiantly dragged himself onto his knees, then planted one foot on the ground in readiness to stand. He spat a large glob of blood onto the floor, then wiped his mouth with the back of his hand.

"Stay down," Dillon repeated through gritted teeth.

"Go fuck yourself, pig," Casper growled, before launching himself forward.

Dillon had thought the fight was all but over. He didn't understand how the albino could even talk after taking a hit like that, let alone continue fighting.

With a crazed roar, Casper lunged at him, arms extended for a rugby tackle. They went down hard, as Dillon had known they would, and he felt the air being violently expelled from his lungs as the albino's great bulk crushed him.

Dillon flexed his muscles, straining every sinew, but there was no escaping the crushing bear hug that Casper now held him in.

Dillon was struggling to breathe. Unless he could free himself quickly, positional asphyxia would set in, and then gravity would finish the job off for Casper. But the albino was too stupid to realise this, and he willingly surrendered the advantage the bear hug was giving him for the satisfaction of clamping his hands around Dillon's throat.

With Dillon's arms no longer pinned against his sides by Casper's great bulk, he was able to move again. Placing his feet flat on the floor, Dillon violently arched his back in an attempt to buck Casper, but for all the good that did him, he might as well have been trapped beneath a car.

Panic began to set in as the giant crushed his windpipe. In

desperation, Dillon reached up and grabbed hold of Casper's wrists. He clawed at them, trying to drag the man's fingers from his throat, but the albino was far too strong, even for him.

Unable to breathe, Dillon could feel his strength ebbing away. He slammed his palms into the other man's ears, hoping to perforate the drums but, with his range of movement severely restricted, he couldn't generate the power he needed. He tried raking his nails down the side of Casper's face, but the giant just elbowed his hands away.

Dillon could feel the life being choked out of him. For the first time ever, he began to consider the unthinkable; that he might not win this fight.

Above him, a cruel smile spread across Casper's face, reflecting his growing confidence. He sensed that victory was his, and he intended to enjoy it.

The gloating smile infuriated Dillon, injecting new purpose into his flagging body. There was no way that he was just going to lay there and let the smirking bastard kill him. Ignoring the nauseating wave of dizziness spreading through him, Dillon blindly groped the albino's face with both hands, seeking out his eye sockets. As much as it sickened him to do it, Dillon gouged his thumbs into Casper's eyes, banking that the other man would rather let him go than risk losing his sight.

Realising what he was trying to do, Casper tilted his head back and shook it violently, doing everything he could to thwart Dillon.

Dillon was becoming disorientated. He needed air. Pouring all his energy into one last effort, he plunged his thumbs in deeper. He really didn't want to maim or disfigure the other man, but if it was a choice between doing that or dying, then it was a no brainer.

He suddenly felt one of his thumbnails rip through the membrane lining in the albino's eye socket, and a warm, sticky liquid gushed over his thumb and trickled down onto his palm. At the same time, Casper screamed in excruciating agony. Releasing his grip on Dillon's windpipe, his hands flew up to his left eye, covering it protectively.

Able to breathe at long last, Dillon gasped in air.

Casper's screaming grew louder. Clasping his damaged eye with one hand, he began clubbing Dillon's head with his free hand.

The first blow caught Dillon on the side of the face, making his ears ring and blurring his vision. It was like being slapped by a full grown grisly. He managed to intercept the follow up punch, catching Casper's wrist and twisting it to the side, at the same time thrusting his free hand upwards at great speed, striking Casper on the point of the chin with the heel. The albino's head snapped backwards, and his teeth slammed together. There was a satisfying snapping noise, like something had just broken. Dillon immediately followed up with another heel strike, but this one didn't connect as cleanly as the first. However, it did force Casper to redistribute his weight, which finally enabled Dillon to throw the heavier man off him.

As Casper flopped onto his stomach, Dillon rolled over twice, putting some distance between the two of them. He rose to his feet unsteadily, then leaned forward. Resting his hands on his knees, he hungrily gulped in fresh air.

A few feet away, Casper was floundering on the floor, trying to gain the purchase he required to stand. With a gargantuan effort, he somehow managed to stumble to his feet and square off against Dillon. His left eye was completely closed, and it was bleeding badly. One side of his jaw was sagging down at an unnatural angle, and Dillon realised that it was broken.

As Casper stumbled forward on unsteady legs, Dillon held up a hand. "Enough," he panted. "It's over. You've lost."

Casper's face was suffused with raw hatred and, even though he looked like he was going to topple over at any second, there was a defiance in his body language that told Dillon he wasn't beaten yet.

"Don't make me hurt you unnecessarily," Dillon warned.

Casper laughed. "Look what I just found." As he spoke, his right hand came up, and it was holding the Browning.

For a moment, Dillon didn't know whether to laugh or cry.

It was over; the albino had won.

A feeling of resignation washed over him as he tensed for action.

If he was going to die, he wasn't going to go quietly, or without a fight.

Out of the blue, an image of Imogen Askew's sleeping face popped into Dillon's head. The thought of her grieving for him, and the pain that caused him, surprised him even more than the unexpected appearance of the gun.

Dillon took a deep breath to oxygenate his body, then threw himself at Casper.

Casper smiled triumphantly as his finger tightened on the trigger. "Game over," he boasted.

A single shot rang out, striking its intended target in the head and dropping him like a felled tree.

36

Nellie the Elephant

Tyler huffed moodily. He had just fielded a call from a stroppy custody sergeant who had informed him that, having been examined by the FME at the station, the man they now knew as Mickey Mulligan might have a fractured wrist, and would therefore need to attend hospital so that X-rays could be taken and a cast fitted if necessary. Said custody sergeant had then made the mistake of demanding to know how long it would take Tyler to drum up the escorts, complaining that Mulligan's constant whinging was getting on his nerves.

It had been a red flag to a bull, and Tyler had furiously chewed the sergeant's ear off for the best part of a minute, pointing out that his detectives had far better things to do than sit around a hospital all night waiting for a prisoner to be examined. He had then told the sergeant, in no uncertain terms, to stop bothering him and organise the escorts himself, in accordance with MPS standard operating procedures. With his tail firmly between his legs, the custody sergeant had apologised profusely, hanging up as quickly as he could to avoid incurring any more of the angry detective's wrath.

Tyler checked his watch. It was getting on for an hour since Dillon had set off after the van containing Fred Wiggins and Casper Wright, and they still hadn't heard from him.

Imogen Askew had tried ringing him numerous times since then, as had Tyler and Bull, but there was never any reply. Imogen was frantic with worry and, although he had gone out of his way to reassure her that everything would be okay, and that Dillon would call in as soon as he could, he was secretly very concerned. In fact, he was so worried that he had recently instructed Reg Parker to have the TIU ping Dillon's Job phone. In addition, he had Dean Fletcher running the pool car's registration number through the ANPR system, to see if there had been any activations, and he had requested that the registration number be circulated on the Main-Set, with instructions for all patrolling officers to be actively on the lookout for it.

Tyler's phone rang, and he snatched it up, hoping it was Dillon.

"Boss, I've found the car that those keys you gave me belonged to," Jim Stone informed him. *"It's a Ford Scorpio, and it's parked between the two buildings opposite the warehouse. You might want to pop over and see what I've found inside."*

After securing the crime scene, Murray had searched the warehouse office, hoping to find the keys to Willard and Wiggins' cars. He hadn't found either set, but he had stumbled across the keys to a Ford, and Tyler had tasked Jim Stone to check if the car was parked nearby.

Glad of a chance to grab some fresh air, Tyler informed Juliet Kennedy that he wouldn't be long. Logging out with the cordon officer, he nipped across the service road to where Stone was waving at him from the entrance to a narrow alley between two dilapidated buildings.

It was still raining heavily, but getting soaked through was infinitely preferable to being cooped up inside a stuffy room that reeked of a toxic mixture of burnt flesh, petrol and disinfectant.

Imogen Askew and Bear were standing with Stone, having filmed him searching the area for the car.

"Any news from Tony?" she asked as Tyler walked over, his shoulders hunched against the downpour

Tyler shook his head, pensively. "Not yet, but I've got people actively trying to find him."

Biting her lip, she stared up at him with worried eyes, but said nothing.

He squeezed her arm gently, then followed Stone over to a black Ford Scorpio.

The boot was open.

Stone pointed inside, where the spare wheel had been removed from its cavity. In the gap it had occupied, sat a large self-sealing plastic bag. This contained a smaller velvet bag with a long drawstring, and two large stacks of cash.

Tyler peered in, raised an eyebrow. "That's an awful lot of money," he observed. "Any idea what's in the velvet bag?"

Stone shook his head. "Thought I'd wait for you to arrive before opening it."

"Well, I'm here now," Tyler said, indicating for him to carry on.

Stone was wearing two sets of nitrile gloves. He removed the plastic bag, placed it on the rear wing of the car, and carefully undid it. Reaching in, he removed the velvet bag and gave it a little shake. The contents jingled. He looked at Tyler, shrugged. Pulling the drawstrings open, he peeked inside, then let out a little whistle. "I'm no expert," he said, holding the bag out for Tyler and Askew to see for themselves, "but I'd say they were diamonds."

Tyler looked in, nodded. "That's a *lot* of diamonds," he said.

"That's a lot of very expensive diamonds," Imogen added.

"Do we know who the car's registered to?" Tyler asked.

The detective nodded. "We do. It belongs to Darren McCullen."

Tyler frowned. "What's his car doing parked across the road from Willard's warehouse?"

Stone could only shrug.

Tyler opened his mouth to speak, then closed it without saying a word as he experienced a lightbulb moment akin to having an epiphany. What if Darren McCullen's criminality extended beyond committing ram raids? What if it also included robbery and murder?

Perhaps McCullen wasn't out of the country as they had been led to believe; perhaps Willard's men had grabbed him and brought him here? Could the body they had found wedged into the steel drum belong to Carrie's older brother?

It made perfect sense.

It would certainly explain why his car was parked nearby, and it potentially explained where the jewels and cash had come from. If Kyle had been looking after them for Willard, and McCullen had stolen them, Willard's retribution would be swift and terminal.

"I need to speak to Andy Quinlan," he said, reaching for his mobile. Quinlan would know whether any gems had been reported stolen during the robbery.

―――

The left side of Casper's head exploded outwards as the bullet passed through his skull, killing him instantly. Blood and bits of dura mater flew through the air in a crimson mist as Casper staggered edgeways a step, a look of confusion appearing on his face. Then, his eyes went blank, and he toppled sideways, landing in the mud with a loud squelch.

For a moment, all Dillon could do was stare at him in open-mouthed shock. The albino's life had just been snuffed out with no more effort than someone would have used to extinguish a match.

He spun in the direction the shot had come from to see Casper's killer propping himself up on one elbow. The pistol in his hand was still smoking. Looking Dillon straight in the eye, he managed a weak smile, exposing blood-stained teeth. Then his eyelids fluttered and he dropped the gun. Sliding backwards, he came to rest in the soft mud. Almost immediately, he began coughing violently, and a frothy jet of blood erupted from his mouth.

Although badly injured, he was conscious and breathing, whereas Wiggins was face down and unmoving.

Dillon hesitated for a split second, then ran over to Wiggins and rolled him onto his back. There was a gaping hole in the centre of his chest, and he was staring up at the sky through unseeing eyes.

"Shit," Dillon breathed, checking for a pulse.

Nothing.

"Shit," Dillon said again.

Behind him, the gun battle's sole survivor let out a long, painful wail, then resumed his coughing.

Dillon ran over to him, slipping and sliding in the mud. Up close, his injuries were even worse than Dillon had imagined. He was clutching his abdomen, writhing around in agony, and his right knee was a shattered, pulpy mess. Even with the tourniquet applied tightly, his entire lower leg was coated in a slimy film of blood.

Ignoring his protestations, Dillon carefully pulled the man's hands away, then grimaced at the sight of the jagged stomach wound. The entry was just above his navel, and the bleeding was severe. The exit was higher up, and to the right, making Dillon think the bullet had hit bone and ricocheted around inside his body.

Skin deathly white from blood loss, lips blue from cyanosis, the injured man's breathing was worryingly weak, and becoming shallower by the second. As Dillon looked on, more blood bubbled over his lips and ran down his chin.

Although he had been gut shot, Dillon suspected that he also had a lung injury, and was slowly drowning in his own blood. Whether this was a result of the bullet bouncing around inside him, or an earlier beating, Dillon had no way of telling.

Like all serving police officers, Dillon had undergone extensive first aid training, but these injuries were so catastrophic that he didn't even know where to begin. He knew he needed to roll his patient into a recovery position, so that the blood filtering into his lungs could drain off, but the injuries to his stomach and leg were so severe that Dillon was almost afraid to move him.

Not for the first time since the shooting had started, Dillon cursed himself for having surrendered his phone to Tyler.

"Is he... is he dead?" the man suddenly asked, indicating the albino with a flick of his eyes. His voice was a weak rasp, so frail that Dillon could barely hear the words.

Dillon nodded. "Yes, he's dead."

The man coughed again. "What about... what about Fred? Is he... is he dead, too?"

Dillon glanced behind him at the unmoving form of Fred Wiggins. "I think so," he said, preparing to roll the injured man onto his side.

Through the pain, he managed a weak smile, then whispered, "Thank God. Now Carrie can rest in peace."

Dillon stiffened. "What do you mean?"

"Had to... had to..." His voice broke off as he launched into another coughing fit, spraying blood all over his chest. "Had to kill the bastards to avenge her... had to..."

The words tapered off as he drifted into unconsciousness.

"Wake up," Dillon said, shaking the other man's shoulders.

His eyes flickered open, and he stared up at Dillon. It took him a moment to focus.

"How does killing Fred Wiggins and Casper Wright avenge Carrie?" Dillon asked, his voice full of urgency.

The injured man frowned, as if he was having trouble processing the question. "They killed her," he whispered. "The bastards killed my sister."

It was only then that Dillon realised the injured man was Carrie's older brother, Darren, the man they had all thought was on holiday in Tenerife.

"Why would they have done that, Darren?" he asked, speaking softly, cajolingly.

Darren licked his lips. "Because... because she gave me the information about Frank the Tank, told me... told me about the cash and diamonds... in his house."

It took Dillon a moment to make the connection, but then he realised that Darren was referring to the botched robbery Andy Quinlan's team were dealing with. "Darren, did you kill Frank Kyle?" he asked, conscious that he was probably receiving his dying declaration.

"I–I…" Darren shuddered, coughed up more blood. His head came off the floor as he gasped for air. Screwing his eyes shut, he rolled onto his side and clutched his abdomen as a spasm of pain ran through him.

Dillon quickly placed a protective hand on the back of his head, to stop it from smashing into the ground.

Darren seemed to be fighting for his every breath as Dillon rolled him into a recovery position. He tried to speak, but nothing came out. Then, he let out his last gurgling breath and went still.

"No, no, no!" Dillon said, hurriedly feeling for a pulse.

He tried the wrist first, then the neck.

Nothing.

Pulling Darren onto his back, he began to perform CPR, singing the words to *Nellie the Elephant* in his head to get the rhythm right, just as they taught him during his first aid training.

Whatever crimes he had committed, Darren McCullen had just saved Dillon's life, and he was determined to repay the compliment.

"HELP!" he shouted into the night air. "SOMEBODY, ANYBODY, PLEASE HELP ME!"

Behind him, the incessant pounding of the rain on the shed's roof was the only noise he could hear; a million little taps all happening at once.

As anyone who has had to do it for real will tell you, performing cardiopulmonary resuscitation – trying to make another person's heart reach the 100 beats per minute target to achieve effective blood circulation – quickly becomes utterly exhausting.

As seconds turned into minutes, Dillon's breathing became increasingly laboured and his limbs began to shake from the effort. Ignoring the fatigue, he carried on relentlessly, pausing only to call out for help every few seconds.

He continued until he could barely move, praying that someone had heard his calls for help, and that skilled medical assistance would arrive in time to save the day.

If only he still had his phone, he could–

A thought occurred to him, bursting through the fog of exhaustion like a brilliant ray of sunshine, and he cursed his stupidity for not having thought of this sooner.

Breaking off the CPR, he hurriedly patted Darren's pockets down, hoping to find a mobile phone.

Drawing a blank, he stumbled over to the albino, repeated the process. Again, no phone. Either Casper didn't possess one or he had left it in the van.

Dillon staggered back to Darren for another minute of CPR, then dragged himself over to Wiggins, went through his pockets, discovered a little Nokia in his inside jacket pocket.

Pulling it out with shaking a hand, he frantically dialled 999.

37

SUNDAY 14TH OCTOBER 2001

That'll make a good soundbite on the telly

It was the morning after the night before, and what an eventful night it had turned out to be.

The rain had gone, replaced by glorious sunshine. The sky was cloudless, a picture-perfect canvas of cerulean, so vibrant and intense that, had it been depicted that way in an oil painting, critics would have complained that the artist had gone overboard with the colours. It was hot out there, too; T-shirt weather again, not that Tyler was in any position to enjoy the resurgent Autumn sunshine.

He sat in his air-conditioned office, huddled over his desk, where he had been since returning from the warehouse crime scene in the early hours. Shirt sleeves rolled up, collar undone, tie hanging loose, Tyler felt hot and grubby. He longed to take a break, to soak his tired, aching body under a hot shower for a few minutes, and to put on some fresh clothes. But he simply didn't have the time for such indulgences.

There was still so, so much to do.

Taking a break from writing up his Decision Log, Tyler ran a weary hand over his stubbled chin. He let out a cavernous yawn, then shook his aching fingers to dispel the cramp that was setting in. He looked at his knuckles, which were red and bruised from the previous night's fighting, and wondered if Basher's face looked that bad. As an afterthought, he snatched a sip of lukewarm coffee, grimaced at the taste. With a sigh, he resumed writing.

Things were a little clearer this morning, but not by much.

The body in the steel drum remained unidentified, but at least they now knew it didn't belong to Darren McCullen. After the record photography had been completed, and the relevant samples had been taken in situ, the body had been removed from the steel drum with painstaking slowness under the watchful eye of Juliet Kennedy, the Crime Scene Manager. The on-call FME had attended to pronounce life extinct. A wet set of fingerprints had also been taken from the corpse, before the head and hands were bagged, and they had been rushed up to New Scotland Yard for urgent comparisons. It was hoped that, as long as the mystery victim was in the system, they would have his identity within a matter of hours. DNA swabs had also been taken from him, and these would be sent off for identification purposes if the fingerprints failed to yield a result.

It had become clear that Andrew Quinlan's investigation was deeply entwined with Tyler's own, so Holland had suggested that they combine their teams and share the workload. As it seemed likely that the man in the steel drum had been killed by Willard and his thugs, it was looking like he and Andy were going to retain that investigation as well, and not get away with farming it out to another team.

After being X-rayed, Mickey Mulligan had been discharged from hospital and returned to Plaistow police station. It seemed his wrist was badly sprained, but not fractured, so he was fit for detention and interview, much to his displeasure. Having been returned to police custody, Mulligan had been placed straight into a mandatory sleep period, and he would be interviewed later that morning.

Gregory 'Basher' Nolan had been kept in hospital overnight,

suffering from concussion. He was due to be seen by the doctor later that morning, and the Ward Sister anticipated he would be discharged by lunchtime. A cell had already been reserved for him at Barking. There had been space at Plaistow, where Mulligan was, but Tyler wanted the two men kept apart.

Jonas Willard had been picked up a mile away from the warehouse, his clothing ripped, his hands and face badly lacerated from fighting his way through the dense undergrowth of the land abutting his warehouse. His clothing had been seized, gunshot residue swabs had been taken, and he had been placed in a cell. He was to be interviewed about Stella's kidnapping and the dead body at his warehouse later that morning. His solicitor, a slimy weasel called Oliver Clarke, from the decidedly dodgy firm of Cratchit, Lowe and Clarke, had arrived at the station a half-hour earlier, and he was already making a nuisance of himself by all accounts.

At least Stella Carter hadn't been admitted to hospital as an inpatient. After being examined at A&E, and undergoing X-rays, she had been released into police custody. She was currently being held at Hackney police station. Her solicitor had already arrived, and he had been provided with initial advance disclosure. Carter was now locked in consultation with him, and the interviews would commence as soon as that had finished.

It promised to be a very busy day for everyone connected to the enquiry. Willard and Mulligan were to be interviewed about Carter's abduction and the murder of the man whose body had been crammed into a steel drum, as indeed Nolan would be when he was released from hospital later that day.

Stella Carter was to be interviewed about Carrie's murder.

And, as if all that wasn't enough, Darren McCullen's flat would have to be searched in relation to Frank Kyle's murder, the botched robbery at his house, and all the ram raids he had been involved in.

Casper Wright and Fred Wiggins had been pronounced dead at the scene, and Tyler was firmly of the opinion that neither man's demise was a loss to mankind. The allotments where they had been shot were currently being processed by Sam Calvin, with Dick Jarvis serving as his Advanced Exhibits Officer. The record photography had been completed overnight, and their bodies had been bagged and removed to Poplar mortuary. The Special Post Mortems wouldn't take place until the following day, but that was of no consequence as the detectives already knew exactly how they had died.

In due course, a specialist search team would carry out a fingertip search of the allotments for the discarded shell casings and whatever it was that they had gone there to dig up. There was even talk of calling in a Ground Penetrating Radar team if necessary. The Police Search Advisor in charge, more commonly known as a POLSA, anticipated that, to do justice to it, the search would probably take a good couple of days.

Miraculously, and against all the odds, Darren McCullen had still been clinging onto life when the HEMS helicopter arrived. Supported by paramedics, a ballistic trauma specialist had worked something of a miracle to stabilise him at the scene, and he had eventually been airlifted to the Royal London Hospital, where he had undergone hours of surgery.

Now in ICU, Darren was sedated and on a ventilator. It was touch and go whether he would last the day, let alone recover, and there was a significant chance of there being brain damage if he did, due to the length of time he had gone without oxygen.

The door to Tyler's office opened and Dillon barged in carrying two Styrofoam cups. His unshaven face was gaunt, and there were huge bags beneath his eyes. "There you go," he said, placing a latte in front of Tyler.

"What the hell are you doing back here?" Tyler demanded, lowering his pen and leaning back in his seat. While running disapproving eyes over his partner, he massaged a crick in his neck.

When Dillon had finally returned to Hertford House, after completing his notes and being grilled by the on-call DI from complaints about the shootings, Tyler had sent him straight home, with explicit instructions to take the day off and get some rest.

Dillon blew out his cheeks and flopped down into the seat opposite Tyler's. Ignoring the withering look his partner was giving him, he took a sip of his cappuccino, and sighed appreciatively. "No point my staying at home. It's not like I would have been able to sleep, so I thought I'd come back in," he said with a wan smile.

Tyler opened his mouth to protest.

"Relax," Dillon said, beating him to it. "I've had a long, hot shower – something you could do with from the smell of you – eaten some breakfast, and changed out of my poor ruined clothes. I'm good to go."

Tyler stared at him for a long moment, evaluating his condition, worrying about his welfare. "Well, if you're sure," he said, reluctantly.

"Yes, I'm bloody sure," Dillon said, irritably swatting his friend's concerns away. "It'll be better for me to keep busy and I–"

The office door flew open and Imogen Askew swept in like a cyclone. "Oh, Tony," she said, rushing over to give him a crushing hug. "I was so worried about you."

Tyler rolled his eyes, but the ghost of a smile materialised across his lips. "Oh, for goodness' sake, get a room, you two," he said with mock severity. Having seen just how worried Imogen had been about the big lug, his attitude towards her had mellowed somewhat.

Dillon blushed, disentangled himself from her embrace, said, "Don't worry, I'm fine."

Imogen grabbed his hand, squeezed it hard, and it struck Tyler that his friend made no effort to pull free.

"After what you went through, how could you possibly be fine?" she asked, still clinging to his hand

Dillon winked at her. Then, to Tyler's surprise, he raised the back of her hand to his mouth and kissed it gently. "It's all in a day's work for a roughty-toughty cop like me."

She was staring at him like a lovesick schoolgirl.

"Did you actually want something?" Tyler asked.

It was her turn to blush now. "Oh, er, yes. I was just wondering if it would be okay for Bear and I to accompany the officers assigned to search Darren McCullen's flat?"

Tyler thought about this for a moment, but couldn't see any harm in it. "I'm sure that will be fine," he said. "I'll have a word with Sam Calvin and Kevin Murray, let them know you'll be tagging along." If nothing else, it would prevent her from following Dillon around all morning, and fawning over him like she was now.

"This interview is being tape recorded," Paul Evans said, reading from the idiot card Sellotaped to the desk in front of him. "At the conclusion of the interview, I will give you a written notice explaining what will happen to the tapes should you subsequently be charged." He looked up, smiled first at Stella, then at her solicitor, a mild mannered podgy man in his mid-thirties, with a neatly trimmed beard and a scruffy suit. Neither smiled back. "Long story short, you or your solicitor will be given copies."

"Am I going to be charged, then?" Stella asked, leaning forward in alarm.

Evans smiled reassuringly. "No decisions have been made yet," he informed her. "We're still in the process of gathering all the facts."

"But I *didn't* kill her," Stella blurted out. Tears were beginning to well in her eyes, and her bottom lip was trembling.

Evans and the solicitor simultaneously held up a hand to discourage her from speaking further.

"Stella," Evans said, kindly. "I very much want to hear what you have to say, but we need to go through the formalities first."

When she nodded her understanding, Evans resumed reading from the prompt card. He stated the day, date, time and location of the interview, formally introduced himself for the purpose of the tape, and then asked everyone present to do likewise.

"My name's David Owens," the solicitor said primly. He spoke in a deep baritone, and his Welsh accent was much stronger than Evans'. "I'm here in my capacity as Ms Carter's legal representative. My role is to protect and advance her rights and entitlements, and to ensure that this interview is conducted in accordance with the Police and Criminal Evidence Act 1984. In this role, I will be forced to intervene if I feel any line of questioning is inappropriate or unfair."

When he had finished his little speech, Evans thanked him, then cleared his throat and cautioned Carter. "Stella, you do not have to say anything, but it may harm your defence if you fail to mention when questioned something that you later rely on in court. Anything you do say may be given in evidence. Do you understand what that means, or would you like me to break it down into layman's terms for you?"

Stella responded with a jaded shake of her head. "I've been interviewed before. I know exactly what it means."

Evans studied her for a moment. There was a massive hand shaped bruise on one side of her slender face. The ugly graze on her chin was starting to scab over, but it still looked very sore. He knew from reading the FME's report that her body was covered in bruises from where she had been given a shoeing by the gangsters while being held captive. He was also aware that she had received a couple of head injuries and had been treated for mild concussion, although she had been deemed fit for detention and interview.

"How are you feeling?" he asked.

"Like shit," she told him, truthfully.

He nodded, sympathetically. "I'm sorry we have to conduct this interview now, while you're not at your best, but we just don't have the luxury of being able to put it off. That said, if you feel unwell or need to take a breather at any stage of the process, just say so and we will immediately take a break."

She nodded, gratefully. "Thank you, but I've got nothing to hide, and I really want to get this over with."

"Okay. Let's start with you telling me about your relationship with Carrie McCullen. Take your time, don't leave anything out."

Stella blinked, and a tear ran down the side of her face.

Evans reached into his jacket pocket, withdrew a packet of paper tissues. "Here," he said, handing them over.

She took one and went to hand them back, but he told her to keep them.

"Thank you," she said, dabbing her eyes.

Her hands were shaking badly, Evans noticed.

When Stella had composed herself, she told Evans how she had met Carrie, how their romance had blossomed, and how their time together had been the happiest of her life. She described her heartbreak when Carrie had ended the relationship, and her ongoing efforts to win the woman of her dreams back.

Her take on what she described as a 'perfect and harmonious relationship' was very different to the train crash that Carrie's family and friends had all described. Stella was going to great pains to portray herself as a loving and considerate partner, and didn't once mention her bad behaviour or unreasonable conduct towards Carrie. Maybe, she was deliberately withholding that side of their relationship from him, afraid that it might incriminate her further? Maybe, her subconscious mind had simply buried all the painful memories because, deep down, Stella couldn't bear to face the truth about herself?

"Carrie's family and friends tell us you took to stalking her after the relationship ended," Evans said. "Is that true?"

Stella shook her head, and her mouth became a thin, angry line. "No. That's absolute rubbish," she insisted. "I mean, I contacted her a few times, in the hope that we might be able to reconcile our differences and give it another go, but I *never* made a nuisance of myself." She tried to sit still, but her agitation made her fidget. "And for anyone to suggest that I was stalking her is absurd."

Evans said nothing to challenge this. That would come later.

"When was the last time you saw Carrie?" he asked.

Stella glanced sideways at her solicitor, who gave an almost imperceptible nod for her to continue. "I, er, I bumped into her in Pitfield Street on the Friday night," she said, breaking eye contact for the first time since the interview had begun.

Evans made a mental note of the non-verbal tell that had just signalled she was lying.

"She was coming home from a night out with some mates," Stella continued. "We had a brief chat, then went our separate ways."

"I see. And you say this was an accidental meeting?"

Carter nodded again, vigorously this time. "Absolutely."

"Did you argue or fight during this meeting?"

Carter was still avoiding eye contact and, every now and then, the side of her mouth twitched nervously.

It was another tell, Evans noted, thinking that Stella Carter would be a rubbish poker player.

"We had a brief chat. I asked her how she was getting on. We spoke for a few minutes, then went our separate ways. It was all very amicable."

Evans nodded, said nothing. She was telling him so many porkies that he was surprised her nose hadn't grown a foot longer. "Stella, I'm going to play you a short CCTV compilation. I want you to watch it carefully."

"I object," Owens said, looking flustered. "No mention was made of this in the advanced disclosure I was served. Before you show her any footage, I need to know what's in the film and what questions you intend to ask my client."

No," Evans responded, calmly but firmly. "You don't. There is no obligation to provide you with a list of questions, or tell you the content of every clip of CCTV in advance. Under advanced disclosure rules, I'm required to provide you with sufficient information for you to consult with and advise your client. I'm satisfied that I have complied with that obligation. If you want to know what happened that night, may I suggest you ask your client, not me. After all, she *was* there."

Owens' face was becoming flushed, and he squirmed uncomfortably in his seat, starting to feel the pressure. "I really must insist that—"

"Your objections have been noted on tape," Evans cut him off. "Should this case go to court, your client's barristers can make representations to the trial judge for this interview to be excluded if they feel so inclined. I very much doubt they will get anywhere with that, but they are very welcome to try. Now, I'm going to play the compilation." He turned to Stella, gave her a brief, business-like smile. "I want you to watch it carefully. I'll be giving a commentary as it plays, to help you understand the significance of what you're being shown. Afterwards, I'll invite you to pass comment and answer any questions I may have."

Evans removed a VHS tape from his briefcase, inserted it into the portable TV-video combo he had arranged to be placed in the interview room in advance. It had a fourteen-inch screen. Not the biggest, but good enough for their needs.

Evans arranged the TV so that Carter and her legal representative could see it clearly, then pressed play. "This is exhibit CF/10," he explained. "It's a compilation of video clips from the evening of Friday 5th October, 2001. The first clip is from inside *The Merry Fiddler* public house near Broadway Market, and is timed at 19:00 hours. The woman who has just entered, wearing black trousers and a red blouse, and carrying a bag, is Carrie."

Stella's hand flew to her mouth to stifle a gasp. Her solicitor placed a warning hand on her arm and shook his head to stop her from saying anything.

The screen flickered and cut to a street scene.

"This is the view from outside the pub in Westgate Street, timed at 19:28 hours. You can see the pub entrance on the left of the screen, about halfway up. To the right of the screen, you can see London Fields." He leaned between them and tapped the screen with his biro. "See the person sitting on the moped at the entrance to London Fields? Well, that's you."

"That could be anyone," Owens objected. "The rider's wearing a crash helmet. How can you possibly–"

As he spoke, the rider removed her helmet and ran a hand through her short dark hair. It was undeniably Stella.

Evans looked at him, smiled sweetly. "You were saying?"

Owens' face was glowing red. "I really should have been told about this footage before you showed it to my client," he said, folding his arms huffily.

"For the purpose of the tape," Evans continued, "Stella Carter has removed her crash helmet and looked straight at the camera. Now, she's placed her helmet on the seat of the moped, crossed to the pub, and gone inside."

They watched in silence for the next two minutes, staring at the pub entrance, until Carter reappeared.

"Stella has now emerged from the pub and has returned to her moped." Evans said.

The screen flickered again, switching views to the same camera inside the pub that they had seen Carrie enter via earlier.

"Stella entered the pub at 19:30 hours," Evans continued with his commentary. "I would suggest that she looks very angry. She stands there, clenching and unclenching her fists for several seconds. She appears to be staring straight at Carrie during this time, then she about turns and storms out of the pub."

"I'd hardly say she stormed anywhere," Owens said, quickly.

"Well, I guess, we'll have to let the jury decide that, if the case goes to trial," Evans retorted tartly. "We have footage of Stella sitting outside the pub on her moped until closing time. I'm not going to play that now, because there would be no point, but copies will be provided if charges are brought."

The screen flickered again, returning to the street view outside the pub. It was timed at 23:00 hours.

Evans cleared his throat, continued his narration. "At eleven o'clock, which is closing time, we can see a group of women leaving the pub. Carrie's amongst them. They all say goodnight to each other and go their separate ways. You'll notice that Stella's still sitting on her moped, watching them."

Stella groaned, buried her head in her hands. She knew where this was going.

"Most of Carrie's friends head off towards Well Street," Evans explained. "But Carrie and a woman called Trish walked off together to get a taxi from the cab office in the market. Note that Carrie has just slipped an arm around Trish's waist, and they appear to be laughing and smiling, really enjoying each other's company. As you can see, a few moments after they disappear from sight, Stella starts her moped and follows them."

Evans leaned forward and switched the TV off.

"I object," Owens bristled, wagging a forefinger in the air. "That's pure conjecture on your part." He spoke as if they were in court, and he was appealing to the trial judge for an adversary's comment to be struck from the record.

Evans smiled, knowingly. "Actually, it's not," he said, smugly. "I have another compilation, which I'll play for you after we take a quick break. It shows Stella's moped following the cab that Carrie and her friend took from Broadway Market all the way to Pitfield Street." He looked Stella straight in the eye. "Having viewed the compilation, is there anything you want to say about it before we take a quick break?"

Stella swallowed hard, shook her head. Her face had drained of colour and she had gone a little green around the edges.

"Okay, in that case, we'll stop the interview so that you can consult with your solicitor. For your own sake, I want you to think very carefully about what you say when the interview resumes. The footage we've just watched shows, beyond a shadow of a doubt, that you knew where Carrie was going to be that night, and that you stalked her from the pub to her home. It shows that your meeting was anything but accidental. It shows that you lied to us, Stella. And, if you've lied about this, what else have you lied about?"

Evans turned the tape recorder off and stood up.

As she left the room, ushered away by her solicitor, Stella Carter was looking totally shell-shocked.

Armed with a search warrant, the detectives forced entry to Darren McCullen's flat in Oberon House, Ivy Street. Sam Calvin and Kevin Murray went in first, both clad from head to toe in full barrier clothing. Bear, also wearing white coveralls, and complaining to anyone who would listen that the crotch was far too tight, had been given permission to accompany them, so that he could film the initial flash search as it happened. He had a point, to be fair; the paper overalls he'd been given by Calvin were creaking at the seams, fighting a losing battle to contain his substantial bulk.

"Just for your information," he whispered as they crossed the threshold, "the camera is now running."

Leading the way, Calvin responded with a thumbs up.

They checked the ground floor out first, passing through the hall and into the kitchen. They opened all the cupboards in the kitchen, looked inside, then on top. Then they flicked through the bills and letters on the windowsill.

"What exactly are we looking for?" Bear asked. The question would be dubbed over by the show's presenter, Terri Miller, in due course, so that viewers would hear her voice, not his.

"We're looking for evidence relating to the murder of Frank Kyle, and the robbery at his house, along with anything that might have been used in, or stolen during, the ram raids we now know he was involved in," Murray explained, looking over his shoulder to speak into the camera lens. Imogen had asked him if he would mind doing this, and he had jumped at the chance, eager to have his fifteen minutes of fame when the show aired.

They wandered along the hall into the lounge. Bear stood in the doorway, filming while Calvin and Murray lifted cushions, pulled chairs away from the wall to look behind, then tilted them up to look beneath. They checked through the magazines on the coffee table, and then looked behind the TV and inside the video cabinet.

Back in the hall, there was a storage cupboard. This contained a Hoover, a mop in a red plastic bucket, an assortment of coats and shoes, but nothing of interest to the detectives.

After a cursory glance in the downstairs loo, they trekked up the stairs to check out the top floor. "This is only a preliminary search for anything obvious," Murray told the camera when they were all standing on the landing. "The place will be checked properly after we've conducted a forensic sweep and taken any samples we need to get."

Calvin stepped into the bathroom. Stopped dead. Sniffed. He looked at the others, his brow furrowed in thought. "Someone's recently done a heck of a deep clean in here," he announced.

Murray peeked in, sniffed, shuddered. "Bloody hell," he said. The smell of bleach was overpowering. He looked around the room. The tiles, lino, bath and sink surfaces were gleaming; it was a stark contrast to the levels of cleanliness they had found elsewhere in the flat.

Calvin returned to the hall. "We'll check out the rest of the floor first, then we can explore what's gone on in the bathroom a bit more thoroughly."

There were two bedrooms; a double and a single.

The double was very cluttered; it contained an unmade queen-sized bed, a large wardrobe, a chest of drawers, and there was a large Samsung TV on a stand at the bottom of the bed.

Clothing was strewn across the floor, like someone had left in too much of a hurry to clear up after themselves.

They had a quick rummage through the wardrobe and chest of drawers, which were jammed full of clothes, looked under the mattress, then moved into the spare room.

This appeared to have been transformed into a dressing room for the lady of the house. There was another large wardrobe, two chests of drawers, one stacked on top of the other, a full-length vanity mirror and, located at the far end of the room beneath the window, a white dressing table with a rectangular mirror that was surrounded by Hollywood LED lights.

Murray entered the room first, and his eyes were immediately drawn to a velvet trouser suit with bell bottom flares that dangled from a hanger on the wardrobe door. The garment looked like a throwback to the seventies, and he wondered who in their right mind would choose to go out in public dressed in that?

A wig of long brown hair was draped over one of the wardrobe's handles. Murray unhooked it and placed it on the dressing table. The velvet number followed. When he opened the wardrobe's double doors, the smell from inside hit him at once, and he automatically recoiled.

"Fuck me, that's rank," he said, almost choking on the pungent odour of decomposing flesh.

Calvin stepped into the room behind him, peered into the wardrobe, pointed to a hat box sitting on the bottom shelf. "That awful pong appears to be coming from whatever's in there," he said, stating the obvious.

"You think?" Murray replied, fanning his nose.

The hat box had been placed inside a clear LBH recycling bag, but the top of the bag had unwound, allowing the rancid odour to filter out.

Holding his breath, Murray knelt down and studied the hat box for a moment. There had been some leakage at the bottom, and a horrible red gloop had congealed between the box and the plastic bag. He stood up, turned to Calvin. "Sam, I attended the scene when Carrie McCullen's torso was pulled out of the canal," he said, "and it was wrapped in a clear London Borough of Hackney recycling bag, just like that one."

Calvin raised an eyebrow. "Is that so?"

Murray nodded, grimly. "The only part of her that's still outstanding is her head."

Both men stared down at the hat box again.

"A head would fit nicely inside that box," Calvin observed.

"I suppose we'd better take a look inside, then," Murray said.

The sound of dry heaving came from the doorway.

"Sorry," Bear said as they both turned to stare at him. "But that smell is–" The sentence was left unfinished as he retched again, then swallowed down bile.

Calvin pointed a warning finger at him. "Do NOT throw up inside my crime scene," he warned.

Bear turned on his heels ran towards the bathroom.

"No!" Calvin yelled. "Go outside if you need to puke. If you spew your guts up in this house, I will personally cut your nuts off."

Hand tightly clasped across his mouth, Bear ran down the stairs, along the hallway, and out of the street door.

Behind his mask, Murray grinned. He had never seen the Crime Scene Manager so animated; truth be told, he hadn't thought he had it in him. "You're going to cut his nuts off, are you? That'll make a good soundbite on the telly," he said, amused.

38

Everyone loves a trier

"Okay, so I haven't been completely truthful with you," Stella said when the interview recommenced. Head bowed shamefully, she was worrying at the patches of dry skin on her palms, peeling sections off like little strips of wallpaper. "On the Friday morning, I bumped into a mutual acquaintance of ours at the Tesco store in Morning Lane. Her name's Sharon, and she's a bit of a Nosey Parker." A humourless laugh. "Anyway, she told me that Carrie had met another woman, and that they were going out together that night. It really shocked me. Deep down, I'd always believed we'd find a way to get back together, and the thought of Carrie starting a new romance hit me hard, like a kick to the stomach." A pathetic shrug. "It made our split seem so… so final."

Evans nodded, said nothing. It was important not to interrupt her while she was speaking freely.

Sitting to Stella's right, Owens was looking pretty miffed with her, and Evans suspected that this was because she was ignoring his advice to go 'no comment.'

Stella dabbed at her eyes with a tissue. "I know it was wrong of me, but I was desperate to speak to her, so I waited for her outside her work, hoping to have a word with her when she came out."

"And did you?" Evans asked. He already knew the answer to that one, and in due course he would play the CCTV footage of Stella speaking to Joan Spinney. First though, he wanted to see how economical she was going to be with the truth.

Stella's shoulders slumped in defeat. "No. I bumped into a woman she worked with, and she told me that Carrie had left early that day, so I went home."

"What did you do after that?" Evans asked.

Owens slouched down in his seat, folded his arms and gave her a hostile sideways glance, then pursed his lips in disapproval.

Evans smothered a smile, resisted the urge to gloat.

"Later that evening, I went round to her house, hoping to speak to her before she went out," Stella said, quietly. "I knew I was taking a big risk. That albino bastard had warned me what he would do to me if I ever bothered her again, but I—"

Evans reluctantly raised a hand. "Sorry to interrupt," he said, "but can you expand on that for me? Are you saying that someone warned you off from having any further contact with Carrie?"

Stella was still staring down at her lap, still actively plucking dead cells from her flesh, but she managed a slow, ponderous nod.

"After we first split up, I got a bit..." She swallowed hard, choked down a sob. "...Needy, I suppose you'd call it."

She supposed wrong. Stalker was the word that Evans would have used, but he refrained from correcting her.

"Carrie kept telling me I was making a nuisance of myself, but everyone loves a trier, so I kept chipping away at her, hoping to wear down her resolve. You know how it is."

Evans didn't, but he doubted she would appreciate him saying so.

"In the end, she got so fed up with me that she had a word with a bloke called Fred Wiggins. He's the head of security at Willard Betting, and he's a right nasty bastard. He had this giant albino called Casper pay me a visit to scare me off, and let me tell you, it bloody well worked." Stella shuddered, as she did every time that she recalled the incident.

Owens was obviously feeling pretty redundant, because he was sitting there with a bored expression on his chubby face, and he had taken to doodling on his legal pad. There was an umbrella, a smiley face, a little dog, and… Was that an ejaculating penis? A self-portrait, no doubt, Evans thought, smiling inwardly.

"So, what happened when you went to Carrie's house?" Evans asked.

Stella shook her head, dejectedly. "Nothing. Both her and Aidan were out." She looked up at him, bit her lip. "I didn't know what to do," she said. "I couldn't stand the thought of Carrie being with another woman, so I went looking for her. I figured that *The Merry Fiddler* was as good a place to start as any; after all, it was one of her favourite pubs, so I rode over there on my moped and waited to see if she showed up. I got lucky, I guess." She paused long enough to give him a bittersweet smile. "Or at least I thought I had. Knowing what I do now, I wish I'd never found her."

'So, you saw her arrive at the pub, then followed her in?"

Stella nodded.

"This is an audio interview, not video, so I really need you to answer," Evans said, apologetically.

"Yes, that's right," Stella said, meekly.

"Were you angry when you saw Carrie with her friends?"

Stella nodded again, then remembered that she was supposed to be giving verbal responses. "Yes," she said quickly. "Yes, I was. I felt betrayed, and I was furious."

Beside her, Owens groaned, shook his head in despair.

"So, you went back outside and waited for her to leave?"

"Yes," Stella said, sounding thoroughly miserable. Her face screwed itself into a bitter smile. "I sat on that fucking moped and tortured myself by thinking about Carrie having fun with another woman. When they left, I followed them."

"Why?" Evans asked, amiably. "You must have known that no good could possibly come from doing that?"

Stella shrugged. "When you love someone as much as I loved Carrie, you lose the ability to think straight," she said, trying to justify her actions. "There was a horrible void in my life after she left me. The pain was indescribable, like nothing I had ever known before. It was so bad that I would have traded my very soul to get her back."

Evans believed her. The tortured look on her face, the agony in each word she uttered, left him in no doubt that she was telling him the truth.

"I swear I didn't intend her any harm," Stella was saying. "All I wanted to do was talk, make her see sense before it was too late."

"So, what went wrong?" Evans enquired, keeping his face impassive, his voice neutral.

Stella dry washed her face, then ran her hands through her short hair. She rolled her neck muscles and let out a long sigh, seeming to shrink in size as she did. "The cab dropped them off outside Clinger Court," she began. "I'd been terrified that Carrie was going to take her back to her house and, you know, spend the night with her, but they just had a kiss and a cuddle, and then Carrie set off towards her place."

Evans paused a beat, then said, "How did that make you feel, seeing the woman you loved kissing another woman?"

Stella's face darkened, her breathing quickened, and her eyes burned with anger. She gripped the top of the table so tightly that the whites of her knuckles showed through.

"Stella, can you answer the question, please?"

For a moment longer, she sat there, staring daggers at him but saying nothing.

"Stella…?"

"How do you think it made me feel?" She shouted, hammering her fist against the top of the table so hard that Owens jumped. "It made me feel sick to my stomach." Her fist came thundering down again. "It was like having a knife stuck in my heart. I wanted to cry. I wanted to scream. I wanted to kill them. I …" She stopped speaking as it dawned on her what she had just said. "Not literally, of course," she added quickly, staring at Evans in alarm.

Owens palmed his forehead, gave a little sigh of exasperation.

"What happened next?" Evans asked.

"I followed her, pulled up next to her as she reached the top of her road. We talked, we argued. She called me names, said such hurtful things."

"Did you hit her?"

"It got a little out of hand. I–"

"Did you hit her, Stella?"

Her face sagged, then crumpled completely. She stared at Evans through eyes that were welling with tears. The first one escaped as soon as she blinked, opening up a deluge.

She was on the verge of confessing. He could feel it.

Stella nodded once, a shallow dip of her head.

Evans held his breath.

Come on, admit it…

"Y–yes," she said a moment later, almost choking on the word. She opened her mouth, and what started off as a low moan quickly intensified into an anguished howl of pain.

Evans sat still, letting her vent her emotions, knowing it would be cathartic for her.

When she had cried herself dry of tears, Stella dragged an arm across her face, leaving behind a long snail-trail of snot.

Evans tried not to stare at it. "When you're ready, tell me what happened," he said, softly.

Stella nodded, wiped her face again, getting rid of the snotty eyesore in the process.

"She was calling me a nutjob, a stalker, saying that I wasn't right in the head, and that I should be locked up," she sobbed, hiccupping the words out. "She–she said she would rather die a lonely old spinster than get back with me. I–I don't even know how it happened. One moment she was right in my face, shouting at me and poking me in the chest; the next, she was lying on the floor, clutching her face from where I had punched her." She closed her eyes, shook her head as the memories came flooding back. "I swear, I didn't set out to hurt her."

"Go on," Evans encouraged. "What happened next?"

"Nothing happened," Stella told him indignantly. "I helped her to stand up. She was a little unsteady on her feet, but I assumed that was because she was a bit pissed."

"Did you hit her again?"

"No, of course not," Stella said, shaking her head to emphasise the denial. "She had bitten her lip, and it was bleeding. I tried to apologise, but she pushed me away. I begged her to forgive me, but she told me to fuck off before she called the police."

"Did you?"

Stella shook her head, guiltily. "No. I was worried about her. I put my arm around her and offered to walk her home. The back of her head was bleeding, where she had banged it when she fell."

"She didn't fall; you punched her to the floor."

Stella buried her head in her hands. "I know. I'm so sorry." She lowered her hands, stared at him imploringly. "You have to believe me when I say it was out of character for me."

Evans didn't believe her, not for one second. "Had you ever been violent towards Carrie before?" he asked, casually.

Stella opened her mouth, closed it again, then fired a nervous look towards Owens, who responded with a disinterested shrug. The look on his face said, 'It's a bit late to be looking to me for advice'.

Stella licked her lips, swallowed. "N–no," she said, timidly. Then, with more assertiveness, "No, never." The look of guilt that flashed across her face told a very different story.

"That's interesting," Evans said, reaching into his briefcase and withdrawing a statement. "I took a statement from Carrie's best friend, Abigale Stanwick. She says that she found you controlling and manipulative, and that you were insanely jealous, accusing Carrie of having affairs with all and sundry, even with her at one point."

Stella's eyes widened, and what little colour was left drained from her face.

Evans ran his eyes over Stanwick's statement, until they came to rest on the section he wanted to quote from. "She states that Carrie would often go round to her place after you two had fought, and that she would be in tears."

"She's lying," Stella said, her voice trembling.

Evans raised an impartial eyebrow. "She also says that Carrie often had black eyes, bruised ribs and the like, from where you had punched and kicked her."

Stella screwed her eyes shut, let out a little cry of anguish. "No," she said, shaking her head. Tears began to roll down her cheeks.

Were they tears of guilt, Evans wondered?

"Did you murder Carrie?"

Stella gasped as if she had been shot, and a hand flew to her chest. "No! I swear I didn't. I started to take her home, but she saw the lights were on, so she asked me to walk her over to her brother's flat in the block opposite."

Evans' eyes narrowed suspiciously. "Why would she do that?"

"Because she hates Aidan, and she didn't want him to see her like that. That's bloody well why."

Evans considered this. Everyone he had spoken to during the enquiry said that the twins detested each other, so it kind of made sense that Carrie wouldn't want her brother to see her in a state of distress. "How did she get in?' he asked.

"Carrie had a spare key for the flat," Stella told him. "So that she could keep an eye on it if Darren was ever away."

That made sense too, Evans allowed grudgingly. "What happened when you reached the flat?"

Stella shrugged. "We went inside. I washed the cut at the back of her head for her, then we talked." A mirthless smile. "Well, we argued more than talked to be honest."

"Did you hit her again?"

Stella's cheeks flushed with righteous anger. "No," she said, frostily. "I told you, that was out of character, and I only did it because she provoked me."

"How long did you remain there with her?" Evans asked.

A despondent sigh. "Not long. It quickly became clear that my stupid temper had ruined any chance we might have had of getting back together. She stared at me with such hatred that I knew it was finally over, and I was beside myself. I wanted to jump under a bus."

"And yet you didn't," Evans said, drily.

Stella flinched as though she had just been slapped. "No," she said quietly, "I didn't."

"So, you're telling me that you left Carrie alive and well?"

Stella nodded. "Yes. She had a cut lip and a bump on the back of her head, but nothing serious."

"And you were happy to leave her alone after a bang to the back of the head, were you?"

"I never said I left her alone," Stella said.

Dillon stared at the decapitated head that was looking up at him from inside the hat box, grimaced at the gruesome sight. He had been called down as soon as it had been discovered, and he was most definitely not enjoying the experience. Even with a liberal amount of Vick's nasal gel rammed up each nostril, he was still getting occasional whiffs of decaying flesh.

"Can't we open a sodding window?" he asked Sam Calvin, irritably.

Between all the dismembered body parts he'd been forced to watch being sliced and diced during the seemingly never-ending series of Special Post Mortems he'd attended over the past week or so, and now this, he would be spoilt for choice when it came to having nightmares.

The CSM shrugged, grumpily. "I suppose so," he said, crossing the room to let some air in.

Dillon was feeling exceedingly tired and crabby, and he was having trouble getting his head around what Carrie's decapitated head was doing inside a wardrobe in her elder brother's flat. There was no doubt in his mind that Darren McCullen genuinely believed Fred Wiggins and Casper Wright had murdered his little sister, and that they had probably been acting on the orders of Jonas Willard, so why was her head in his wardrobe?

"I just don't get it," he finally said, looking around the room as if he might find the answer written on one of the walls.

"Don't get what?" Calvin asked.

"The head being here," Dillon said, pointing at the hat box. "We know a woman disposed of the body. We've got CCTV and witness evidence to that effect, not to mention the blood we found in the boot of the cab that took Lucinda to the canal."

"We know a woman disposed of the body parts," Calvin corrected him. "That doesn't necessarily mean that a woman *killed* her. McCullen's got a partner, hasn't he? Perhaps, after he topped his sister and chopped her up into little pieces, he persuaded his other half to get rid of the various body parts for him."

Dillon snorted. The idea was preposterous. "And why would she do that?"

Calvin gave the matter some thought, shrugged when he couldn't come up with a valid reason. "I don't know. Why does anyone do anything? Maybe, she did it to give him an alibi or something."

Dillon considered this for a moment. "Yes, I see where you're going with that," he allowed, sounding impressed. "It's a very good hypothesis."

"See, I've solved the case for you," Calvin said, treating him to a rare smile.

Behind his Victoria mask, Dillon pulled a 'not so fast' face. "Only one slight snag with your brilliant theory, Sherlock," he said, folding his arms across his chest.

Calvin raised an eyebrow in challenge. "Oh? What's that then?"

"Darren McCullen and his other half flew to Tenerife on the morning of Friday 5th October, and Carrie was still very much alive when they left the country."

Calvin frowned. "If that's the case, how did her head end up here?"

Dillon performed a theatrical eye roll for the CSM's benefit. "That's what I'm trying to establish," he said, as though addressing a simpleton.

Kevin Murray wandered into the room. "I've just finished

carrying out some presumptive tests for blood traces in the bathroom," he informed them.

Calvin stared at him expectantly. "Annnnnnnd...?" he asked, stretching the word out, turning it into a sentence.

"And every single one of them was positive," Murray said with a triumphant grin. "Looks like we've found our dismemberment site."

"Kevin, are there any signs of a forced entry to the flat?" Dillon asked.

Murray shook his head. "Nope. All the doors and windows are intact, and there's no evidence of anyone tampering with any of the locks."

Dillon grunted his thanks. If this was the dismemberment site, it was almost certainly also the murder scene. He looked at each of the others in turn. "We know that Darren McCullen and his partner didn't kill Carrie, so we need to find out who had access to this place while they were away."

Murray didn't answer straight away. He was staring at the velvet trouser suit and the wig. "Boss, can you remember what that Lucinda woman in the cab office CCTV looked like?" he asked, walking over to them. "Only I read the cab driver's statement the other day, and I'm sure he made a remark about her wearing a velvet trouser suit and looking like a throwback to the seventies."

Dillon reached into his coveralls, withdrew his mobile. "Now that you mention it, that description does sound familiar. I'll give Colin Franklin a bell, get him to take a quick gander at the footage for us."

"So, what happened next?" Tyler asked. He had been going through the latest forensic reports when Paul Evans rung him with an update regarding Stella Carter's interview.

"She claims that there was a knock at the street door, and that Carrie went off to answer it, leaving her alone in the lounge. Stella reckons she could hear raised voices, but they were muffled, so she couldn't tell how many there were or whether they were male or female. She didn't know Darren McCullen and his

missus were out of the country, and her first thought was that it was them, returning from a night out. She assumed the raised voices were a result of them getting angry when they saw the state of Carrie's face. With discretion being the better part of valour, she decided to slip out the back way rather than face them."

"Why would Darren need to knock at the door when he lives there?" Tyler asked, pointing out the obvious flaw in Carter's account.

"I asked her that, and she said she wasn't thinking straight at the time, and just assumed they had forgotten their key."

Tyler ran a hand through his hair, stifled a yawn. "Did you play the footage of her speaking to Joan Spinney?" he asked.

"*Yep, sure did,*" Evans confirmed. "*She readily admitted that it was her in the clip, said she was wearing a wig to disguise herself because she couldn't risk Fred Wiggins or Casper Wright recognising her.*"

Tyler opened his daybook, started making notes. "What about the CCTV of Lucinda from the cab office on the Saturday night? Did you play that as well?"

"*Of course,*" Evans assured him. "*I played the clip, then read out the descriptions of Lucinda that the minicab office staff gave in their statements. Then I played the clip again and pointed out that Lucinda looked very much like Stella had when she met Joan Spinney.*"

"How did she react to that?"

"*Honestly? She didn't seem remotely fazed when I played her the minicab office clip. She just looked at me blankly, as if to say: what's this then? When I asked if she was Lucinda, she seemed genuinely surprised, and laughed at me. She didn't get defensive or anything. In fact, she even agreed that Lucinda's hair was very similar to the wig she wore outside Willard Betting, and that their builds were similar.*"

"Where did she say she went after leaving Stella?"

"*She reckons she rode her moped straight home, parked it outside her flat, and then remained inside for several days, drowning her sorrows in alcohol. She claims that she didn't even find out that Carrie was dead until about a week later.*"

"What, she didn't talk to anyone, she didn't read any newspapers, she didn't watch TV or listen to the radio for a whole sodding week?" Tyler's voice was dripping with scepticism.

"That's what she says."

Tyler could almost hear the shrug in Evans' voice. "Yeah, well, it sounds like a load of old bollocks to me," he said.

Silence.

"I take it that you believe her, then?" Tyler said, irritably.

"I'm not saying that, but she comes across as very credible," Evans said, hedging his bets.

Tyler sighed. He would be glad when this job was over.

39

What happened to your face?

"So, what's the plan, here?" Dillon asked Calvin. Having been on the go now for more than twenty-four hours, sleep deprivation was starting to take its toll on him, making it hard for him to see straight, let alone think clearly.

Calvin looked around the bedroom, where Nerdy Ned, the police photographer was snapping away under the direction of Kevin Murray. "Okay, once the record photography's complete, we'll get the velvet jumpsuit and wig bagged and rushed up to the lab for microfibre and DNA testing. Apart from wearer DNA, there's a good chance we'll pick up some trace evidence from our victim, blood spots and the like, which will irrefutably connect the two of them. Then, we'll start swabbing this room. I'll also get the door handles, mirrors and any other shiny surfaces fingerprinted."

After reviewing the video clip of Lucinda at the cab office on their behalf, Colin Franklin had called Dillon straight back to describe the jumpsuit in great detail. The description matched the item they had found perfectly. Franklin had also described the bomber jacket that Lucinda had been wearing and, to their delight, an identical coat had been found hanging on a hook on the back of the bedroom door.

Surveying the room, Calvin's eyes settled on a large holdall tucked away beneath the dressing table. "I haven't examined that holdall yet, but a pound to a penny says the killer used it to transport Carrie's limbs to the canal, one at a time."

Dillon pulled a sour face. "What a charming thought."

Calvin frowned. "I wonder why she didn't dump the head as well?" he said, his eyes wandering back to the hat box.

"I really wish I knew," Dillon said, but the truth was he was just as perplexed as Calvin.

Was it possible that Carrie's killer had planned to place it in a formaldehyde filled jar and keep it as a ghoulish trophy?

Dillon shuddered at the thought.

The killer hadn't disposed of the clothing or the wig she had worn to the cab office either, which made him think that the most likely – and least sinister – explanation for the head's presence was that Casper had kidnapped Stella before she could finish disposing of the evidence.

But what if Stella Carter wasn't the killer?

As preposterous as it sounded, what if she was actually telling them the truth when she claimed to be innocent?

Excusing himself from the others, he walked out of the flat and dialled Tyler's number.

"On the off chance that Stella Carter's not our killer," he said as soon as Tyler picked up, "is it worth withdrawing from McCullen's flat and putting it under surveillance?"

"Why would we want to do that?" Tyler responded in a tone that screamed, 'Are you stark raving mad?'

"Well, it just occurred to me that, if Carter didn't murder Carrie, the chances are that the real killer's going to come back to finish the clean-up operation before Darren and his missus get back next week."

There was a long silence as Tyler thought this through. *"Dill, that* scene's a gold mine of forensic evidence, so there's no way we can just walk away from it."

"I'm not suggesting that we should," Dillon bristled. "What I'm proposing is that we remove Carrie's head, along with the other evidence we've found, then lock the place down and put it under surveillance for a day or so. With any luck, if Carter's not our girl, then the real killer will come back and we'll catch her red handed."

"*Dill, last night's shootout at the allotments is all over the news this morning. I've just had a right earful from George Holland for letting you go there without armed backup. The media have released McCullen's name, and declared that we're treating his flat as a crime scene. If Carter isn't responsible, the real killer will know by now that the game's up.*"

Dillon's face crumpled. He hadn't considered that the shootout would make the news, and he really should have. Tiredness was obviously taking its toll on his thought processes. "Yeah, fair enough," he conceded, feeling silly. "Let's just hope that Stella Carter really is as guilty as we all think she is."

As he turned to walk back into the flat, a van pulled into Ivy Street. It was a Sky News outside broadcasting unit, and it stopped right outside Oberon House. Dillon told the PC guarding the door to make sure they didn't get anywhere near the flat, then walked inside.

———

Hanging up, Tyler turned to Kelly Flowers and Debbie Brown, who were sitting opposite him. Unlike him and Dillon, they had managed to grab some sleep, and were looking much healthier for it.

Kelly had thoughtfully brought him in some clean clothes, which he still hadn't had a chance to change into yet, and she had been running around him like a mother hen since her arrival. It was really quite touching, the way she pampered him when he was too busy to take proper care of himself. She had kept his coffee cup topped up, and she had even popped down to the canteen earlier, to order him some breakfast, insisting that he would make himself ill if he didn't eat.

Ignoring the worried looks she kept giving him when she thought he wasn't looking, he smiled at each of them in turn. "You've got to visit Aidan and Annie this morning to inform them that we've found Carrie's head, and to update them regarding Darren's condition. While you're there, see if they have any idea who, apart from Carrie, might have had legitimate access to Darren's flat while he's been away."

"How much can we reveal about what Darren's been up to?" Debbie asked. So far, Aidan had been told that his brother had been shot during a gun battle with Fred Wiggins and Casper Wright, and that he was in a critical condition in hospital, but nothing had been said about his suspected involvement in the ram raids, or about his murdering Frank Kyle. "From a FLO perspective, they haven't been an easy family to establish a relationship with, and I don't want to risk alienating them further by withholding information from them."

Tyler grunted. He really didn't give a toss about alienating Aidan. "For the time being, don't say anything."

Debbie nodded obediently, but she didn't seem terribly happy about withholding the information.

"What time are you seeing them?" Tyler asked.

"I've just spoken to Annie," Kelly said. "We're going round to her place as soon as we finish this meeting. Aidan's at work, so he'll be a little delayed, but he's agreed to meet us there as soon as he can get away."

"Remind me where he works," Tyler said.

"He works for a warehouse in the city," Debbie told him.

"I offered to pick him up," Kelly added, "but the miserable git reckons he would rather get a bus than be given a lift by us."

Tyler frowned. "Why's he getting a bus? Hasn't he got a car?"

Debbie shook her head. "I know it's hard to believe in this day and age, but neither Aidan nor Annie possess a driving licence."

"Okay," Tyler said, rapidly losing interest. "Leave him to make his own way home. In the meantime, speak to Annie. From what I can gather, she's the more reasonable of the two anyway. In the meantime, I need to get some fresh air, so I think I'm going to pop down to Darren's flat and see how Dill's getting on."

"Maybe we can meet up for coffee afterwards?" Kelly suggested, hopefully. "There are a couple of really nice cafes in Hoxton Market."

Tyler nodded approvingly. "Sounds like a plan," he said with a weary smile.

Kelly paused in the doorway after Debbie left the room. "One last thing before I go…"

Tyler raised an eyebrow. "And what would that be, my beautiful fiancée?"

Kelly beamed, as she did every time that he reminded her that they were now engaged, and her eyes involuntarily flicked down to the ring on her finger. "Have a shower and change into some fresh clothes before you go out."

Tyler lifted an arm, sniffed at his armpit. "Are you saying I smell?" he asked with a scowl.

Kelly's smile broadened. "You smell lovely," she assured him. "But you look like shit. A shower and a clean shirt will make you look and feel much better."

―――

When Annie opened the door, the detectives were shocked by the state she greeted them in.

Her left eye was all swollen and puffy, and the area around the socket was covered in an ugly mass of black and purple bruising. Her face was pale and drawn, as if she had been having trouble sleeping, and her clothing was dishevelled, like she hadn't changed it in days.

"What happened to your face?" Kelly asked as Annie moved aside to let them in.

"Go on through to the kitchen," Annie responded, avoiding the question. "I put the kettle on when I saw your car pulling up, and it should have boiled by now."

Inside the small kitchen, the detectives slid onto the narrow bench seats on either side of a pine table that had been crammed into the far corner.

Annie prepared the coffee in silence, then joined them. She seemed unable to settle, and couldn't stop fidgeting. As soon as she rested her hands on top of the table, her fingers began drumming a staccato beat. When she caught the detectives staring at her, she rammed her hands under her thighs. Almost immediately, her legs started bobbing up and down, so she crossed them tightly, interlocking her ankles to keep them still.

They had never seen Annie so jittery, and Kelly wondered what had happened to bring on such weird behaviour.

Had she been taking drugs?

Her eyes were red, and the pupils were dilated, so it was possible, but being stressed and overtired could also account for all the traits Annie was currently exhibiting. As could being on the receiving end of a punch in the eye from her boyfriend, Kelly thought, cynically.

Debbie took a sip of her coffee, smiled appreciatively. "That looks painful," she said, nodding at Annie's black eye. "How did it happen?"

Annie self-consciously raised a hand to her face, and a blush started at the base of her neck. It continued upwards until it disappeared into her hairline. "It's nothing," she said, dismissively. "An accident. I'm such a clumsy cow at times."

"How did it happen?" Kelly persisted. It was the third time they had asked her, and they were yet to receive an answer.

Annie took a sip from her cup, let out a strained laugh. "Well, if you must know, I opened a cupboard the other day, banged myself straight in the face with the edge," she said, unconvincingly. Wilting under the intensity of their stare, she lowered her cup and performed a comical mime, hoping the infusion of humour would defuse the situation.

Debbie's eyes narrowed. She wasn't buying that flimsy excuse for one second. "You're seriously telling us it was an accident?"

A lame shrug. "Like I told you, I'm clumsy."

The detectives shared a knowing look. They had both been in The Job long enough to recognise the signs of domestic violence.

On impulse, Debbie reached across the table and grasped Annie's hand supportively. "We're not silly, love," she said, kindly. "Why don't you tell us what *really* happened?"

Annie stiffened, withdrew her hand, folded her arms defensively. When she spoke, her voice was cold, verging on angry. "I told you, it was an accident."

Kelly stared at her for a moment. "Look, we're not here to judge you," she said, trying a different approach, "but we're not stupid either, so don't insult our intelligence by treating us as such."

Annie opened her mouth to protest, but Kelly silenced her with a stern look. "If you want to make an allegation of assault, we will take it very seriously. If you don't, we'll find some other way of supporting you. It's obvious that you're finding things very tough at the moment, which is to be expected after losing a loved one in such terrible circumstances. I suspect Aidan's struggling to cope, too. Am I right?"

Annie hesitated, then nodded slowly.

"How have things been, between the two of you?"

"Things have been... strained," Annie admitted, staring down at her lap.

"Have you been arguing?" Debbie asked.

Another nod, more animated this time. "It's been really hard, having this hanging over our heads, and..." She wrung her hands together. "Well, let's just say that Aidan isn't always the easiest person to speak to. At times, he can be... he can be—"

"A bit of a dick?" Debbie suggested, earning herself a reproachful look from Kelly.

Annie smiled, and the tension between them receded slightly. "Yes, he can be a bit of a dick," she admitted.

"Speaking of dicks," Debbie said, leaning forward conspiratorially. "I've always thought life's a bit like my husband's dick..."

Kelly spluttered, almost choked on her coffee.

Debbie carried on, unperturbed. "...sometimes it's up, sometimes it down, but no matter how hard it gets, it never stays that way for very long."

Annie couldn't help but laugh.

"Seriously though," Debbie said when the moment had passed. "If you need to talk to us about anything, you can. We're very discreet."

Annie nodded, gratefully. "Thank you," she said. "I'll bear that in mind."

They sat there for a few minutes, making pointless small talk while they finished their drinks.

After a while, Kelly checked her watch, wondering how much longer Aidan would be. "There's been a development in the investigation," she said, solemnly. "We've found Carrie's head."

Annie gasped, and her hands flew to her mouth to stifle a sob. Closing her eyes, she swayed in her seat. For a moment, Kelly thought she was going to faint. Then Annie surprised her by taking a deep breath, and sitting up straight. She let her hands drop into her lap with a dull plop. When she looked up at them again, there was a strange air of resignation about her.

"When did you find it?" Annie asked, her voice eerily calm.

It was strange, Kelly thought, that her first question should be when, not where.

Inside Darren McCullen's flat, Murray had just noticed an old rucksack that had been thrown up on top of the wardrobe. Dillon had gone outside to get some air, and Sam Calvin was tucked up on the phone, arranging for the Luminol team to come out and treat the bathroom the following day, so he asked Nerdy Ned to take a shot of it in situ, then pulled it down.

"Wonder what we'll find in there?" Ned said. "Are we still any body parts adrift?"

Murray shook his head. "Nah, we've recovered all the interesting bits now, so this'll probably just be a load of shit."

"Oh, pity," Ned said, sounding genuinely disappointed. Then

his face brightened up. "Maybe it'll contain the murder weapon," he suggested, hopefully. "Or whatever tools the killer used to dismember her body."

"Maybe," Murray allowed, but he didn't think so. The bag was full to bursting. "I definitely wouldn't get too excited," he said, unclipping the top fastener and pulling the flap back.

The bag was crammed full of VHS video cassette cases. Murray held it out for Ned's benefit, turned his nose up. "See, nothing but home movies."

He pulled a few out, opened them up, but there was no labelling on any of the tapes. Then he noticed the brown A4 envelope wedged against the spine of the bag to keep it crease free. He gave it a tug, but it was tightly wedged in, so he emptied the rest of the cassettes out, then removed it.

"What's in there?" Ned asked, peering over his shoulder inquisitively.

Murray frowned. "Looks like colour photos," he said, pouring them onto the floor.

They weren't photos. They were glossy cover inserts for the VHS tapes, and they all featured two women cavorting about on a bed together.

Murray picked one up, grinned like a deviant. "Well, well, well, look what I've found."

"Is it evidence?" Ned asked.

"Oh, it's much better than that," Murray said with a pervy leer. "It's porn."

He scooped up one of the tapes and set off towards the door. "Well, come on then," he said, impatiently.

Ned scratched his head, confused. "Where are we going?"

"Duh! We're going to sneak downstairs to find a video player so we can check this out," Murray explained, wondering if Ned was really that stupid.

Ned took a step in Murray's direction, then hesitated. "Shouldn't we continue processing the scene?" he asked, clearly conflicted.

Murray shook his head in growing exasperation. "It'll only take us five minutes to fast forward through this," he said, then added in a sly voice, "And it would be very remiss of us to ignore it."

Ned frowned. "It would?"

Keen to take a sneak peek at the porn film before Dillon returned and kyboshed the idea, Murray's face took on a calculating expression as he thrust the video cassette towards Ned's face.

"What if this tape doesn't contain a porno?" he asked in his best conspiracy theory voice. "What if those covers are merely a front to deceive people? This tape could be a snuff movie of Carrie's murder, or it could show the killer chopping her body up? There's big money in that kind of thing."

"Oh," Ned said. He hadn't thought of that. "Is that likely?"

"Absolutely," Murray lied.

As Murray walked out of the door, Ned bent down, retrieved the cover that Murray had dropped, examined it dubiously. "Lusty Lucinda," he read aloud.

A moment later, Murray thrust his head back through the door. "What did you say?" he demanded.

Ned held the cover up for him to read. "The porn film, it's called Lusty Lucinda."

Murray snatched the cover from his hand, read the title for himself, studied the picture a little closer. "Oh, shit," he said.

40

What's on your mind?

Tyler pulled up outside Oberon House, slotting into a gap behind a Sky News outside broadcasting unit. He slipped his sunglasses on and ambled over to join Dillon, who was leaning on the railings, watching the world go by. "Are you okay?" he asked, noting the lugubrious expression on his friend's face.

Dillon nodded. "Yeah, just thinking."

"I wondered what that burning smell was," Tyler said with a wry grin.

"Very funny," Dillon said, flatly.

The melancholy response was most unlike Dillon; he would normally have come back with a witty retort, which would have triggered a round of quick-fire banter between them.

"What's on your mind?" Tyler asked, realising that something was bothering his friend.

The big man shrugged. "I think I might be developing feelings for Imogen," he mumbled, as if confessing that he had recently received a terminal diagnosis.

Tyler stared at him, unsure how to respond. Over the years, Dillon had acquired a well-deserved reputation for being a ladies' man. Putting it kindly, Tyler thought that his relationships were probably best described as tidal; as soon as the old one was swept out, the new one rolled in. He had a roving eye and a short attention span or, to put it another way, he wasn't big on long-term commitment.

Now that Tyler thought about it, Dillon hadn't dated anyone, not in the true sense of the word, since splitting up with Emma Drew, a couple of years back. The big man had always tried to gloss over the split, playing it down as no big deal, and saying that there were plenty more fish in the sea but, even though they had never discussed it, Tyler knew just how badly her loss had hurt his friend.

"Okay," he said, cautiously. "No big deal. I mean, falling for someone isn't such a bad thing, is it?"

Dillon turned to look at him, all puppy eyed and doleful. He threw his arms out wide and shrugged. "Honestly, I don't know. I'm pretty sure she feels the same way about me, but I don't know if I'm ready to lock myself into another serious relationship, not after…" he looked away, fidgeted uncomfortably, then took a deep breath. "Not after the way I felt when things didn't work out with Emma."

It suddenly occurred to Tyler that Imogen should have been there, at the scene with them. She and Bear had accompanied the team down to the flat, and he had agreed to let Bear go inside under Calvin's watchful eye, although no such permission had been granted for Imogen Askew. "Speaking of Imogen, where is she?" he asked.

"Oh, she was called back to the office for a sit-down meeting with George Holland and Terri Miller," Dillon said. "She left before I arrived."

Tyler placed a hand on his shoulder, gave it an affectionate squeeze. "Dill, there's lot of truth in that old poem by Tennyson, the one about it being better to have loved and lost than never to have loved at all. Our relationships are part of what defines us. My advice, for what it's worth, is that, if you like her, give it a go. What have you got to lose?"

Dillon shrugged again. "Oh, I don't know, my heart maybe, or my happiness?"

Tyler sighed, resisted the urge to tell him not to be so bloody melodramatic. The German philosopher, Friedrich Nietzsche had once said, 'That which does not kill us makes us stronger.' Tyler wasn't sure if that was true, but it was the advice his father had given him years ago, and he had done okay by following it.

"There's always a risk that a relationship won't work out, that it'll end badly and you'll get hurt but, even if that happens, you'll be a better, stronger person for the experience."

Dillon looked at him, nodded slowly. "Yeah, you're probably right." He let out a jaw splitting yawn. "Anyway, don't pay any attention to my ramblings, I'm just being a bit maudlin because I'm so tired."

Tyler's phone rang.

"I'd better get inside, see how they're getting on," Dillon said, leaving him to answer it.

The caller was Colin Franklin.

Tyler had tasked him to review the Trelawney Estate footage from the camera covering Stella's front door. If she had told Evans the truth during interview, about locking herself away in her flat for the best part of a week, the footage would exonerate her; if she was lying, it would hang her out to dry. Either way, he needed to know as a matter of urgency.

"Blimey, Colin," he said with a wry grin. "Don't tell me you've reviewed all that CCTV already?"

Franklin chuckled. *"I wish! No, I've farmed all that out to some of the people Mr Holland gave us to assist with the viewing. Hopefully, they'll have the answer by early afternoon, but there's an awful lot of footage to look at, so it'll take a fair bit of time, even if they whizz through it on fast forward."*

"Fair enough," Tyler said, feeling marginally disappointed. "But, if you're not calling about that, what *do* you want?"

"I don't know if you remember but, at the start of the enquiry, when we

asked the family for some photos of Carrie, they gave us one of her posing with Aidan and his girlfriend, Annie Jenkins?"

Tyler frowned, shook his head. "Can't say that I do," he admitted. "Why?"

"Well, I've just been reviewing the footage from a camera in Hoxton Market for the evening of Friday 5th October," he explained. "And I'm pretty sure I've just spotted Annie Jenkins walking towards the top end of the market."

"Okay, and why is that relevant?"

"Because, in her statement, Annie reckons that she didn't go out that evening. Clearly, she did, and I've got to say, with her long hair and slender figure, she looks an awful lot like Lucinda."

Tyler felt his heart rate climb.

Could Annie be Lucinda?

Could she be the killer?

Annie would have known that Darren and Janice were away for a couple of weeks, and she might well have had a spare key for their flat. But what would have been her motive for killing Carrie? There was nothing on record to suggest there were any bad feelings between the two of them. He felt excited, energised by the news, but he warned himself not to get too carried away. One thing was for sure, it merited further enquiries.

"Thanks for letting me know, Colin," he said, still trying to process the implications. "I'm only around the corner from Annie's place. I think I'll pop round there now, and have a quiet word with her."

"Do you want me to arrange some backup?" Franklin asked.

"No, it's okay," Tyler said. "It's probably just an oversight on her part, but Kelly and Debbie are already round there, updating the family about our finding Carrie's head."

Shit!

If Annie *was* the murderer, how would she react to that news? Unless she was a complete fool, she would know that they would carry out a detailed forensic sweep of the flat, and that the trace evidence they recovered would link her to the crime.

Would she stick or twist?

Panic and run, or stay put and try to bluff it out?

As he walked back to his car, deep in thought, Dillon came running out of the flat, waving his hand to get Tyler's attention.

"Jack, wait! You need to see this."

Conscious that the film crew were starting to show an interest, Dillon didn't say anything further until he reached Tyler's side. Using his body to shield them from view, he handed Tyler a VHS tape.

"Kevin found a stack of these in a rucksack in the room Carrie's head was in," he said, breathing heavily. "It's basically a low-grade porn film called Lusty Lucinda. He's had a quick peek at it, and it features two women going to town on each other with an assortment of dildos and strap-ons. Either of them could be the woman in the cab office CCTV."

Tyler's eyes widened. "You think Lucinda's a porn star?"

"I think Lucinda's the name that one of the girls in this tape uses as her porn name, and when we find out which one of them it is, I think we'll have found our killer."

Would that be Stella Carter or Annie Jenkins, Tyler wondered?

Surely, it had to be one of them?

He turned the tape over in his hand. There was no label, no information of any kind. "It's a pity we don't know which studio made the film," he said. "If we had that information, we might be able to pressure them into revealing her real name."

"Ah, well, I might be able to help you with that," Dillon said with a grin. "Along with all the tapes, there's a stack of glossy covers waiting to be inserted into the cassette sleeves prior to distribution. The bumf on the back says the film was produced by an outfit called Pete Phallus Productions."

Tyler dug out his phone, rang Dean in the office. "Dean, I need you to drop whatever you're doing and find out everything you can about a porn studio called Pete Phallus Productions. I want to know who runs them, where they're based, and anything else you can rake up."

"That's funny. Kevin Murray called me a few minutes ago and asked me for exactly the same thing."

"Really? What have you found out so far?"

"I couldn't find anything on any of the intelligence databases, so I rang a mate who works on the Obscene Publications Squad, pulled in a favour," Dean said. "He reckons the company's a shyster outfit based above a video rental shop in Dalston. It's run by a small time sleazeball called Pervy Pete Simpkins. I thought the name sounded familiar, so I got Chris Deakin to run it through HOLMES. Turns out he's Annie Jenkins' boss. She works behind the counter for him in the video store."

Tyler's heart missed a beat, and he gripped the phone tighter. "Are you sure?" he asked, trying to remain calm.

"Guv!" Dean said, sounding mildly offended. "When have I ever not been sure?"

Tyler blew out his breath, thanked him, hung up. "Have you seen the two girls in the porn film?" he asked Dillon.

"I had a quick look, not that I could make out either of their faces, what with their hair covering it. Why?"

"Could either of them be Annie Jenkins?"

Dillon frowned, shook his head. "I don't know," he said with a shrug. "I've never seen her in real life."

Tyler recanted the information he had just received from Dean, and then told his friend about the earlier call from Colin Franklin.

Dillon let out a low whistle. "But why would Annie want to kill Carrie?"

"I don't know," Tyler said, "but I'm going straight round there to find out."

It only took Tyler a couple of minutes to drive from the crime scene to Annie's flat, which was located at the other end of the market, in Crondall Street. Annoyingly, there were no parking spaces outside, so he was forced to drive all the way to the other end of the road, until he found one outside St. John's Estate. Fuming at the time he had wasted, he marched back to the market end and began searching for Annie's flat.

For a while, he thought he was going to be thwarted at the first hurdle, because there was a security door with an intercom system controlling entry, and Annie Jenkins wasn't responding when he pressed the buzzer for her flat. Nor were any of her neighbours. He was about to ring Kelly, and ask her to come out and let him in, when it occurred to him to try the tradesman button. To his surprise, with a dull metallic click, the security door popped open.

Tyler knew that Annie's flat was on the ground floor, so he walked along the landing slowly, checking the numbers as he went.

He pressed the bell on the pristine blue door but, like the external buzzer, it wasn't working, so he banged instead. As he was waiting for it to be opened, Aidan McCullen came bowling along the landing, red faced and clearly agitated.

"Who are you?" he demanded, aggressively.

Like I could be anything other than a police officer!

Keeping the thought to himself, Tyler produced his warrant card. "I'm DCI Jack Tyler, the Senior Investigating Officer for Carrie's murder. I'm sorry that I haven't been able to meet up with you before now," he lied, secretly wishing that he could have postponed the meeting for even longer.

Aidan studied the photograph on warrant card far longer than was necessary, made a point of comparing it to Tyler's face several times over, then snorted. Impatiently motioning Tyler aside, he inserted his key into the lock and gave it an angry turn. "Where are you, babes?" he shouted as soon as the door flew open.

"We're in the kitchen," Annie called back.

Tyler followed him through to the cramped kitchen, where he found Kelly and Debbie sitting with Annie. The latter looked as though she had recently been crying.

Were they tears of sadness, he wondered, or tears of fear?

The two FLOs looked up, surprised to see him standing there.

"Annie, this is DCI Tyler, the Senior Investigating Officer," Kelly said, recovering first.

As he offered his hand, Tyler noticed the nasty black eye that Annie was sporting, and wondered how she had come by it. A little gift from Aidan, perhaps? From his limited experience of the man, Tyler had no doubt that Aidan McCullen was the type of man who would be quick to lash out at a defenceless target, but would instantly back down if confronted by someone who could look after themselves.

Aidan leaned against the door frame, crossed his arms truculently. His face was covered with perspiration, and he stared resentfully at the two FLOs, giving Tyler the impression that their presence offended him. "Come on then," he said, aggressively. "What's so urgent that you had to drag me all the way home from work to tell me?"

"T–they've found Carrie's head," Annie said, locking eyes with Aidan. "They... They found it at Darren's flat this morning."

Was it Tyler's imagination, or did a knowing look pass between them?

In an instant, Aidan's cockiness seemed to evaporate. He swallowed hard, and the colour drained from his face.

For a split second, Tyler thought he was about to burst into tears.

Tyler glanced at Kelly, gave her a surreptitious smile. Her eyes widened as they met his, silently communicating that something was amiss.

"Annie, we never mentioned where we had found Carrie's head," Kelly said, staring at her intently.

Annie blanched, looked from Kelly to Debbie, then back again. "What? Y–yes, you did. You must have. How could I have known, otherwise?"

"That's what I'd like to know," Debbie said, softly. "Because we never said we'd found it at Darren's flat."

Her mouth opened and closed several times in rapid succession. "I–"

"You heard it on the news, didn't you?" Aidan cut in quickly.

"Yes," Annie said, grabbing the lifeline he'd thrown her. "That's it, I remember now."

"The fact that we were searching Darren's flat has been on the news," Tyler confirmed. "But that was in relation to other matters, not Carrie's murder. The media don't know that we found Carrie's head."

Annie's trembling hand rose to her mouth, and she bit down on her forefinger. Big fat tears ran down her cheeks.

"Annie Jenkins," Tyler said, taking a proprietary hold of her arm, "I'm arresting you on suspicion of the murder of Carrie McCullen." As he began reciting the caution, she snatched her arm away.

"No," she said, shaking her head vehemently. "I didn't kill Carrie. I swear I didn't." She looked up at Aidan, imploring him to say something, but he just stood there, looking at her with dead eyes. "Aidan, say something," she pleaded, "tell them I didn't do it. Aidan—"

"Just shut the fuck up," he shouted, yelling so loudly that the veins on his neck stood out and his face turned the colour of puce. "Don't say another word until you've spoken to a solicitor."

Pushing her chair back, Annie jumped up, tried to run.

By now, Tyler had regained control of her arm, and he squeezed it tighter this time, preventing her from going anywhere. She was screaming at him hysterically, lashing out with her free hand and attempting to break free.

Kelly and Debbie were on their feet in an instant.

As Kelly pulled her Quick-Cuffs from her bag, Debbie inserted herself between her colleagues and Aidan, who had grabbed hold of Tyler's shoulders and was frantically trying to pull the bigger man away from his girlfriend.

Things were going downhill rapidly.

Still resisting arrest, Annie made a grab for something shiny on the work counter.

It was a carving knife, Tyler saw. Reacting quickly, he twisted her arm behind her back.

Kelly quickly moved the knife out of reach, then passed him her handcuffs.

He applied the first to Annie's right wrist before dragging her left around to join it.

Aidan took a punch at Debbie, but it was clumsy, and she easily evaded it. "Cut it out," she snapped, pointing an angry finger at him, "or you'll be nicked, too."

Kelly appeared by her side and, grabbing one arm each, they manhandled him out of the room. He was still shouting and swearing at them, but the threat of arrest had been enough to deter him from doing anything silly.

Annie's neurotic wailing was hurting Tyler's ears. "Calm down," he told her. "Acting like this won't help your cause. If anything, it'll just make things worse."

Tears streamed down Annie's cheeks; snot gushed from her nostrils. All of a sudden, her knees buckled, and she collapsed onto the bench seat.

Tyler supported her down.

"I didn't do it," she repeated over and over again, until her voice was so hoarse that all she was capable of was a strangled rasp.

Knowing that he needed to get her away from the flat as quickly as possible, before she got her second wind and kicked off again, Tyler pulled out his phone, dialled 999 with his thumb, and requested the attendance of a van on blues and twos.

Tyler could hear Aidan gobbing off in the lounge, but he was full of hot air, and unlikely to cause them any real trouble.

What a day, he thought as the faint sound of an approaching siren reached his ears. It was just what he needed to round off the week from hell.

Tyler watched the station van containing Annie Jenkins drive off. She was being taken to Shoreditch police station, and Debbie had gone along as her escort. Behind him, Kelly was speaking to Aidan, who had now calmed down considerably, explaining what would happen to his girlfriend when she arrived at the station.

A uniformed constable was standing guard outside the flat, with strict instructions to admit no one without Tyler's express permission. It would have to be treated as a crime scene, which meant being forensically examined and properly searched.

Aidan had nearly blown a gasket when he'd been told he wouldn't be allowed back inside until the police were finished.

As the van disappeared from sight, Tyler strolled over to join them.

"Where am I supposed to go in the meantime?" Aidan demanded. "All my things are either inside my house or in there," he said, pointing towards Annie's flat.

"I appreciate that," Tyler said with forced patience. "And I'm sorry for the inconvenience, but it really can't be avoided."

Aidan's shoulders slumped in resignation. "Can you at least let me grab some clothes?"

Tyler shook his head. "I'm sorry but I–"

"This is shit," Aidan snapped, cutting him off mid-sentence. "I'm going to make a complaint about this."

Tyler shrugged. "You must do as you see fit," he said, indifferently. "But you're not going back inside until the flat is released."

Spinning on his heels, Aidan stormed off, swearing repeatedly and energetically under his breath. Tyler watched him go in stern faced silence, then turned to Kelly. "Well, all things considered, I think that went rather well," he said, treating her to an ironic smile.

41

The devil is in the details

"Look, Annie, we've been over this several times now," Debbie Brown said. "Why don't you just be honest with us and tell us why you were walking along Hoxton Market towards Ivy Street on the evening of Friday 5th October?"

They were sitting in a windowless interview room that smelled as though something had recently died in it; the last interviewing officer's will to live, Debbie suspected, if her own experience was anything to go by.

"No comment."

Debbie pinched the bridge of her nose, surreptitiously checked her watch. The digital display told her it was 20:46 hours. "Were you making your way to Carrie's house when you were caught on camera?"

"No comment."

"Did you go into Carrie's house?"

"No comment."

"Did you go to Darren's flat?"

"No comment."

"Did you murder Carrie?"

Annie performed a theatrical eye roll for the benefit of her brief, who was staring at her sympathetically. "No comment."

"Did you then dismember her body?"

An overly dramatic sigh this time. "No comment."

"Did you subsequently dispose of her body in the canal?"

Anne let out an ill-tempered groan. "No-bloody-comment."

Her solicitor tutted, not at her, but at the heartless officer asking such brutal questions of his poor, misunderstood client.

Debbie resisted the urge to flip him the finger.

"Earlier today, we showed you some CCTV footage of a woman wheeling a suitcase into the offices of Easy Cars in Hoxton Market. As I pointed out at the time, the woman bore a striking resemblance to you. She identified herself as Lucinda McLean. Are you the woman who featured in that footage? Are you Lucinda?"

Annie snorted, as if the idea was just too ridiculous for words. "No, of course I'm bloody well not," she said angrily, then remembered her instructions. "I mean, no comment."

"What route did you take back to your flat after you left Darren's place?"

"No comment."

"My client has never admitted going to Darren's flat, or to Carrie's house for that matter," the solicitor interjected, primly.

"She hasn't said that she didn't go there, though, has she?" Debbie pointed out cattily.

The old man stiffened at the rebuke.

Debbie gave Annie a crocodile smile. "If you'd gone home via the market, you would have been captured on camera, but you didn't. Why didn't you?"

Annie cast a sideways glance at her elderly solicitor, who just shook his head.

"No comment," she replied, wearily.

"If it's not too much trouble, I'd like to have a consultation with my client," the solicitor said. His name was Simon Perkins. He had lank white hair, loose jowls, and he sported a pair of cheap, wire framed reading glasses, the sort that could be purchased for a fiver from any local chemist. He also had an irritating habit of tugging at the loose skin beneath his chin, stretching it downwards as far as it would go, as if its fading elasticity was a constant shock to him.

Perkins had spent most of the interview dozing, and Debbie suspected that he was only asking for a consultation because he needed the loo again. The man obviously suffered from a weak bladder, because he had been popping in and out of the restroom like a bloody yo-yo for most of the day.

"Of course," Debbie said, sitting forward in weary resignation. At this rate, they would never be finished. "It's now 20:50 hours, and I'm going to suspend the interview in order for Annie to have a consultation with her legal advisor. I'm sure we could all benefit from a toilet break as well."

Not picking up on the sarcastic innuendo, Perkins smiled, gratefully. "Indeed," he said.

"Would you like a hot or cold drink before we come back?" Debbie asked as they all stood up.

"I don't need a drink," Annie said, snubbing the offer.

Debbie stared daggers at her.

Ungrateful cow.

With Jim Stone bringing up the rear, Debbie led Annie back through to the custody sergeant, informed him what they were doing, and then placed Perkins and his sullen client into one of the vacant consultation rooms.

At that point, Murray wandered into the custody office and began looking around. When he spotted them, he grinned and walked over to join them. "I've just finished documenting what happens in the porn film," he announced, handing over several sheets of A4 paper. "As you can see, I've made a detailed list of every scene."

Debbie read through the notes, blushed.

Murray smiled, wickedly, enjoying her discomfort.

A look of distaste crossed Debbie's face as she passed the notes to Stone for his perusal. "I can't read *that* out," she said.

"Don't, then," Murray responded with a shrug of indifference. "If you don't appreciate all my hard work, you can just play the tape and ask any questions that come to mind as you go along."

Debbie groaned out loud.

"Tell you what," Stone said, taking pity on her. "Why don't me and Kevin handle the next interview while you grab something to eat?"

Murray seemed surprised by this. "I don't usually get to do many interviews," he said.

There was probably a very good reason for that, Debbie thought. The man was about as subtle as a brick through a window. "I'm pretty sure the DCI would want to keep to the same interview team, for continuity reasons," she said, hastily.

"That's okay," Stone said, not picking up on the hidden message. "I'll take the lead, and Kevin can just deal with the questions relating to the porn tape. That okay with you?" he asked Murray.

Murray shrugged. "Fine by me."

The consultation room door opened, and Simon Perkins appeared, followed by Annie.

Murray leaned in to Stone, said none too quietly, "She's definitely one of the women in the porno."

"Why don't you pop along to interview room number one," Stone suggested. "You can be setting the video up while I book her back out for interview."

As Stone turned towards the custody officer, Debbie grabbed his arm. "Are you sure it's a good idea letting Kevin do this?" she asked, worriedly.

Stone smiled at her. "Relax. It'll be fine," he assured her.

"Sure, it will," Debbie said to herself as he walked off. "With Captain Tactful by your side, what could possibly go wrong?"

Having been deprived of sleep for the best part of two days, Tyler was starting to feel as though he were living in an alternative reality.

He was really struggling to concentrate, and he had noticed a decline in his balance and coordination. Reaching for his mug earlier, he had misjudged how far away it was, and sent the scalding liquid sprawling all over a report he had been reading. As he had tried to snatch the papers to safety, he had knocked his in-tray off the desk, scattering the contents all over the floor.

The endless supply of coffee had perked him up for a while but, as the day progressed, the accumulation of caffeine had made him feel hyperactive and jittery without improving his cognitive functions. He had switched to water a couple of hours ago, hoping to flush it from his system. Unfortunately, in his eagerness to do so, he had consumed so much of the stuff that he now found himself having to rush to the toilet every half-hour.

Speaking of which…

With a sigh, he stood up and pushed his chair back. It was time to point Percy at the porcelain again.

Franklin popped his head around the door. "Got a minute?" he asked.

Sitting back down, Tyler beckoned him in. For the sake of his bursting bladder, he hoped that whatever Franklin wanted, it wouldn't take long. "What can I do for you, Colin?" he asked, forcing a welcoming smile onto his face.

Franklin unscrewed a bottle of mineral water, took several large swigs, reinforcing Tyler's need to pee.

"We've finally finished viewing all the footage from Trelawney Estate and the cameras either end of Belsham Street," Franklin told him.

"And…?"

Franklin shook his head, yawned, took another gulp of water.

To Tyler's annoyance, Franklin began swishing the remaining liquid inside the plastic bottle around. Crossing his leg, he tried to blot the sound out.

"Looks like Stella Carter was telling the truth," Franklin said a moment later.

Tyler leaned back in his chair, massaged his neck. "Are you sure?"

Franklin nodded. "Absolutely positive. There's no way that she could have left her gaff without being picked up on camera."

As Franklin left, Dean Fletcher appeared in the doorway. "You look like shit," he informed Tyler.

"I feel like it, too," Tyler admitted. "What can I do for you, or did you just come here to insult me?"

"Nah, that's just an added bonus," Dean said with a chuckle. "I've just spoken to a contact at Social Services, and it turns out that Annie Jenkins is applying to have visitation rights to her kid reinstated. The poor little mite was taken into care a few years ago, when Annie was on the game. Apparently, she was bringing clients home and shagging them while the baby was lying in her cot beside the bed. To feed her drug habit she was also performing in low grade porn films, and would go out and leave the baby unattended for hours at a time."

Tyler sat up straight, his tiredness and the urgent need to urinate temporarily forgotten. "You're joking."

"Au contraire," Fletcher said with a sad smile. "If she's drifted back into the porn industry, as the films we found in Darren's flat would tend to suggest, you can bet your pension that Social Services would take a very dim view of it."

"Most definitely," Tyler agreed, wondering if they had just found their motive for the murder. "If Carrie discovered what she was up to, and then confronted her…" he left the rest unsaid, letting Dean join the dots for himself.

"Yeah, I reckon the thought of Carrie grassing her up to Social Services, and the fear of them turning down her application on the basis that she's still an unfit mother, would be a pretty strong incentive," Dean suggested.

Tyler checked his watch.

21:05 hours.

Wondering whether Debbie and Jim were still tied up in interview, he dialled the number for Shoreditch custody office. They needed to be told about this development because, with the CCTV corroborating Stella Carter's account, Annie Jenkins was now their only viable suspect.

"Okay, so here's the thing. The production company I work for has two rooms reserved at a three-star hotel in Barking," Imogen informed Aidan. "However, we're only using one of them at the moment, so I've spoken to my producers, and they are more than happy for you to use the unoccupied room for a few days, free of charge, until the police release your house or Annie's flat, whichever happens first."

"*That's very kind of you,*" Aidan said with uncharacteristic humility.

Up until this point, Aidan had repeatedly rejected her requests to film an interview, but Imogen was nothing if not persistent, and she had reached out to him after his eviction from Annie's flat earlier in the day, sensing an opportunity.

"Of course," she said cagily, "in exchange for our help, we'd expect you to film that exclusive interview for our programme I've been asking you for."

Aidan's laugh was harsh, cynical. *"Everything in life comes at a price, right?"*

Imogen said nothing, waited for him to make his decision.

"Yeah, okay, why not?" he said, after a moment's reflection. *"But I'm going to need some expenses to pay for my food and stuff."*

"I'm sure that can be arranged," Imogen said. She had been expecting a demand of this nature from him.

"Alright then," he said gruffly. *"In that case, we've got ourselves a deal."*

"Excellent," Imogen replied, trying not to let her delight creep into her voice. She gave him the hotel's address. "Why don't you make your way over there, and I'll meet you in, say, a half hour?"

"Yeah, that sounds good," Aidan said.

Hanging up, she went in search of Tony Dillon.

She found him deep in conversation with Tyler. Their faces were very serious, she noted. "Has something happened?" Imogen asked, pulling up a chair.

Dillon smiled at her. "It looks like Stella Carter was telling the truth about staying in her flat for a few days after Carrie's death"

Imogen's mouth formed a tight moue. "So, I guess that means you're pinning all your hopes on Annie Jenkins now?"

"We are," Dillon confirmed. "And I'm pleased to say that the case against her is slowly coming together. Not only do we have her on CCTV walking towards Carrie's house on the night of her disappearance—"

"Which is particularly relevant because she said in her statement that she stayed in all night," Imogen cut in, just to show that she had a grasp of the investigation.

Dillon responded with an indulgent smile. "Yes, that's right. Today, when the FLOs revealed that Carrie's head had been found, they never mentioned where, yet she already knew." He paused, waiting to see if she wanted to make any observations, but she just stared at him, so he continued. "We've since learned that Annie had an infant taken into care three years ago, because she was a drug addict and a prostitute, and she's currently trying to get visitation rights."

"Why is that relevant?"

"We found copies of a low budget porn film in the same room as Carrie's head," Dillon explained. "They were made by a company called Pete Phallus Productions, which has a studio above a video rental shop in Dalston. It's run by a bloke called Pete Simpkins. Annie works for him."

"So what?" Imogen performed a lackadaisical shrug of her shoulders. "That's hardly a reason for Social Services to reject her application, is it?"

"The film's title is Lusty Lucinda, and Annie's one of the performers in it."

Imogen stiffened. "Lucinda? As in the same Lucinda who killed Carrie?"

Dillon nodded. "We think Carrie found out about this and confronted her, and that's why Annie killed her."

"Does Aidan know about this yet?"

Dillon shrugged. "He knows she's been arrested, obviously, and that she knew where the head was before we told her, but as for the rest?" He threw his arms out expressively.

She checked her watch. "I've got to go," she said, standing up. "Bear and I are meeting Aidan at our hotel shortly. We've offered to let him use my room for a few days, seeing as I won't be needing it. In return, he's agreed to let us interview him."

After going through the introductions and repeating the caution, Jim Stone explained that they were going to show Annie a video film. "We won't play it all," he explained. "There would be no point, seeing as you were involved in the making of it."

That elicited a worried frown from her, and her eyes suddenly became guarded.

Stone smiled inwardly. *That's got you thinking, hasn't it?*

"As we go along, my colleague, who has watched the film in its entirety, has some questions that he would like to put to you about the film, or more specifically about the two people who star in it."

"I object," Perkins said, bristling with anger. "I haven't been given any disclosure in relation to this."

Stone responded with a saccharine smile. "If you'd like to revisit the previous written disclosure you were served, you'll see it specifically states our intention to show your client a number of video tapes, all relating to the woman known as Lucinda."

Perkins opened his mouth, closed it, then bent down to retrieve his briefcase from the floor. Pulling it open, he rummaged around for the document he had been served upon his arrival, many hours earlier.

Murray impatiently drummed his fingers against the table. "Take your time," he said, sarcastically. "We've got all night."

Perkins face reddened. "Give me a moment," he snapped. He finally found the disclosure document, skimmed through it, let out a little grunt of disappointment.

"Satisfied?" Stone asked, keeping his voice neutral.

"I suppose so," Perkins said, still glowering at Murray, who responded by winking at him.

"Let's crack on then, shall we?" Stone said, nudging his colleague's arm.

Leaning forward, Murray pressed the play button. "For the benefit of the tape, I am now playing a low budget, poor quality porn film featuring two women having sex with each other in a variety of positions with the aid of sex toys. I've turned the volume down so that our voices can be heard clearly above all the fake moaning. The film's title, which is Lusty Lucinda, has just popped up in big red letters, filling the entire screen. Interestingly, the I in Lucinda has been replaced by a penis." He glanced at Annie, whose face had completely drained of colour. Staring at the TV monitor in horror, she looked like she was going to throw up.

"Again, for the benefit of the tape," Murray continued, jauntily, "the title has now been replaced by the performer's names, which are Lucinda and Sin. As was the case with the title, the I in both names has been substituted by a penis." He pressed the pause button, and the blurred image on screen began flickering. "Which one are you, by the way?" he enquired of Annie. "Lucinda or Sin?"

She said nothing, but her bottom lip was trembling, and a solitary tear ran down one cheek. She wiped it away, angrily.

"Why would you assume that my client is either of these women?" Perkins asked, handing her a tissue.

Murray pressed the play button. The contemptuous look he fired in Perkins' direction implied it had been an incredibly stupid question. "In a minute or two," he said, staring pointedly at Annie, "we'll get to see some close ups of your client's face. In fact," he added with a nasty sneer, "we'll get to see close ups of a few other places as well, won't we, Annie?"

Annie cringed, let out a low moan of embarrassment, and began squirming uncomfortably in her seat.

Murray raised an enquiring eyebrow. "Do you need the loo, or are you just adding your own sound effects to the movie because I turned the volume down?"

Annie stiffened at the jibe, then stared at him hatefully.

"The credits have now finished," Murray continued. "The opening scene features a woman with long brown hair hanging down over her face, who's kneeling on a four-poster bed. She's wearing a PVC suit with the arse cut out of it. A second woman, who we can clearly see is Annie Jenkins, then comes into view from behind. Annie's dressed in lacy underwear, stockings, suspenders and high heels. The strap on dildo she's wearing is bigger than my forearm. For the tape, can you confirm that you're the woman wearing the strap on?" he asked her.

"No comment," Annie mumbled without even looking at the TV.

"Annie, I know this is uncomfortable for you," Stone interjected, "but I need you to at least look at the person on screen before answering the question."

She glanced up, shuddered at the sight that met her eyes, looked away quickly. Her shame was palpable. "No comment," she said in a strangled voice.

"Oh, come on," Murray said, his tone scornful. "Take a proper look. You're wearing a dildo the size of a pneumatic drill. Surely you remember doing that? I mean, the bloody thing's so big that I'm surprised you didn't put your back out lugging it around."

Annie's eyes returned to the screen for the briefest of moments, then she looked away, feeling humiliated.

"Okay, for the benefit of the tape, Annie has now climbed onto the bed and positioned herself behind the other woman," Murray continued in a bored monotone. "She has now inserted the dildo into her anus." He shuddered as they started to have intercourse. "Jesus," he said, glancing sideways at Annie and wincing. "You definitely got the better deal, being the giver rather than the receiver. I bet she couldn't walk straight by the time you'd finished with her."

Annie was crying now, but Murray felt no sympathy. She had either killed and dismembered Carrie McCullen, or she was protecting the person who had, which, in his eyes, made her just as bad.

Over the next few minutes, he played a series of clips all featuring Annie using different sized sex toys to perform anal penetration on her very willing partner. Then the two women reversed roles, and Annie laid on the bed while the other woman went to town on her vagina using a throbbing red vibrator the size of a large cucumber.

Murray paused the picture every time that a good quality close up of Annie's face appeared on screen, asked her to confirm that she was the woman they were looking at.

Interestingly, they were never afforded a clear shot of the other woman's face, and it seemed as if she was deliberately obscuring her features to ensure that she could never be identified.

"Who's the other woman?" Murray asked for the umpteenth time.

Annie had stopped speaking by this stage, and she was no longer even bothering to say 'no comment.'

When the tape finished, Murray switched the TV off and nodded to Stone, indicating that he was done.

Taking a deep breath, Stone leaned forward. Speaking softly, he said, "How's your application for visiting rights coming along, Annie?"

Annie reacted as if she had been slapped. With a frightened gasp, she looked up at him, and the desperation in her eyes told Stone that she knew the game was up.

Stone nodded, confirming her fears. "That's right, we know all about Anabel. We know she was taken into care when she was only three months old. We know you've been denied access to her over the past three years because of your chaotic and unstable lifestyle, and we know that you have an application pending for visiting rights to be reinstated." His voice became gentle, sympathetic to her predicament. "I assume that your long-term plan is to prove that you've turned your life around and that you should now be granted full time custody of her?"

Without realising she was doing it, Annie nodded. She looked utterly crestfallen, as though her world was about to come to an end.

Maybe it was, Stone thought, taking no pleasure from it. "For a while, we struggled to work out what possible motive you could have had for killing Carrie," he said. "But then all the pieces started falling into place, as they inevitably do. Did Carrie discover that you were making porn films again? Did she threaten to tell Aidan, and go to Social Services with the information? How would that have affected your chances of getting your daughter back?"

Annie was shaking her head with increasing agitation. "No," she said through the tears. "No, no, no."

"We've examined your phone records," Stone told her. "We know you received a call from Carrie during the early evening of Friday 5th October. Yet you never mentioned that when you made your statement, did you?"

Annie was still shaking her head. "I didn't kill her," she sobbed.

"Course you did," Murray said, bluntly.

Stone shot him an angry look, warning him to keep quiet.

"If you didn't kill Carrie, why did you lie about staying in your flat all evening? If you didn't kill her, why did you refrain from mentioning that she called you on the night she disappeared?" Stone noticed that Annie's hands were trembling the way an alcoholic's do when they come off a long drinking binge and start getting the DTs. "Annie…?"

"I–I…"

Perkins reached out, placed a restraining hand on her arm. "I must remind you of my earlier advice to exercise your right to remain silent and not answer any questions at this time," he said, firmly.

"Mr Perkins is quite right," Stone conceded. "As I explained when I cautioned you, you don't have to say anything. That means you can sit there in complete silence if you so choose. However, as I also explained, if you don't mention when questioned something you later rely upon at court, it may harm your defence. In layman's terms, that means that the trial judge could allow the jury to draw an inference from your silence. They could conclude, for instance, that any defence you subsequently come up with was a pack of lies and, if it had been true, you would have said so during interview."

Annie was looking confused, conflicted, as though she wanted to speak to him, but didn't want to go against her solicitor's advice.

Stone changed tact. "I'm not trying to put you under any pressure," he assured her. "In fact, if you're guilty, making no comment would probably be the most sensible thing to do. But…" he let the word hang in the air for a moment or two. "… if you're *not* involved in Carrie's murder, or in the subsequent disposal of her body, then you're really not doing yourself any favours by remaining silent."

Annie shot a worried glance in Perkins' direction, and he responded with a stern shake of his head.

Stone leaned back in his chair, conveying an attitude of relaxed indifference. "We know that Carrie was murdered and dismembered at Darren's flat. We know that a woman calling herself Lucinda McLean stuffed her torso into a suitcase and, on the evening of Saturday 6th October, she took a minicab from Easy Cars in Hoxton Market to Regent's Canal. We have CCTV footage of her in the cab office, and more footage of her wheeling the suitcase along the canal path after she was dropped off. We know that Lucinda is one of the two women in the porn film we've just shown you." He was pleased to see that she was now hanging onto his every word, hoping for a lifeline to be thrown her way. "Earlier today, we recovered the holdall that was used to transport Carrie's limbs to the canal, and the clothing and wig that Lucinda wore when she took the minicab. I'm confident that the forensic evidence from these items will identify Carrie's killer, along with anyone who helped her." He leaned forward, resting his elbows on the table. Staring into Annie's eyes, he said, "If you killed Carrie, or helped to dispose of her body, then by all means remain silent. It won't change the outcome in the long-term, but at least you won't be incriminating yourself. If, on the other hand, you had no involvement in Carrie's murder, or in the disposal of her dismembered body, you need to understand that, by withholding information from us, you could end up facing charges of concealing a death and attempting to pervert the course of justice. If convicted of that, you're likely to end up doing jail time. How will that affect your chances of getting Social Services to approve your request for visitation rights with your daughter?"

Sobbing uncontrollably, Annie buried her face head in her hands.

Stone sat in silence until the crying stopped, then said, "Annie, if you've been withholding information from us because you think admitting your involvement in a porn film will damage your chances of getting access to your daughter, I need to make something very clear to you." He waited until she looked up at him before continuing. "As we sit here, officers are en route to speak to Pete Simpkins, whose studio I believe you used to make the film at. Rather than have Obscene Publications go over his operation with a fine-toothcomb, I suspect he'll fall over himself in his eagerness to cooperate with us."

He paused to let her ponder what he had told her, and was pleased when she responded with a little nod of resignation. She knew as well as he did that Pervy Pete Simpkins would sell them out to save his own slimy skin.

"Why make things any worse for yourself than they already are?" he asked, amiably. "Tell us what we want to know now, before it's too late, because once we get what we want from Simpkins, we won't need your help, and there will be no reason not to charge you."

42

Hello, Lucinda

Imogen was halfway through recording her interview with Aidan McCullen when a loud knock at the hotel room door startled her. Annoyed by the untimely distraction, she turned to Bear, who was standing behind his video camera, which had been set up on a tripod in the far corner of the room. "Did you order anything from room service?" she asked, staring at him accusingly.

Peering over the top of his camera, Bear shook his shaggy head, looking more like Captain Caveman than ever. "No, but that's not a bad idea," he said with a wonky grin. "I'm absolutely famished."

"I'm hungry, too," Aidan announced. He was sitting on the edge of the double bed, facing them.

"We'll discuss food once the interview's over," Imogen said, firmly. It was going very well, and she had no intentions of allowing the proceedings to be interrupted by talk of food.

Striding across the room, she opened the door, expecting to be greeted by a hotel employee. Someone from housekeeping, perhaps? To her surprise, she saw Jack Tyler and Tony Dillon standing there, looking solemn. They were flanked by two stern faced detectives she didn't recognise.

"What are you two doing here?" she asked, making no move to invite them in.

From the way that Aidan had ranted about Tyler's earlier treatment of him, she knew that the strong-willed SIO wasn't exactly the flavour of the month, and she really didn't want her star witness being unsettled before the interview concluded.

"Is Aidan still in there with you?" Dillon asked, sounding apologetic.

The question threw her. "Yes, we're halfway through our interview." A frown of suspicion marred her pretty brow. "Why, what's happened?" Before Dillon could tell her, she raised a hand to her mouth. "Oh, my God. It's Darren, isn't it? Has he died?"

Dillon shook his head. "Not as far as I'm aware."

"Oh, I see," Imogen said, sounding vaguely disappointed. Having the police break the news of Darren's death to Aidan on film would have made great TV, she thought.

Tyler stepped forward. "We need to speak to Aidan," he said, making no effort to conceal the impatience in his voice.

Imogen stood her ground. "Can't it wait? I haven't finished the interview yet?"

"I'm afraid it can't," Tyler said, indicating for her to move aside.

Dillon followed him in, leaving the two detectives who had accompanied them outside. "You might want to film this," he discreetly whispered to Imogen as he walked past her.

When Aidan saw Tyler, he jumped to his feet. "What's he doing here?" he demanded of Imogen, who was speaking through a cupped hand into Bear's ear.

"We're here to see you," Tyler said.

Aidan scoffed at him, folded his arms belligerently. "What, are you going to evict me from here now, as well?"

Tyler grinned. "Actually, yes."

That wiped the smile from Aidan's face. "What?" Alarmed, his eyes sought out Imogen. "Tell him, he can't do that," he implored. "I haven't got anywhere else I can stay."

"That's okay," Tyler said, enjoying the moment. "We've got a nice cosy little room arranged for you, and it won't cost you a penny. In fact, I suspect we'll be supplying you with rent free accommodation for the next thirty years or so, don't you, Dill?"

Removing a set of handcuffs, Dillon smiled, malevolently. "That about sums it up," he said, walking purposefully towards Aidan.

"I don't understand," Imogen blurted out. "What's going on, here?"

"We've just interviewed Annie Jenkins," Tyler said. "She's told us who killed Carrie." He turned from her to face Aidan, who had backed himself into a corner, and was now looking at the detective fearfully.

"Hello, Lucinda," Tyler said.

Glancing sideways, Imogen anxiously checked to see that Bear was following her instructions.

This is dynamite! Please tell me you're getting it on film…

To her relief, Bear's eye was glued to the viewfinder, and the little red light was flashing, indicating that the camera was recording.

"This is a mistake," Aidan was shouting. "Annie killed Carrie, not me."

"Aidan McCullen, I'm arresting you for the murder of your twin sister, Carrie McCullen," Dillon said, grabbing his skinny wrist and slamming a cuff over it.

Aidan stood there in stunned silence as Dillon applied the other handcuff and cautioned him.

"Let's go," the big man said, taking hold of Aidan's arm and guiding him towards the door.

"Are you sure about this?" Imogen asked him.

He nodded. "Oh yeah, I'm sure."

At the door, Dillon handed Aidan into the custody of the two detectives who had waited outside, and told them to drive him to the station. Then he re-joined the others inside. "Is that thing turned off?" he asked, checking the camera to see if the red light was glowing.

"It's off," Bear said, looking as mystified as Imogen.

Hands on hips, Imogen glared at the detectives, and her lips compressed into an angry thin line. "You just completely ruined my interview," she informed them. "Could it not have waited five more minutes? It's not like he could have run off."

Tyler glanced sheepishly at Dillon, who shrugged. She had a point, he supposed. They could have waited, but Tyler had been awake for something like thirty-nine hours, and his powers of reasoning weren't as sharp as they usually were. "Sorry," he said, guiltily. "I suppose we could have given you a few more minutes."

Imogen's face softened. "Don't worry," she relented. "We'd already covered all the important stuff and, if he's guilty, we filmed his arrest, which is pure gold as far as TV goes." She broke into a grin. "The look on his face was priceless, by the way."

Tyler agreed. It had been very satisfying to watch.

"So, how confident are you that he did it?" she asked. "No offence, but he's the third person you've arrested for her murder so far."

Dillon cringed, shot a nervous look in Tyler's direction. To his surprise, Tyler laughed good naturedly.

"That's true," he admitted. "In fairness though, we had good reason to arrest Carter and Jenkins. We didn't just pluck their names out of thin air."

It was Imogen's turn to laugh. "Granted, but I thought Carrie's killer was a woman, so why arrest Aidan?"

Tyler flopped down on the bed, closed his eyes. "Jenkins broke down in interview a little while ago," he said with a lengthy yawn. "She basically told us everything. It's a long, convoluted story, but the bottom line is that Aidan's the killer."

Sitting on the bed beside him, Dillon prodded the mattress, then laid down beside his partner. "This is really quite comfortable," he remarked.

The pair of them lapsed into silence.

Imogen folded her arms. "So, Annie fingered Aidan, did she?"

Tyler laughed, wickedly. "Oh, so you've already seen the porn film, have you?"

Imogen giggled. "Seriously, Jack, how do you know she's telling the truth, and not just lying to save herself?"

It was a reasonable question, he allowed. "Jim Stone interviewed her. He's a pretty sharp cookie, and he's convinced that she's telling the truth. I must say, I'm inclined to agree with him."

"Do you mind," Dillon said in mock irritation. "Some of us are trying to sleep."

"But what exactly is the truth?" Imogen persisted.

Sitting up, Tyler propped a pillow up behind his back and made himself comfy. "Aidan likes dressing up as a woman and having Annie insert large dildos up his back passage," he said, cheerfully. "Apparently, there is a niche market for this sort of thing in the porn industry, which Annie was aware of thanks to her previous experience as a performer. She came up with the idea of making a couple of porn films so that she and Aidan could pay off their debts, and she persuaded Pervy Pete Simpkins to distribute and market the films for them, in return for a significant share of the profits, of course."

"Of course," Imogen said. As Aidan had recently told her, nothing was for nothing in this life.

"Naughty Lucinda was their first attempt," Tyler continued. "Unfortunately, Carrie found a copy of it, and she went ballistic when she saw what they were getting involved in."

'So, he killed her to silence her, did he?" Imogen asked.

"Apparently not."

Imogen scratched her head. "So, why did Aidan kill her?"

"If Annie's to be believed, she didn't realise that Aidan was the killer until Kelly and Debbie popped round to show them the clip of Lucinda dragging the suitcase into the cab office on the Saturday night. After the FLOs left, she confronted Aidan. He denied it at first, but then broke down and admitted responsibility. He was suffering from paranoid delusions that Carrie and Darren had talked their parents out of leaving him a share of their house so, that night, not knowing that Darren and Janice had flown to Tenerife, he decided to go over and have it out with Darren once and for all. To his surprise, Carrie answered the door. Pushing his way in, Aidan started an argument, which quickly got very heated. Halfway through, he lost his rag and smashed her over the head with a heavy ashtray."

"But why would she stay silent over something like that?" Imogen asked.

Tyler gave her a mirthless smile. "Ah, well, apparently, Aidan told her that, if she grassed him up, he would claim she was the one who had killed Carrie, and that he had merely cut the body up and disposed of it to help her out."

"Maybe that's what really happened," Imogen said, massaging her temples. "My understanding is that you can't even see the face of the second woman in the porn film, so how can you prove it was him?"

Standing up, Tyler removed a small notebook from his jacket pocket. He wrote the name Lucinda McLean in capital letters. "That's Aidan's porn name," he told her.

Imogen glanced at the paper, then shrugged. "You've only got Annie's word for that."

"That's true," Tyler said. He then wrote Aidan McCullen in capital letters. "What does that say?" he asked, holding it up for her to read.

Imogen frowned, not understanding where this was going. "It says Aidan McCullen," she told him.

Tyler smiled. "Also true." Using his biro, he drew connecting lines between the thirteen letters of each name.

Imogen looked at the lines he'd drawn between the names, and then at the letters they linked. For a moment, she frowned in puzzlement, then her eyes went wide. "Oh, my God," she exclaimed as the penny dropped. "The two names are an anagram of each other!"

"Yep," Tyler said with a smile. "He's going to have a hard time explaining that one at court."

"When did you work *that* out?" Imogen asked, staring at him with grudging respect.

Tyler chuckled. "I wish I could take credit for it," he admitted, "but the truth is, Annie told Jim Stone during interview. It seems that Aidan got a big kick out of hiding his name in plain sight."

Behind them, on the bed, Dillon began snoring loudly.

43

WEDNESDAY 17TH OCTOBER 2001

Now that the dust has settled

"Mind if I join you?" Tyler asked. Without waiting for a reply, he sat down next to Andy Quinlan in the canteen at Hertford House. It was lunchtime, and he had ordered the spaghetti bolognese. While waiting in line, he had heard someone complaining that the spaghetti was a little undercooked, but his looked fine and it smelled delicious.

Maybe he was less fussy than them; maybe he was just too hungry to care.

A few moments later, Dillon slid into the chair to his right, carrying a plate of fish and chips. "Move over," he said, flexing his massive shoulders. "You know I need lots of elbow room when I eat."

Tutting at the inconvenience, Tyler dragged his seat sideways a couple of feet to give the big lug some more space.

Pushing his glasses further up his nose, Andy Quinlan smiled at them affectionately. "You know, you two really are like an old married couple."

Tyler snorted. "Who in their right mind would marry *him*?" he asked, thinking he'd be a rich man if he'd received a pound for every time that someone had said that to them over the years.

"For your information, Mr Picky, plenty of women would kill to have a husband like me," Dillon said, adopting an indignant pout.

Tyler gave him a dubious sideways glance. "You mean, plenty of women would kill a husband like you," he corrected with a grin.

Quinlan speared some tuna with his fork, popped it into his mouth. "So, now that the dust has settled, how's it all going with Aidan McCullen?"

Tyler groaned. "We're taking him back to Thames Magistrates this afternoon to apply for an extension on the warrant of further detention."

The police were initially allowed to keep a suspect in custody without charge for twenty-four hours. This could be extended by an additional twelve hours with the authority of a Superintendent not directly involved in the investigation. To go beyond that required a warrant of further detention issued by a Magistrates Court, who could authorise continued detention for a period not exceeding ninety-six hours. The initial WOFD they had already obtained was due to expire later that day, so Aidan and Annie were going back before the Magistrates for it to be extended.

"I take it he hasn't confessed, then?" Quinlan enquired with a cynical smile.

Tyler grimaced. "Of course not."

"But I take it everything is going to plan?"

Tyler took a deep breath. Where did he even begin to break down all that had happened over the past couple of days?

Since his arrest, Aidan had strenuously denied being responsible for his sister's death and had taken to blaming Annie at every opportunity, insisting that she had acted entirely without his knowledge.

During the first round of interviews, Aidan had been shown the footage of Lucinda entering the cab office, dragging the suitcase behind her. He had dismissed as laughable the suggestion that it was him, dressed in women's clothing and wearing a wig. He had been equally contemptuous of the CCTV depicting a woman dragging the suitcase along the canal path after the minicab had dropped her in Dunston Road.

"Surely this proves a woman killed my sister?" he had shouted, angrily. "You should be grilling Annie about this, not me."

Evans had then dropped the bombshell that they knew he liked dressing up as a woman, backing up the accusation by showing him snippets from the Lusty Lucinda porn film.

"That's not true!" Aidan had protested, angrily.

Evans had gone on to explain that the cab office and canal CCTV had been reviewed by an expert in gait analysis, who had concluded that it was the same person in both clips.

"It might be," Aidan had replied bullishly, "but it's not me."

At which point Evans had revealed that the gait analysis expert had also viewed covert recordings they had made of Aidan walking around the custody office following his arrest, and he was supremely confident that the person it featured was the same one he had watched in the previous clips, albeit now dressed as a male.

In subsequent interviews, Paul Evans had disclosed that Lucinda's wig, along with the clothing she had worn to the cab office, had been discovered inside Darren's flat, and that preliminary findings from the Forensic Science Services laboratory indicated a perfect match between the wearer profile obtained from the them and the DNA sample taken from Aidan upon his arrival at the police station.

Finally, Evans had played the CCTV footage of Aidan purchasing a SIM card from a mini-market in Hoxton on the Saturday morning, before outlining how Reggie had skilfully established that the SIM card had been used in Carrie's mobile phone that evening to order a cab under the name of Lucinda McLean. Lucinda McLean, he had then pointed out, was an anagram of Aidan McCullen.

At that point, Aidan's solicitor had hastily stepped in to demand the interview be suspended in order for him to consult with his client in private.

When the interview resumed, Aidan had sheepishly told them

that he wanted to change his account. Although still adamant that Annie had murdered Carrie during a heated argument over the porn film, he now reluctantly accepted that he had helped her to dispose of the body.

At least they had cleared up the mystery of why he hadn't disposed of the head, or the clothing and wig he had worn to he cab office. Having run out of time and energy over the weekend, he had intended to dump the head on the Monday night. However, Abi Stanwick had scuppered his plans by dragging him off to the police station to report Carrie missing. She had put the mockers on him again on Tuesday evening, by coming over and staying there till late. He would have dumped the head on Wednesday evening, but that was the day the torso was discovered, after which getting rid of Carrie's head became problematic. As for the clothing, well, that belonged to Janice, and he was worried that she would notice if it was missing when she returned from holiday. Aidan had shrugged when asked about the wig, admitting that he had never intended to get rid of it as he figured it would be needed again when they made their next porn film.

In addition to the lengthy interviews, a massive amount of work had been carried out since Aidan's arrest.

When Darren's flat had been treated with Luminol, the non-visible blood staining in the bathroom had been completely off the charts, confirming it was, without doubt, the dismemberment site.

A Special Post Mortem had been carried out on Carrie's head by Dr Tolpuddle at Poplar mortuary, and this had concluded that the cause of death was blunt force trauma. Carrie had been struck a single, powerful blow with a heavy, pointed object, and this had resulted in a depressed skull fracture.

Now that Carrie's body had been recovered in its entirety, the services of a forensic anthropologist had been enlisted. Professor Suranne White, considered one of the leading experts in her field, had examined Carrie's remains the previous day.

Her findings had made for grim reading.

The professor had concluded there was a mechanical fit between Carrie's head, torso, and all four limbs. She had indicated that the dismemberment had occurred in confined conditions; Carrie had been lying face down when her head, left shoulder and left leg were removed; the head had been removed between the C3 – C4 joints; Carrie had been facing upwards when her right shoulder and right leg were severed.

Prof. White observed that the removal of the limbs from the left side of Carrie's body was considerably neater than the corresponding removal of the limbs from the right side of her body. There were two potential explanations for this, she had explained: It could have happened because Aidan's technique had improved as he'd gone along, making him more efficient; conversely, the efficiency of the dismemberment could have deteriorated because he was becoming increasingly tired.

She concluded that no power tools had been used during the dismemberment process, and estimated that, from start to finish, it would have taken Aidan between three and four hours to complete. A sharp knife had been used to de-flesh the body, pairing the muscle and soft tissue away from the bone. A cleaver had then been used to hack through the bones. The kurfs (splintering of the bones) on the left side were only small, but the kurfs on the right side were far more pronounced and jagged.

The professor was able to say that the legs had been severed by working from the inside out, and she had made specific reference to a noticeable mark on one of Carrie's inner legs. This, she explained, was consistent with a heel mark being caused by the pressure of Aidan's foot as he pushed back against one leg while cutting through the other.

Lastly, the POLSA search team had recovered a load of plastic blood-stained sheeting and a set of equally bloody overalls from a shed down at the allotments, which they had stumbled across while searching for the discarded shell casings following the shootout between Darren McCullen and Fred Wiggins. It transpired that the shed had once belonged to the late Mrs McCullen, who had rented one of the allotments for many years prior to her death.

Tyler paraphrased all of this for Quinlan's benefit, finding it slightly surreal that they were discussing such a morbid and harrowing subject over lunch.

"What about your job?" Tyler asked, having brought Quinlan up to speed. "How's that coming along now that we've solved it for you?"

Beside him, Dillon chortled. Lowering his fork, he leaned over and high-fived his partner.

"Ha-ha," Quinlan said, drolly. "I'll have you know there was still an awful lot to do after that."

Tyler wondered if he had accidentally hit a nerve. After all, this wasn't the first case that he and Dillon had inadvertently solved for Quinlan. "Which is why I'm so keen to know how you're getting on," he said, smiling placatingly.

Quinlan took a moment to compose his thoughts. "We identified the body in the drum through his fingerprints," he began. "His name was Terry Marshall, and he was a mechanic from Stratford. He had a few convictions, but nothing major. Turns out, he was a good mate of Darren McCullen's, and he was looking after the garage for a couple of weeks while Darren and Janice sunned themselves in Tenerife."

"Do we think this Marshall character was involved in the robbery at Frank Kyle's place, along with Darren McCullen?" Dillon asked through a mouthful of chips.

Quinlan shook his head. "There's nothing to suggest that was the case, but Willard and his cronies obviously thought otherwise. From what we've pieced together so far, Wiggins and three of his goons, that's Casper Wright, Basher Nolan, and Mickey Mulligan, abducted Marshall and another grease monkey called Paul Pickford, aka Fingers, from McCullen's Garage on Friday 12th October. Believing them responsible for Kyle's murder, they took them to the warehouse, intending to kill them."

Dillon chuckled. "Fingers? What a great name! I take it he's a dipper?"

Quinlan shook his head. "With a name like that, I can see why you would assume he's a pickpocket, but he's not." He raised his left hand and wiggled his fingers. "No, the poor bugger lost a couple of pinkies in an accident a few years back, so his mates took to calling him Fingers."

Dillon found this highly amusing.

"Has Darren McCullen corroborated any of this?" Tyler asked, attempting to twirl a slithering pile of spaghetti around his fork. Kelly always made this look so effortless, but he had never mastered the knack. In the end, he gave up, and rammed the few strands he'd been able to snare into his mouth.

Against all the odds, Darren McCullen had somehow survived his horrific injuries. He was still in the ICU, and would remain there for some time, but he was off the ventilator and fully conscious, showing no signs of the brain damage his doctors had feared he would be left with.

"He's far too ill for us to formally interview him yet," Quinlan said, pulling a face that suggested Darren's medical condition was a great inconvenience. "But he did tell the hospital guard that Marshall wasn't involved in any criminality, and was just looking after the garage for a couple of weeks."

Tyler winced. That meant that Marshall had died purely for being in the wrong place at the wrong time. "What did the SPM show as cause of death?"

Quinlan shook his head sadly. "I'm afraid he didn't die nicely. Before killing him, the bastards set fire to his lower legs. Then they threw him into a cold, empty room and left him to suffer in what must have been the most excruciating agony imaginable, without any pain relief."

Tyler grimaced. He couldn't even begin to imagine how horrible it must have been. "Poor bastard," he said, feelingly.

Quinlan nodded. "I know. It's barbaric, but he might have survived the burns if Casper Wright hadn't subsequently reduced his head to pulp."

"Can we prove he was the one who did that?" Tyler asked.

"We can," Quinlan confirmed. "Even after traipsing through the allotments, the soles of Casper's boots had large segments of flesh and gore trapped in the grooves, and a tooth had become imbedded in the rubber. Plus, the legs of Casper's trousers were covered with blood spatter, the pattern of which was consistent with the injuries inflicted on Marshall."

Tyler thought for a moment. "In that case, I'm glad the bastard's dead. It'll save the taxpayer from having to fork out for his incarceration over the next thirty years."

"He's no loss to humanity, that's for sure," Quinlan agreed. "Obviously, we're planning to charge Willard, Nolan, and Mulligan with Pickford, Marshall, and Carter's abduction, and with a conspiracy to murder all three of them."

"How did your people get on with interviewing Stella Carter?" Tyler asked, trying to rid himself of the disturbingly graphic images of Marshall's suffering, which had become lodged in the forefront of his mind.

"Oh, Stella's been very helpful," Quinlan said, allowing himself a smug smile. "Willard was convinced that she'd topped Carrie, which is why he wanted her dead, and he told her that he was going to do her the honour of snuffing her out himself."

Tyler raised a surprised eyebrow. He hadn't imagined Willard as being the type to get his hands dirty.

"Willard was uncharacteristically loose lipped with Stella," Quinlan chuckled. "I suppose he thought she wouldn't live to repeat anything he told her."

"Looks like he was wrong there," Dillon observed with a wry grin.

"Indeed," Quinlan acknowledged. Pushing his plate aside, he dabbed his mouth with a paper napkin.

It was amazing how all the various pieces of the story were coming together, Tyler thought, and how interlinked everything was. The synchronicity was quite staggering.

"I'm confident we can prove Darren McCullen and Paul Pickford stole Jonas Willard's diamonds from Frank Kyle's house, killing him in the process," Quinlan was saying. "And, thanks to Darren spilling the beans to Tony after he'd been shot, we now know that Carrie provided the information. It seems that Willard somehow discovered their identities, then had them rounded up and taken to the warehouse. I don't suppose we'll ever know whether they mistook Marshall for Darren, or just didn't want to leave any witnesses behind, but they systematically tortured him in front of Pickford until he revealed where the diamonds were buried. After that, they tossed Marshall into a cell for a while, then brought him back out so that Casper could jump up and down on his head." A deep frown appeared on his forehead. "I wonder if they made Pickford watch that as well?"

"Have you managed to find Pickford yet?" Tyler asked.

"Regrettably, not," Quinlan said. "Since doing a runner from the allotments the other night, he seems to have disappeared off the face of the earth. Still, he'll get his comeuppance in the end; they always do."

Tyler didn't doubt that. "These diamonds that Willard mentioned," he said, rubbing his chin thoughtfully. "Would I be right in assuming they're the stones we found in the back of McCullen's car?"

Quinlan chuckled. "You most certainly would be. We've had them valued by an expert from Hatton Garden, and he reckons they would probably fetch as much as 1.5 million pounds on the open market. On the black market, their value would probably drop to just over the million mark."

It was an awful lot of money, but was it worth a man's life?

Darren McCullen had obviously thought so, as had Willard, who would have willingly ended the lives of three men to get them back.

"Are the gems stolen?" Tyler asked.

Quinlan chuckled. "There must be something dodgy about them and, as Willard can't prove ownership, the diamonds will be confiscated under the Proceeds of Crime Act."

Tyler laughed. "There is an exquisite irony to that, isn't there?"

"I think so," Quinlan concurred.

"Can you connect either of the guns that were recovered from the allotments to Kyle's murder?" Dillon asked.

"We can," Quinlan beamed. "Both pistols still had their serial numbers on them, and we were able to trace them to a batch that went missing from a military installation in Germany at the same time as Darren McCullen was stationed over there in the army. The gun that Darren used to kill Casper was also used on Frank Kyle, and I'm overjoyed to report that we found a mixture of Darren's fingerprints and DNA on the gun itself, on the magazine, and on some of the bullets."

"Sounds like he's well and truly screwed," Tyler observed. "Well done, mate."

Dillon nudged Tyler's arm. "Sorry to interrupt," he said, tapping his watch, "but time's pressing on and, if we want to get to court in time to speak to our brief before the application is heard, we need to get going."

Tyler groaned. "Dill's right," he said, standing up. "I'll catch up with you later, Andy."

"Good luck," Quinlan said, waving them off.

44

I want to be there when the charges are read out

The uniformed gaoler unlocked the door leading from the custody suite to the rear yard of Shoreditch police station. Holding one arm each, Paul Evans and Kevin Murray led their prisoner through the caged area towards the station van that was waiting to take him to court.

Aidan squinted into the bright sunshine. His hands were cuffed behind his back, and he was still wearing the same grubby grey tracksuit they had provided him with after seizing his clothing on Sunday afternoon. On his feet, a pair of black plimsoles that were two sizes too big for him were slipping on and off like a pair of cheap flip flops.

"I look like a complete fucking loser in this getup," he complained.

"Trust me," Murray said with a condescending smirk. "You were a complete loser long before you put that lot on."

The uniformed driver ambled over to join them at the back of the van. He was a short, overweight man with a military buzz cut, several chins, and a bulging belly that had taken him many years to grow. The utility belt containing his baton, Quick-Cuffs, CS spray and first aid kit was worn cowboy style, with one side hanging down lower than the other. Unlocking the rear doors, he indicated for Aidan to get in. "Mind your head," he said, more out of habit than because he actually cared.

Aidan was about to step in when he caught sight of the other prisoner. "What the fuck is she doing here?" he demanded, trying to back away.

"Get in," Murray said, giving him a firm shove in the back.

With no choice in the matter, Aidan took a seat in the cramped caged area at the rear of the van. Facing him, Annie Jenkins looked equally uncomfortable to see him. Like Aidan, her hands had been cuffed behind her back, forcing her to sit hunched forward.

"Hello, Aidan," she said, coldly.

Aidan stared out at the two detectives, who were watching him impassively. "What's Annie doing here?"

"We're taking you both back to the Magistrates Court in order to request an extension to the warrants of further detention we were granted yesterday morning," Evans explained.

Licking his lips nervously, Aidan looked with uncertainty from the detective to Annie, then shifted uncomfortably in his seat. "Can't we go in different vehicles?" he asked.

"We don't have a limitless supply," Murray said with an ill-tempered sneer.

A moment later, the rear doors slammed shut with a loud clunk, and they found themselves trapped in such close proximity that their knees rubbed.

After a short conversation with the detectives, the driver climbed into the van, which rocked up and down on its springs under his weight.

The engine started.

Every time Annie attempted to initiate conversation with Aidan during the stop-start journey, he angrily shushed her. The metal bars and wire mesh of the caged area they were sitting in rattled non-stop, making a considerable racket, so they could probably have spoken freely, but he was too paranoid to risk it.

A half hour later, having been delayed by heavy traffic, the van pulled into the rear yard of Thames Court and came to a juddering halt. A middle-aged man wearing the uniform of a court security officer approached the driver, spoke to him for a few seconds, and then walked away.

Cursing the inconvenience, the van driver reversed back into a space by the far wall, then switched the engine off.

"What's going on?" Aidan enquired. The last time he had come here, the van had been driven straight inside the secure area.

The driver grunted, then addressed Aidan over his shoulder. "There's a problem with the shutter mechanism, so we've got to wait out here for a few minutes till they fix it." A few seconds later, he let out a long sigh. "It's far too hot to sit in here," he said to his mate. "Let's go and stand in the shade till they're ready for us."

Both men opened their doors.

"What about us?" Aidan shouted after them. "We're hot, too."

The driver shrugged his indifference. "Not a lot I can do about that," he said, closing his door behind him.

Aidan watched them through the windscreen as they walked away from the van, laughing and joking. "Wankers," he muttered under his breath. When he was sure they were out of earshot, he turned on Annie, baring his teeth in a snarl. "Right, you scheming cow, we haven't got much time, and I need to know what you've told them."

According to the officers who had interviewed him, Annie was being very cooperative, and she had told them everything she knew, which included the confession she had wrangled out of him.

"I didn't tell them anything they didn't already know," Annie said defiantly.

Anger flared in him.

Lying, two-faced cow.

He tensed his shoulders, leaned forward aggressively. "I mean it, Annie," he growled. "I want to know exactly what you told them."

She looked up at him, and there was a hardness to her face that he had never seen before. "What did you tell them about me?" she shot back.

Aidan hadn't expected her to take the offensive, and her outright aggression caught him off guard. "Nothing," he said, hastily. "Why would I say anything about you. All you did was cover for me when I told you what had happened."

"I should *never* have done that," she said, bemoaning her folly. "I should have gone straight to the police and told them what you'd done. I would have too, if you hadn't blackmailed me into staying silent."

A crafty smile crossed Aidan's face. "Yeah, well, you always were weak."

Her face flushing with anger. "You disgust me," she snapped. "I don't know how you can live with yourself, after murdering your own sister."

"I told you, I didn't intend to kill her. I didn't even know she was in the poxy flat, did I? I thought I was going to have it out with Darren. When Carrie opened the door, I was as surprised to see her standing there as she was to see me." The oppressive heat inside the van was giving him a rotten headache, and he could feel little pinpricks of perspiration breaking out on his forehead. "You know what she's like. The selfish cow just went on and on at me until I lost my temper and hit her." A lame shrug. "She must've had a weak skull or something." He shrugged again, and when next he spoke, his voice was full of self-pity. "Honestly, Annie, I was gutted when I realised that the stroppy cow was dead. You've got to believe me." He sniffed, shook his head ruefully. "I only hit her the once."

"You seem to think that makes what you did okay," Annie said, shaking her head in disgust. "If you had a shred of decency in you, you'd put your hands up to what you've done, but you won't because you're a selfish bastard, and you only ever think of yourself."

"And you're not selfish, I suppose?" he scoffed. "Yet you sold me out to save your own skin."

"I was trying to clear my name because you tried to stitch me up!" she hissed.

Aidan shrugged. "What was I supposed to do?" he demanded, petulantly.

Annie leaned forward so that she could look him straight in the eye. "I'm begging you, Aidan," she sobbed. "Please tell the police the truth. Please don't take me down with you."

Aidan watched dispassionately as the tears streamed down Annie's gaunt cheeks. He had never loved her, and he certainly had no intention of throwing himself on his sword to save her. "You don't get it, do you, you stupid, braindead cow?" he snapped, wishing his hands were free so that he could slap her. "I'm not trying to take you down with me."

She seemed confused, then cautiously hopeful. She tilted her head to one side, while trying to blink away the tears that blurred her vision. "You're not?"

"No," he said with a cruel, vindictive smile. "I'm trying to send you down *instead* of me."

It was five o'clock, and Tyler was lounging at his desk, nursing a cup of coffee to his chest. Dillon, Bull, Evans and Murray were all sitting in a tight semi-circle around him, their brows knotted in concentration. The extension of the warrant of further detention had been granted without any hitches, so they now had until the following morning to question Aidan and Annie. Having just listened to the short audio recording that Evans had played for him, Tyler was satisfied that the extra time was now superfluous. With a contented smile, he leaned forward, rewound the tape for several seconds, then pressed the play button.

Aidan's gruff voice immediately came through the speaker, clear and crisp. *"What was I supposed to do?"*

Between sobs, Annie said, *"I'm begging you, Aidan. Please tell the police the truth. Please don't take me down with you."* The desperation in her voice shone through.

Aidan again, openly ridiculing her. *"You don't get it, do you, you stupid, braindead cow? I'm not trying to take you down with me."*

"You're not?"

"No… I'm trying to send you down instead of me."

Tyler pressed the stop button, ejected the tape. "I take it everything went smoothly?" he asked, addressing the question to Paul Evans.

"Like clockwork," Evans grinned. "The van driver and his operator played their parts perfectly, even though they didn't have a clue why we were asking them to do it. So did the security guard at the court. Neither Aidan nor Annie suspected that the whole thing was a set up."

That was good to hear, Tyler thought, feeling vindicated for all the stress and hard work he had caused his team. The operation to have a covert microphone installed in a station van at short notice had taken a lot of organising, and there had been so many hoops to jump through along the way that it had very nearly failed to get off the ground.

Tyler had come up with the idea the previous day, believing it was the only way they would ever get to the bottom of who had done what. After speaking to the Duty Officer at the Technical Support Unit, he had instructed Steve Bull to complete the appropriate forms, which were incredibly arduous and time consuming. When they were done, they were electronically submitted to the Covert Authorities Bureau at New Scotland Yard, whose eagle-eyed staff had carried out the necessary quality control checks before arranging an appointment for Tyler to attend The Yard that evening.

Making an in-person presentation to an Assistant Commissioner was always a nerve-wracking affair, and he had gone into the room knowing that he would be expected to provide a compelling business case that demonstrated how the covert deployment he was seeking to carry out was proportionate to the seriousness of the offence under investigation, and why it could not be obtained by less intrusive methods.

Once the operation had been green lighted, the TSU were able to go to work. That morning, Murray had collected the van they were going to be using from their base in South London. Taking it to Shoreditch, he had then set about briefing the van crew, and arranging for the shutters at the court to develop a 'temporary fault'.

So much could have gone wrong. The various actors could have fluffed their lines; the recording equipment could have failed to work, or produced a poor-quality product that was totally inaudible; Aidan and Annie could have sat there in stony silence, saying nothing.

Tyler leaned back in his chair, smiled at them like a proud father. "You all did a fantastic job getting this organised in the short space of time we had," he declared, encompassing everyone in the room with a sweep of his arm. "I can't begin to tell you how grateful I am for all the hard work you've put into this over the last day or so."

Being roughty-toughty homicide detectives, they all tried their best not to look too chuffed but, in the end, they just couldn't help themselves.

"Thanks boss," Murray said, his pigeon chest swelling with pride.

"Yeah, it's really nice of you to say so," Evans said, blushing.

"Now what?" Dillon asked, after they had all finished patting themselves on the back.

Tyler grinned. "Fancy a trip over to Shoreditch?" he asked his partner. "I want to be there when the charges are read out."

―――

"Aidan McCullen, there is one charge against you today," the custody sergeant informed him, speaking in an officious tone.

The custody area had been cleared so that Aidan was the only prisoner there. He was flanked by his solicitor. Several detectives, including Tyler and Dillon, were watching on from the side lines.

Behind the raised dais, the grim-faced custody sergeant peered at Aidan over the top of his reading glasses. "The charge is that, on or before Wednesday 10th October, 2001, within the jurisdiction of the Central Criminal Court, you did wilfully kill Carrie McCullen." Because they couldn't establish the exact date of Carrie's death, the charge was required to show that it had occurred on or before the day that the body had been found. "This is an offence contrary to Common law." He then proceeded to caution Aidan, who made no reply.

The custody officer checked his watch, then announced, "Charged, charge read over and cautioned at 18:30 hours. No reply made."

Aidan's solicitor and Paul Evans, who was acting as the charging officer, noted the time and lack of reply in their respective daybooks.

Clearing his throat, Aidan's solicitor stepped forward and gave the custody officer a saccharine smile. They were about the same age, but where the custody officer was trim, smartly turned out, and in good shape, the solicitor looked haggard, overweight and like he had slept in his suit.

"Sergeant, I'm Mr Freeman, and I'm Aidan's solicitor. I'd like to make representations for bail on his behalf."

Removing his reading glasses, the jaded custody officer regarded him with weary resignation. They both knew the solicitor was wasting his time, and that Aidan was going nowhere, but the game had to be played out. "You can make as many representations as you like," he said, picking up his pen to note them.

Once Aidan had been safely returned to his cell, where he would spend the night before being shipped back to Thames Court the following morning, and his solicitor had been shown the door, Evans fetched Annie from her cell.

As she was ushered into the custody office, Tyler was staggered by the contrast between her current appearance and how she had looked when he'd arrested her on Sunday. Her long auburn hair was all dirty and matted. The bruising and swelling around her injured eye had started to fade, but the area was still noticeably darker than the waxen skin surrounding it. Her eyes were red rimmed from all the crying she had done, and her nails had been chewed down to the quick.

Looking more like a broken doll than a human being, Annie listlessly shuffled up to the custody officer's desk, her eyes constantly flitting between the uniformed sergeant sitting behind it and Tyler.

As he walked forward to engage her, he wondered if her rapid deterioration was down to the fact that she was resigned to spending the next thirty years behind bars, or because she believed she would never see her daughter again.

"How are you feeling?" he asked.

She responded with a forlorn shrug that seemed to drain what little energy she had left. Leaning on the counter, she wiped her runny nose with the back of a trembling hand.

"DC Evans told me you just charged Aidan with Carrie's murder," she said, her voice quivering with fear. "Is it... Is it my turn now?"

Tyler smiled at her, then shook his head. "You're not going to be charged with her murder," he said.

Annie frowned, perplexed by the statement. "W–what do you mean?" she stammered, wrapping her arms around her scrawny body.

Tyler gave her a sympathetic smile. "There have been some new developments this afternoon," he explained. "I can't go into any details at this point, but suffice to say we now know that you didn't kill Carrie, and that you had absolutely no involvement in the subsequent dismemberment and disposal of her body."

Annie gasped, and if Paul Evans hadn't stepped forward to grab hold of her arm when he did, she would have collapsed on the floor.

Tyler took her other arm. Between them, they guided her over to the wooden bench that ran along the far wall. Once she was seated, Evans shot off to get her some water.

"I don't understand," she said, peering into Tyler's eyes.

"Annie, I'll have to submit a report to the Crown Prosecution Service, seeking their views on whether you should be charged with attempting to pervert the course of justice by withholding the information you had about Aidan's involvement in Carrie's death, but I'm satisfied you only did that because he put pressure on you and threatened to implicate you. I know about your application to get visiting rights with your daughter, so I can completely understand why you didn't come forward." He shrugged, pragmatically. "It'll be the CPS's decision in the end, but my recommendation will be not to press any charges against you."

Her bottom lip quivered and, as she blinked, a tear ran down the side of her face. "Really?"

"Yes, really."

It took a moment or two for his words to sink in. When they did, her face seemed to light up, becoming animated for the first time since she had walked into the room. "Thank you," she said, reaching up to squeeze his hand.

"Relax," he told her, placing his other hand on her shoulder and giving it a little squeeze. "It's all over. The custody sergeant's just completing the paperwork, and then we'll get someone to drive you home." Her flat had now been released as a crime scene, so she would be free to return to it.

"It's really over?" she asked, half expecting there to be a catch.

Tyler nodded. "It really is," he confirmed. "Of course, we're going to need a detailed statement off you regarding Aidan's confession, but that can wait for another day."

EPILOGUE – ONE WEEK LATER

DS Jim Cuthbert knocked on the door to Derek Peterson's office in the Command Corridor.

"Morning, Del," he said, popping his head around the door. "When I arrived for work a few minutes ago, my DCI told me to come straight down to see you, wouldn't say what it was about." A conspiratorial smile. "I'm not in the dog house, am I?" He was trying to act nonchalantly, doing his best to give off a cheeky chappie kind of vibe that proclaimed he wasn't remotely concerned, but the truth was, he was bricking himself.

"Morning, Jim," Peterson said, stony faced. "If you'd like to follow me, I'll show you straight through."

Cuthbert swallowed hard. The normally bubbly Staff Officer had given him a decidedly frosty reception, so something was obviously amiss, but what? He had been so careful, there was no way that anyone could suspect him of any wrongdoing. He made another attempt to be friendly. "Don't tell me I've incurred another parking ticket, have I?"

"No," Peterson said. "This isn't about outstanding parking tickets." As he made to walk out of the door, Cuthbert placed a restraining hand on his arm.

Epilogue – one week later

"What the fuck's going on, Del?" he demanded. "You're giving me the creeps, cold shouldering me like this. Do I need my Fed Rep or something?"

Peterson shrugged his hand off, gave him a withering look that conveyed a very simple message: *Touch me again, and I'll knock your block off.*

"They're waiting for you in the second room on the right," Peterson said, pointing.

Worried now, Cuthbert walked along the corridor, stopped outside the door that Peterson had indicated. He took a moment to smarten himself up, noting that Holland's staff officer was watching him like a hawk, waiting to make sure he went into the room and didn't do a runner.

Cuthbert's mouth was suddenly very dry. Taking a deep breath, he rapped on the door, ignoring the tremor that had developed in his hand.

"Come," a stern voice announced from inside.

Opening the door with some trepidation, he gingerly stepped inside.

Two men in dark suits were standing on either side of the door like sentries. Their faces grim, they stared at him through suspicious eyes.

Rubber Heelers, he thought with a sinking heart.

There were three more men in the room, all sitting at a long table in front of him. He recognised the first two as DCIs Jack Tyler and Andy Quinlan, but the third was a mean looking stranger. In his early forties, he had a square jaw, a grizzled face, and he wore his salt and pepper hair in a military type buzz cut. Dressed in a simple black suit and tie, with a crisp white shirt, he had the intimidating appearance of a Gestapo officer from one of those old war films. He was staring at Cuthbert with black eyes, which seemed to drain all the energy out of the room.

Cuthbert felt his knees go weak, and his sphincter twitch.

"DS Cuthbert?" the stranger enquired in a voice that sounded like he had swallowed gravel.

Epilogue – one week later

Cuthbert nodded nervously. "I was told to come straight down here when I arrived for work this morning."

"Yes, I know," the stranger said. "It was I who gave the order."

Cuthbert tore his eyes away from the stranger's mesmerising gaze before the man sucked his soul out of his body. "What's this all about?" he asked, directing the question at Tyler and Quinlan in the hope that he would get a friendlier reception from them.

Quinlan, who always reminded Cuthbert of a university professor with his mop of black hair, tortoiseshell glasses, and academic demeanour was sitting with his arms folded. His lips were compressed into a tight line, and there was an air of disappointed anger about him.

He knows.

As the realisation kicked in, Cuthbert felt an urgent need to empty his bowels.

Tyler, the so-called golden boy of the command, the man everyone said got a kick out of taking on the difficult cases that all the other SIOs ran away from, looked furious.

"These gentlemen are from the Complaints Investigation Bureau," Tyler said. "They're here because of some worrying anomalies that have come to light over the past couple of weeks."

Cuthbert frowned. "Anomalies? What does that mean?"

"It means you answer questions, not ask them," the stranger said in a chillingly scary voice.

Putting on a bravado he didn't actually feel, Cuthbert turned to face him. "I'm sorry, who are you exactly?"

The stranger's predatory smile made Cuthbert think he was in very deep trouble. "My name is DCI Peter Frank, and I'm the man who will decide whether you get to keep your job and your freedom."

Cuthbert swallowed hard, opened his mouth to respond, but just couldn't find the words.

Frank stood up, wandered around the table to stand next to him. Of medium height, he was broad and solid, without being too big. "DS Cuthbert," he said, running his eyes over Cuthbert from top to

Epilogue – one week later

bottom, as if deciding which bones to break first, "what is your connection to Fred Wiggins and Jonas Willard?"

Cuthbert shook his head. "I don't have a connection," he said, trying to inject some confidence into his voice but failing miserably.

Frank smiled. It was a cunning smile that warned him to tread carefully. "Are you sure?" he asked. "Do you know either of them on a professional or social basis?"

"I–" Cuthbert stopped himself. He had been about to deny having any connection to either of them, but then he realised that people like Frank didn't often ask questions they didn't already know the answer to, at least not in the early stage of an investigation. His shoulders slumped, and he let out a sigh of defeat. "I went to school with Fred," he admitted, knowing it would look bad, and that he should have disclosed that information to Tyler as soon as Willard and Wiggins' names came up in the investigation.

"Ah, I see," Frank purred. "Have you been in contact with either of them during the investigations into the murders of Frank Kyle and Carrie McCullen?"

Cuthbert opened his mouth to deny this, but Frank cut him off with a raised hand.

"I want you to think very carefully about your answer," he warned, "because what you say next will determine how I proceed." He raised an eyebrow, inviting Cuthbert to speak.

"I haven't had any contact with either of them," Cuthbert said, praying that they couldn't prove otherwise.

"Very well," Frank said, returning to his seat.

Cuthbert watched on in confusion.

Was that it?

Had he passed the test?

Leaning back in his chair, Frank sniffed the air like a bloodhound, then turned towards his fellow DCIs. "Can you smell that?" he asked them.

Looking bemused, Tyler and Quinlan shook their heads in tandem.

Frank smiled. "It's the smell of bent cop." With an impatient wave of his hand, he signalled to the two men standing by the door.

Epilogue – one week later

They immediately walked forward, coming to a halt on either side of Cuthbert.

"James Cuthbert," Frank said formally, "I am arresting you for malfeasance in a public office, and on suspicion of conspiring to abduct and murder Darren McCullen, Paul Pickford, Terry Marshall and Stella Carter." He recited the caution, but Cuthbert was no longer listening.

His head was spinning. How could this be happening? How could they have discovered what he had been up to?

"DI Manning and DS Roberts will now escort you up to your office to search your desk," Frank informed him. "Before you go, I will require you to surrender your work and personal phones to DI Manning for examination."

The man standing to Cuthbert's left held out a hand.

Feeling like he was about to throw up, Cuthbert handed over the phones. He had deleted every text that he had ever sent to or received from Wiggins, so there shouldn't be anything on there to incriminate him. He knew that Wiggins had always used an unregistered burner phone to communicate with him, so even if they obtained his call data and then carried out subscriber checks on the numbers that came up, they wouldn't be able to link him to Wiggins.

He had to be strong. As long as he didn't crack, it would all be okay in the end, and he would be able to bluff his way out of this mess. At least that was what he told himself. Deep down, on a subliminal level, he wasn't so sure. "You're making a big mistake," he said, as his escorts led him away.

Frank smiled knowingly. "I think you'll find the mistake is all yours," he parried.

After Cuthbert had been led away, Frank's demeanour changed completely, and he became more human, less monster. "Can I buy you gentlemen a coffee in the canteen?" he enquired, pleasantly.

Tyler and Quinlan declined with thanks, saying that they had far too much work waiting for them. They didn't need to add that no

Epilogue – one week later

one wanted to be too closely associated with a senior Rubber Heeler.

"Very well," Frank said, offering them his hand to shake. "I'll keep you both updated, of course, but I'm confident there will be more than enough evidence to charge Cuthbert with all of these offences."

Cuthbert's involvement had initially come to light when Wiggins' phone was examined after his death. The dedicated phones officer on Quinlan's team had read through the messages it contained, then gone running to his boss to raise the alarm. While Cuthbert had deleted all the text messages between them, Wiggins hadn't, and the content had been truly damning.

Although none of the messages contained any names, their content had made it painfully obvious that Wiggins had a police officer involved in the enquiry on his pay role. Swearing his phones expert to secrecy, Quinlan had ordered an urgent subscriber check be carried out on the number that Wiggins had been liaising with. To everyone's horror, it had come back as belonging to Jim Cuthbert.

Quinlan had informed Tyler, and they had gone straight to Holland, who had ordered them to contact CIB. The Rubber Heelers had quietly gone to work in the background, putting Cuthbert under covert surveillance, researching his financial situation, ordering his call data and having his phone cell sited. They had also run his personal and Job cars through ANPR to establish their movement history. The analyst assigned to review the material had identified that a lot of the messages and calls that Cuthbert had made to Wiggins were timed only a few minutes after Tyler's regular team meetings concluded. It soon became very clear that he had been passing Wiggins classified information that had endangered the investigation and people's lives.

CIB had also looked at the phone traffic between the rest of the firm, and they had forensically examined the mobile phones seized from Jonas Willard, Casper Wright, Basher Nolan, and Mickey Mulligan. They had all been as lax as Wiggins. There were numerous messages between Wiggins and Willard referring to 'his

Epilogue – one week later

man on the inside' and the constant stream of information he supplied. In one sequence of undisciplined banter, Basher and Mickey had openly joked about Wiggins' mate from school, the one with the gambling habit, who was now in the Old Bill, and who had been passing him information for several years in return for regular payments.

A forensic accountant had gone through Cuthbert's finances, and had identified monthly payments from an unidentified source located outside the UK. The CIB Financial Investigators had eventually made the connection between the holding company concerned and Willard Betting.

"I still can't believe someone like that infiltrated the command," Tyler said, shaking his head sadly.

"Me either," Quinlan admitted, sounding equally glum.

Frank placed a hand on each man's shoulder, gave it a little squeeze. "Look on the bright side," he told them. "Your outstanding hard work and unquestionable integrity has helped us to remove a cancerous growth from the organisation. Cuthbert was part of a well-established organised crime network run by Jonas Willard, which has now effectively been dismantled, with all the main players either dead or in custody. It's a fantastic achievement, and you should be proud of yourselves, as should all your staff."

Quinlan shook his head. "We had a rotten cop in our midst, someone we liked and trusted. You know as well as I do that the world will tar us all with the same brush, even though scumbags like Cuthbert are extremely rare, and the overwhelming majority of police officers are completely honest and trustworthy."

"He's right," Tyler said, morosely. "I know we've had a good result, but it still feels like a kick in the teeth."

Frank nodded his understanding. "I know exactly how you feel," he assured them. "I do this job to weed out corrupt bastards like Cuthbert, shitbags who betray us and everything we stand for. Getting a result like this always brings me satisfaction and sadness in equal measures, but it never makes me happy. We all know the Met will be heavily criticised by the media and various self-serving politicians when this story comes out, that's inevitable, but I'd rather we

Epilogue – one week later

went through a little pain and recrimination now than allowed a loathsome creature like Cuthbert to continue, hidden amongst our ranks."

He was right, they both agreed, but they still left the room feeling deflated.

———

Arthur Brownlow was half cut as he staggered out of *The Black Horse*. He would have stayed there till closing time given the chance, but he had just spent the last of his money on the slot machines, so he couldn't afford to buy himself another drink.

Inhaling deeply, the aging Teddy Boy ran a leathered hand through his Brylcreemed hair, then carefully pulled the forelock of his quiff down so that it hung at a jaunty angle. "Still got it, old son," he slurred as he studied his reflection in the door window.

Turning his collar up, Arthur set off towards the railway viaduct.

He had only taken a dozen steps when he became aware of someone coming up behind him at speed. He wasn't overly worried; most everyone in the area knew him, including all the young scallywags who committed street robberies, and they knew he didn't have a pot to piss in.

"Hello, Arthur," a voice said, slightly out of breath from where its owner had been jogging.

Turning around, Arthur nearly lost his balance before managing to steady himself. He frowned at the skinny man with the spotty face, trying to recall his name.

And then it came to him.

"Hello, Fingers," he said with a lopsided smile. "Haven't seen you in a while." A sudden thought struck him. "Fancy buying an old mate a drink?" he asked, wrapping an arm around the younger man's shoulders and trying to steer him back toward *The Black Horse*.

Fingers shrugged him off. "Get your hands off me," he growled.

Arthur was confused by the strange reaction. "Don't be like that, lad." He could tell that Fingers' nerves were on edge. The boy was

Epilogue – one week later

constantly looking all around him, as if afraid of being seen. A crafty smile crept across Arthur's wrinkly face. "What you been up to?" he asked, conspiratorially. "Not got yourself in a spot of bother with the law, have you?"

Fingers stepped forwards and punched him straight in the face.

Caught unawares, Arthur fell back against the wall and slid down to the floor, landing heavily on his backside. Dazed, he stared up at Fingers in shock. "What did you do that for?" he whined, rubbing his jaw.

"You grassed us up, didn't you?" Fingers demanded angrily.

"Grassed you up? I don't know what you're talking about," Arthur protested, trying to stand up at the same time.

Fingers kicked his legs out from under him, then booted him in the stomach for good measure.

Arthur screamed out in pain, then curled into a foetal position and began retching.

Fingers kicked the old man again. "You sold us out to Fred Wiggins. Terry Marshall's dead, and Darren McCullen's on life support in hospital, and that's all because of you."

Arthur threw up, covering the pavement in dark frothy liquid. The night air quickly filled with the acrid stench of vomit and regurgitated alcohol. "I didn't sell you out," he cried. "I would *never* do something like that to a mate."

Fingers kicked him in the lower back, eliciting a scream of agony. "Someone grassed us up," he insisted, "and it could only have been you or Vlad."

"Well, there you are, then," Arthur sobbed. "It must have been Vlad. I've never trusted that Russian bastard."

Fingers' face twisted with rage. "You lying piece of shit," he snarled, kicking the old man twice more, and targeting his thighs this time. "I know it was you. You didn't even have the brains to keep your mouth shut, did you? Word on the street is that you've been bragging about coming into a bit of money for some information you supplied to Wiggins."

Arthur let out a low, pitiful moan. "I–I'm sorry," he sobbed as he

Epilogue – one week later

lost control of his bladder and a wet patch spread out from his groin to cover his upper legs. "I was desperate for the money."

Leaning over him, Fingers spat in his face. "You're lucky that I'm not like Wiggins and his savages," he snarled, "because you deserve to die for what you did."

"Pleeeease!" Arthur wailed, fearfully covering his face with his arms. "Don't hurt me again."

When he peered out a moment later, Fingers had gone.

Tyler sat opposite Kelly in the dimly lit restaurant. They had come out to celebrate the successful closing of the case. The meal had been Tony Dillon's idea, a foursome with him and Imogen, who it seemed he was now formally dating. The others hadn't arrived yet, so Tyler was making the most of having Kelly all to himself for a little longer

She looked stunningly beautiful in a tight-fitting, off the shoulder scarlet dress that accentuated the soft curves of her body, and he felt incredibly lucky to have her.

"Stop staring at me," she told him, self-consciously peering at him from above the menu.

He watched her lips move as she spoke, thinking how much he enjoyed kissing them. "I can't help it," he told her with a guilty grin. "You're the most amazing woman I've ever met."

She blushed at the compliment. "I bet you say that to all the girls."

He laughed heartily. "No, that line is reserved exclusively for you," he said with undisguised adoration.

She smiled, then lowered the menu. Her face suddenly became serious, and she lowered her voice so that he could barely hear it above the background music that was playing. "Jack, there's something I need to tell you."

Tyler stiffened. "What is it?" he asked, hoping that nothing was wrong.

Epilogue – one week later

Kelly carefully scanned the dining area to make sure that they couldn't be overheard. "I'm late," she murmured.

Tyler frowned. "What for?"

Kelly rolled her eyes. Men could be so stupid. "My period. It's late."

Tyler's eyes widened. "Oh," he said, lamely. "How late?"

She pulled a face. "Two weeks."

Tyler frowned, wondering if he was missing the point. "But you're on the pill," he said, stupidly.

She nodded. "I am but… it isn't always foolproof."

Tyler leaned back in his chair and let out a low whistle. "Does that mean… Are you?"

She shrugged. "Honestly, I don't know. I don't feel any different in myself, so it could just be a glitch because we've been working such long hours and my body clock is a little out of whack. I could come on any day now or…"

"Or?"

A wan smile. "It could mean that you're going to be a dad."

Tyler sat there for a couple of seconds, processing what she had said.

"Say something," she pleaded, staring at him intently.

Tyler reached across the table and took her hand in his. "I think this is wonderful news," he said, breaking into a goofy smile. "I mean, we would have to get married first, my parents are funny about things like that, but I'm absolutely blown away by the news, and I couldn't be any happier."

Kelly let out a long sigh of relief. "So, you're not angry or disappointed?"

His eyes widened. "Are you kidding me?" he said, squeezing her hand tighter. "I'm over the sodding moon."

"Me too," Kelly admitted, shyly. "Of course, I haven't done a test yet, so I don't want us to get too carried away, only to find out that I'm not actually preggers."

Tyler pulled her hand to his mouth, kissed it gently. "Kelly, my darling. If you are, you are. If you're not, that's fine too. We've got

Epilogue – one week later

our whole lives ahead of us and, as far as I'm concerned, we can start having children as soon as you feel ready for them."

"I think that might be now," she said, demurely.

Tyler gave her a tender smile. "In that case, if it turns out you're not already pregnant, maybe you should come off the pill and we should start trying for a baby."

"I would like that very much," she said, feeling her heart swell with love.

FURTHER READING

TURF WAR

May 1999.

An out of town contract killer is drafted in to carry out a hit on an Albanian crime boss.

That same evening, in another part of town, four Turkish racketeers are ruthlessly gunned down while extorting protection money from local businessmen.

As the dust settles, it becomes apparent to DCI Jack Tyler that the two investigations are inexorably linked, and that someone is trying to orchestrate a gangland war that will tear the city apart.

But who? And why?

The pressure is on. can Tyler can find a way to stem the killings and restore order to the streets, or will this be the case that destroys his career?

JACK'S BACK

October 1999.

When a horribly mutilated body is discovered lying beneath a taunting message written in its own blood, it quickly becomes apparent to DCI Jack Tyler that he's witnessing the birth of a terrifying new serial killer.

With the relentless media coverage causing panic on the streets of Whitechapel, Tyler is put under increasing pressure to bring the case to a rapid conclusion, but the murderer is scarily smart; a ghost who always seems to be one step ahead of the police.

Tyler knows that this case could make or break his career, but he doesn't care about the bad press, or the internal politics; all he's interested in is finding a way to stop the killer before he strikes again…

But what if he can't…?

THE HUNT FOR CHEN

November 1999.

Exhausted from having just dealt with a series of gruesome murders in Whitechapel, DCI Jack Tyler and his team of homicide detectives are hoping for a quiet run in to Christmas.

Things are looking promising until the London Fire Brigade are called down to a house fire in East London and discover a charred body that has been wrapped in a carpet and set alight.

Attending the scene, Tyler and his partner, DI Tony Dillon, immediately realise that they are dealing with a brutal murder.

A witness comes forward who saw the victim locked in a heated argument with an Oriental male just before the fire started, but nothing is known about this mysterious man other than he drives a white van and his name might be Chen.

Armed with this frugal information, Tyler launches a murder investigation, and the hunt to find the unknown killer begins.

UNLAWFULLY AT LARGE

January 2000.

When DCI Jack Tyler put Claude Winston behind bars, he was convinced the psychotic killer would never breathe fresh air again. Then the unthinkable happened and Winston escaped, leaving behind a trail of death and destruction.

Recapturing Winston won't be easy. He'll be better prepared this time around and, due to the bad blood that exists between them, he'll be itching for another chance to see Tyler lined up in the crosshairs of his gun.

Tyler doesn't care. With a colleague dead, this case has become personal, and he'll do whatever it takes to see justice done, even if that means putting his reputation and his life on the line.

THE CANDY KILLER

July 2001.

When DCI Jack Tyler is called upon to investigate the murder of a man killed while trying to protect a girl from an aggressive drunk, he thinks the case is going to be fairly straightforward. He should have known better.

Recently released from prison, a convicted rapist is desperate to track down the love of his life and rekindle their relationship, but she has very different ideas, and would rather die than have him come anywhere near her.

When a kidnap plan goes wrong, those involved begin to turn on each other.

As their fates all become increasingly entwined, not everyone will survive the fallout.

WOLFPACK

It's bonfire night, and Gabe Warren, a fourteen year old runaway from Bristol has just arrived at London's Victoria coach station. He is homeless, penniless and friendless, which makes him ripe for the plucking.

When Gabe accepts the offer of a hot meal and a place to sleep for a few nights, he is unaware that he is about to set foot along a dark and twisted path that will lead to murder.

That same night, two young boys are snatched from a busy fairground in Chingford.

DCI Jack Tyler is tasked finding the boys, but he knows that time is against him. If they were taken by a paedophile, as seems increasingly likely, the chances of them being found alive diminishes with every passing minute...

ACKNOWLEDGMENTS

Edited by Yvonne Goldsworthy

Cover design by Darren Howell

As always, I'd like to say a very special thank you to my brilliant team of Beta Readers, not only for taking the time to read the first draft of the manuscript, but also for all the fantastic feedback they provided. They are: Clare R, Danny A, Cathie A, and Darren H.

GLOSSARY OF TERMS USED IN THE JACK TYLER BOOKS

AC – Assistant Commissioner
ACPO – Association of Chief Police Officers
AFO – Authorised Firearms Officer
AIDS – Acquired Immune Deficiency Syndrome
AMIP – Area Major Investigation Pool (Predecessor to the Homicide Command)
ANPR – Automatic Number Plate Recognition
ARV – Armed Response Vehicle
ASU – Air Support Unit
ATC – Air Traffic Control
ATS – Automatic Traffic Signal
Azimuth – The coverage from each mobile phone telephone mast is split into three 120-degree arcs called azimuths
Bacon – derogatory slang expression for a police officer
Bandit – the driver of a stolen car or other vehicle failing to stop for police
BIU – Borough Intelligence Unit
BPA – Blood Pattern Analysis
BTP – British Transport Police
C11 – Criminal Intelligence / surveillance

Glossary of terms used in the Jack Tyler books

CAD – Computer Aided Dispatch
CCTV – Closed Circuit Television
CIB – Complaints Investigation Bureau
CID – Criminal Investigation Department
CIPP – Crime Investigation Priority Project
County Mounties – a phrase used by Met officers to describe police officers from the Constabularies
Cozzers – Police Officers
CJPU – Criminal Justice Protection Unit (witness protection)
CRIMINT – Criminal Intelligence
CPS – Crown Prosecution Service
CSM – Crime Scene Manager
(The) Craft – the study of magic
CRIS – Crime Reporting Information System
DNA – Deoxyribonucleic Acid
DC – Detective Constable
DS – Detective Sergeant
DI – Detective Inspector
DCI – Detective Chief Inspector
DSU – Detective Superintendent
DCS – Detective Chief Superintendent
DPG – Diplomatic Protection Group
DVLA – Driver and Vehicle Licensing Agency
ECHR – European Court of Human Rights
Enforcer – a heavy metal battering ram used to force open doors
ESDA – Electrostatic Detection Apparatus (sometimes called an EDD or Electrostatic Detection Device)
ETA – Expected Time of Arrival
(The) Factory – Police jargon for their base.
FLO – Family Liaison Officer
FME – Force Medical Examiner
Foxtrot Oscar – Police jargon for 'fuck off'
FSS – Forensic Science Service
GP – General Practitioner
GMC – General Medical Council
GMP – Greater Manchester Police

Glossary of terms used in the Jack Tyler books

GSR – Gun Shot Residue
HA – Arbour Square police station
HAT – Homicide Assessment Team
HEMS – Helicopter Emergency Medical Service
HIV – Human Immunodeficiency Virus
HOLMES – Home Office Large Major Enquiry System
HP – High Priority
HR – Human Resources
HT – Whitechapel borough / Whitechapel police station
IC1 – PNC code for a white European
IC2 – PNC code for a dark skinned European
IC3 – PNC code for an Afro Caribbean
IC4 – PNC code for an Asian
IC5 – PNC code for an Oriental
IC6 – PNC code for an Arab
ICU – Intensive Care Unit
IFR – Instrument Flight Rules are used by pilots when visibility is not good enough to fly by visual flight rules
IO – Investigating Officer
IPCC – Independent Police Complaints Commission
IR – Information Room
IRV – Immediate Response Vehicle
JL – Leyton police station
JS – Leytonstone police station
KF – Forest Gate police station
KZ – Hertford House, East London base of the Homicide Command, also known as SO1(3)
Kiting checks – trying to purchase goods or obtain cash with stolen / fraudulent checks
LAG – Lay Advisory Group
LAS – London Ambulance Service
LFB – London Fire Brigade
Lid – uniformed police officer
LOS – Lost or Stolen vehicle
MIR – Major Incident Room
MIT – Major Investigation Team

Glossary of terms used in the Jack Tyler books

MP – Radio call sign for Information Room at NSY
MPH – Miles Per Hour
MICH/ACH (Modular Integrated Communications Helmet / Advanced Ballistic Combat Helmet)
MPS – Metropolitan Police Service
MSS – Message Switching System
NABIS – National Ballistics Intelligence Service
NADAC – National ANPR Data Centre
NFA – No Further Action
NHS – National Health Service
Nondy – Nondescript vehicle, typically an observation van
NOTAR – No Tail Rotor system technology
NPIA – National Police Improvement Agency
NSY – New Scotland Yard
OCG – Organised Crime Group
OH – Occupational Health
Old Bill – the police
OM – Office Manager
OP – Observation Post
P9 – MPS Level 1/P9 Surveillance Trained
PACE – Police and Criminal Evidence Act 1984
PC – Police Constable
PCMH – Plea and Case Management Hearing
Pig – Derogatory slang expression for a police officer
PIP – Post Incident Procedure
PLO – Press Liaison Officer
Plod – Slang expression for a police officer, usually a uniformed officer on beat patrol
PM – Post Mortem
PNC – Police National Computer
POLACC – Police Accident
PR – Personal Radio
PS – Police Sergeant
PTT – Press to Talk
RCJ – Royal Courts of Justice

Glossary of terms used in the Jack Tyler books

RCS – Regional Crime Squad
Ringer – stolen car on false number plates
RLH – Royal London Hospital
Rozzers – the police
RTA – Road traffic Accident
RT car – Radio Telephone car, nowadays known as a Pursuit Vehicle
QC – Queen's Counsel (a very senior barrister)
Rubber Heelers – Police officers attached to Complaints Investigation Bureau
SCG – Serious Crime Group
Scruffs – Dressing down in casual clothes in order for a detective to blend in with his / her surroundings
SFO – Specialist Firearms Officer
SIO – Senior Investigating Officer
Sheep – followers of Christ; the masses
Skipper - Sergeant
SNT – Safer Neighbourhood Team
SO – Specialist Operations
SO1 – Homicide Command
SO8 – The Flying Squad
SO11 – Criminal Intelligence / surveillance (formerly C11)
SO19 – Met Police Firearms Unit
SOCO – Scene of Crime Officer
SOIT – Sexual Offences Investigative Technique
SPM – Special Post Mortem
SPOC – Single Point of Contact
Stinger – a hollow spiked tyre deflation device
Tango – Target
TDA – Taking and Driving Away
TDC – Trainee Detective Constable
TIE – Trace, Interview, Eliminate
TPAC – Tactical Pursuit and containment
Trident – Operation Trident is the Met unit investigating 'black on black' gun crime
TSG – Territorial Support Group

Glossary of terms used in the Jack Tyler books

TSU – Technical Support Unit
VODS – Vehicle On-line Descriptive Searching
Walkers – officers on foot patrol
Trumpton – the Fire Brigade
VFR – Visual Flight Rules are regulations under which a pilot operates an aircraft in good visual conditions

AUTHOR'S NOTE

Diamonds and Death is the sixth story I've written in The DCI Tyler Thriller series, and I have to admit that it took me far longer to complete than I'd originally anticipated. This is partly because it was a complicated tale, with lots of different strands to weave together, and partly because I'm always overly optimistic when it comes to setting myself writing targets. Anyway, now that you've had a chance to read the book, I really hope you enjoyed it, and that you think the end result was worth the wait!

Dismemberments are still incredibly rare in the UK. During my ten years on the Homicide Command, I only ever dealt with three such victims, and two of those were killed by the same person.

One of the cases was fairly easy to solve, and we had pretty much worked out who was responsible by the end of day one. Of course, knowing and proving are two very different things, and it still took a lot of leg work to gather the relevant evidence together and get the case trial ready.

The other case was far less straightforward, and the investigation proved incredibly challenging for everyone involved.

Striking several weeks apart, a middle-aged white male called Derek Brown lured two female strangers he had met on the streets

Author's note

of Whitechapel back to his flat in Rotherhithe, where he proceeded to kill them before dismembering their bodies and disposing of the various parts.

Brown's first victim was a twenty-nine year old female called Xiao Mei Guo. An illegal immigrant from China, Ms Guo was a mother of two who scraped a meagre living by selling counterfeit DVDs on the streets of Whitechapel. She was last seen alive on 29th August 2007.

Brown's second victim was a twenty-four year old female named Bonnie Barrett. A local prostitute, Ms Barrett had gone missing on 18th September 2007, just twenty-one days after Ms Guo's disappearance.

On 6th October, 2007, following many weeks of intense investigation, Brown was finally arrested. Using Luminol, blood from both victims was found in the kitchen, corridor and bathroom of his flat. DIY equipment, including a hacksaw and heavy-duty bin liners were found at the flat. Brown pleaded not guilty when his case appeared before The Central Criminal Court at Old Bailey the following year. It took the jury just three hours to reach a verdict, finding him guilty of both murders.

Sadly, the bodies of Brown's victims were never recovered, depriving their loved ones of the closure they so desperately needed.

Although the DCI Tyler thrillers and all the characters who feature in them are entirely fictional, I am often inspired by my real-life knowledge and experiences of murder investigations, which is why I had to chuckle when my wife passed a comment about one of the scenes in Diamonds and Death while reading the first draft of the manuscript.

Basically, she found it hard to believe that Kevin Murray could possibly have found minute traces of Carrie's blood in the back of the mini-cab that Lucinda had taken down to the canal, seeing as Carrie's torso had been wrapped in two plastic sacks and hidden inside a suitcase. I had to laugh, because that is something that really did happen in one of the dismemberment cases I worked on, and it just goes to show that fact can indeed be stranger than fiction!

If you've enjoyed reading Diamonds and Death, I would very

Author's note

much appreciate it you could spare a few moments of your valuable time to leave a quick, honest review on Amazon for me. It doesn't have to be anything fancy or prolonged; just a couple of lines to say whether you enjoyed the book and would recommend it to others. I really can't stress how helpful feedback like this is for indie authors like me. Apart from influencing a book's visibility, your reviews will help people who haven't read my work yet to decide whether it's right for them.

I'll sign off by saying that if you haven't read them yet, why not give the other books in the DCI Tyler Thriller series a try? And, while you're at it, feel free to pop over to my website, www.markromain.com, and grab yourself a free copy of The Hunt For Chen.

Right, time to start working on Tyler's next big case!

Best wishes,

Mark.

ABOUT THE AUTHOR

Mark Romain is a retired Metropolitan Police officer, having joined the Service in the mid-eighties. His career included two homicide postings, and during that time he was fortunate enough to work on a number of very challenging high-profile cases.

Mark lives in Essex with his wife, Clare. They have two grown-up children and one grandchild. Between them, the family has three English Bull Terriers and a very bossy Dachshund called Weenie!

Mark is a lifelong Arsenal fan and an avid skier. He also enjoys going to the theatre, weightlifting and kick-boxing, a sport he got into during his misbegotten youth!

You can find out more about Mark's books or contact him via his website or Facebook page:

Mark Romain – author

Markromain.com

Printed in Great Britain
by Amazon